E T

Border
Region

KHAM
PLATEAU

LHADRUNG

BURMA

BONE
MOUNTAIN

Also by Eliot Pattison

Skull Mantra
Water Touching Stone

BONE
MOUNTAIN

Eliot
Pattison

St. Martin's Minotaur
New York

For my mother

www.minotaurbooks.com

ISBN 0-312-27760-1

First Edition: September 2002

10 9 8 7 6 5 4 3 2 1

ACKNOWLEDGMENTS

Much of the information and inspiration for this book derived from quiet, confiding conversations with Tibetans and Chinese during the past twenty years, some of whom took risks in just speaking with me. I will always be indebted to them. For their sage guidance and steadfast support I am deeply grateful to Natasha Kern, Michael Denneny, and Kate Parkin. Special thanks also to Ed Stackler and Lesley Kellas Payne.

CONTENTS

Part One
SALT

CHAPTER ONE

"Sift the sand to find the seeds of the universe."

The voice that came to Shan Tao Yun through the night was like wind over grass. "Let them reach the original ground then plant them," the lama said as Shan's gaze drifted from the white sand in his palm to the brilliant half moon. He knew his teacher Gendun meant Shan's original ground, the seedbed of his soul, what Gendun called Shan's beginning place. But on such a night he could not shake the sense that Tibet itself was the true original ground, that the vast remote land was the world's beginning place, where the planet, and humankind, never stopped shaping themselves, where the highest mountains, the strongest winds, and the most rugged souls had always evolved together.

Ten feet farther down the river's edge Shan's old friend and former cellmate Lokesh chanted quietly, beads entwined in his fingers, his mantra almost indistinguishable from the rustle of the water. Shan breathed in the fragrant smoke of the juniper branches they had brought to burn at the water's edge and watched as a meteor flew over a low distant shimmering in the sky, the only hint of the snow-capped mountains that lined the horizon. It seemed he could reach out and touch the moon. If the earth had a place and a season for growing souls this was surely it, the chill moonlit spring of the high Tibetan wilderness.

Shan watched as though from a distance as Gendun gently opened Shan's fingers and lifted his hand toward the moon, then lowered it and turned Shan's wrist to empty the sand into the small clay jar they had brought from their hermitage ten miles away.

"*Lha gyal lo,*" a voice murmured on Shan's opposite side. It was the caretaker of the hermitage, Shopo, his voice cracking with emotion. "Victory to the gods." They had arrived at the river at dusk, and only now, after the lamas and Lokesh had spent two hours speaking with the *nagas,* the water deities, had Gendun decided Shan could begin collecting the special white sand.

"Lha gyal lo!" an excited voice echoed halfway up the slope behind them. It was one of the four *dropka*, Tibetan herders, who had escorted them to the river and now stood guard, nervously watching the darkened landscape. Gendun and Shopo were outlawed monks engaged in an out-lawed ritual, and the patrols had grown aggressive.

Without even sensing the movement, Shan found his hand back in the water, and when he lifted it out it was full of the white sand again. In the moonlight he saw Lokesh's eyes widen and gleam with excitement as, slowly repeating the motions Gendun had shown him, Shan washed the sand in the moonlight then emptied his palm into the jar.

Gendun's face, worn smooth as a river stone, wrinkled with a smile. "Each of the grains is the essence of a mountain," the lama said as Shan's hand dipped into the water once more, "all that is left when the mountain has shed its husk." Shan had heard the words a dozen times during the past two months as they had ventured into the night to collect sands from places known only to Shopo and the herders. In their turn each of the vast peaks that lined the horizon would be reduced to such a grain, Gen-dun explained, and so it would be for all mountains, all continents, all planets. It would all end as it began, in such tiny seeds, and humankind in all its glory could never match the power reflected in a single grain. The words were a way of teaching impermanence, Shan knew, and of showing respect for the nagas from whom they borrowed the sand.

Shan sensed a distant drumming noise in his ears and the moon seemed to edge even closer as he gathered another handful for the jar. His hand reached toward the clay jar then froze in midair as a frantic voice split the stillness.

"*Mik tada*! Watch out! Run!" It was one of the dropka sentinels on the ridge above. "The fire! Dowse the fire!"

Shan heard feet scrambling over the gravel of the slope above and looked up to see two men silhouetted in the moonlight, realizing in the same moment that the drumming was not in his head. It was a helicopter coming in low and fast, the way Public Security operated when raiding Tibetan camps.

One of the guards, wearing a black wool cap, darted to the water's edge, futilely pulling on Lokesh's shoulder, then moving to Shan's side to tug on his collar. "You have to go patch that god!" the man shouted. "We must flee!"

Shan let himself be pulled to his feet, his spine chilling as he looked first toward the helicopter, then at the lamas, who only smiled and con-tinued their homage to the river. Gendun and Shopo were accustomed to risking imprisonment for simple acts of reverence. And though Shan and the dropka might be disturbed by the increased pressure from Public Se-curity, there was only one mystery that ever concerned Gendun, the mys-tery of growing and strengthening souls.

"If it is Public Security they will drop soldiers over the ridge to sur-round us!" the sentinel groaned as he kicked sticks from the small fire. "They will have machine guns and devices to see in the night!"

Shan studied the man in the black cap warily. He had more than a mere herder's grasp of Chinese weapons and tactics. Shan suddenly realized that he had not seen the man before, that he had not been part of their escort.

Gendun replied by raising a finger to his lips, then gestured toward the water. "There are nagas," he observed quietly.

"The sand will be useless if you are arrested," Shan whispered, his hand on Gendun's shoulder.

"There are nagas," the lama repeated.

"It's only sand," the stranger argued, casting a tormented glance in the direction of the approaching helicopter. Public Security had its own ways of teaching impermanence.

As Gendun turned back to the water Lokesh was suddenly at the stranger's side, pulling him away from the lama. "We are creating something wonderful with that sand," Shan's old friend whispered, the white stubble of his whiskers glistening in the moonlight. He placed his hands on the man's shoulders to be sure the young Tibetan was listening and gazed into his face. "When we are done," he explained in a solemn, confiding tone, "it will change the world."

The man in the black cap illuminated an electric lantern and aimed the beam into Lokesh's face as if doubting he had heard the old Tibetan correctly, then, as the sound of the helicopter surged to a crescendo, he snapped off the light and dove to the ground. A moment later the machine was gone. It had skimmed the ridge above but had been traveling too fast to deploy troops.

The man in the cap lit his lantern and muttered under his breath, casting an accusing glance at the other guards, who had gathered behind Lokesh with sheepish, even embarrassed expressions. He aimed the light beam into each man's face, settling it on Shan's, which he studied with a frown. "You are supposed to be delivering an artifact," he said to Lokesh, his voice heavy with impatience. He did not move the light from Shan.

"We are," Lokesh agreed. "We are preparing for the journey," he added with a gesture toward the two lamas, who continued to speak over the swift dark river.

"Preparing?" the man scoffed. "What have you been doing for two months? You're not preparing, you're taking root! You will ruin us!"

Shan stepped beside Lokesh and pushed the man's lantern down. "Those who brought the artifact agreed that the lamas will decide the proper way to return it." He knew now the stranger, like those who had brought the sacred artifact to Shopo's hermitage, was a *purba*, a member of the secret Tibetan resistance.

"You mean Drakte agreed."

"Drakte is one of you," Shan asserted. He and Lokesh had met Drakte nearly a year earlier aiding prisoners in the gulag camp where they had served. It had been Drakte who had intercepted them two months ago and taken them to Shopo's hidden hermitage. "We will go when the lamas

5

and Drakte are ready. He is coming to show us the way. A few more days at most."

"We don't have a few more days," the purba groused. "And don't expect Drakte. He's not keeping his appointments."

"Missing?" Shan noticed a bulge under the man's jacket, at the waist, and looked back at Gendun. If the lamas thought the man had a gun they would insist he leave.

The purba shrugged. "Not where he was asked to be."

"And you've come in his place?"

"No. But I was hoping to find him at that hermitage. There is news. And I brought something he had asked for," he added in a peevish tone. "He said the lamas needed it. He said if we did not agree to retrieve it he would go himself, all the way to India if necessary." The purba lowered a long, narrow sack from his shoulder and produced an eighteen-inch-long bamboo tube, which Lokesh eagerly accepted.

"What news?" Shan asked.

Before he replied the man pointed to one of the herders, then to the top of the hill where the guards had been watching the road beyond. The herder sprang up the slope. "A man was killed. An official, in Amdo town," he said, referring to the closest settlement of any size, nearly a hundred miles away. "Public Security will sweep the hills and detain people. When they interrogate, they will learn of the hermitage." He cast another frown toward the lamas. "You may call it sacred, what you are doing, but they will call it a crime against the state." He took a step toward Gendun as though to try again to drag him away, but a herder in a fleece vest stepped forward with a hand raised in warning.

"Do you have any idea how dangerous this is?" The purba's hands clenched and unclenched repeatedly. He seemed ready to do battle with them. "No one told us you would wander around the mountains like this. You could go to prison, all of you. For what? You can't fight the Chinese with sand and prayers."

Lokesh uttered a hoarse sound that Shan recognized as a laugh. "I have known Chinese prisons," the old Tibetan said. "Sometimes sand and prayers are the only way."

The purba fixed Shan with a bitter stare. "You are the famous Chinese who fixes things for Tibetans. You know better, but still you let them do this."

Shan paused to study Gendun and Shopo. "If these lamas asked me to jump into this river with my pockets stuffed with rocks," he said quietly, "I would thank them and leap in."

"Lha gyal lo," the herder in the vest whispered, as if to cheer Shan on.

Lokesh touched the warrior's arm. "It is difficult for one so young to understand these things," the old Tibetan said. "You should return with us to the hermitage and see."

"Unlike Drakte, I obey my orders," the man snapped. "I am needed elsewhere."

Lokesh raised the bamboo tube in his hand. "Then look now," he suggested, extracting a roll of cloth from the tube. As Lokesh straightened it Shan saw that it was an old *thangka*, one of the cloth paintings used to depict the icons of Tibetan Buddhism.

When the purba's light hit the painting the man grimaced and retreated a step. One of the dropka guards moaned loudly. It was the image of a fierce demon, with the head of a bull garlanded with human skulls, surrounded by swords and spears and arrows, holding a cup of blood. The flayed skins of its victims lay at its feet. Lokesh studied the image with a satisfied grin, then motioned the purba forward.

"Look carefully," the old Tibetan said, pointing to the head of the terrifying image. "This is what we are doing. This is how we win without violence. This is how the artifact will be returned, how that deity is going to be repaired. Because this is what he is becoming."

"Who?" the purba asked, the anger in his voice now tinged with confusion.

In the dim light Shan thought he saw surprise on Lokesh's face, as though the answer were obvious. Then Lokesh gestured from the skull-clad demon to Shan. "Our friend. Our Shan."

The spell cast by the words silenced the purba and the dropka, all of whom stared uneasily at Shan. Shan searched Lokesh's face for an explanation, but his friend just grinned back expectantly, as if he had given Shan a great gift.

Suddenly another desperate cry split the air. The guard at the top of the ridge frantically stumbled down the slope. "A patrol! Knobs!" he cried, meaning the soldiers of the Public Security Bureau. The purba and Shan leapt up and moments later gazed down at a troop transport half a mile away, edging its way slowly toward their position.

"That helicopter spotted us," the purba said. "Last month they used infrared to find an old hermit who only came out at night to pray." Shan sensed the fierce determination rising in the warrior's voice and shuddered.

At the river three of the dropka were in a cluster around the lamas, facing outward, as if preparing to engage the knobs with their staffs. The fourth, the man wearing the fleece vest, stood apart, staring into the black water. As the purba marched purposefully toward the lamas the herder in the vest spun about and hurled himself on the purba, shoving him to the ground, then just as abruptly pulling away. In his hand was a large automatic pistol.

"You fool!" the purba spat. "They have to be taken away! We can't fight those knobs."

Shame crossed the herder's face as he looked at the pistol in his hand, and he held the weapon clumsily, fingers around only the grip, not touching the trigger. "You see that one," he said, nodding toward Gendun, who still communed with the river. "My mother stays at that tent by the hermitage. She calls him the Pure Water Lama. You know why? Not just because he never registered with the bastards at the Bureau of Religious Affairs, but because he took his vows more than fifty years ago, before the invasion. Before the Chinese scoured our land and changed it forever. He has never gone into exile, never been captured. His words are uncontaminated, my mother says, because they flow from a stream the Chinese never discovered." The man spoke slowly, with a tone of wonder, as if he had forgotten the knob patrol. Beside him two of the herders knelt at the river and began collecting pebbles.

"I need my gun," growled the purba, still sprawled on the ground. He was scared, Shan saw. Sometimes traditional Tibetans hated the purbas as much as the Chinese. "We need to get them out of here."

The herder shook his head. "I have never done anything with my life," he said in a hollow voice. "The Chinese would not let me go to school. They wouldn't let me travel. They wouldn't let me get a job. I'm like a little stunted tree that can never grow, and that one, the Pure Water Lama, he is like the towering survivor of a forest where everything else was leveled."

He cast a smile toward Gendun, then looked at the purba, his face hardening. "Here is how we protect such men," he said, and he threw the gun into the black water. The two herders at the river's edge rose and stepped to his side, pulling slings from their pockets. "We have heard how to do this from others. We will smash their searchlights and fill the air with stones. If we are lucky they will not see us. Chinese soldiers get scared in the night. They hear stories of demons." He glanced at the thangka, still in Lokesh's hand, then at Shan. "The lamas must fill the jar," he said to the purba, "and then you will take them back. My younger brother knows the way," he said, gesturing toward the remaining herder. "If we do not stop the patrol, you are the one who best knows how to evade the soldiers."

When the man lifted his sling his hand shook. "Patch the deity," he said in a rushed whisper to Shan, then faded into the shadows with his companions.

As Shan helped the purba to his feet the man looked into the darkness, in the direction the herders had gone, a mixture of anger and awe on his face. "That artifact," he said in a hollow voice, "I hear it's just a little piece of stone."

The events of the night haunted Shan during their long trek back toward the hermitage, and stayed with him as he lay restlessly on his pallet finding it impossible to sleep. It was nearly dawn when he stepped into the little chapel of the hermitage, the *lhakang*, and settled cross-legged before the altar. Before its cracked wooden Buddha, flanked by butter lamps, sat a jagged piece of stone, six inches long and curved along its front, where a faint circle of red was centered, a dim remnant of an eye that had once been painted there. Just a piece of stone. But it was why the dropka had risked their lives the night before. It was why Lokesh said Shan was becoming the demon, why the purbas were so upset that Shan and his friends lingered at the hermitage, why they had gone to such lengths to bring Shan there.

He and Lokesh had been slowly returning from a pilgrimage to Mount Kailas, in southwestern Tibet, walking on remote trails, sometimes daring to ride an hour or two on trucks bound for central Tibet. One night the truck they had been traveling on had been abruptly stopped by a horse cart drawn across the road. Several young men sprang from the surrounding rocks, running not toward the driver but toward the cargo bay, closing in on Shan and Lokesh before their feet were on the ground. Shan recognized Drakte instantly, a tall lean Tibetan with a double looping scar on his forehead, received from a knob riot squad that had wrapped barbed wire around their truncheons.

"We've been looking for you," Drakte had announced and studied the two men peevishly, as though Shan and Lokesh had been deliberately avoiding him.

"We've had a pilgrimage," Lokesh offered brightly. "We're going back home, to Lhadrung."

"No, you're not," the purba had insisted. He spoke briefly with the driver, handed the man a *khata*, a prayer scarf, and as the man sped away Drakte had gestured them into a smaller truck that emerged from the rocks.

For three days they had driven through the rugged mountains and valleys northwest of Lhasa, skirting the town of Shigatse on roads that were little more than rutted game trails, then heading north through small barren villages and onto the *changtang* plateau, the vast wilderness land of north central Tibet, before turning east at the mining town of Doba. As they sat around their campfires Drakte had spoken of his beloved changtang, and many other things, but never of the reason he had intercepted them or where he was taking them. On the fourth day, when they had been met in a canyon by dropka horsemen leading two mounts, Drakte watched Shan leave with a strange longing in his eyes.

"Do this thing for all of us," the young purba said to Shan as they parted. "When it is time, I will come to take you," he promised, and Shan had thought he had seen the stirring of friendship in the man's eyes.

For two more days they had ridden, the dropka never speaking of their destination, until finally they had crested a high windswept ridge to find a group of ragged buildings in the small hollow below. Three of the largest had been repaired in a patchwork fashion, with plywood, tin, and cardboard fastened to the packed earth and stone walls of the original construction. Inside the compact stone building that housed the lhakang, he had discovered Gendun. Along with a middle-aged lama and a nun he sat at the altar before the jagged eye, reading long narrow sheets of text, unbound pages from a traditional teaching book. Gendun, whom Shan had last seen over four months earlier hundreds of miles away in the western Kunlun Mountains, acknowledged him with a serene smile and gestured for the two men to sit in the empty space beside him, as though they had been expected. It had been more than two hours later, as a meal of roasted barley and buttered tea was being prepared, when Gendun had finally introduced Shopo, and Nyma, a sturdy woman of perhaps thirty.

Nyma had burst into an excited greeting. "We've waited so long," she exclaimed, "and now at last you have come. All these years," she sighed.

"Years?" Shan asked in confusion as he had studied the young woman's leathery face and strong shoulders. But for her robe he would have taken her for another herder. "The purbas found us last week."

The nun laughed and pointed toward the lhakang. "Many decades ago it was lost—stolen and taken out of Tibet as a trophy."

"The eye?" Shan asked, remembering what he had seen on the altar. "That broken stone?"

Nyma nodded enthusiastically, moving up and down on her toes, barely in control of her emotions. "From the deity that guards our valley. Only five years ago did it return to Tibet, and only a few weeks ago was it freed from Lhasa," she said, as though the stone had been in prison. "We knew he must have his eye returned, we always knew it would come back eventually. But no one could find the way back for it. Now we have you. The things he will see," she added ominously. "The things he will do then."

After they had eaten that first night Shopo had explained that three months earlier, before news of its recovery had even reached the valley, an oracle in the Yapchi Valley, where the eye belonged, had declared that the eye could only be returned by a virtuous Chinese, a certain Chinese of pure heart. Gendun had been on his way to Lhadrung when this news had reached him, and he had instantly changed his direction to find those who had been debating the words of the oracle. He had known whom that Chinese must be.

Shan had not pressed the Tibetans with questions. The story of the stone had to come out at its own pace, in its own way. He had learned long ago that there usually were no words for the things most important to the Tibetans, and even when they might find words, they were wary of speaking them. To people like Gendun and Lokesh words were treacherous, imperfect things, capable of connecting people in only the most tenuous ways. If the eye were truly important, they would teach Shan not about the eye as such but about how to think about the eye, how to fit the eye into his particular awareness.

Yet after so many weeks with it, Shan thought he would have understood it better. The stone eye seemed to mock him, still caused an ache in that part of the old Shan that would not die, the investigator who could not stop asking questions. Why were Tibetans willing to die for the stone?

Outside, a voice shouted in excitement, then another. In an instant Shan was at the doorway. The middle-aged dropka woman who watched over the hermitage with her brother was on the ridge above, pointing over the buildings to the opposite slope. Several of the dropka who had pitched a tent two hundred yards away had taken up the call. Shan darted to the back of the building and to his relief saw a familiar figure in a long brown robe.

It was Nyma, who had left the hermitage the week before to retrieve the special vermilion sand that was found only in the bed of a spring near one of the high glaciers. Nyma turned and swayed as she descended the trail. She did not believe anyone was watching, Shan realized, and she was dancing; dancing because, he sensed, she was filled with joy, because she was bringing the last of the sands they needed.

Nyma could not stop smiling as the inhabitants of the hermitage sat with her ten minutes later, encircling the pouch of sand she had brought from the glacier. "The stream was frozen," she said, explaining why she had been gone several days longer than expected. "So I sat and waited." Slowly, ceremoniously, she used both hands to remove the derby that covered the braids she kept pinned over her crown, set the hat on the ground and folded her hands over her lap. "On the second day a warm wind came, and the ice began to melt. On the third I watched as a hole opened, just big enough for my hand to fit through."

Shan gazed about the circle at the three men who sat with them. Lokesh offered his lopsided grin, made crooked years earlier when the boot of a knob had broken his jaw. He looked from Lokesh into the smiling countenance of Gendun, who solemnly nodded at Nyma, then at Shan, as if to confirm that yes, this would be the night, yes, despite the torment raging elsewhere in Tibet, in their little remote outpost all was right with the universe.

Beside them, in a tattered maroon robe, sat Shopo, who had tended the illegal hermitage since being driven from his monastery twenty years earlier. "It has all become the right thing," he observed serenely. Nyma's contribution was the perfect offering for completing their work, made all the more powerful by the reverence she had shown the mountain. She had not taken the vermilion sand, but had waited for the ice to melt, had waited for the mountain to offer it to her.

Shopo lifted the pouch and reverently poured its contents into a clay pot. As he raised the pot toward the sky, a tall man with a narrow, downcast face appeared around the corner of the nearest building, carrying a large leather sack over his shoulder. It was Tenzin, who had been at the hermitage when Shan and Lokesh had arrived, carrying his day's collection of the yak dung they used for fuel. Tenzin stared woodenly at the clay pot, placing one hand over his *gau*, the silver prayer amulet that hung from his neck, then nodded and continued toward the hut where he stored the fuel.

"Lha gyal lo!" Shopo called toward the heavens in a joyful voice. "Victory to the gods!" He rose from the blanket, both hands cradling the pot, and carried it into the compact stone structure that housed half a dozen meditation cells and the hermitage's lhakang, Shan and his companions close behind. Silently acknowledging the Buddha on the altar at the rear wall, Shopo set the pot on a cedar plank that held ten similar pots and several long, narrow bronze funnels, then turned toward the multicolored, seven-foot circle that covered the center of the stone floor, a reverent awe filling his face.

It was called the Vajrabhairava, the Diamond Terrifier, one of the rarest forms of the intricate mandala sand paintings that had been part of Tibetan ritual for centuries. It had frightened Shan at first, when he heard Gendun explain that the deity they were invoking was one of the fiercest of all the Tibetan deities, and he watched now as the dropka woman halted and grimaced at the old thangka of the Diamond Terrifier, which Lokesh had hung in the lhakang. Some may have thought it meant Shan and his friends were on a path of demons and destruction but Shan had learned how such severe images were used by the lamas as symbols of higher truths, and he knew now not to see violence in the image, but hope. The Diamond Terrifier was the form wisdom assumed to challenge the Lord of Death when it sought to take humans before they achieved enlightenment.

At first Shan and Nyma had listened for hours every day as Gendun orally painted the complex mandala, describing it inch by inch from memory. Finally, a month earlier, Shopo and Gendun had laid out intricate chalk lines on the stone floor, outlining the foundations of the wheel. It had been thirty years since Gendun had helped create this particular mandala, taught to him by a lama who had been ninety years old at the time, but he recalled its many symbols perfectly. The mandala held dozens of symbols, each made by pouring a few grains of sand at a time with the *chakpa*, thin five-inch-long funnels. Indeed, every image, even every color, was a symbol, and each symbol had a teaching associated with it. Shan gazed upon the grounds of the symbolic palace at the center, divided into intricate quadrants. The white east held the wheel of dharma, the yellow south wish-giving jewels, the red west the lotus of purity, and the green north a flaming sword.

After a quarter hour, buoyed by the joy of the Tibetans, Shan drifted outside to the circle of earth in an outcropping above the buildings where he had passed many hours in meditation during the past weeks. Gendun would want him to contemplate the lesson of the sands on this final day, but suddenly Shan felt too full of life, too content with the knowledge that he had, after the ordeal that had been his life thus far, finally found a place in the world.

As he watched the clouds, letting his contentment push back the fear he had felt when sitting by the jagged stone, Shan discovered an unfamiliar nervousness. For tonight, instead of filling the chakpa for Gendun as the lama painted the mandala, Gendun would fill the chakpa for him, so Shan could create the cloud and mountain images along the perimeter of the painting.

For hours the lamas had taught him the proper posture of the hands, and mind, in applying the sand, until Shan sensed he was not so much holding an implement for art but offering a prayer with sand. Then together they had practiced the cursive pattern Shan would create with the white sand along the outer perimeter of the circle.

"Follow the curve a lark makes in its flight," Gendun had explained, referring to the long graceful dip made by the bird between wing beats, and the lama had expressed wonder about the strange blend of excitement and sadness that had appeared on Shan's face.

"It's nothing," Shan had whispered, after floating for a moment on a tide of memory. His father had used almost the same words, almost the same voice, speaking of birds and willows and the wind, drawing patterns with his brush in the air, when he had taught Shan how to create his first Chinese ideograms.

Suddenly Shan became aware of someone sitting beside him. He turned from the clouds and looked into Gendun's serene face.

"We will have mountains to climb," the lama observed abruptly. He was sitting beside Shan in the lotus fashion, his legs crossed, as if he had been spirited there from a meditation cell. The words were Gendun's way of asking if Shan was ready, not for the mandala, but for the journey they would begin afterwards, for it was because of that journey they had undertaken the mandala. Just as others might methodically assemble supplies and study maps to prepare for arduous travel, the lamas had been methodically strengthening Shan, Lokesh, and Nyma with images of the Diamond Terrifier. Or perhaps, as Lokesh had chillingly suggested, preparing Shan to do the work of the Diamond Terrifier.

"I am ready for mountains, Rinpoche," Shan said, using the term of address for a revered teacher.

Gendun's eyes twinkled as he studied Shan's face. More often than not the two did not need words to communicate. "And there will be more than just yak chips to watch for," the old lama added.

Shan studied his teacher in confusion. "I thought Tenzin would stay here, Rinpoche," Shan said. Tenzin had not spoken a word during the two months Shan had known him, but Shan had recognized the man's sad, broken nature, and the way the dropka warned him away from roads. He was an escapee from the gulag, Shan had realized, another fugitive trying to revive himself, to discover the spark inside after having had so many, for so long, try to extinguish it.

"He is going north. Someone died."

13

The remnants of Shan's grin vanished.

"No," Gendun added quickly. "Not that way," he said, meaning not one of the violent mysteries the old Shan had been obsessed with solving. "Nothing to do with the stone or any of us. He's just going north and I worry about him."

Although Tenzin usually ate with them and shared their chores, he had stayed away from Shan, denying Shan the chance of knowing him better. Despite all their weeks together, Tenzin was as great an enigma as ever. At first Shan had taken his manner for an aloofness tied to the oddly aristocratic air he projected, even when carrying his dung sack. More than once Shan had wondered if Gendun or Shopo had given the man penance, in punishment for something. Sometimes such men committed violence in making good their escape. Gendun might not condemn him for killing a jailer, but would worry about the damage such an act would cause to his inner deity. The tall, silent Tibetan left at dawn each day with his leather sack and returned at dusk, having filled it with yak dung, a meager haul for a day's work. But even with a single sack a day he had filled one of the smaller huts to the ceiling with fuel for the hermitage.

"I will help him if I see how, Rinpoche."

Gendun nodded. "I worry sometimes that he goes beyond seeing." The lama was not referring to Tenzin leaving their sight, but to the dangers of drifting into deep meditation and losing awareness of one's immediate surroundings while moving about the treacherous landscape. Monks sometimes broke legs, even necks, when traveling alone in the mountains.

Shan studied his teacher. Gendun knew something about the melancholy man that Shan did not, or at least sensed something that Shan had not seen. Tenzin had never helped with the mandala, but watched its creation with a child-like fascination, steadfastly attending Gendun and Shopo with tea and replenishing all the lamps when the dropka brought skins of butter. Although Shan had never seen him meditate, never seen him show interest in what the Tibetans might call the Buddha within him, he remembered the single sack of dung brought back each day. The sack could be filled in two or three hours time. Did Tenzin spend the rest of his day sitting on the high ridges in meditation? Once, Shan remembered, after Shopo had carefully described how to commune with the river nagas, Tenzin had come back with black sand for the mandala and reverently presented it to Gendun. Another time Shan had discovered him alone, in the middle of the night, hovering at the edge of the mandala with his eyes full of tears, his hand cupped in the air over the image of a hermit monk.

"When he grows his tongue," the lama said, "it will be better. A few more months perhaps."

It was how Gendun described the silence of such broken men, how Gendun had referred to Shan's own dark silence in the weeks after he left the gulag. When the man finally found the spark that had been Tenzin before imprisonment, before the torture of the gulag, the fire of his spirit would reach his tongue and he would be ready to speak with the world. Perhaps, Shan thought, it was why Gendun was asking him to watch over Tenzin, because before he met the lamas Shan, too, had once consisted only of mute, confused fragments.

Sift the sand to find the seeds of the universe. The words echoed in Shan's mind as he sat by the mandala four hours later with the pot of white sand by his feet. The sun had set, their last night of work on the mandala begun. A fingertip touched his arm, light as a feather.

"It is time," Gendun said, and from a sleeve of his red robe he produced a chakpa, extending it toward Shan.

Shan hesitated. From the darkened corridor that led to the chamber he heard the moan of the wind as it played with the crumbling stonework of the hermitage, creating an eerie harmony with the mantra murmured by Lokesh, who sat beside Tenzin at the wall behind them. He slowly raised his hand to accept the narrow chakpa from Gendun, filled with the white sand. The lama handed him a second, empty chakpa, to be used to tap the sand out of the first. Shan's gaze drifted toward the small wooden altar, toward the jagged eye, then he glanced back at Gendun with a fleeting sense of guilt. The eye was there, always watching. But part of the discipline Gendun had imposed on Shan was not to think about the mysterious eye, to immerse himself instead in the mandala. Not since the first day at the hermitage had anyone spoken about the eye, except Lokesh, who had soberly whispered to him one night that Shan need not worry, because wherever Gendun and the stone traveled, that place would be a sanctuary. Lokesh seemed to think of the upcoming journey as a pilgrimage, in which holy men would return a holy stone, and that the world would part to offer a peaceful path for such pilgrims.

Shan watched Nyma finish a flame shape along the outer ring, then he leaned forward to begin outlining the image of a cloud with a tiny line of white sand. He lowered first the sand-filled chakpa, then the empty funnel, but quickly lifted them away. His hands were trembling. No one spoke. He collected his awareness for a moment by gazing upon the palace at the center of the circle, where wisdom and compassion reigned. His hands steadier, he began to tap the white sand chakpa, loosing a white thread onto the outer rim of the mandala. The tapping of his metal funnels became a tiny muffled bell, a sound that had become part of the nightly ritual, each ring announcing the planting of a few more seeds into the little universe the lamas had created.

As Shan finished the image, he nodded to Nyma, who would continue the pattern by applying vermilion sand in the shape of a tree, then stood and stepped away from the circle, wary of breathing deeply across the delicate sand images. As he turned he saw a stranger squatting by Lokesh, arguing in a low voice. The man wore a heavily stained fleece hat and a

15

chuba, the heavy sheepskin coat favored by the nomads who inhabited the sparse landscape, but he was not one of those from the dropka encampment above the hermitage.

The man's eyes widened as he stood and stabbed an accusing finger toward Shan. His chuba opened with the movement, revealing a long knife at his belt. Lokesh, marking his rosary in the tight grip of two fingers, rose and used his free hand to push down the man's arm as Shan approached.

"You're crazy," the stranger muttered, and as he twisted away from Lokesh his fleece cap fell away, revealing a head shaved completely bald. Shan was wrong, he realized, as he studied the man's strong, boney features, his smooth scalp and long thin moustache. The stranger was not one of the local herders, he was a Golok, from the far northeast of Tibet, perhaps the most untamed of all the Tibetan peoples. "He's Chinese!" the Golok barked loudly.

Shan glanced uneasily toward the mandala. Nyma and the lamas were ignoring the man.

"It's Shan," Lokesh countered, still holding the man's arm as if he thought the Golok would attack Shan. "He's the one."

The intruder cut his eyes toward Lokesh, then examined Shan. His anger faded, replaced by scorn. "I don't think so. The one that's going to patch the god? He's a criminal. Hard as nails they say. All the other Chinese hate him."

Lokesh glanced apologetically at Shan. "Not a criminal, a prisoner. Four years *lao gai*," he added, referring to the hard labor gulag camps run by Beijing. Until the year before, Shan and Lokesh had both served in the 404th People's Construction Brigade, one of the most notorious camps in China's slave system.

"This one," the Golok said as he surveyed Shan's heavily patched coat, his tattered work boots and the cracked, frayed end of the vinyl belt that jutted from his waist, "he looks like a shopkeeper. A failed shopkeeper," he added, fixing Shan with a sneer, then surveying the others in the chamber with a frown. "There are supposed to be purbas, supposed to be warriors. No chance you'll make it. You have no idea," he said haughtily, turning back to Shan. "You could die a hundred ways. Better men than you have tried and died."

Shan silently returned the Golok's stare. If the Golok, who was certainly no purba, knew about their secret plans, he wondered, how many others knew that they were going to return the jagged eye? Why did he seem to know more than Shan? And why, when he so obviously didn't belong at the hermitage, had the dropka who guarded the buildings let him in?

Lokesh sighed. "Yes," he said, as if he had heard such warnings before. He took the man's hand and pulled him forward. "You need to study the sacred circle," he advised in a patient tone. The words had the sound of

16

a healer's advice, and Shan decided the man must be one of those bitter, angry Tibetans who were brought to the hermitage by the older herders to witness the mandala and reflect on the power that compassion could exercise over hate and fear.

The Golok cocked his head at an odd angle toward the mandala, as if seeing the lamas and the circle of sand for the first time. He frowned, then bent to his knees, briefly lowering his forehead toward the floor in reluctant homage. As he rose he muttered in surprise, his gaze having fallen on the altar. He quickly stepped past the mandala to stand in front of the stone, staring at the jagged eye, crouching in front of it. He was far more interested in the stone fragment than in the lamas or the mandala.

Shan had known Goloks during his years in prison. No, not known them, for they had refused to speak with him, always just stared with the silent malevolence reserved for their enemies. Even many of the Tibetans avoided them, for the Golok tribes had been known for centuries as a wild and brutal people notorious for their banditry. The Goloks would have tried to kill Shan had he not been protected by the monks who shared his lao gai barracks. He knew of two Chinese prisoners who had been attacked by Goloks, one found in his bunk with a screwdriver driven into his brain, the other castrated with a sharpened spoon. During his early days in the slave labor camp, Shan would have welcomed death by such men. But that had been a different Shan, a different incarnation—the Beijing Shan who had entered the gulag had wanted nothing more than to be released from the constant pain and fear that had seized him after weeks of Public Security interrogation.

Gendun turned and looked toward Shan expectantly. Nyma had finished her tree on the sand wheel. Shan returned to the lama's side and accepted the chakpa, refilled with white sand. He closed his eyes a moment, leaned forward and began tapping the funnel, this time to make three curving mountains. Shan worked in silence, Nyma and the lamas contemplating the nearly completed wheel, the wind moaning over the rooftop, the butter lamps flickering, Lokesh's whispered mantra rising and ebbing like the wind. He focused his entire being on the grains of sand falling from the chakpa. They seemed to glow; white like fresh snow, white like the deities who lived in the clouds. Finally, finished with the mountains, Shan pushed himself away and stepped back to sit beside Lokesh and Tenzin as Shopo raised a chakpa of blue sand to paint a monk sitting in Shan's mountains.

Shan labored to keep his focus on the mandala. But the Golok moved restlessly about the rear of the chamber now, looking at the jagged eye one moment, then leaning forward, staring at Shan. Shan knew what the man was thinking. Shan had shared the same question for weeks now. Why Shan? "Because you know the ways of the demons that wish to keep the deity from seeing again," Nyma had declared when he had asked her, meaning, Shan sadly realized, that he knew the ways of the Chinese government. "It is your reward," she had added. "People know how you have restored the balance when violence has taken it away. You find that which has been lost."

But surely the local people must know where the eye belonged, Shan had suggested to the nun one morning when they had gone for water together. No, Nyma had replied, with round, sad eyes. Once the deity had been blinded it had retreated deep into the mountains. Yapchi Valley, where it had resided for centuries, was over two miles long and a mile wide with great ridges surrounding it on three sides, ridges riddled with chasms and caves. The deity could be waiting anywhere.

Four more times Shan took the chakpa of white sand, four more times he added images of clouds and mountains, then watched as the others worked on the wheel. Time passed without measure. Tenzin silently relit sticks of incense. For a brief moment hail rattled on the tin roof. Lokesh kept up his mantra, without ceasing, until it seemed just one more tone of the wind. The Golok settled cross-legged before the altar, his head constantly in motion, twisting and turning as if trying to see the eye better.

But Shan refused to let the Golok's strange behavior disturb him. He felt an unexpected warmth and tried to remember the last time he had felt such contentment. It would have been before his years of lao gai imprisonment, before he had been made Inspector General of the Ministry of Economy, before he had married a senior party member and started working for those who ran the government in Beijing. This was an important night, he realized, an initiation of sorts, a night of discovery. A night, Lokesh would say, when they were all living close to their inner deities. A night when he could tell himself with confidence that in all the universe, here was where he was meant to be, here among the lamas who could forget that a million Tibetans had been killed by his Chinese countrymen, could forget that nearly all their treasured monasteries had been crushed under Beijing's boot, could forget that still—after fifty years— they lived in an occupied land, could forget all the suffering because here, in this lonely, forgotten, wind-battered hermitage, a few reverent souls endured to complete a mandala dedicated to compassion and wisdom. And now, as they began the final round of painting with the chakpa, they had entered the perfect hour of this perfect night.

As he looked up into Gendun's eyes, a grin tugged at Shan's face. Perhaps he had been reading too much into their strange quest to return the eye, perhaps this was all it was about, keeping such moments alive, protecting the lamas and the traditions, preserving the seeds. Suddenly he couldn't imagine anything more important in all the world than returning the eye to its deity.

Gendun's head twisted and the lama bent an ear toward the outer wall. The wind had turned sharper, rising into a long hollow tone that had a strangely metallic quality. Shan sensed sudden movement and glanced away from the mandala to see the Golok rise on his haunches, looking warily toward the door. The long hollow sound came again, pitched lower this time. Shan heard a scramble of feet in the corridor. The old herder who was guarding the lhakang was running outside.

The herdsman and his sister alternated shifts, one in the hermitage, the other on the ridge to the west, overlooking the valley that led to the outside world, armed not with a gun but with an ancient, dented *dungchen,* one of the long telescoping horns used in temples. The new sound wasn't the wind, Shan realized, but the dungchen, sounded in warning. The Golok stood and shot out the door, his hand on the hilt of his long knife. Shan rose and took an uncertain step in the same direction. Lokesh paused in his mantra and tilted his head as though to listen, then cast a weary glance toward Shan and continued his prayers, at a slightly faster rate. The horn sounded again, more urgently, but the lamas gave no sign of having heard. The knobs could come. They could bring machine guns. They could bring truncheons and the electric cattle prods they used to subdue Tibetan crowds. They could bring manacles for a lao gai prison, where Gendun and Shopo, as unlicensed monks, would be certain to serve at least five years. Nothing would rob the lamas of their joyful moment. Their mandala was almost complete.

The Golok reappeared, breathing hard, and grabbed Shopo by the shoulder, trying to pull him away. But the lama seemed immovable, as though he had taken root in the stone flags of the lhakang floor. The Golok muttered angrily, and tried Gendun, likewise without effect. Shan took a step toward the door, listening for the metallic rumble of a helicopter, even the pounding of knob boots. Shan would not be arrested as an illegal monk but as a lao gai fugitive, for his release from his Lhadrung prison had been unofficial, a favor from the local commander. The knobs would only have to check the number tattooed on his arm to discover that while Beijing had condemned him to lao gai, it had not approved his release.

As the horn stopped sounding, Shan stared at the alarmed Golok, who cursed now, confusion and fright in his eyes, his hand still on his knife hilt. He paused for a moment, wondering why the Golok did not simply flee, then stepped beside Lokesh and slowly sat down, cross-legged, forcing himself to gaze upon the painting. The lamas continued to work on the mandala. It would be time for Shan's white sand soon.

Suddenly the herder who had been in the corridor reappeared, panting, but wearing a pleased expression. The Golok quieted, and stepped toward the shadow by the wall, his hand still on his knife. The sturdy woman who had been stationed on the ridge stepped in behind her brother, followed a moment later by a tall thin man who crept around the doorframe, holding it, leaning against the wall as he stepped inside.

The man's face was clenched tight as he gazed about the chamber. Shan recognized the ruin of the man's forehead, the looping slash of scar tissue above his eyes. It was Drakte, the purba who had delivered Lokesh and Shan to the dropka with the promise that he would return. Drakte, who had been missing. But it was a pale, hollow Drakte, without the hard, proud glint that Shan had always seen on his features before.

"That one is coming," Drakte declared in a hoarse, strained voice. "There's no time." The young Tibetan seemed overcome with fatigue. He pressed his right hand against his abdomen and stepped toward the circle on the floor, turning his head back and forth as though searching for someone in particular. He looked into the shadows where Tenzin sat and paused for a moment, before he settled his gaze on Shan. "Take the eye," he said with a rush of breath. "Take the eye and run."

Nyma sighed and continued with her chakpa, outlining a mountain with blue sand. But Shan saw that Gendun stared at Drakte, his head slightly cocked, his eyes drawn, as if there was something about the purba he could not comprehend.

Lokesh stood and took a step toward Drakte, who raised his palm, arm outstretched, to warn the old man away.

"He doesn't care who has to die," Drakte groaned. "He wants to find the stone. He kills the thing he is. He kills prayer. I saw him kill. He can't be stopped. Just run," he repeated, the words coming out like a sob. "All you can do is run now. Save the eye. Save yourselves." He looked plaintively at Shan with these last words. "I'm sorry," he moaned, as though he owed Shan something.

Shan stood, chilled by the purba's words, uncertain what to do, and stepped to the edge of the sacred circle. He was about to reach out and steady the purba, to offer to take him away for a bowl of tea so they could speak more calmly about his fears, when the dropka woman gasped and dropped to the floor on her knees, bowing her head close to the floor in the direction of the door. The Golok groaned and darted behind the circle, toward the altar. Nyma looked up and let out a muffled cry, forgetting her chakpa, blue sand spilling in a small heap onto the mandala.

A grotesque creature stood on two legs in the doorway, its huge frame filling the entire space, its eyes wild and glaring at the purba. It was a man, Shan told himself, or had once been. He was so accustomed to Tibetan tales of demons, so familiar with the lamas' efforts to visualize deity demons, that for a moment he was not wholly certain whether the thing he saw was real. The second dropka called out the name of blessed Tara, protectress of the faithful, and dropped to the floor.

The intruder had a huge head in the shape of a man's but somehow bestial, with blackened cheeks and greased hair tied in a tight bob at the crown. The thing's shoulders were wider than the doorway and it had to twist and bend as it entered the chamber. One arm, protruding from a sleeveless brown robe, was wrapped above the elbow with a red cord, its hand holding a long staff nearly as thick as Shan's arm, ending above his shoulder in a gnarled knot of wood.

Shopo stood and extended his hand, palm outward, as if to greet the intruder. But before the lama could speak the stranger lashed out with his staff, striking Drakte in the belly and shouting at the purba. He spoke fast, and so loud his voice drowned out the wind. The dropka clamped their hands over their ears. The old schools of Tibetan Buddhism taught that there were evil mystics who spoke words of power that could enslave those who heard.

But the huge black-faced intruder seemed not to notice the dropka or even the lamas. He continued shouting at Drakte in his deep demonic voice, stabbing at the purba with his staff, hitting the young Tibetan in the belly, the arms, the thighs. Shan tried in vain to understand the words. They were Tibetan, but unintelligible to him. Perhaps it was old Tibetan, like that used in ancient teachings, or one of the many dialects spoken in Tibet's remote regions. He understood only the name of Yamantaka, Lord of the Dead.

Drakte's face drained of the little color it had left. The anger that filled his eyes for a moment was quickly replaced with fear. His hand went to his chest and he stepped back, trying to avoid the reach of the staff until, as Nyma gasped, Shan saw that the purba was standing in the center of their fragile mandala. Shan desperately looked about the room for a weapon that might be used to defend the purba. Drakte, his lips trembling, his eyes fixed on the demon, began reciting the mani mantra, invoking the Compassionate Buddha.

Abruptly, the intruder stopped speaking and stared malevolently at Drakte, shaking his staff in short jerking motions. The only sound in the room was that of the purba's mantra, until it tapered off into a low whimper. Drakte began to sway, as if a strong wind blew upon him. Shopo turned toward the young Tibetan and Drakte began to raise a hand as if to ask for help. But the hand trembled and slowly fell, and Shopo moaned. Shan followed the lama's gaze toward the mandala and shuddered. It was changing before them, its colors mixing, a dark cloud spreading over the intricate pattern as though something evil had overtaken it.

Struck dumb by the sight, unable to comprehend anything that had happened in the last few moments, Shan could only stare as Nyma, then the dropka, uttered forlorn cries and pointed at the swirling mandala. With a sudden stab of pain Shan understood. It was blood. Dark red blood was pooling around Drakte's feet, streaming out of his right pant leg, covering their precious mandala.

Shan took a hesitant step forward, then another, to reach out and help Drakte. The purba seemed to sense his intention and turned his hollow, confused eyes toward Shan. But in the next moment the swaying man toppled, dropping to his knees, then falling heavily onto his face, his jaw making a sickening crunching sound as it slammed against the stone floor.

Shan looked back toward the door. The demon had disappeared.

"It's no good," the dropka woman sobbed loudly. "We are ruined." Tears streamed down her face as she stared at the mandala, over which they had labored for two months. She meant the sacred painting was contaminated. The mandala was ruined. The deities would abandon it, and perhaps abandon them.

Lokesh darted past Shan and knelt by Drakte, cradling the purba's head. The old Tibetan's face sank, and with a low rapid murmur he began a different kind of prayer. Lokesh had recognized what Shan had seen in the young purba's glazed, unfocused eyes. Drakte was dead.

CHAPTER TWO

"The basic nature of your mind is luminosity and emptiness," Gendun intoned softly as he sat beside the young Tibetan's body. "It dwells as a great expanse of light beyond birth or death." He had begun reciting the Bardo ritual the instant he had seen Drakte's face, quietly offering the ancient words as the two dropka reverently straightened the body on the floor. There was no time to lose. The Tibetans believed Drakte was now sensing a great falling, a rush of wind, and the flashing of brilliant colors. He had not been prepared for the loss of his body and would be confused.

"Rinpoche," Nyma said to Gendun in a numbed voice, "the mandala for the—"

Gendun paused a moment, surveying the ruined mandala, the jagged eye, then Tenzin, who had rushed forward to kneel by Drakte, before finally settling his gaze on the dead man. "This is where the Compassionate Buddha has taken us," he declared, and continued the ritual. "You will leave this body of flesh and blood and know you are at peace," the lama recited from memory, his eyes nearly closed.

The dropka produced a blanket, onto which they lifted the body. With Gendun walking alongside still reciting the death rite, Lokesh and Tenzin slowly carried the dead man into the hut next door. As Nyma lit butter lamps they arranged the body in the traditional fashion, in a sitting position, leaning against the wall. Shan sat for a moment with the lama, his heart still pounding loudly, desperately trying to understand what had happened. Then he rose and stood at the door, looking outside. The Golok and the two herders were nervously pacing the perimeter of the small compound, the dropka woman was calling to the adjacent encampment, spreading the alarm. Shan looked back inside the hut. It appeared in the dim light that Gendun and Drakte were conversing.

In the lhakang Shopo began a second ceremony at the mandala. One by one, with Nyma and Lokesh sitting on either side, the lama began to address the images invoked in the sand painting, uttering to each a low prayer that had the sound of an apology. Shan sat with them for nearly thirty minutes; then, his confusion giving way to fear again, he stepped outside, to the doorway of the second hut, where Gendun still spoke to Drakte. He stared at the dead man, recalling the first time he had seen him in the Lhadrung valley, gathering food for families of prisoners. Drakte had worn the robes of a monk for several years before being forced out of his *gompa*, his monastery, when Beijing's Bureau of Religious Affairs had established strict limits on the number of active monks. In another age Drakte would have passed his life in a robe, learning and teaching the ways of compassion. But those who controlled the world Shan and Drakte lived in had told the young Tibetan he was not allowed to sit in a gompa and share the wisdom of the lamas.

He had been wrong, Shan told himself, to think they could be safe in their hidden hermitage, wrong to have let himself be drawn so deeply into the mandala ritual when danger lurked so near. Perhaps it had even been wrong for him to have become so focused, obsessed even, with the mandala and the hope it embodied. Shan had often listened as the lamas spoke with men like Drakte about the importance of letting compassion become the weapon of their struggle. Most of them replied that if they tried to defend their cause only with compassion, eventually all the compassionate would be dead.

He found himself wandering, walking as if in a daze, finally reaching his meditation place by the rocks. A cloud passed over the moon. The terrible scene kept playing again and again in his mind's eye: Drakte's life blood oozing over the mandala, Drakte staring helplessly at Shan. He restlessly watched the dimly lit horizon, then ventured toward the death hut again, thinking of entering. But the door was closed, and as he stepped closer he heard the Bardo, not in one voice but in two. The second voice was not that of Nyma, or Lokesh, or Shopo, all of whom remained in the lhakang. Someone else, a stranger, had joined Gendun. The second voice was almost like an echo of Gendun's soft, seasoned voice, but deeper—the voice of someone long schooled in the traditional ways, the voice of a teacher like Gendun. Shopo had told him other lamas sometimes came to meditate in secret at the hermitage. Or perhaps one of the dropka from the encampment knew the ceremony. Shan backed away. He could not bear to interrupt. Somehow he felt he had made it hard for Drakte to live. He didn't want to make it harder for him to die.

At dawn Shan asked the dropka woman to take him to the ridge and show him where she had first seen Drakte the night before. He followed her in silence through the grey light, up the steep switchback trail that connected the hermitage to the outside world. At the crest the dropka sank to the earth and warily inched herself forward to survey the valley beyond, as if expecting an ambush. After a long moment the woman pushed herself up and signaled for Shan to join her, but she did not wait for him. She jogged along the path at the crest for two hundred yards to the highest point of the ridge, where a rock cairn had been raised. When Shan caught up with the woman, she was busily adding rocks to the stack. The base of the cairn was ancient, thickly covered with grey-green lichen. But during the past weeks, while the dropka had been standing guard on the

24

ridge, the herders had added several rocks a day, building it to a height of over six feet, to gain the attention of the local deities. Now the woman was gathering rocks at a feverish pace, her face drawn with worry. If the dropka were not permitted weapons at the hermitage, at least they could add rocks to the cairn.

Shan lifted a large rock as he approached and set it near the top of the stack. A sad smile split the woman's leathery face and she pushed back the red braided headband she always wore, then silently retrieved another stone.

"I can't stop thinking that I caused it," she said at last, studying the valley with a haunted expression. "Maybe what I did brought that thing that killed him. I blew the horn when I saw Drakte coming, before I recognized him." She stared at the horn, laying on a cloth near the cairn. "Maybe my dungchen attracted it somehow."

"No," Shan said, trying to sound more certain than he felt, "this thing was already after Drakte, already after the stone. Drakte came to warn us." But the purba had also been coming to help them start their journey with the stone eye. The purba's last words haunted him as much as the image of the young Tibetan's blood soaking the mandala. Had he apologized to Shan for something he, Drakte, had done? Or because the journey would be impossible now? Perhaps both, because he had unleashed the demon on them.

"And died for it," the herder said. She grimaced in pain and clutched her chest, as if something inside had torn. "I knew Drakte. He was born in this county, to herders living only a day's walk from here. His mother was so proud when he became a monk. He helped rebuild this hermitage years ago. He always knew which families had members imprisoned, and brought others like him to help in their places. Drakte even brought me messages from my son, who is in prison near Lhasa for sheltering a monk years ago." She touched the headband, braided of red cloth. "He brought me this from my son, made from the robe of a monk who died."

The woman stared out over the long valley as the dawning sun washed over it. "But the thing he came to warn us about did not harm us," she said in a confused tone. "It just killed him and left. It could have taken the stone but it didn't. I heard Drakte say it will kill for the stone. We saw it kill him." The dropka searched Shan's face. "It must be waiting somewhere in the mountains to return. Now that it knows. Tonight. Does it only do its killing at night?"

Shan only shook his head sadly. He extended a hand toward the head of the valley. "How did you see Drakte in the dark? You must have sounded the horn because you saw him. Was it only him?"

"There was nearly a half-moon. I have sat with our herds on many such nights, watching for wolves and snow lions with my sling. In such light, without clouds, I can see a great distance. I knew someone was coming. By the time he reached the valley floor I could see him plainly where he passed through patches of snow. Only him. But first I heard the dogs."

"Dogs?"

"From down the valley. Dogs barked from where the valley bends, where there had been no dogs for all these weeks." She pointed toward a large set of outcroppings nearly a mile away. "I began to watch more closely. At first I thought it might have been Tenzin."

"Tenzin?" Shan asked in surprise.

"He goes away at night sometimes. Two nights ago, and one night last week. I think he goes to places where he can pray in the moonlight. There are prayers that should only be said at night, and things that are perhaps best said only to the moon." She looked at Shan pointedly then shook her head and looked back down the valley. "I never suspected it was Drakte. I wouldn't have sounded the warning. He would always stop to talk with dogs he met, they wouldn't bark like that. And I knew his gait. He always walked straight, proud, like a warrior. But last night he acted so strange, trotting in plain sight in the moonlight, then sometimes stopping at rock outcroppings, as if trying to hide, like for an ambush."

"Or to see if he were being followed." In his mind's eye Shan replayed Drakte's entry into the chamber, followed moments later by the intruder. No, the purba had been shocked to see the huge man with the staff. He had not expected the intruder, had not expected to be followed. There had to be another reason he had been pausing at the rocks, another explanation for his strange behavior.

"When he finally climbed the ridge and he saw you what did he say?"

"I recognized him when he reached the crest, and waved. He said nothing, just pointed toward the hermitage. I went down with him, because I had blown the horn and didn't want the others to be alarmed, to think trouble was . . ." The words choked in the woman's throat. She had gone down from her post to assure them no one dangerous was coming after all. But while she was away from her post something very dangerous indeed had come.

"That thing. It was a powerful demon, to make us see the spear that way." The woman's voice was nearly a whisper.

"Spear? There was no spear."

"Of course you didn't see it, none of us did. But we all saw how Drakte was stabbed. That demon made the rest of us see it as just a staff."

Shan stared at the woman, considering her words, until he saw that the dropka had begun to stare past his shoulder. He turned to see Shopo cresting the ridge, walking down toward the long valley below, a cloth bundle slung over his shoulder.

"Blessed Buddha," the woman said in her mournful voice. "The sand." She touched the gau on her neck as she spoke. "He has to return the sands to the nagas, to the water deities."

"But in daylight he can be easily spotted by the patrols," Shan said in alarm, taking a step forward as he considered whether to run and stop the lama. "He could be arrested. Can't he wait?"

The dropka looked at Shan, gazing plaintively toward the mountains across the valley, as if asking the deities why she had to be burdened with such a Chinese. She shook her head. "All that blood. And just as they were finishing, after all the weeks of prayers. At least it hadn't received the final consecration," she said heavily, as if an even greater catastrophe had been narrowly avoided. She gazed down at the solitary figure descending into the empty valley, and shook her head. "When they had finished Shopo would have gone to thank the nagas and tell them what a beautiful thing had been done with their gift, how it had been used to begin patching a god. Think of what he'll have to say to them now," the woman whispered, and a tear rolled down her cheek.

Shan watched the lama's retreating figure a moment in silence. "If there were dogs," he said, "maybe herders were at the head of the valley last night. Maybe someone could find them, and ask them what happened. I must stay with Gendun, but we need to know what happened out there last night."

When the woman gave no sign of hearing, Shan wandered back toward the switchback trail, leaving the forlorn dropka alone, stacking rocks again. He paused before beginning the descent to the hermitage, surveying the vast rugged landscape. Beyond the low spine of mountains on the far side of the valley he saw another range, higher again, the air shimmering behind it, its peaks snowcovered and lit a dazzling white by the early sun. It was how he felt. No matter how he tried, how hard he climbed, whenever he reached a new height, a new understanding, a new connection with his teachers, another mountain rose up, another obstacle presented itself, another mystery blocked his path. Once Lokesh had described it to him as the burden of being Shan. "Things we see as inevitable turns in the path of our lives, you see as enigmas you must stop to understand. It is the way you have of teaching yourself," his friend had added with a tinge of curiosity in his voice. But teaching implied learning, advancing with new knowledge. And Shan's path seemed to be relentlessly telling him how much he did not know.

As he began to turn toward the hermitage he caught movement on the valley floor. A black figure moved impossibly fast along the trail—on foot—so fast another pang of fear stabbed through Shan. Was it the same unnatural creature that had caught up with Drakte in the lhakang? Shan crouched in the low grass and watched in alarm as, far below, Shopo stopped and stared at the approaching figure. The dropka at the cairn groaned loudly and grabbed her horn, then stared at the figure in confusion. Old Tibetans told tales of mystic runners called *lunggompas* who could travel hundreds of miles in a day by summoning superhuman strength and training their bodies to ignore fatigue.

The figure slowed momentarily as it passed Shopo, then resumed its unnatural gait to ascend the ridge where Shan stood, toward the hermitage. The dropka lowered the horn. The intruder had not harmed nor even challenged the lama with his bundle of sand. Shan sat down on a rock near the path and waited. The runner, clad in a black-hooded sweatsuit, saw Shan from fifty feet away, slowed, then silently approached and sat across from him, cross-legged. After a moment the stranger produced a water bottle from a belt under the sweatsuit, briefly drank, and flipped back the hood.

It was a young Tibetan woman with a thin face and intense black eyes. "You must be the Chinese." She spoke in a stern voice, breathing deeply, though not panting as she should have been after such an arduous climb. After studying him a moment, she reached back to release two braids of hair which had been pinned close to her ears and arranged them, as if suddenly concerned about her appearance. "I am looking for Drakte."

"You're a purba," Shan suggested.

"I am a schoolteacher," the young woman shot back.

"There are no children here," Shan observed quietly.

The woman fixed Shan with a cold, challenging stare. "The Chinese said go to university to become a teacher, become a model for Tibetan youth," she said when he silently returned the stare. "So I went to university. They said run on the track team so we can have a Tibetan endurance runner to compete in China. So I did. I won medals in Beijing and I returned to my home district to be that model citizen." She spoke loudly. She was relating the story to taunt him. "But after a year of teaching they said no more classes in Tibetan. Only speak Chinese, only use Chinese books. And I said no, I will speak to Tibetan children in their own tongue. That is what a model Tibetan citizen does." She raised the bottle and drank deeply. "One day I came to my school and a Chinese teacher had taken my class. They had emptied my office, even took all my medals." She gazed down at the hermitage, then looked back at Shan. "But they didn't take my legs."

"So now you run for the purbas."

"I can go places horses and trucks can't."

"A purba lunggompa."

The woman gave an impatient shrug and pursed her lips in a frown, as if to emphasize that she was not impressed with his wit. After a moment she glanced back at the trail she had climbed.

"Are you being followed?" Shan asked.

"I need to see Drakte," she said.

"He's—" Shan's tongue seemed to grow heavy. He looked toward the buildings below.

Without waiting for another word the woman sprang up, bottle still in hand, and descended the steep ridge with the long leaps of an antelope.

Shan caught up with the woman in the death hut. She was leaning against the wall, drained of color, clutching her belly as she stared at the dead man. Her water bottle lay by her feet, its contents trickling onto the floor. Lokesh and Tenzin sat by the body with a bowl of water and a cloth, reverently washing Drakte's limbs. The brother of the woman on the ridge was lighting sticks of incense. Gendun sat in the shadows, softly continuing the Bardo rites, his eyes closed.

Shan lifted the water bottle. "Did you have a message for him?" he asked in a near whisper.

The woman did not reply. She approached the corpse and knelt, then slowly extended her fingers toward its face, as though to touch Drakte's cheek, but pulled them back before reaching his skin. "Who?" she asked in a cracking voice. "Who saw this happen? Who did this?" Her eyes shot toward Shan. Everyone knew who killed purbas.

"We all saw him killed," the dropka said with a shudder. "A curse was put on him and his blood poured out."

"No one," Shan disagreed. "No one saw him killed. We just saw him die. An intruder came and hit him in the belly with a staff. But not hard enough to make him bleed that way." He returned the woman's icy stare, until she raised a hand to wipe away a tear. "Our sentry above said Drakte was acting strange," he said more softly, "stopping along the valley floor. I think it was because he was already hurt." Shan approached the body and knelt by Lokesh, then lifted the bloodstained shirttail. He had been too shocked to investigate the body the night before. But now he had to understand. He raised the shirt and folded it back to expose the right abdomen. A four inch gout of tissue lay open, surrounded by a stain of congealed blood that ran down his hip. Now he remembered how, when he helped lift Drakte onto the blanket the night before, the purba's abdomen had felt unnaturally hard. Because he had been hemorrhaging internally.

"He was stabbed!" the woman groaned.

"Not last night," Shan said, and pointed to several threads extending from the sides of the wound, where it had been crudely sewn together. "This wound was made earlier, slicing deep into his organs." The makeshift sutures had burst apart, no doubt when the intruder pummeled Drakte with his staff.

The woman made a wrenching sound—half groan, half cry—then cut it off by clenching a knuckle between her teeth. "Last year," she said after a moment, her voice trembling, "Drakte slashed his arm when we were climbing some rocks above an army base." She knelt and rolled up Drakte's left sleeve, exposing a rough six-inch scar on his forearm. "He laughed when I said, Go to a doctor. He said it was too hard to find a good Tibetan doctor. He said bad things happened to Tibetans in Chinese hospitals. So he just sewed it up himself. No painkillers. Just a big needle and some yak hair thread he borrowed from a dropka who was repairing his tent."

Shan remembered how weak Drakte had appeared when he had arrived the night before, how he had leaned against the wall for support before stumbling toward the center of the room. The dropka guard said he had lingered at outcroppings as though watching for someone. He hadn't been watching, Shan was certain now, he had been resting, nursing his wound, summoning his strength to reach the hermitage. Drakte had thought he was free of his attacker, had even taken the time, hours earlier, to sew up the wound.

The purba runner leaned closer to Drakte's head and seemed to whisper something in the dead man's ear. When she straightened more tears were streaming down her cheeks. Shan remembered how she had tended to her braids on the ridge.

They sat in silence, watching as Lokesh gently washed the blood from the wound and replaced the shirttail. Tenzin continued to help, holding a bowl of water, but then he suddenly halted, his breath catching, and he set the bowl down with shaking hands as he studied the dead man again. He pushed back and leaned against the wall, grief abruptly twisting his face. The woman's eyes glazed and she seemed to forget the rest of them. Her hand rose again and she traced with one finger the long curving scar on Drakte's forehead, cupped her palm around his cheek then absently traced the scar once more. The motion had an intimate air, like a gesture of affection Drakte might still recognize.

"You would have been such a lama," Shan heard her whisper. "You would have lived to be a hundred and carried on the true ways." She laid her palm on his cheek. "Who will be the old ones when you should have been old?" she asked the dead man. Slowly her hand dropped, and when she turned, though her eyes brimmed with moisture, her voice was cool and steady. "What do you mean he was cursed?" she asked the dropka.

"A demon came and spoke words of power," a voice interjected from behind Shan. The Golok stood in the doorway. "We know why," he said in a taunting tone toward Lokesh and Gendun. "It's because that demon won't have another Chinese taking the eye."

Shan's gaze shifted from the Golok to Lokesh, who seemed as confused by the words as Shan himself. Lokesh shrugged at Shan, looked at the man and frowned. "Not a demon," he said. "A *dobdob*. If it were a demon he'd be back for someone like you, who speaks with such disrespect around the dead."

Shan gazed with surprise at his old friend. It was not like Lokesh to rebuke anyone. The Golok answered with an exaggerated wince then stepped back and left the hut.

They finished cleaning the body as best they could, lit more butter lamps, and went outside. Shan lingered for a moment at the door, longing to speak with Gendun, to make certain the lama would be ready to flee with them. But Gendun continued the Bardo, staring now at one of the flames near Drakte. Gendun had lived in a hidden hermitage, carved inside a mountain, almost his entire life. The first Chinese he had ever met had been Shan, the year before. The first time he had left his own hermitage in decades had been only four months earlier. The thing he could not get used to about the outside world, he had sadly confided to Shan, was how many good people died without having prepared their souls, as if they had not taken their gift of human incarnation seriously.

As he stepped outside, Shan was relieved to see the Golok preparing a short grey horse for travel. The dropka guard squatted at a small fire between two of the buildings, protected from the wind, working a churn to mix buttered tea, casting anxious glances toward the ridge where his sister still stacked stones. Lokesh, Shan, and the purba runner squatted by the man as he poured out bowls for each of them.

"I don't understand," Shan said to Lokesh. "You know who that was last night? A dobdob you said. It is not a word I have heard before."

"Not who, but what he was," Lokesh said with wide eyes. "A monk policeman. A dobdob enforces virtue, enforces respect for the lamas. All the big gompas had them when I was a boy. First time I saw one I thought it was a monster, too. The cheeks darkened with ash. The big shoulders. They put special boards on their shoulders sometimes, under their robes, to make them look bigger than life. I hid behind my father, that first time, until the dobdob was gone. I hadn't seen one for forty years at least," the old Tibetan added with a distant gaze. As a former member of the Dalai Lama's government Lokesh had spent nearly half his life in a gulag prison. "They kept order in the ranks at large assemblies. Enforced rules of the gompa's abbot. Helped monks adhere to their vows with their staffs and their yaktail whips." He raised his fist and brought it down with a sudden jerking motion. "If a novice was speaking out of turn, one tap with a staff on his skull would shut him up fast."

"But here," the purba said. "Last night? It's impossible. They don't exist anymore."

"The ghost of a dobdob," the dropka said, not with fear, but a certain awe. "He just appeared, punished Drakte, and evaporated, the way spirit creatures do at night. He doesn't want us here. Next time," he said to the runner in a somber tone, "next time the purbas need watchers here, they can ask someone else."

"A ghost didn't slice open his abdomen," Shan said. "A ghost didn't attack him and chase him over the mountains."

"Drakte warned us, said he saw him kill," the herder whispered. "We saw the one he meant, and minutes later Drakte himself was dead."

The purba woman gazed into her bowl. "Drakte was the one who had the idea about runners," she said in a distant voice, as if she owed him a eulogy. "He arranged for me to train others. He had been in prison for leading a demonstration in Lhasa on the Dalai Lama's birthday. I met him that day, sang songs with him, saw him get dragged away by the soldiers. Later I visited him in prison, and was there the day he was released. For the first month all he did was find food and bring it to the families of each of his cellmates." She looked up from her bowl. "What will happen to him?" Her eyes brimmed with tears again.

"We are making arrangements." The dropka put a comforting hand on her shoulder. "There is a *durtro* on top of a mountain overlooking the sacred lake. When the time comes we will take him there."

A durtro. The herder meant a sky burial site, a charnel ground where the *ragyapa*, the body breakers, would cut the body up and feed it to vultures. Three days after death, when the body was properly blessed, Drakte's remains would be carried to the durtro and chopped into pieces to be returned to the circle of life. Even his bones would be pounded into a paste to be eaten by the birds.

"Don't let the Chinese get him," the purba said in an urgent, pleading voice. "Don't let them know."

The dropka nodded gravely.

The woman stared at Shan but quickly looked away as he met her eyes. "My name is Somo," she said nearly in a whisper. It was her way of apologizing, he realized, to show that despite what she thought about other Chinese, she would trust him with her name because Drakte had done so.

"I am called Shan."

She nodded. "I heard about you even when you were in prison."

"Were you with Drakte in Lhadrung?" Shan asked.

Somo shook her head. "Usually in Lhasa. He spent much of his time there, and the lands north of here, where he was born."

"When were you last in Lhasa with him?"

"Nearly three months ago, the last time," the woman said warily. It had been more than two months ago when the eye had been brought to the hermitage, and weeks before that it had been stolen in Lhasa. "Drakte said you did things in prison to help the old lamas there. There was an old official from the Fourteenth's government you got released."

Lokesh gave one of his hoarse laughs and looked at Shan with amusement.

Somo studied the two men a moment. "You?" she asked Lokesh in disbelief.

The old man nodded. "I was going to die in that prison," he said, still grinning, "but Xiao Shan found a different path for me." Xiao Shan. Little Shan. It was Chinese, but Lokesh sometimes used the term of affection from Shan's childhood, one used traditionally by an older person addressing a younger one, as Shan's long-dead uncles once had done.

Shan stared into his bowl. "I was already dead, and they brought me back to life," he said, and gazed back at the hut where Gendun still sat with Drakte. The Bardo had to be recited for twenty-four hours after the purba's death. In their lao gai prison, when an inmate died the oldest lamas took shifts of four hours each, even while breaking rocks on their road crews, reciting the words from memory. Always the oldest, because the

32

younger monks had had their education cut short by the Chinese and did not know all the words.

"There is no one else," Lokesh said, as if reading Shan's mind. "I only know the first hour of the ritual. We have no text to recite from."

"I heard someone else, last night," Shan said. "We can't wait a day."

"There is no one else," Lokesh repeated.

Shan looked toward the death hut in confusion. It was true. He had seen no one else. Had it been some strange echo, or Drakte trying to reach out to Gendun?

"But you can't stay," Somo protested. "Whatever Drakte was trying to warn us about—" she glanced at Shan, "it's too dangerous. That's what he was telling you last night."

As if in answer, Lokesh rose and walked into the small lhakang. Shan followed him inside. Nyma was there, praying by the altar in a low, nervous voice. It sounded almost as though she were arguing with the eye, which had been pushed to the front edge of the altar toward a small wooden box, lined with a felt cloth, which lay open on the floor below.

When the nun saw Shan her eyes brightened and she rose to stand by the altar, gazing expectantly at him. When Shan did nothing she gestured at the box.

"Are you scared to touch it?" Shan asked.

"Yes," the nun said readily. "I pushed it with a chakpa to the edge," she explained, as if that was the most she could be expected to do.

Lokesh sighed and bent to pick up the box. Shan stepped forward, glancing uncertainly at the nun, and set the jagged piece of stone in the box. Lokesh folded the felt to cover it and closed the lid.

"But we have time," Shan said. "Rinpoche will not be done until late tonight."

Lokesh stepped outside without reply, still clutching the box. The Golok was near the door, tightening the saddle on his sturdy mountain horse. He was leaving, and Shan had never understood why the man had come. But then, to Shan's dismay, the Golok stepped to a brown horse that now stood beside his own, opened its saddlebag and extended his hand toward Lokesh just as Tenzin and one of the herders rounded the corner of the farthest hut, leading more horses.

"We should have left at dawn," the Golok said with an impatient gesture for Lokesh to hand him the box. "Didn't you listen? The killer is out there, he's coming for the stone, that purba said so. And you wait around like old women."

Shan looked pleadingly at Lokesh as the Golok set the box in the open saddlebag.

"I do not understand much of this," his old friend said with a despairing shrug. "But I do understand we must go."

"But Gendun," Shan protested. "He must come with us."

33

Lokesh shook his head sadly. "What he must do now is stay with Drakte. He will go to the durtro, then if the deities permit, he will join us." He turned and pulled something from the saddle of one of the horses, extending it to Shan. It was a broad-rimmed felt hat, Shan's traveling hat.

"I am staying with Drakte also," Somo announced, her tone strangely defiant. "I will see that your lama is safe. The herders from that camp above are making piles of yak dung in a ring around the hermitage. Tonight they will surround us with fires."

As the dropka extended the reins of the brown horse to Shan, the Golok stepped away from his own horse and, arms crossed over his chest, fixed them with a pointed stare as if they had forgotten something. "I was going to be paid," he said sourly. "A guide has to be paid. That boy who died said I would be paid. So far I haven't received a fen."

Shan stared at the man with a sinking feeling. The Golok had finally explained why he had come to the hermitage.

"I have nothing," Nyma said in alarm. "Drakte had nothing, nothing but an old account book and a shepherd's sling." They had found the battered ledger in a pouch hanging from his belt, with entries that had the appearance of accounting reports. "It must mean those at your destination will—"

"I told that Drakte," interrupted the Golok. "I don't face patrols unless there's profit."

Somo reached into her small belt pouch and produced an object wrapped in felt, extended it toward the Golok. "Here," she said in a reluctant voice. She shook the cover away to reveal a finely worked silver bracelet set with lapis. "Drakte gave this to me last month," she added. Her gaze shifted to Nyma, then Shan. "He would want your journey to continue. That was why . . ." She looked back toward the death hut without finishing the sentence.

The Golok grabbed the bracelet and studied it with a frown. "Hard to convert this to cash without going to a damned city," he complained, even as he stuffed the bracelet into his pocket. "I'm not going to a city again for a long time."

The purba runner reached into her pouch again and produced a complicated pocketknife with many blades, even a spoon folded into one side. "I got this for Drakte," she said in a tight voice and extended the knife toward the man.

The Golok snatched the knife and the reins of his horse almost in one motion.

"We don't even know your name," Shan ventured in a hesitant voice. He saw that something else had appeared in Somo's hand, out of her pocket: a small turquoise stone which she began kneading with her fingers. Something else given her by Drakte, Shan suspected, something she would not part with.

"Dremu." The Golok fixed Shan with another frown. "My mother

34

called me Dremu," he said, as if he had been called many names in his life. Shan and Lokesh exchanged a worried glance. Dremu was the name of the great brown bear that had once freely roamed the Tibetan ranges. Hunted to near extinction by the Chinese, it was a symbol in Tibetan folklore of one who harms himself through excessive greed, for the animal would tear into the burrows of its main prey, marmots, pulling out stunned animals and piling them behind it until the burrow was destroyed. More often than not, the marmots would recover their senses and flee while the bear still dug, leaving it still hungry and angrier than ever. Sometimes the Tibetans used the term for the Chinese.

As Tenzin and Nyma led their horses toward the trail, Shan poured a bowl of tea and stepped inside the hut where Gendun sat with the dead man. He stood for a moment in silence until the lama looked up and acknowledged him with a small nod. After another minute's recitation, Gendun rose and stepped back from the body.

The lama accepted the bowl and drank deeply before speaking. "It wasn't anguish he felt at the end," Gendun declared, looking at the body. Shan had never known a voice like Gendun's. The lama's words often came in a whisper, but his whispers were as clear and powerful as a great bell. "It was only sadness at leaving important things uncompleted. It is very difficult for him to give up." The Tibetans believed that there was a period after death, sometimes lasting days, when a spirit was confused and would not accept that its incarnation was extinguished, when it might struggle to reanimate the lost body, to continue unfinished work.

"Rinpoche," Shan said, "the stone eye is packed on a horse." His gaze lingered upon the dead man. "But I cannot do this thing without you."

"Drakte will learn to leave his body behind, my friend. So must you."

"Drakte lost his life. That thing, that dobdob, could come back." Shan looked away, into one of the small flames, and felt a sudden sense of desolation. Only hours before he had decided there could be nothing more important than returning the stone, for he, like the Tibetans, had come to see it as one of the seeds to be planted to keep the wisdom and compassion alive. But everything had changed when Drakte had arrived at the lhakang. Although Gendun and Lokesh would resist, would say Shan was denying his own deity, he had to solve the mystery of Drakte's death. Because as important as returning the eye may be, there was something else, something he would sacrifice even his inner deity for, and that was keeping the old Tibetans safe.

"And a valley of people lost their deity," his teacher replied. He let the words hang in the air a moment, until Shan looked back into his eyes. "It will be your greatest test. Look forward. Look inside. Not behind you. You must stop being the seeker you were and become the seeker you want to be."

It was a topic of many conversations between them. Shan's biggest spiritual handicap was his obsession with the workings of what Gendun called the fleeting, unimportant mysteries of the surface world when he should be looking to the mystery of his soul.

"You must stop being a seeker of fact and become a seeker of truth," Gendun said. "That is how deities are repaired."

"Rinpoche, after the durtro, don't try to find us," Shan said abruptly. Gendun looked at him, and Shan's face flushed. The words sounded like Shan was bargaining, as if he were asking Gendun to at least acknowledge the danger that he always ignored. "You must go back to Yerpa," Shan said, referring to the secret hermitage inside a mountain above Lhadrung, where Gendun was the principal teacher to a handful of monks. "Please."

"My boots." Gendun nodded toward to his feet, where the soles of his old work boots had split open at the toe. "My boots are tired," he said, as though agreeing. "But first I must deliver the earth part of Drakte back to the earth," he said quietly, looking at the dead man a moment before turning back to Shan. "May the Compassionate Buddha watch over you," he whispered.

A single dried, brown leaf blew into the doorway. They watched in silence as the wind carried it out again, past the cluster of buildings and up into the air, until it soared out of sight. They both stared at the empty place it had been; then, as if the leaf had been a signal, Gendun turned toward Drakte, pausing to fix Shan with a brief gaze that somehow expressed worry and hope at the same time. "Beware of the dust and air," he said with a note of finality, then sat and began reciting the Bardo again.

Beware of the dust and air. It was one of Gendun's customary farewells, a way of saying pay attention only to the essence of what you encounter.

But something made Shan turn back as he reached the door. Gendun paused and slowly brought his eyes back to Shan's. There was an exquisite silence between them for a moment, and Shan fought the urge to go to Gendun's side and not move until the Bardo was done.

"The deity you find, Shan, will be the one you take with you," Gendun said quietly, punctuating the words with another long stare before he turned back to Drakte.

As Shan stepped outside he realized the hairs on his arms were standing on end. He stood perfectly still a moment, looking at his hands, which trembled. Slowly, stumbling over his own boots, he stepped toward his horse, ignoring the Golok's impatient gestures for him to mount. As he lifted the reins he looked back at Somo, who stood at the door to the lhakang now. "You never did tell us what it was, the message you were carrying for Drakte," he said.

The woman frowned. "It was a purba message."

"It was about the eye," Shan said, "if you were coming here."

"The lamas. The government is sweeping the mountains for unregistered lamas."

"No. We knew that already."

She glanced back toward the death hut, then hesitantly stepped to Shan's side. "All right. We didn't think Drakte knew. He had to be warned before he started for that valley with you. They're moving north, a head-quarters unit from Lhasa," Somo declared cryptically. "That was my message. A small unit." She bit her lower lip. "Platoon strength, that's what I was to say to Drakte."

"I'm sorry," Shan said, his throat suddenly bone dry. "I don't understand."

"I guess it means you must move quickly now. This Golok must know secret trails." She saw the confusion in Shan's eyes and glanced at Nyma. "No one told you about the struggle over that old stone eye? Someone else thinks they own it. It was taken from them in Lhasa. They want it back."

"Who?" Shan asked with a sinking heart.

Somo bit her lip again, then answered slowly, in a chill tone. "The 54th Mountain Combat Brigade of the People's Liberation Army."

Chapter Three

They rode not north, as Shan expected, but west, climbing the high ridge on the far side of the long valley, then descending toward the second snowcapped range of mountains beyond it. As he rode over the crest and out of the valley that led to the hermitage, Shan reined in his horse and watched Dremu trot off to scout ahead. He looked back to the ridge where the dropka had stacked rocks to protect the lamas, toward the hermitage. Gendun had been sheltered inside his own secret hermitage above Lhadrung until Shan had discovered it. Gendun might never have been exposed to the outside world except for Shan.

"When we arrived there, before the mandala began, I talked with Shopo," said Lokesh, at his side. The old man had an uncanny ability to read Shan's emotions. "They didn't know Gendun. He just arrived and sat in the lhakang for hours contemplating the stone eye. Then he drank tea with Shopo and said he knew that eye now, and he knew who would return the eye, as certain as if he had read it in a book where the future is written. Shopo said he hadn't been sure himself, but Gendun would not be swayed. He knew it had to be you. He said not only did you have a pure heart, you had a big heart, so big it was a burden to you."

So big its pain almost overpowered Shan. If the killer was stalking the eye he had no choice but to take it away from the lamas. And going with it was the only way he would find the killer. He could only protect the lamas by leaving the lamas.

Shan cast an awkward glance at Lokesh, who grinned back, leaned over like a mischievous uncle and pulled Shan's hat brim down over his eyes, then trotted away toward a clump of flowers. It was how Lokesh always traveled, not in a straight line but from flower to flower, or rock to rock, stopping to examine the shapes of nature in whatever form might capture his curiosity. He turned toward the Golok, who was moving so quickly away he seemed to be fleeing them. He did not trust the man. But Drakte had, or at least Dremu wanted Shan and the others to believe he had. Dremu knew about the eye but none of the others left alive knew about him. Drakte had apparently known him, but from where? The only logical answer seemed to be from prison. Shan checked the binding on his saddlebag, then reluctantly urged his horse forward.

Three hours later Dremu waited for them at the crest of the lowest ridge in the second range, their mounts following a winding goat trail through patches of snow. The air beyond still shimmered, as Shan had seen from a distance, and as they reached the crest he discovered the reason.

"Lha gyal lo!" Lokesh called out with a boyish glee as he rode up behind Shan, pointing to the vast flat expanse of turquoise that dominated the landscape below them. "Lamtso!"

Shan stared at the distant water. It looked like a long jewel inlaid between the mountains. Lamtso was one of Tibet's holy lakes, its waters known as the home of important nagas, its shores a favorite grazing ground for the dropka herds.

From a bag tied to his horse the Golok produced a large plastic water bottle filled not with water but with amber *chang*, Tibetan barley beer. He did not open it, but quickly surveyed the faces of his companions. "We sleep there tonight," he announced with a gesture toward the water. "If we move fast enough," he added with a frown toward Lokesh. The Golok paused and squinted toward the horizon behind them. Shan followed his gaze toward the valley they had just traversed. A small band of horsemen was pursuing them. Or perhaps not pursuing them, he realized, for they had stopped as well and had spread out, watching behind them.

"Those dropka," Dremu said. "They are worried about you, Chinese. They think they can try to guard your back but they don't know the kind of trouble that follows. How many Tibetans are you worth, comrade?" he asked, aiming a bitter glance at Shan, then kicked his horse into a gallop and disappeared around a bend in the trail.

They caught up with him a quarter hour later, waiting at a huge outcropping of rock, a leg draped over his horse's neck, nearly half the bottle gone. As Nyma and Tenzin began to ease their mounts around him, the Golok raised a hand in warning. "Wouldn't if I were you."

"I think we can find the lake from here," Nyma declared impatiently.

Dremu pointed toward a small dust cloud on the rough track in the low rolling hills that led toward the lake. Shan reached into the drawstring sack tied to his saddle and produced his battered pair of field glasses. He focused on the cloud a moment and sighed, then handed the glasses to the nun.

"Army!" Nyma gasped.

"One truck," the Golok grunted. "No more than five or ten soldiers."

With a sudden tightening in his stomach Shan studied the approaching vehicle. It was still over two miles away, speeding not toward them but toward the lake. As he watched, however, the truck stopped. The nun cried out and bent down as though to hide behind his horse's neck. "I saw a glint of something. I think they're searching the mountains with binoculars!"

The Golok scowled at the nun. "That's what soldiers do. Could mean a hundred things. Could be escorting a birth inspector," he said, referring to the hated bureaucrats who enforced China's birth quotas. "Could be out hunting wild goats. Could be searching for something stolen from them," he added with a meaningful gaze at Shan, then reached for the glasses. "The way that truck is painted in shades of grey, could be mountain troops," he added in a tone like a curse. "I'd rather go against the damned knobs."

Shan looked back down the trail. Lokesh had lingered behind again, stopping his horse to stare down at a pattern of lichen on a rock face. Since their pilgrimage his old friend had particularly sought out self-actuated symbols of the Buddha—meaning elements of nature that had assumed the shape of a sacred object. More than once he had abandoned a piece of clothing or some food from his own drawstring sack in order to make room for a rock with lichen in the shape of a sacred emblem, or a weathered bone shaped like a ritual offering.

The Golok pointed with his bottle toward a shadow below an outcropping a hundred feet away. Nyma sighed with relief and pushed her mount toward the opening.

Shan doubted there was any land on the planet with more natural caves than Tibet. Certainly there was no land where caves were so integrated into the story of its people. There were cave hermitages, cave shrines, even entire gompas built around caves. Centuries before, Guru Rinpoche, the most revered of the ancient teaching lamas, was believed to have deposited sacred objects and scriptures in caves throughout Tibet. Tibetans still kept watch for forgotten caves that might harbor some of the Guru's sacred treasures. And many of the local protector deities that watched over valleys and mountains were said to make their homes in caves.

Although the cave was low and wide at its mouth, it quickly narrowed into a small tunnel. The horses seemed to understand what was expected of them, and as soon as their riders dismounted the animals scurried to the back of the entrance chamber. Lokesh arrived and began helping Tenzin loosen the saddle girths, speaking in comforting tones to the animals as the Golok and Nyma settled onto rocks at opposite sides of the entrance. Dremu lifted his bottle and gulped noisily, not offering it to anyone else.

"You knew about the army having the eye," Shan said to Dremu and Nyma. "Both of you knew."

"I told you," the Golok said with a wide grin that exposed several of his yellow-brown teeth. The only thing Dremu had told Shan was that he could die a hundred ways.

"Why would the army want an old stone eye?" he asked Nyma.

"Most people in the northern changtang know about the army and the eye."

"I don't. I'm not sure Gendun did."

"It was a long time ago. From an invasion," Nyma offered in a reluctant voice.

"You mean the stone was taken as some kind of trophy fifty years ago," Shan said, referring to the arrival of the People's Liberation Army.

"Not that invasion," Nyma sighed.

Shan sensed movement behind him and saw Lokesh standing at his shoulder now.

"It was when a Chinese army came to drive the Thirteenth out of Tibet in the Year of the Female Water Hare," Nyma explained. She meant the invasion early in the twentieth century. When, Shan recalled, imperial troops had marched into Lhasa, leaving a bloody swath across eastern and northern Tibet in an effort to unseat the Thirteenth Dalai Lama.

"Terrible things happened," the nun continued in a brittle voice. "Chinese soldiers under a General named Feng razed gompas and buried the monks alive, hundreds of monks. Butcher Feng, they called the General. After several years the Tibetan army finally organized a defense and pushed Feng back. There was a terrible fight at the Turquoise Bridge in Lhasa, where the Lujun Combat Division was driven into retreat by Tibetan soldiers. The Lujun were the crack troops of the Chinese army. They were humiliated and wanted to avenge themselves. But the generals ordered the Lujun home because their Empress Dowager had died and more soldiers were needed to keep order in Beijing. The troops marched up the old northern route—the Changlam, it was called—annihilating gompas, killing all monks and nuns they encountered on the way." Nyma hesitated a moment, studying a dark black cloud that had appeared on the horizon. "They were on the Changlam, two hundred miles north of Lhasa when they learned that the home of the senior officer of the troops that defeated the Lujun in Lhasa was a village only twenty miles to the west. They marched on the village and when they found the villagers treating wounded soldiers, they set up cannon and destroyed it. Only one house survived."

The nun stood, staring more intensely at the black cloud, which was rapidly approaching. Suddenly she bent and darted to the edge of the outcropping. The Golok belched toward the nun, then raised his bottle in salute.

After a moment Nyma walked back to the cave. "They haven't moved," she announced. "That's good, right?"

When no one replied, she continued her story. "That village, or the valley where the village was, was the home of the Yapchi deity. For centuries that deity had lived in a self-actuated statue, a rock shaped like a sitting Buddha. Two eyes had been painted on it in ancient times, so it could better see the world and to remind those who lived in the valley that it was always watching."

"And the soldiers took the statue?" Shan asked.

"Not exactly," Nyma said in a melancholy tone. "When they finished shelling, the Tibetan soldiers were dead, for they had been too weak to flee. The surviving villagers ran to the deity in the center of the valley, about fifty of them, mostly women and children and old men. The Chinese officer of the Lujun laughed and called for them to surrender. If they agreed to be their porters, to carry the soldiers' equipment to the Chinese border, he would let them live. When they refused he selected ten soldiers and sent them with swords among the villagers. They slaughtered the people like goats, cut them into pieces, laughing like it was great sport. No one from that Tibetan officer's family survived."

She turned suddenly and stared at the blackness at the back of the chamber, as if she felt she were being watched from inside the mountain. "Only those few who happened to be away from the village survived. A caravan from the village was away at the holy lake. And there was a girl with sheep up on the slopes who watched it all. But the soldiers found the girl trying to reach the bodies. The officer made her watch as he smashed the deity into tiny pieces with a hammer. Then he took the only piece big enough to recognize, the single eye, the *chenyi*," she said, meaning the right eye. "The officer said the eye had witnessed the vindication of the Lujun and he would give it to his general as a trophy."

Nyma's voice drifted off and she looked toward the menacing cloud again. "They ordered the girl to find her mother among the bodies, then bound her to her mother's dead body, face to face, and left her there. Monks from the gompa on the other side of Yapchi Mountain found her there after three days."

There was a long silence as Shan studied first Nyma, then the dark cloud.

"And your people recorded the story," Lokesh said over Shan's shoulder.

"That little girl, she was my grandmother. She helped to bury them. Our people don't give the dead to the birds. We give them back to the soil. She helped put them in a big grave. When I was young she used to sit at the grave and recite all the names of the dead to me."

The Golok had his chang bottle in midair as Nyma made the announcement. He lowered the bottle, stared at it for a moment. "The bastards," he offered, as though to comfort the nun, then packed the bottle away.

"Afterwards," Nyma added, "people kept watch for the chenyi stone. It was kept in an army museum near Beijing for many decades and a man from Yapchi obtained special charms from lamas and traveled there to bring it back. But the Chinese shot him as a spy. The eye disappeared after the communists came. But we found out that parts of the Lujun were reconstituted into the People's Liberation Army."

"The 54th Mountain Combat Brigade," Shan suggested.

Nyma nodded. "After they were assigned to duty in Tibet, people kept a close watch on them. Another man from the village went to speak with the army but he was arrested and went to lao gai, where he died. A secretary saw the chenyi stone on the desk of the colonel of the brigade in Lhasa and sent word. After a few months a letter was sent to Lhasa, signed by all our villagers, asking that it be returned. But the only thing that happened was that the township council sent back the letter and demanded extra taxes from us. Then last year when the Chinese celebrated August First in Lhasa that colonel had it taped to the turret of a tank in the parade." August First was the day reserved for celebrating the People's Liberation Army. "The soldiers laughed and pointed at it to taunt the Tibetans. Someone took a photograph and brought it to us."

"Purbas," Shan said, not expecting an answer. "Drakte stole it back."

"Someone else, I think. I don't know for certain. Purbas know how dangerous it can be to share secrets. We don't want to know. People get captured. The Chinese use drugs that unbind their tongues."

"But you were in Lhasa and brought the chenyi stone to the hermitage," Shan suggested.

Nyma shook her head. "I was working in our valley," she said enigmatically. "One day our oracle spoke about a Chinese returning the eye. I thought she meant the army would bring it back one day. Only afterwards, when I went to speak about it with some purbas, did I know the eye had already been recovered from those who had stolen it from us."

Our oracle. The nun spoke as if every community still had its oracle. But until arriving at the hermitage, Shan could not recall ever having heard a Tibetan speak of an active oracle. Even Lokesh, who clung so steadfastly to tradition, spoke of oracles as part of some distant past.

The nun looked inquiringly toward the black cloud, which was nearly over them now. Dremu watched it too, with suspicious, worried eyes, and retreated deeper into the cave. "I spoke about what the oracle said, and later Drakte sought me out and asked me many questions, all about the eye and the village. Later people came and took me to the hermitage."

Shan studied Tenzin, who had stepped forward to study the strange cloud, then turned back to Nyma. "Why would the purbas be so interested in returning the eye?"

The nun shrugged again and cast a small frown toward Shan. She was speaking of things that seldom were spoken out loud. "The purbas want justice," she ventured. "It is the right thing to do."

There was a rumble of wind—not thunder, but a roaring rush of air that brought an abrupt darkening, as if night had fallen. Hail began to drop, small kernels at first, but soon balls nearly half an inch in diameter. The nun nodded toward the sky, as though she understood some secret about the hailstorm. Lokesh stared back at the tunnel that extended toward the heart of the mountain, where the local earth deity might live.

Sometimes in Tibet hailstorms came with such violence and such large stones that crops were destroyed in seconds, people even killed. The Tibetans treated such deaths with particular reverence, as if the victim had been summoned by a sky deity for a special purpose. Shan extended his hand out into the storm. The hail stung his palm but he kept it extended, collecting the stones.

At his side he sensed Nyma moving, and turned to see her trying to pull Tenzin back from outside the cave. The tall Tibetan had removed his coat and stepped into the open, bending his back to the storm, protected only by his thin shirt, letting the stones lash at him. A sudden gust whipped stones into Shan's face, stinging his cheeks. He dropped the hail in his hand and retreated into the cave. Sometimes it was difficult not to believe in the earth deities.

But, incredibly, Tenzin pulled away as the nun reached for him, stepping further into the storm and kneeling, curling his head into his knees, his hands wrapped around his neck. It was as though he were being flogged, as though he were inviting the deities to punish him. Tenzin seemed to understand something about the storm as well, but it was different than what Nyma sensed. Or perhaps the secret Tenzin understood, Shan thought, was just about himself.

As she pulled at Tenzin's shoulder, Shan ran toward the nun and grabbed Tenzin's other shoulder. Together they dragged him inside. He did not seem to notice their grip at first, then looked at them with wild, surprised eyes. His shirt was torn, and there were several tiny red spots where the stones had pierced his skin.

As Nyma wrapped Tenzin's chuba around his shoulders, Dremu gasped in fright and pointed into the storm. An unearthly wail rolled down the slope, and a wraith-like shape emerged through the greyness, a figure mounted on a small black horse. The rider was hunched over in the saddle, the horse galloping, futilely trying to escape the hail. The sound was the crying of the horse as the stones pummeled its flesh. Shan sensed Nyma shudder, then retreat deeper into the cave, followed quickly by the other Tibetans. But Shan took a step forward, watching in fear. The animal, its rider limp in the saddle, could run off a ledge in such a frenzy. He pulled his hat low and darted into the storm. The horse whinnied louder as it saw him, then slowed as Shan extended a hand. A moment later, one hand on the bridle, Shan was running back to cover with the frantic creature.

The rider was a woman, although the cuts and welts on her face made it difficult to discern her features. Blood mixed with rain streaked down her face. She was not unconscious, but her wild, unblinking eyes were little different than those of the inconsolable horse, who paced back and forth among the other mounts, its flanks quivering, unwilling to be touched.

Then the woman glimpsed Shan and she clamped her hand around his arm. "I found them, those herders you needed to know about." Shan recognized the weary voice, and the braided red cloth she wore around her head. It was the dropka woman from the ridge, the guard who had blamed herself for letting the dobdob through to Drakte. Lokesh gently wiped the blood from her cheeks. "They had a terrible fright," the woman gasped. "There was just an old man and woman, with a small herd and dogs," she said. "They never saw Drakte, they said, but an old lama was with them, just for the night, and he was attacked." Tears mixed with the blood that still trickled down her face. She forced a smile for Lokesh as he wiped her cheek again, then continued. "The knobs want that lama. They have been chasing him, those herders say."

"What lama?" Shan asked in alarm, leaning over her. Surely she did not mean Gendun, or Shopo, both of whom had been in the hermitage the night before.

The dropka shook her head. "I don't know. Those old people didn't make sense, they were so scared. They were shy of speaking about him. A ghost lama, they called him. Sometimes ghosts are real, they said. They were very upset. The lama disappeared before dawn. The old man said the knobs must have taken him. But the woman insisted otherwise. She said ghosts always fade away when the sun rises."

The wind blew harder, screeching around the outcropping. The woman stared at her palm, where a drop of blood had fallen. Shan looked up in surprise, searching for its source, then she lifted a trembling hand and touched his cheek, her fingers coming away bloody.

"You're injured," she said softly.

"It's only hail," Shan said.

The woman's eyes cleared, and she pulled away the rag Lokesh was using to clean her own face to clean Shan's. "I didn't understand," she continued. "But you said you needed to know. I had to find you, because of the danger it may mean for the eye." She paused and clenched Shan's arm again. "It was knobs who wounded Drakte, it must have been. Our Drakte, he would have fought knobs to protect a lama." She twisted to see her horse. "And that," she said, pointing to the crude wooden saddle. "I wanted you to have it. We couldn't keep it because those knobs are coming and maybe some night that thing . . ." She swallowed hard and looked away, as though unable to speak of the dobdob.

Shan stood and lifted a pouch from the saddle, the pouch Drakte had carried to the hermitage the night before, the pouch with the sling and ledger book.

Suddenly the storm was over. The air cleared, and sunlight burst across the barren landscape. But the woman's words hung over them like a portent of another, far worse storm.

Nyma looked to Dremu, as if expecting him to lead them on. But the Golok was gazing with hooded eyes, shifting from the dropka woman to her horse to Tenzin. When he felt the nun's stare he forced a thin smile, then ventured around the corner of the rock with the field glasses. "Soldiers kneeling on the hood of the truck," he reported a moment later. "Maybe the windshield was shattered. They'll probably give up for the day."

45

"Go," the dropka woman pleaded. Threads of blood still streaked her cheek. "I will watch Shopo and the Pure Water Lama."

Tenzin dumped a small mound of yak dung beside her and ignited it. As she gestured for them to hurry, they reluctantly climbed onto their horses.

Shan paused as the others rode away. "Tell those riders behind us to go back," he said. "Tell them to help protect the lamas."

When Shan emerged around the outcropping the truck was moving back in the direction it had come, toward the south. "Was it the 54th Mountain Brigade?" he wondered out loud.

Dremu grunted but offered no answer. Nyma stared at the ground, her lower lip between her teeth. The Golok circled his horse about them, looking not toward the lake but behind them, before setting off down the western slope. Shan settled his horse into a slow walk at the back of the column, keeping Lokesh before him. The army was in front of them but there was no turning back, for behind were the knobs and the furious dobdob.

In another hour they crested the last of the low hills that surrounded the lake and gained an unobstructed view of the vast turquoise waters. The twenty-five-mile-long lake seemed alive as the waters shivered in the wind and sun. Nyma pointed out several low dark shapes scattered along the distant shoreline, mere dots on the horizon, the heavy felt yurts of the dropka clans who had brought their sheep to the rich spring pastures.

They rode through meadows dense with spring growth, splashing through countless rivulets of runoff from the mountains, until they reached the lake and dismounted near a huge raft of black and white geese that floated offshore, their white crowns gleaming in the sun. Bar-headed geese the Tibetans called them. The wind ebbed and their chattering filled the air.

Suddenly Lokesh leapt past him, arms extended, and ran into the cold waters of the lake, laughing like a child, pushing through the water until it reached his knees. "Aw! Aw! Aw!" he cried toward the birds, then turned toward Shan with a huge grin. "It's a sound my mother used to make to geese. It's good luck, she always said, to see so many geese resting on water. It means the spirits of the air are in harmony with the spirits of the water."

His mother. Lokesh almost never spoke of his mother, who occupied a special, sacred place in his heart, much as Shan's father did in his. Lokesh's mother had died in 1940, the year that the young Fourteenth Dalai Lama had arrived in Lhasa, a year of great celebration and affirmation of the old ways. She had led a perfect life, Lokesh once said, and died at the perfect time, for afterwards came the decades of darkness and destruction.

The old Tibetan bent and splashed water on his face, then gestured for Shan to join him. Shan hesitated only a moment, then stepped into the lake beside his friend. "Aw! Aw! Aw!" Shan cried toward the geese, hands upraised.

Lokesh laughed heartily. "Lha gyal lo!" he called out joyfully toward the birds.

Shan washed his face in the frigid water, then cupped some in his hand to drink.

"No," Lokesh warned, touching Shan's arm. "Too salty. Drink from the streams."

Shan tasted a drop on his finger and confirmed Lokesh's words, then surveyed the landscape again. Lamtso was one of the great basin lakes that were spread across the eastern changtang, lakes that had no outlets and therefore concentrated the salts and other minerals that washed off the surrounding mountains.

The Golok found a boulder and sat, drinking his chang as Nyma and Tenzin collected rocks for a small cairn to honor the nagas before moving on. "Auspicious start," Nyma observed repeatedly as she worked, then paused to watch Tenzin. The mute Tibetan, whom she had stayed beside since the hailstorm, put a frantic energy into building the cairn. Her face clouded with concern, Nyma stepped to her horse pack, reached in, and extracted a *mala*, her spare rosary, which she extended toward Tenzin.

Tenzin looked at the beads but his eyes seemed unable to focus on them. His jaw worked up and down as if something inside was trying to speak, perhaps trying to remember the mouthing of a mantra. Ever since Drakte's death he had been more distant than ever, more withdrawn into his strange personal anguish. Shan knew survivors of the gulag often lived this way. An event would trigger a door inside and some nightmare from his imprisonment would be relived. Nyma pressed the beads into his hands and led Tenzin to his horse as Dremu trotted away.

They had followed the lakeside trail for only twenty minutes when Dremu halted at the top of a hill and dismounted, staring down the far side with a worried expression.

Shan dismounted and followed the Golok's gaze toward a white vehicle, a heavy compact minibus of the type sometimes used to convey passengers between Tibet's cities. It had apparently arrived from the southeast by means of a narrow dirt road, and had just turned onto the rough track that paralleled the shores of the lake. Two men sat on a large flat rock in front of the vehicle, one in the maroon robe of a monk, the other dressed like a businessman in a white shirt and tie, while three men in monks' robes struggled to free the left rear wheel, which was mired in mud.

"Better to go around," Dremu warned.

But Shan was already striding down the hill as the Golok spoke.

The men on the rock watched Shan with disinterested expressions as he approached. With his broad-rimmed hat and tattered coat, he looked like just another dropka. The man in the tie was a middle-aged Han, bald on the top of his head, his remaining hair thin and long on the sides, combed back. The small black eyes that looked out of his wide, fleshy face seemed as brightly polished as his shoes. A cigarette dangled from the man's lips. The Tibetan he sat with had thick, neatly trimmed hair, and wore a robe unlike any Shan had ever seen, for it was fringed with gold and appeared, implausibly, to have a monogram embroidered over its left breast. Between them on the rock was a bottle of orange drink and what seemed to be a plastic bag of sunflower seeds.

The Han exhaled a long plume of smoke toward Shan as he approached the rock, as though to warn him away. Shan offered a hesitant nod and stepped around the two men, slowing to read the six-inch-high Tibetan and Chinese characters painted on the side of the bus. New Beliefs for the New Century, they said, and below them in smaller letters an adaptation of a familiar slogan: Build Prosperity by Breaking the Chains of Feudalism.

He looked back toward his companions. Lokesh and Nyma followed, but Dremu and Tenzin had retreated, so that only their heads were visible above the crest of the hill. Nyma approached the rock with the two men, then froze and cast a nervous glance up the hill as if thinking of fleeing. Shan saw a small legend stenciled on the driver's door: Bureau of Religious Affairs.

"Howlers!" Nyma whispered in alarm as she reached him. It was what many of the purbas called the members of the Bureau, for the strident way they often addressed Tibetans. At first the howlers had screamed at *tamzing*, the criticism sessions that had long been the Party's favorite tool for political correction. Now, with tamzing losing favor in Party circles, they continued to be howlers, just in subtler ways, fervently preaching to Tibetans about the socialist sins of traditional Buddhism.

Shan's throat went bone dry as he glanced back at the Han in the tie. These were the men who granted, and revoked, the licenses of nuns and monks; the ones who anointed gompas based on the political correctness of their inhabitants; the ones who opened or shut monasteries with the stroke of a pen and granted the right to practice spirituality as though they were courtiers granting political favors.

Nyma pressed her hat low over her head and stepped close to Shan. The chuba she wore hid her makeshift robe.

The three monks were struggling to free the wheel, a small trowel and a long jack handle their only tools. Two of the men, spattered with mud, knelt by the wheel as the third, a stocky monk with the thick arms and broad hands of a laborer, carried stones from the hillside to the mired wheel.

"A flock of sheep was on the road," the broad-shouldered monk explained as he dropped the stones by the bus. The other two monks, both younger than the first, cast sharp glances at the man as though warning him not to speak. "They couldn't wait, so they drove around them, off the road. I don't know which made them angrier, getting stuck or the way all of those sheep stopped and stared at them after we went into the mud." Nyma gave a small sound of amusement and nervously looked back at the men on the rock.

"Digging around the wheel just moves the mud around," Lokesh suggested to the mud-spattered monks. "You need to make the wheel grip something," he said, pointing approvingly to the stack of rocks collected by the third monk, then followed the stocky man toward the hill to collect more.

They were a mobile education unit, the monk explained as Shan joined them on the hillside, bringing news of government programs to the local population. "Counting the barley fields," the monk added.

Shan stared out over the landscape. It was a land of herders. He doubted there was a barley field within fifty miles. "But you're from a gompa," he observed.

"Khang-nyi." It meant Second House. "The only gompa for a hundred miles." He paused and looked at the men on the flat rock. The wind had died, and a cloud of cigarette smoke hung about them. A puzzled expression crossed the monk's face, as though the two men on the rock confused him. He bent to retrieve another stone.

"What kind of government programs?" Shan asked.

The monk looked at Shan uncertainly. "Build Prosperity by Breaking the Chains of Feudalism," he recited in the formal tone of a mantra, as though to correct any wrong impression he may have made, and carried away his stones.

Ten minutes later, the vehicle freed, the men on the rock stretched lazily and stepped toward the front doors of the minibus. As Nyma and Lokesh hurried back up the hill, the one wearing the elegant robe reached inside the bus and pulled out several pamphlets, handing one to Shan.

"Have you come to understand, comrade?" the man asked abruptly. His eyes burned brightly above a hooked nose that gave him a hawk-like appearance. His companion stepped closer and pointed sternly to the words on the cover of the pamphlet: Serene Prosperity.

Shan stared at the men uncertainly. For some reason he remembered being stopped years earlier on a Beijing street by an earnest young woman in a brilliant white blouse, who handed him a pamphlet and asked, "Do you believe?" This team from Religious Affairs were also missionaries of a sort, for the godless agency that regulated the deities of Tibet.

Serene Prosperity. He stared at the words. They had the sound of a cruel joke played on the Tibetans. Suddenly Shan realized the man in the white shirt, the howler, was staring at him. "This is a land for herders," the man observed. "The ones they call dropka." He seemed to have suddenly recognized Shan as a fellow Han. His small black eyes moved restlessly back and forth, scanning the hill behind, though his head did not turn.

Shan sensed the muscles of his legs tensing, as if something in him expected the howler to coil and strike.

"You have companions who are hiding from us," the elegant monk observed in a casual tone. "So shy, like pups, running when a vehicle comes." His voice was smooth and refined, an orator's voice. "These people need to understand," he added, as if enlisting Shan's aid, "they need our help." Then he handed Shan the pamphlets remaining in his hand. "I am their abbot. Khodrak Rinpoche."

Shan found himself staring at the man. He had never heard a monk introduce himself as a revered teacher.

"They need our protection," Khodrak said. "Are you a school instructor?" The government sometimes sent Han instructors among the nomads, riding circuits through the vast pasture lands. "They don't understand what is at stake," he continued, not waiting for an answer. "The Bureau of Religious Affairs is the key to their prosperity. Misinterpretation of events is dangerous."

Shan didn't understand a word the men were saying. The Han in the white shirt acted anxious, on the edge of anger; the abbot as if engaged in some form of political dialectic with Shan. They both assumed they could confide in Shan. In their world Han did not travel with Tibetans on the remote changtang voluntarily, so he must be on government duty.

"News comes slow this far away from the highway," Shan ventured.

The two men exchanged a puzzled, uncertain glance. "Director Tuan suffered a terrible loss," Khodrak said, indicating his companion with a nod. "His deputy, a man named Chao, was murdered in Amdo town. We all must work to prevent the wrong kind of reaction."

"A Deputy Director in Religious Affairs was murdered?" Shan asked the question slowly, fighting the chill that crept over his limbs. The purba at the river had said an official was killed but had not known it was a howler. It was the worst possible news, the kind of news that brought martial law to a district, for Religious Affairs was a favored child of Beijing, its most important political vehicle in Tibet.

Khodrak nodded gravely. "Killed in a stable near his office. Deputy Director Chao is a martyr to our noble cause. You must be watchful. Important things will be happening."

A senior howler had been killed and the reaction of his superior and the abbot was to distribute propaganda among the herders. Shan tried to make his bone-dry tongue move. He raised the pamphlets Khodrak had given him. "I will do what I can," he said, and backed away.

The stocky monk lingered a moment at the rear of the vehicle, wiping mud from his hand with a tuft of grass as the others climbed inside. Shan offered him the rag he carried in his back pocket as a handkerchief. The man declined with a grateful nod, then leaned toward Shan. "Be careful with their words," he said in a low, confiding tone. "The abbot is really looking for a man with a fish."

Shan studied the monk in confusion. "You mean the killer? From the lake? A fisherman?" It made no sense. The Tibetans of the region almost never ate fish, would never take fish from a holy lake.

"Warn the dropka, warn my people," the monk said urgently, then quickly joined the others. He had not even fully shut his door when Director Tuan gunned the engine and the minibus roared away.

Shan stared at the minibus as it disappeared down the track that ran along the shoreline. Had the monk been suggesting that a man with a fish was connected to the killing? But Religious Affairs did not conduct murder investigations, Public Security did. And the knobs were chasing an old lama. Did they think the lama was the murderer?

He handed one of the pamphlets to Lokesh as they reached the top of the hill. Inside was a photograph of the Chairman of the Communist Party, crudely interposed over the image of the Potola in Lhasa, above several paragraphs of small print. Dremu reached out and grabbed the brochure from the old Tibetan, inserting it in his pocket without opening it. "Firestarters. The howlers always have good paper for burning."

Shan quietly scanned his own brochure before folding it into his pocket. It was a polemic about the economic disadvantages of devoting resources to religious reconstructions, complete with tiny graphs. He glanced back at the words at the top of the paper: Serene Prosperity. Below them was the full official title of the campaign: Religious Serenity Must Be Built on Economic Serenity. A perennial gripe of political officers was that Tibetans undermined the economy by giving a disproportionate share of their meager incomes to the reconstruction of gompas. Where contributions were limited to no more than two percent of income, one chart purported to demonstrate, prosperity soon followed.

Shan stared back in the direction the minibus had taken. Have you come to understand, the strange monk with the gold fringed robe had asked him. Shan understood nothing. The stocky monk seemed to be warning Shan, suggesting that Tuan and Khodrak were engaged in a subterfuge, that they were actually looking for a man with a fish. In all his years in Tibet Shan had never even seen a fish.

By mid-afternoon the five riders crested a small knoll to see a long rolling plain that gleamed white from salt encrusted on its surface, at the center of which lay a busy camp containing four white tents and three black ones. Dremu told them to wait as he rode toward the camp. They watched as a man in a derby emerged from one of the white tents, shouted at the Golok, then picked up stones and threw them at him. Dremu wheeled his horse and trotted back.

"This is the place," he declared with a satisfied tone, and gestured for Shan to lead the way toward the yurts.

It was a salt camp, Lokesh explained excitedly, as they dismounted amid several small children who darted among the horses, rubbing their noses and helping Tenzin loosen the saddles. Shan untied his saddle bag and relinquished his mount to a beaming girl whose cheeks were smeared with red *doja* cream, one of the dropka's defenses against high altitude sunlight. As he took a tentative step into the camp a sweet pungent scent wafted by, the smell of yak butter being churned.

Several men and women worked at the shoreline, using short wooden pestles to break the rough crust of salt into coarse pieces, then pushing the salt into piles with crude rakes. Others were packing the salt into small colorful woven pouches which were fastened together in pairs with stout cords. Like saddlebags, Shan thought as he noticed a woman sewing the bags shut, though too small for horses.

The man in the derby who had yelled at Dremu stood at the flap of a white tent near the center of the camp, a brown and white mastiff at his side, motioning them toward the fire that lay smoldering in a ring of stones by his feet. Shan and Lokesh passed a stern grey-haired man in a tattered chuba sitting at the entrance to one of the tents, a heavy staff across his legs. A dropka woman wearing a bright rainbow-pattern apron sat by a solitary yak, tethered to a stake, working a long wooden cylinder with a handle protruding from its open top, a *dongma*, one of the churns used to mix the tea, butter, and salt for the traditional Tibetan beverage. Her hair was arrayed in dozens of braids, each ending with a bead, a style that had been worn for centuries by devout women, always using one hundred eight braids, one for every bead of the Buddhist rosary. She acknowledged them with a casual, disinterested nod. Shan surveyed the little village and realized it was actually a series of camps, separate fires and separate tents brought together by the salt.

The man at the white tent eagerly searched the line of new arrivals as they walked toward his fire, his brown eyes gleaming with anticipation as he lifted his hat, revealing a head of shaggy black hair streaked with grey. A birthmark in the shape of an inverted, slanted U was conspicuous on his neck above a necklace of small turquoise stones that supported a large silver gau. Suddenly his face lit with a smile. "Nyma!" he exclaimed as the nun dismounted and darted to him. "Blessed Buddha, it is true!" They embraced tightly before Nyma gestured toward Shan. The man straightened, suddenly very sober, and silently inspected Shan.

Shan removed his own hat and returned the man's steady gaze.

"You are the virtuous Chinese," the man observed skeptically. He abruptly raised his hand and gripped Shan's chin in his calloused thumb and forefinger, turning his head from left to right as though measuring Shan for something.

"Just a Chinese who was asked to help," Shan replied impassively. He was accustomed to being greeted with taunts by unfamiliar Tibetans.

The man frowned in apparent disappointment. "I was expecting someone taller."

Shan found a grin tugging at his face.

"His back used to be straighter," Lokesh offered in the same dry tone used by the stranger, "before they forced him to build lao gai roads."

The man acknowledged Lokesh with a solemn nod, then called out, cupping his hands toward one of the salt teams, to announce their arrival. "I am called Lhandro," he said, smiling now, and gestured toward the small knot of men approaching the white tent. "We from the Yapchi Valley offer you welcome."

"Yapchi?" Shan asked in surprise, and found himself glancing toward the saddlebag that contained the chenyi stone. "But it's more than a hundred miles to the north."

Lhandro just kept smiling, letting Nyma introduce her companions as another man emerged from the tent, holding a dongma of fresh tea. Shan studied the tents as the Tibetans exchanged greetings. They were all of the traditional yurt style, but only the heavy black felt ones were for dropka, those who lived year-round on the plains. The white tents were of canvas, of the kind used by those who lived in settlements but occasionally camped in the mountains or high plains. Lhandro and his companions were not herders. They must be *rongpa*, Shan realized, farmers who tended crops in the Yapchi Valley.

As bowls of frothy tea were distributed Lhandro pointed toward the white, crusted plain. "Our people have been coming here for centuries. The government gave us little boxes of Chinese salt, with pictures of pandas on them, and said we were slaves to feudalism for coming here." He shrugged. "But Chinese salt makes you weak. We said we like the taste of Lamtso salt." He squatted with Nyma and began speaking in low, confiding tones. Lhandro was not giving her good news, Shan saw. Nyma stared at the farmer in dismay, uttered something that had the cadence of a prayer, and hung her head in her hands. The nun seemed to remember something and it was her turn to speak in a grim tone to Lhandro. The rongpa's face sagged and he glanced back in alarm at Shan. She had, he knew, explained about Drakte's death, and the purba's strange warning before he died. At last, as Nyma began speaking with the others from her village, Lhandro stepped back to the fire, his face clouded with worry. The nun spoke loud enough now for Shan to hear snippets of her conversation. She was speaking of their encounter with the white bus. One of the men hurried away, apparently spreading a warning among the other tents. Howlers might come. Several of the salt breakers stopped and darted into their tents. The dropka sometimes kept things on their altars the howlers did not approve of. A woman ran to the man who sat like a guard with his staff, and he stepped inside his tent momentarily, then reappeared, standing, staff at his side like a sentry.

An adolescent girl wearing her hair in two braids, her eyes nearly as bright as her red doja-smeared cheeks, approached the ring of stones with a small drawstring bag. She had a conspicuous limp, and her left leg seemed to twist below the knee. For a moment she and Nyma exchanged huge smiles, then silently, fiercely embraced. When they finally separated, the girl dropped her bag by the fire and opened its top. Tenzin stepped over and prodded the load with an approving nod. It was dung for the fire, and the mute Tibetan held up a piece with the air of connoisseur, as if to confirm it was yak dung, the best of the fuels typically used on the high plateau. Unlike sheep or goat dung it did not need the constant work of a bellows to keep a flame. Tenzin emptied the girl's bag, silently raised his own leather sack, carried from his saddle like a treasured possession, and walked out toward the pastures. Shan watched the enigmatic man. It was as if collecting dung had become the escapee's calling in life, as if the Tibetan with the aristocratic bearing had decided that his role in society would be to keep other people's fires burning.

Shan saw that the red-cheeked girl with the braids was watching Tenzin, too. She finally turned and cast a shy, sidelong glance toward Shan, then limped toward a man in a ragged fox-fur hat who was digging with a shovel fifty yards from camp. The man was surrounded by several small piles of earth.

"I thought the salt was taken from the surface," Shan said in a perplexed tone. As soon as the girl arrived at his side, the man handed her something and she turned in excitement to run with a crooked, shambling gait to the tent where the old herder stood guard.

Lhandro followed his gaze, then gestured in the opposite direction. Shan turned to see an old woman sitting on a hill above the camp.

"Tonde," Lhandro said, referring to the sacred objects that Tibetans sometimes retrieved from the earth. They could be arrowheads or shards of pottery or carvings in the shape of ritual objects. Once a prisoner in Shan's camp had found a corroded bronze buckle he had proclaimed to have belonged to Guru Rinpoche, the ancient teacher, and built an altar for it out of cardboard.

"Holy men have been coming to this place for a thousand years. That old dropka woman, she found a piece of turquoise carved into a lotus flower which she says has great power. Yesterday she said a Chinese airplane came and she used the tonde to scare it away," he said solemnly, then shrugged. "But she's nearly blind with cataracts."

"Our Anya," Lhandro continued after a moment, nodding toward the limping girl, "Anya saw her waving her fist at the sky and said it was just a goose that had lost its way from the flock. Now the old woman says if the soldiers come close she'll call another hailstorm against them."

Shan and Lokesh exchanged a glance. The army patrol they had seen had been many miles from the camp. The people of the changtang always seemed to have their secret ways of knowing things.

"Don't underestimate the tonde," a voice interjected from behind them. They turned to see the woman in the rainbow-colored apron carrying a leather bucket past their tent. "Some are just pieces of pretty stone, perhaps. But others," she studied Shan a moment then stepped closer. "They say it was a tonde in the hands of a monk that destroyed that Chinese mountain."

"Destroyed a mountain?" Shan asked.

"In the far south, near Bhutan," the woman said with a nod. "One of the army mountains. Their slaves had dug it out, and soldiers had arrived with their machines." The woman meant one of the massive military installations that gulag prisoners were often forced to construct for the People's Liberation Army, carving out vast networks of tunnels inside mountains, mostly along the southern border. Some had become barracks for entire divisions of Chinese troops, some depots for equipment, others sophisticated listening and command posts.

"That mountain, they filled it with computer machines and radios and army commanders. But they didn't know one of the prisoners was an old monk with a tonde that had belonged to that mountain deity. He could talk to that deity and explain what had happened. When that deity finally understood, the mountain fought back," the woman declared with a satisfied air.

Shan gazed at her expectantly, but she spoke no more.

"There was some kind of collapse," Lhandro said, glancing uncomfortably at the woman. "The newspapers said nothing, but people talk about it everywhere. The tunnels fell in, the machines were destroyed. Some soldiers were trapped and killed, and many Tibetan workers. Afterwards the army went on alert, rounded up local citizens for questioning. But experts from Beijing came and said it was just the wrong mountain to use. The Himalayas are unstable, they said, and something inside shifted."

"The wrong mountain," the woman repeated with a knowing nod.

At his side Lokesh grunted. "What do they expect, when they have soldiers for combating mountains?"

Shan looked at his old friend. Lokesh had strangely misunderstood what a mountain combat brigade was; he had taken the words too literally. Shan opened his mouth to explain, but then realized that maybe Lokesh wasn't far from wrong. Some said Beijing's ultimate campaign in Tibet was against nature, for all the mountains it gutted, the wooded slopes it deforested, the valleys laid waste with open pit mines.

Shan pressed Lhandro and the woman in the apron for more news, asking them if they knew of Public Security or military crackdowns between Lamtso and Lhasa. They shrugged. "Only the usual," Lhandro said. "That Serenity campaign. Howlers are appearing everywhere, more often than ever, all over the district." He shrugged. "It's just more words for the same thing, like always, another way of saying it." The campaign, he meant, was just another political initiative for eroding the influence of the Buddhists.

The woman, however, sometimes took wool to Amdo town, the nearest settlement of any size, and read newspapers there. A famous abbot was fleeing south to India, with Public Security and howlers racing to catch him. A manhunt was underway for two terrorists, one a recent Dalai Cult infiltrator from across the border, the other the notorious resistance leader called Tiger, a general of the purbas, who had been sighted in the region. The troops were telling people they would be imprisoned for helping him, she announced, and in the next breath offered a quick prayer for the man. Heroes of the army and model workers were being assembled in Lhasa for the biggest May Day parade in years. Shan listened closely to the woman, who seemed bursting with news and rumors. But she made no mention of a stolen stone eye or killers of purbas.

"Has there been word of the murdered Religious Affairs official?" Shan asked. The question silenced everyone within earshot. Alarmed faces stared at Shan. "His name was Chao, from Amdo town."

Nyma appeared from inside Lhandro's tent. "I knew of Chao," she said with a worried expression. "Those howlers from Amdo come over our mountain into Yapchi sometimes. He was the only one who did not examine private altars when he visited homes, never ordered people to open their gaus. He was Tibetan, but had taken a Chinese name." It was a practice the Chinese encouraged among young Tibetan students.

"That monk spoke to you about the murder?" Shan asked. He remembered the ride from their encounter with the minibus. Nyma had been unusually quiet, sharing none of Lokesh's excitement over seeing more flocks of geese.

"Only briefly." Nyma kept her eyes on the ground as she spoke. "It was very violent, very bloody. Chao was stabbed in the back. It happened in a garage that used to be a stable, at the edge of town, just two nights ago."

Shan stared at her.

"Is that important?"

"Two nights ago was probably when Drakte was attacked," Shan explained. "The wound that killed him was inflicted many hours before we saw him."

Nyma's eyes welled with moisture and she turned away for a moment, looking at the lake. "You don't know that for certain," she said.

"No," Shan admitted. But he was almost certain. He had seen many stab wounds in his Beijing incarnation.

"Drakte? Drakte!" a woman gasped behind Shan. He turned to see the woman in the brightly colored apron, her hands at her mouth. "Our Drakte!" she cried, and the other dropka in earshot pressed closer as she told them the news in low, despairing tones.

Shan patiently answered their questions about the purba's death, then asked his own.

"He was here only last week," the woman explained, "talking with us, asking us questions, playing with the children. One afternoon he took all the children and made a new cairn on a hill." Shan followed her gaze toward a tall grass mound half a mile away crowned by a small tower of stones. The woman slowly sank upon a boulder by the fire.

"What questions? What did Drakte ask?" Shan inquired, squatting beside the woman.

"The number of sheep and goats we have," the woman said woodenly. "Who has yak and who has goats. Where the nearest fields of barley might be. How much fodder we cut for the winter."

Barley. Shan stared at the woman, then at Lhandro and Nyma. The abbot and the Director of Religious Affairs had been counting fields of barley. Counting them on the changtang pastureland, where no barley grew. He darted to his blanket and unrolled it to find the pouch the dropka woman had brought through the storm. They leafed through Drakte's book together until they found a page near the end captioned Lamtso Gar—Lamtso Camp—dated the week before. There was a column for barley, marked none, and others for sheep, yak, and goats.

"This camp is our home for much of the year," the woman explained. "Everyone else just visits for the salt." She pointed to the columns with obvious pride. One yak, eighteen sheep, five goats read the entry for Lamtso Gar. And two dogs.

If it made no sense that the abbot and a senior howler were collecting such data, it made even less sense Drakte would be. But Drakte had not only collected the data, he had certified it. At the bottom of the page were signatures, and beneath the signatures a note Shan suspected was added later. Last year, Drakte had written, a two-year-old girl died of starvation here.

Shan leafed through the following pages and pointed to entries that had no signatures, only circles or X's.

"Even those who could not write had to sign," the woman explained. "He insisted there be an entry for every family, every home. He said bad things until they made their marks," she added in a low, perplexed voice.

"Bad things?"

The woman hung her head, as if embarrassed. "He was tired, and worried. He was a good boy."

"What things?" Shan asked again.

The woman stared at the ground and whispered so low Shan had to lean toward her to hear. "He said sign or else all your children will grow up to hate you." She shivered and folded her arms over her breast.

Shan stared at the woman, then at the ledger.

Suddenly a loud curse echoed through the camp. Dremu was yelling at a middle-aged woman who was throwing pebbles at him and encouraging the children to do likewise. The Golok raised his fist threateningly, but turned and broke into a fast stride toward the fire. When he reached the ring of stones he paused, looked at Lhandro, then stepped behind Shan. Lhandro, the soft-spoken rongpa, had thrown stones, too.

"This Golok is not welcome," Lhandro said stiffly.

"You would welcome me . . . ," Shan said in confusion, not needing to ask the obvious question: Why would Lhandro welcome a Chinese but not another Tibetan?

"I don't mean all Goloks," Lhandro explained in a heavy voice. "But this man's clan were bandits. Once that band raided many camps and villages between here and the ranges in Amdo the Goloks call home. They attacked many innocent clans, stole many herds and bags of barley."

"Those bandits died a long time ago," Dremu muttered. "Caught by Public Security and executed."

"Is this man still a bandit?" Lhandro demanded of Shan.

Dremu gave a grunt-like laugh, as though to say, if only he could have it so good.

"You don't need this man," Lhandro said when Shan did not reply. "You are going to Yapchi with us."

"But the purbas arranged it," Nyma interjected. "I think they wanted someone who knows the mountains, knows the hiding places, knows where patrols look. We aren't used to knobs. Drakte arranged it," she whispered soberly, as if it settled the matter.

"I don't understand," Shan said. "Who else is going to Yapchi Valley?" Their trip was supposed to be a secret.

"We have been waiting for you," Lhandro said, sweeping his hand toward the white tent where the men had begun sewing a mound of the filled salt pouches shut. "Those from my village who came to the salt camp. Five of us from Yapchi, and forty sheep. We leave at dawn." As though to ease Shan's doubt, the rongpa produced a tattered map from his pocket and unfolded it, showing Shan the lake, a large oval blue shape at the edge of the changtang. Then he traced a route east along the shore and north through the mountains into Amdo, the part of Tibet that Beijing called Qinghai Province. Shan studied the map. It was surprisingly rich in detail, including a fifty-mile-wide sector of red hash marks along the far shore of Lamtso. Along the top of the map was a large legend. *Nei Lou.* It meant classified, a state secret. He glanced up at Lhandro, who returned his gaze with challenge in his eyes, then pointed to the red marks. The legend over the marks said Toxic Hazard Zone.

"An army base?"

"No," Lhandro sighed. "Worse. There are places in this region where special weapons were tested. Things that caused disease, or killed everything with chemicals. Some say they were used on herds of wild animals. Some say on bands of nomads who refused to be registered. But no one

58

goes in the places with red marks, not even the army. Sometimes people find things, canisters on the ground, or a herd of sheep that has died for no clear reason, and the army comes and declares a new zone. The army puts signs up, and fences sometimes."

Shan looked at Nyma, then the sturdy farmer. "You planned this with the purbas? The salt caravan?"

Lhandro smiled. "My village has always done a caravan to Lamtso, every spring. The purbas learned about it," he said with a glance toward Nyma. "They said it would be a way of making you and the stone inconspicuous." He stepped away to help sew the salt bags shut.

Nyma began to move among the other tents, speaking in gentle, reverent tones, straightening prayer flags that had been strung from tent lines. She sat by the old dropka woman with cataracts and began reciting her beads. Dremu stared warily at the people walking about the camp, who either refused to acknowledge him or glared at him with obvious resentment. He cursed, then stepped toward his horse. Shan assumed the Golok was going to groom the animal, but suddenly he was mounted. He ran his horse out of camp and disappeared into the hills. The man had been paid already. Shan doubted they would see Dremu again.

Shan and Lokesh wandered about the camp, Shan watching for any sign of a man with a fish, or anything to explain the monk's cryptic warning. They lingered by a fire where a woman was frying sweet dough for the dropka children until Lokesh decided he should join the search for tonde. His old friend was always seeking the little treasures and, like many older dropka they had met, he tried to keep nine in his possession at any one time, a number that was said to bring powerful luck.

Shan watched as Lokesh walked toward the slope where the man in the fox hat dug, then he circled behind the tents, intending to approach the back of the tent where the old man stood guard with his staff.

But Tenzin stood at the water's edge, looking forlornly across Lamtso, his new beads dangling from his fingers. Shan paused, stepped to his side, and sat on a boulder. The grief the mute Tibetan had shown in Drakte's death hut seemed to have returned to his face.

"When I was in prison," Shan said after a long silence, "there was a man in my barracks for hitting a Public Security officer. His spirit was so troubled he could barely speak and everyone feared he would take his own life. Finally the lamas were able to get him to speak about the burden he carried inside. He confessed that he had killed a Chinese whom he had caught stealing sheep. The Chinese had beaten his wife unconscious and drawn a pistol on the man. No one, not even his wife, knew that they had struggled and that the Chinese had been killed. He had hidden the body and it was later that he hit the knob, when the man refused to give a ride to his injured wife."

The only sign that Tenzin heard him was a lowering of his gaze to the ground by Shan's feet.

"A lama gave the man a pebble and had him focus on it." Shan lifted a large pebble in his palm. "He told the man to push his guilt into it. Then he had the man throw the pebble into a river. The man was healed after that."

Tenzin looked at the stone, fixed Shan with a brittle gaze, then stepped several feet away to retrieve a heavy rock nearly a foot in diameter. He paused, looked pointedly at Shan, threw the rock into the water, and turned back to stare at him.

Shan returned the stare for a moment. Shaken, he turned away. What had it been, to cause such anguish? Something had been pulling at his memory. The dropka woman said that Tenzin had been away the night before Drakte died. The night Chao had been murdered. He looked at the ripples where the heavy rock had fallen. A pebble had been enough for a single killing.

Shan backed away from Tenzin and turned toward the yurt. The old herder squinted at him as he approached the entrance, then raised the staff threateningly.

"The girl brought you a tonde," Shan said tentatively.

"Not me. Go away. This is my family's tent. People are sleeping."

"You guard them when they sleep?"

From the corner of his eye Shan saw several more figures approaching in haste.

"There is fresh tea!" the woman in the bright apron called from a hundred feet away, gesturing Shan toward her fire. But Shan quickly put his hand on the man's staff to deflect it and stepped inside.

An old woman with no teeth, the sole occupant of the tent, groaned as he appeared. "No!" she cried and rose, lowering the prayer wheel she had been spinning. "Chinese!"

Shan sensed figures moving behind him. He tensed, expecting to be dragged away, until a soft voice called out from the shadows at the back of the tent. "He is a friend of the lamas," a woman said, and the man behind Shan halted, lowering his raised staff.

"Nyma?" Shan asked, stepping toward the shadows, where two felt blankets had been strung to create dressing chambers inside the tent. A hand appeared between the blankets, pushing one aside, and Shan bent to enter the dark, cramped space.

Nyma sat in the dim light of a single butter lamp beside a pallet, holding the hand of a woman of perhaps thirty years. The woman's face was beaded with sweat, her breathing labored. She seemed to be trying to smile through a mask of pain.

"Lokesh," Shan said, "he studied with medicine lamas."

"She fell from a ledge three days ago, running from a patrol in the night. I think she broke ribs," Nyma said.

"Then she needs a doctor," Shan said urgently. Arranged along the pallet was a dirt-encrusted bell and several dirty beads.

"No doctor!" shouted the old woman, now standing over them, her hands holding back the blankets.

"Some herders from the east of here rode in last week and told everyone to beware of new doctors, to hide the sick, and not speak of any Tibetan doctors to any Chinese." Nyma raised her eyebrows toward Shan as though to express her frustration. "I don't know why. No one really does."

"But you can't hide someone injured so badly," Shan said. "What if her organs are bleeding? A hospital . . ."

"We don't need those doctors. They aren't real," the woman said, then bent and wrapped the injured woman's fingers around the little bell.

The woman on the pallet stared up at Shan, pain and confusion in her eyes. Shan sighed. "Lokesh knows medicine teas," he said and turned away, striding past the old woman and four grim-faced herders.

He found his old friend near a freshly turned pile of earth, explained about the injured woman, and watched as Lokesh rose and hurried to the tent. Then Shan turned and studied a grassy hill half a mile away. Ten minutes later he stood at the five-foot-high cairn Drakte had made with the children. Shan walked around the stack of rocks several times, then sat before it. Drakte had been on urgent business, in the middle of making final arrangements for the chenyi stone, but he had taken the time to build a cairn for the local deities. And he had planned to return to the salt camp with Shan and the stone. Shan stood and studied the wide, flat stone that covered the top. He lifted it and lowered it to the ground. The narrow openings between the stones underneath were so dark he almost missed the piece of brown yarn wedged between two of them. He pulled on the yarn and a small felt pouch rose out of the shadows. Inside was a mala, a rosary of exquisite ivory beads carved in the shapes of animal heads. It was a valuable antique worthy of a museum. Why, he wondered, as he slipped the rosary back into the pouch, would Drakte have wanted it hidden? Because it was too dangerous to carry the week between his visits to the camp? Or because he had meant for someone else to retrieve it? Shan pocketed the pouch.

"This is how Chinese help the deities?" a flat voice called out from behind him.

Shan slowly turned to see Dremu, sitting on his grey horse thirty feet down the slope, on the side opposite the camp. There was no surprise on the Golok's face, only a sinister amusement. He lifted a leg and rested it on his horse's neck.

Shan silently replaced the capstone. "I want to ask you something. Where did you meet Drakte? Where did he hire you?" he asked.

"In a city."

"Lhasa?"

Dremu's eyes half closed as he examined Shan. "Lhasa," he confirmed in a low voice. "I learned things there not even the purbas knew."

"What kind of things?"

"You can die in this country for telling too many secrets."

"Or for being too secretive," Shan shot back. Had the Golok seen the priceless rosary? "Why? Why did Drakte select you to help? You're no purba. You're not welcome among the people of Yapchi."

Dremu's lips curled up as if he took satisfaction in Shan's words.

Shan studied the Golok, who returned Shan's stare inquisitively, running his finger along his moustache, his other hand on his knife. Abruptly Shan stepped away, dropped to his knees by a large rock, and pulled it up on one edge. He pointed to Dremu, then to the cairn. The Golok frowned, but silently dismounted and helped Shan carry the rock to the top of the stack. Shan offered a mantra to the Compassionate Buddha and the Golok hung his head with a deflated expression, as if Shan had earned himself unexpected protection. He marched to his horse and rode away. Shan fingered the rosary in his pocket, suddenly remembering that Drakte had brought nothing to pay the Golok. Had the beads been intended for Dremu?

As Shan approached the camp he found Lokesh back at his excavation. "She is sleeping now. I told them of a tea they can make, for the pain. I will check her later," the old Tibetan explained.

"Did they explain why suddenly they want no doctors?"

Lokesh and Shan exchanged a knowing glance. Every Tibetan knew stories of Chinese doctors performing unwanted surgeries on Tibetans, usually sterilizations, and even of Tibetans dying mysteriously when under Chinese medical care. But the woman's fear was more urgent, more directed. Riders had come to camp to warn about doctors.

Lokesh shook his head. "They are scared. The howlers in this district are ruthless." They worked in silence for several minutes, Shan digging with a flat stone.

"I heard you speaking with Lhandro and that woman about Drakte dying," Lokesh said abruptly. "And that man Chao."

Shan looked into the old man's eyes, which did not show inquiry, but frustration.

"We know how to work in storms," Lokesh said quietly. It was a phrase from their gulag days, when the lamas exhorted the prisoners to ignore suffering and other distractions, and only work on their inner deities.

Shan's mouth went dry. "You and I saw monks die in prison because they decided to do nothing but work on their inner deities," he said after a moment.

Lokesh replied with a disappointed frown.

"What if Drakte's killer is following us?" Shan asked. "How can we avoid the killer, how can we get safely to that valley with the chenyi stone if we do not understand this killer?"

Lokesh shook his head. "By appealing to our deities. When there is a deity to repair there is nothing more important. All that work we did at the hermitage, it was like a vow. I am bound. And if that stone wants a piece of my own deity to help it heal, I will gladly give it."

Shan recognized his friend's words as a challenge. Although Lokesh usually supported Shan's quest for truth in all its forms, this time everything was different. There were no rules for healing deities, but Lokesh knew that trying to understand a killer was probably the opposite of trying to understand a deity. He conceded by bowing his head. "I am bound," Shan said in a solemn whisper. "I can work in storms."

They dug again until Lokesh gave an exclamation of triumph and extracted a small grey stone. "A very good one," he said with satisfaction and handed it to Shan.

Shan had seen the shape in the rock before. It was indeed a rare find. "A fossil," he announced. "A trilobite that lived when these lands were under a sea millions of years ago."

Lokesh gave a patient sigh, as if Shan had missed the point. "A powerful tonde," he said, "because it took the combined action of the water and earth deities to make it."

They were walking toward the lake half an hour later, when Lokesh paused and held his hand to his ear. "A song," he declared, "a song is coming from the earth." He firmly believed in the ability of inanimate objects to become animated when inhabited by a deity. Lokesh studied the landscape, then pointed toward a small knoll. They were proceeding toward it, pausing every few steps to listen, when Lhandro called out for them to stop.

"Leave her alone," the Yapchi farmer warned as he trotted to their side. "She needs this time."

When he saw their confused expressions, Lhandro gestured them forward with a finger to his lips, stopping when they could see a girl sitting in the shallow depression on the far side of the hill. It was Anya, the crippled girl with the braids and red cheeks. She had a lamb on her lap. The animal's tongue was out of its mouth, its breathing heavy.

"Anya is an orphan, like the lamb," Lhandro said. "The lamb's mother was killed by wild dogs a few days ago. No other ewe was in milk. She tried to feed it goat's milk but it wouldn't drink. It will be dead by nightfall." He looked out over the lake. "Sometimes she speaks the words of deities."

In the silence they listened. The girl was singing to the lamb in a high voice that came like a whisper on the wind. Shan could not understand the words, but they were strikingly beautiful, somehow eerie yet soothing, so natural it seemed to Shan that if the lamb's mother had been there and could express her sorrow, this would be her sound.

Lokesh cocked his head toward the girl and closed his eyes. Others were listening, too, Shan saw. Tenzin sat in the spring grass at the top of the opposite knoll, gazing sadly at the girl. Near Tenzin sat one of the big mastiffs, looking just as forlorn. Shan gazed at the girl, then the sky over her head. When he looked back at Lokesh a tear was falling down his cheek, and the old Tibetan nodded knowingly at Shan as if to say yes, it was a deity who was singing after all.

"When I was young my mother used to sing like that," someone said behind Shan, "just go sit out on a ledge and sing." It was Nyma, staring at the girl. "First time I heard her I thought she was crying. But she said no, she was trying to call the Yapchi deity back, to tell the deity it wouldn't be blind forever. When she died she said to me she was praying for the deity to forgive her, because she had lied to the deity, that it would have to get used to being blind."

"But now it will be different," Lhandro said, fixing his gaze on Shan. "Now they will be made to understand about the land."

Shan looked in confusion at the farmer. "They?"

"All those people who lost the understanding of earth deities."

"I don't know what—"

"Our valley," Lhandro said with a distant gaze toward the northern mountains. "It's full of Chinese and foreigners who plan to take the blood out of our earth."

"Blood?" Shan turned to Nyma for help.

"The earth's blood," Lhandro said.

"Oil," the nun offered in a hushed voice, lowering her eyes, as if the word frightened her, or she was embarrassed not to have told Shan before. "They destroyed the home of the deity and now they are drilling in our earth. They say they will find oil soon, then our valley will be destroyed." She looked into his eyes with a pleading expression. "But now, Shan, you are coming," she said, and hope lit her countenance. "You and the Yapchi deity are going to fix the land for us. You are going to make them leave."

Chapter Four

The crust of the earth under Tibet is twice as thick as elsewhere on the planet. Shan had heard that fact twice in his life. First from a professor in Beijing, who had emphasized that because plates of the earth had piled up on themselves in Tibet the land was constantly rising, causing many dangerous, unpredictable seismic events. But the point had also been related to Shan by an old lama in prison, who had explained that it meant the power of the land deities was more concentrated in Tibet than anywhere else on earth, that the roots that connected the land with its people ran much deeper, that the land expressed itself in more powerful ways.

As they left the next morning Shan remembered the words of the lama, for the earth was indeed expressing itself in powerful ways. A small but violent squall raced over the peaks to the north, one moment enveloping them in the white curtain that meant swirling snow, the next breaking to let the sun brilliantly illuminate a patch of slope. To the south clouds were scudding over another range, washing peaks with swaths of shadow that shifted so rapidly that the mountains themselves seemed to be in motion. And in between, the air over the great lake was clear and crisp under a cobalt sky. During the night the geese had gathered close to the salt camp, and Lokesh was standing close to the shore, speaking with them, or perhaps his mother, as he waved a farewell. The night before, his old friend had decided not to sleep. As the moon had risen over the holy waters, he had announced that he felt closer to his mother than he had in years, and he wanted to experience the sensation as long as possible. It was the geese, Lokesh had decided, and he wanted to stay near them all night.

As Shan had watched his friend settling onto a rock at the darkened shoreline he, too, decided to begin a vigil of sorts, atop a small hill, hoping for one of the rare moments when he connected with his father, when he would suddenly sense the smell of ginger and hear a hoarse, throaty laugh down some long empty corridor in his mind. But after an hour he had given up, realizing his father would never approach when the vision of Drakte's death lingered so close to Shan's consciousness.

Nyma, too, had been moved by the moonlight on the lake, for he found the nun sitting on a white rock, the water lapping against it. Fearful of disturbing her, he had been about to move on when she spoke.

"Once," she said in hollow voice, "the village would have visitors from gompas several times a year. Now no one comes. No monks. No nuns. Maybe that's all it is, maybe we have drifted so far away that no deity is interested in helping."

Shan wasn't even certain she was speaking to him until she paused and turned to stare at him. "They have you," he offered awkwardly, stepping closer. He saw that for the first time since he had known her, she had let her hair down. It was long, nearly to her waist, and she absently ran her fingers through it.

"A real nun, I mean. I'm not a real nun," Nyma said in a matter-of-fact tone.

Somehow the words seemed to hurt him more than her. "I think you're a real nun," Shan said.

In the moonlight he could see the trace of a sad smile on her face. "No," Nyma sighed. "They closed the convent where I was training and sent away all the real nuns. I had nowhere to go but to my village." She raised her face to the moon. "When I go to towns, I wear the clothes of a poor farmer. I do not have the courage to wear a robe in towns," she confessed to the moon. "I don't even cut my hair short like a nun. Lhandro says it could be too dangerous if howlers came."

"And what good would you do for Yapchi in prison?" Shan asked, for that was where she would go if plucked off the street in an illegal robe.

Nyma did not answer, or did not hear. A solitary goose called out.

"I remember someone sitting waiting for ice to melt for days, to get some sand," Shan said after studying the moonlit water a long time. "That woman was a nun."

"It was me acting like a nun. I can act like a shepherd, or a farmer, too."

Shan sat on a nearby rock. "Why are you so hard on yourself?" he whispered, feeling an unexpected helplessness. There were thousands of Nymas all over Tibet, men and women who had aspired to be monks and nuns and been denied the opportunity. Some just gave up, resigned to the notion that such a life would have to wait for a future incarnation. Others struggled on, trying to learn how to be a nun or monk without the benefit of regular teachers or role models. You must carry your gompa on your back, Shan had heard Gendun say to a despairing former monk.

"It feels like a lie, what we've done to you," Nyma blurted out. "A nun who understands the path of compassion would have done different, I am sure. You didn't know about the soldiers and the chenyi stone. We didn't tell you about the Chinese and Americans drilling for oil at Yapchi. I could have told you at the hermitage about the oil but I didn't, for fear of scaring you away. Now a killer is following us and that crazy Golok is watching the eye and all I feel is guilt over what we have done to you.

And fear. When Drakte said that demon kills prayers he was right. I have been unable to pray, not truly pray in my heart, since that thing walked into the chapel. All day I have felt such fear. Terrible things are going to happen, I can feel it. You must think we have betrayed you. You must think we are so foolish, so reckless. Letting the oracle's words bring us to this."

"I would have come," Shan said. "Even if you had told me it all, I would not have understood, but I still would have come. If the lamas asked me to go to the moon I would tie a hundred geese together and give it a try."

In the moonlight Nyma's sad smile reminded him of an old Buddha statue in ivory.

"Do you still have family at Yapchi?" Shan asked after another long silence. The woman had never spoken of her connection to the village.

"I call Lhandro uncle sometimes, but he is only a cousin. I have no close family left. He has only his parents. He was going to be married many years ago, but the woman who was intended for him was sent away for reeducation and never came back. My mother's house is there. I have a home."

Home. For a moment Shan was shamed because of the envy he felt for the Yapchi villagers, despite all the trouble in their valley. They had a home and a bond among them, roots in the land. He had no one, except Lokesh and Gendun, and a son who had disowned him and no doubt thought his father dead.

Shan had awakened to find Lhandro, Nyma, and Anya with two of the sturdy men from Yapchi arranging the small tandem salt sacks on a blanket. As Lhandro finished counting forty sets of pouches, Anya led a sheep forward and Nyma, her cheeks now smeared with red doja cream, quickly arranged the sacks on the back of the animal, tying the loose cords around the sheep's belly so that each animal appeared to be wearing a woven saddle. The men from Yapchi worked quickly, some bringing the animals one at a time, others waiting in turns with the bulging sacks. When all the sheep were loaded, except a sturdy brown ram, Nyma called Shan to the ram's side and opened one of the pouches, the only one that seemed to be empty. As Lhandro appeared with a leather bucket of salt, the nun pointed at the saddlebag which Shan carried in his hand, the bag he had brought from the hermitage. Shan hesitated, then opened the bag and extended it to the nun. But Nyma shook her head, as if still afraid of the bag's contents, and gestured toward the pouch as Lhandro poured a handful of salt into it. Shan pulled out the cedar box and lowered it into the pouch, watching it with an unexpected sense of foreboding as Lhandro covered it with salt, produced a long needle, and began sewing the bag shut. The pouch was woven in a multicolored pattern with a round red circle in its center surrounded with white. Like an angry, watchful eye.

As the red-eyed pouch was loaded on the brown ram, Lhandro began watching the lake trail to the south, the trail Shan and his friends had arrived on the day before. A solitary figure, jogging along the trail, appeared on the crest of the nearest hill and waved to Lhandro. Shan saw that it was one of the Yapchi men he had met the day before, looking exhausted, an old muzzleloading rifle in his hand. He had been watching over them, guarding the trail in the night, Shan realized.

The other inhabitants of the salt camp gathered by the trail that opened to the north, watching with strangely solemn faces as Lhandro surveyed the line of loaded sheep and his companions, then nodded toward Anya, in the lead. The girl settled her chuba on her shoulders, whistled to the dogs, and began walking with her crooked gait, singing one of her eerie songs, the sheep and dogs following the girl as if under a spell.

"Lha gyal lo!" a woman by one of the dropka tents cried out, and the call was taken up by others, to Lokesh's obvious delight. The old Tibetan echoed the words back to the camp as the caravan left the salt gatherers behind, Tenzin and the Yapchi men leading horses laden with equipment.

Yapchi had been sending salt caravans to the lake for as long as people remembered, Lhandro explained to Shan as they walked together— meaning not simply as long as the farmer and his family remembered, but for centuries, even before Buddha and the dharma path came to Tibet. More than twelve centuries. For much of the morning Lhandro walked beside Shan and spoke of those older caravans, recalling names and events from fifty, a hundred, even five hundred years earlier as if they had just happened. A Yapchi farmer named Saga had once found a dying Western priest, a Jesuit, near the lake, and had stopped for a week to carve one of his god's crosses out of rock for his grave, since no wood could be found. Once, when there had been terrible sickness during the winter, the entire village had come to bathe in the healing waters of the lake. Another time a wild yak, white as snow, had followed a caravan all the way home and settled on the mountain above Yapchi where, for twenty years afterwards, it would be seen every year on Buddha's birthday.

The tales echoed in Shan's mind throughout the morning as the long empty miles of grassland seemed to put their dangers behind them. A sense of timelessness settled into Shan as they led the sheep along the eastern shoreline then into a long grassy valley that rose toward a pass over the first range of mountains. What had changed? he wondered. The Tibetans had taught him many ways to look at the world. One of them was to perceive the strange way that most humans viewed progress, even the very thing called civilization. He had evolved more as a person in four years in prison, enslaved, than he had in all the previous three decades he had spent in Beijing, accumulating the meager belongings by which most people judged a life's progress. And now, carrying salt to Yapchi, walking by the sheep with the serene, joyful Tibetans under a cobalt sky rimmed with snowcapped peaks, a simple drawstring bag holding all his earthly possessions, Shan felt he had perhaps reached the pinnacle of civilization.

Had anything really changed since those first caravans, he wondered. The herdsmen still ventured by foot over the rough, rocky landscape, still broke the salt crust with their wooden pestles, slept in tents made of yak hair and packed their salt on their sheep in bags woven from wool taken from the same animals, still rejoiced over the sweet taste of milk from animals that grazed on the spring blossoms. Nothing had changed. Or everything, he thought sadly as he glanced at the short, sturdy ram carrying the bag with the red circle. For this time one of the sheep bore the eye of a deity, stolen by those who had massacred a village. And a killer was stalking the eye. A killer and a platoon of mountain troops. And perhaps even someone else. The more he replayed Drakte's last moments in his mind the more he wondered whether Drakte had been warning about someone else, not the dobdob. If he had known the dobdob intended them harm, or if it had been a knob or soldier standing there, the Drakte Shan knew would have flung himself at the intruder to defend the lamas. But Drakte had just stood there when the dobdob arrived, frozen with the same confusion Shan and the others had felt.

He paused and waited for Lokesh, who had been walking at the rear of the caravan. "If you saw that dobdob in your mind again," Shan asked his old friend, "would you see a real dobdob or someone dressed to look like one?" It was possible, Shan knew from his own experience, for a killer to don the old costumes to intimidate and confuse his victims.

Lokesh gazed toward a juniper tree that grew at the top of a nearby hill, the only tree visible anywhere in the landscape. "I see him. I see him when I try to sleep at night. I see him when I wake in the morning," he said heavily and turned back to Shan. "It was not a pretend thing. It was a real monk policeman."

"But you said they hadn't been seen for decades."

"Not by me. And I think not by anyone else. Almost anyone else."

"To a dobdob, a Religious Affairs official would be an enemy," Shan suggested. The coincidence still troubled him. Drakte and the man Chao had probably been attacked the same night.

"To a howler, a dobdob would be an enemy," Lokesh said, correcting Shan. He stepped away as if to discourage further questions. A monk, Lokesh was saying, a true monk, would not perceive enemies at Religious Affairs, only people whose awareness had been stunted.

But a real dobdob would take orders only from a lama or senior monk. Had Drakte infuriated a lama?

Shan became aware of a robed figure walking far to one side of the caravan, gaze on the ground, almost as if wandering, unaware, of the caravan. When he saw Lhandro watching the figure with a worried expression he stepped to the village headman's side.

"When she was with you," Lhandro began, "did she always..." He struggled to find words, then turned with inquiry on his face. "She was going to run away to India last year, to find a convent there. I convinced her not to go. But now I think I was wrong."

"She has always been a great help," Shan offered, uncertain what Lhandro was asking.

The rongpa seemed relieved. "She was only fifteen when the government closed that convent of hers. She had gone away two years before. Not long after, her mother died. She had no hope of finding another convent so she took her robe off and tended the village sheep. But then one day three years later she found Anya lying on a rock, shaking, reciting old scriptures none of us had even heard before. It disturbed Nyma more than it did Anya herself. She said the fabric of our deity was being unraveled, and she put her robe back on. She and Anya made a little chapel in a small canyon behind the village and would stay there meditating for hours, for entire days. She asks me, how would a nun do this, what would a nun do about that, what was it like when monks used to come to the valley."

He sighed and took a step forward as Anya called out to Nyma, and the nun began walking toward the head of the column. Then he paused and looked back at Shan. "But it has been many, many years since monks came to us. My father said to her once, you need not worry about studying the Compassionate Buddha, just study the Compassionate Nyma." He offered a strained smile then stepped on a boulder to look behind the column, his face clouded with worry again.

At least the other villagers showed no concern about a killer or the dangers of the chenyi stone. Their spirits seemed to lighten as the day progressed, and they sang songs sung by salt trekkers for centuries, sometimes teaching them to Shan and Lokesh. As they sat at midday and ate cold *tsampa*, Lhandro and Nyma described the beautiful valley where they lived. For long miles Shan let himself be absorbed into the simple carefree joy of the others. At nightfall, after they had made camp in the shelter of a large rock outcropping miles beyond the first pass, where the villagers had stockpiled yak dung on their journey to the lake, Lokesh sat facing the south. His old friend chanted his beads, squinting as if searching for something beyond the mountains. Sunrise would mark the third day, when Drakte would arrive at the charnel ground for his sky burial. Perhaps they had already left the hermitage by now, Gendun, Shopo, and Somo, bearing the dead purba up and down the mountains with the help of the dropka.

Shan sat beside Lokesh, facing the same direction, and made a *mudra*, arranging his fingers in one of the traditional forms to invoke a ritual symbol or teaching. He closed the fingers of each hand, with the thumb out, extended up, then put the right hand on top of the left thumb. It was called the Banner of Victory, invoking the triumph of compassion over ignorance and death. As he sat contemplating first the mudra and then the distant mountains where Gendun traveled with Drakte's remains, the

70

pain he felt over Drakte's killing surged through him again. Not simply because the purba had been steadfast and brave and selfless but because Shan's confusion over his death only seemed to grow, and with greater confusion came greater fear for those he traveled with. Gendun would have said Shan's awareness was being distorted by his emotion, for death never had a reason, only an appointed time, that Drakte was always meant to end this particular incarnation at that particular hour. There was no cause and effect in such a death because, Gendun would say, the world was never so orderly as Shan seemed to imagine. But even the Tibetans accepted that all things in the universe were interrelated, and a stone dropped in a remote lake caused ripples that changed, however subtly, the contour of the world. Something had happened in Lhasa, more than just a simple theft, and its consequences were catching up with those who had the chenyi stone.

Shan looked back toward the sheep, which were settling into sleep for the night. Despite the danger, despite the apparent urgency surrounding the eye, those responsible for taking Shan and Lokesh to the distant valley had chosen the slowest possible course.

"You could just say no." The words were spoken to him so abruptly, so unexpectedly, Shan turned to see if someone had crept behind him before he realized it was Lokesh who spoke. "Tell them no, that you are not the one," his old friend sighed, "and go back to that durtro. You can return to Lhadrung with Gendun. Go no further if you have doubt. Go no further if you can only think about killers. There would be no dishonor if you return. I will go on with the salt. I am going north anyway."

Shan was silent a long time. He realized his fingers had formed a new mudra, hands clasped together, fingers intertwined, the two middle fingers raised, pressing against each other like a small steeple. Diamond of the Mind, it was called, used to help focus awareness. At first he thought his old friend was again helping him focus on his responsibility to the broken deity but then he saw the expectation on Lokesh's face. "Going north anyway?" Shan asked.

Lokesh nodded solemnly. "Last night those geese helped me find my mother. I told her of the sadness in the land, of how people have lost the way of compassion and how we are taking the chenyi stone home. She said what we are doing is for the broken deities everywhere. She said afterwards I must find the true heart of those who oppressed us and shine a light of compassion on it."

Shan searched his friend's face for an explanation.

"I should have thought of this long ago," Lokesh said with a sense of wonder. "It took my mother. He is flesh and blood, he has a heart like any other man. He has a deity that has been broken, too."

"I don't understand."

"I am going to Beijing," Lokesh announced, his eyes glistening now. "I will travel north like a pilgrim, to gain merit. And my destination will

71

be the home of the one they call the Chairman, in the capital."

At first Shan wanted to laugh, but then he saw the determination in the old Tibetan's eyes, and a chill rose inside him. He clenched his jaw and stared at his mudra again. "You cannot."

Lokesh shrugged. "I have strong legs. I just go north for perhaps two months, then east for another three or four."

"I mean you will never be permitted. You could not make it," Shan said, with a sound like a moan.

"I must go alone, my friend," Lokesh said, as if Shan had offered to accompany him. "This is a thing for my deity, not yours. And it is too dangerous for you in China."

"They will never let you within half a mile of him," Shan said, and for a moment found himself short of breath. His Tibetan uncle wanted to sacrifice himself to the same people who had killed Shan's father and his blood uncles.

Lokesh put a hand on Shan's back and held it there, as if trying to get the sense of his heart. "I am not telling you to frighten you. I told my mother I would go and speak with the Chairman, so he understands the truth of things here. I wanted you to understand, for when the time comes for us to separate." He pointed out a solitary goose flying toward the setting sun. Shan watched him, then the goose, until Nyma called them to eat.

At the camp Lhandro revealed a bladder of fresh yogurt, a gift from the dropka at the lake, and a skin of cream which, having been jostled all day on one of the pack saddles, had become thick, sweet butter. The rongpa rolled the butter with their tsampa into little balls and enthusiastically consumed them with bowls of tea. As the others arranged the heavy felt blankets about the floor of the tent, Shan took his blanket outside and lay studying the night sky, fighting a bleakness inside. Some of the Tibetans believed struggling souls passed through many levels of hell before freeing themselves. In his particular hell he alone could see the torment and suffering approaching those he held closest to his heart, but could do nothing to prevent it.

He awoke suddenly, not aware until that moment that he had been asleep. With a catch in his breath he realized that a meteor had passed overhead, close by. But he had no memory of having seen it. It was not the first time this had happened in recent months. He had told Lokesh about a similar incident during their pilgrimage, and his old friend had seemed to find it cause for celebration, saying it was a sign of new awareness. "If your awareness experienced it within," Lokesh had said, "is it not as real as if your eyes had seen it from without?" But then, as now, the experience unnerved Shan. Holding on to reality was difficult enough in his world, without having his Tibetan friends try to teach him it came in many different forms.

Wide awake now, he lay watching the moon rise over the mountains and gradually was able to push back the pain that obscured the way he saw Drakte's death in his mind's eye, so he could replay it slowly, again and again, searching for a clue, for a hidden meaning. He saw Drakte's chin rise and his brow tighten as the dobdob had appeared. Though the purba had carried a belt knife his hand had gone not to the knife but to his prayer amulet. Drakte's reaction had not been that of a warrior defending those he had vowed to protect. But the purba's other hand had been doing something else. He played the scene again and again. Drakte's left hand had been pushing his bag back, hiding the drawstring sack with the sling and the ledger book with the innocuous entries about the dropka.

Shan became aware of a strange ebbing and flowing in the gentle breeze, then realized it was a low sound, rising and falling, a moan. He sat up. Not a moan. A chant, even a song.

Slowly, stealthily, he followed the sound over a hillock. A dark shape blocked the path. Lhandro had set a guard, he knew. But he froze as he saw it was one of the mastiffs. The animal simply raised its head toward him and turned toward a rock ten feet down the slope, as if directing Shan's attention there.

Anya sat on the rocks staring at a brilliant star on the horizon. The sound Shan heard, louder now, was coming from her lips, though he couldn't say what it was. Not a song exactly, but a sound like some of the old lamas made when using their voices in meditation, a sound that grew out of a mantra but became, at least to the untrained ear, a resonation that communicated not to the ears but some other sense, a folding of sound that could not possibly have come simply from the tongue and vocal cords.

He had heard such a sound before. Shan had asked Lokesh about it once when they had found a hermit making the same low wrenching sound on a high ledge. Lokesh had shrugged, as if the answer were obvious. "It's what you get, when you strip away the flesh of words," he had said earnestly. "It's just the way a spirit sounds when it's not communicating with humans."

He sat beside the girl and watched the stars. If she was not communicating with humans, he wondered, who was it she was trying to reach?

At last Anya's voice drifted off and they sat in silence.

"It's a long way we have to go," the girl said.

Although he felt strangely close to the girl, Shan realized it was the first time she had spoken to him. "Nearly a hundred miles to Yapchi," he observed quietly.

"No, not that," the girl said slowly, in the patient tone of a teacher, "if you and I are to bring the old eye into focus, there are many shadows to explore first, many knots to untie."

Shan considered the words for a moment. "You and I?"

"When it said this in me," the girl said cryptically, "I didn't understand at first. But I believe it now."

"I'm sorry," Shan said with a chill in his belly. "Who said something to you?"

"I was in a barley field turning earth with a hoe when it found me the first time. Nyma found me, shaking on the ground. It's only happened four times before. They say when I'm older they may need to keep me in a nunnery, if they can find one. They said in the old days I would have been sent to live in the convent after the first time."

Shan stared at the girl hard, trying to piece together the puzzle she had spoken. Then, he recalled Lhandro's words, how Anya had been found lying on a rock, reciting strange scriptures. And before, at the lake. She spoke the words of deities, Lhandro had said. "The oracle," he whispered. "You are the oracle."

The girl gave a thin laugh. "Not the oracle," she explained in a patient voice. "Some call me that, but an oracle is not in human form. Oracle deities just use certain humans as vehicles sometimes."

The words made Shan sad somehow. Maybe it was the hint of help-lessness in Anya's voice. Maybe it was because he remembered stories from the monks about the mediums who had once resided in the large gompas near Lhasa. They had been nervous, often frail creatures, usually short-lived, because when they were taken over by the oracle they suffered ter-rible fits and spasms, like seizures, that could last for days and exacted a terrible toll on their bodies.

Anya studied the stars, then abruptly turned to him again. "What if the valley was locked for some reason and the eye was its key? What if we opened it without understanding why it was locked?" The words came in an urgent rush, as if she had been contemplating a long time how to ask him.

"All I know," Shan said after another silence, "is that when I begin a long journey my mind is often plagued with doubt over where it will lead, about what comes after the one thousandth step, or the ten thousandth. So I try to make myself concerned only with the next step, then the next after that, so that eventually the ten thousandth becomes just another next step. By then we will all understand the eye better." His own words sur-prised him. He was speaking like the Tibetans, as if the chenyi stone were alive.

The girl nodded vigorously, as if it were exactly the answer she needed. Behind her, the dog stood, then she stood, as though the dog's movement had been a signal, and she stepped with the animal into the darkness.

Shan looked after her, not sure he had understood any of their con-versation. In fact, the more he learned of the people from Yapchi the more it seemed he didn't know. They seemed to have been cut off from the world for so long a wary, feral spirituality had overtaken them. But in his heart he knew they weren't that different from many other Tibetans he had met, each of who seemed comprised of many layers of mysteries and perceptions. The land itself was such a rich, vast tapestry of people and beliefs that the term Buddhism often seemed a meager label for the com-plex ways Tibetans viewed their world.

A low rumble rose over the blackened landscape. Shan searched for thundercaps but saw none in the clear night sky, instead spying a cluster of four red lights soaring across the heavens. Chinese fighter jets on high altitude patrol. As he watched the planes a deep sense of grief welled up within him, and stayed with him long after the planes disappeared over the horizon.

The caravan had been underway for two hours the next day when Shan, leading a packhorse, noticed a flicker of movement on the slope a hundred yards above them. He stopped and stared, finally discerning a man standing with a horse in the shadow of a large boulder.

Lhandro, behind Shan, whistled sharply, halting the caravan. "Damned Golok," he muttered.

As the figure on the slope stepped into the sunlight Shan saw that it was indeed Dremu, who seemed to search the caravan, then began waving at Shan, gesturing for him to come closer.

"Don't," Lhandro warned. "He could have friends hidden in the rocks. A man like that can't stop being a bandit."

Shan ignored the advice, but found himself watching the surrounding rocks warily as he jogged toward the Golok. "I didn't expect to see you again," he called out when he got within earshot.

"I got paid, didn't I?" Dremu snapped back. "Paid to get you through to Yapchi. Not to share tea with the likes of them," he said with a nod toward the caravan. "I go where the eye goes," he said in an oddly fierce tone.

"They're good people," Shan said.

Dremu frowned. "There's something," he said, "someone—" He glanced over his shoulder. "I don't know what to do with her," he said in a low voice, as though he did not want the rongpa to hear. He pulled his horse about and stepped behind the boulder onto a game trail that led toward the top of the low ridge. Shan turned to see Lokesh climbing the slope toward him, then slowly followed Dremu up the trail. He caught up with him just beyond the crest, where Dremu was kneeling beside a short, stunted juniper growing in the lee of a boulder.

Shan stepped past Dremu and discovered a small, frail-looking woman sitting against the rock. Perhaps fifty years of age, she wore a ragged grey wool scarf on her shoulders, over which hung several necklaces of coral and turquoise. Two small, tough hands extended from her heavily patched chuba, one clutching a mala, a rosary, the other a prayer scarf. On the ground beside her, resting on a piece of cloth, was a small copper prayer wheel.

Shan bent over the woman. *"Ku su depo yinbay?"* he asked in Tibetan. How are you?

"La yin, la yin," she replied with a weak smile. I'm fine.

But she wasn't fine. Her eyes had a sickly yellow cast, and Shan saw now that the hand with the khata, the prayer scarf, was pressed against her side, as if trying to touch the scarf to a pain in her abdomen. The woman gazed past Shan with a determined glint, as if trying to will him away.

"She was sitting here when I rode by," Dremu said. "Didn't even seem to notice me. She just kept staring down the trail," he said, gesturing toward the trail that climbed along the far side of the ridge, coming from the south.

Shan looked down the trail. "As if she's expecting someone." It was a remote, inhospitable landscape. Weeks could pass without a human entering the small, high valley the woman was looking into. He sensed movement behind him, and Lokesh appeared, his face creased with worry, his palm extended to touch the woman's head. He lifted her hand with the beads and placed three fingers, spread apart, inside the wrist. Once Shan had heard Lokesh bemoan how little he knew about healing despite his years with medicine lamas, but Gendun had rejoined that the most important aspect of healing was the moral quality of the healer, and in that aspect Lokesh was an adept.

After listening to the woman's pulses at both wrists Lokesh straightened and placed his fingertips on her cheek. "We must restore you," he said quietly.

The woman stared a long time at Lokesh, studying him, as if perhaps trying to recognize him, then she offered her weak smile again. Her hand with the mala reached out and touched the prayer wheel.

"Come with us," Lokesh said. "We can make you comfortable."

"Are you truly one of the old ones?" she asked, still studying Lokesh intently.

Lokesh rubbed the white stubble of whisker on his chin and looked at Shan as though uncertain how to reply. "We have horses," he said. "You could ride a horse."

The woman shielded her eyes with one hand and stared at Lokesh's face. She offered another strained smile, then settled her gaze on the trail again. It was as if she were expecting a healer, but had decided that Lokesh was not the healer she was waiting for.

"How long have you been here?" Shan asked.

The woman shrugged, without moving her gaze from the slope. "Two days I think." She slowly turned and searched Shan's face a moment as though she were about to ask him what day it was.

"Can you walk?"

"Of course," she said with a slightly impatient tone, then was seized by a fit of coughing. "I got here," she added hoarsely when the coughing had passed.

Shan sighed and exchanged a frustrated glance with Lokesh. "You should have a hat for the sun. What happened to your hat?"

"It blew away," she stated flatly and watched the trail again. Some Tibetans clung steadfastly to the old belief that once a hat blew off it was bad luck to retrieve it.

Shan removed the brown, broad-rimmed hat he had been wearing for the past three months and placed it on the woman's head, tugging it down for a tight fit. The woman slowly lifted her hand and touched the brim, as though about to pull it off.

"A monk gave me that hat," Shan said, "near the sacred mountain, Kailas. He said I looked cold. I'm not cold anymore."

The woman's yellow eyes blinked at him, as if to express gratitude, and the hand dropped into her lap.

Shan left her with Lokesh, passing Dremu, who still hung back watching nervously, and retrieved a bag of tsampa and a water bottle from the caravan. When he returned no one seemed to have moved, except Lokesh was holding his own beads now, reciting a mantra.

"Who is coming here?" Shan asked as he stuffed the food and water between the woman and the rock. "Who do you expect?"

"The one who understands it all," she said in a new, serene voice. Her gaze still did not leave the trail.

Shan touched Lokesh on the shoulder and the old man reluctantly rose, fumbled in his pocket, then placed the fossil rock in the woman's lap. "It's a powerful tonde," he said, "from Lamtso."

But she did not seem to hear, did not acknowledge the gesture, or shift her gaze from the trail as they stepped back over the crest of the ridge.

"Right," Dremu said. "The one who knows it all. Uncle Yama, that's who she expects, he's the one who knows." Dremu meant the Lord of Death, Yamantaka. "Waste of food and water," he groused. "Just her way of ending things. Hell, with the leopards and wolves in these hills, she won't even need to be taken to the body cutters." He mounted his horse and trotted away to the north, still keeping the caravan at a distance.

The image of the feeble woman alone on the side of the mountain haunted Shan most of the day as they wound their way toward the pass over the second of the four ranges of mountains that separated them from Yapchi. The woman had been waiting for someone coming from the south, coming along the difficult, unlikely trail that followed the crest of the ridges. But the ones most likely to come from the south were not healers.

As they stopped for lunch, Lhandro unfolded his tattered map on a flat stone and with his finger traced the course they would take for the seventy miles remaining to Yapchi Valley. It was not the most direct route, but a remote path that kept them far from the north-south highway and even away from the few low valleys at the edge of the changtang that held farming settlements. It would take two or three days longer than the traditional route of the salt caravans, Lhandro explained, but it would almost guarantee they would not be observed. Shan had seen Nyma speaking with Lhandro on several occasions, pointing south, scanning the horizon. As Lhandro folded his map Shan saw a solitary figure on a ledge, also looking south. Lokesh joked sometimes that Tenzin must be worried about leaving behind all the yak droppings they were passing in their travels. But Shan saw the worry etched on the mute Tibetan's face, and remembered the anguish he had evidenced over Drakte's death.

Tenzin turned at Shan's approach and began to step off the ledge, but Shan stopped him with a hand on his arm. "Did Drakte help you escape from your prison?" Shan asked. Tenzin tried to pull away with a resentful glance but Shan would not let him go, fixing him with a level stare until the emotion left the Tibetan's face. Tenzin nodded soberly, then pulled from Shan's grip.

After another hour on the trail they rounded a bend to find Dremu squarely in the path, sitting in his saddle with his left leg on his horse's neck, lazily cutting an apple with the elaborate knife the purba runner Somo had given to him.

Shan hurried to the front of the column.

"Pass is blocked!" the Golok called out loudly, as if he preferred that they keep their distance. "Snow avalanche."

"Not likely," Lhandro called back, just as loudly. "It was clear when we came through. Supplies are hidden there. Food for the sheep. There is no grass that high in the mountains."

"Spring melt shifted the slopes. That pass is under twenty feet of snow now," Dremu declared, and pointed toward the pass, still miles away. Its outline was visible, but its details obscured under the shadows of low clouds. But when Shan handed Lhandro his field glasses the rongpa studied not the pass but the alternative trail that could be seen leading toward the east, circumventing the tallest of the peaks. He suspected the Golok's motives, Shan realized, and was studying the trail for signs of unwelcome strangers. After a long moment the village headman gazed at the Golok with a sour frown, then motioned for the caravan to continue north.

Dremu pulled his horse to the side of the trail, watching with a sullen expression as the column of animals passed him, then wheeled his horse and galloped to the top of a small hill that overlooked the junction with the eastern trail, where he dismounted and made a conspicuous show of throwing his blanket onto the grass, languidly stretching upon it.

An hour later the sky cleared over the mountains and Lhandro examined the range once more with Shan's glasses. He stared hard, constantly shifting the focus, then handed the glasses to Shan, pointing between two peaks. The pass was gone, replaced by a large wall of brilliant white, at the top of which were great ragged blocks of snow that indicated an avalanche.

"The bastard," Lhandro growled, as if Dremu had caused the avalanche. He called for the caravan to reverse its course.

Shan studied the pass and the steep forbidding mountains that flanked it. "You came through there on the way to the lake?"

"Supplies were hidden there."

Shan examined Lhandro's face. "Are you saying someone else put supplies there?"

The rongpa did not reply.

"Purbas," Shan ventured.

"He liked climbing the high lands," Lhandro said after a moment. "He said he had a friend he would bring back and they would run up the mountain together."

"Drakte? Drakte was there?"

"He said everything was secret, that it was dangerous to speak about him or anything he did." Lhandro looked back into Shan's eyes. "But I guess now the danger for him is over. He was at Yapchi over two months ago. He said lamas were preparing for the return of the eye, but he had to find a safe way to get it north, a way no one would suspect. When we agreed on the salt caravan Nyma went away with him."

Drakte had been here, or near here. Shan began surveying the landscape. It was as though Shan was retracing the last days of Drakte's life, in reverse. "Did he travel with you and the sheep?"

"No. But he came to our village three times. Once, just after it was recovered in Lhasa, after Nyma told about the oracle's words. Then that time two months ago, and again last month, when he asked about details of the salt caravan, and he gave me his map so we would know the places where he left supplies, so we could avoid going near any settlements. He said when you came you would be on horses. He said we could keep the horses." Horses were prized possessions, beyond the reach of many herders and farmers.

"At the lake the herder spoke about the purba general the knobs are hunting. The Tiger. Did he help? Is he involved with the stone?" It might explain much. Perhaps the army and knobs were not after them at all. The scent of such a senior resistance leader would make the soldiers ravenous.

"I don't know. Maybe. One night Drakte met someone in the rocks above our village. I followed, to help keep guard. Drakte would not let me close. But I could hear a voice like I have never known. Deep like a growl but not exactly. Like someone roaring in a whisper. Drakte wouldn't say who it was, but later I found out that this Tiger had something broken in his voice box once, by a knob baton."

Dremu was sitting on his blanket as they approached the eastern trail. He did not greet them, did not pause to gloat, but simply tied his blanket to his saddle and trotted toward the east, ahead of the caravan.

It was midafternoon when a cluster of houses, animal sheds, and ragged fields came into view, a small rongpa village at the head of the narrow gravel road that the caravan would need to follow for several miles to reach the next pass to the north. Both the Tibetans and the animals seemed to quicken their pace as they approached the village, as if in anticipation of a warm meal and perhaps shelter from the steady, chill wind that had begun to blow.

But the village was abandoned. Tables in front of two houses held bowls of cold tea and tsampa. A blanket was spread on the dirt track in front of another, littered with the remnants of walnut shells. A small fire smoldered by the door of another of the decrepit buildings, its sheep dung fuel left to smolder when someone had dropped the crude leather bellows at its side. A large mastiff tied to a post barked loudly, not at the strangers arriving in the village but toward the eastbound road.

Lhandro halted the caravan, his eyes filled with alarm, then quickly ordered them back up the trail, behind the cover of the hillock they had just crossed, until he and Shan explored the empty village. At the first house, Lhandro stopped and called out a greeting, then stepped into its open door when no one answered. He moved into its shadows and reappeared a moment later wearing a grim expression, staring at a frame of sticks, ten inches square, that hung from the doorframe. Yarns of many colors had been stretched across the sticks, and it twisted in the wind. It was a spirit catcher, meant to trap evil spirits that wandered too near the house.

"No one," Lhandro said, as he scanned the remaining houses, then the surrounding hills. "Not even that damned Dremu," he added, as if now he blamed the Golok for emptying the village. "Bandits could do this, take the people until they ransom themselves."

The sudden sound of footsteps from behind caused Lhandro to spin about, crouching as if to meet an attack. Lokesh emerged from between two houses, followed a moment later by Nyma. Lokesh walked past them silently, his head cocked in curiosity.

"Not bandits! Don't you recognize it?" the young nun cried. "It's what the knobs do sometimes," she added in a tormented tone. "If they suspect someone of subversive activity, they just round up all his neighbors and question them, keep them locked up while their animals are starving and crops are dying. Eventually someone remembers something to implicate the suspect, true or otherwise."

The four of them walked uneasily down the track that led out of the village, moving in shadows when they could, following the rough road around a huge outcropping where they discovered a red utility vehicle parked, empty, at the side of the road. It was the kind of truck few Tibetans could afford, the kind primarily used in government service. As they stared uncertainly at the vehicle a scream echoed over the rocks. Shan hesitated, not certain where the sound had come from, then saw Lokesh jogging toward a narrow, two-foot-wide gap in the huge rock ledge that lined the road. Shan quickly followed as another loud cry split the still air, Nyma and Lhandro close behind.

The short passage opened into a natural, grassy bowl where slopes intersected at the base of the ledge. They had found the inhabitants of the village, and Shan realized the cries had not been from fear or pain, but excitement. Nearly fifty people sat on the slope or stood along the edge of the small flat clearing at the bottom of the bowl. Someone shrieked in surprise, another laughed. Not at Shan or his companions, for no one had seemed to notice their arrival. The population of the village was watching a man mounted on a huge, angry yak, one hand in the air, the other clutching a leather strap that had been fastened around the belly of the creature. The animal was bucking and twisting and, as Shan watched, it reared its broad head with a loud bellow that caused several children to run toward the back of the crowd. The animal was magnificent, probably not far removed in its breeding from the *drong*, the massive wild yaks that still roamed the Tibetan wilderness.

But Shan's eyes did not linger on the powerful creature, for as surprised as he was to see the rampaging yak, he was even more startled to see its rider. The man was long-boned and lean, with straw-colored hair that hung over his ears. The rider seemed to be conversing with the yak, for each time the animal bellowed the man yelled out strange syllables. "Ya! Ya!!!!" the man called for no apparent reason, then "Yi ha!" and "Yo!"

"Listen to him," Lhandro said at his side. "The man must be in great pain. Who would make a *goserpa* do such a thing?" he asked in alarm, as if it were a form of torture. "Goserpa." Nyma repeated the word twice, gaping at the man. It meant yellow head, one of the terms Tibetans used for Westerners. To most of those in the region, Shan knew, seeing a Westerner would be as rare as seeing one of the nearly extinct wild yaks.

Suddenly the Westerner was thrown clear of the furious animal, his legs flying in the air in front of him, as if he were sitting. But somehow his hand still clutched the strap, and when he dropped he found his seat on the yak again. Three large men stood anxiously at the front of the crowd with ropes, as if trying to find a way to capture the yak. A small pale Tibetan in a dark suit, white shirt, and tie stood by a large boulder at the far side of the clearing, every few seconds scrambling behind the rock then slowly reappearing, staring at the rider with a terrified expression, timidly raising his hand every few seconds as though to get the foreigner's attention.

With a sudden mighty heave the yak arched his back and the rider was off, shooting in a long arc through the air, arms and legs still working frantically as if the Westerner expected to return to the animal. But as the crowd watched in abrupt silence he soared across the little bowl and slammed into the ground with a loud groan. He lay flat on his back, without sign of life, as the three men with the ropes frantically closed around the yak. The little man in the suit produced a pair of spectacles from his pocket and slowly stepped forward to retrieve a black cap from the ground. Shan took a hesitant step toward the limp Westerner as Lokesh rushed past him.

The Westerner began convulsing. His hands clutched his belly and his chest began heaving. The little Tibetan in the suit shouted angrily at the three men with ropes, not in Tibetan but in Chinese. "Public Security will know about this!" he screeched, suddenly assuming an important air, shaking the black hat toward them. "You fools! People from Lhasa will have to come! You'll see what happens when a foreigner—" the man stopped as he stared at the blond man on the ground. Lokesh, too, stopped, the worry on his face evaporating. The Westerner was laughing.

"Yeee–esss! Oh mama, yes!" the man shouted in English, the first words from him Shan understood, and his hands shot up in the air as if in celebration. He sat up, laughing so hard one hand returned to his belly.

The biggest of the Tibetans with the ropes, a burly man with three front teeth missing, hesitantly approached and pulled the Westerner to his feet. Immediately the Westerner embraced the Tibetan, then studied the man's companions, who had the yak secured with two ropes around its thick neck. The tall, lean man pushed back his long hair, and grinned at the crowd.

The villagers were laughing now, some pointing with derision at the man in the suit, who stood with a surly expression, arms akimbo, staring at the Westerner as though deeply disappointed the man had not died. The blond man's gaze settled on Shan a moment, his head cocked in curiosity, then he pushed another strand of his hair from his eyes and looked toward the man in the suit, the Tibetan who had shouted in Chinese at his countrymen. The Westerner paused for a moment, frowning, as if about to speak to the nervous little man, then his eyes drifted toward the yak and the joy returned to his face. Strangely, the animal returned the man's gaze, its wide brown eyes seeming full not only of wild energy but also inquiry. The Westerner stepped in front of the animal and suddenly, before the yak could react, reached out, grabbed its head, and kissed the animal on its wet nose. The villagers broke into a cheer. The Tibetan in the suit lowered his head and covered his face with one hand.

"How much would it take, to buy this king of beasts?" the Westerner asked the three men loudly, in perfectly intonated Tibetan.

The men stared at him in confusion but after a moment quickly huddled to confer. "A thousand RMB," the tall one announced solemnly. The animal was clearly a prized possession. The price, though not much more than a hundred American dollars, was probably more than many of the villagers earned in a year.

To the obvious astonishment of the three men the stranger produced a wallet and counted out the asking price. When he had finished he studied the assembled villagers and approached a young woman. In a loud voice that carried through the hushed crowd he offered to buy one of the two red ribbons that bound her braids. She blushed, then nodded excitedly. He filled her palm with coins, accepting the ribbon with a small bow, then tied the ribbon tightly to a lock of the yak's mane. With the ease of one accustomed to working with animals he slipped the ropes off the yak's neck, then slapped its flank with one of the rope ends. The animal burst away, shooting through the shocked crowd and galloping up the slope like a young stallion. It did not stop until it reached the top of the first ridge where it turned and gazed defiantly over the hushed villagers, who suddenly burst into another wild cheer. The Westerner had not only given the magnificent beast its freedom, the ribbon meant that he had marked the animal as one ransomed, a mark of protection to honor the deities. Typically ransoming was for beasts marked for slaughter and such a ribbon would free them from the butcher, assuring them a long life. The ribbon on the yak meant it was freed from labor and could not be used by men again without offending the gods.

Half the villagers gathered excitedly around the three men who stood staring at the vast bounty they had suddenly received. Many of the others ran to the Westerner, some just reaching to touch him, some thanking him for his act of homage, others praising his riding of the yak. Still others held back, working their beads as they watched the foreigner with round, awed eyes.

After a few moments the stranger took a tentative step toward Shan. "If you are hurt," Shan ventured, "we could look to your injuries."

The man reacted with an amused smile. He studied Shan, and Lokesh, with the same cocked head and curiosity as before, then turned to gaze back at the yak, which still surveyed them from above. "With an animal like that, I could get rich back in Oklahoma," he observed, in his perfect Tibetan, his blue eyes sparkling.

"I don't understand what you were doing," Shan said.

The man smiled again and surveyed Nyma, Lokesh, and Lhandro, nodding at each one as they returned his gaze with looks of bewilderment. "It's that impermanence thing," the stranger declared, extending his right hand to each of them. "Shannslow," he repeated, and when he took each of their hands he covered it with his left hand, not shaking it but squeezing it like a tiny embrace as he heard and repeated each of their names.

"Why would you ride that animal?" Shan tried again.

Winslow ran his hand through his hair. "I told you," he said, and spoke toward Lokesh. "It's just like your *chod* ritual," he said matter of factly, "except that cowboys do it by riding bulls."

Shan stared at the man in astonishment. Chod was one of the rituals Gendun had often discussed with him. It was usually conducted only late in a monk's training; the monk sat for hours alone with the bones at a sky burial site, often overnight, to experience and contemplate the frailty of human existence. It was a brutal ordeal for most, from which some returned babbling incoherently.

"Cowboys?" Nyma asked slowly. Winslow had used the American word, for which there was no Tibetan equivalent. "What is cowboys?"

"Mostly you ride horses around mountains, looking for cows and singing," Winslow said with another grin.

Nyma nodded, slowly at first, then quite vigorously, as if now she perfectly understood about cowboys. Shan realized that somehow the American had made it sound like a pilgrimage.

A young girl appeared between Lokesh and Lhandro, holding out a blue ribbon toward the American. Winslow squatted by her, a hand on her shoulder. "The yak just needed the one," he said in a gentle tone. He unfastened the button that fastened his shirt pocket and pulled out a photograph, printed on heavy stock, half the size of a postcard. He extended the photo in both hands, like a gift, and the girl accepted it with wide eyes. She cried out and turned, unable to contain her sudden joy. Those near her crowded close and called out in turn. They seemed just as excited as when the American had released the yak.

The photograph, Shan saw, was of the Dalai Lama. In years past Tibetans had suffered imprisonment for mere possession of such a photograph. The pictures were still officially banned and routinely seized by the authorities. In the campaigns of repressions that periodically surged through the land they were used as evidence of political unreliability. But Tibetans treasured such photos, and Shan had seen many displayed on the portable altars used in dropka tents.

He studied the strange American as the man lifted the girl, who called excitedly for her mother now. Shan had encountered such foreigners before, men and women who roamed Tibet looking for adventure, or enlightenment. Lokesh called them wanderers, which made them all sound lost. Shan always kept his distance from them, for they seldom had the proper travel papers and always attracted the attention of Public Security or army patrols. The real danger wasn't for the foreigner, who, if picked up would simply be deported. Those found with such foreigners would be detained and questioned, because talking with foreigners evidenced dangerous propensities.

The girl pointed toward the gap in the boulders that led to the road, as if she had decided that was where her mother had gone, and wiggled out of Winslow's arms. The American smiled as he watched her disappear. "You're not from the village," he said to Lhandro in a conversational tone, then shifted his grin toward the distant yak, which was standing at the crest of the ridge. As he did so Shan noticed movement far up the slope opposite the animal. A man on a grey horse.

"We came with a caravan," Lhandro replied.

The horseman looked like Dremu, Shan realized, and the Golok seemed to be waving at them.

The American's head snapped back toward the rongpa. "From the north? West? Not on the road?" He glanced at Shan. "All of you?" When Lhandro nodded, Winslow quickly produced a map from his hip pocket. "Show me," he said with a new, urgent tone. "Tell me who you saw, where exactly you were. I need to know if—"

A frightened cry split the air. The little girl shot back out of the gap, frantically crying for her mother. In her hand was a jagged piece of paper that showed a man's smiling mouth and chin. Someone had ripped away the top half of her treasured photograph. Shan looked back up the slope at Dremu, who had stopped and dismounted. The Golok wasn't waving at them, Shan realized with a chill, he was frantically trying to call them away, to warn them.

But in the next instant Nyma darted into the gap in the rocks, Lhandro at her heels. Lokesh pulled on Shan's sleeve as though to restrain him, to keep him from following. "Go," the old Tibetan urged, pushing Shan toward Dremu. "Get to the Golok."

People were scattering, running up the slope in every direction. When he looked back Lokesh was gone. Without a second thought Shan ran through the gap toward the road.

He stepped into the brilliant sunlight to find a body lying on the gravel. It was Lhandro, moaning, holding his scalp. Blood oozed between his fingers. Nyma knelt over him. Lokesh stood nearby, his arms pinioned behind him by two large Chinese in the green uniforms of the People's Liberation Army. A dozen more soldiers stood deployed in a V-shape facing the opening in the rock to trap anyone emerging from the far side. Two grey troop trucks were parked on the road behind them, each with a fierce looking snow leopard painted on the front door. Between the heavy vehicles, sitting on a folding metal chair, was an officer watching with satisfaction as his trap filled. A cigarette dangled from his mouth. As Shan watched the man began writing on a clipboard balanced on one knee, with the casual, amused air of a scorekeeper at an athletic event.

Someone grabbed his hand roughly and Shan suddenly realized he had been bound to Lokesh, his left wrist fastened to Lokesh's right wrist, not by manacles but by a thin piece of wire, its ends twisted tightly together so that any movement was painful.

They were prisoners again.

Part Two

ASHES

CHAPTER FIVE

More than twenty villagers were lined up against the rock, all wearing expressions of defeat, hands at their sides, waiting as two soldiers checked their identity papers. Their faces told Shan the villagers had been through such checks often. Some suppressed anger, some fear. All suppressed indignation at being treated like outsiders in their own land. "Where's *your* papers?" Shan had heard a Tibetan boy shout out at a knob at a Public Security checkpoint just three months before. The knob had shackled the boy and in an hour's time the youth had been on the way to a year's imprisonment.

The villagers moved slowly when asked to reach inside their clothing to produce their papers, and watched not the sergeant who barked orders at them but a second soldier, behind the first, who held a semiautomatic rifle, an AK-47, barrel pointed down, hand on the trigger guard. It was impossible to predict what would happen when Public Security or the army came to such a place. More often than not any Tibetans who had their registration papers would be released. But if the patrol had a mission beyond merely sweeping for illegals, even those with perfect papers might be detained. In slow seasons some enforcement officials were known to pick up innocent Tibetans and detain them until they offered up an accusation. "Everyone is guilty of something," an interrogation officer had once declared to Shan, "we just don't have time to investigate them all."

Nyma pulled Lhandro into a sitting position. Blood trickled down his left temple, where he had obviously been struck, probably by the butt of a rifle. The nun put her arms around him, like a protecting mother, and glanced at Shan with moist eyes. She knew about such patrols, too. The villagers might be left alone, but Nyma, who had insisted she was not a real nun, could still be sentenced to prison for wearing the robe of a nun without a license from the Bureau of Religious Affairs.

"That yak, it ran like an antelope," Lokesh said quietly, toward the sky. The nearest soldier made a growling sound and raised the butt of his gun, warning Lokesh to be silent.

Shan looked at his old friend. At least they had been able to see the American with the yak, Lokesh meant. It was a prisoner's game Shan and Lokesh had often played during their years in the gulag. Fix an image in your mind and let it fill your awareness, blocking out the pain and hunger and fear. Shan remembered once coming back in a prison truck from a road construction site where several old monks had collapsed in weakness and been beaten and dragged away by the guards, too weak to do their work because their breakfast and lunch had consisted of a thin gruel made of ground corncobs and water. "I saw a snowflake land on a butterfly today," one of the battered lamas suddenly said, and earned a blow to his skull from a guard's baton for breaking the rule of silence. But by the time they had reached the prison every man in the truck had been smiling serenely, their minds filled with the image of the butterfly.

They would be taken to an army prison first, Shan suspected, then he would be separated from Lokesh. Lokesh's only crime was not having papers to travel outside Lhadrung, where he had been released from prison. But once they focused on Shan they would quickly discover the tattoo on his arm, and check it with Public Security computers. They would treat Shan as a fugitive from the gulag, and to such men a fugitive was like fresh meat thrown to starved dogs. He fought the temptation to look back toward the hills beyond the village, where another fugitive, without a tongue, hid.

The man in the chair tossed his cigarette to the ground, stood, and stepped toward the team checking papers. He impatiently ordered the soldiers to stop, then surveyed the expanding line of villagers. After he rose he strutted along the line with an imperious air, pausing to light another cigarette with an elegant gold lighter, and tapped the shoulders of several of those in line, ordering them away with a gesture of his index finger. A middle-aged woman a few feet down the line suddenly stepped forward and pointed to Shan and his three companions.

"They aren't from our village," she shouted, "just remember that, we never saw them before. We never helped them!"

Shan sighed. He didn't resent the woman's words. No doubt she had been before security squads before, had learned from the Chinese that the best way to protect herself and her family was to deflect official attention to others. But he felt sorry for the way she would feel later, and the way her neighbors would look at her.

The officer paused and stared at Shan, as if noticing him for the first time, taking the cigarette out of his mouth and blowing a stream of smoke in Shan's direction before he turned back to the line. He was finished in another minute, having dismissed all the women and children, and all the younger men. Every man remaining in the line was at least thirty years old, Shan guessed. The officer walked along the line again and dismissed two more men. They were older but short, less than five and a half feet tall, the shortest in the line.

At a snap of the officer's fingers the two soldiers who had been checking papers sprang back into action, scrutinizing the papers of the six men remaining with louder voices and rougher actions than they had used before. The officer paced impatiently as they worked, finishing his cigarette in three long inhalations, then lighting another from its butt. They were at the fifth man in the line when he lost interest and stepped inside the two lines of soldiers that still guarded the boulders. They weren't a patrol, Shan realized. They were what the purbas called a snatch team. They were looking for someone in particular.

"She said you're outsiders," the officer observed in a thin, slow voice, blowing smoke into Shan's face.

Shan and Lokesh looked at the ground. He felt strangely removed from the scene, as if he observed himself from afar. A part of him had never doubted he would one day return to the gulag. The yak ran like an antelope. He thought of the joyful American wanderer, hoping the man had escaped. It had been an impossible task, foolish to think Shan could help save their valley. Maybe in another hundred years the Tibetans could find a truly virtuous Chinese.

The sergeant held something up for the officer to see, the torn half of the Dalai Lama photograph. He flipped the card in his fingers when he caught the officer's attention. It was part of what soldiers did when they saw such photos, one of the thousand mannerisms of oppression ingrained in soldiers and knobs. Sometimes on the reverse of such photos a Tibetan flag was printed, which would guarantee arrest, and worse. This photo was blank on the reverse.

"My name," the officer announced abruptly, "is Colonel Lin of the 54th Mountain Combat Brigade." He spoke slowly, a strange anticipation in his voice. He surveyed the line of villagers before turning to Shan and his companions. "I will ask questions. You will give answers."

Shan looked into the Colonel's face, hard and gnarled as a fist. The 54th Mountain Combat Brigade had caught up with them. He fought the temptation to look toward the village again. Surely someone in the caravan had seen, surely they would all be fleeing into the mountains by now. He glanced at his companions. Nyma looked at the ground, the color gone from her face. Lokesh looked at the sky. Lhandro, still on the ground, blood trickling down his face, glared at the colonel with a mix of fear and loathing. He was looking at the Lujun Division, the soldiers who had massacred his ancestors.

Colonel Lin reached out suddenly and pulled a baton from the belt of the nearest soldier. He stepped to Shan, who had fixed his gaze on the little pool of blood beneath Lhandro, then silently placed the end of the baton under Shan's chin and lifted his head with it. Their eyes met and Lin studied him for a moment.

"Han," Lin observed under his breath, like a curse. Lin was Shan's age, slightly shorter than Shan, with a metallic cast to his eyes. The officer hesitated a moment, as if wondering whether he saw challenge in Shan's face, frowned, dropped the baton, gesturing his sergeant forward as he turned to Lokesh. Lin examined the old Tibetan much more intensely than he had studied Shan. Shan barely noticed as the sergeant padded his pockets. He was watching the end of the baton, tensing his legs to leap and take the blow if Lin raised it to strike Lokesh. But the colonel took Lokesh's free hand by the wrist and turned it over to study the palm.

"Nothing," the sergeant spat.

Lin's eyes lit with an icy gleam as he looked back at Shan. "You have no papers?" he asked quietly.

"Just a brochure to teach me serenity," Shan said.

Lin seemed to welcome his defiance. A thin smile creased his face, and he pointed the sergeant toward the clipboard on the chair. "You will give me your name."

Shan looked back at the pool of blood.

Lin dropped Lokesh's hand and presented his raised palm toward the old Tibetan.

"Do you have papers, comrade?" Lin asked in Chinese.

What had he been looking for in Lokesh's palm? Lin was not looking for a piece of stone. He was looking for a specific person, a person with what on his palm: The calluses of a hard labor fugitive perhaps? Or not calluses? Scars? Did it mean Lin knew who had stolen his stone?

Instead of presenting his Lhadrung registration paper, Lokesh offered his lopsided grin, which seemed to amuse Lin. The colonel studied Shan again, then bent his head to gaze with interest at Lokesh's grizzled jaw, which obviously had been broken, as though he were a connoisseur of fractured jaws. He looked into Lokesh's eyes, then lifted up the old man's arm and pushed up his sleeve. Six inches up the arm, on the inside, was a tattooed line of numbers.

"Lao gai," Lin announced with a tone of satisfaction, and called out the number to the sergeant, now standing at his shoulder with the clipboard. "We asked his name," the colonel said to his sergeant, for Shan's sake, then sighed and lifted Lokesh's hat from his head, handing it carefully to the nearest soldier. He studied the crown of Lokesh's head and tapped the baton in his palm.

"My name is Shan," Shan said, watching the tip of the baton.

"A Han traveling with a Tibetan criminal," Lin observed in an accusing tone.

Lokesh's head shifted upward. Shan followed his gaze toward a line of birds flying low, approaching the village. A dozen bar-headed geese, bound, Shan suspected, for Lamtso.

As the colonel twisted his head and saw the birds his eyes lit with a new hunger and he snapped out a sharp syllable. A soldier ran to the first truck, opened the door painted with a fierce, leaping snow leopard, and retrieved a heavy gun, a long semiautomatic rifle. Lin grabbed the weapon, waited a moment, and when the line of birds was fifty yards away, no more than thirty high, he jerked the rifle to his shoulder and fired half a dozen rounds. Nyma cried out. Lokesh gave a small, disbelieving groan.

Two of the big geese tumbled to the earth, a third somersaulted in the air, dropping low to the ground, but kept flying. Several of the soldiers cheered, and one darted away to fetch the dead birds. Lin returned the gun to the soldier who had retrieved it for him and turned back to his prisoners, his icy expression unchanged.

Lhandro was on his knees now, blood trickling down his cheek. As Nyma began to help him to his feet the soldier beside her pulled her away. When she resisted the soldier slapped her hard across the cheek. Shan watched in horror as the nun recoiled, then pushed back as though to strike the soldier, who lashed out with his hand again, grabbing her necklace, twisting it until it choked her, until it broke and the large gau it supported dropped free into his hand. He glanced at the amulet then slammed it against the rock wall. Nyma groaned and seemed about to jump for the prayer box, but froze as if she realized she should not draw the soldier's attention to it. She had once opened her gau to show Shan the treasure inside, covering her prayer. A photo of the Dalai Lama, with the Tibetan flag on the reverse.

Lhandro struggled to his feet, reached into his shirt pocket and with a shaking hand pulled out his papers.

Lin seized them before the sergeant reached Lhandro. "Yapchi," he read with sudden interest. "Yapchi," he repeated in a meaningful tone. His eyes flared, first with anger, then satisfaction. A murmur spread through his soldiers, several of whom raised the barrels of their weapons toward Lhandro. "Over fifty miles from your fields, farmer," the colonel observed, then surveyed Nyma, Shan, and Lokesh. "All of you from Yapchi?" He growled, his fingers clenching, the knuckles white. "Why here? Why so far away?" His lips curled to reveal a row of teeth stained with tobacco and Lin paused, as if relishing the moment. His eyelids seemed to droop. It was an expression Shan had seen in many such officials, a casual, patient cruelty hidden in a languid face.

"It's too early to weed our barley," Lhandro ventured weakly.

Lin gestured to the sergeant, who trotted to the cab of the first truck and marched back with an expectant gaze, holding a foot-long metal object in both hands.

"Have you been to Lhasa?" the colonel asked, gripping Lhandro's arm tightly. "Where's your bags? Your packs? I must see them!" The sergeant snapped his heels together and extended the object to Lin. Something frigid seized Shan's stomach. It was Public Security's favorite import from America, an electric cattle prod.

Nyma also recognized the instrument. She gave a high-pitched moan and stepped in front of Lhandro. Shan stared at the colonel in confusion. The prod was something the knobs used, seldom the army. It was for interrogation cells, not a remote roadside at the edge of the changtang. The colonel was desperate to extract information from his prisoners.

As Lin shot an amused glance toward Nyma and accepted the prod from the soldier a loud, bold voice rang out from the rocks.

"Yo, General, your majesty! My friends and I were having a peaceful picnic. No one invited the Boy Scouts." Shan turned to see the American at the split in the rocks. He spoke in Mandarin. His mouth was turned up in a grin but his eyes were cool, and fixed on the colonel.

The colonel's lips pursed in a silent snarl, and the officer stepped closer to the American. A green nylon rucksack hung from one of Winslow's shoulders. In his hand was a water bottle, from which he drank with a casual, unconcerned air as several soldiers closed about him.

"You've made a serious mistake," Colonel Lin growled. Lhandro's papers, still in his hand, disappeared into the pocket of Lin's tunic.

"Someone has," Winslow agreed, in English, and slipped his free hand into a pocket of his rucksack. The nearest soldier lifted the barrel of his gun. The American produced a thick carrot, leveled it at the soldier as if it were a weapon, then raised it to his mouth and loudly bit off the end. Several of the freed villagers, watching now from beyond the army trucks, laughed.

"You have no idea," Lin said icily. With a gesture of his hand two soldiers sprang into action, one leaping to each side of the American, pinning his arms behind him. The rucksack and water bottle dropped to the ground. The carrot flew through the air and landed at Shan's feet.

Winslow seemed not to notice the rough treatment. "Not much," he agreed, in Mandarin, grinning at Lin as the soldiers, still holding his arms, pressed him against the rock wall.

The sergeant jammed his hand into the breast pocket of the American's shirt and pulled out a bundle of papers, with half a dozen photographs of the Dalai Lama, which he dropped in disgust, grinding them into the soil with his boot. The American looked forlornly at the ruined photos. "You know," he sighed, "they say that man is the reincarnation of the Compassionate Buddha." His gaze drifted toward Colonel Lin, and Shan shuddered. The American was deliberately badgering the colonel. Lin returned the American's stare, then pointedly looked at the cattle prod. With a nod from him the soldiers began dragging Winslow toward the first truck.

Lin spat a curse under his breath and turned back to Lhandro, the prod still in his hand. The American was but a momentary distraction. A clanging of metal rose from the rear of the second truck and a soldier began tossing leg manacles onto the ground.

Lin stepped back to Lhandro and abruptly hit his face with the back of his hand. "Answer my questions!" he snarled, and hit him again. The farmer gave a small, surprised whimper, then swayed. Lin looked at his hand and frowned again. There was fresh blood on it. A metallic snap punctuated the momentary silence. The sergeant had fastened the manacle on Lhandro's ankles.

As Shan watched Lin, the icy knot in his gut grew tighter and more painful. Everything—first Lhandro's evasiveness, then the American's appearance and his disrespectful attitude, and finally the stain of blood on Lin's fingers—had only served to fan the flames of Lin's rage. His hand made a tiny, almost imperceptible motion toward his belt, snapping open the holster that held a small automatic pistol.

"You are going to write statements," Lin barked. "Every detail of how you arrived at this place, why you are traveling so far from your home, who else is with you, whom you encountered on the way, where you have been for the past three months." As he spoke, the soldier who had produced the manacles held up a roll of heavy, wide grey tape. It would be used, Shan knew, to seal their mouths as they wrote. "You will write them separately, and if your reports do not perfectly match you will be charged with conspiracy to obstruct administration of the people's justice."

"Hell, General, you're not Public Security," Winslow said in a loud, glib voice. Never in his life had Shan encountered anyone so foolish as to deliberately mock a senior PLA officer. "Just the damned army." One of the soldiers twisted the American's arm behind him, and pain erupted on Winslow's face. But as the soldier kept twisting the American forced his mouth back into a grin.

Suddenly the short Tibetan in the business suit emerged from the rocks. He stared in dismay at the American, and seemed about to shout. He turned to the colonel and opened his mouth, but still no words came out. Then his shoulders sagged and he stared at the black cap in his hands, stepped toward Winslow and placed it on the American's head. Everyone stared, confused, except Winslow, who laughed.

An instant later the sergeant gave a cry of alarm and darted to Lin's side, handing him Winslow's documents. As Shan stared in confusion the colonel's eyes grew round, then he threw the papers on the ground with a look of disgust and barked out a series of orders so quickly Shan could not understand them. The men behind Winslow released him. The soldier holding Lokesh's hat threw it at the old Tibetan and followed the others of the squad into the second truck. The sergeant released the manacles from Lhandro and threw all the chains, and the colonel's chair, into the rear of the truck.

Colonel Lin stepped backwards toward the first vehicle, silently watching Lhandro and Lokesh, fury back in his eyes. In another thirty seconds he had climbed into the lead truck and both vehicles were speeding down the road. As the Tibetans watched in disbelief Shan unwrapped the wire from his wrist, then bent and picked up the carrot and the papers. He studied the American's passport a moment and looked up, more confused than ever. The passport in his hand said that Shane Winslow was an American diplomat.

"It was just a piece of paper," Nyma said in confusion as she watched the American and the short Tibetan jog toward their own truck. Winslow had said nothing after the soldiers sped away, only cast a satisfied grin toward Shan and his companions before gesturing his nervous escort toward the red truck. They seemed in as much a hurry to leave as Lhandro, who had sent Nyma to run and bring the caravan to the road.

"But it had powerful words," Lokesh suggested in a tentative voice.

Shan glanced at his friend, who had been taught that there were adepts who could write special, secret words that would unleash powerful forces upon those who read them. In a sense Shan knew Lokesh was right. He could not imagine any paper a foreigner could show a man like Colonel Lin that would cause him to reverse his behavior, except the very paper Winslow had produced. Lin would gleefully help deport a troublesome foreigner, and would not hesitate to detain suspicious citizens in front of a foreigner. But whatever he had had in mind for Shan and his companions, he would not do it in front of a foreign government. And Winslow's paper said he was the U.S. government, or at least its only representative for probably hundreds of miles.

Still, that did not explain why the American was in such a hurry to leave. It was as if, although not concerned about confronting the ruthless colonel, he was nonetheless worried that Lin would report his presence to other authorities. Perhaps, Shan suspected, his own American authorities. Shan could not imagine a reason why an American diplomat would be in such an unlikely place, a forgotten village in a remote corner of the chang-tang wilderness.

Winslow tossed his rucksack into the back of the truck amid a throng of villagers who were quietly offering their gratitude, some pressing forward to touch him for good luck again. He opened the passenger's door as the nervous Tibetan, still in his suit coat, started the motor, then reached into his rucksack and produced a stack of the Dalai Lama photographs, the first of which he handed to the young girl whose photo had been destroyed by the soldiers. Shan stared at the strange American as he distributed a dozen more photos to the eager villagers. Whatever his official duties might be, Shan was certain they did not include passing out contraband photos of the exiled Tibetan leader.

As Winslow raised a foot into the truck the first of the caravan sheep appeared, trotting with Anya and Tenzin down the dirt track that ran through the center of the village. The American paused, as if the sheep reminded him of something, and he turned toward Shan. He hesitated a moment, pulled a map from the dashboard of the truck, and trotted to Shan's side. Suddenly Shan recalled the American's inquiries just before Lin had arrived. He had been asking about their travels through the mountains.

Winslow held the map, folded to show the region north of Lhasa into Qinghai Province. "You came from the west?" he said. "Can you show me? How close to the Kunlun?" he asked, referring to the vast range of mountains that divided Tibet from the Moslem lands to the north, running his finger along the provincial border. "Which way? What route?"

"South, we came from the south," Nyma volunteered, from behind

Shan. Winslow nodded energetically, and his gaze shifted from the map to the sheep.

"Those bags," he said in a surprised tone. "Salt? I've heard that in the old days caravans—by god it is, isn't it?" he exclaimed to Shan, in a tone that almost suggested envy. The American's fingers began roaming across the map. "That means one of the big lake basins, right?"

"Lamtso," Nyma answered enthusiastically.

The American nodded slowly, and traced his finger along the space between the lake and the village.

"You are looking for someone?" Shan asked.

Winslow nodded. "An American woman. Missing for several weeks. Presumed dead."

"We saw no Americans," Lhandro interjected from Shan's side. The rongpa cast a glance of warning at Shan. "We thank you for your help," he added hurriedly. "We will watch for her." Lhandro pressed Shan's arm, as though to push him way.

The American paused and studied the two men. "Your route is to the north," he said with a speculative look in that direction. "But you turned onto the road to the east."

Lhandro stepped away and gestured for Shan to follow. "Thank you," the Tibetan said again.

Winslow grinned, held up his hands as though in surrender and backed away. He climbed into the truck and the nervous little man behind the wheel put it into gear and sped down the road, away from the village and toward the northern highway that would take them to Lhasa.

As Shan watched the truck an animal brushed his knees, and he looked down. The ram with the red-spotted pouch was at his side, looking up at him with frightened eyes.

Every creature in the caravan, from the silent Tenzin to Anya to the sheep and dogs seemed to sense an urgency that afternoon. They moved at a half-walk, half-trot, not pausing for food or drink. After an hour Lhandro stopped and unloaded one of the horses, redistributing its cargo among the other four horses as he nervously watched the road. His eyes heavy with worry, he gave the horse to one of the Yapchi men, who trotted away to scout ahead, and in the adjacent hills. Dremu had not appeared since their encounter with the army.

When they had covered the ten miles of road two hours of daylight remained. Lhandro pushed them on, up the trail to the north until it curved, blocking the road from view. As the others rested Shan and Lhandro studied the steep, rough track that led north, looking for any sign of soldiers. Lin sent the man on the horse into the hills ahead. Everything seemed to have changed since the village. Colonel Lin, from whom the eye of Yapchi had been stolen, now knew about a band of travelers from Yapchi. He knew Lokesh was from a lao gai camp. He had lost them as prisoners only because of the American's intervention. But Lin would not give up, and his soldiers were trained for setting traps in the rough mountain terrain. Such men could easily elude the caravan scout, or trick him into thinking the path was safe.

"The colonel doesn't know our path," Shan said to Lhandro. "And he doesn't know about the sheep." In the hours on the road Lhandro had seemed to transform from the spirited, energetic rongpa to a man carrying a heavy burden of fear. The colonel had taken his papers and kept them, had discovered he was from Yapchi. He had felt Lin's manacles and for a few terrible minutes Lhandro had no doubt believed that he would spend his remaining years in a Chinese prison, losing everything, even, or perhaps especially, losing the chenyi stone.

"I didn't have to bring Anya on the caravan," the farmer said. "It should have just been me and the older men. And we shouldn't have involved Nyma. She wants to be a nun so bad.... She needs to be a nun.... This is not a nun's work. Some of us would gladly ..."

"Somehow," Shan said, "I don't think Anya or Nyma would have let you deny them the opportunity."

Lhandro offered a weak smile, then whistled sharply and began moving up the track with long, determined strides. At first only the dogs followed him, but he did not call out, he did not turn, he did not gesture for the others. The largest of the mastiffs paused when Lhandro had gone a hundred feet, then turned and barked once. The sheep raised their weary heads and began to follow. Anya stood and extended her hand to Lokesh. The two walked by the sheep, hand in hand, and Anya began to sing one of her songs. Slowly, groaning as they lifted their exhausted limbs, the others of the caravan silently rose and followed.

After a mile Lhandro gestured Shan to his side and pointed up the trail. Shan raised his hand to shield his eyes and saw their scout, two hundred yards away, unmounted, facing them with his hands raised above his waist, open, as if in an expression of chagrin. Lhandro and Shan jogged toward the man.

As they approached the scout disappeared behind a large outcropping. Lhandro halted and led Shan off the trail, around the backside of the outcropping. They edged around the rock to see the back of a large man in a bright red nylon coat and black cap sitting before a tiny metal frame that hissed and produced a small blue flame. Their scout squatted beside the man, drinking from a steaming metal cup. As Shan ventured forward the man in the red coat turned.

"Only have two cups in my kitchen," Winslow declared, extending a second mug toward Shan. "You're welcome to share. No butter, no salt. Just good Chinese green." Shan accepted the mug, savoring the aroma of the green leaves for a moment. He saw the others staring at him, then self-consciously extended the mug to Lhandro. He blinked for a second, something blurred in his mind's eye, and he saw his mother, sitting with him, patiently watching a steaming porcelain pot as green leaves infused the water. The pot had a picture of a boat on a river by willow trees. It was the way his memory sometimes worked now, after the knobs had used electricity and chemicals on him. His early years lay down a long dark corridor, where doors sometimes, but rarely, were unlatched by a random, unexpected event. Not events as such, but smells, or other sensations, even the inflection in someone's voice.

"Wasn't hard to figure," he heard Winslow saying. "You were going north from the lake and suddenly veered east, to the road. If you had been intending all along to go east you would have taken the road from the lake to the east. So you were blocked unexpectedly from going further north. The pass you intended to take got blocked by a snow avalanche or rock slide, I figure. If you were on the road it was just to get to the next pass." He gestured toward the high northern peaks. "Up there. The Tangula Mountains they call them, a spur from the Kunlun."

"I don't understand," Shan said.

"My government will pay a transportation fee if you want," Winslow said, and grinned as he saw Shan's confusion. "I'm going with you."

Lhandro stared woodenly at the American, then quietly asked the scout to make sure the caravan kept moving.

"You don't know where we're going," Shan pointed out.

"Sure I do. North. Same direction I'm going."

"To look for the missing woman," Shan said.

"They say she's dead," Winslow said, and left the words hanging like an unfinished sentence.

The announcement silenced Shan and his friends. Shan took a step back, as though to better see the American. He glanced at Lhandro, who shrugged, as if to say he knew nothing of dead Americans.

"He saved us from that colonel," Lhandro observed to Shan after a long silence.

"With a piece of paper," Shan recalled. "Could I see it again?"

The American stared at Shan coolly for a moment, unzipped the breast pocket of his nylon coat and produced the passport. Shan studied the document, not knowing what he was looking for. Benjamin Shane Winslow, it said, with a home address in the state of Oklahoma. It had over twenty entry stamps for the People's Republic of China, and many more for countries in South America and Africa.

Winslow took the mug, now empty, from Lhandro and refilled it from a pot on his tiny stove. "Just how would you go about identifying a fake diplomatic passport, tangzhou?"

Tangzhou. It meant comrade. It was the American's way of taunting Shan, he suspected, or perhaps any Chinese he met.

Shan handed the passport back to the American. "I've met several diplomats in my life, Mr. Winslow. None were remotely like you. And my name is Shan, not comrade."

Winslow made a great show of looking into his pack and rummaging through its contents, then looked up. "Damn. Forgot my black tie and patent leather shoes," he declared with exaggerated chagrin.

"Perhaps you would share with us what's in the bag," Shan said.

"You want my dirty underwear? Sure, welcome to it. Light on the starch please." Then Winslow studied Shan's stern countenance and his face hardened. "I've taken enough shit off Chinese today," he said. "You don't even have a uniform."

"You're the only one claiming to work for a government." As Shan spoke the herd of sheep appeared around the outcropping and the caravan began marching past the rocks. Moments later Lokesh appeared, then Nyma and Anya. They stepped toward the American with uncertain expressions, sensing the tension in the air.

"You had a driver and a truck. Where are they?" Shan asked.

"Sent them back to Lhasa. I didn't like him. When the embassy asks the Chinese government for drivers you can be sure they work for Public Security."

Shan considered the American's words and realized he was right, which meant the knobs would soon know all about the confrontation at the village, and the caravan.

"This man saved us at the village," Nyma said to Shan in a low voice that had a hint of pleading. "You especially should know what it would have meant if that colonel had taken us back with him."

The nun's words caused Winslow to look at Shan with a sudden intense curiosity.

"I only asked him to show us what he is carrying in his bag," Shan declared quietly.

"He's American," Lokesh said.

"He works for the American government. The government in Washington cultivates relations with Beijing, not with Tibetans."

The American seemed pained by Shan's words, but he offered no argument. He raised his open palms to his shoulder, then extracted an expensive-looking camera and a compact set of binoculars before turning his rucksack upside down, spilling its contents onto the ground. Shan squatted to study the items. A large plastic bag of raisins. A grey sweatshirt rolled into a ball. A box of sweet biscuits. A small blue metal cylinder that matched the one fueling the stove. Two pairs of underwear and two pairs of socks, knotted together. Half a dozen bars of chocolate. A one liter bottle of water. A tattered guide book on Tibet, in English. A tiny first-aid kit. And a small black two-way radio.

"You could call your driver on that?" Shan asked, pointing to the radio.

"The driver, or the office he is assigned to. It's how I get back."

"You said the driver works for the knobs."

Winslow grimaced.

Shan realized that Nyma had stepped behind him now, with Lhandro. They were frightened of the little black box.

"It's my lifeline for Christ's sake," the American protested. "You think I'm trying to interfere with your caravan, maybe steal your animals?" he said impatiently, then studied Shan and the others for a long moment. His eyes widened. "Christ. You're illegal. That's why you were so scared about Colonel Lin. You have no papers or—" the American looked back at the animals as they wound their way up the slope "—you're carrying something illegal."

No one spoke, which was answer enough. The wind moaned around the corner of the rocks. The little stove continued its low hiss. In the distance sheep bleated.

The American looked into his hands with a pained expression. "The missing woman is named Melissa Larkin," he explained. "People seem to have given up on her. She is presumed dead. You'd be surprised how many Americans die in Tibet," he added. "For tourists, it's an expensive destination that takes a long time to see, which means many of the tourists are senior citizens. Then there's the dropouts who don't understand about bandits in remote places or the diseases they would never catch at home, or how altitude sickness can kill them overnight. You can die of things here that would never kill you in the States, because medical treatment can be so far away." He looked up with a frown. "It's the embassy that has to get the bodies home for burial."

"But surely the Chinese authorities must help when foreign bodies have to be collected," Shan stated with a pointed glance at the American.

Winslow bent to turn a knob on the stove. The hissing stopped. "This Larkin woman is different. Thirty-five years old. A scientist. Geologist, seismologist. Worked in the North Sea, Alaska, Patagonia. Someone who can handle herself."

"You mean she was working in Tibet?"

"In old Amdo for the past year," Winslow nodded. "Southern Qinghai Province, just across the border from the TAR," he said, meaning the Tibet Autonomous Region, Beijing's misleading name for what had been the central Tibetan provinces.

"A snow avalanche. Rockslide. Bandits," Shan said. "Just because she was independent didn't mean she could avoid bad luck."

"Right. That's what they all say. I had to argue with my boss just to get the right to look for her." Winslow spoke with an odd note of challenge in his voice. "I have two weeks, then off to a conference in Shanghai."

No one spoke. Shan and Lhandro exchanged sad glances, and Shan knew the Tibetan and he were sharing the same thought. They had been brought up in a world where people went missing all the time, where almost no family was exempt from the pain of losing someone. People might walk into the mountains and never come back. People were dragged off to prison without warning, without announcement. People might come back from prison and find that all those they had known had vanished. Shan himself was missing, although he doubted his former wife or even his son cared, and would prefer to assume him dead. Shan saw that his companions were all staring at the American. Winslow lived in a truly different world.

The entire caravan was visible above them now, climbing up a switch-back trail on the slope above.

"I don't know these mountains," Winslow said in a softer, pleading tone. "I just need a way in, so I don't waste my time finding the right trail."

Still no one spoke. Suddenly the American sighed and handed Shan the radio. Shan held it in his hands a moment, then laid it on a flat rock, the American watching uncertainly. The Tibetans inched away. Shan grabbed a large stone, raised it over his head, and, as Nyma uttered a small surprised cry, slammed it down on the device. He hammered the radio once, twice, three times, until the case burst and bits of broken circuit board and wiring fell into the dirt.

"Dammit," the American growled. "You could have just taken the battery."

Shan ignored him, silently gathering the pieces of the radio and throwing them into a narrow cleft in the rock. "I still don't understand something," he said as he turned to face the American. "Why this pass? This woman could be anywhere in the mountains."

Winslow stared at the hole where the shards of his radio had disappeared, shook his head, and turned to Shan. "I spent four days looking around her base camp to the north and found nothing. Her company had other field teams out searching for her body. I thought I would work from the south up. But I didn't know where exactly. Then today after that yak and I met, I stopped to study the map with my driver, on the road below this spot."

The American hesitated a moment, pushing his hair back with a self-conscious expression. "A large bird, like a grouse, with white in its plumage, landed on a boulder nearby while I was working with the map. It kept staring at me. I walked over and it kept staring until it flew to another boulder a little way up the trail." Winslow shrugged and looked up sheepishly. "Like something was waiting for me up the trail."

Lokesh nodded solemnly. Shan studied the man. When speaking of the day's events, he had not mentioned meeting Colonel Lin, only meeting the yak.

"A bird," Nyma whispered soberly, to no one in particular.

"Where is this base camp exactly?" Shan asked. "How far north?"

"In one of the valleys where they are drilling. There's a mountain called Geladaintong, which holds the headwaters for the Yangtze. This place is twenty miles west of there, inside the ridges of another huge mountain. It's called Yapchi Valley."

Lhandro let out a gasp of surprise. Lokesh began nodding his head, as if it all made perfect sense.

Winslow stared in confusion as Shan replayed what had happened at the village. The American had emerged from the rocks to confront Lin after the colonel and Lhandro had spoken of Yapchi. He had not heard them speak of the distant valley.

"The Yapchi oil project," Shan said.

"Right. She works there."

Shan sighed, looking into his friends' expectant faces. There would be no denying the American now. The Tibetans would say it was predestined that the American travel with them. He knelt and helped the American repack his bag.

They camped that night below the pass in a field of boulders where the wind blew incessantly and they could light a fire only after building a small wall of rocks to shield the flame. The American offered to cook on his little stove but Nyma simply pointed to a figure climbing along the slope above them. It was Tenzin, who still seemed unable to complete a day without gathering dung.

"It must have been a bad thing he did," Lhandro had observed when he had first seen Tenzin with his sack, exchanging a knowing glance with Shan. The rongpa, like Shan, had guessed that Tenzin was performing penance. Shan remembered Tenzin's strange behavior in the hailstorm, and later at the lake. Drakte had freed him from prison and he was going north because someone had died.

Winslow studied the silent, stooped figure with a bewildered expression. "I don't think a cowboy could be a cowboy," he said slowly, in English, to himself, "if he had to collect cow shit every night."

"Keeps you close to the earth," Shan offered in the same tongue.

The American looked up in surprise. "You speak American well."

"My father taught me English before he died."

Winslow contemplated Shan, as if sensing a story in Shan's words, but did not press. "Don't see my bird," he said, switching to Tibetan as he gazed back over the slope. "I never believed in signs, until I started coming to Tibet. First couple trips, no big deal. Flew into the airport to meet the coffin of a former governor who had a heart attack climbing the Potola steps. Second time, I just went into Lhasa for a mountain climber who had died of altitude sickness. But the third time I was on the road to Shigatse and told the driver to stop for a monk who was looking for a ride." He paused, seeing the others had closed around the fire and were listening. "An hour later I told him to stop again," Winslow continued. "I got out without knowing why and stared at this high hill. Not really a mountain but big and steep, all rock and heather. I had to climb it. I still don't know why, it was like a dream. Afterwards, I thought maybe it was the medicine I was taking. But I started walking. Took almost an hour to get to the top."

"What was there?" Nyma asked.

"Nothing. Not a thing. Except an old piece of cloth jammed under a rock. An old square of silk with Tibetan writing on it. At the time I didn't even know it was one of those wind horses, a prayer flag. But I freed it so it flapped in the wind. Then I picked up a rock, a small red rock, and I threw it far down the slope without knowing why. It just struck me that the rock didn't belong there, that it needed to be thrown. Afterwards, when I got to the truck I told the two Tibetans. The monk nodded with this wise expression and said that clearly it had to be done, and thanked me for coming to Tibet to do it."

The Tibetans at the fire nodded knowingly.

Nyma filled her bowl with buttered tea, then shaped three butter balls and set them on the edge of the bowl. Shan had often seen dropka do the same thing, reserving the morsels for the deities. "I'm sorry," the American said. "I know I don't make any sense."

But Nyma and Lhandro seemed not to be listening. Lhandro was pointing. There, thirty yards up the slope, a grey shape rested on a boulder. A large bird, watching over the camp.

"It can't be," the American muttered, but he stared long at the creature, then turned away with an unsettled expression, as if he could not decide if the bird had come to guide him or haunt him.

Movement caught Shan's eye and he saw Tenzin emerge from some rocks not far from the bird, his sack on his shoulder. A second figure came into view above him, leading a horse, extending a yak chip toward the mute Tibetan. They had not seen the Golok since the village.

"He's with you?" the American asked. "He was riding above that village."

Lhandro looked at Shan as though for help. "He's part of the caravan," Shan said, and was struggling to find more words to explain the Golok when Anya suddenly stepped close to the fire, wedging herself in a sitting position between Winslow and Shan. The American shared his mug with the girl and she drank heavily as Shan and Winslow gazed at the bird again.

"I understand the sheep carrying salt," Winslow said after a few minutes. "I understand that some of you don't have papers. But," he said to Shan, "I still don't know what you are doing here."

"The Chinese forced him out of China," Anya blurted out. "And now," the girl made a gesture toward the mountains, "now he has to be here."

"Forced him out?"

"He has a tattoo," Nyma said with a loud whisper, leaning toward the American.

"Jesus," Winslow muttered. "Lao gai." The American seemed to understand much about Tibet, or at least about China's role in Tibet. He studied Shan with pain in his eyes. "How long?"

"Four years. Not so bad."

"Not so bad? Christ! You were in slave labor for four years?"

Shan looked at Lokesh, who was gazing with a look of wonder at the stars that were appearing over the mountains. "Not as bad as thirty."

Winslow followed Shan's gaze toward the grizzled old Tibetan and his mouth opened. But all that came out was a small moan.

As Shan studied the strange American again he recognized the awed, confused feeling that Shan, too, had experienced years ago when arriving in Tibet. Winslow was not just visiting the country, or encountering it like a stranger. The land was drawing him into it, beginning to change him in the deep, mysterious ways it had changed Shan. And no one, not Anya, not the lamas, certainly not Shan, could predict what Winslow would be when Tibet was done with him.

The next morning the Yapchi farmers offered the American a horse for the steep climb up the pass, but Winslow refused it. The American took his place behind Shan, near the end of the line, leading one of the pack horses as they climbed through a thick snow squall for thirty minutes, then broke into brilliant sunlight as they entered the high pass.

No one spoke as they wound through the dangerous passage. A twenty-foot-high ledge of ice and snowpack, rendered unstable by the spring winds, loomed close on the left, leaning over the trail. A nearly vertical wall of splintered shale rose on the right, and down the center of the high winding trail ran frigid melt water, turning the path into a long narrow track of cold mud.

When they cleared the pass Shan turned to see the American had paused and was staring back at the treacherous wall of snow that seemed about to collapse. "Geologists sometimes set off explosions," Shan observed. "Avalanches can happen."

Winslow nodded his head solemnly. "Especially oil geologists. There's probably a thousand places like this where she could have died in an accident."

"Why would she be alone?" Shan asked as he gazed out over the barren landscape they had passed through. There were indeed a thousand places to die. And a thousand places for the dobdob or Lin's troops to hide. "Geologists need a team for support. People to collect and carry samples. People to take measurements. People to watch people," he added, meaning that if a foreign scientist was wandering the mountains Public Security would be interested.

Winslow nodded again. "A team of four or five. She took two Tibetan assistants up a slope five miles from the field camp and sent them off to collect rocks at a ledge she saw through binoculars, told them to meet her in three hours at another ledge. She never showed up. They backtracked. They called in a company helicopter the next day. They even took dogs to search. Nothing." Winslow paused, turning to stare at the long high plain the pass had led them to. Suddenly he pointed. Something was moving across it, a rider galloping toward them, raising a long plume of dust behind him.

Lhandro, at the front of the column, raised his hand for them to halt, then jumped on a rock to better see the rider as the others anxiously gathered around him for a report. But Shan did not need to be told. He knew it was Dremu, and the Golok was frightened.

Dremu wheeled his horse around Shan. "He's out there," the Golok said, gasping, shaking his head as though in disbelief. "It must be that demon again." He extended his hand and pulled Shan up behind him as Lhandro began stripping the bags off the lead packhorse.

They rode hard out onto the plateau, Shan not understanding what to look for, part of him fearing the Golok had led them into a trap. But when they had gone less than a mile the horse stopped so abruptly that Shan almost flew off. A body lay on the path, a man in a red robe.

Shan and Dremu leapt off, the Golok circling the man, facing outward, his long knife in his hand. Shan knelt by the man's side. The monk lay outstretched, his arm extended toward the south. One leg was bent under him as if he had been crawling when he had collapsed. The short-cropped hair on his scalp was matted with blood. His mouth lay open against the earth, a trickle of fresh blood running onto the soil.

CHAPTER SIX

Shan turned the monk over. He was breathing, but barely. A long tear in the side of his robe exposed a green-black welt along his ribs. Another long bruise ran almost the entire length of his forearm. His hands and arms had several long cuts and scratches, from which thin lines of dried blood ran. Shan could find no other injuries. The man had been savagely beaten, perhaps even flogged, but not stabbed or shot.

As Shan pulled off his coat and placed it over the monk a second horse wheeled to a halt, carrying both Lhandro and Lokesh.

"A holy man!" Lhandro gasped.

Lokesh knelt by the battered man and lifted his left hand, arranging his three fingers along the man's wrist to take a pulse, then touching his neck. "He has had a terrible shock to his system," Lokesh declared after a few moments. "A violent beating. But he is young. His blood is strong."

"Who is he?" Lhandro asked in alarm, then began walking around the man, pulling his hat low as he surveyed the landscape. "What is a monk doing up here?"

Shan lifted the man's right hand. There were black smudges on his fingers, and similar smudges on the bottom of his robe. He touched one and pulled his hand away, rubbing his fingers. It was soot. But there was no sign of a fire. And there were no other monks, no minibus from Religious Affairs, no vehicle of any kind, not even a horse. The monk must have been on a retreat, or perhaps a solitary pilgrimage.

Lokesh produced a bottle of water and began to gently wash the monk's face, speaking in soft tones, first telling the man he was with friends now, then beginning a mantra to the Compassionate Buddha. Lhandro began clearing a circle of bare earth and collecting rocks. He was going to do what Shan had always seen herdsmen and rongpa do when someone was injured. Lhandro would light a fire and make buttered tea.

As Shan knelt opposite the limp form of the monk the man's eyes fluttered open and he jerked his hand from Lokesh. "You will need weapons! You must have weapons to stop the thing!" he groaned. His eyes widened, and he squinted at Lokesh as though trying to recognize who, or what, the old Tibetan was. Then he faded back into unconsciousness.

Moments later the caravan began to arrive. The Yapchi villagers rushed to the monk's side, murmuring excitedly, confusion and fear twisting their faces. No monk had come to their valley for many years, Lhandro had said. Tenzin quickly produced the sack of fuel carried by one of the packhorses and helped Lhandro ignite a fire in the circle of rocks. The American pulled the sweatshirt from his rucksack to make a pillow for the man, then produced his first aid kit, from which Lokesh selected small squares of sterile gauze to dab at the worst of the monk's wounds.

Shan pulled out his battered fieldglasses and stood on a flat boulder to survey the high plateau. The land was surprisingly fertile, carpeted with the spring growth of plants, many of which were unfamiliar to him. He carefully studied the entire terrain without seeing any sign of life, then began again with the northwest side of the plain, the direction from which the monk seemed to have been crawling. For a moment he thought he saw a wisp of smoke in the distance, then it was gone.

"What kind of bastard would do this?" a deep voice near Shan asked. "A harmless monk." Winslow was aiming his compact binoculars in the direction Shan had been looking.

"I thought I saw smoke," Shan said.

"Smoke?"

"The monk has soot on his hands and robe."

Shan turned back to the caravan. A pan was being unpacked, with a kettle and churn. Lhandro had decided to make their midday camp early, to cook tsampa and check the bindings on the sheep packs. Shan caught Winslow's eye and motioned toward the two empty packhorses that now stood grazing on the sparse spring growth.

"If the monk does not strengthen we will stay here tonight," the rongpa headman said when he saw Shan and the American leading the horses away. "But if we are not here when you return, ride to the grove of junipers at the far side." Lhandro pointed to the high ridge that defined the northeast side of the plain, perhaps ten miles away. "On the other side is a ruined gompa where there is better shelter."

Shan and Winslow trotted side by side over the rough terrain, stopping to follow a flash of movement on the side of the high ridge they had passed through that morning. After a moment they saw in their glasses that it was a family of goats. As they started again Winslow raised his hand. The sound of pounding hooves made them turn. Dremu was bearing down on them.

"You have to stay with it," Dremu growled in a scolding tone to Shan as he pulled his horse to a sudden halt.

"It?" Winslow asked.

The Golok replied with a frown. "You're looking for that fire?" he asked.

"Did you see a fire?" Shan asked.

"No, but I smell it. Not yak dung. Not wood," he said, and kicked his horse into a trot toward the northwest corner of the plateau.

A quarter hour later Shan and Winslow dismounted behind Dremu, who stood at the edge of a shallow bowl perhaps fifty yards wide, marked by a two-foot-high cairn covered with lichen. The bowl differed from the rest of the landscape because it was lined with a uniform growth of a short grey-green plant, ten inches high, that Shan had not seen growing elsewhere on the plain. But half of the small hollow was blackened, the spring growth burned to the ground. A pungent smell, at once sweet and acrid, filled the air.

"Why a fire here?" Winslow wondered. "Lightning?"

"A campfire," Dremu interjected, and pointed to a low, dark six-foot-long mound on the far side of the bowl, adjacent to the scorched earth, ten feet from the cairn of rocks.

They walked their mounts slowly around to the mound, their pace slackening the closer they approached, each man glancing warily toward the slope above. Shan could not escape the sense that they were being watched, but he saw no sign of life on it other than a family of pikas scurrying over the rock talus.

The three men halted half a dozen paces from the mound. It was covered in black nylon cloth, and beside it was a yellow nylon vest. A red wool cap nearby was singed black by the fire. Shan and Winslow exchanged a grim glance. The black mound was in the shape of a body.

Dremu tossed a pebble onto the black cloth, with no effect. Then the Golok spun about and studied the slope intensely. His hand closed around the hilt of his knife.

Shan stepped forward reluctantly and lifted one end of the black nylon. It was a sack of some kind, a long bulky sack, and extremely light. He lifted the end to his waist with a sigh of relief. There was no body, only the sack, stuffed like a quilt.

"Sleeping bag," Winslow said with a confused tone, and bent to pull the yellow vest from the ground. It was large enough to fit Shan and looked new. Under it, in a pile at the head of the bag, was a pair of blue denim pants with an American label. In a small nylon pouch were a black metal compass with a red cross and a dozen bars of something called high energy protein, labeled in English and Chinese.

"There's no campfire." Shan gestured toward the scorched bowl. There was no ring of rocks, no cleared circle, no stones stacked for cooking. No campfire that had gone out of control. "And if lightning struck there would be a gash in the earth, some sign of a violent burst of heat."

Winslow nodded slowly. The brush had been set on fire deliberately. "To burn the whole damn plain, you think? To keep someone away, maybe scare off pursuers? But air doesn't circulate in the bowl. The flames crept down and smoldered away."

Shan bent and broke off one of the grey-green plants from a patch at the edge of the bowl and held it to his nose, detecting the same smell that hung in the air. As he pushed the sprig into his pocket Winslow bent over the bag and vest. "Expensive stuff," the American observed. "And all the labels are American, not just the jeans."

"Your geologist?"

"That's what I'm thinking," Winslow said as he examined the pockets of the jeans and vest. In the vest pocket was a government issued map of the region. The jeans yielded a plastic cigarette lighter, a pencil stub, a metal whistle on a lanyard—a device field teams might use to stay in contact when radios were not available. The American stuffed the vest, jeans, and singed hat into the sleeping bag, rolled it all into a tight bundle and tied it to his horse.

They rode halfway up the slope, along a trail that arced along the ridge into a maze of huge boulders that soon became impassable for the horses. Dremu produced short lengths of rope and hobbled their mounts, letting them forage in the thin growth, then pointed out a goat path leading up the mountainside he would scout while Shan and Winslow explored the field of rocks.

They searched futilely for half an hour, then climbed onto one of the boulders to scan the long plain again with their glasses. In the middle of the rolling green landscape was a blurred line of color. The caravan was moving northeast, as Lhandro had suggested, toward the grove of trees on the opposite side of the plain.

"Sometimes in Tibet," Winslow said, "when it gets really quiet, in a place like this, I hear things. Like a groan or a shudder. Only bigger. My grandfather would have said it was giants talking in the mountains."

Shan said nothing, but studied the landscape; first the plain again, then the slope around them. He couldn't shake the feeling of being watched.

After a long silence the American sighed. "You don't trust me, do you, Shan?"

"I don't believe you are what you say."

"Call the embassy. Call Washington. I'll loan you my passport for verification."

"I know something about working for governments. The Foreign Service is a career job. You should be halfway through your career."

"Right."

"And you are sent to collect the bodies of dead Americans? It's the job of a very junior officer at best."

Winslow offered no reply.

"And looking for the missing woman, that's a law enforcement job. Your government would ask the authorities in Beijing to find her. You say you came for that woman's body, but there is no body."

Winslow silently stared over the plain. "I guess you could say I've been reincarnated into a lower life form by Foreign Service standards." He lifted a pebble and tossed it from one hand to the other, then glanced back at Shan with a frown. "Two years ago I was Deputy Commercial Attaché in Beijing, engaged to be married to another Foreign Service officer, a cultural attaché in Beijing. I had always been a high achiever, collected languages like some people collect coins. Marked for fast advancement because I was the only one who spoke all the major languages of China. I had an apartment outside the embassy compound.

"There was a Chinese woman who did my cleaning. Over sixty years old, a real delight. Like the gentle old grandmother I never had. My fiancée and I started going to her home after we knew her a year, took her family out of the city for picnics at the Ming Tombs and the Summer Palace. After a while we noticed she wouldn't eat much of the food we brought for her and she always asked if we minded if she would take her share away. Eventually we found out she was giving it to orphans at a school run by one of those religious groups the government hates so much. The government support for the school had been dropped because the group had publicly demonstrated for freedom of religion. So the children were living on two bowls of rice a day. One day she didn't come to work and I found out that she had been arrested, along with all the teachers at the school. It took me a week before I could find her in a jail. They had beat her and ruptured her spleen, trying to get her to disavow her belief in her religion." When he looked at Shan there was pain on the American's face. "I never had much religion, but like my fiancée said, people have a right to find their god, and worship it in their own way," he said quietly, looking into his hands now.

Shan nodded. In the end it was all that the Tibetans wanted to do.

"I used my diplomatic credentials to go to the Ministry of Justice and make inquiries about her, ask for her release. The Ministry told the ambassador and the ambassador ripped off my stripes and broke my sword."

"I'm sorry?"

"Did everything but fire me, because I had no authority to make such inquiries, because the U.S. keeps its hands off the way China treats her citizens. Said I'd be cleaning embassy bathrooms for the rest of my career. So my fiancée and I decided to quit. She left and got a teaching job in Colorado, and I went back on leave to get married and buy a house with her. Two months later I returned to interview for a job at the same university."

"But you didn't quit," Shan pointed out.

"No," Winslow said heavily, and looked out over the plain again before speaking. "It was winter when I flew back, in a bad snowstorm. The house was up in the mountains. On the way to the airport to pick me up she slid off the highway and into a river. Took them two days to recover her body. The morgue called me to ask if I knew she was two months pregnant." Winslow watched a hawk fly overhead. "I hadn't, but by then I had gone to the house. She had bought a set of baby furniture and had tied balloons all over it, to surprise me."

Shan studied the American's face. Winslow didn't seem the same ebullient man he had seen riding the yak the day before.

"I had nowhere to go, no roots anywhere, no family left alive. So I came back. Started volunteering for every shit job nobody wanted. Just to get away. Recover all the bodies for shipment home. Clean up after the ambassador's poodles."

Shan felt an emptiness welling within. Somehow the American's words made him remember his father, who had been taken from him by the Red Guard, after stripping him of his beloved job as a professor because he taught Western history and had friends in Europe and America.

"They shouldn't have arrested that old woman for helping orphans," Winslow said in a voice grown hoarse.

"What happened to her?"

"Died. She died in that jail and they sent her family a bill for cremating her."

Shan stared at the American's hollow face. Winslow's woes had started with government service in Beijing. Everything that happened in life was connected, Lokesh was fond of saying.

"But still," Shan said. "You came here without a body to collect."

Winslow offered a melancholy grin. "I lied to them, to my boss. The oil company had sent a copy of their personnel file on Larkin when she went missing. We figured there would be a body later, just not yet. I read the file. Same age as my wife. Marked by the company as a high achiever. Had been engaged to another company geologist, but he died in an avalanche in the Andes four years ago. After that she asked for the most remote assignments possible."

"So you felt"—Shan searched for words. "Lokesh might say you were on similar awareness paths."

Winslow's sad smile reappeared. "I told them I had a call, that her body had been sighted in the mountains. Only a little lie really. I'd be the one they would send eventually anyway."

They sat watching the wind wash the spring growth on the plateau. Finally Shan sighed and stood. "I've heard that noise, too, when the land speaks like a groan. A lama told me it happens sometimes, when the earth senses its impermanence. It just groans." Strangely, Shan remembered sifting grains of white sand in his hand. He felt an intense longing to be with Gendun, or at least to know he was safe.

As if on cue the land rumbled. The thunder came in three overlapping peals from the far distance. It seemed to be coming from the huge snow-capped mountain on the far side of the plain, the mountain that separated them from Yapchi Valley. But there were no clouds in the sky.

As the sound faded a shrill shouting replaced it, a torrent of furious Tibetan. Winslow pointed to a figure two hundred feet below on a rock spur that overlooked the plain. It was Dremu, his knife raised over his head, brandishing it toward the far side of the plain as if he were answering the strange rumbling.

The distance was too great for Shan to make out individual words but the anger in the Golok's voice was unmistakable. Anger at first, then a hint of fear, and finally what may have been desperation. Shan eased himself over the ledge they stood on and began climbing down.

Dremu was squatting when they reached him, throwing stones in the direction of the northern mountains. He spun about at their approach, then sheepishly looked in the direction of the horses. "All right, we can ride. Lhandro is taking that monk to the water by the trees," he said, and tossed a stone toward a pile of cans in the shadow of the boulder. "I found those up the slope at a campsite," the Golok said. "With a lot of bootprints, new boots. Expensive boots. Nothing else. It was a week old."

There were three empty cans, one of peaches, one of canned pork, and one of corn. Not Tibetan fare. The labels on the pork and corn were in English, the peaches in Chinese. Stuffed into one can was an empty wrapper for one of the protein bars they had seen below.

"How far are we from Yapchi Valley?" Shan asked.

"Maybe fifteen miles," Dremu replied.

"But why would the Americans be so far away from their oil project?" Shan wondered out loud, surveying the high ridge above them that defined the northern end of the plain. "What's beyond this? On the other side?"

"Nothing. A river. Steep ravines. Places only goats can walk."

Shan studied the Golok. "Who were you so angry with? Was it because of that sound?" He still knew very little about the fiery, bitter man, other than that the purbas had asked him to help.

"You wouldn't understand," the Golok said after a long silence.

"I think that sound made you angry. That sound like thunder."

"Thunder?" Dremu snapped. "You think it was thunder? Without a cloud in the sky? It was that damned Yapchi Mountain." He stood and raised his knife again, stabbing it toward the snowcapped peak. "It's the damndest mountain in the world. There's no mountain like it anywhere. Some say there's treasure buried in it, but I say it's full of demons." He had the air of a warrior about to do battle.

Shan looked back toward the horizon. The mountain, and the valley beyond, was their destination, the home of the chenyi deity.

"You speak like it was alive," Winslow said uneasily.

Dremu winced and rolled his eyes at Shan, as though asking to be saved from foreigners who were ignorant about mountain deities, then turned and started down the trail.

"The man you made a bargain with is dead," Shan said to his back. "You've been paid. It's not far now. Lhandro and Nyma can take me the rest of the way."

The Golok slowly turned, anger back in his face. But an odd melancholy quickly replaced it.

"I have little of value," Shan said, fighting the temptation to touch the ivory rosary in his pocket. "These old binoculars are the most valuable thing I own. But you can have them, and ride on, leave us. Just tell me one thing. Why are you angry at that mountain?"

Dremu walked to the edge of the ledge they stood on, facing the mountain that dominated the northern horizon. "I spent a month there once with my father."

Shan stepped to his side.

"Those Lujun troops," Dremu said with a much quieter voice, "after what they did in Yapchi Valley they passed through my family's lands. In those days Goloks were to be feared. The Chinese knew they had to show respect or they would lose men. So like everyone else they paid their respect and moved on. They had orders to hurry home."

"You mean they paid tribute," Shan suggested.

Dremu nodded. "It was a tax everyone paid. So Goloks wouldn't shoot from the top of gorges, and would make sure others didn't. It was just a business. But my people didn't know what those Chinese had done in Yapchi. A week later when we learned of the massacre, my family was shamed. We wouldn't have taken that gold if we had known," he said, speaking as if it had just happened. "So my grandfather's father rode out to find those Chinese, to get the eye back or return the gold piece he had taken from the Chinese." He fixed Shan with a sour expression. "To claim his honor back," he added in a defiant tone, and began fingering a small leather pouch that hung beside his prayer gau.

"It was very brave," Shan replied solemnly.

"They shot him. The general did it himself. They had Tibetans helping with horses who saw. Shot him in the head and laughed. Then they hired a dropka to take the body back to us. They had sewed the gold into his pocket. Later monks came and made my family go to Yapchi and apologize to the survivors, and help them build new houses. Even other Goloks hated my family afterwards. There were stories about how old monks came in the summer to Yapchi, and sick Goloks once would go there to be healed. But all the healing stopped after that because the people there hated the Goloks so much." He gazed toward the horizon again. "Of course we rode with bandits after that." He kicked a stone off the ledge.

"Those Lujun soldiers destroyed my family," he said. "My uncles rode away with bandits, or disappeared in cities. My father took me to that mountain one summer, looking for a monk, any monk who could help our family out of the blackness that had come over it. But by then there were no monks to be found anymore, so he meditated for days and days, trying to reach that Yapchi deity. But it only made him more sad. He knew the mountain was punishing him. He died not long after and my mother went to work in a city scrubbing Chinese floors. I was fourteen and had my own horse," Dremu added, as if it explained why he had stayed behind.

114

The three men stood with the cool wind washing over them. It was mingled with the vaguest hint of flowers, like a subtle incense wafting over the plain. The Tibetans used incense to attract deities. Perhaps it was simply something in the air, Shan thought, that had caused first Winslow, then Dremu to speak of their tragedies. Shan was certain the Yapchi rongpa knew nothing of Dremu's story—and he had no idea of how they would react if they did know. He suspected that Winslow seldom shared his tale with anyone, even other Americans.

"What do you mean the eye?" Winslow asked Dremu. "You said something about an eye. And the Lujun?"

The Golok gestured at Shan, who winced. He began to explain about the eye and the valley. But it seemed the closer he got to Yapchi the less he understood about the eye.

The story brought the sadness back to Winslow's face. He gazed at each of his companions in turn, and seemed about to speak, to ask something, but finally he turned and began slowly walking down the slope toward the horses.

"How did the purbas find you?" Shan asked Dremu as they began following the American. "They chose you not just as a guide, but because you know about the eye."

"Find me? I found them," Dremu said in a low voice, leaning close to Shan as if wary of the rocks overhearing. "Others knew the fifty-fourth had it, but I was the one who discovered exactly where. I found the Tibetan worker the soldiers paid to clean their damned toilets and sometimes he loaned me his identity card. I found it on that colonel's desk. That bastard Lin. I made plans, careful plans, but one night some purbas caught me outside the army headquarters and asked me what I was doing. When I told them I was going to steal the stone they laughed, but kept me in a house for two days. That Drakte came and said no, don't steal it, not if you really want to hurt the Chinese. Just tell us how to get inside Lin's office then meet the eye at that hermitage and help get it to Yapchi. Drakte said they would pay me for what Goloks always did best, watching in the mountains and avoiding troops. They didn't want me in Lhasa. Because they had someone else who had to steal it."

As if it had been listening, Yapchi Mountain replied with another of its ominous rumbles.

CHAPTER SEVEN

They rode at a brisk trot over the high plain, their horses seeming eager to catch up with the caravan. Perhaps, Shan thought, the animals were unsettled by the plain, experiencing the same sensations he did, a vague presence, an expectation in the air. He could find no words to describe the feeling. It wasn't fear, although Dremu frequently rose in his stirrups to look about as if wary of pursuit. There were moments when Shan even felt an unexpected exhilaration as they loped across the wild, remote plain. The high ridges that bounded it on three sides gave it a remote, secret air, a sense of being a world untouched and apart.

As they closed with the caravan he slowed his horse and dismounted, letting Dremu and Winslow catch up with the others as he walked behind. He studied the column of animals and people stretched out over the wind-blown plain and realized how, during the more peaceful moments of the past few days, he had come to think of their journey as a pilgrimage. He considered the odd assembly. The young girl who spoke for the deities. Nyma the uncertain, illegal nun. The rongpa who thought a jagged piece of stone would protect them from the Chinese. Dremu the bitter warrior, who searched for a way to restore dignity to his family. Perhaps they were more like fugitives than pilgrims. Tenzin the escapee. The American, fleeing from a life and career of disappointment. Perhaps even the Yapchi villagers themselves, now that Colonel Lin had glimpsed Lhandro and Nyma and confiscated Lhandro's papers.

As the caravan entered the little grove of trees, Nyma and Anya, at the back of the line, paused to study a pattern of stone shapes visible on the slope beyond the trees. They trotted into the shadows as if eager to investigate further. Lhandro waited as the sheep and horses gathered around the small stream that coursed through the grove, then gestured Shan and Winslow down a path that led to the far side of the grove. Shan looked for Lokesh, found him helping the villagers untie the packs from the sheep, then followed the two men through the trees.

Shan had seen many ruined gompas in Tibet, the work of the army and, later, the Red Guard, who together had destroyed all but a handful of Tibet's six thousand monasteries and convents. But as he stepped out of the grove he realized that never—except for the huge complexes near

116

Lhasa and Shigatse that had been the most conspicuous symbols of traditional Tibet—had he seen such total annihilation. Dozens of large buildings had once extended up the slope and out onto the floor of the plain to the edge of the stream. Nothing was left of them but ragged shards of foundations and, in a few piles, the shattered remains of stone walls. A line of stones extended around the perimeter, along the line of a thick high outer wall that survived only at the nearest corner, where a section nearly ten feet high towered over the ruins.

"Someone's planning to build something?" Winslow asked at his shoulder.

Shan glanced in confusion, then understood. Scattered among the old foundations were rectangles of small, precisely laid rocks. To the casual observer it might not appear to be so much a ruined gompa, but someone's plan for a new gompa.

"I forgot what it was like. I was just a youth last time I was here," Lhandro said in a hushed tone as he joined them. The village headman walked slowly along the line of the outer wall, as if frightened of crossing the line of rocks. "The army came with big cannons, led by Mao's children."

Mao's children. It was a euphemism for the Red Guard, the fanatical waves of Chinese youths unleashed by Mao Tse Tung during the Cultural Revolution. The Red Guard had destroyed libraries, universities, hospitals, and any other establishment identified with the reviled four "olds"—old cultures, old customs, old thought, and old habits. Sometimes they had commandeered entire units of the military for their campaigns of political cleansing.

"We all thought there must be rebel soldiers hiding in the mountains. Even the monks came out and stood on top of the walls as though curious to see how far into the mountains the guns would shoot. But the soldiers turned the guns on the gompa. They didn't warn the monks. Just began shelling. Soldiers set up machine guns and shot into the gompa. Like a war, though no one was fighting back. Some of the old buildings had cellars, temple rooms carved into the rock below them. It took two days before the soldiers decided no one could still be alive in the cellars. Then the Chinese conscripted everyone they could find for miles to work. Every man, woman, and child."

"Even the monks?" the American asked.

"The monks?" Lhandro asked, looking at the American with a melancholy expression. "That day, when they started shelling, was the last time I saw a monk for years. When they destroyed the gompas in this region they never gave the monks a chance to flee. Many here went to the lhakang, the main temple, and prayed until the end. Some went to the shrines underground. I was with the first group of workers sent here. We were slaves really, slaves for the army." He stared at the ruins with a hollow expression. "There weren't any whole bodies left, just body parts. But they made us put all the parts, all that was left of the monks, in two of the big holes that were the remains of the underground shrines. Then we had to cover them. There were no machines to use. We had shovels and hoes only. We buried the monks, then for six months we burned all the timbers and hauled away the rocks."

"The rocks?" Winslow asked.

"The building stones. Nearly every loose stone was put in trucks. So the gompa couldn't be rebuilt. The gompa was over five hundred years old, and the old books said it had taken fifty years to construct. Fires were lit and kept burning for days, with paintings and altars and books for fuel. Everything that was not metal or rock was burned. There were a lot of stones. Some went to be crushed for Chinese roads. Some to an army base fifty miles from here. We were sent to use them to build barracks there for the Chinese invaders. That took another six months. Everyone was a slave to the Chinese in those years." He spoke in the distant, matter-of-fact tone Tibetans usually resorted to when describing the tragedies of the Chinese occupation. Lhandro had to distance himself from the events or he would be unable to speak of them at all. "When we were done here we had to rake the ground smooth," he added in a near whisper. "They made us spread salt on the soil, so not even a flower would grow again."

"Christ," Winslow muttered, his face drawn in pain. His eyes settled on a circular depression of blackened earth thirty feet away. It was, Shan realized, a small bomb crater. "It's like it just happened."

But not entirely. New rocks had been brought, or dug out of the soil, and arranged to outline several of the old foundations. And four small buildings had been rebuilt among the ruins. Three of them were at the far side of the old compound, over three hundred yards away, and had the appearance of painstaking reconstruction. The fourth Shan saw only as he stepped closer to the surviving section of outer wall: a small sturdy stone and stucco structure consisting of two new walls built into the surviving corner section of outer wall. In front of its door sat a young boy, playing with pebbles. As Shan appeared the boy's jaw dropped and he darted away toward the restored buildings in the distance.

In the same moment Lhandro touched Shan's arm. He turned to see Lokesh standing, slightly bent, holding his belly as he stared at the ruins, as though he had been kicked. As they watched, the old Tibetan turned, or rather staggered about, to study the trees and then the slope above with an anguished expression. He faced the ruins again and stumbled forward, slowly at first, then more quickly until, with a sound like a sob, he broke into a trot toward the center of the ruins.

He ran with a curious gait, repeatedly slowing, looking about, turning left, then right, then jogging again, once even stopping to squat and lift a handful of the sandy earth, gazing at it forlornly as the particles trickled through his fingers, then lowering his hand until it touched the earth. At several places where Lokesh turned, Shan saw there was a narrow line of stones that recalled former foundations. But at most of his turns the earth was bare, although Lokesh seemed to perceive something. As if, Shan realized, he saw the buildings that once stood, as though he were navigating around them.

Suddenly his friend stopped, close to the slope, more than halfway across the ruins, and dropped cross-legged onto the ground. Shan took a few steps forward to join him. But then a figure emerged from the buildings at the far side, walking hurriedly toward them, the boy at his side.

"The keeper," Lhandro announced with a tone of relief. "He will help us. He will help the monk." The rongpa stepped forward and met the man a hundred feet away. Together they hurried off toward the injured monk, now lying on a blanket by the stream.

Shan stepped into the ruins, wandering along a long line of rocks before pausing near the center of the vast ruin by two low oblong mounds. A small cairn had been built on each, and along the perimeter of each were stones inscribed with Tibetan letters, some carved, some painted, with the mantra to the Compassionate Buddha: om mani padme hum. *Mani stones*, they were called. As he studied the first mound a deep sadness welled within him. Between the two mounds was a square, eight feet to the side, three feet high, made of stones and mortar. Someone was building a *chorten*, one of the seven-stage shrines, capped by a balloon dome and spire, that were often used to mark sacred relics. How many had there been, he wondered, how many monks at such a large gompa? Three hundred perhaps. Even as many as five hundred.

He felt weak and sat, facing the mounds, and found his right hand extended over his knee, the palm and the fingers extended toward the ground. They had formed a mudra, the earth witness mudra, calling the earth to bear witness.

When he finally stood he saw that Lokesh had not moved. Shan walked to his friend's side and sat again. Lokesh's hands were bent in a mudra as well, the thumb and index finger of both hands touching to form a circle, the remaining fingers of each hand extended upward. Shan studied it a moment, confused. It was the *dharmachakra*, the wheel-turning mudra, a mudra used by teachers to invoke the union of wisdom and action which was the goal of Buddhist learning.

"I didn't know," his friend said after several minutes, his voice cracking with emotion. "No one mentioned a name for this place where we were going. Rapjung gompa is its name. That plain is a holy place. Metoktang it is called." It meant the Plain of Flowers.

"You were here before?"

Lokesh nodded. "I didn't recognize it. Who could have recognized it, after what they did?" He shook his head forlornly. "I always came on a trail that led from the south, not from the west like we came. There were so many buildings, beautiful buildings. And the slopes were covered with trees then, beautiful tall evergreens and rhododendron. I heard the Chinese

119

had taken the forests. I didn't know they meant like this. Not a twig left except that little grove of junipers."

"Did you come for the government?" Shan asked.

"Before that. Rapjung was famous for its medicine lamas," Lokesh said, his voice cracking again. "Not just doctors, but scholars of medicine, those who first found awareness in Buddha and then dedicated their lives to understanding the connection between the health of men and the natural world around them. This plain has great spiritual power. Students came from all over Tibet, from Nepal and India even, to learn about herbs and mixing medicines. There was one lama who taught only about the hour of mixing."

Shan remembered the strange haunted feeling he had experienced out on the plain. "The hour?"

Lokesh nodded his head solemnly. "There were times of the year when certain medicines should never be mixed, times of the day when certain mixtures were best made, when they would be most potent, certain places where mixing worked best." He stared down at the barren earth at his feet. "Special medicine plants grew here, on the grounds and out on the plain and in the mountains nearby, that grew nowhere else," he said, surveying the stark ground of the ruins with haunted eyes. His mouth opened and shut several times, but no words came, and his eyes grew moist. The Chinese had poisoned the earth with salt.

"It was such a joyful place in the summers," Lokesh continued after a moment, an intense longing entering his voice. "The lamas took us on the plain or into the mountains and we pitched tents so we could collect wild plants and study them, and sometimes collect big sacks of herbs to send to the medicine makers. There were special songs they sang to invoke the healing power of the plants and special foods they ate. When I was here there were a dozen lamas of over one hundred years. I asked one of them whether he lived so long because of the special herbs here. He grew very solemn and said, no it wasn't the herbs, it was the songs, because the songs kept them connected to all the deities that lived in the land here. They knew teaching songs that would be sung all day without repeating a verse."

Teaching songs. Lokesh meant special recitations of ancient texts, memorized by the lamas, sometimes done to the accompaniment of horns and cymbals and drums.

"They're lost now, you know," Lokesh said in a small voice. "Some of them are lost forever." His voice shook, and he looked up to Shan as if asking why. "Gone," he said, his voice cracking with emotion.

The songs were lost, Lokesh meant. Because the lamas who had memorized them had been killed, with no chance to teach them to another generation.

"Why here?" Shan asked after a moment. "You came to this particular spot."

Lokesh looked up with a sad smile. "There was a lama here, named Chigu. A hundred and five when I last saw him. He had been abbot for many years but had left office when he was seventy-five to spend all his time meditating and making medicines. There was a small courtyard here, with wisteria vines"—Lokesh paused and pointed in the direction of the reconstructed buildings—"where he taught the drying and chopping of herbs and roots. There were big cleavers, and sometimes students lost fingers." Lokesh paused again. He was adrift in a flood of memory. "Each summer he and I would go out on the plain, only the two of us, walking on game trails, for a week at a time. We gathered herbs and prayed and at night stared at the heavens. There were places high up on flat rocks where we sat, where you could see nothing of the earth, only the heavens, so that we called it sitting in the sky. He told me things his own teacher had told him. His teacher had been one hundred fifteen when he died, in 1903, the Water Hare Year. Chigu Rinpoche told me things from his lips that his teacher had told him from his lips, of things he experienced in the years of the Eighth Dalai Lama," Lokesh said, wonder in his eyes now. The Eighth Dalai Lama had died in the eighteenth century. "To sit in the night, in the wilderness, and to be connected to the years of the Eighth by a chain of only two tongues, it burned something into my soul," he said, looking into the patch of empty earth before him. "This is where he lived, these are the chambers where I would come to meet him when arriving each summer." The last words choked in his throat as Lokesh was overcome with emotion.

They sat a long time, silent, listening to the wind. Shan let his awareness float, experiencing the holy place, thinking more than once that he heard the deep, spine-pinching sound of a mantra recited by monks in assembly. He closed his eyes and imagined the smell of fragrant juniper burning in a *samkang*, one of the ceremonial braziers that would have been scattered across the grounds of such a gompa, then became aware that he was alone and stirred back to full wakefulness to see Lokesh walking slowly toward the three restored structures.

Five minutes later Shan caught up with his friend, standing inside the small three-sided courtyard formed by the buildings, wearing his lopsided grin. Shan had not imagined the scent of juniper. A four-foot-high, four-legged iron samkang sat at the open end of the courtyard, juniper smoldering inside it. Under the overhanging roof of the center building was mounted a keg-sized prayer wheel crafted of copper and silver. A young Tibetan girl, no more than six, her cheeks smeared with red doja cream, stood at the wheel, turning it with a solemn expression. The building had a heavy door of expertly joined wood, painted a dark ochre enamel. As Shan watched, Lokesh gave the door a tentative push and stepped inside. He followed him into a small assembly room, a *dhakang*, lined with smooth flag stones and containing three tattered old thangkas, cloth paintings, depicting scenes from the life of the revered teacher Guru Rinpoche. One of the paintings was ripped and crudely sewn back together. Another was so faded the images were almost impossible to discern.

Shan thought of the barren land surrounding the ruins. Small as the buildings were, their erection had constituted a mammoth task. Every board, every stone flag, every nail had to have been brought in, from outside, from down in the world, probably from one of the towns on the northern highway, if not farther.

They explored the two adjacent buildings and found one to be a *gonkang* shrine, for a protector deity, the other a small lhakang, a chapel. Both structures were built with the same fine attention to detail as the dhakang. In the chapel was an altar made of split logs, bearing an eight-inch-high bronze statue of the Compassionate Buddha and the seven traditional offering bowls, all different, all carved of wood except one of chipped porcelain. At the back of the gonkang was a half-completed statue of Tara, the protectress deity, one of her hands resting on a lotus blossom. Wood chips were on the floor beside it, and a mallet and several chisels lay on a nearby bench. Shan remembered the man who had been brought from the building by the boy when they had arrived. The caretaker.

As they left the building they discovered a new visitor. Tenzin was standing in the smoke of the samkang, his eyes closed, as if trying to be washed by the purifying smoke. They watched as his eyes opened and he stepped toward the child, who showed signs of exhaustion. With a gentle motion of his hand Tenzin offered to take over, and the tall silent Tibetan took up the repetitive motion as the girl stepped away with a grateful nod, not letting the wheel miss a single rotation. Shan and Lokesh had passed by a remote house in western Tibet where an old man and his wife turned a similar prayer wheel, salvaged from a ruined gompa, spinning it in four hour shifts, twenty-four hours a day. They had been doing so for ten years because, they solemnly explained, when they had turned the wheel for twenty years the deities would become so pleased they would bring the Dalai Lama back to Tibet.

Lokesh touched Shan's arm and nudged him away, around a corner of the building, so as not to disturb Tenzin. They left him spinning the wheel, the girl sitting against the wall of the lhakang, the solemn Tibetan exchanging a tiny smile with her.

The sheep of the caravan were lying contentedly along the bank of the small stream that flowed through the juniper grove, watched over by the mastiffs and Anya, sitting beside Winslow, who lay napping in the thick grass. They found the Yapchi villagers by the small house built against the wall, standing by the open door with bowls of tea. To Shan's great relief the monk was sitting upright on a straw pallet inside the simple structure, a bowl in his hands, attended by Nyma and the caretaker, who stood with his back to Shan, speaking in low, gentle tones as Nyma washed the monk's wounds.

Shan turned and silently stepped out of the doorway and around the corner of the house, where he found Lhandro on a roughhewn bench set against the wall studying his map. As he approached the rongpa Nyma rushed around the corner. "It was him!" she cried. "That dobdob! He says he was meditating when a huge man appeared, a crazy man dressed like a demon, with blackened cheeks. He began beating him for no reason with his long staff, and threw fire at him." The nun stared at Shan with a confused, frightened expression.

Lhandro called out to one of the Yapchi men, who darted to one of the horses and rode away. Even here, in the wild, remote Plain of Flowers, they needed to guard the chenyi stone.

"How would he know?" Lhandro asked. "That demon follows the eye as if it speaks to him."

Not follow, Shan thought. The dobdob had come from the hermitage to the Plain of Flowers ahead of them, as though he had known they would come this way. Had he caused the avalanche that blocked the pass, to be sure they would detour across the plain? Had he attacked the monk and burned the plain in an effort to stop them, or slow them? Or had he been waiting and felt the need to slake his appetite by attacking another of the devout?

"Lokesh said a dobdob enforces virtue," Nyma said in a low voice, as if scared of being overheard. "But this one attacks the virtuous. It's like he's the opposite of a dobdob, or some dobdob crazed with evil."

She looked from Lhandro to Shan for an answer, then sighed when both men stayed silent. "At least he's going to be all right," she said as Shan sat down on the bench. "His eyes are clear. He is hungry. His name is Padme. He told us where his gompa is," she added, as Lhandro produced his map and she pointed to a dot labeled Norbu at the end of a road that extended east to the north-south highway. Lhandro traced his finger from the dot to a point a few miles below them on the plain, then outlined a trail that led east along the high slope above them, north into Qinghai Province, toward Yapchi Valley. "We have heard of this Norbu, one of the gompas permitted to open five years ago. My father wants me to go there some winter, to bring back blessings. It would be only ten miles off our path. Five of us will take him tomorrow—four to carry the blanket, one for relief." He fixed Shan with an uncertain gaze. "We can't leave a monk in the wilderness," he added in a plaintive tone.

"We can't," Shan agreed, and looked over the ruins. Tenzin had not emerged from the reconstructed buildings where he had been turning the prayer wheel. It was the first time the mute Tibetan had not departed with his leather dung sack as soon as they made camp.

"You take him," Shan said, "let me go on to the Yapchi Valley alone. Lokesh and I."

"Impossible," Lhandro protested. "The chenyi stone—the caravan. We are entrusted to escort you."

"I fear what could be there waiting," Shan said. "The Colonel. His mountain commandos. They know where the eye came from originally. They must know that is where it will return."

"It is our home," Lhandro declared with a determined glint. "I live in the house built by my family generations ago. I will not let soldiers keep me from my home."

"You must understand something," Shan said in a sober tone. "Bringing the eye back now is more likely to cause your people harm than good."

"No," Lhandro insisted, the doubt gone from his voice. "Of all the paths that are possible, that is not one of them. We must take the stone back, at any cost, even if it means facing the army, or that dobdob. We will get rest tomorrow, then—"

Lhandro was interrupted by the appearance of a Tibetan woman in a frayed red tunic with a long yak hair belt and several heavy turquoise and coral necklaces around her neck. She cast a worried glance at Shan, then looked back toward the house. "You should go tend those sheep," she said in a low, hurried voice.

Lhandro stood, looking with alarm toward the flock. The sheep lay peacefully on the banks of the stream, a hundred yards away.

The woman glanced back at the fire, where two children tended a small bellows. She lived here, Shan realized, was probably the caretaker's wife.

"I'll go with you to your sheep," the woman offered. "We should go now."

Lhandro took a step forward, staring at the animals again.

"Not you," the woman said to Lhandro pointedly. She was wringing her hands.

Shan stood, not understanding either the woman's words or her nervousness. "Do you need to speak with me?"

"No," the woman began, then groaned as the caretaker appeared around the corner of the house. He was a big-boned man, slightly taller than Shan, wearing a broad-rimmed brown hat and one of the wool fleece vests favored by the dropka. He froze, glared at Shan with a look that seemed to be something like horror, then came at him like a bull, not speaking, giving no warning as he abruptly shoved Shan back into the bench, slamming him against the wall so hard the wind was knocked out of him.

"No one asked you here, Chinese," the man spat with cold fury. "You're not welcome."

Shan stood on wobbly knees, trying to regain his breath. The man slammed him back against the wall. Shan felt dizzy. He became aware of the woman running away toward the fire. He heard the sound of a horse cantering and saw movement in the direction of the trees.

Lhandro put a hand on the man's arm but the caretaker twisted and hit the rongpa with an elbow, in the process knocking his own hat off. Shan stared at him in confusion. The caretaker was Chinese.

124

"Take your murdering ways and leave!" the man spat. "There is no room for blasphemers!" As he stepped toward Shan with his fist raised, a horse wheeled to a halt in a cloud of dust and in a blur of speed its rider launched from the saddle onto the caretaker's back. It was Dremu, throwing his arm around the man's neck, pulling him backward, twisting, forcing him to the ground.

The woman screamed. The caretaker pulled a chisel from his belt and, still sitting on the ground, lashed out at Dremu as the Golok leapt back and crouched, hands floating in the air, as if about to spring again. As Shan stood Nyma appeared, then Anya, crying out in alarm. Suddenly Dremu's knife was in his hand.

"It is not the way, father," a patient, youthful voice called out. The boy who had first run to bring the caretaker from the reconstruction site repeated the words as the woman pushed the boy forward, as though the boy were the only means she had to stop Shan's attacker.

The hand holding the chisel seemed to droop. The caretaker seemed unaware of Dremu now. He looked venomously at Shan then back at the boy.

"These two men," a calmer voice declared from behind Shan. "They found me when I lay wounded on the plain." Shan turned to see the monk at the corner of the building, leaning on Lokesh.

The caretaker seemed to go limp. He looked at the monk, the woman and the boy, and folded his arms around his knees, dropping the chisel to the ground. He pressed his head into his knees. After a moment he looked up with a sullen, resentful expression at Shan, then turned to Lhandro. "You should have told me a Chinese was coming," he spat, but there was more sorrow in his voice than anger.

The boy stepped cautiously to the man's side and extended an arm to help him up. For a moment, as he rose with the boy's help, the caretaker seemed old and unsteady, then his eyes flared again and as he retrieved the chisel and replaced it in his belt he fixed Shan with a baleful stare.

"He's not one of—" Lhandro began, searching for words. "He's like you, Gang."

The man reacted with a resentful snort, as if to say no one was like him, but, as his son took his hand, he seemed to deflate again. His gaze drifted toward the ground and he let the boy lead him back across the compound.

Shan staggered to the bench and sat down, then watched as the man walked toward the shrines. Gang. It meant steel, a name given by members of what his father would have called the Mao Cult during one of the Chairman's fanatical campaigns for steel production more than four decades earlier.

"My husband is not—" a strained voice started near Shan. He turned to see the woman with the child beside him. "Gang isn't like that. . . ." She looked toward the strange angry man and seemed about to cry. "My hus-

125

band built those shrines," she offered in his defense, then asked the boy to bring Shan a bowl of tea. "It's taken him nearly ten years."

Lhandro stepped past Shan to help the monk back inside. "Gang has bad memories," the farmer said in an apologetic tone, looking at Shan, then the monk. "I'm sorry. I had not seen him in years. I had forgotten that." Bad memories. It was a catch phrase, another part of the odd language developed by all those who had lived under the shadow of Beijing, a way to explain the torment suffered by those who had been caught up in the bloody terror that nearly annihilated their world.

The caretaker Gang had bad memories. But of what? Shan had never heard Tibetans speak of Chinese having bad memories.

"I've read reports of the rumor in the mountains, about a Chinese who builds temples," the monk said in a weak but smooth, well-educated voice. He looked across the field of ruins at the caretaker, who was nearly at the reconstruction site. "But up here," he said in a quizzical tone, shaking his head. "We never thought the rumors were true. No one comes up here. The winds are so cold. We thought this was just ruins and wilderness." He put his hand against the wall, as if suddenly dizzy, and Nyma helped him back to his pallet.

Gang's wife collapsed onto the bench beside Shan. "He came with the People's Liberation Army, a teenager then, in 1964." The woman quickly explained that Gang had arrived as a young corporal with the occupation forces and after serving his term had accepted land from the army, and won a bonus for marrying a Tibetan woman. "It was my sister he married," the woman explained in a sad tone, "and they settled near the northern road to Amdo. They had a son and there was much happiness. Gang became a Buddhist. Once, when his son was very sick, a medicine lama from Rapjung gompa came and saved the boy's life. After that, Gang came to help the lamas with the special herb plantings whenever he could, always a week or two in spring to ready the earth and a week in the autumn to help with the harvest and drying.

"But then those children came" the woman continued, "after they had destroyed Rapjung. The Red Guard," she said ominously. "Gang's wife had feared for our father and went with their son to help the family flee into the mountains. But the Guard caught up with them. They held a trial on the spot and condemned the family for being members of the oppressive landowner class." She glanced at Shan and looked toward the ground. "Those judges pronounced sentence and made my nephew carry it out," she said in a near whisper.

Shan's head slumped down. He held it, elbows on his knees, fighting a choking sensation in his throat. The woman meant the Red Guard had forced the young boy to execute his mother and grandfather.

"Then they took that boy away," she added in a hollow voice.

Such survivors of political undesirables, if not killed immediately, had often been sent back east to special political indoctrination schools, so they could join the Chinese proletariat. "We never saw him again."

"They say Gang went crazy," Lhandro continued the story, "that he started ambushing and killing Red Guard. No one knew for certain. But the Red Guard became scared of certain places in the mountains and began pulling back from the area. The sister of his wife returned," he said with a sad glance at the woman, "and was assigned to the collective that took over their old family estate. Gang came down from the mountains after a couple of years and worked there. Eventually they became husband and wife. When the collective broke up they came here, to be alone and because of the debt Gang felt he still owed the healers who had lived here." Lhandro cast his look of apology toward Shan again. "I forgot about Gang and his problem with the Chinese. We never . . ." His voice drifted away.

Nyma completed the sentence for him. "In Yapchi we never had a Chinese friend before."

By the next morning Padme was alert and talkative, hungry enough to eat two bowls of tsampa.

"You saved my life," the injured monk said to Shan and Lhandro several times. He sat by the fire, a blanket over his shoulders against the chill morning wind, sometimes intensely studying the reconstructed shrines, making notes in a pad he kept in his belt pouch, sometimes staring at the flock of sheep that grazed by the stream. "But I don't understand why you bring your herd here," Padme said to Lhandro. His gaze fell upon Winslow, who was walking along the stream.

"We were going north when we found you," Lhandro said. "You could not travel so we sought water and shelter."

"That young girl with you, she said those bags the sheep carry are filled with salt." Padme kept staring at the American as he spoke.

Lhandro nodded. "From Lamtso."

The young monk searched Lhandro's face. "That is a very old thing," he said in an odd, uncertain tone. It almost sounded like he was chastising Lhandro. "It could be contaminated if you just take it from the soil."

Lhandro looked at the monk, perplexed, even worried, wondering, Shan knew, if in all their years without monks the Yapchi farmers had forgotten something important. "It is good salt," the rongpa said. The monk shrugged, and accepted another bowl of tea from Gang's wife.

"But there are rules about salt. There is a government monopoly on salt," the monk said in his tentative voice. "I would hate to see you accused of—" he paused, then shrugged and did not complete his sentence. "If there was no caravan I may not have been found for many hours." He turned and gazed at Shan.

"Why?" Shan asked. "Why were you on the plain? Were you expecting to meet someone?"

Padme explained that he and a group of monks from Norbu sometimes roamed the lands neighboring their gompa looking for religious artifacts. They had not visited this remote plain before and when they arrived upon it they had realized that they would need to split up if they were to explore it all. Padme had walked to the far end of the plain and had just come upon a small cairn and was examining the area when he was attacked by the giant with the staff.

"Did you see who left this?" a deep voice interjected in Mandarin. Winslow appeared in front of them, holding the yellow vest left by the American woman. "Did you see an American?"

"No," Padme replied slowly. "It was just there. By that little cairn."

The American sighed and handed it to the monk. "Take it. Might as well do someone some good."

Padme extended his arm hesitantly, dropped his blanket, and pulled on the vest. "Has this foreigner been gathering salt, too?" he asked Lhandro in Tibetan.

"Just along to enjoy the fresh air," Winslow quipped in Tibetan, and the monk stared at him, his eyes wide with wonder.

"An American who speaks Tibetan?" he exclaimed, and looked back, with intense curiosity, at Lhandro and Shan, as though the news somehow changed his perspective on the party.

They would stay at the ruins until the next day, Lhandro announced, while the Yapchi men probed the surrounding land by horseback. The next morning the caravan would continue north while some of the party returned Padme safely to his gompa. The monk expressed his gratitude and led the Yapchi villagers to the base of the wall, out of the wind, where he sat to lead them in mantras to the Compassionate Buddha.

A quarter of an hour later the Yapchi riders trotted away, each in a different direction. Nyma stepped to the door of the house, speaking to someone inside, then bent to tighten the laces of her shoes. Gang's wife appeared and pointed to a worn dirt path that ran along the outside edge of what had been the outer wall of the old gompa. No, not to the path, but to someone on the path: Tenzin, walking at a slow, contemplative pace toward the far end of the ruins.

"A *kora*," Lokesh said as recognition lit his eyes. It was a pilgrim path. Many old shrines and gompas had such a kora, for circumambulation by pilgrims as a way of acquiring merit and paying homage to those who resided there, or had resided there.

"Past the wall at the north, to an old hermit's cave," Gang's wife explained, gesturing past the reconstructed buildings as if the wall still existed, "then up past the drup-chu shrine," she said, meaning a shrine by a spring of what the old Tibetans called attainment water, believed to impart blessings and health on those who drank from it. Lokesh bent and tightened his own laces, looking up expectantly at Shan. Shan grinned and stepped away to retrieve a water bottle from the stack of blankets by the

128

wall, where the caravan party, except Dremu, had slept. The Golok, as usual, had chosen to sleep apart, hidden somewhere, but close.

When he returned Lokesh was staring in confusion at Lhandro, Nyma, and Anya. The three Yapchi villagers had begun to walk down the kora path, but to the east, to the right, in a counterclockwise direction. Lokesh twisted his head in curiosity. From behind Shan heard a disappointed sigh and saw Padme in the doorway, bracing himself with an arm on the frame, staring after the trio.

"Why didn't we know this?" Shan wondered. Only as Lokesh turned to him did he realize he had given voice to his question.

Lokesh smiled. "There are many paths," he said, with a satisfied tone. Many paths to enlightenment, he meant. Traditional Tibetan Buddhists, no matter which of the major orders of Buddhism they worshiped with, always conducted themselves clockwise along a kora circuit. It was part of the tradition, meaning part of the reverence to be shown.

But there was another faith in Tibet, older than Buddhism, based on animism. The Bon faith, though it had been largely subsumed into Buddhism and followed most of its teachings, still had its distinctive practices; one of which was that kora pilgrims walked counterclockwise.

"We should have known," Shan said, answering his own question. It might explain much, especially why the farmers of Yapchi clung so fervently to their hopes for the stone eye and their land deity, why they had been so forlorn for four generations over its fate.

As Shan and Lokesh started the clockwise circuit, Lokesh began quietly reciting one of his pilgrim's verses. Minutes later they heard footfalls behind them and turned to see Winslow running to catch up. He extended the bottle he kept for water, now empty. "I need attainment." He grinned. "Boy, do I need attainment."

Two hours later they had completed three-quarters of the path and stood at the drup-chu shrine on the slope above the gompa, Winslow filling the water bottle after each of them knelt and drank deeply from the tiny spring of sacred water. Shan and Lokesh had passed many pleasant hours at such springs in their travels, pursuing Lokesh's burning interest in understanding the particular reason each of the springs was special. Lokesh was fond of pointing out that just understanding such reasons would tell much of the story of Tibet. Like many, he believed the land was not sacred just because devout Buddhists had inhabited it for so many centuries. The land drew them to such springs, Lokesh often declared, and every spring had a tale not just of the devout Buddhists who had identified it, usually centuries earlier, but of the ancients who had come before. At a spring in central Tibet that had been surrounded by crushed rock and gravel amid what were otherwise slopes of solid granite, Lokesh had decided that thousands of years earlier, when air deities traveled in the form of giants, the giants had favored the spring and crushed the earth by landing beside it so often.

129

As they rested by the spring Winslow scanned the Plain of Flowers with his lenses.

"Have you decided what they were doing, why oil geologists would be out on the Plain of Flowers?" Shan asked.

Winslow didn't lower the binoculars, just shook his head slightly. "The oil concession ends at the Qinghai border, at least five miles north of here," he said and glanced back at Shan. Dremu had found empty cans of American food, on the far side of the plain, even farther from the concession.

"Why would she leave a vest and sleeping bag?" Shan wondered out loud.

"I don't know," the American said in a hollow voice. "Maybe the thing that attacked Padme found her, too. Maybe it's not sure who has the stone eye, and it's just attacking anyone on the northern trails." He packed his binoculars and knelt at the spring a moment, dipping in his cupped hand once more. He studied the water in his palm, lifted it and emptied it over his head. He closed his eyes and let the water drip down his head, and when he opened his eyes Shan saw a flash of deep emotion. Desperation, he thought, or profound sadness.

"There was a letter from her, to her mother, in the company files," Winslow said abruptly, as if the water had freed the memory. "Her manager showed it to me, he hadn't mailed it because he wasn't sure if it would be too painful, their not knowing for sure about her. He said the company instructed him to open it, to see if she had been suicidal. Her mother is a professor in Minnesota. They talk about things in their letters, I guess." Winslow stared into the water, or past it, as if he were speaking to something below, at the underground source of the sacred water.

"I mean big things. She said she wished all of her assignments could be in Tibet, that although the Chinese wouldn't say so, Qinghai Province was really Tibet, that people in the mountains were teaching her things. She said she loved Tibet but was hating what the company was doing to the land. That Tibetans told her that the most important thing for maintaining the human life force was connection to the land, and that the world had become divided between people whose lives were severed from that life force and people who lived close to the land. That those who lived close to the land had a sacred duty to protect the life force." Winslow looked up from the water. "And she worked for an oil company." Something like pain seemed to cross his face again, as though the paradox had been deeply troubling him.

"At the end of the letter she said that some Tibetans had told her that a geologist was really like a special kind of monk who studied the behavior of land deities." Winslow looked back into the dark patch where the spring emerged from the earth, as if waiting for such a spirit to emerge and explain. "She said her Tibetan friends wanted to take her to hidden lands." He turned to look at Lokesh. "What did she mean?"

Lokesh needed no time to consider his reply. "A bayal. They meant a bayal. It means hidden land. Some people believe there are hidden portals to special lands, like heavens, where deities roam freely." He glanced at Shan. Some people. Like the followers of Bon who lived at Yapchi. Lokesh sighed, then stood and stepped with a deliberate pace to a low pile of rocks ten feet from the spring. Although Shan expected him to add a rock to the pile, Lokesh began pulling the pile apart, until he had exposed a square of solid granite, two feet to the side. "There was a little chorten here," he said in an urgent, awed voice, as if the memory had just washed over him.

"A shrine with a relic underneath, the foot bone of an old hermit who had walked all over Tibet collecting herbs, more than five hundred years ago." He stared at the square stone and the way it was encrusted with lichens that joined it to the ground. "The Tibetans who did this," he said excitedly, meaning those who had been forced to destroy the gompa, "didn't move this base, didn't move the relic." Lokesh looked up with a hopeful gleam. "We would sit here for lessons sometimes, and the lamas would explain how the spring was connected to the center of the earth. They would wash herbs in this water and send clay jars of it to healers all over Tibet. I remember listening for hours here while Chigu Rinpoche taught us how the power of plants came from the power of the earth and their power to heal came from the ways they connected humans back to the earth."

Winslow stepped to the slab, knelt reverently by Lokesh, his eyes wide with wonder. "I read somewhere that doctors say they could heal anything if they just knew how the human animal evolved, how to trace the human body back to where it rose up out of the mud. Because everything we're made of came from the earth." When he looked up at Shan his eyes held a strange fervor. "It's a different way of saying the same thing, isn't it?" He placed his fingertips near the lichen of the rock, but not on it, as though it were too holy for him to touch. Then he looked up sheepishly and began helping Lokesh to replace the stones, not in a pile, but in a square, like the base of a chorten.

After they had laid the first layer of stones Lokesh paused and picked a sprig of the plant that grew around the stone slab, looking at it quizzically. "Chigu Rinpoche said that the whole function of the healers was to translate the power of the earth into the life force of the human."

Winslow studied Lokesh a long time, then slowly picked up a rock and continued building the little stack of rocks as Shan began carrying more stones from the slope above them.

Lokesh paused again. "We learned how to dig roots in the reverent fashion here, at this spring, learned how to push aside the soil a little at a time, taking time to coax the earth, always leaving some so the plant could grow back. Chigu Rinpoche said we learned about ourselves by digging into the soil. He said we should dig inside the earth to find the earth inside us." Lokesh raised some soil in his hand and let it trickle into his other palm. "It was a teaching mantra he used. Inside the earth, for the earth inside."

When they had finished Lokesh nudged Shan and pointed toward the top of the ridge above the ruins. "People are up there," the old Tibetan announced.

Shan studied the slope and saw nothing except a large black bird circling high overhead, riding the updraft. Winslow glanced up the hill with a skeptical expression, then scanned the top of the ridge with his lenses.

"You see them?" Shan asked in a slow, careful tone. His old friend's senses, like his emotions, were usually in a delicate balance. What he might have sensed was a memory of people on the slope, decades earlier, or perhaps he had seen the back of a fleeing antelope. Not infrequently Shan had followed his old friend when Lokesh had sensed the presence of a spirit creature, only to sit and contemplate a rock where Lokesh insisted the creature had taken refuge.

Lokesh rubbed his grizzled jaw then turned with a sheepish grin toward Shan and continued down the trail. Shan silently followed, knowing that once they completed the circuit they would be climbing back up the slope.

An hour later, after having returned to the camp and consumed a meal of cold tsampa rolled into balls, they were nearly at the top of the slope when they paused at a flat rock that overlooked the long plain. Winslow, who had refused Shan's suggestion that he remain at the camp and rest, pointed to two small clouds of dust at the southern and western ends. "Those scouts from Yapchi," the American said.

"The Tara Temple, the Maitreya Chapel, the Samvara Temple," Lokesh said suddenly, and Shan saw that he was pointing at empty places among the ruins, speaking of what he had seen, or maybe still saw, at the gompa. "The chora," he said, referring to the debating courtyard, "the inner herb garden, the north garden, the north kangtsang and the barkhang," he added in a contemplative tone, referring to a hall of residence and the printing press.

Lokesh's finger hovered in midair as if he had forgotten something. "All those prayer flags in the trees," he said in a distant voice. "It's like a festival."

Shan looked back down on the ruins. There were no prayer flags except for a single modest strand by Gang's shrines, and no trees except the small juniper grove outside the gompa grounds. Lokesh was in another time, another place. Shan was never embarrassed for his friend, or fearful of his sanity. But today Shan felt a certain envy for the old Tibetan.

He put his hands inside his coat pockets. Something brushed his left hand and he pulled out the sprig of brush he had taken from the burnt patch of earth, and extended it to Lokesh. The old Tibetan took it and placed the sprig under his nose. He looked at Shan with surprise in his eyes. "Thank you," he said with a grateful smile.

Shan studied his friend as Lokesh clasped the sprig inside his cupped hands and pushed his hands against his nose, his eyes closed. "It's medicine?" he asked.

Lokesh nodded, his eyes still closed. "Not ready for picking, but from a healthy plant. Chigu and I would gather this sometimes out on the plain. It's called birds foot, for the way the stem branches out."

Shan pictured the scene as he and the American had found it, where he had plucked the stem. The plant had been growing only in the protection of the shallow bowl. Maybe the dobdob had not tried to burn the plain. Maybe he had only tried to burn the medicine plants. But why? He remembered the salt camp, where the herders were hiding the injured woman from healers. And the woman on the trail, who had rejected Lokesh's offer of healing.

They reached the top of the slope to find a long rolling meadow that extended nearly a half-mile across the crest and at least two miles to the east and west. Above them, only a few miles away now, loomed the huge shape of Yapchi Mountain, standing guard over the Plain of Flowers to the south and Yapchi Valley to the north.

Shan and Winslow stepped aside for Lokesh to lead them into the maze of game trails that crisscrossed the meadow. But his friend shrugged and stepped backwards, gesturing for Shan to continue in the front. It was an odd dance they had done often in their travels. It didn't matter who led, Lokesh was saying, for they would always find what they were meant to find, and eventually arrive where they were meant to be.

Shan felt an unexpected exhilaration as they moved along the rolling meadow. The wind blew steady and cool, but not uncomfortably so. Small pink flowers grew close to the earth. From across the meadow came the trill of a lark.

They walked slowly along the rolling meadow, Shan randomly selecting new paths where the game trails intersected, until they came to a long low ledge of rock that bordered a large meadow, protected on the north by a towering wall of rock. The bowl, nearly three hundred yards across, was filled with a low heather-like plant, and larks—more larks than he had ever seen in one place, fluttering among the growth. As Shan led his friends through a gap in the ledge he heard the hushed, urgent sound of voices and a hand came out of the shadow of the rock to hold his arm.

He pulled back with a shudder, imagining the dobdob had found them again.

"You have to get down," a woman whispered.

Shan bent to see five Tibetans—three middle-aged herders, a slightly younger woman, and a boy—sitting in the shadow made by an overhanging ledge. "If they see you they will run," the woman said. She did not seem surprised to see three strangers, only concerned they might

133

frighten away the objects of their attention. Wild drong, Shan suspected, or maybe some of the rare blue sheep that roamed the mountains.

The Tibetans wore the thick chubas of dropka, heavily patched with swatches of leather and red cloth. Two of the men wore dirty fleece caps, the other the quilted, flapped green cap issued to soldiers for winter wear. The woman clutched a large silver and turquoise gau in one hand, with the other on the arm of the boy, who watched the meadow with round, expectant eyes.

Not even the appearance of the lanky American distracted the dropka for long. They stared quizzically at Winslow for a few seconds, and the boy pulled on the woman's shoulder to make sure she saw the goserpa. But when Lokesh and Winslow settled in beside the herders, as if they, too, had come to see the creature the dropka awaited, the boy's attention shifted back to the meadow.

Shan sat beside Winslow, his back to the rock, covered in shadow, then leaned forward to speak. But no one returned his gaze, nor seemed to even notice him. It was more than expectation in their eyes, Shan saw, it was a deep, even spiritual excitement. They sat, the wind fluting around the rocks, larks calling, brilliant clouds scudding across an azure sky. Two of the men began low mantras, fingering their beads. Suddenly the boy pointed toward the far side of the meadow, near the wall.

Shan saw nothing, though the dropka uttered tiny gleeful cries. The two men increased the pace of their mantras, joined now by Lokesh. He became aware of movement at the edge of the wall's shadow, a great hulking shape standing on four legs near the shadow. From so far away he could not tell whether it was a yak, a large sheep, or even a bear. Then a second shape, a human figure in a red robe, emerged from the shadows, and the first shape rose up on its hind legs. The man's features could not be seen from such a distance, but the stranger walked in short steps, leaning on a tall staff. Shan sensed the man was not merely old, but ancient.

Lokesh had stopped his mantra. His face was as excited as the boy's, tears streaming down his cheeks. "I recognize this place now," he whispered in a very still voice. "We would come here in summers. Pitched a white tent and stayed many days, a week sometimes. Chigu Rinpoche said the larks sang the herbs here."

Sing the herbs. An image of larks offering lullabies to young plants flashed through Shan's mind.

"It's true," a child's voice said. But Shan turned to see that it was the woman speaking, with the tone of a young girl. "It's all true, isn't it?" she said to Lokesh, and a tear rolled down her cheek. "Remember this," she added solemnly to the boy and hugged him. "Remember that it was spoken that this was one of the places where they came in the old days, that today you saw one of them come."

Sometimes, Shan's father had told him, people can live eighty or ninety years and only briefly, once or twice at most, glimpse the true things of life, the things that are the essence of the planet and of mankind. Sometimes people died without ever seeing a single true thing. But, he had assured Shan, you can always find true things if you just know where to look.

It was one of those rare true things they were glimpsing now. An ageless medicine lama gathering his herbs, a medicine lama who shouldn't exist, in a field that had been forgotten for half a century, rising up like a ghost to confirm that once there had been wise, joyful old men who gathered plants so they could translate the magic of the earth to its people.

They watched, the sound of the whispered mantras becoming almost indistinguishable from the low sound of the wind on the rocks. The low, bent shape in the shadows did not move, and Shan realized it might be a helper, a protector for the old one, crouching, on guard against the world outside. The medicine lama wandered among the flowering plants, stooping sometimes, sometimes rising with a sprig and looking skyward, as if consulting with the air deities about his find.

Then suddenly, with a low moan, as if struggling mightily to contain himself, the boy burst up with his hands in the air. "Lha gyal lo! Lha gyal lo!" he shouted with joy, just twice before his mother pulled him backwards and clamped a hand over his mouth.

But the sound had carried over the meadow, echoing off the rock face, and the lama and the hulking shape darted toward the deeper shadows. The old man halted for an instant, peering toward the rocks where they sat. Then, like a deer at the edge of a wood, he merged into the shadows and was gone.

They waited a quarter hour for the ghost lama to return, exchanging uncertain glances, as if none were sure now of exactly what they had seen. Then the herders rose and silently filed away from the rock, following one of the game trails that led southward down the wide ridge.

It was impossible, Shan kept telling himself as they slowly walked back to Rapjung. The medicine lamas had all died. The soldiers had cleared out the surrounding hills years earlier. With all the patrols, all the pacification campaigns, it did not seem possible even one could have survived. Lokesh offered no suggestion, no theory of how now, after decades, one of the old lamas could appear in the hills. He just followed Shan, lost in a strange reverie, or perhaps in his memories of Rapjung as it had existed fifty years earlier. Several paces behind Lokesh, came the American, also silent, seemingly numbed by what he had seen.

Again and again Shan replayed the scene in his mind. It wasn't that a lama had survived all these years in the mountains, he realized; the dropka had come because of something new, because they had heard of a miracle. Someone else had seen a ghost lama, he suddenly remembered. The herders by the hermitage the night Drakte had died. One of the old lamas had arrived, had returned. From where? Why? And why now, when the eye was on its journey, when Drakte had died and the army was scouring the land, when a dobdob, protector of the faith, was attacking devout Buddhists, when an American had gone missing?

Shan had no answers. He had only foreboding. Although he knew little, he knew enough to be frightened.

No one asked where they had been when they arrived at the camp. Several of those who had completed the kora had just returned themselves, having meditated at the hermit's cave or the drup-chu shrine. As the Yapchi men went to check on the sheep, Nyma sought Shan out.

"It happened again," the nun said. "The poor girl." Shan looked up from the sheep whose pack he was tightening. "She just fell over on the trail and began shaking, and beating the earth with her hands and feet."

"Anya?" Shan asked, realizing he had seen the girl lying under a blanket by the fire.

"Nothing happened. No words. Sometimes it's like that," Nyma murmured.

The words chilled Shan. She was talking about the oracle.

"I told that monk, hoping he could help," Nyma continued. "But he seemed angry at my words. I think his head is still hurt from that attack."

Shan followed the nun's gaze toward Padme, who sat resting against the ruins of the wall, at a place apart, writing in his small notepad.

They ate in silence and drank tea as the sun set, the company in quiet contemplation after a day on the kora.

Lokesh did not speak until he spread his blanket near Shan to sleep.

"It is a good sign, a wonderful sign, for a medicine lama to appear in the herb meadow," the old Tibetan said, in a tone that said he was still not certain the man had been flesh and blood. "And a monk on the Plain of Flowers. That dobdob will not hurt us. Things will get better, you'll see."

But in the early hours of the morning, a scream woke Shan. He sat up as Lokesh gave an agonized groan. The restored shrines of Rapjung were engulfed in flames.

CHAPTER EIGHT

The dry, brittle wood of the elegant little lhakang cracked and spat, burning as hot as a furnace, throwing off sparks that spiraled far into the night sky. No one could get close to the flames, or even close enough to the adjacent assembly hall to keep the fire from spreading to it. Gang's wife held the caretaker back, tears streaming down her face, the young boy holding his father's left wrist out as though trying to show it to someone. The skin on Gang's palm was a mass of welts, the back of the hand scorched red and black. A small soot-stained figurine lay at his feet. He had saved the little Buddha from the altar.

The stream was two hundred yards away, and they had only two small leather buckets and the cooking pots from the house to carry water. They ran back and forth from the stream for a quarter hour, then Lhandro raised his palm and lowered his empty bucket to the ground. They could do nothing but watch as the conflagration, having already destroyed the lhakang, consumed the assembly hall and spread to the small deity chapel beside it.

"Like a giant samkang," Nyma said with a whimper. Incredibly, Gang, through years of effort, had constructed the buildings of cedar and juniper, the kind of fragrant wood burned in samkangs to attract deities.

Suddenly the nun cried out and ran to the other side of the lhakang, Shan at her heels. Winslow was bent over, gasping, hands on his knees, beside a large block of wood. Tenzin sat on the ground nearby, his face smudged with soot. As the flames flared up in a gust of wind Shan saw the block more clearly. The two men had saved the half-completed carving of the protector deity. Beyond them in the shadows another figure sat, Gang's young daughter staring with vacant eyes at an object between her legs. It was the prayer wheel. Her hands lay open on either side of the wheel. The skin was burned away from the palms, exposing raw flesh where she had grasped the searing metal. Nyma gasped and bent over the girl, calling for the last pail of water to wash the terrible wounds.

Shan found Lokesh with his back to the fire, deep pain in his eyes, watching the sparks as they flew into the night. As Shan stepped to the old Tibetan's side, he was unable to find words. It could not have been an accident. There had been no campfire near the cluster of restored buildings, and Gang would never have burned his little samkang, consuming scraps of his precious wood, at night, unattended.

"Someone came from outside," Shan said in a low voice. "That dobdob tried to burn the plain. It must have been—" something cracked into the side of his head and Shan found himself on his knees, blinking, unable to focus his eyes. Something sharp hit his shoulder, then Lokesh cried out and threw himself over Shan.

"Oppressor!" a voice shouted angrily, and a stone bounced off Lokesh's leg. "Tyrant! A Chinese comes and ruin follows!"

There was a struggle behind them. Shan twisted about on his knees to see Lhandro and Nyma pulling Gang backwards, dragging him away from Shan. His injured hand reached out toward Shan like a claw, as the other was pushed downward by his wife, a stone dropping from it. As the others pulled her husband away Gang's wife hesitantly stepped toward Shan, her cheeks stained with tears and soot.

"You must understand," she said in a rush of breath, like a sob. "All these years. Since our first child was born, all that time." Tears streamed down her cheeks. "In the winter waiting for snow so he could drag the wood down from the mountains. In the summer covered with sawdust. Working in the moonlight even, working on festival days. Never even taking time to play with his children." A wall crashed down, sending splinters of smoldering timbers flying in an explosion of sparks. A piece of charred, smoking wood landed at her feet, and she knelt by it, studying it as if she needed to understand where it had belonged in the lhakang.

"Sometimes he had to make his own tools," she said, in a remote tone now, as she lifted the wood and struck it on the ground to shake off the embers. After a moment she stood and carried the fragment to a row of stones, then carefully laid it on the ground. She found another, nearly two feet long, struck away the embers, and silently laid it alongside the first. Tenzin appeared, carrying another fragment to lay beside those collected by the woman. A pile of salvaged wood. The first step in building again.

They spent the rest of the night and much of the next morning combing through the ruins of Gang's buildings, collecting the remnants of wood, gathering up nails and straps of metal from the ashes, many twisted with heat.

As they worked Gang lay on a pallet that had been brought for him, sometimes gazing morosely at the smoldering ruins, muttering something that might have been a prayer, other times glaring toward Shan, throwing pebbles and curses at him whenever he approached. Again, the only person able to restrain him seemed to be his son, who sat holding his father's good hand, gripping it tight when emotion flared inside Gang.

"It's so remote," Winslow said as he gathered nails in one of the cooking pots. "So empty here." A moment later he looked up with a puzzled expression. "It could only have been that man who attacked Padme. He burnt that little meadow."

"Lightning," Lhandro reminded them. "Lightning could have struck the rooftop. It is a way the deities have of speaking," he added, looking back to Gang, as if suggesting that the deities may have perceived that the shrines had been reconstructed perhaps as much out of hate as faith.

They left for Norbu gompa, Padme's home, late in the morning as Gang and his daughter were led to the stream to bathe their scorched hands. The caretaker stared with glazed eyes as the sheep began filing away from the bank of the stream. He hadn't invited the caravaners, hadn't even welcomed them, and now they left with ten years of his life's work destroyed.

"We will pray for you," Nyma said to Gang's wife as she watched Gang. Then she followed Shan onto the trail.

After four miles they reached the junction with the trail to the north, the trail the caravan would take over Yapchi Mountain to Yapchi Valley. It was another ten miles southeast to Norbu, and they had agreed that the sheep would continue with the other Yapchi villagers on the north trail as Lhandro, Shan, Lokesh, Tenzin, and Nyma carried the monk to Norbu on the blanket litter. They should expect to stay at Norbu, Padme insisted, at least long enough to receive the thanks and blessings of his gompa.

"I'm going up," Winslow had said as the two groups began moving along their separate paths. Shan studied the American, puzzled. Winslow was leading one of Lhandro's horses. Then he saw Dremu waiting on the slope above. The American meant he and Dremu were going higher in the mountains to look for the missing woman. The Golok wheeled his horse back and forth, staring at Shan with worry in his eyes. Dremu seemed troubled by the splitting of the party. As the last of the sheep turned onto the northern trail he trotted to Shan's side. "He can walk," the Golok said loudly, within earshot of Padme. "Don't go. Let that one walk home."

Nyma shot Dremu an irritated glare. "We know how to take care of injured holy men," she declared curtly. The monk moaned and held his head, giving no sign of having heard.

Dremu returned her stare. "Ask him to tell you how monks mingle with the sky deities," the Golok barked, then cantered away.

Shan studied the caravan as the dogs pushed the sheep up the trail. Dremu's strange connection with the chenyi stone seemed to have made him resentful of anything, anyone, that caused a delay or detour in its return. But the Golok would soon see that the red bag was staying with the caravan. Shan and the others would be gone just a few hours. After that it would be only another two days to Yapchi.

Shan's worry soon faded, replaced by an unexpected sense of antici- pation as they crossed the ridge that walled the plain on the south side, then descended through the low hills that led to the broad rolling plain below. He had been to very few gompas, at least gompas that practiced in the open, legally, with a full complement of teachers and student monks, and he missed the serene voices of lamas. Looking at the faces of his Tibetan companions, he realized that Padme's promise of blessings from the Norbu holy men somehow felt important to the Tibetans as well.

It was midafternoon when they crested the last of the long, low ridges and looked down on a complex of buildings surrounded by a ring of poplar trees in spring bud. Most of the structures appeared to be of stone and pressed earth construction, with neat grey tile roofs, the walls painted a pale cream color, all within a square outer wall of stone painted white, perhaps two hundred yards on each side. Three large buildings lay in the center of the neatly groomed complex, their walls sloping slightly inward at the top, all painted in the same cream color to a point just past the center of the second floor windows, then maroon above, the color of a monk's robe. Lhandro and Nyma, at the front of the litter, gave simultaneous exclamations of joy, and encouraged the weakened Padme to gaze upon his gompa.

"I never thought to see so many buildings!" Lhandro exclaimed. He offered a look of encouragement to Nyma. "The world is changing, you see."

But just as they were about to lift the litter again Nyma pulled a length of yak hair rope from the sack on her shoulder and tied it around her waist, giving her robe the appearance of a dress. Shan stared in puzzlement a moment, until Lhandro looked from Nyma to the gompa and nodded soberly. He took off his vest and handed it to her as she unpinned her long braids. Even though the world was changing, even though it was a gompa, it still meant Nyma was going down into the world, or at least its nearest outpost, where even a casual observer might quickly surmise she was a nun and inquire about her registration.

After half a mile, only a few hundred yards from the gompa, Lhandro looked back with frustration at Lokesh and Shan realized his friend, at the rear of the litter, had slowed, impeding their progress.

"The gompa," the Yapchi headman reminded Lokesh energetically. Lokesh offered a weak smile in reply, then quickened his pace. The old Tibetan's companions had become familiar with his habit of gazing off at some distraction in the landscape. But Shan studied his friend. There was something else about Lokesh his new companions didn't understand, something Shan himself had taken years to recognize. Just as Lokesh occasionally had outbreaks of deep emotion, he also had outbreaks of what, for lack of a better word, Shan could only call intuition. He could be like a horse, innately sensing something approaching on the far side of a hill, or the rock pika jumping out of its hole and screeching for two minutes before an avalanche tumbled down from the mountain above.

Once, three months before, Lokesh had stopped Shan as they began to cross an ice-covered river after they had crossed three such rivers that very day. The old Tibetan had not been able to answer Shan's confused questions, had only stood and made a hoarse croaking noise, even when he looked into Shan's eyes. They had stood there for ten minutes before Shan's spine began to tingle because he realized that the river was croaking, too, echoing Lokesh with a deeper but somehow similar sound. Then abruptly the river ice had split apart and a long wide gap appeared in the center, revealing black, fast-moving frigid water underneath.

Was that what Lokesh was feeling now? Was that what Dremu, the feral Golok, had sensed at the trail turnoff when he had seemed to be asking Shan and the others to leave Padme behind? Shan kept studying his friend as Padme began to stir in the litter. Lokesh was not staring at the gompa now, but beyond it to a thin grey ribbon that led toward the horizon. Toward the northern highway, perhaps thirty miles away. A road meant patrols.

They were only four hundred yards from the gompa when Padme weakly raised his arm for them to stop. "I will not go in like this," he said in a strained, brave voice, and rose from the litter. He zipped up the yellow vest and began to walk, feebly at first, with visible effort, then with longer, more confident strides. A monk on a ladder, adding whitewash to the outer wall, stopped brushing and called out excitedly. Moments later several monks ran out of the gompa to greet Padme.

"Rinpoche! We were going to send out searchers!" the first to reach him called, then cried out in dismay as he saw the injuries on Padme's face and arms.

Men in robes quickly surrounded Padme, supporting him at each shoulder as they escorted him past a small collection of rundown habitations and through the two tall square pillars on either side of the gompa gate. Shan and his friends stared toward the monastery uncertainly, then with a blur of movement a small brown dog was at Tenzin's feet, barking in a shrill, high-pitched frenzy, tugging his pant leg, tearing it. Tenzin bent to put a hand on the dog's head, and the dog bit it. Suddenly a stone flew through the air, hitting the dog on its side. The animal yelped and scurried away around the corner of the gompa wall.

Lhandro stepped to Tenzin, who held up a bleeding finger, and produced a water bottle to wash the wound. Shan surveyed the small buildings by the gate. In front of one crumbling packed-earth house a man with shaggy white hair and leathery skin sat under a crude awning, bent over a foot-powered sewing machine, working on what appeared to be a monastic robe. Another man, nearly as old, his head heavily bandaged, leaned against a rusty metal barrel, asleep. An old woman in a heavily patched chuba, her eyes glazed with cataracts, sat in the doorway of another house, little more than a hut, spinning a small prayer wheel. No one looked up. No one showed a victorious smile after witnessing Padme's return, or even after driving away Tenzin's attacker.

There was a single new construction outside the gate, a long narrow open-faced shelter of cinderblocks with a tin roof and a dirt floor. It was a familiar fixture of Shan's prior incarnation; they were called newspaper huts in Beijing or, by some, Party shithouses. Inside, on the back wall, a long glass-enclosed case displayed a recent copy of the official newspaper published in Lhasa, in Chinese. Shan looked back at the Tibetans scattered around the buildings. He doubted any of them spoke, let alone read, Chinese. Hesitantly stepping into the hut, he gazed down the row of newspaper pages, at the end of which was a board on which local announcements had been pinned. He quickly scanned the pages. A speech on foreign relations from the Chairman in Beijing was reproduced in its entirety, taking up three pages. A company from Shanghai, whose name he recognized as an entity owned by the People's Liberation Army, was building a hotel for tourists at the base of the Potola. Production of timber in eastern Tibet continued to surpass all records. The beloved abbot of Sangchi gompa, one of the largest in Tibet, previously reported to be defecting to India, was now known to have been kidnapped by members of the Dalai Cult—one of Beijing's favorite labels for those who resisted the party line in Tibet. A new hydroelectric facility had been dedicated southeast of Lhasa. A senior leader of the Dalai Cult, the notorious Tiger, was now believed to have killed Chao Yu, the heroic Deputy Director of the Bureau of Religious Affairs in Amdo town. Shan read the story twice. There was no reported evidence, just a statement from Public Security about the Tiger's record of violence and treason. The Tiger, the reviled reactionary puppet of the Dalai Cult, an accompanying article reported, would soon be cornered by Public Security forces and would meet the people's swift justice. A Tibetan school in Qinghai had sent the Chairman a map of China constructed entirely of rice. A Chinese school girl had saved a drowning lamb in Shigatse. There was a photograph of the lamb.

Shan paused at the last panel, half of which was taken up by a single announcement from Norbu gompa and the council that administered the township. A May Day festival would be conducted at Norbu, where the economic progress of the township would be celebrated in coordination with the holiday activities held in Beijing in honor of the global proletariat. Citizens were expected to participate, and a sheet with numbered lines was stapled below the proclamation for families or work units to sign up to display the fruits of their labors. The date was ten days away. Only one line had been filled in. Lhalung Pelgyi Dorje, it said, in the hurried scrawl of a prankster. It was the name of a Tibetan who, over a thousand years before, had killed a king who had almost extinguished Buddhism with campaigns of terror so severe they had not been seen again until the communists arrived. The hero was coming to Norbu, the writing said, and would bring one stale dumpling to honor the Chairman. No one else had subscribed to the May Day celebration. Shan studied the weary Tibetans who sat outside the gate. It was as though some of the local population were trying to embarrass the gompa, and others were scared of it.

"If we left now, we might reach the sheep by dark," Nyma suggested in a near whisper, as though she suddenly had doubts about receiving the blessings of the lamas. But before anyone could reply a middle-aged monk in an elegant gold-fringed robe emerged from the gate, smiling, his arms open in greeting, followed closely by two boyish monks.

Shan froze for a moment, and glanced with worry at Nyma. He recognized the monk, whose nose was long and hooked. It was Khodrak, the one who called himself abbot.

"Forgive us," Khodrak said. "We were so overjoyed at the return of our Padme that we neglected you." Shan looked over the monk's shoulder, past the gate. Over the ornate front door of the central building was a small banner in elegant Chinese script. Serene Prosperity, it proclaimed. "Those who saved our Padme are welcome in Norbu gompa," Khodrak proclaimed in a gracious tone, gesturing them toward the gate.

As Khodrak and his nervous young attendants escorted them across the neatly raked earth of the courtyard it became obvious that the rebuilding effort had been confined to only certain elements of the gompa. The three central buildings appeared to be of sturdy new construction but along both sides, parallel to the outer walls, were several long single-story buildings of wood and pressed earth, most of which were neither new nor well-maintained. They would have been built to house the monks, Shan knew, and for the many meditation cells and minor deity chapels common to traditional gompas. They were all framed in wood, with small, empty porches where rows of prayer wheels would have traditionally hung. The first of these buildings on each side of the main courtyard had been restored to resemble the newer central buildings, giving an elegant atmosphere to the entry courtyard, and each had a long red plank bolted over its doorway, bearing the mani mantra in recessed gold letters.

The abbot led them under the sign of the low building on the left, then excused himself, announcing that one of the young novices would guide them around the compound. The nervous novice showed them pegs where they might hang their belongings and explained that Norbu was the main gompa of the region, with thirty-five monks and novices, boasting one of the highest Religious Affairs scores in all of Tibet.

"Scores for what, exactly?" Shan asked the novice as he led them outside, past the first two central buildings, the first of which he had quickly identified as the administration building, the second as the site of the dining hall and instruction rooms.

The youth gave a short grimace. "Proper conduct," he said, staring straight ahead. "Serenity," he added in a strangely somber tone, and quickened his pace. In the southeast corner of the high wall stood a long wooden building and a stable, both in severe disrepair. They seemed to be huddling together, the last survivors of an older, different monastery, resisting the bigger, more modern construction in the center of the gompa. Shan studied the buildings, which were made of planks joined with pegs. Shovels and rakes were laid against them. A pile of tattered baskets, with thick shoulder straps and padded loops extending out of their tops were stacked against the stable. Shan knew such baskets, for he had carried one nearly every day for four years, the long loop on his forehead, hauling rocks and gravel for government road builders. Past the buildings in the corner of the outer wall was a four-wheeled wooden cart and a huge pile of dung, more than ten feet high. Towering above the dung pile in the shade of the poplar trees that grew outside the wall was a tall, thin pole on which were fastened a long radio antenna and a satellite dish.

Nyma darted toward a huge cylinder hung in a scaffold near the center of the rear wall, a beautifully-crafted prayer wheel. But as she reached to touch it the novice called her away, and quickened his pace again to lead them past a row of vehicles parked along the wall, one a large van with the markings of an ambulance. A stern Han man in a sky blue uniform stepped around the end of the van, studying them intensely as he lit a cigarette.

"A special medical team from Lhasa," the novice explained in his nervous boyish voice. "They travel the countryside to help the local people. They have been on an extended assignment for weeks, coming from the south, near the Indian border, visiting local villages and camps. Seldom do the people get to see real doctors."

Real doctors. Lokesh looked back at Shan. Once there had been a college for real doctors, on the Plain of Flowers.

Tenzin had lingered by the mound of dung. As he approached, Shan saw that he had spread some of the mound's dry, dusty contents on his cheeks and pulled his hat low.

As they continued around the southwest corner a line of perhaps twenty Tibetans came into view inside a line of wooden stanchions threaded with rope. Half a dozen more men and women, mostly Han, all wearing the light blue uniforms, were grouped at the door of a small building, studying the Tibetans in line. The rongpa and dropka in line all wore the same anxious look as the young monk. They did not look sick. They just looked worried.

A man wearing a fleece vest called Lhandro by name, gesturing him closer as though he feared stepping out of line. But when Lhandro took a step toward the man the novice touched his arm to restrain him. "The doctors don't like anyone interfering," he said in an earnest tone. Shan heard one of the men in blue remind the Tibetans to have their papers ready for inspection.

The third of the central buildings was a longer lower structure that did not share the polished look of the first two structures. Patches of stucco were falling off the rear wall. Two red pillars straddled a thick wooden door, ornately carved with images of the Historical Buddha's life, that appeared to have been salvaged from an older building and set into a metal frame. They stepped into an entryway of rough plank flooring into a large chamber with a concrete floor. Half a dozen monks sat on cushions on the cold, hard floor, facing an altar topped with yellow plastic laminate on which sat a four-foot-high plaster statue of the Historical Buddha, Sakyamuni, painted in garish colors. Beside the Buddha was a small table with offering bowls and a smoldering cone of incense.

"Our lhakang," their guide explained. The gompa's main chapel.

Lokesh took one look at the statue and sat down among the monks. Their escort raised his hand as though to protest, then Nyma sat, and Tenzin.

"There are so few temples in the mountains," Shan observed pointedly.

The monk studied Shan and opened his mouth with an inquisitive glint, then, as Lhandro, too, joined the others on the floor, he shrugged. "Please be with us for the evening meal," he said. "Listen for the bell." He turned and stepped out of the chapel.

Shan sat with his friends for half an hour, breathing in the fragrant incense, studying a row of freshly painted thangkas on the wall, folding and unfolding his legs. But he could not find the mindfulness of meditation and finally stood and stepped outside, walking along a low abandoned wall that ran between the second and third buildings. It had once been a thick wall of stone, the foundation of a substantial building. He slowly circled the other two central buildings, noting with satisfaction the ropes of prayer flags that connected the upper corners of the first two buildings, then found himself before the prayer wheel at the rear of the grounds. It was beautifully crafted, six feet high and nearly three across, made of finely worked copper and brass. He touched it and, to his surprise it spun freely, turning almost an entire revolution. It was hung with heavy ball bearings, as though an engineer, not a monk, had designed it. Under it he noticed a plaque in Chinese and Tibetan. He had sometimes seen similar plaques, declaring that a wheel or statue had been donated by a youth league, or the friends of a gompa. But this one, like the giant wheel itself, was unlike any he had seen before. Operating hours 8 A.M. to 8 P.M., it said. He stared at it, not understanding, then heard someone at the old stable by the giant pile of dung. Stepping tentatively toward the sound he discovered a stocky monk speaking to a huge shaggy black yak that stood beside the wooden cart. The monk was shoveling dung from the pile into the cart, addressing the yak in a conversational tone as he worked.

After a moment Shan realized he had seen him before. He slipped into the shadow along the wall of the stable and watched the man, who was so absorbed in his work and discussion with the yak that it was five minutes before he noticed Shan. He acknowledged Shan's presence only by pausing a moment, ceasing to speak to the yak, then continuing his labor of transferring the dung to the cart.

"I hope you didn't get stuck again that day," Shan ventured.

The monk turned and grunted as he studied, first Shan, then the empty grounds beyond him. He offered an uncertain nod. "Twice more," he replied. "They canceled the schedule and came back here." The words caused Shan to turn and study the gompa grounds himself. "The Bureau of Religious Affairs is here?"

"Everywhere," the monk replied in a reluctant tone, shoveling more dung into the cart. People didn't talk about the howlers, just as they didn't talk about knobs or other demons.

"Someone worked hard to bring all that fuel here," Shan observed.

"Someone did," the monk agreed once more, eyeing Shan warily. He turned away and continued shoveling. "Local farmers, and herders. Sometimes it is all they can afford to give. Once they would go without their hearthfires to bring fuel to the gompa."

"You said you came from Khang-nyi gompa," Shan recalled.

"Right. Second House, it's the old name, the original name for this place. There was a big gompa, the First House, up on the high plain to the north. This was a station for those traveling there, or those waiting for lamas to come down."

Shan found a shovel leaning against the stable, an old handmade implement with a wooden blade, and began helping the monk. "I did this once before, only wet," he said after a few minutes.

The man paused with his shovel still in the pile. "Wet?"

"Rice paddies," Shan said. "In Liaoning Province. I wasn't given any choice."

The man nodded and kept working. "You mean they forced you?"

Shan threw another shovelful on the cart. "Soldiers," he confirmed. "They mostly stayed away because of the smell. Just came close to beat us with bamboo canes when we stopped working."

They labored on in silence. From somewhere came music, the singsong strains of Chinese opera.

"The smell?" the monk asked, after he seemed to have considered Shan's words for several minutes.

"The soldiers were from the city," Shan said with a sigh.

The monk contemplated Shan, resting his shovel, one hand stroking the back of the big black animal. "Yak dung doesn't smell bad."

"This was human. Night soil, from the cities, too."

The man worked a moment and stopped again. He slowly put his hand on the handle of Shan's shovel and pushed it down. "I am called Gyalo. I am just a rongpa at heart. They wanted some monks from the local farm laborer class two years ago, and my grandmother had always wanted me to be a monk. They gave me a license. They like to take me to see other laborers now." He looked at Shan expectantly. It was Shan's turn to explain.

"It was an agricultural reform camp, when I was only a child. My family was sent because my father was a professor. A small army of workers brought the night soil in big clay jars on bicycle racks. Usually we just poured it into the rice fields. But there would be times when the jars stood in the sun and dried, so they would dump it in long piles, or make us scrape it out with our hands. What I remember most of all was how, when it rained, everything turned wet and smelly and too soft to put on a shovel."

The monk contemplated Shan a long time. "This isn't like that at all," he said, very seriously. Shan stared back, and the man's stern expression slowly warmed to a grin.

"Is the gompa delivering this to the villagers?"

"The gompa is just getting rid of its stockpile. Too old-fashioned they say, reminds them of the olds. Doesn't set the right example. We must show the people what prosperity means," he said in the tone of a political officer. Gyalo gestured toward the shadows where the stables abutted the outer wall. Several large metal gas cylinders were lined up along the wall.

"The medicals brought you in?" he asked Shan after throwing a few more shovelfuls on the cart. He made it sound as if the doctors were arresting their patients.

Shan shook his head. "I was still in the mountains with my friends. We found a monk named Padme on the Plain of Flowers. He had been attacked by someone and needed our help."

Gyalo studied Shan carefully again and seemed about to ask him something. "May the blessed Buddha watch over Padme Rinpoche," he said instead, quickly, in his stiff tone. "Prayers were offered for him in the chapel." Shan looked at the monk, and wondered why he, and he alone, was shoveling the dung. Was it a punishment? Gyalo didn't say he had offered prayers for Padme, only that prayers were offered. And why did he and the monks at the gate call the young monk Rinpoche, a term usually reserved for older, venerated teachers?

"Do those doctors come often?" Shan asked.

The monk frowned. "Not these, these are special," he said, and leaned on his shovel, studying Shan again. "Where did you learn to speak Tibetan so well? Only Chinese I've known who spoke Tibetan worked for the government."

"I did work for the government. Building roads. I carried one of those," Shan said with a gesture toward the stack of baskets.

The monk winced then pointed toward the clinic at the opposite corner of the compound. "This region was once full of medicine lamas. Famous for healers. It meant people were slow to change their ways, slow to retreat from religion, slow to embrace the Chinese doctors. The government wants to be sure people don't get sick."

"You mean don't get healed the wrong way."

Gyalo fixed Shan with a pointed gaze.

Shan considered the monk's words again. "So you mean those people waiting aren't sick?" He had seen sick people, he recalled; one hiding from doctors in the salt camp, the other waiting on the trail—the woman who had refused Lokesh's offer of help.

147

"They were told to come down from the mountains to be checked. For innoculations. For papers."

"Papers?"

"Those doctors arrived two weeks ago, and just stayed. Mostly they have meetings in the offices. Sometimes a knob officer with a pockmarked face comes, a man with dirty ice for eyes. And they all have radios like soldiers. Not everyone wearing one of those blue suits is a doctor," Gyalo warned in a low voice. "And even the real doctors are issuing new health cards, like identity cards. Everyone has to record exactly what doctors they have seen in the past five years, including Tibetan healers. And they have to sign papers that come from the office. When that knob comes he makes people read."

"Read? Read what?"

"Anything. A paragraph from a Serenity Campaign pamphlet. A line from the medical forms." Gyalo frowned toward the far corner, where several of the Han in blue could still be seen. "Some people came willingly at first. But now, most don't come on their own. Soldiers provide trucks. Or men like soldiers, wearing white shirts," he said, with a meaningful glance at Shan.

Shan stared at the monk. Howlers wore white shirts sometimes, but howlers were not soldiers, howlers were the political officers of modern Tibet. "You mean there are Public Security soldiers posing as howlers? As doctors?"

"Norbu gompa is like a border post, at the edge of the wilderness, hidden from the rest of the world. A place for experiments."

Shan eyed the monk closely. "You mean this county is experimenting somehow? With politics?"

"The authority that controls us is the Bureau of Religious Affairs. The county council ignores us. Norbu District of the Bureau, that's who we are, a district bigger than the county, running north across the mountains even, into Qinghai Province. All run by Religious Affairs in Amdo town and by those who sit in those offices," he said, nodding toward the first of the two-story buildings.

Shan worked in silence for several minutes. "If those doctors came two weeks ago, then they're not here because the Deputy Director was killed."

Gyalo nodded, rubbing the yak's head. "That Tuan, most people just know him as head of Religious Affairs. But he spent twenty years in Public Security first. The perfect credential for running Religious Affairs in such a tradition-bound district," Gyalo said bitterly, then looked up at Shan. "Not all the people they want to bring here will come. Some just hide and wait. I used to go and help the herders and the farmers when I could. Now they seldom give me permission to leave without an escort."

"But Padme was far away, by himself," Shan said slowly. "A day's walk from here, without even a water bottle."

"Padme doesn't need permission," Gyalo said into the yak's ear, in a loud whisper. "And he never walks far."

"But we found him. No horse. No cart. Like a hermit, we thought."

Gyalo, grinning, seemed to think Shan had offered a good joke. He stopped looking at Shan, and conversed only with the yak now. "If you study enough, and find the right awareness, an old lama told me, you can learn to fly," he said to the animal, and flapped his arms like a bird's wings.

Shan looked at him uneasily. "Was he also looking for that man with a fish?"

Gyalo bent over the yak's head. "Maybe this one doesn't know about dropka and sacred lakes. Maybe he doesn't know what swims in sacred waters."

Shan looked skeptically from the monk to the yak, wondering about the man's mental condition.

The monk turned his back and Shan returned the shovel to the stable wall. But as Shan stepped away the monk spoke once more. "He shouldn't let that nun go upstairs," Gyalo said to the yak. When Shan turned the monk was bent over the yak, straightening a tangle of the animal's long black hair, as if he had said nothing, as if Shan had already gone.

Shan moved slowly back toward the chapel and found it empty. Don't let Nyma go upstairs. Shan wandered toward the first of the two-story buildings, the one nearest the gate, the one with the banner. There were wooden plaques he had not read before along the front of the building. They weren't religious teachings, he saw now with a chill, although they were done with the graceful embellished Tibetan script used for such quotes. Use Buddha to Serve the People, one said. Endow the Words of Buddha with Chinese Socialism, read another.

He circled the building slowly, examining the two ropes of prayer flags that connected it with the adjacent structure. One line were mani flags, inscribed with the mantra to the Compassionate Buddha. But he had been mistaken about the second line. It consisted of minature red flags bearing one large star in the upper left corner, with an arc of four stars beside it. The flag of the People's Republic of China. He paced slowly along the western wall of the compound and watched as four dropka entered one of the decrepit buildings in the center of the western wall. He followed them through a door of dried cracked wood down a corridor of creaking floorboards into a small chapel, no more than twelve feet long and eight wide. The room was crowded with over a dozen Tibetans, sitting worshipfully before a small bronze statue of the teacher Guru Rinpoche. On the wall, on either side of the statue were old faded thangkas of Tara, eight in all, the eight aspects of the deity, which offered protection from eight specific fears. Shan recognized several. There was one that protected the devout from snakes and envy, another that shielded them from delusion and elephants, one more that provided protection from thieves. Above the statue was a much smaller thangka, also old and faded, of a deity Shan did not recognize at first. A dropka woman made room beside her and he sat, studying the thangka. Suddenly with a start he recognized it. It was not an old thangka, only cleverly crafted to look old to disguise it. It was a representation of a lama with a peaceful smile, mendicant staff over his shoulder, hand raised with the index finger and thumb touching in what was called the teaching mudra. It was the Fourteenth Dalai Lama, Tenzin Gyatse, the current Dalai Lama.

After half an hour he moved back into the courtyard, toward the front of the administration building, his gaze surveying the yard in confusion, trying to reconcile the mani prayers over the side doorways and the doctors who acted like knobs, the giant prayer wheel and its admonishing rules, the reverent paintings of deities and the red emblems of Beijing.

He stepped into the entry hall of the building to find it empty, adorned only with two large, modern paintings, stylized imitations of thangkas, and another Serenity campaign banner. Below the banner was a printed notice pinned to a large bulletin board. It was a chart for a scoring system. Religious Affairs districts would be graded according to the economic advancement made as a result of each district's efforts to turn religious inclinations to economic activity. There was a table of economic criteria, with current statistics and averages for the five years ending the year before: number of sheep; number of domesticated yaks, goats, horses; acres of barley; number of children enrolled in approved schools; number of vehicles; and production of felt, wool, and dairy products. Shan quickly scanned the column listing prior years' activity. The local district had to be one of the poorest in Tibet, judged by such standards. Or judging by Drakte's own ledger. Surely Drakte hadn't been compiling data for the campaign?

There was a handwritten note at the bottom of the notice, in a careful, practiced script. We will have serenity, and we will have it now, it said. It was signed by Chairman Khodrak. Beside the notice was a smaller note, stating that all monks were expected to attend the upcoming Workers Day celebration on May first.

Shan ascended the simple wooden stairway at the end of the hall, not knowing what to expect. The atmosphere of the upstairs corridor was of a government office. A door at the top of the stairs opened into a chamber where a monk sat beside a man in a business suit, both of them typing rapidly on computer keyboards below monitors displaying Chinese ideograms. Above them were two photographs, one of Mao Tse Tung and another of the chairman who currently sat in Beijing. On a table beside the men was a facsimile machine and a large telephone with buttons for multiple lines. On one wall was a map, with the familiar words *Nei Lou* boldly printed at the top. Below the map was a typewriter with a letter in it. His eyes lingered on the machine. He and Lokesh had seen a typewriter in a herder's hut when traveling with Drakte. The purbas had grown quite agitated when they realized Shan had seen it. Typewriters were still treated like secret weapons by the knobs. More than one dissident had been convicted simply on the evidence he or she possessed their own typewriter.

Shan stepped past the open door and paused at a large poster on the wall, printed in Chinese only, with the words Bureau of Religious Affairs in bold type across the top. Qualifications for admission, it stated at the top, with ten criteria listed. Shan clenched his jaw and read.

The candidate must be at least eighteen years old, said the first. Tibetan families had practiced a centuries old tradition of sending their oldest boy at a much earlier age to be educated at gompas, for the formal education process could easily last more than twenty years for those aspiring to the ranks of geshe, the highest rank of monastic training.

The candidate must love the Communist Party, said the next line. Shan read it twice to make sure he had not mistaken the words. Love the Party. The Candidate's parents must be identified, said the third, and demonstrate their approval.

The Candidate's work unit must approve the transfer to the monastery unit, meaning not only were gompas considered just another type of work unit but also that young men had to embark on a different life, a different job, before applying to the political leaders of their work units, who more likely than not would be Chinese immigrants.

Local authorities must consent, and the county authorities must consent. Then, both the candidate and the candidate's parents must have an acceptable political background.

The candidate must come from an approved geographic area. There were still areas, where Tibetan resistance had been greatest, where local citizens were prohibited from taking a robe under any circumstance.

Finally there were two brief standards. Committee Approval, the poster said, and approval of the Public Security Bureau.

Shan stared at the poster, fighting an acrid taste on his tongue that seemed to be spreading to his belly. Beijing's Bureau of Religious Affairs established a strict cap on the number of monks at each gompa, usually a fraction of the original population. Gompas where two thousand monks once served might have only fifty authorized by the howlers. Even when an opening arose, a candidate could take years to satisfy all the necessary approvals. Once applicants might have sat with lamas and recited scriptures learned at home or spoken of how a growing awareness of the Buddha within was calling them to put on a robe. Now for the best chance of winning a robe, an applicant should sit with a commissar and recite scripture from little red Party books.

Past the poster, on the opposite wall, was a sheet of paper whose handwritten words were almost as large as those of the poster. Never Again a Monk, it said, with five names below it, each with a date from the past two years. On the wall, in chilling proximity, hung five robes with names on labels pinned over each. Above them was another sign. *Walked Away from Buddha*, it read, and under it a quote, *Once you walk away*

151

Buddha will not embrace you again, over the embellished signature of Chairman Khodrak. The line of pegs continued down the corridor with another dozen pegs, all empty, except for the last two, from which hung lush foxfur caps. Past the caps, at the end of the hall, was a set of double wooden doors, one of which hung partially open.

Shan heard voices and stepped toward the gap in the doors to see Nyma, Lokesh, Lhandro, and Tenzin seated in front of a heavy wooden table in rigid straight-back chairs. On the far side of the table were three much larger chairs, wooden but with padded backs, upholstered in red silk. Two of the chairs were occupied, by Khodrak and the Han with long thinning hair Shan had seen at the lake. Director Tuan of Religious Affairs, who had qualified for his job by having a prior career in Public Security. An elegant set of porcelain tea cups sat on the table, and a young monk was refilling those in front of Shan's friends. The monk disappeared from view and a moment later the door flung open. The monk gestured Shan toward one of the empty chairs beside his friends.

"Excellent, excellent," Khodrak said. "Take a moment with us, Comrade Shan." Behind him, leaning against the wall, was a long ceremonial staff, a mendicant's staff with an ornate head of finely worked white metal ending in a point. "We were expressing our gratitude and our pleasure that you will be able to join us tonight for a meal with the assembly."

Shan stole a glance at his friends. Only Lhandro returned it, with a small, forced smile. The others stared uncertainly at the dainty, steaming cups in front of them. Shan hesitantly took a seat beside Nyma. Khodrak had learned his name. What else had he asked about?

"This kind of heroism should not go unrewarded," Khodrak said. "Common people, agricultural laborers even, sacrificing themselves to save the life of a representative of the religious establishment. Here at Norbu, a model of right conduct amidst so many reactionary thinkers, we especially applaud your contribution."

It was Shan's turn to stare at his cup of tea, placed there by the young attendant, for he feared what he might say if he fixed eyes with Khodrak or Director Tuan. Khodrak had assumed the Tibetans were all herders or farmers. Agricultural laborers were the most revered of classes in the hierarchy the Party had created for its classless society. Shan's mind raced. Images of the signs in the hall flashed before him, and the Chinese flags, the stalwart Gyalo alone with the yak dung, and the office outside that looked like the operations center for a government agency. He ventured a look up at the empty chair. Khodrak had called himself chairman. The signs outside did not refer to him as an abbot, or kenpo, the traditional head of every Tibetan gompa. When Gyalo had spoken of the authority inside the gompa he had used the plural 'they'. Because, Shan now knew, Norbu was a model of the truly modern gompa, run not by a lama abbot but by a Democratic Management Committee.

Once, during a winter storm that kept them confined to their prison barracks, Shan and his cellmates had listened to a young monk who had just begun a five-year sentence. The monk had explained that his crime was refusal to sign a statement swearing to patriotism and pledging never to protest against the policies of Beijing, a pledge required by those who ran his gompa. What the older monks hadn't understood, and what the new prisoner had had to explain repeatedly, was why abbots and lamas would request such a pledge, and how they could send him to a Chinese prison for refusing to accept it. The reason, the monk patiently explained, was that a new body had taken over administration of his gompa, a Democratic Management Committee. The Committee tested monks on their knowledge of correct political thought, and would call upon monks in assembly to recite Chinese versions of Tibetan history, in addition to their sutras—the version that said Tibet had always been Chinese and that Tibetans were descended from Chinese stock.

The attending monk appeared by Khodrak with a stack of slender, six-inch-long boxes. "Please," Khodrak announced, "you deserve something in honor of your contribution." He said it in a gracious tone, speaking slowly and loudly, as if he were accustomed to public speaking. The young monk distributed one of the boxes to each of them and gestured for them to open their gifts. Inside was a heavy red plastic dorje, the thunderbolt symbol used in many Tibetan rituals. The monk showed Nyma how to push one end so it clicked. A ballpoint pen. Along the bottom was inscribed, in Chinese characters, Bureau of Religious Affairs.

Shan looked up, his throat dry. Khodrak was smiling broadly, studying each one of them with intense interest now as his hand absently straightened the monogram on his robe. Shan had heard somewhere that members of Democratic Management Committees were paid salaries by the Religious Affairs Bureau. He gazed out the window. It was getting dark, too late to leave the gompa.

"Perhaps an extra one for our special friend?" Khodrak said to the attendant, in the tone of an order.

"Yes, Chairman Rinpoche," the monk replied woodenly.

The young monk appeared at Shan's side, another of the pen boxes extended toward him. Shan looked at Khodrak. His special friend. Because Shan was Han. "Thank you, no," he said to the monk in a taut voice. "Unfortunately I can write only with one hand."

Khodrak chuckled, then laughed loudly, and Director Tuan took up the laughter, followed by the attending monk. Shan's friends offered strained smiles. Abruptly Khodrak stopped laughing and clasped his hands, the index fingers extended together. Not a mudra. He was pointing with the fingers, pointing at Tenzin.

"Perhaps your friend should see a doctor. We have specialists here, all the way from Lhasa."

See a doctor. The expression sparked a flash of pain in Shan. The words had been a code in the gulag, a threat used by the guards for

153

recalcitrant prisoners like Shan who were sometimes taken to knob specialists with cattle prods and small hammers and needle-nosed pliers.

"Have you had your affliction long?" Khodrak asked Tenzin in his solicitous tone. He seemed to be studying Tenzin's hands. Shan recalled the rongpa village, where Colonel Lin had studied Lokesh's hands. What was it? Was there something special about Tenzin's hands? They were not, Shan realized, the rough calloused hands of a rongpa or herder.

"We told you," Nyma interjected. "Tenzin was struck by lightning. He doesn't speak. We don't mind. He is a good worker."

Khodrak tossed the napkin by his cup across the table. Tenzin still wore the dust from the dung pile on his face. "You should wash," he said in an offhand tone. He studied the faces of the others at the table.

Shan watched Tenzin and Khodrak with a chill. Tenzin kept his gaze on the table with studied disinterest, then pulled his hands from the table and folded them on his lap where Khodrak could not see them. But Shan could. They formed a mudra, with the little fingers linked, the middle two fingers of each hand bent inward, and the tips of the index fingers and thumbs touching. It was called the Spirit Subduer, and it seemed aimed at Khodrak. Suddenly a light flashed, and Shan looked up to see the attendant with a camera, busily snapping photographs of Shan and his companions.

"Perhaps you have heard," Tuan said in an oily voice, "that my deputy was assassinated."

Tenzin stared at his hands a moment, his gaze drifting slowly toward Khodrak. The two men exchanged a hard, challenging stare. Shan watched the exchange in confusion. Tenzin had disappeared the night of Chao's killing. But surely they didn't suspect him or they would have seized him already. Suddenly he recalled Gyalo's words to his yak. Shan didn't know what swam in sacred waters. Gyalo had meant nagas. Khodrak might have been searching for a man connected to the water deities. Tenzin had gone from the hermitage once to get black sand from the nagas. He could have been seen by an informer as he performed a ceremony at a river. The howlers despised nagas as symbols of the Tibet's oldest traditions. If they were to detain Tenzin and interrogate him about his interest in water deities, even if they had to wait for the mute Tibetan to write his confession, they would eventually find out about the hermitage, about Gendun and Shopo.

"Was that the reason Padme Rinpoche was walking on the high plain?" Shan asked abruptly, trying to deflect Tuan's attention. "Helping restore public order?"

Tuan looked at Shan intensely, but without showing emotion.

Nyma and Lhandro frowned at Shan and fixed him with an annoyed stares. Shan was implying that Padme had been engaged in something other than religious pursuits.

But Khodrak seemed to find nothing extraordinary about the inquiry.

"Everyone must be vigilant in times like these," the chairman suggested, with an appreciative nod toward Shan. "When so much important progress is at hand, that is when reactionaries are most apt to strike. Murder. Kidnapping. At least it validates our work."

"Kidnapping?" Shan asked.

"Surely you heard about the abbot of Sangchi. The blessed leader of such an important institution. A model of right thinking for all Tibetans. Creator of the Serenity Campaign. Another martyr of our cause."

"The newspapers say the abbot of Sangchi is being taken to India."

"We know now the abbot was kidnapped by the most radical elements of the resistance," Tuan interjected. "Possibly the same ones who killed Deputy Director Chao not fifty miles from here. They will doubtlessly try to harm the abbot as well."

Shan looked at the table, trying to steady his nerves. What were they suggesting? That they knew the infamous Tiger was in the vicinity? That the lost abbot was imprisoned by the Tiger somewhere nearby? Surely not, or the region would be saturated with Public Security troops.

"Dinner," Khodrak announced abruptly, smiling smugly. "Dinner will be served soon, in the assembly hall. Take a moment. Enjoy our hospitality." The Chairman rose and left the room, Tuan following close behind. Shan looked after Khodrak. Take a moment. The words seemed to be an idiom for Khodrak, a signature. The chairman spoke them gently, even graciously. But Shan had heard those words before. They were also an idiom of tamzing, the struggle sessions where correct thought was beaten, figuratively and literally, into wayward citizens. Take a moment, a tamzing leader would say to show his or her good nature. Take a moment to reconsider before we resort to more painful means to wrench you back to the Party's true path.

Shan lingered at the top of the stairs by the office, tempted to venture inside. As the monk called for him to join the others and he slowly descended, voices were raised in anger in the chamber beyond the office, but he could make out no words. He followed the others to what appeared to be a rear door opening to the courtyard between the buildings, and had almost reached Lokesh, when a hand closed around his arm.

"Comrade Shan," a stern voice said behind him.

Shan turned to look into the black, pebble-like eyes of Director Tuan. Tuan gestured toward an open office door. Shan hesitated, watching his friends disappear out the door. His chest tightening, his throat bone dry, he entered the chamber.

A small metal desk was pushed against the window to make room for four overstuffed chairs arranged around a low table with a long lace doily. Tuan closed the door behind them, lowered himself into one of the deep chairs and motioned for Shan to do the same. "Comrade," he repeated, like a cordial greeting this time.

Shan sat on the edge of the chair opposite Tuan and nodded slowly.

On top of the lace were several stacks of the Serenity pamphlets he had seen at the lake.

Tuan drummed his hand on the arm of the chair as he examined Shan, looking at his tattered boots and patched clothing. "It must be difficult for a man like you," he began.

Shan nodded again. They knew his name. But surely they had not had time to find out who he was, that he was still officially a lao gai prisoner.

"How long have you been in Tibet?" Tuan pulled a pack of cigarettes from his pocket and placed them on the wide arm of the chair.

"Five years."

Tuan seemed to welcome the news. "Most don't last a year. I salute you. People like you are the real worker heroes. Anyone could work back home in a factory. But you are here, in the front lines of our great struggle." He picked up the cigarettes and tapped them on the arm of the chair. Shan had met Religious Affairs officials before. Most were soft and bureaucratic, biding their time before rotating back to a better office in eastern China. But Tuan was different. Tuan was like a hard-bitten soldier. Tuan had already finished one career at Public Security.

"Your friends said you were traveling north, and came out of your way to bring Padme home. Padme said you were traveling with salt."

Tuan wasn't asking about nagas, or Yapchi and Lhasa, none of the questions asked by Colonel Lin. Indeed, Tuan didn't seem to be interrogating him so much as testing him somehow. "It's a tradition they have," Shan said.

"There are taxes to be paid to the salt monopoly," Tuan observed. "You could get a bounty for reporting them. I could arrange it, even have it deposited somewhere. They need never know."

Shan forced a small conspiratorial smile which caused Tuan to raise his hand, palm outward. "You've thought of it. Excellent." He lifted the cigarette pack to his nostrils and inhaled, lit one of the cigarettes, and carefully set it in the ashtray on the table. "You could not be blamed for the companions you acquire when traveling. A man like you has the opportunity to meet all types of Tibetans."

Shan clenched his jaw. "My companions brought an injured monk here," he reminded Tuan.

The Director's lips curled in a thin smile as he inhaled the smoke drifting from the table. It was as if he were using the tobacco as incense. "It's an untamed land, this region. Criminal elements in hiding on every mountain. The one who killed Deputy Director Chao is out there. He must have attacked Padme."

"You make it sound as though you know who it is."

"Of course. It is the same war that started when the liberation army arrived. It has never really concluded, it's just less visible."

"You mean you don't care who it is."

156

Tuan shrugged and leaned toward the smoke. "Do they? They take one of us, we take one of them," the Director said in a disinterested tone, then smiled icily. "There will always be more of us than of them."

Shan studied Tuan as the Director smoothed the long hair on the side of his head. Was Tuan so disinterested because he had already taken one Tibetan to balance his equation, because he knew he had already fatally wounded Drakte?

"There will be an accounting soon," Tuan said. "In less than two weeks. But meanwhile someone like you, a Han among them, will be in constant danger. Let me help you."

"I am not afraid of them." But Shan was scared of Tuan and the strange game he was playing. Tuan was going to account for Chao's murder in two weeks. He made it sound like one more item on his busy schedule.

Tuan leaned forward. "Things are changing in this district. A Han who knows how to deal with these Tibetans could have a bright future. We can use a man like you. We'll be looking for someone to manage all the other teachers. You will need to decide soon. Glory is coming, and there will be enough to share."

Shan almost asked him to repeat himself. Glory is coming? "Other teachers?"

"Special knowledge is coming to Norbu. A new world is coming for the people here," Tuan said.

Shan stared at the piece of lace. He usually recognized the special language of senior officials, but Tuan seemed to have developed a code all his own. "But for now all those doctors," Shan said tentatively. "They are frightening the people. Surely you do not need them to catch the killer."

Tuan offered an appreciative smile. "They have orders from Lhasa. National security is at stake. A senior Cult leader has infiltrated from India."

"We're more than four hundred miles from India."

"He's giving them a good chase."

"But why doctors? Why would disrupting the local people help the effort?"

"National security," Tuan repeated.

The Director glanced at his watch and stood. He reached into his pocket and produced a business card, extended it to Shan. "I know things. When we win, after May Day, give me a call." He tossed the cigarettes on Shan's lap and left the room without looking back.

Shan stared after him. I know things. The words probably meant nothing, just the idle words of an arrogant bureaucrat. But they made Shan recall the terrible night at the hermitage again. *He doesn't care who has to die*, Drakte had said, with nearly his last breath. *He kills prayer. He kills the thing he is.* Tuan was the senior official responsible for religion, and he killed religion.

157

Shan dropped the cigarettes on the arm of the chair, and found his friends outside waiting with the young monk under the fluttering flags.

"What was it?" Nyma whispered nervously.

Shan shrugged. "I don't know," he said truthfully. "He wanted to give me some cigarettes."

The monk led them into the adjacent structure and a large white-washed chamber, where twenty monks waited at two long plank tables. Some acknowledged their visitors with polite but restrained greetings, others looked away nervously. Gyalo was not present. An old monk, the oldest present, rose and recited the opening text from one of the early teachings, what the Tibetans called the Heart Sutra. His words, or perhaps his deep, resonant voice, had a calming effect on the assembly. But Shan could not relax. He fought the temptation to grab Lokesh and run. He could make nothing of his strange audience with Tuan. Tuan and Khodrak were going to win something, and glory would follow.

At last Khodrak, holding his mendicant's staff like a scepter, arrived with Tuan a step behind, each of them adorned in a fox-fur hat. The two sat at a smaller table at the head of the long ones, and moments later two young monks appeared with a huge steaming pot of *thugpa*, noodle soup cooked with vegetables. The attendants quickly served out the soup, then distributed bowls of steaming white rice. They ate quickly, with little conversation, the monks restlessly watching both their visitors and the two men at the head table. At the end of the meal, as Chinese green tea was served, Khodrak stood to explain how Comrade Shan and his companions had saved Padme. Comrade Shan. Khodrak had turned Padme's rescue into a political parable of the selfless Han saving a troubled Tibetan.

When they had finished, a monk led them first to retrieve their belongings, then to the gompa's guest quarters, a dormitory-style room with eight beds in one of the low single-story structures, gesturing Nyma toward a similar room on the opposite side of the hall.

"We saw an old stable," Shan said. "We would prefer to sleep there." His friends said nothing. Lokesh moved his head in a small, tight nod.

"They said here," the monk protested. "Surely the beds would be more comfortable."

"Not for us," Shan said firmly. "Our bones are accustomed to sleeping on the ground."

With a reluctant sigh the monk turned and led them to the abandoned stable, only a few paces from the cart Shan had helped fill. Beyond the cart in the deep shadows of the wall he sensed, more than saw, the big yak watching them.

The monk pulled open the heavy timber bar laid across the door on iron straps, and handed Shan the candle lantern he had been using. They stepped into a small musty chamber with half a dozen stalls, straw covering half the floor. Above the stalls was a low, half loft, where fodder had once been stored, with a small loft door for loading the hay.

158

Lokesh and Lhandro were already pulling straw together for bedding as the monk bid them a good night and pushed the door shut. In a few minutes Shan was listening to the slow, relaxed breathing of his companions, and he quickly followed them into slumber.

He awoke just before dawn, invigorated by the night's sleep, surprised at how sound it had been. He quickly brushed the straw from his clothes and stepped to the door. Hearing what sounded like a heavy truck outside, he paused for a moment, then pushed lightly on the door for a glance into the compound. The door would not move. The truck seemed to stop and he heard the sound of heavy boots on the earth outside. He pressed his eye to a narrow slit in the door. One of the medical trucks was there, its lights flashing as if for an emergency. A whistle blew, followed by an order. Shan could not make out faces in the dim light, but with a sinking heart he saw a line of white shirts.

There was movement behind him and Lhandro appeared. The Tibetan tried his luck with the door, to no avail. They pushed together. It did not move. The bar had been lowered into place. Someone had imprisoned them, and the guards were surrounding the stable.

CHAPTER NINE

Shan quickly woke the others, explaining in urgent whispers that they were prisoners. Nyma rushed to the door and pushed it, without effect, and turned with fear clenching her face. Lokesh sat on his pallet and offered a mantra to Tara, protectress of the devout, as orders were barked outside.

Lhandro leaned his ear against the wall as Nyma used the tine of a pitchfork to pry splinters from a small crack in the old wood, trying to see outside better. "That ambulance," Nyma reported as she bent to the crack. "Maybe the doctors just wanted—" she turned back and saw Shan's confusion as he stood in the rear shadows where Tenzin had slept.

"They took Tenzin!" Nyma cried in dismay as she rushed to his side.

They quickly searched for any sign of the silent Tibetan, or evidence of his departure. Shan and Lhandro paced along the walls of the stable. There were no loose boards, no other doors, no ladder to the loft where the small door opened to the outside.

"He's just a . . ." Nyma began forlornly, and her voice drifted off.

A what, Shan wondered. A dung collector? None of them really knew who Tenzin was. Just a fugitive, like so many others. Sometimes, if you were not to be taken in by what Beijing was doing to Tibet, all you could do was be a fugitive, always moving, always shying away from settlements and crowds. Shan recalled the strange exchange between Khodrak and Tenzin the day before. Had Tuan and Khodrak truly known something about the man or had it just been Tuan's instincts, honed by twenty years in Public Security? Tenzin was guilty of something, and by the political accounting that governed them, Tuan and Khodrak would get credit for taking him.

Suddenly there was a scraping sound, the sound of the bar of being dragged out of its iron straps, and the door flew open, casting such a brilliant shaft of sunlight inside that Shan and his friends threw their hands up to shield their eyes.

Director Tuan walked in, followed by a middle-aged Han in one of the light blue uniforms. A stethoscope hung from the man's neck, a small radio protruded from one of his tunic pockets. Tuan took in Shan and his companions with a quick glance, then stepped into the shadows at the rear of the stable as the physician stood silently at the door, watching with anticipation on his face. Two younger men in the light blue uniforms hovered outside the door, as though standing by to assist the doctor. Shan stepped sideways and saw that a stretcher, collapsed, leaned on one man's shoulder. He heard, but could not see, the heavy boots again, several pairs. Soldiers seemed to be pacing anxiously somewhere near the ambulance. Someone angrily snapped an order. But he could see no soldiers, only men in white shirts with epaulettes or medical uniforms.

A slight, small-shouldered man suddenly stepped into the doorway, silhouetted by the brilliant sunlight. Shan recognized the man's boots before he saw the man's grey uniform. A chill crept down his spine as he looked up into a face that seemed to be pounded out of corroded steel. The man might have been in his early thirties, but he had already acquired the cold machine-like demeanor which would likely stay with him for the rest of his career—the frigid, permanent sneer that Shan had seen so many times in the gulag. The man in grey was a Public Security officer, the pockmarked one Gyalo had spoken of, the one with dirty ice for eyes.

The knob studied Shan and his companions with a cold glare. Looking at Tuan, he uttered a low growling sound. It could have been anger, or disappointment, or the rumbling, expectant sound some predators made before a long-awaited feed. The doctor looked at the knob officer with a frustrated, impatient frown and held up four fingers. Four prisoners, he must be saying, when there should be five. Not four fingers exactly, for curiously, the doctor had pushed his little finger down and held up three fingers and a thumb. The officer replied with something like a snarl, and a fist raised a few inches in the air.

Something extraordinary was happening at Norbu gompa. It wasn't just that the gompa was in the hands of political commissars, or even that Shan and his friends had been seized. There was something else, something to do with the way the Religious Affairs officials acted like Public Security soldiers, the way they were being detained by a howler, with only the single knob officer present. Maybe the howlers were looking for Tenzin because of his work with nagas, but Public Security wanted him for something else. There was another possibility that had so frightened Shan he had not mentioned it to his companions. The knobs were desperately searching for a man with a croaking, growling voice—the notorious Tiger, whose broken voice box made a sound like no other. The knob officer had been forcing people to read to him. The only way a man could hide such a voice was to stay mute. Wheels spun in Shan's mind. Tenzin had left the hermitage the night Chao died. The government thought the purba leader Tiger was the likely murderer. Tenzin certainly knew purbas. Was their entire journey an elaborate ploy by the purbas to keep the Tiger hidden?

Shan closed his eyes, trying to calm himself. He took a step back, to stand in front of Lokesh. Here was the way it ended, or ended again, in a dark musty stable while their captors waited for them to cower, or invite a beating by a hint of resistance. If Tuan and the knobs thought they had been harboring the Tiger, no mercy would be shown. A strange sensation surged through him, a floating distant feeling that he recognized, because he had seen it in others' eyes at execution grounds. This was how firing squads often worked when the political officers had decided against a public exhibition, putting their victims against a wall early in the day, before most people awoke. It was how they would treat the Tiger when they caught up with him. And perhaps any of those who sheltered him. Surely they wouldn't do such a thing in a gompa. But this was Khodrak's gompa, an instrument not of Buddha but of the howlers. And a doctor would have syringes that would preserve the quiet, and be even more effective than any bullet.

He saw that everyone was looking at him, and knew he must have made a sound, a small utterance of fear. He turned slowly to Lokesh, whose eyes, assuming the cast of a prisoner, had also grown distant. He could push his friend deep into the shadows and charge the officer, maybe distract them long enough for Lokesh to escape. At least the chenyi stone was still safe in the mountains, a voice whispered in the back of his mind.

Someone moved at Lokesh's side. Tuan stepped back into the light, looking expectantly at Shan, pausing, as if waiting for Shan to say something. But then a shadow crossed the door and another figure entered. Khodrak, holding his staff, and behind him, Padme, in a clean robe, his arm in a sling. The Chairman's eyes flared, not at Shan but at the doctor and the knob officer. No one moved. The knob and the doctor seemed confused.

Shan studied the monk they had brought from Rapjung. Padme stood straight, in no apparent pain now. His arm was in a sling, although he had not complained to them of his arm hurting. His robe was not only spotless, it was fringed with the same narrow strip of gold thread that Khodrak and the other committeeman wore. Shan recalled the third chair at the Committee table and the way the others had called the young monk Rinpoche. It had been Padme's chair.

"Some of the old ones can turn themselves into smoke and drift away," Padme said, casting a thin smile toward the knob officer, who replied with a sour frown and marched out the door.

Khodrak sighed and studied the loft and its little portal. Someone tall, and strong, and lean might have climbed out. He put his hand on Tuan's arm and seemed to push. One side of the Director's mouth curled down. He relented, stepping back out of the stable followed by the doctor.

"There is a mistake, Chairman Rinpoche," Padme said to Khodrak. He looked at Shan. "These people are our friends. Our heroes. We cannot allow them to be abused."

Shan stared in confusion. Public Security and Religious Affairs had

162

been about to unleash their wrath on them but Khodrak and Padme had turned them away.

"Where is he?" Nyma cried out. "You have Tenzin. Why? You can't just—" Nyma looked from Padme to Khodrak, then to Shan, and her words choked away.

Khodrak seemed not to hear her. "Take a moment," he said, and gestured toward the ground. Padme hitched up his robe and sat on the stable floor, cross-legged, pulling out his rosary. He gestured for Nyma to follow, and in a moment all of them but Khodrak were sitting in a small circle. Padme began reciting the mani mantra, waving his hand to encourage the others to join in as Khodrak paced around the outside of the circle, tapping his staff in front of him like an old beggar.

It was a strange, unsettling ceremony. Padme stopped speaking after a moment but kept waving his hand, directing the others like a choir, Nyma and Lhandro chanting awkwardly as Lokesh and Shan uneasily watched the young monk. After perhaps two minutes, Khodrak halted and Padme abruptly rose, brushing off his robe, the words of the mantra slowly fading.

"Will we find their friend?" Khodrak asked Padme.

"We will find their friend," Padme replied quickly, as if reciting more of the ceremony. Then Khodrak turned and moved out the door, his staff resting on his shoulder.

Padme turned to address Lhandro. "There are no words to express my shame," he said to the rongpa. "There was a mistake." The monk looked back at the door and nodded, then turned to Shan. "It's an old shed used for little other than storage. Someone could have mistakingly inserted the door bar, that's all," he said tentatively, as if suggesting that was how they should explain what had happened. "The medical team is overzealous. They are trained to act extremely, for the containment of disease." He stood, waiting, as the ambulance pulled away, then turned back to them. "The kitchen will give you some food for the trail," Padme suggested. "I will see to it myself." With a gesture for them to follow Padme stepped out into the sunlight.

Tuan stood in front of a white utility vehicle beside half a dozen men in white shirts. Shan studied the seasoned faces of the men. But for their shirts he would have said they were a special Public Security squad—a boot squad, the purbas called them—one of the squads reserved for use against particularly stubborn political threats, which, to those responsible for public security in Tibet, typically meant purbas and other troublesome Buddhists.

The guards stared at Shan and his friends as they filed out of the stable, several glancing back at Tuan, whose eyes found, and stayed on, Shan. They watched Shan intensely, not accusing but calculating. When Tuan saw Shan return his stare Tuan nodded pointedly. You will have to decide soon, Tuan had told Shan. An accounting was coming.

"These are confusing times," Padme observed as they approached the gate ten minutes later, Lhandro holding a paper sack of dumplings and apples from the kitchen.

"May the Compassionate Buddha protect you," Lokesh called tentatively as they walked out of the gate.

Padme's head jerked back and he nodded. "Exactly," he said, in an odd, offhanded tone. "And you." Then he straightened and spoke more loudly, as though for an audience. "May the Compassionate Buddha protect you," he called out, and smiled toward the ragged group of Tibetans who sat among the houses outside the gate.

They walked for an hour without speaking, Lhandro in the lead, walking so rapidly Nyma had to trot sometimes to keep up. Finally, when the gompa was far out of sight behind the hills they stopped at a small stream.

"Who is that Tuan?" Lhandro blurted out in a low, urgent whisper, as if the question had burned his tongue since leaving the gate, and he still feared being overheard. "Why did they—what have they done to poor Tenzin? He never hurt anyone."

"Chao's murder," Nyma said slowly. "A murder like that would have everyone acting strange. They must have thought Tenzin could have information. They confused him with someone. The fools. All that time he was with us at the mandala."

Shan looked up from where he drank but he found no words to reply. Tenzin had not been at the mandala all the time. And there was something else he had almost forgotten. When Drakte had entered the lhakang, moments before dying, the first person he had looked to had been Tenzin.

Shan sighed, and watched as Nyma shifted her gaze to Lokesh, who had removed his coat and rolled up his sleeves nearly to his shoulders. He was vigorously rubbing his arms with the white sand of the streambed. Lhandro began to do the same. Lokesh rubbed his face. Shan and Nyma stripped off their coats, too. No one had words to explain anything that had happened at the strange gompa but they all felt the need to be cleansed. Nyma held some of the sand cupped in her hand for a moment, and glanced at Shan. They had seen such sand before, had seen it sanctified by the lamas and later washed with blood.

Lokesh lit a stick of incense and sat.

"We have no time," Nyma protested, but then hesitantly followed Shan and Lhandro as they folded their legs and watched the wisps of fragrant smoke. They had to calm themselves, to brace themselves against the frightening, confusing forces that seemed to be against them.

When the stick burned out, Lhandro rose with a deliberate air and reached into his sack. He produced the small scrap of cloth he sometimes used as a towel and laid it flat on a rock, setting his red plastic dorje pen on it. "It isn't a real thing," he said as he stepped to Shan with the cloth spread between his hands. Shan quickly dropped his own pen onto the cloth. None of them wanted the tokens of the gompa, he knew, but Lhandro's words referred to the plastic the dorjes were made of. He had known other Tibetans who reacted the same way with any implement made of plastic. It wasn't wood, or cloth, or stone, or bone—not of the earth—and somehow they didn't trust the plastic, as if it were one more of the tricks the Chinese played on them. They were just shadow things, a herder had told him once, you could tell just by feeling them. He had known a dropka who kept in a leather sack whatever plastic items he was given or found by roads, and left them in a small pile whenever he visited a town. The man wasn't sure what they were exactly, but he knew they belonged down below, which was how dropka often referred to towns.

An hour later they stopped suddenly as Lhandro, about to lead them over the crest of a ridge, raised his hand. "It's one of them," he said with a weary tone. "We'll have to wait."

Shan followed the rongpa to the crest of the ridge to see a loaded cart moving slowly along the trail ahead of them pulled by a sturdy black yak. A stocky man in a robe walked alongside the yak, his hands moving as if he were conversing, trying to make a point to the animal.

"He's so slow," Nyma said, now at Shan's side. "We will waste half the day waiting."

"I have no fear of a man who speaks with his yak," Lokesh announced from behind them and pushed past, continuing down the path.

In a quarter hour they were close enough to see that the cart's cargo was yak dung and moments later the yak halted and twisted its massive head in their direction.

"It's a long way to go, to dispose of all this fuel," Shan observed as he reached Gyalo.

"No one said how far to take it," Gyalo observed. He surveyed Shan and his friends and studied the trail behind them.

Shan introduced the others, and Lokesh offered some of the food from the gompa. The monk ate two momo dumplings, then offered an apple to the yak.

"Where are you bound?" Shan asked.

The monk shrugged and gestured to the sky. "It's a good day in the mountains," he said, and began to massage the yak between the ears. "Jampa here will let me know when we get there."

Jampa. One of the names of the Future Buddha.

Shan studied the man a moment as Gyalo took a long swallow from Lokesh's water bottle, then walked around the cart. The old wooden shovel Shan had used lay on top of the load. He turned the shovel and saw that the wooden blade covered a depression in the pile, a hole.

"No one is following," he said quietly.

"What's that?" Gyalo called out, cupping his ear toward Shan.

"Just speaking to our friend," Shan said and, as Nyma gasped in sur-

165

prise, a hand emerged from the pile of dried dung. Shan took the hand and steadied the figure that rose up in the cart.

"Tenzin!" Lhandro cried, as the tall man stood and cast an anxious smile toward his friends before he climbed down.

"Where did you—" Nyma blurted out, then ran to embrace the mute Tibetan. "How did you—How could you have known? Why did they—" the questions rushed out as she held Tenzin at arm's length. Tenzin looked at Shan as though for help, then the nun grinned and laughed at herself for asking for explanations from the man who could not speak. She began wiping the dirt from his face with one of her sleeves.

"I was sleeping with Jampa under the moon," Gyalo explained. "I thought if I woke up in the night I would just leave," he said, stroking the shaggy yak again. "We don't mind the night. We talk about the stars. Last night, in the early hours—maybe two, three o'clock—Jampa put his nose in my ear. I cuffed him at first but he pushed harder and I sat up and moaned because there was this ghost by the cart. Jampa and I knew he needed help, though he didn't say a word. Jampa and I knew what needed to be done. We loaded him—Tenzin, you say?" he asked in an aside to Nyma. "We loaded Tenzin in and slipped away. Not a soul moving anywhere. An hour later, as we cleared the first ridge, one of those soldiers' trucks drove in from the highway." He looked at Shan with questions in his eyes.

Shan studied Tenzin a moment longer, sighed and looked toward the northern mountains. "We will go on, ahead," he said to the monk. "Thank you for helping our friend." He studied the cart a moment. "Near the end of the plain there is an old ruin of a gompa. A family lives there now. They have much to do and little time to look for fuel. This could last them many weeks."

"Rapjung," Gyalo said with a nod. "I know it. The old First House." He glanced back toward the south, as though to be certain no one else was listening. "Norbu was not just a traveling station in the old days, it was also a hospital where people from far away came to consult the healers who descended from the high plains and mountains. But after Rapjung was destroyed, the hospital was torn down and the new buildings put up," he said sadly, looking at Shan. Shan recalled the old foundations he had seen by the chapel.

"What is it you are trying to escape?" the monk asked in a slow, measured tone, and studied each of them in turn. He had the sound of an old lama.

"We don't know," Nyma answered in a haunted whisper.

"There are birds up there," Lokesh said in a tentative voice, "that have never seen the world below." He gestured toward the tall peaks, wearing his crooked grin. His tone was earnest, and pointed, almost urgent. "This month they are hatching babies. If things go well their babies will never need to see the rest of world either."

166

As if it understood Lokesh, the yak twisted its huge head toward the mountains. It seemed to be looking for birds. Gyalo rubbed the tuft of hair between the animal's ears, following its gaze. After a moment he turned with a troubled smile. "Go with Buddha."

They reached the trail junction in another hour and Lhandro led them up a steeply ascending path, newly churned with the hooves of sheep. The long Plain of Flowers disappeared behind them and new landscapes to the north and east opened to their view. They sat and ate cold dumplings on a flat rock that commanded a view of miles over a ragged brown and grey landscape of rock and gravel through which ran narrow lines of shrubs, marking the courses of small rivers that wound eastward toward a patch-work of tiny squares in the far distance, fields green with sprouting barley.

Lokesh pointed out a thin, high waterfall that cascaded over a steep rock face more than two miles away. He was tracing the course of the narrow river it fed as it tumbled down a gorge when Lhandro gasped.

"Tara protect us!" the rongpa moaned, and motioned to a point farther down the river, where it flowed out of the gorge. "The deities are truly angry!" He paled and clenched his gau.

As Shan followed Lhandro's arm in confusion, first Lokesh, then Nyma groaned. The water in the river was red. Not the entire river, but a long patch of the water was bright crimson. Shan quickly calculated the distance and size of the patch. It was sixty or seventy yards in length and covered the entire breadth of the stream.

Nyma turned to Shan with fear in her eyes. "What is it?"

But Shan had no explanation. "Sometimes," he said weakly, "there are algae that make the ocean look red."

Lokesh and Lhandro nodded, not because any of them thought it could be algae, Shan knew, but because it offered the suggestion that there could be a natural explanation.

They watched the red patch in silence until it disappeared behind a bend in the river.

Lokesh raised his finger again and traced the course of the river from the waterfall to where it had disappeared. With a hollow expression, he turned and followed a frightened Lhandro, who had begun jogging up the trail. The rongpa, Shan knew, had taken it as an omen of something terrible to come.

Nyma lingered beside Shan as Lokesh moved on, watching the river with a grimace of pain. "The mountains are bleeding," she said, then turned and followed Lokesh. Shan took a step toward the trail, where he saw Tenzin kneeling at the overhang, near the edge. He had constructed a small cairn of stones and as Shan watched in silence the Tibetan poured water onto a patch of earth. He stirred the little pool and used the mud to write on the rock face beside the cairn. *Om amtra kundali hana hana hum phat*, he wrote. It was known as one of the fierce mantras, a powerful invocation of cleansing.

Tenzin stared at the words, then gazed out over the low ranges to the east. He seemed to have forgotten Shan was there.

"It was a mistake," Shan said quietly, "going to that gompa." It occurred to him that perhaps Khodrak and the howlers knew more about Tenzin than he did. He knew the reticent Tibetan would not answer.

But suddenly Tenzin drew in a breath. "When the soul suffocates," he said in a deep, melodic voice, "and only revives on the last gasp, it is never the same soul again." He did not break his gaze from the distant ranges and spoke the words so quickly that Shan thought he had imagined them. The Tibetan turned to Shan and searched his face. "Your lama Gendun said sometimes it is possible to be reincarnated in the same body, in the same lifetime. He said you know about that."

Shan stared. Tenzin had grown his new tongue.

"I am not the man they think they are looking for," Tenzin added. There was torment in his voice.

Shan studied Tenzin's tormented face, trying to understand the strange words. "What is it?" Shan asked. "Why do they seek you? Did you kill someone?"

But Tenzin had receded into his silence again. He stared out at the river that had been bleeding. "Once I did things I hate myself for," he said after a long time, "then I did things they hate me for."

"In Lhasa?" Shan asked. "Were you in Lhasa?"

"That abbot who is missing. I was there."

"The abbot of Sangchi? You saw him when you escaped from prison? Drakte was with him?"

But Tenzin touched his fingertips to his lips with a confused expression, as if just realizing he had been speaking, and fell silent.

Suddenly Shan remembered the awful night again, and the sound of the voices in the death hut. "It was you with Gendun and Drakte," he said. "I heard your voice. You were chanting the Bardo with Gendun." It was not a rasping voice, not one with a broken voice box.

Tenzin only sighed in reply, and melancholy settled over his face.

It was late afternoon when they saw the first sheep, grazing in the distance on the sparse grass that grew in the shelter of boulders, all wearing their brightly colored packs. A high, lilting sound caused Lhandro to stop and hold up a hand. After a moment he relaxed, then led them around a bend in the trail, and halted again with a smile. A small campfire could be seen two hundred feet up the trail, in the lee of a huge slab of rock that had sloughed off the cliff above. Three of the Yapchi villagers stood at the fire. But Anya sat closer to Lhandro, her back to the trail, singing to half a dozen sheep. The animals seemed to listen to the girl with rapt attention, as if about to join in her song at any moment.

"She's communicating with them," Nyma said in an awed tone. The travelers stood in silence, listening, not daring to move an inch—perhaps, Shan thought, under the same spell as the sheep. Then one of the villagers

168

saw them and called out. Anya turned and the magic was broken.

The caravaners were full of questions, and Shan and Lokesh let Lhandro and Nyma give all the answers. Yes, Padme had recovered and was walking about the gompa when they departed. Yes, he lived at a reconstructed gompa, the old Second House gompa. Yes, the monks had given them blessings. Yes, there were even novices there, learning to be monks like the old days. The villagers were pleased with the answers, and though Lhandro looked to Shan and Nyma for help, no one volunteered anything else about what happened at Norbu. The headman squatted by a pile of blankets on which someone had placed the red-circle pouch, the pouch with the eye inside. Lhandro silently rubbed the pouch, as if the chenyi stone somehow needed comforting.

It was nearly sunset when one of the dogs began barking. Two of the Yapchi men shot into the rocks above the trail. Lhandro jumped up on a boulder that provided a view down the side of the mountain, and a moment later motioned for Shan to join him.

A man and a yak were coming up the mountain. As Shan watched they stepped into a pool of light from the setting sun. The man was wearing a robe.

"You'll be expected back at Norbu tonight," Shan observed in a tentative tone as Gyalo led the big, broad-backed animal toward the fire.

"It's an odd place, that gompa," the monk said in a distant voice. "The Committee says only thirty-five monks can be there, though there's room for three times that number. The Chairman stopped our class on the teachings of the Rapjung medicine lamas and started a class on the integration of socialist thought into the teachings of Buddha." He scratched the broad shoulders of the black yak as he spoke. "We have to sign a paper pledging not to criticize the government and recognizing the authority of the Bureau of Religious Affairs over all we do. If you don't sign, you can't be a monk anymore, they told us," he said, shaking his head as if in disbelief. "Some of the monks said we were lucky, that at some gompas monks had to sign statements renouncing the Dalai Lama, or be sent to a Chinese jail."

Lhandro stepped forward, his face heavy with worry. "You have to be at your gompa. They will send people to look, after what happened to Padme."

"For the last month I have slept only every second night. The other nights I have gone out by that dung pile," Gyalo said with a glance at Shan, "and recited my beads." He was saying he had been in spiritual crisis, Shan realized. He was saying he had been trying to make an important decision. "When I left to live at Norbu my uncle said to pay attention to the lamas who ran the gompa, because the senior lamas could be emanations of the true Buddha. But there were no Buddhas, there were only committeemen. They get paid by the government," Gyalo said, his brow creasing, "but Jampa and I, we don't think you can be a lama and be paid by Beijing. The closest thing to Buddha at that place was right here," he said, and placed his hands on either side of the yak's head. There seemed to be deep meaning in the stare exchanged by the monk and the animal, and everyone stood perfectly still as they watched. The yak seemed to look at each of them in turn, then it breathed heavily, like a sigh.

A murmur spread through the Yapchi villagers, and several of them nodded solemnly, as if they knew about Buddha yaks.

"Jampa was at that place, too," Gyalo said, as though he couldn't bear to say Norbu's name now. "The committee was going to get rid of him, as soon as all the dung was hauled away. He was deciding to leave all these past months. Now," Gyalo said with a shy smile, "they still have all that dung, but they don't have us."

"We can find you clothes," Lhandro said, and bent toward one of the horse packs.

"No," Gyalo replied quickly, then spoke in a slow, deliberate voice. "No. I am a monk. I am just a monk between teachers." He knew, as did all of those present, the significance of his words. He would be an unregistered monk, an illegal monk. If the knobs found him he would have no defense, and would be shown no leniency. He would be sent to a lao gai prison for many years. And after release he would be forever banned from serving in a gompa.

Nyma stepped forward, her beads held conspicuously in her raised hand. "There are mantras to be said," she suggested. Gyalo replied with a pleased nod and Lokesh stepped forward, beads in hand, followed by two of the villagers.

The monk followed Nyma toward a large flat rock near the fire. He paused and surveyed the others in the camp. "My name is Gyalo," he said. "This is Jampa. And the other's name is Chemi," he added with a gesture down the trail. "She wanted to sit and watch some clouds for a while."

Shan looked up to see a woman emerging out of the shadows, one of the mastiffs at her side, wagging its tail.

"She was at that ruined gompa, helping them sift through those ashes," Gyalo explained. "But she said she was on her way north, too, to her home."

The woman smiled shyly as she approached the fire, and Nyma handed her a bowl of tea. She leaned back against a boulder and explained to Lhandro she was returning to her family in the hills above Yapchi Valley. Nyma and Lhandro welcomed her warmly, explaining to Shan they knew her family, who lived in a compound of five small houses only four miles from their own village. Lokesh sat beside her and began speaking with her in low tones as if he knew her, and then suddenly a wind blew and she put on the hat she had been carrying in her hand.

Shan stared in disbelief. It was his hat, or had been his hat. She was the woman Dremu had found on the trail, sick and too weak to stand. He knelt beside Lokesh. "That tonde," she was saying to the old Tibetan. "It was a good one, I think." Shan remembered the fossil Lokesh had

170

given her, and the confused way she had looked at Lokesh when he had first placed it in her hand. He saw now that there was still weakness in her face, but her color was back and her eyes bright.

Shan stepped to her side. "What happened? Who came that day?"

The woman offered a thin smile. "I am better now," she said, and her hand moved to the mala at her yak-hair belt. She began a mantra, her way of avoiding Shan's questions.

He stared at her, then at Lokesh. She had been waiting for someone that day on the trail, alone and sick but so confident the one she awaited was coming she had resisted their offer of help. A healer had come to her in the mountains, and Shan and Lokesh had seen a healer, at least the ghost of a healer, in the mountains two days later.

They ate their meal in the twilight, Lokesh and Shan sitting with Lhandro in the shelter of a rock with a candle, studying the rongpa's tattered map. They would be out of the high mountains in a day, and in Yapchi the day after. Shan stared at the map in silence, as in a trance, thinking absently that it might show him where a deity might reside if only he knew how to read it.

Chemi fell asleep beside the fire under a heavy felt blanket. Lokesh and Gyalo sat watching the moon. Tenzin settled onto a flat rock nearby, silhouetted against the night sky, saying his silent rosary, seeming to have lost his tongue again. When the wind ebbed Lokesh and Shan sometimes gazed at the mute Tibetan and shared a meaningful glance. They had been used to such scenes in the gulag, where monks learned to do their rosaries in their bunks without violating the strict curfew rules against speaking. After years of living in such barracks Shan had begun to discern something like a sound from the monks. At first he had thought it was simply the sound of their lips touching, but later he had begun to hear more: a strange low noise like a rolling, constant moan, as if his ears had become attuned to a different range of sound that the monks were using to reach out to their deities.

Suddenly a dog barked. Lhandro was up at once, one of the heavy staffs in his hand. "Someone's coming from above," he warned, and motioned Shan to take cover in the rocks.

"Is it you, Yapchi?" a strained voice called out from the darkness. Lhandro dropped more fuel on the fire and stepped to the trail as two horses came into view. There were two men, but both were mounted on the lead horse.

"The Golok," Lhandro announced quietly, then called out to Dremu. "What did you do to our horse?"

"The horse is fine," Dremu said wearily. "It's the American."

Shan shot forward to help ease Winslow's limp form out of Dremu's saddle, where he had been riding in front of the Golok, as though he needed support.

"Something in his head," the Golok reported. "I knew he had to come down, fast. He kept asking to go higher. He thought he saw someone higher. But it was too high for him. He's from America."

Altitude sickness, Dremu meant. As they lay Winslow on a blanket by the fire the Golok explained that in the late afternoon the American had seen something, a reflection of bright light, as though from a piece of metal, from equipment, but when they had stopped on a ledge to study it in the binoculars, the American had acted drunk, staggering about the ledge, almost tumbling off the edge.

It was a common problem for visitors to Tibet and could strike even seasoned mountain climbers without warning. Winslow himself had told Shan about the American tourists who died every year of the sickness. It could be an embolism, or edema in the lungs or the brain. Usually the only treatment was significant and immediate descent.

Winslow's eyes fluttered open. "Pills. I have pills," he said in ragged gasps. "I left them with the pack horses."

Shan quickly found the American's rucksack among the caravan packs and located a small glass bottle labeled Diamox. He gave two of the white tablets to the American with some tea, and a few minutes later Winslow opened his eyes and raised his thumb and index finger in a circle, the American okay sign.

Shan and Lokesh sat with him as he gulped down a bowl of tea. "Sorry," Winslow said. "It happens. No big deal really. Except I was at a five-hundred-foot drop off when it hit me. This guy," he said, pointing to Dremu. "He saved my life."

The words seemed to confuse Lhandro, who had never lost his distrust of the Golok. The rongpa stood hesitantly, poured a bowl of tea and handed it to Dremu. The Golok slowly extended his hand and accepted the tea with an uncertain expression.

As if he had to prove his point, Winslow reached for his pack and ceremoniously unpacked his little metal stove. He called Dremu to his side and handed the device to him. "I've only got the one extra fuel tank," the American said apologetically, and handed the Golok the little blue tank Shan had seen in the pack.

Dremu gazed wide-eyed at the stove, smiling one instant, then looking solemnly at the American, then smiling again. "You saved my life," the American said again, loudly, as if he wanted to be certain everyone in the camp heard. "I was looking out over the cliff and suddenly everything was spinning. Next thing I know I'm leaning over the abyss and Dremu has me by the belt, pulling like a yak. He saved me for certain."

Unexpectedly, a sense of contentment fell over the camp. The American had recovered from near death. Chemi, a new friend, was healed and heading home. The brave monk Gyalo had chosen to spend the first night of his new life with them. Shan, Lokesh, Winslow, Lhandro, and Gyalo sat huddled in their blankets, watching the moon again, exclaiming every few minutes over shooting stars.

172

Suddenly a low agonized groan resonated through the darkness. Winslow pulled his electric lamp from his pocket. Lhandro grabbed his staff. Lokesh grabbed his mala.

Shan darted toward the sound. It was Nyma. She was rapidly uttering a mantra, with the sound of crying, bent over Anya.

"She was feeling strange all afternoon, she told me, said she stopped once by the trail, shaking all over, then it passed. She said it was okay now, that sometimes it didn't mean anything, that he might not be waking up, that sometimes it was like this, and nothing happened, as if he had dreamed something, or had a nightmare, but was still asleep."

A chill crept down Shan's spine. Nyma meant the oracle, the deity that spoke through the young girl.

"But look at her . . ." Anya was shaking visibly, convulsing, her arms and legs jerking off the blanket she lay on. One of the girl's hands was clenched around one of Nyma's. A trickle of blood ran down the back of Nyma's hand. The girl's fingernails were digging into the nun's flesh.

"Christ!" Winslow cried with a helpless glance at Shan. "She must be epileptic. It's a seizure. Grand mal they call it. Put something in her mouth," he gasped, "to protect her tongue."

"Above all," Lhandro said in a solemn tone with a hand raised as though ready to deflect the American, "you cannot block her tongue."

Shan pulled Winslow away and tried to explain to the American what the Tibetans thought was happening.

"An oracle!" Winslow cried out, anger in his voice now. "Dammit, she's a little girl. You can't believe—" His words choked off as he studied the Tibetans, half a dozen now, sitting around the girl with grave, even scared expressions, not trying to help Anya despite their affection for her, only waiting. Lhandro darted to the packs and returned with a pencil and paper.

"Christ almighty," Winslow whispered in frustration. He stared uncertainly at the Tibetans, who gathered around the girl with butter lamps. "Jesus, Shan, you can't believe . . ." His voice drifted off and he stepped closer to the convulsing girl, as though he still might intervene to protect her from injuring herself.

Shan didn't know what to believe, except that he knew what the Tibetans believed about the girl. All he and the American could do was watch.

Gyalo sat near Anya's head. "My grandmother was visited, too," he declared in a soft voice. "We should make a welcoming place," he said, and began a quiet mantra. The others joined in immediately. Shan found that his hand was clasping his own gau.

"In my mountains," Anya suddenly said, "in my heart, in my blood." It sounded like Anya, Shan told himself, though a weary, distracted Anya. It could be a dream of some kind. Perhaps the girl had simply been exhausted from the trail, perhaps she had collapsed in slumber and was singing one of her spirit songs in her sleep.

Anya stopped trembling and seemed to stiffen, then grew very still as she spoke again. "Deep is the eye, brilliant blue eye, the nagas will hold it true." A chill crept down Shan's spine. Winslow gasped and stepped back. This wasn't Anya's voice. It was a cracked, dry voice, an old person's voice. It sounded hollow, like it was coming down a long tube.

There was movement at Shan's side. Lhandro was busily recording the words of the oracle. The voice echoed in Shan's mind. The eye, the oracle said. But the eye was not blue.

"Bind them, bind them, bind them, you have to wash it to bind them!" the voice croaked on. "So many dead. So many to die," it said in a mournful tone. A chilled silence hung over the camp and Lhandro, his face ghastly pale, looked up from his writing.

"Who will give voice when the songbird is gone?" the voice said, then spoke no more. With these final words Anya, though lying flat, somehow seemed to collapse. They waited in silence, no one moving, as though the words had somehow paralyzed them. Nyma stared into Anya's eyes, as though searching for the girl. Lokesh kept slowly nodding, and Nyma began rocking back and forth on her knees. Gyalo washed the girl's face from a bowl of water. No one spoke. Lokesh began his mantra again. Lhandro stared at the words he had written, then handed the paper to Shan as if Shan would know what to do about them. Shan stared uncertainly at the hurried scrawl, unable to read the handwriting. But he had watched, and knew Lhandro had not written the final words of the oracle. Who will give voice when the songbird is gone? the oracle had asked.

They sat for almost an hour, until Anya revived, rubbing her eyes as though coming out of a deep sleep, then suddenly pointing upward. A brilliant meteor shot through the sky, so close they heard it.

"The deity of Yapchi, the one whose eye you have, and that oracle," Winslow said in a small voice, still shaken by what he had witnessed, "they are the same? I mean I know there can't really be . . ." The American's words drifted away. There can't be a deity in the valley, he was about to say, just as, a few minutes earlier, he had been about to say there could be no oracle.

"I don't know," Shan replied hesitantly. "I don't think so."

Neither man seemed able to put their feelings into words. Because what they mostly felt, Shan suspected, was confusion.

After a long time Shan borrowed the American's light and went out with the red-circle pack among the sheep. He found a flat rock and salt in a pool of moonlight, cutting the threads away, reaching in for the chenyi stone. It was the first time he had looked at the stone since the day it had been sewn into the salt pack at Lamtso. He sat with the eye in front of him and stared at the dim outline in the rock, not knowing why. At least it might help him focus, might help him reach into his awareness in the way Gendun had taught him.

A loose pebble rattled behind Shan. As he turned, a shadow leapt forward and something hard pounded into his skull. He fell forward and drifted toward unconsciousness, quickly, yet still slow enough that before the blackness took him he realized dimly, like observing it from afar, that someone was kicking him in the ribs.

Chapter Ten

The eye of Yapchi was gone. In a fog of pain Shan squinted into the patch of moonlight where he had set the eye and reached out with one hand, futilely groping for the stone. He braced himself on one arm to peer into the shadows around him, fighting a stab of pain in his ribs. There was a glimmer of movement in the distance. He threw himself onto his feet, took a step—but the world spun about and he found himself on his knees, then on the ground. Blackness overtook him again.

When he awoke he was by the fire, on a blanket beside Anya. The girl, propped against a rock, offered a weak smile. Lokesh was on his other side, dabbing a bloody cloth against Shan's forehead. "It's gone," Shan said in a forlorn gasp. "I lost the eye."

"They're out there," Lokesh said softly. "Our friends are looking." He lifted Shan's hand and pressed it firmly, keeping it in his grip a moment.

As Shan tried to sit up blood roared in his ears. His eyes fluttered closed in another spell of dizziness. He became vaguely aware of people approaching, and urgent words in low voices. He heard hoofbeats, and in the distance, someone calling to the dogs. His mind went somewhere like slumber, but not slumber, and suddenly he was awake.

Hours had passed. The moon was setting. It was perhaps three in the morning. The villagers had used all the spare fuel to make half a dozen fires in a circle around the camp. A rider was dismounting. Lhandro was with the sheep, checking their harnesses. One sheep sat beside Anya, alone, without a pack, the brown ram that had carried the red-circle pack. The girl was stroking its head, as if to comfort it, as though it, too, shared their anguish.

Lokesh brought a bowl of tea and at last Shan was able to sit up. The old Tibetan shook his head grimly.

"There is no sign," Lhandro said when he approached Shan minutes later. "The eye is gone. The pack it was in is gone. We had a guard out but he was on the trail, watching for anyone following. The thief did not come up the trail. We searched the slopes in every direction. The moon was bright enough that we could scan the slopes with field glasses. Nothing," Lhandro concluded wearily. "That thing burns temples and tries to kill monks," he said, as though to explain his hopelessness. His face seemed

176

to have aged many years. The eye was gone. He had failed his people. He looked up the slope, then jogged away into the darkness.

"It is my fault," Shan said, "I took it away from camp." Had it indeed been the dobdob? He tried to remember, but the memory was only of night, and pain. He touched the knot on his head. Something hard had hit him. It could have been the gnarled end of the dobdob's staff.

"No!" Nyma protested. "You probably saved others from injury. A thief like that would just have brought his violence to the rest of us if you hadn't taken the eye aside."

The searchers returned one by one over the next two hours, the last coming by horseback from the trail above. Some shook their heads, others just shrugged. Only Dremu, the last rider, from the slope above, had anything to report. A wild goat had run past him on the trail as though frightened by something above.

"The army," Winslow sighed. "If it was the army . . ." he began.

"How could it be the army?" Nyma asked. "If it had been the army, if it had been that Colonel Lin, they would not care about stealth, they would have just pounced on us, taken all of us away in chains like he tried to that day."

Some of the villagers murmured agreement. But Winslow and Shan exchanged a glance. Lin might have acted quietly, sending only one of his commandos for an ambush, if he had known the American was present.

"If the army took the eye," Shan said, "then it is gone, out of our reach. But if the army did not take the eye," he said with an expectant look at Lhandro, "then the eye may still be in our grasp." Lhandro shook his head, but seemed to ponder the words and looked up at Shan with interest.

"What would be the other reasons to take it?" another voice asked from the shadows. Gyalo appeared. "Nyma explained things to me," he said in an aside to Shan, before he turned to the others. "Shan is saying we must know the why of this theft."

"To destroy it," Nyma suggested. "So the valley could not be saved. Or to hide it."

"That would mean it could be those who wish to use your valley," Gyalo observed.

Lhandro nodded. "The oil crews. The geologists who work for the petroleum joint venture."

"And if not to destroy it or hide it?" Shan asked. "Perhaps the thief wants it back in Yapchi, too, just in a different way."

"Return it?" Nyma asked, creasing her brow. "Someone else . . . someone who didn't believe we would make it to Yapchi," she said in a hollow voice. "Maybe someone who didn't understand the oracle," she added with a quick glance toward Shan. "Or someone who just thought they could acquire merit somehow."

"That goat that ran from up the slope, it could have been someone climbing above who spooked it. Someone taking the eye over the mountain," Winslow observed.

"The army wouldn't take it over the mountain," Lhandro said quietly. "They would take it back to Lhasa."

"If the army didn't take the eye," Shan said, "then we must get to the valley, and quickly. Someone attempting to return it to the deity might be conspicuous. Maybe we can find the thief before the army does." It was a slim chance, he knew. But it was the only one they had.

"The oracle," Nyma said with a glimmer of hope, looking at Shan. "It didn't say how the eye would get to the valley, only how it would be returned to its true place."

"There is a secret trail over Yapchi Mountain," a new voice said from the shadows. They turned to see Chemi standing by the big yak. "A high trail, very narrow in spots, very dangerous. I took it once when I was a girl. I've seen old goats on it. Not for horses, not for sheep wearing packs. The caravan will have to go around the base of the mountain to the valley. But on foot, some of us can go over it and be in the valley before dusk tomorrow, if we leave at daybreak." She searched the faces of the villagers. "I know about that eye," she said, looking at Shan. "My grandfather's father was from Yapchi. He was away on a pilgrimage when those Lujun soldiers came. He never went back after that."

"I'll go," Winslow said quickly, then, in response to Shan's worried glance, shrugged and gestured toward his pack. "I'll take my pills. She might be up there."

There was movement at Shan's side. Lokesh was kneeling now, tightening the laces of his tattered boots. Shan put a hand on his shoulder and Lokesh pretended to ignore it. "Old goats," he said. "You heard her. It's for old goats."

The Yapchi villagers laughed.

"The four of us then," Shan declared. "At dawn."

Lhandro surveyed the caravaners. "Someone from the village should go. Shan may need help in understanding the valley before we arrive with the sheep. Only one. We cannot spare more and still drive the sheep."

Nyma seemed about to step forward when a diminutive figure pushed through from the shadows behind her. "It needs to be me," Anya said solemnly. Her voice seemed small and brittle. It was the first Shan had heard her speak since the oracle had visited.

Lhandro's chest pulled in, as if he were about to protest that the girl's twisted leg would make it too dangerous, but the headman only sighed and stared at the girl in silence.

An owl called from somewhere.

In the blur of events since he had been attacked Shan had almost forgotten about the strange words of the oracle. Had the oracle somehow been warning that the eye would be lost? Did Anya somehow feel responsible?

Gyalo, squatting by the fire, raised his wrist to his mouth as if biting something on it, then stood, extracting a grey strand from his hand and extending it to Anya. "It's a yak-hair bracelet," he said. "From Jampa. My mother always made me wear one in the high mountains. She said a yak-hair bracelet would make you as surefooted as a yak. Good for high places."

Anya studied the bracelet of woven hair. She seemed reluctant to take it.

"We are going to help with the sheep, Jampa and I. We want to see this Yapchi Valley. You can return it to me there."

They started when the eastern sky was the color of juniper smoke, the high peaks above them lost in purple and grey shadow. A cry of a bird echoed from above and Winslow cocked his head, listening. A moment later, a sheep bleated toward them, as though in reply to the bird. Another sheep called, and another, until a dozen or more were calling at once. It sounded as if they were mourning the loss of the jagged eye.

Chemi led the way, not on a trail at first, but up a series of ledges and steep gravel slopes that would reach the trail in an hour, she promised. After a few minutes she turned and pointed to a rider urging his horse along the lower trail, the caravan route. Dremu was riding out ahead of the rongpa. Shan stared at the Golok as he disappeared around an outcropping. Dremu was on Yapchi Mountain now, the mountain he hated.

It was rough going. More than once Lokesh slipped and fell to his knees on the loose rough slopes. The American stopped several times and held his head but each time continued, matching Chemi's hurried pace. It seemed as if they were fleeing from something. More than once he studied the line of figures in front of him. Winslow, who had almost died the day before of altitude sickness. Anya who had been seized by the oracle. Chemi who had seemed more dead than alive when they had seen her on the trail the week before. Some of the older Buddhists would have said the wheel of their karma was moving quickly.

After an hour, as they followed Chemi around a sharp turn up a steep switchback trail a movement below caught Shan's eye. Another figure was climbing behind them. Tenzin. Somehow Shan wasn't surprised. Of all of them, perhaps Tenzin had the most urgent reason to flee.

They reached the main trail and climbed for another hour before Chemi paused to rest, on a ledge that overlooked several high, broad ridges to the south that led to the Plain of Flowers in the distance. Chemi pointed between two of the northern peaks to a brown swath of land in the north. "Amdo Province," she said with a flash of defiance in her eyes. "Our people never call it Qinghai, that's only for Chinese maps. On the far side of the mountain," she said, looking at the massive rock wall that towered before them, the pinnacle of Yapchi Mountain, "there is a long twisting path down a gully that opens on a shelf of land where my family lives. An hour beyond that, over the next ridge, is Yapchi Valley."

Shan stared at the monolithic face of stone towering above them, recalling how the huge mountain had dominated the horizon even from the far side of the plain, how Dremu had cursed it from afar. The entire mountain, with its series of outrider ridges reaching toward the main Kunlun range, was nearly twenty miles long. On the north side it reached into Amdo and cradled the valley of the rongpa.

Winslow produced his binoculars and swept the ridges below. Anya stood close to the American, fingering her yak-hair bracelet.

"There is a goat path along the rock face," Chemi said, pointing to the massive rock wall, a seemingly impassable barrier. "It is a difficult path to find—" She was interrupted by a distant sound. The shot of a heavy rifle, Shan thought at first, but then as he heard a second identical sound he knew it was something bigger. Explosions, like an artillery barrage or grenades. Again the sound echoed and Winslow pointed toward three puffs of smoke on one of the ridges below, perhaps a mile away. Instantly Shan and the Tibetans dropped to the ground, fearful of being seen. Whether artillery or grenades, explosions meant the army. Anya reached out and tugged on Winslow's pant leg. The American was frantically working his binoculars, adjusting the focus knob, sweeping the lenses back and forth across the ridge where they had seen the smoke.

"Three people, maybe four," Winslow reported, as Shan sat up and pulled his own field glasses from his bag.

He quickly found the distant figures, jogging toward the deep shadow cast by an adjoining ridge. He saw no vehicle, no helicopter, no troop carrier. But even stranger, he saw no burning building, no old chorten, no shrine that might have attracted a demolition crew. He glanced back at Anya, who had edged up so she could see the ridge below.

"Sometimes the army still finds resisters," Chemi declared in a remote voice. "Sometimes they refuse to be taken alive. And there are bandits," she added, in a tone that almost sounded hopeful. Did she mean Dremu? Had she somehow recognized Dremu? Shan had not dared give voice to his first suspicion after his attack. Could it have been the Golok, riding somewhere below them, who had stirred up the troops, the Golok who had his own interest in the eye, and his own strange war with the mountain?

At Shan's side, Tenzin grimaced. He looked at Shan with pain in his eyes. Tenzin was being aided by the purbas, which probably meant that somewhere on the way to Yapchi purbas would be waiting for him, maybe traveling to meet him now. Tenzin looked past Shan in puzzlement and Shan turned to see Lokesh beside him, his finger raised in the air again. The old Tibetan appeared to be tracing an imaginary line through the landscape. Shan watched as he pointed toward the long grey line of mountains on the horizon that defined the provincial border, then downward toward Rapjung and a closer landscape, to the high broadtopped ridge that flanked Rapjung's northeast side, then to the series of ridges that ended in the deep gorge below them.

Shan's old friend reached into his pocket and pulled out a piece of paper, one of the Serenity Campaign pamphlets. As the others watched in silence he began working the paper in a series of folds. After nearly a minute he held the paper up, not toward his companions, but toward the mountain, toward the very top of the mountain. It was a horse, a paper horse, and Shan had helped Lokesh make many such horses during their travels. As Chemi and Anya nodded knowingly, the old Tibetan spoke to the horse in a whisper and released it into the wind.

As they watched the paper shoot out over the abyss below and slowly drift toward the ridges, Shan turned to Winslow, who was watching in confusion. "A spirit horse," he explained. "There is a tradition that such a horse, if released with a prayer, will reach a traveler in need, and when it touches the earth it will become a real horse."

Shan studied Lokesh again, and with a new surge of alarm he understood what his old friend was thinking. There may not be purbas in the mountains below them, but Shan and Lokesh knew of someone who was. The medicine lama was out there. Not a ghost, for Chemi had met a real healer, the old one she had expected. He looked at the small sturdy woman who was their guide. She had offered no explanation of what had happened to her on the trail that day, but pain was in her eyes now, and for a moment her face seemed to take on the frail appearance Shan had seen that day on the trail. Suddenly Tenzin pointed upward, and they looked up to see a *bharal*, one of the rare blue mountain sheep that roamed the mountains, seemingly suspended two-thirds up the face of the vast rock wall before them.

A calm strength filled Chemi's face. "It's showing us the way," she said in a reverent tone, and continued up the trail without looking back. Long after the others were out of sight, Shan lingered with his field glasses, scouring the ridges below. A raven flew over the gorge. A large dark animal, probably a wild yak, ran across the top of another ridge. But there was no sight of a medicine lama and no sign of soldiers.

They walked ever upward. Snowflakes swirled about them sometimes, even though the sky overhead was bright blue. Twice Anya's crooked gait caused her to slip, and pebbles spilled over the edge of the narrow trail, dropping downward for what seemed an impossibly long time.

The trail constantly changed in width and direction, sometimes dwindling to little more than a gap between walls where a wild sheep might just squeeze through. Now it disappeared altogether at a nearly vertical wall of rock. Chemi continued, pulling herself upward with meager handholds, jumping from one outcropping to the next, guided by nothing more than an occasional worn spot in the rocks that may have been caused by sheep leaping at the same point, over the course of centuries. Winslow stopped often, drinking, twice taking his pills. They passed fields of snow, and once a brilliant white bird burst out of a crevasse.

"Christ," Winslow repeated often, sometimes when he was pausing to press his palms against his temples, at other times when he stopped to consult his map. "Fifteen damned thousand feet," he reported in disbelief, but did not complain when Chemi took them still higher. Every five minutes he had to stop, panting heavily, to catch his breath. He answered Shan's anxious glances by grinning and shaking his head, then moving on with a spurt of energy as though to prove his vigor. They were on the long unprotected trail where they had seen the bharal, a path no more than thirty inches wide, above a thousand-foot drop, when the American stopped and leaned against the wall of rock. Anya, closest to him, turned back and put her hand in Winslow's as Shan inched closer.

"It's all right," he heard the girl say, softly, in the voice she used with the sheep, "hold my hand and the yak bracelet will protect us both." The American turned toward Shan, his head sagging, his eyes rolling as if he were dizzy. Anya squeezed his hand hard, as though to remind him she was with him, and the American straightened. With a sober expression he let the girl lead him onward.

They were two-thirds of the way along the treacherous, unprotected goat trail when Chemi moaned and threw up a hand. They all froze as she cupped her ears toward the north and slowly began backing up. Moments later they heard it, too, a harsh metallic thumping that was rapidly growing louder.

"Helicopter!" Winslow shouted, and suddenly Anya was pulling him toward a shadow in the rock face. Not a shadow, Shan saw, as first the girl and then the American turned sideways and stepped inside it. It was a narrow cleft in the rock, perhaps big enough to hide them all until the helicopter passed. It was why Chemi was backing up, he realized, because she, too, had seen the cleft. The thumping grew much louder, and Chemi turned and began running along the narrow trail. Tenzin paused at the cleft, helping Lokesh inside, then disappeared himself as Shan approached the shadow.

Shan waited a moment, until Chemi was only thirty feet away, then the noise of the machine drove him inside. He could see none of his companions, even though they had entered the cleft only moments before. His eyes adjusting to the dim light, he saw that the gap was more than a split in the rock—it was a narrow winding passage that led steeply upward. He followed a small trail, worn from the hooves of mountain creatures. After fifteen feet he discovered that he was inside a narrow fissure in the cap of the mountain, with walls that opened near the peak hundreds of feet overhead.

"It wasn't military," a voice said behind him. Chemi was there, looking out into the daylight as she spoke. "And it was low, below the trail, like it was searching the ridges where the bombs went off."

Shan took another step forward. There was still no sign of his friends. "Did they fall?" Chemi asked in alarm. "They can't just disappear."

A shaft of sunlight lit the ground thirty feet in front of them. He stepped toward it uneasily as Chemi called out Anya's name. There was no reply. There was no sound at all. No wind blew in the chasm. No bird flew. No water fell. Chemi pulled his sleeve and pointed with alarm toward the pool of light which lit a wide crack in the floor. They stepped to the edge of the crack. It seemed to have no bottom. He kicked a pebble over the side and heard nothing.

"One of them could have slipped in and the others fell trying to help," Chemi said in a tight voice. "A place like that, they would just fall," she added, as though the chasm would have no bottom.

Shan stepped back without thinking, as though recoiling from the thought.

"They're gone," Chemi moaned, and she looked up mournfully toward the patch of sky at the top of the chasm.

Shan steadied himself by holding onto a pillar of rock. After a moment he realized his fingers were touching striations in the rock. He bent and blew into the tiny cracks, packed with dust, then pulled out his water bottle and poured some of the liquid over the pillar. Instantly the cracks took on definition, darker lines against the grey surface. They were Tibetan script, intricately carved into the pillar. Remember this, he read, we are made of nothing but light. It was a version of an ancient teaching, that the essence of life is luminosity, meaning awareness.

He looked up from the pillar in confusion. Beyond the pool of light the trail curved away toward a darker patch of shadow. He heard a small sound, the murmur of an animal, and ventured along the curve toward the darkness, following the trail up a short embankment beside which lay a row of small rocks on the ground. They were strangely smooth and flat, appearing as if they had been melted and folded. He knelt beside one and touched it. It wasn't rock, but dust he touched, dust the color of the rock. He lifted the object, still puzzled, and froze as he saw that it was a dust encrusted piece of cloth. It was a *lungta*, a prayer flag, made of silk, once red, painted with the mani mantra and a small horse. The dust fell away in flakes under his fingers, like a layer of ice, and he wondered, awed, how many decades it might have taken in the windless chasm for such a crust to accumulate. Not decades, more likely centuries. The flag had been sewn onto a strand of yak-hair rope, expertly woven, that had rotted away at each end. He looked at the line of tiny mounds, each another encrusted lungta. They pointed to the pillar with the writing. They had been tied to the pillar, he suspected, and affixed to the wall beyond him, in the darkest part of the shadow; not to flap conspicuously in the sky, but perhaps, in another age, to guide visitors. He turned and stepped further into the shadow, toward the wall where the line of flags would have ended. The darkest point was where two walls came together. There was something like a shadow inside the shadow. And the animal sound again.

He stepped into the blackest part of the shadow and found himself in the narrow entrance of a cave, which he followed, Chemi a step behind, feeling with his hands for eight feet as it curved sharply. Dim light appeared ahead of him, and suddenly he stumbled, nearly falling over Anya, who sat on the stone floor, murmuring softly in the detached voice he had heard her use for her animal songs. Beyond her stood the American, his electric lantern in his hand, shaking his head as he stared at the wall in front of him. Only Lokesh moved. The old Tibetan was circling the chamber they had discovered, uttering syllables of glee, his eyes shining with excitement. On a rock ledge that ran along the far end of the cavern, twenty feet from Shan, sat over two dozen elongated objects, in four stacks, each capped top and bottom with wooden slabs and bound together with cloth and strips of silk. The caps on those on top of each stack were made of rosewood, and carved with intricate patterns, some of flowers and leaves, others of wild animals.

As he stepped to Lokesh's side his old friend lifted the top of one of the box-like objects and with shaking hands pulled back the straps and cloth that covered its contents. It was a *peche*, a Tibetan book, in the traditional form of long unbound leaves of paper printed with wood blocks. "The Gyuzhi," he read in a whisper, then looked at his companions and explained that the Gyuzhi, or Four Tantras, was the most renowned of the ancient medical texts, written a thousand years earlier. He lifted the first leaf and read in silence for a moment, then pointed to the lines in the center of the page. "Possession of Elemental Spirits is caused by performing repeated sins, opposing thinking worthy of honor, failure to control the torment of sorrow." He looked up and grinned. "The causes of insanity, it means."

The excitement on his face was slowly replaced with solemn reverence as he replaced the leaf and the cover and repeated the process at the next peche, then two more. Winslow stepped forward and silently held the light at Lokesh's shoulder as the old man described the contents. "A teaching on medicinal stones," he said of the first, then explained that another was on medicines from fire elements, and the third about the use of stars to determine the most effective dates for mixing pills, written the year that the construction of Rapjung had begun.

At last Lokesh looked up and swallowed hard. "They thought—we didn't—" he began, his voice swelling with emotion again. His hand closed around the gau that hung from his neck and he cast a grateful glance back at the thangka that hung directly over the peche. On it was a Buddha figure painted blue, holding a begging bowl, the right hand outstretched in a gesture of giving. Vaidurya, the Medicine Buddha. "We thought some of these books were dead."

The purbas maintained a chronicle of Chinese atrocities they called the Lotus Book, which they had shared with Shan more than once. It listed details of lost gompas, lost lamas, lost treasures, and of those Chinese who had been known to commit the acts which had annihilated so much of traditional Tibet. Tibetan peche were listed too, sometimes, for the texts were always hand printed, and therefore never in wide circulation. Some texts were unique to the gompas which had produced them, and such texts and the wood blocks they were printed from were often among such gompas' most revered treasures. When the People's Liberation Army and the Red Guard had destroyed Tibet's gompas they had destroyed the peche within, destroying not only the texts but those who knew the contents of the texts. The Lotus Book recorded that huge bonfires had been made consisting only of the wooden printing blocks of ancient texts, and how the peche themselves had often been transported for use in the soldiers' latrines. Those peche known to be lost were listed in the Lotus Book as dead, with a summary like an obituary, often the last mention of the last work of a scholar who may have lived centuries before.

On the wall beside the peche hung a row of four more thangka, suspended from a plank jammed into a crack in the cave wall. Lokesh sighed again, and explained each one to the American in a reverent whisper. "The King of Lapis," he said of the first one, explaining that it was another emanation of the Medicine Buddha, who was often called the King of Lapis Lazuli, a gem highly valued in traditional Tibet as a healing stone. Tsepame was the next, the Buddha of Immortal Life. There was an astrological chart, of the kind used to diagram and treat disease; an anatomical chart of a human back, with vertebrae marked; one of the medicine trees used to describe the interrelationship of diseases. The last was an image of a simplistic mandala circle with claws extending from it, a head of flame at the top, and a curled tail of beads at its bottom. Shan had seen such images before, drawn by lamas in prison when no medicine was available for the sick. It was a scorpion charm, a token to drive out the demons that caused illness. Or perhaps, he thought as he saw the empty space where he knew the name of the sick was to be inscribed, a chart for teaching scorpion charms.

As Lokesh gazed upon the hangings, Winslow stepped around the chamber to each of the walls. There was another thangka—much larger than the others, hanging to the floor on one wall—another image of the King of Lapis. Beside it on another small ledge was a row of small dorjes, the scepter-like ritual objects used to symbolize the indestructible reality of Buddhahood. There were over a dozen dorjes, and though most were encrusted with dust they all seemed to be different. Some were of wood, some of iron, one had the gleam of gold. One seemed carved of lapis stone.

Shan sensed movement behind him and turned to see Chemi and Anya. The girl was standing by the woman. But Chemi wasn't trying to comfort the girl. It seemed Chemi was using the girl for support, as if the woman had grown unsteady on her legs.

Lokesh and Winslow noticed, too. They stopped, Winslow lowering the light so it made a white pool on the floor, like a small fire. They stood in silence, none of them seeming able to speak, until suddenly a woman's voice broke the spell.

"It wasn't day when he came," the voice whispered, "but not night either." Shan looked up in surprise, searching the chamber, before he realized it was Chemi. She stared wide-eyed at the thangkas, speaking to the Medicine Buddha. "It was the time just between, when the sun is gone but the night has not come. I wanted so much to believe he was coming. I had to believe it. I was so sick that believing it was all I had left. But it seemed so impossible." Her voice trembled. "I had an uncle. Before he left for India I promised him I would trust in the old ways, stay out of a Chinese hospital if I got sick. Sometimes Tibetan women go to sleep in Chinese hospitals and when they wake up terrible things have happened." She glanced at Shan, then her eyes dropped to the floor. "Part of me never expected him to come. Then he was just there. I had closed my eyes because my belly hurt so much. When I looked up all I saw was his smile. He was such a frail old thing, it seemed he might blow away if the wind grew. I was so tired, I wasn't sure if I was dreaming. This couldn't be the great healer, I thought, for he looks so frail himself. But when he touched the top of my head I felt such energy. The wind wasn't cold anymore and I just smiled and he listened to my pulses. When he asked me things I just smiled and told him, but it wasn't my voice, it was the voice of a little girl." Chemi took a step toward the thangkas, twisting her head as though trying to see them better.

"What kind of things?" Shan asked softly.

"Not about my sickness. Not at first. What time of year was I born. Had I ever taken a pilgrimage to Mount Kalais. He asked if I had ever flown a kite as a child, and did I know how to make a whistle out of a stick. How my family fared in the great struggles with the Chinese. Whether I still felt the Buddha within me. He gave me some little round brown pills and told me to drink from his bottle of drup-chu water. Then he lit some incense that he said was made of aloe wood and we talked a long time." She raised her hand as though to touch the thangka of the blue Medicine Buddha but instead she paused with her hand hanging in the air as if she were greeting the ancient image. "He wanted to know about places, about Rapjung and the plain, even about Yapchi." She slowly turned to Shan and Lokesh, as if she expected them to ask a question. "We talked about how you could smell the spring flowers at night now, and he asked why I carried a dark spot in my spirit."

Chemi's voice grew even fainter. "That's when I told him about an old woman who had lived in our village who always yelled at me for having loud dogs and how when some soldiers came long ago I told them how she kept a photograph of the Dalai Lama and prayed for his return. They took her away and no one ever saw her again. I told him I could not sleep at night, that she always appeared to me, the sight of her being dragged away by the soldiers." She paused to look in each of their faces. "He said the soldiers would have found the photo anyway and not to blame myself anymore. He said it was time to surrender the guilt, that a woman who loved the Dalai Lama would hold no blame for me. Then he put his hand on my belly and my skin burned, and my belly contracted and I think he drew something black out of my abdomen. Something changed inside me. I fell asleep and when I awoke the sun was dawning and no one was there except a little pika that just kept staring at me. I felt different; light and strong again. But there was no sign anyone had been there, and at first I thought it was a dream. But I could remember every word that lama had spoken and my weakness was gone. I stood, and I jumped in the air. That pika should have run, but it didn't move, not until I began to walk away. Then it ran to a rock and chattered, like it had to tell the world that I had lived. That maybe it had seen a miracle," Chemi added in a low voice, staring at the outstretched hand of the blue Buddha, and pushing her fingertips close to the blue fingers, just above the surface of the old cloth.

"But even now, today, I was wondering if maybe it had been a dream after all. Because I think the medicine lamas were from one of the other worlds." Other worlds. Chemi meant one of the bayal, the hidden worlds, thought to be accessed through secret portals in the earth. "They can't exist here, I was telling myself, they don't exist. They are like some of the spirit creatures in another age that were hunted down and killed by demons. I must have been carried to some bayal. But look—" She swept her hand toward the line of thangkas. They had found a place of the medicine lamas. In this world.

Each of them, even the American, wandered about the chamber in silent reverence. Lokesh kept returning to the small row of dorjes on the ledge. Nearly all were double ended, with symmetrical scepters at each end, but two consisted of a scepter at one end and at the other end a purba, the ritual knife for which the resistance was named.

"It's been so long," Lokesh said as he touched an unusually long dorje made of sandalwood. "But this one, it seems like I know it." He ran his fingers along its worn, burnished top but seemed reluctant to lift it. "My teacher, Chigu Rinpoche, had one like this," he declared in a puzzled tone. "The only one I ever saw."

"Sometimes they put treasures away," Chemi explained, "when they knew the breakers were coming."

Shan looked at the woman. Breakers. Some villages, some clans, had their own vocabulary about what had happened during the past fifty years.

"They stored treasures," Shan agreed, but looked uncertainly at Lokesh. Tenzin bent to the base of one wall where there was a long low mound of dust. He probed it with his fingers and pulled out an end of fabric with threads of bright color. Above it, over their heads, was a gnarled limb with two pieces of yak-hair twine frayed at the end. A thangka had hung there, and fallen away. He looked at Shan, then reverently lowered the cloth. Tenzin understood, too. This was not simply a cache of treasure hastily secreted when the army came to destroy Rapjung. This was an ancient retreat cave of some kind, perhaps a place for a special, secret ritual whose purpose had been lost to time.

Finally, Chemi reminded them of their destination and they followed her quietly outside. Shan lingered at the stone pillar for a moment to look toward the shadow that marked the cave entrance. "How could they survive? How could any lama endure," he wondered. "The army would have searched the mountains."

"Survived?" Chemi said bitterly. "They sterilized the mountains. For a while they even had patrols with rifles that had telescopes. They killed anything that moved. They put up posters that warned all of us to stay out of the mountains for three months. Every goat, every wild yak was shot, because when he was dying a monk had said all the Tibetans killed by the Chinese would come back as mountain animals until they could live as humans again. Nothing survived up here."

"Then how would one of the old medicine lamas be here?" a voice asked over Shan's shoulder. The American had been listening.

Chemi shrugged. "Sometimes things grow back," she said, as if someone had planted seeds and a crop of old lamas had emerged. "Sometimes they find a way to step between worlds." As she turned into the cleft that led to the trail outside Shan studied the sturdy woman. She hadn't explained everything, hadn't explained why she had gone south, days away from her home, to reach the healer, waiting on a particular trail. How had she known where to find him, how had the dropka known to watch the herb meadow? A medicine lama was in the mountains but so was the dobdob who was attacking Tibetans, even monks.

Outside, on the side of the mountain, there was no sign of the helicopter, no evidence of activity on the ledges below. They hurried along the exposed trail into a series of deep gorges, walking sometimes in chasms so narrow that they moved through water a few inches deep, the runoff from the rocks above. They navigated along a row of rock pinnacles that towered like sentinels along the Qinghai border until they reached an open ledge that commanded a view of many miles to the north and east.

Chemi pointed to the next high mountain to the east in the long line of snowcapped peaks that defined the border. "Geladaintong," she explained. "Where the Yangtze River begins. And there," she said, turning west to point to a long flat-topped ridge that lay to the west. "Three miles past there, that's my village." She said it with an air of satisfaction. "We will have hot tea and tsampa. And noodle soup. My sister always has a kettle of noodle soup."

Shan lingered a moment looking at the rugged peak Chemi had pointed out. He had forgotten that the source of the Yangtze was in Amdo. For a moment he pictured the mighty river flowing through Chinese cities and farmland, powering so much commerce, feeding millions of Chinese, emptying into the East China Sea near Shanghai. It all began with one Tibetan mountain.

They circled a massive outrider of the mountain, like a huge granite rib, and found themselves hovering at the edge of a cliff over a patch of greyness below, a cloud along the base of the rib. It seemed as though a piece of the sky had fallen and been trapped in the rocks.

"Always like that," Chemi explained as Lokesh stared in wonder at the strange fallen cloud. "They say a demon lives there; when there is no wind you can hear it roar. Hermits used to come to this ledge to meditate, I've heard, because it was a connected place."

"Connected?" Winslow asked.

"For humans to connect with something deep in the earth. Where land deities were connected to sky deities." Chemi leaned out from the overhang, so far Shan stepped forward in fear that she would fall. "My uncles used to walk over this ridge to come visit us. They said it was the place where clouds are made," she added, then stepped back with a triumphant smile as a small grey wisp drifted up the gorge and floated toward the southern ridges.

They descended on a narrow switchback trail and in an hour began to cross the ridge under an afternoon sky so clear it shimmered. When the wind ebbed birds could be heard in the distance. Lokesh, for the first time in many days, began to sing one of his traveling songs, a song that pilgrims sang when they rested at night.

Coming down the high mountain onto the ridge underscored the sense of arrival into the land of the Yapchi villagers. The landscape was largely comprised of lichen-covered rocks, with long steep gravel slopes, and deep gorges falling between fingers of the mountain, full of the stark beauty that Shan had grown accustomed to in Tibet. He was in Qinghai now, a new land. He recalled hearing from a prisoner that there was more tolerance in Qinghai, that the destruction of traditional Tibetan institutions had not been so complete in what had once been Amdo, because there had been no real centers of population in the land, no obvious targets for the army.

As they emerged into a broad open field of gravel and low heather, Lokesh called out softly and pointed at a small flock of grouse-like birds, dappled with the white remnants of their winter plumage, that were browsing on the field two hundred feet away. "Lha gyal lo!" Lokesh called softly.

Then the birds exploded.

Gravel, plants, and birds burst into the air with a deafening blast. Chemi shouted and dropped to the ground. Tenzin grabbed Anya and pulled her behind a boulder as Shan pushed Lokesh in the same direction. The American did not move, but stood, cursing loudly in English as the rubble tumbled to the ground. As Winslow took a step forward, pulling out his binoculars, another patch of ground fifty feet beyond the first erupted with the same violence, blasting stones far into the sky. Winslow retreated to the rocks beside Shan, still cursing, and a third explosion ripped through the still afternoon air.

Abruptly, there was silence. Tiny bits of soil began to shower down on them, and three small columns of smoke drifted upward from small craters in the meadow. Three explosions, in a line, evenly spaced. Like the ones they had witnessed from the heights of the mountain that morning.

Chemi rose, terror in her eyes. Tenzin stepped to her side, his eyes upward, watching something white drift down toward them. It was a feather, and they all watched it in silence until it touched the ground in front of them. Lokesh began a mantra in a low, sorrowful tone.

"What would the army . . ." Chemi began, and rubbed her ears.

Shan realized his own ears were ringing. "Not the army," he heard Winslow say, as if from a distance, and the American pointed toward the far end of the clearing.

Several figures were emerging from the outcropping at the far end of the field. They wore helmets, but not the helmets of soldiers. Their helmets were red and silver, the kind construction workers sometimes wore. Shan motioned the others back into the rocks. He stepped hesitantly into the clearing and waited.

The fury of the man in the lead was evident. Even though he was still out of earshot they could tell he was shouting and pointing at them, pointing at the small craters, even turning to wave his fist at the small party that followed him. As he reached the crater nearest them the man halted and examined Shan, then removed his silver helmet and marched quickly forward, his hands clenched, his mouth curled in anger. For a moment Shan thought the man was going to throw the helmet at him.

"Just walking across the ground could have ruined the test!" he shouted as he advanced.

The stranger replaced his helmet as he reached Shan, as though to say he was prepared for violence. He was a Han, slightly taller than Shan, square-shouldered, with knuckles that bore the scars of having been laid open many times. He wore a green nylon coat that bore the emblem of a golden oil derrick on the left breast.

"We could have been killed," Shan said quietly.

"You could have ruined our test *and* been killed," the man shot back loudly, his eyes still blazing.

"You did kill some birds." Anya appeared a few feet behind Shan.

The words, or perhaps just the soft, disappointed way Anya spoke them, seemed to deflate the man. He frowned. "Walking in the test quadrant, so close to the charges, can distort the results," he growled, his anger seeming to ebb into frustration.

"How could we know?" Shan asked.

"Know? All you need to know is that the whole area was off-limits.

Don't you read? Posters in every village below, with dates for testing in each quadrant. Only a fool would—"

As he spoke another man approached, a short man wearing dark glasses. His heavy cheeks and compact features had the look of a Mongolian. A number of instruments hung from his neck. A small, expensive camera. Binoculars. A compass, and a small black-cased device that may have been an altimeter. He wore a red nylon vest and, rather than a helmet, a red American-style cap with a broad front visor, that also bore the image of a golden derrick. The hair exposed below the cap was long, but trimmed and oiled. He looked surprisingly well-groomed for climbing the mountain trails.

"We didn't come that way," Anya announced.

Again her words seemed to take the strangers by surprise. The man in the sunglasses studied Anya, then Shan, and looked behind them. Chemi stood there, and Tenzin stepped out of the shadows. The man in sunglasses turned to the first man, who cocked his head as if suddenly very curious. He pulled a map from his pocket and studied it intensely.

"Which way then?" the man in the helmet asked.

"Sometimes sheep get lost in the hills," Shan interjected, taking another step forward.

"You have no sheep," the man observed.

"I said they were lost," Shan shot back.

There was a sudden mechanical clicking. The second man, with the sunglasses, was shooting photographs of them, rapidly pressing the shutter and winding as he aimed the device at each of them. An instant later a similar clicking and whirling answered the first, and Shan turned to see Winslow photographing the oil crew, answering each of the man's shots with one of his own. The man with the dark glasses lowered his camera and glared at Winslow; Winslow lowered his camera and the man saw the American's face. He straightened and stepped closer, then twisted about and ordered the rest of the work crew back, leaving only the man in the green jacket by his side.

"I am the foreman," the man in green hesitantly announced, looking to the second man as though for a cue. "Team leader for this field study. For the Qinghai Petroleum Venture." He looked from Shan to Winslow and back again, obviously uncertain which to address. "There must have been a misunderstanding." He studied Shan's frayed clothes and decided to look at Winslow as he spoke. "You should have been warned about the blasting zone."

"Why would you look for oil so high in the mountains?" Winslow asked in an offhand tone, taking off his hat and pushing back his hair.

"Not oil, not here. The blasting is monitored by seismometers positioned in the mountains and in the valley where the exploration is focused. These are very complex geologic formations. We need to record the way the vibrations travel through the rock to define the geologic structure, so we can understand how large the deposit of oil is, how economic it would be to extract."

"And?" Winslow asked, still in his disinterested tone.

"So far the results are inconclusive. It will depend on what the drilling strikes in the valley," the geologist said with a thin smile. "Our models suggest a strike big enough to justify at least a ten-year project here."

"Were you blasting three days ago, on the south side of the mountain? Or this morning?" Winslow demanded. "Have you been on the ridge on the far side of that big plain?"

The foreman glanced at his companion again. "No. We do not operate outside our concession area."

Winslow studied the two men. "Qinghai Petroleum," he observed, "has American partners."

"Italian," the foreman replied, "French, British. And American. We work with Americans on this project."

"So you know Melissa Larkin."

The geologist's expression froze, and he threw a pleading glance toward the man in the sunglasses.

"A horrible thing," the short man observed in an earnest tone. "Tragic, so far from home. So sudden." He removed his glasses and fixed Winslow with a steady gaze. There was sympathy in his words, but not in his eyes.

"You knew her?" the American asked. "I was at Yapchi. I didn't see you."

"Zhu Ji is Director of Special Projects for the entire company," the foreman said. "He works with the foreign experts."

The short, sleek man called Zhu nodded slowly. "But I haven't met you before," he said pointedly. "You are not with the venture. I would know."

Winslow sighed, then pulled out his wallet and handed a business card to Zhu.

It was printed in Chinese on one side and English on the other. Shan saw the image of an American eagle, in blue ink, and gold stars. Zhu stared at it a long time, before handing it to the geologist, who repeatedly turned the card over in his hand, seeming to read it each time, as though the lettering might change when he turned it. "I heard someone from your government came," Zhu said dryly.

"Are you suggesting Miss Larkin suffered an accident?" Winslow asked.

"Miss Larkin is dead," Zhu said abruptly. "She fell off the mountain into a river. I saw it happen."

Shan heard a sharp intake of breath from Winslow. "You were there?"

"I saw it, but not close. You know she had stayed out in the field without properly clearing it—supposed to be on a three day mission but never returned. We had been watching for her, because her superiors were quite angry about it. Her team had expensive equipment and was gathering important data. Only two of her team came back, only the Chinese, who said they had become lost. The others with her were Tibetans," he observed in an accusing tone. "I said maybe she was just lost as well. It is so easy to become disoriented in these ranges. We watched for her when we were traveling in the mountains, and saw her through binoculars on a ledge high above us. I think she was delirious from hunger. Or maybe the altitude. Foreigners often have trouble with the altitude."

"Why wasn't I told this when I visited the camp?"

"I was in the mountains. When I returned I reported it. Forms have been sent to Beijing. And to her American employer."

It was Winslow's turn to fall silent. He sat on a flat rock and surveyed the barren landscape. "Is her body at the camp?" he asked after a long moment. "I need to take the body."

"No body," Zhu said soberly. "Into the river, washed away. It happens. Sometimes people are found floating hundreds of miles away."

"You mean the Yangtze?"

"No. We were on the crest of the long ridge, on the provincial border. She fell on the southern side. The Tibetan side."

"I have to have a body," Winslow declared quietly, to a cloud over the northern horizon. "It's my job. The U.S. government must account for all of its taxpayers." He sighed and unfolded his map. "Show me where."

Zhu pulled a pencil from his pocket, studied the American's map for a long time, then pointed to an area of rugged terrain nearly fifteen miles to the west, where the topographical map showed the sharply compressed lines of a steep wall. Below was a thin blue line that drifted south on the map, into Tibet. Zhu followed the blue line with his pencil tip to a larger blue spot over a hundred miles away. "To a lake," he said in a victorious tone, as if it proved his point. "Probably one of those sacred places."

Winslow's gaze moved slowly up and down the man. "I'll need those papers you filed," he said in a cool voice.

"At Yapchi. Ask for the manager."

"Jenkins. I met him."

"Right," Zhu agreed in his slow, oily voice. "Mr. Jenkins was very upset, too. We all liked Miss Larkin. Very pretty. She told jokes. Spoke Tibetan. Not Chinese," he said pointedly, "but Tibetan." The foreman turned away, as if Zhu's words were a cue to leave.

"Stay on the main tracks," Zhu advised as he took a step backwards. "Safer for everyone." He studied the steep slope behind them as though trying to discern how they might have descended. "Otherwise we can't guarantee your safety." As he spoke the Special Projects Director stepped past Shan to the rocks behind them, walking warily along the edge of the field as though he suspected others might be hiding. He circled back and stood behind the foreman again. "You have no dogs," Zhu said, looking at Shan suspiciously. "Shepherds have dogs."

Shan returned his steady gaze. "Sometimes dogs have to choose when sheep stray. Go to the shepherd or stay with the sheep. This time they must have stayed with the sheep."

Zhu replied with another narrow smile. "A Han shepherd with Tibetan sheep. Difficult," he said, and nothing more. He spun about and the two men marched away to join their crew, back on the far side of the long rock-strewn clearing which now resembled a battlefield. Shan recalled another crater, the one he had seen at Rapjung. The land took long to heal from such wounds.

Shan watched the Special Director until he was out of sight, trying to persuade himself Zhu was only what he had said he was. But he had known too many men like Zhu, as colleagues in Beijing, and later as his handlers in the gulag, for him to dismiss Zhu so easily. Zhu was more than what he had claimed to be. A Party member, almost certainly. The political commissar of the oil project, most likely. Perhaps a special watcher from Public Security.

He weighed Zhu's words, trying to make them fit with what they had seen earlier that day. No oil crew had been authorized to work on the other side of the mountain but the explosions they had heard that morning had been seismic charges, identical to those they had just experienced. The helicopter Chemi had seen had been civilian, and the only civilian helicopters in the region probably belonged to the oil venture. Zhu had said a helicopter had searched for Larkin. But why would it search on the far side of the mountain? And if Zhu had already reported Larkin dead, what was it searching for?

As the oil crew disappeared from sight, Winslow kept staring at his map. "Jesus," he said as Shan approached. "Over a cliff." He was remembering, Shan suspected, that he had almost fallen the same way the day before.

"I always get a body," the American said absently, staring at the map.

"Maybe later we could find the river," Shan suggested, "and say some words."

"I didn't know her," Winslow said, in a tone that sounded like protest.

"A rebellious American," Shan observed, "who leaves her normal duties, her normal life, to wander about Tibetan mountains, perhaps to look for something bigger."

Winslow grunted. The small grin that rose on his face slowly angled downward into a frown. "You make it sound like she and I have been looking for the same thing."

Shan did not reply, but kept staring at the American. Winslow returned his gaze for a moment, grimaced and looked away.

The landscape greened as they descended into Qinghai Province. The hills were still largely the same rugged, gravelly slopes they had encountered on the south side of the range, but the gullies where the spring melt ran contained more vegetation. Juniper and poplar trees could be seen in the lower elevations. There even seemed to be more pikas running in and out of the tumbles of rock scree that covered many of the slopes.

Lokesh seemed intensely interested in every stream and rivulet they encountered. Whenever they were within reach he paused to taste the water. Where one came into view in the distance he pulled his hat low to shield his eyes and studied the water. He offered no explanation, but Shan knew Lokesh was thinking of the patch of blood red water they had seen the day before. Shan still did not understand it, but he did understand that the healers Lokesh had trained with believed the health of the land and the health of the people who inhabited it were inextricably linked. To Lokesh and his teachers it was impossible to treat a human illness without addressing the state of harmony in the human's spirit, and it was impossible to address the harmony in a human spirit without also considering the harmony in that part of the earth where the human lived. To Lokesh the crimson patch might have indicated a tear in the fabric that bound them all together.

They followed Chemi down a long steep gully for half an hour before Winslow paused, map in hand, and called out to her. She pointed to their location on the map, then to the narrow gorge they were about to enter. Where the gully opened onto the lower slope of the mountain was her village, she said with a smile of anticipation. Winslow stooped for Anya to climb onto his back. Chemi's pace quickened, and although she usually remained at least fifty feet in front of their small column as they moved down the gully, Shan thought he heard her singing.

The gully ended abruptly and Chemi stood in a pool of sunlight in front of them. The sharp, sudden sound she made seemed to start as a greeting. But then she sank to her knees and held her belly, and the sound became a long painful groan. He ran to her side but she seemed unable to speak.

Her home had been there, Shan saw, less than two hundred feet from a small stream that emerged from the mountain near the mouth of the gully. Between the stream and the site of the tiny village there had been trees, but now these were twisted, smoking stumps. And beyond the stumps were the smoldering remains of four houses.

CHAPTER ELEVEN

The sound of engines and clinking metal broke through their stunned silence. Chemi did not hesitate, did not look back, just ran for the cover of the outcroppings that lined the slope beyond the ruined village. Shan grabbed Lokesh and pulled him into the same rocks as Winslow threw Anya onto his back and followed. Only when they had run nearly a hundred yards did Chemi stop. She seemed unable to speak, not because of her exertion but because of the emotion that twisted her face. She bent into the rocks and retched. When she turned back Shan glimpsed the sick woman again, the frail creature they had encountered on the trail.

It wasn't battle tanks, as Shan feared, but two bulldozers that appeared from around the high rock wall that sheltered the southern and eastern sides of the village. One of the machines did not slow, only lowered its blade and began carving a swath through the ruins of the village, sweeping through the remains of the buildings, throwing before it a rolling wave of debris. A chair flew into the air, the shards of a window and a bed, then something swollen and white that could have been the body of a dog.

The second bulldozer pulled a two-axle trailer from which at least a dozen men climbed down. They quickly unhitched the trailer and, as the second earthmover crawled forward, began unloading building materials.

"The petroleum venture," Anya said in a pained voice. "Only they have such equipment."

Her words seemed to say it all, or at least there seemed to be nothing else anyone could say. Anya took Chemi's hand and led them through the rocks. Yapchi Village, Chemi had said, was only an hour's walk past her home.

Shan had never understood the subtleties of traveling by foot, the many ways one could walk, the messages of human stepping, until he had come to Tibet. Lokesh had once reminded Shan that Tibet had known the wheel for many centuries, as long as China and India, but for most of its existence Tibet had used the device not for transportation, but only for prayer wheels. Tibetans liked to walk, Lokesh said, for it kept them connected to the earth and gave them time to contemplate. But there were many ways of walking in Tibet. There were pilgrim's steps, the slow reverent pace of those bound for holy places. There were caravaners, who moved firmly and steadily, eyes fixed on the horizon or their animals. There were prisoners, who moved in short shuffling steps, heads bowed, sometimes even, by habit, long after they were released. Now Chemi assumed another, an uneven stuttering pace that involved frequent steps to look nervously over the shoulder or to simply sigh and let a wave of emotion break and ebb before moving on. It was the walk of the refugee. It pained Shan to see Chemi fall into it so readily.

They walked in silence, until Anya led them to a narrow ledge of rock that opened with views to the north and west. They stood on a saddle of land that rose up to separate the grey rolling hills to the east from a small fertile valley, bounded on three sides by a long high curving outrider of Yapchi Mountain. The walls gave a symmetrical shape to its curving sides, so that the valley, lush with spring growth, had the appearance of a green oval bowl. Except for the open grass-covered saddle of land they stood on, the sides of the bowl were trimmed with a swath of conifers perhaps a quarter-mile wide. Above the trees were cliffs and towers of rock. Below them were pastures, and fields concentrated at the end nearest them—some crudely terraced, some of them a warm willow green, the color of sprouting barley, others the deeper green of pastures used for sheep.

Anya pointed excitedly to the small cluster of buildings at the south end of the bowl and pressed her rosary to her chin as if in silent prayer. Her village was intact. The girl glanced up at Chemi with an apologetic air and reached for the grim woman's hand. Chemi seemed to be in shock. Shan was not certain her eyes even saw the valley below them. "You'll stay with us. You'll like Yapchi," the girl said. "Soon we will have Lamtso salt for our tea," she added, and led them back onto the trail.

Winslow lingered, scanning the far side of the valley with his binoculars. Shan saw his frowning expression and reached for his own field glasses. As he adjusted the focus another village came into view at the far end of the valley, more than two miles away, where a dirt road descended into the valley from a gap at the end of the high saddle of land. A line of heavy trucks were parked beside two rows of box-like structures.

"They bring in offices and quarters on the back of trucks. Long trailers," the American explained. Shan nodded as he swept the valley with the lenses. He had seen oil convoys in Xinjiang, the vast arid province to the northwest. Once he had encountered one over a mile long, waiting at the edge of the highway, trucks of many sizes, and buses, derricks and laboratory vans, a small city on wheels.

On the slope above the oil camp, crews were leveling the forest. A section a quarter mile wide had been clearcut, and the logs were being rolled down to the oil camp. The swath of stumps looked like an open wound on the side of the mountain.

Winslow pointed again and Shan trained the lenses closer, to a point near the center of the valley where a heavy derrick stood with two trucks parked beside it. "An easy place to work," Winslow said. "That's what the manager told me. Very dry. They like dry. Water makes everything more complicated, more costly. Yapchi is so dry they have to bring water in with big tank trucks. No water at the bottom of the valley means they can easily work the center, the lowest point, shortest distance to their target."

Their target. Shan remembered Lhandro's words. The company wanted to take the blood from Yapchi's earth.

Winslow turned to follow the others but saw that Shan still scanned the slopes. "It was a pretty small piece of stone," the American observed.

Shan lowered the glasses with a weak smile. "It's not that I expect to see the stolen eye," he said quietly. "I'm just trying to understand how to look for a blind deity."

The American studied Shan as if trying to decide if Shan were joking, then looked at the derrick with unmistakable resentment. "Where I come from, we were taught if you did something bad enough, your god would come out of the heavens and find you."

"You mean I should look for a wrathful deity?" Shan asked.

But the American just turned and walked on.

As they descended the winding trail through several narrow defiles and along game trails in the junipers, the image of the valley stayed with Shan. He began to understand more clearly the villagers' fierce love of their home. It was such a tiny piece of the world, so isolated it had no electricity, not even anything that could be called a road, a quiet, self-sufficient place that the world had bypassed, where one might be able to forget the outside for weeks, even months. Until the Qinghai Petroleum Venture arrived.

Thirty minutes later they stepped out of a narrow defile under several tall junipers and the village of Yapchi spread out before them, less than a quarter mile away. It was smaller than Shan had expected, no bigger than the little rongpa town where they had first met Winslow. To the right, where a thin growth of trees gave way to the grassy slope, stood an ancient chorten, nearly ten feet high. Shan walked around the shrine, touching the stone. The prayers that had been written around its base had mostly weathered away.

Shan saw Winslow lingering in the shadow of the last tree and realized their companions were not to be seen. He took a tentative step toward the village, then a small stone flew by and landed near his foot. He turned to see Tenzin, behind Winslow, with a somber Tibetan man in a soiled green pullover sweater, beside what once had been a long mani wall, a wall of stones inscribed with mantras. Tenzin gestured for Shan, then moved deeper into the trees with the stranger, behind another of the outcroppings that were scattered about the thin forest. Shan hesitantly followed, but paused at the mani wall, kneeling. He lifted one of the lichen-covered stones. It was centuries old, its carved inscription so embedded with a dark lichen that it appeared that the prayer had been formed by the lichen itself. A self-actuating prayer, Lokesh might have called it.

He leaned the stone against a tree so the prayer faced outward, then followed Winslow, Tenzin, and the stranger down the winding trail toward the sound of voices. The scent of burning juniper floated through the air. They cleared a tall wall of rock and found themselves in a bustling camp. A lean Tibetan youth with a pockmarked face darted forward and grabbed Tenzin's arm, pulling him toward the back of the small blind canyon, followed closely by the man in the tattered green sweater.

Shan lingered near the narrow canyon entrance, surveying the chaotic scene inside. At least forty people were arrayed on blankets or sitting around fires, some of them with bruised faces, some with arms in slings. On one blanket a young man lay prostrate, tended by a grey-haired woman.

Chemi was at the side of the canyon, speaking rapidly with an older woman as she rubbed the hand of a large man who lay beside the rock face, his face swollen and eyes glazed, blood oozing through a sling on his left arm, a bloody bandage around his forehead.

"Ours was the closest village so her family fled here," Anya explained as she stepped to Shan's side. "The company said they had to build a water collection facility at Chemi's home, to install tanks to take water from the stream for the work camp. They said the houses could not stay because it would foul the water needed for the workers. They said the venture would pay compensation. The venture people didn't understand, Chemi's sister told them, they would need to hear from the township council before they could leave their homes. But the company had soldiers to help them."

"The government was there, not just the army," interjected the old woman. "He showed us his card. From some Ministry. It said Beijing. We never expected Beijing to take notice of us. My son always wanted to meet someone from Beijing, because in his school they say many heroes live there. But it was only a Mongolian man with dark glasses."

"Special Projects," Winslow muttered bitterly over Shan's shoulder. Zhu, the Special Projects Director, had been there when the village had been destroyed.

Several of the Yapchi villagers were there to help the injured and spoke excitedly with Anya about the return of the caravan. Some of the villagers looked solemnly toward Shan after speaking with the girl, but soon their gaze shifted toward Winslow as the American began moving about the camp. It was impossible to ignore the tall fair-skinned stranger. He stopped at the pallets and spoke in low words to those lying on them, then reached into his pack and emptied it of its food. A bag of raisins, a bag of nuts, and a bag of hard candy. There were not many children in the camp, only four other than Anya, but all four surrounded the American and gleefully shared out the treasure. Anya watched with a strangely detached expression, as though, Shan thought, she had forgotten how to be a child.

The man beside Chemi groaned, closed his glazed eyes and seemed to sink into unconsciousness. She pulled off her coat, lifted his head, and propped it behind him as a pillow.

"It's my uncle Dzopa," she whispered. "He'd been gone for ten years. He went to India to live."

Shan studied the man. He looked at the woman, perplexed. "Why did he return now?"

"I can't understand him when he speaks," she said, with pools of moisture in her eyes. She nodded toward a woman sitting nearby, churning tea with a sad, distant expression. "My cousin says he was trying to clear out the village when the tank started shooting. Things exploded and hit his head. He had just returned the day before, looking for me. He had heard I was sick. He has no other family. When he was young he was at a gompa and never married."

The big Tibetan appeared to be in his late fifties. His arms were like logs, his neck like that of a bull. "He's a farmer now?" Shan asked.

Chemi nodded. "He sent a letter once. He settled in Dharmasala," she said, referring to the seat of the exiled Tibetan government.

"What do you think, why would he return?"

"Sometimes the Dalai Lama gives speeches, and says the biggest contribution a refugee from Tibet can make is to return. Because those who have crossed over to India have demonstrated their faith, and their strength, and those are the traits needed to keep Tibet alive."

Shan studied the battered man again. His injuries looked severe. The fingers on Dzopa's left hand trembled, a sign of possible nerve damage. "Did he bring something from India? A message perhaps? Was he coming to take others to India?" But Shan looked up to see that Chemi had turned away and was walking toward the back of the small canyon. He found her with Lokesh and Anya, who sat with bowls of tea behind a circle of people reciting a mantra.

"They are not going to stop the mantra until those people leave," Lokesh explained. Beyond the circle was a flat stone with several wooden offering bowls and a charred metal disc where incense had burned. Anya and Nyma had made a chapel in the rocks behind the village, Lhandro had said.

"You mean the bulldozers in Chemi's village?" Shan asked.

"No," Anya said. Her tone was excited, and her eyes wide. "Not until the Chinese and foreigners leave our valley. Night and day they say, they have made a vow to Tara. A mantra chain, for as long as it takes. We will all take turns, when we can."

Shan studied the girl and recognized the fierce light in her eye. There had been an old Khampa warrior in his prison barracks, imprisoned for life for leading ambushes against soldiers, who had always marveled at how the monks resisted by resort to prayer, even when being beaten or electroshocked. "All I could do was shoot guns," the Khampa had often said in a voice that never lost its awe for the holy men. "That's nothing compared to them."

Shan was tempted to sit in the circle himself. Perhaps that was all any of them could do now, just pray. "Why would Chemi's uncle want to have cleared out his village, why warn them now?" he asked the girl.

"Probably because he had met others who had lived near Chinese development projects. He thought the venture would take them away."

"Away?"

"To work for it. Or move the families to a strange place. All the time we have been gone the venture has been torturing our village, harassing it, trying to drive everyone away our people say. The venture took all the young men who were in Yapchi to work cutting trees. They have to stay in that camp, in those metal boxes, that are locked at night. The others are scared to even go ask for them, for fear they will be taken, too." Anya spoke with a defiance Shan had never heard in her voice. But as she returned his stare, confusion crossed her eyes, then fear. "Locked in a metal box," the girl repeated, and she turned away to join the circle.

Thirty feet away, in a corner of the little canyon, Tenzin sat with the two Tibetans who had brought him into the camp, and another man, older, but who wore the same deep-seated anger that etched the faces of the first two. The youngest of the men suddenly turned, stood, and took a step toward Shan, straightening into the pose of a sentry. They were not men who resisted the Chinese merely by reciting mantras. Shan looked beyond the man toward Tenzin, who leaned forward, listening earnestly to the older man. Beside them was a stack of equipment: braided leather ropes; bottles of water; a compass, hanging from a lanyard; a portable shovel, folded into its handle; nylon sleeping bags.

Suddenly there was a wrenching moan from the front of the camp. Shan leapt toward the sound, the purbas at his heels, to find Chemi draped over her uncle's shoulders, trying to pull him back. He was sitting up, holding the wooden handle of a tea churn, savagely beating a small stump. The handle was shredding in his hands. Shan tried to grab Dzopa's arm. The man flung him away effortlessly, then Chemi put her hands on his cheeks. "Uncle!" she cried. "You must stop!" Dzopa paused, and his eyes seemed to find her, though they could not focus.

"Stop them!" he said with another of the chilling moans. "They are burning all the lamas!" He fell back, unconscious, the splintered stump of the handle in his hand.

Still on the ground where the man had pushed him, Shan stared in alarm at Dzopa.

"His head," Chemi whispered, looking at Shan. She reached for the cloth to wipe his brow and froze as she saw those around her. All those within earshot had stopped and were staring fearfully at the unconscious man. Several pulled out their rosaries and began mantras.

Anya did not resist when Shan asked her to take him into her village, despite the protests of the older women. He had to understand the valley, the girl insisted, for the eye was destined to be returned to him and he would have to act quickly when that happened. One of those who listened, a big-boned, ungainly woman in a long felt skirt and red apron, nodded grimly. "If that oil starts coming up," she declared in a defiant tone, as if chastising her fellow villagers, "those Chinese will never leave." Shan pulled his field glasses from his sack and followed Anya and the woman back to the village.

The deity had lived on a low knoll near the center of the valley, the woman explained. Nearly three hundred years earlier a lama had found it living in a rock on the knoll, and the villagers had built a mani wall around it. Lamas from the famous Rapjung gompa had come every year to bless the rock and the people who protected it.

A brown dog burst out of the first house, its loud barking quickly shifting into excited yelps as it recognized Anya. A man with a face blackened with soot, nearly toothless, appeared at the door of the second house and called out affectionately to the girl, who promised him fresh Lamtso salt the next day. A middle-aged man in a tattered derby looked from a crumbling pressed-earth wall that surrounded a third house and asked for news of Lhandro. Shan continued along the broad path that served as the only road of the village as Anya ran from one to another of the few inhabitants who showed themselves. One house, the outermost, was made of substantial timbers and had a loft overhead for storing fodder. It was an old, elegant structure, built in the tradition of Kham, the eastern region where wood had once been plentiful. On its wall hung a large wooden drum, nearly two feet wide and a foot deep, a hide stretched across its top, used for attracting the attention of deities. Shan studied the house, remembering Nyma's description of the attack by the Lujun troops. Only one house had survived. A miniature chorten, two feet high, stood near its door, the kind of shrine made for a sacred household relic. Across from it, inside another pressed-earth enclosure, stood a stable, looking more solid than several of the houses, in which half a dozen sheep and as many lambs lay basking in the late afternoon sun.

He wandered past the village toward a long low mound nearly a mile away, a man-made mound that rose a stone's throw from a smaller, lower-knoll. A few grazing sheep looked up as he walked along the wide path that connected the village to the far end of the valley, the rumble of machinery growing louder with each step. The venture's drilling rig was operating less than a hundred yards beyond the mound.

He studied the path before approaching the mound. It ran along the base of the grassy ridge, passing outside the valley through a small gap at the north end of the valley, by the oil camp. From the derrick to the gap leading to the outside world it had been ripped open, widened by a bull-dozer. An army had come up that same path once, he reminded himself, a vengeful Chinese army, taking a slight detour in its retreat to Beijing to ravage the beautiful valley. He replayed the tale in his mind as he climbed the small hill. It had happened on such a spring day, perhaps in the same month, for Nyma had explained that the salt caravan had been away at the time. The army had shelled the village with its cannons, and the villagers had retreated, not to the mountain slopes, but to their deity on the small knoll for protection. Then the Chinese officer had sent soldiers to work with swords until none of the villagers survived. He looked back along the encircling slopes of the valley. There were ruins of small structures and the outlines of fields not worked for many years. Once the community had been larger. Entire families had been wiped out that day, the day the deity had been broken by the Lujun soldiers.

A low mani wall surrounded the mound, with two strands of prayer flags affixed to weathered posts at each end. On top of the mound, weighted by small stones, were over twenty khatas, prayer scarves, most in tatters. Shan lifted a mani stone and, not certain why, held it out toward the mound, then toward the oil camp. In the same instant a gust of wind snapped the prayer flags, and one of the old tattered khatas worked loose and blew away across the valley floor toward the western slope.

Lokesh would have said it was no coincidence, that Shan was always going to be there that hour, and that the scarf, after so many years on the mound, was always going to blow away in that same moment. The junction of events was woven into Shan's particular tapestry, Lokesh might say. It was why Lokesh and many other Tibetans Shan knew would stop and stare when a hawk flew low across their path, a dried leaf danced in the air before them, or a peculiar cloud scudded across the moon just as they looked up. Acts of nature might to them seem unexpected, but they would never seem random.

He lowered the mani stone and reverently gazed at the mound, at the mass grave of the Yapchi villagers, then did what Lokesh would have done. He followed the khata.

The scarf tumbled across the valley more than a hundred paces away, dropping to the earth one moment, drifting upward the next as if lifted by some invisible hand. He studied the upper rim of the valley as he walked toward the cloth. It was a rocky, ragged landscape, a place likely to hold caves—a place, Nyma said, full of caves—where men, or deities, might hide. He followed slowly, absorbing the Yapchi land, expecting the khata to settle or be snagged on one of the low shrubs where the meadow ended and the steeper slope began. But when it reached the slope the prayer scarf shot high in the air, soaring, tumbling like some caged dove experiencing newfound freedom, gliding toward the edge of the forest to the north.

As Shan watched it speed away he considered turning back. But there was more than an hour of light left, and even in the dark he could certainly find his way back along the path. He needed to understand the valley. He needed to learn where a deity might be hiding. Or at least where an escaping prayer scarf might flee. Several times he paused to study the drilling tower and the oil camp as he climbed to the cover of the treeline before heading in the direction he had last seen the khata. After ten minutes he saw a patch of white hanging in the low branches of a pine tree where the slope curved toward the east.

The wind brought the rumble of chain saws and Shan paused to study with his field glasses the end of the valley that was being civilized by the oil company. There were more trailers than he had at first thought, two rows each containing five of the rectangular units. Metal boxes, the villagers called them, because he knew, to the rongpa they did not deserve the name house. Beyond the trailers were several tents, and trucks of all sizes and shapes from light cargo vehicles to heavy dump trucks, and a large open tent that appeared to be serving as a garage. Above the camp the wide swath of stumps reached all the way to the cliff that defined the upper rim of the valley. As least two dozen men labored there, felling trees at an alarming rate.

Shan retrieved the khata, folding it into his pocket, then wandered closer, more wary, conscious of each tree and rock he might use for cover. He was only two hundred yards from the edge of the camp when he found a thick log, felled by age and not a saw, and sat to study the camp. At the near end a dozen men kicked a soccer ball around a meadow that appeared to have been grazed by sheep. They played hard, yelling but not cheering. Beyond them, close to the tents rose the smoke of several cooking fires. Shan was familiar with the scene. A tentacle, Drakte had called one such camp they had seen when traveling together, a lumber harvesting complex. One of the tentacles that extended from Beijing, the purba had groused. It was the way Beijing reached out to assert itself in the remotest corners of the land, to show its power, to extract riches.

Looking back up to the timber crew, he noticed men stationed at intervals along the work area. What were they guarding against? he wondered. Surely there were not enough predators left to threaten the crew. Then with a shudder he remembered that Yapchi villagers had been conscripted. The men at the edge were not protecting the workers, they were preventing them from escaping. What a cruel torture, he thought, not simply to make the rongpa prisoners in their own valley but to make them destroy the wealth of their own land.

As the sun began to fall below the valley wall he ventured closer to the meadow, hoping to catch a scrap of dialogue, an accent, anything to help him understand more about the Qinghai Petroleum Venture. But as he grew closer he slowed, and a chill crept down his back. Although the soccer players wore tee shirts or undershirts they all seemed to have the same sturdy, trim pants—one side wearing green, the other grey—and all wore the same heavy high black boots, had the same lean muscular build. At the far end of the meadow was a large grey truck with something painted on its door. He raised his glasses, expecting to see the derrick logo of the venture. But it was not a derrick on the door, it was a snow leopard. Beyond the truck were sleek utility vehicles in gunmetal grey. His gut tightened. The soccer players were not oil workers. They were two groups of competing soldiers. Lin's mountain troops were at the oil camp, playing soccer with the knobs.

At dawn the next morning a small band of Tibetans arrived at the camp behind Yapchi Village. Anya ran at the sound of their footsteps, thinking, Shan knew, that the caravan had arrived, but she stopped at the mouth of the little canyon. A woman hobbled forward on a crutch, followed by a little boy who shuffled awkwardly, his feet bent inward, a line of drool hanging from his mouth. There were four others, a woman with eyes clouded with cataracts led by a teenage boy and a sturdy man in a tattered chuba carrying a frail-looking woman, asleep in his arms like a child.

They stood in silence, looking about the sleeping forms on the blankets.

"He's not here," Chemi said softly, apologetically, and suddenly Shan understood. The sick were coming to Yapchi. They must have walked through the night to find the medicine lama. The herder carrying the woman lowered her to a blanket and rubbed his eyes. Shan thought he saw tears.

"But I met him," Chemi added in a hopeful tone. "He healed me."

The crippled woman looked up in disbelief. "The one we seek is from the old days. There were stories from the mountains. But all those . . . they died a long time ago. Sometimes all we can do is follow the stories. . . ." Her voice drifted away and she stared at the ground. "Some people are saying he came to take the chair of Siddhi. Some say he came from a bayal, just to ease our suffering."

"I met him," Chemi repeated, more urgently. "He healed me."

The woman on the crutch stared at Chemi as if just hearing her, her mouth open. "Lha gyal lo," the woman said in a dry, croaking voice, then she began to sway. Chemi leapt forward as the woman collapsed into her arms.

Shan stepped to the small fire at the rear of the canyon and brought Chemi a bowl of tea for the woman. "What did she mean the chair of Siddhi?" he asked as he handed her the bowl.

"It's an old thing," Chemi said in a worried voice, cutting her eyes at him, then looking away.

"Resistance," Lokesh whispered as he suddenly appeared to kneel beside the sick woman. "I heard the purbas talking about it, very excited. They say in this region centuries ago a lama named Siddhi organized resistance against Mongol invaders. He rallied the people like no one ever had and made sure the Mongols never came back to their lands."

"There was a place he stayed in the mountains," Chemi continued, "a small meadow high on the upper slope of the mountain. There is a rock like a chair where he would sit and speak to the people. People have been going there for years to pray. Some say he was a fighter. Some say he was a healer who just gave hope and strength to the people."

Lokesh seemed to recognize the disbelief on Shan's face. "They want to believe in such things," the old Tibetan said, and nodded to another group of new arrivals who sat speaking with the older purba. "They say everyone is talking about Yapchi, for many miles. They say if a real lama would take the chair of Siddhi they could make the Chinese leave Yapchi, could make the Chinese leave the whole region."

Shan returned alone to the village heavy with a strange sense of guilt that had crept upon him during the night, unable to look at the haggard faces that searched his own for explanations. The faces of the sick Tibetans haunted him. He was wrong to have come, for to come had meant giving the people of Yapchi hope, and there was no hope. Beijing had discovered the beautiful valley, and given it to the petroleum company and their American partners. It may as well have been seized by the army for a new missile base, for such a venture would never be dissolved, never be moved. There was only one thing in China more inexorable than the march of the army, and that was the march of economic development. When the venture found oil it would seize the entire valley, drain it of its life force, strip it of everything of value and leave it, years later, soiled and barren. Shan had spent his four years in prison building roads for the economic forces deployed by Beijing, roads to penetrate the remote valleys that had been overlooked in the first wave of Chinese immigration. One of the worst cruelties inflicted on the prisoners had not been forcing them to pound the rocks of high mountain passes into shards, so trucks could traverse the high slopes, but to be forced to watch, from another new road site, as every tree in a newly opened valley was cut down, every seam of coal blasted open.

Yapchi Village was even emptier than the day before. The only sign of life seemed to be the lambs which pranced about in their earthen-walled pen, as though wildly excited that the sun had risen. Then he noticed faces in some of the windows watching him, and watching the path up the valley. The rumble of the drilling rig echoed off the valley walls in the still air, accompanied by the distant whine of chain saws. At the door of the last house, the simple timber house he had admired the day before, an old woman appeared. She offered Shan a quick bow of her head, then slowly, shyly, still standing in the doorway, extended a bowl of tea toward him. He stepped hesitantly through the open gate of the low wall that surrounded the house and nodded, accepting the bowl. The woman retreated silently into the shadow of her house, beckoning him inside.

The house consisted of one large room with a sleeping platform built into the north end and an alcove for preparing and eating food on the opposite side. The finely worked planks that made up the walls and floor bore a rich patina of age. A small wooden altar stood against the rear wall, near the sleeping platform, bearing the seven traditional offering bowls, and a framed photograph of the Dalai Lama, a single smoking stick of incense beside it. The carpet at the center of the room, though worn almost threadbare near the altar, depicted the endless knot, symbol of the unity of all things, and the other eight sacred emblems in rich reds and browns. Everything in the room seemed to be made of wood, or clay, or wool. The chamber was like a clearing in an ancient forest, radiating a natural, soothing tranquility.

The woman smiled awkwardly and sat on a squat stool near the sleeping platform, assuming a somber expression. Shan followed her uncertainly, and saw a figure in the shadows, leaning against the wall, on one of the two pallets unrolled on the platform. The figure turned, rising very slowly, his hand on the wall for support. The aged man moved with obvious effort toward Shan, one hand still on the wall. He sat on the edge of the platform, near the woman, and studied Shan as he smacked his cracked, dried lips together. Silence, Shan suspected, prevailed in the room, a fixture as real as the little altar and the simple benches that lined the wall. In the stillness he became aware of quick, shallow breathing and his eyes fell upon a small shape lying on a blanket in the corner of the platform. A lamb.

"We just wanted to thank you," the man said. His voice was hoarse, nearly a whisper, as though it had not been used in a long time. "I am called Lepka."

Shan lowered himself to the floor in front of the man, balancing the bowl between his legs. "I have done nothing. I lost the eye."

"But you came anyway," the man said, in a lama's voice. "Already things happen. You got the eye closer than it has been for a hundred years."

Things happen. Shan could not bring himself to question the aged Tibetan. What things? The destruction of Chemi's village? The gathering of knobs and army troops in the valley, probably for the first time since the terrible day when the eye was stolen? The distant rumbling of the oil derrick, scraping and grinding deep in the earth? The reckless talk of opposing the Chinese in the valley?

He offered a sad smile and studied Lepka. He had learned to think of such aged Tibetans as one of the treasures that the hidden parts of Tibet offered up, men and women who seemed to defy time, or at least to resist aging, who might live a century or more, and whose most vibrant memories were not of the times since Beijing had arrived, but before. The man's skin was like ancient parchment. He was very old, perhaps old enough to have been alive when the eye was taken from Yapchi. His gnarled fingers, Shan saw, were formed into a mudra, his thumbs pressed together, the knuckles of the first joints above the hands joined, the middle fingers extended and pressed together. With a blush of shame, Shan recognized the gesture. It was an offering mudra, the offering of water for the feet, used for initiating monks or receiving sanctified visitors.

"I went down to that place," Lepka declared. "I leaned on my staff and went down to that Chinese machine." He smacked his lips again and the woman handed him a bowl of water from the side of the platform, which he sipped from before speaking again. "I threw a stone at it." A thin line of water dribbled from his mouth as he spoke. "Sometimes demons make people have visions, make them see evil things that are not really there. But the stone hit metal, and bounced back. The workers laughed and said, 'look at the crazy old man.' " Lepka looked at Shan and grinned. He was missing most of his teeth. "But I can throw rocks good. When I was young I kept wolves away from the herds, with rocks and my sling. I threw another rock, and another, at different places. They laughed some more. But you know what?" he asked, then coughed and made a long wheezing sound before continuing. "I found a place that was a bell," he said with a meaningful gaze. "It didn't look like a bell, because it had been hidden in a different shape. But it sounded like a bell," he declared with a grin. "It was the essence of a bell, hiding there."

Bells, in traditional Tibet, were sometimes used to frighten demons away.

"And they didn't even know," Lepka said, and made the wheezing sound again. Shan realized it was a laugh.

Shan answered with a solemn nod and drank some tea. "Your home," he said, searching for something to say, "is so peaceful. Like a temple."

The woman smiled, and the old man surveyed the chamber slowly, as though seeing it for the first time. "The grandfather of my grandfather built this house," he said. "In the first year of the Eighth." He was speaking of the eighteenth century.

"It has heard many prayers," the woman added quietly. "Our son likes to bring the village here to meet with him on important decisions because he says no one ever speaks rudely in this house, for all the prayers that live in the wood."

Shan gazed back over the sleeping platform. He saw that there was another pallet, rolled, against the back wall, and suddenly he realized whose house he was in. "It's a long journey, to Lamtso."

The old man smiled. "When he was three years old, I took my boy for the first time. He sat on my shoulders as we walked and we would sing. For hours we would sing. And there was a dog, a huge mastiff that let him ride on its back. Sometimes he would lie down and fall asleep on that dog's broad back and the dog would just keep walking. I said it was too dangerous. . . ." The hoarseness was gone from the man's voice, as though the memories had revived something inside.

"But you made all the other dogs work," a voice said softly, behind Shan. "You put packs on all the other dogs when we left the lake. All but that one, so I could ride it home."

"Son!" the woman cried and leapt up to embrace Lhandro.

The village headman looked up from his mother's arms and smiled wearily.

"Lha gyal lo, Lha gyal lo," Lepka intoned quietly, his eyes filling with moisture. "The salt has found its way again."

Lhandro stepped to his father and knelt, opening his hand to reveal a mound of brilliant white crystals. He raised his father's hand and solemnly poured the salt onto the dry, wrinkled palm and closed the gnarled fingers around it. The wheezing laugh erupted again from Lepka's throat, and he pressed the handful of salt against his heart.

As Shan stepped to the door sheep began streaming past the outer gate, salt packs still on their backs, coming from north of the valley. Excited greetings echoed down the central path of the village, but also warnings. He stepped outside in confusion. On the slope above the village, near the trees, several of those from camp stood waiting, some waving, some pointing toward the arriving caravan. Then he saw a figure run from the group, in the opposite direction, as if to hide. He turned and saw that not all the Tibetans had been pointing toward the caravan.

Nyma appeared in the midst of the sheep, worry clouding her face. "They searched all our bags, and made us leave five sheep for them," she blurted out, without a greeting. She looked at the rear of the caravan. Two army trucks were winding their way up their valley, just a few hundred yards behind the last of the sheep.

Lhandro appeared in the doorway behind Shan, raised a hand to warn his parents to stay inside, then swept past Shan, pushing him into the shadows. As Shan took a position just inside the door, the headman stepped out into the central path to wait for the trucks. A knot tightened in Shan's belly as he watched the trucks stop and a dozen soldiers jump out. One of them opened the side door of the first truck, emblazoned with a snow leopard, and a man in an officer's tunic stepped down.

"Good morning, Colonel Lin," a voice called out with false warmth from behind Lhandro. Through the open door Shan watched Winslow walk jauntily to Lhandro's side. The American had washed and shaved, and put on a clean shirt. "Another glorious day for youth league maneuvers."

One side of Lin's mouth curled up as he recognized the American. He turned and spoke to someone behind him, out of Shan's sight. A moment later a soldier marched past Winslow and Lhandro, holding a clipboard as he surveyed the village with restless, hawk-like eyes.

"The American embassy has no authority to meddle in the internal affairs of China," Lin growled as he took a step toward Winslow. He spoke loudly, as if to address a larger audience.

"Of course not," the American agreed in a business-like tone. "The Qinghai Petroleum Venture has an American partner. One of its American workers is missing. Matter of international relations," he added pointedly, in a voice as loud as Lin's.

"Not missing," Lin said readily, as if he had made it his business to know what the American had been doing in the mountains. "Dead. Most unfortunate."

Through the door Shan glimpsed a pair of soldiers advancing around the back of the village, behind the animal pens on the opposite side of the path. They seemed to be searching for something.

"Our village is honored by the presence of the glorious soldiers of the People's Liberation Army," Lhandro said in a flat voice, casting an uneasy glance at Winslow.

"Of course you are," Lin said in an amused tone as he lit a cigarette and shot a stream of smoke toward Lhandro. "And your honor can only increase."

The knot in Shan's gut drew so tight it hurt.

Lin stared at Winslow intensely, as though trying to will the American to back down. "There were others with you before. Tibetans. Two tall men." He paused and stared at Lhandro expectantly, then shifted his gaze toward Lhandro's feet as though reminding Lhandro that Lin had once had the headman in manacles.

"I had a driver . . ." Winslow offered in a speculative tone.

Lin's hand made a quick jerking motion upward, as if he meant to strike the American. But he stopped it in midair and it collapsed into a fist. He surveyed the soldiers moving through the village, then turned back to the American. "But later that day you insisted your driver leave you at the side of the road. Just drop you there and drive away. He was wrong to do that. His report caused quite a disturbance at Public Security. He was punished for his irresponsibility."

"I wanted to walk. Fresh mountain air and all. We call it trekking."

"But how did you get over here?" the colonel pressed. "The mountains are impassable."

"Almost."

Lin frowned. "The petroleum venture is going to bring great wealth to this valley," he observed to Lhandro in his loud, public address voice. "Comrade Lhandro," he added, as if the colonel wanted to remind the village headman that he still knew his name, still held his papers.

"Perhaps," Lhandro offered in an anguished tone, "there isn't any oil."

The amusement returned to Lin's face as he drew deeply on his cigarette. "There's oil. The geologists just have to prove how much. Already there is not enough room in the camp for all the workers, and others will be coming when the oil starts to flow. A pipeline will need to be built. Workers will be stationed here permanently to operate the pumps."

Lhandro stared at the colonel's boots. "We have an empty stable," he said in a hollow tone. "We could convert it, make straw pallets."

Lin's eyes flared, but it seemed as though with pleasure, not anger.

"Please colonel," Lhandro pleaded. "We are simple farmers. We have farmed this valley for centuries. We pay taxes. We could supply food to the workers. . . ." His voice seemed to lose strength. "We have done nothing wrong," he added despondently, still staring at Lin's boots.

"You never explained what you were doing a hundred miles south of here that day."

"Salt," Lhandro said, extending his hand toward the sheep, which the villagers were herding into pens at the far end of the village. "We always go for salt in the spring." Even from his distance Shan saw the hand was shaking.

Lin answered with another frown. "This is the twenty-first century, comrade. You are required to have certificates from the salt monopoly."

Lhandro shrugged morosely, and stepped toward the gate that led to his house. A salt pouch lay on the low wall. He pushed his hand into the open side and extended a handful of salt toward Lin. "We have some money. We could pay the monopoly," he offered.

The colonel sighed impatiently, motioned to one of the nearby soldiers. The man roughly seized the pouch and tossed it on the ground, kicking it with the toe of his boot so that both of the side pockets lay flat. He produced a short bayonet from his belt and probed the contents of the open pocket, then looked up expectantly at Lin, who nodded. The soldier began stabbing the still-sealed second pocket, ripping apart its tight woolen weave, spilling the precious salt onto the ground.

"It is special salt," a woman's voice interjected. Shan saw Nyma step past the door opening to stand by Lhandro. "It could heal you," she declared to Lin, looking straight into the colonel's eyes.

"I'm not sick."

Nyma stared back, as if she didn't agree, but would not argue.

"You should be careful," Lin said icily. "Someone might mistake you for a nun. Yesterday Public Security arrested someone a few miles from here. Under his coat he wore a maroon band on his sleeve. He had a little piece of yellow cloth in his pocket."

Even from a distance Shan could see Nyma swallow hard. Lin meant an outlawed monk had been caught nearby, one reckless enough to carry a Tibetan flag in his pocket.

The tension became a tangible thing, like a frigid cloud in the air about them. Lin cast a gloating grin toward the American. "Even in America, Mr. Winslow," the colonel said, "those who commit treason are sent to prison." He gestured to the headman. "This man Lhandro knows about prisons. He had an old man with him, a former criminal who wore a lao gai registration." Lin's eyes squeezed into tight slits. "Where is that old man?" he barked abruptly. "And the one named Shan, the one who has no papers. They were not with you when you arrived with the sheep. If you are hiding them it will go worse for you when we catch them. And if any of you have something of mine," he said pointedly, "we will consider the entire village guilty of the crime."

There was another long silence as Lin surveyed the village with smoldering eyes. His gaze finally drifted downward, and he pushed the pouch of salt with the toe of his well-polished boot. "I am a simple man," the colonel said in a strangely frustrated tone. "I keep my world simple. There are those who belong to the new order, and those who are trying to. Everyone else," he said in a tone of mock apology, "has no place, and is owed nothing."

Winslow pulled the cover off his camera lens and Lin's face hardened. "The Qinghai Petroleum Venture," he said in a loud voice, as if he were making a proclamation to the entire village, "is prepared to give liberal compensation to all those who cooperate in building the new economy, in building the new valley. We are even honoring it with a new name. We have decided to call it Lujun Valley now," he said with a taunting expression. "I will be issuing orders for the maps to be changed."

Lhandro's head shot up and he lurched forward as if about to attack the colonel, until Winslow restrained him with a hand on his arm. Lin was renaming the valley to honor the Chinese soldiers who had destroyed its people a century earlier.

Lin paused, as if inviting Lhandro to attack, and seemed about to offer another taunt when he was interrupted by a booming noise, a distant, hollow repetitive thumping sound that echoed through the valley. Lin twisted about as though searching the derrick and the oil camp for the source of the noise. But it was not a mechanical sound. It was almost like a heartbeat, slow but steady. Shan found himself inching out the doorway, his eyes searching the outside wall. The deity drum was missing.

Lin's thin lips folded into something like a snarl. He gestured to the soldier who had stabbed the salt pouch, who instantly whistled toward the village. As the soldiers sweeping through the village turned he raised his left arm and clenched his right hand around the left forearm, then pointed to the west side of the valley and made a spiraling motion with his fingers. They were to deploy west, Shan guessed, and climb toward the sound.

"I will need to know about the men I saw with you," Lin said in a low voice to Lhandro. "There can be many ways to ask." He climbed into the nearest truck.

The drumbeat continued. In the distance Shan saw workers on the derrick standing still, looking toward the upper slopes. The few Tibetans who were left in the village had also emerged from their houses and were also gazing at the slopes, some with expressions of hope, others of fear.

The sound of the truck engines starting drew Shan's gaze away from the slopes, and he watched the vehicles drive away, not back down the path but directly to the west, across the fields of sprouting barley. A whimper rose from nearby and he turned to see a small figure huddled inside the earthen wall near where Lin had been standing. Anya had been hiding, listening to the colonel.

She gazed at Shan with wide, afraid eyes, then leapt up and ran down the village path, disappearing into the rocks and trees of the slope.

"Your drum," he asked Lepka as the old man stepped into the sunlight. "Where is it?"

"Gone, disappeared in the night," Lepka said with a shrug, and he placed his hand over his heart and closed his eyes a moment, as if seeking a connection between the drumming and the beating of his own heart.

"You mean someone from the village is up there?"

"No," Lepka exclaimed happily, his eyes wide, as if that were his real point.

Shan and Winslow exchanged worried glances and when Shan began jogging out of the village, in the direction Anya had taken, the American followed a step behind. They found Anya standing alone in the center of the canyon camp with only Lokesh and a handful of the Yapchi villagers. Tenzin and the purbas were gone. The sick strangers were gone.

"Up the trails," Anya said with a puzzled expression. "But these trails are for goats," she said, gesturing toward the end of the short canyon, where the slope was nearly vertical. "So many sick people . . ." she added, her voice drifting off. "They are fleeing. They saw the soldiers. They heard there are knobs at the camp. There is no healing in this valley any longer." The girl's voice faded again as she began staring intensely at a small hole near the base of a large boulder. She limped to the rock, then dropped to her knees and pressed her eye near the hole, as though she expected to see something inside it.

"He's so interested in Lokesh," Winslow said at Shan's shoulder as they both watched the girl in confusion. "Why?"

"When he found travelers from Yapchi coming from the south a former lao gai prisoner was among them," Shan said, his voice heavy with worry. "I think what he really means is that Lokesh could be a convenient suspect, could be arrested if no one else produces whatever Lin wants."

"You mean the eye."

"I don't think it's the eye anymore. Lin wouldn't trouble himself so over a piece of stone. I think what he wants is the one who stole the eye. Because whoever stole it committed a security breach."

"Dremu was going to steal the stone but the purbas stopped him," Winslow recalled.

Shan nodded. "They had other plans. They could have placed someone on the inside. Lin couldn't afford to let such a person escape. There would have been things more important than the chenyi stone in Lin's office."

"You mean Lin thinks the thief stole secrets. You mean they're looking for some kind of spy?"

Spy. The word had not occurred to Shan. But it had doubtlessly occurred to Lin. It would make sense. It would explain why the mountain commandos had come all the way from Lhasa, following a piece of a deity.

A figure rushed past them and bent towards Anya. It was Lhandro, and as he gently pulled the girl up he cast an apologetic glance toward Shan and Winslow. "Sometimes she forgets things," he said, as though the girl could not hear him. When Anya straightened her eyes were hooded, and she searched the landscape restlessly, without any sign that she saw them. "Sometimes all she can do is look for deities. I think it is another way they speak with her," he said awkwardly. "Sometimes we have to go out and search for Anya, with the dogs, like an old monk," he added, referring to the way some old monks might wander away in a spiritual reverie, or lose themselves while meditating on their feet.

Lhandro showed relief for a moment as Lokesh put his arm around the girl and guided her to a pallet. Then his eyes hardened and he surveyed the canyon. "Where is he? Horsetracks led into the valley."

"Dremu?" Shan asked. He had not thought of the Golok since seeing him ride away the day before.

"No sign of the bastard," Lhandro said. "He could be negotiating to sell it back to the soldiers right now."

"The eye?" Shan asked.

"Of course the eye. He knew exactly where it was. He ran away the morning after it was stolen. He knew the mountain trails. And he has helpers. We saw the tracks of three horses, not one." Lhandro looked back at Anya and Lokesh. "He will sell all of us if the price is right."

Shan walked one step behind Winslow as they approached the oil camp an hour later. The American had protested when Shan had said he was going with him to meet the camp manager, but Shan had insisted he would just go alone if the American did not want to accompany him. "Lin will pounce on you," Winslow protested. "He wants you in manacles."

"Lin is in the army camp, in those tents past the oil camp," Shan said in a thin voice. "He doesn't expect me to walk into the camp. And no one else will suspect me if they think I am connected with you."

Winslow had reluctantly agreed, but only if Shan stayed with him, and spoke only English, playing the part of an assistant. For thirty minutes they had worked on making Shan's clothes presentable, finding a nearly new shirt in the village for Shan to wear, over which the American had put his own red nylon coat. Finally, Winslow hung his expensive binoculars around Shan's neck.

The American began to whistle as they approached the derrick, and took several photographs as the workers waved, as though he were a tourist. They were broad shouldered, beefy men, Chinese and Tibetans, who smiled with pride and paused to pose for Winslow, their huge wrenches and hammers raised.

Two hundred yards before the camp was an open square of earth, the size of a large vegetable garden, where two figures knelt. They wore aprons, and one held a large magnifying lens as he studied something in the soil.

"Wasn't there last time," Winslow observed in a voice tinged with curiosity as they walked past the bent figures. "Guess the colonel lost a button."

No one at the camp seemed surprised to see the American. The workers who scurried about the complex of trailers and tents nodded briefly as Shan and Winslow slowly circuited the compound, or made no eye contact at all. Tall stacks of logs lay at the base of the slope where the logging was being conducted, a heavy gas-powered saw on a metal frame whirled and groaned as it cut the logs into long planks.

Shan was watching a huge diesel truck being unloaded of its cargo of heavy pipe, its engine idling loudly, when Winslow pulled him away. A young Han woman, looking out of place in a bright white blouse and neatly pressed blue skirt, had appeared at the door of one of the center trailers. She greeted them with a solicitous nod, then gestured them inside, into the fastidious world of the venture's management. Passing through a short hallway lined with dirt-caked boots and jackets they stepped onto a clean tile floor in a room furnished with two metal desks and a long sofa. Shan might have forgotten he was inside one of the metal boxes, except that all the furniture was bolted to the floor. Black framed, color photographs of famous Chinese landscapes—the Great Wall, the natural limestone towers of Guilin, the Shanghai waterfront—were screwed on the wall above the sofa. The woman opened the door to a small conference room. "I will bring tea," she announced, and left them to sit at the table.

The table was brown plastic, with simulated wood grain, as were the chairs. On the wall hung maps, many kinds of maps. Shan pulled a chair out, then found himself being drawn toward the walls. The oil venture needed precision in its geography. Three maps clearly depicted Yapchi, in sharply different scales, including one large one with a highlighted yellow line that wandered along the base of the nearby mountains to connect Yapchi to a red circle just west of Golmud, the large city more than two hundred miles to the north, the nearest airport and railhead. On a small metal side table there was a stack of single-page sheets that bore a reduced map outlining the route from Golmud to Yapchi, with landmarks highlighted. Shan took one, quickly folded it and stuffed it into his pocket.

"She's dead, Winslow," a gruff voice suddenly announced. "I'm goddamned sorry, but she's dead." The Westerner who spoke filled the doorframe. His hair, though close-cropped, was speckled brown and grey, as was the stubble of whiskers on his face, untouched by a razor for several days. His blue denim pants were held up by bright red suspenders. A cigar in a plastic wrapper protruded from the pocket of his light blue workshirt. The steaming liquid in the mug he set on the table was black coffee.

"My name is Jenkins," he said to Shan, extending a beefy hand.

Shan took the hand and the man squeezed his own, hard. "I am called Shan."

"Shan is helping me," Winslow interjected quickly, as though Shan had already said too much. "Do you know for certain, Jenkins? A man in the mountains said she fell. Said he saw it."

"Right off the edge of the world," Jenkins said, touching the map behind him at the same spot Zhu had shown them. "A thousand feet, she could have fallen." He turned back with surprise in his deep set eyes. "You saw Zhu? Here?"

Shan looked at the American manager in surprise. Had the Special Projects Director not informed Jenkins of his presence?

Winslow stared at the map intensely. "Did anyone try to find the body?" he demanded in a new, sterner tone.

Jenkins sighed. "You have any idea of the work we have to deal with here? I have deadlines. The goddamned banks are coming for inspection. Thieves stole half my garage tools last night. And I've got a horde of bureaucrats ready to descend in less than two weeks to celebrate our oil, even though I haven't struck it yet."

"Did you try to find her?" Winslow repeated.

Jenkins sighed once more and sat down heavily as the woman arrived with two oversized mugs of black tea. "The supply helicopter from Golmud. I asked them to do a flyover as soon as I got the details from Zhu. They saw nothing, and got called back to base. I'll send a team in on foot. I will. I promise I will. But not in the next two weeks. She's not going anywhere. Unless she went into the river, in which case she's gone already."

The big American looked from Shan to Winslow. "I'm sorry, Winslow. But plain talk is the only kind I know. I knew her before. This was our second project together. She was a star. My mother said the brightest stars always burn out early. I've lain awake nights trying to think if I did something wrong. I've written three letters to her family and torn each up. What do I say? Your daughter the trained field geologist, who had led field teams in Siberia, the Andes, and Africa, took a wrong step and fell? One of my Tibetan foremen said maybe she was called by the deities in the mountains," he added in an exasperated tone, and for a moment his head cocked at an angle, looking toward the wall.

"But even before she fell, she was missing," Shan interjected. He studied the room again. On a low shelf in the metal table was a stack of newspapers, the weekly paper published in Lhasa.

Jenkins drank deeply from his mug. "Sort of," he said, addressing his coffee mug. "I learned early on to give her slack. A strong head requires a loose rein. And if she had an excuse to be out of a city and in a camp she'd take it in a second, and likewise for being out of the camp to stay out in exploration. She got close to the Tibetans, started giving them English lessons. Once in a staff meeting she said America needed Tibet, whatever the hell that meant. She loved what she did, said she felt like an early explorer. She loved it here especially, even skipped days off to go back up on the mountain. Making new maps. The Chinese maps are rotten. Deliberate misplacement of locations, for security reasons, they say. Entire regions have never been surveyed. Who the hell knows what's out there?" He drank again. "There's another joint venture camp, a British one, two ranges north of here, about fifty miles away. I thought maybe her radio went dead, and she set out for the other camp. Or maybe one of her team got hurt and it was easier to take him out on the other side of the mountains. Could be a hundred reasons for no contact, I kept telling myself. Trapped in a blind canyon by an avalanche, maybe. When she left here the last time she left a whole pack of food behind, half her rations. Maybe she went to a village for food.

"But there was no doubt after an eyewitness report. Zhu took over, called headquarters from here. Filled out the report, in triplicate. The venture has forms for deaths. With ten thousand workers, people have accidents. Never had an expatriate die though." Jenkins stared into his mug again. "He sent in the form. Got me to countersign and sent it in. Just a damned bureaucratic exercise for them," he grunted. "Only acknowledgment I got was a memo from the company that said they will pay for a memorial stone for her back home."

"Did you speak with Zhu about the details, like how far exactly he was when he saw her fall, what he did to try to recover the body?"

"By radiotelephone. I was in Golmud when he came in. Faxed his report to me. Lucky there was any witness at all. Otherwise her family would be worrying for years. Now they can move on."

"Only Zhu though?" Winslow asked. "I mean didn't others on his crew see something, weren't they listed as witnesses?"

A low rumble erupted from Jenkins's throat. "He's the Director for Special Projects, for chrissakes."

"How long has he been with the venture?" Shan asked.

Jenkins frowned and stared at Winslow before answering. "Not long. Only met him on this project."

"And what exactly do Special Projects consist of?" Winslow asked.

"Whatever the company says." Jenkins shrugged. "He works for someone two or three levels above my pay grade. Someone in the Ministry, I think. Maybe his main job is investor relations."

"Investor relations?" Winslow asked.

"Watching over the foreigners in the venture," Jenkins said in a contemplative tone as he rubbed his grizzled jaw. "Probably wears grey underwear," he observed in a matter-of-fact tone. Meaning, Shan realized, that Jenkins thought Zhu worked for Public Security.

"Zhu brought in these Public Security troops?" Shan asked abruptly, in English. "To look for her?"

The beefy American manager studied him a moment before answering, and shot a peeved glance at Winslow. "Those troops are from Golmud. Sure, maybe Zhu called them. Public Security helps the ventures sometimes, mostly to enforce discipline among the Chinese workers. They never helped us look for Larkin."

"At the other camp," Winslow said, "how many foreigners are there? Would there be other Americans at that second camp?"

Jenkins shook his head. "British. The venture is very regimented. My American employer holds a ten-percent interest in the venture, and the venture has ten exploration camps. So we get to manage one camp. Same for each of the other foreign investors."

"Why here?" Shan asked. "What was it about Yapchi Mountain that got her so interested?"

"She was just a perfectionist," Jenkins said, "and the maps for this area were worthless, lots of holes to be filled in. When she worked a site she made a catalog of everything, wanted to know the surrounding geology for ten miles around and two miles deep. It's a compulsion for oil geologists. In our company they record it all, eventually feed the data into a big computer back home which models the data. Looking for new tracers, similar characteristics, indicators of the presence and type of oil. Geology repeats itself in strange ways. Information about a site in Pakistan might explain a site we're working in Alaska."

"What happened to the others on Miss Larkin's crew?" Shan asked.

"We change field crews all the time. Those who were with her that day, they were shipped back to the main base near Golmud, the operations center. Our hell on wheels."

"Sorry?" Shan said in confusion.

"An old railroad term. Temporary cities spring up around big construction projects. Attract all levels of the food chain, you might say. Booming for a few months, a year, then the whole thing packs up and moves on to be more central to the next set of big projects. We're in an exploration frenzy. Someone came from Beijing and gave a speech in Golmud to all the managers. We're opening China's west, we're the bringers of prosperity. Heroes of the proletariat and all," Jenkins said in a hollow tone. "First the exploration teams, then the drilling camps. Once we finish, pipe fitters move in and the camps move on." Jenkins pulled the cigar out of his pocket. "Mind?"

Winslow and Shan shook their heads, and Jenkins opened the wrapper and ran the cigar under his nose with a small sound of contentment.

"But Miss Larkin's crew," Shan suggested. "You could find them in Golmud, to speak with."

"Me? Hell no. Needle in a haystack. At any one time they have two to three hundred workers rotating through the base. Those men from her team, they could be in four different places now, hundreds of miles away, even shipped off to other provinces. Our Chinese partner has operations all over China."

"Do you have their names?" Shan pressed.

Jenkins lit the cigar, blowing smoke over his shoulder, out the door. He studied Winslow with a disbelieving frown. "You sure you didn't know her? A man might think you and she had—"

"I told you before," Winslow interjected peevishly. "Just doing my job."

Jenkins inhaled deeply on the cigar. "Okay. Some damned computer disc must have some names on it." He rose and stepped to the door, calling out in Chinese to the woman who had brought the tea. They conversed a moment, then he stepped back to the table. He wrinkled his brow and stared into his mug once more, then looked up at Winslow. "A lot of crazy shit goes on here. It's the wild west. It's the end of the world. Everyone is far from home. We're paid to go to some godforsaken place and pump money out of the ground, and we make it happen. Some things I don't totally understand. Not my business. Soldiers come and go. I hear things about people from Beijing coming in for midnight meetings. They tell me not to get involved in politics. So I don't get involved in politics. Nothing criminal about all this, just politics."

It was Winslow's turn to stare into his cup. "Why, Jenkins," he said at last, "would the word criminal come to mind?"

The manager's mouth twisted, as if he had bit something sour. "Just the way you talk. No other reason," he added emphatically.

"But how could you do this to the land when you have no connection to it?" Shan heard himself ask. The words leapt off his tongue before they crossed his mind. As though a deity was speaking through him. It is not your land, the Tibetans would say, and therefore you may ask nothing of it.

"Connection?" Jenkins asked, as if he didn't understand. But then he winced and his eyes drifted downward. "It's my job," he said in a voice that sounded suddenly weary, and Shan knew the American manager understood his question perfectly. "I heard that sound," Jenkins added, almost in a whisper. "It was like a heartbeat." He looked up at Winslow. "You heard it, too, right?"

They sat in silence for what seemed a long time.

"There are two people outside your camp," Shan said, "working on their knees in the earth."

Jenkins snorted and grinned at Shan, as though grateful for the change in subject. "One of the development banks is providing some big dollars for the project. Which means volumes of rules and criteria that have been dreamed up by bureaucrats. One is that we do an archaeological assessment. Someone kicked up an artifact and made the mistake of telling Golmud. Next thing we know two experts arrive with a letter saying we have to cooperate. They will catalog the site, write a report, and move on. Just more red tape."

"What kind of artifact?" Shan asked.

"An old piece of bronze with writing on it. Kind of thing any Tibetan farmer turns up twice a day." As he spoke his secretary appeared with a single sheet of paper with a short list of names. She looked at each of the three men in turn, and handed the paper to Winslow. Then she turned to Jenkins. "Don't tell that Zhu," she said and hurried away.

Jenkins took another puff and looked after the woman with worry in his eyes.

"If Public Security is here, why would you need the army too?" Winslow asked offhandedly.

"PLA often helps with relocations," Jenkins grunted. "They say it is good training for the soldiers."

A shiver ran down Shan's spine. Training for the soldiers. It was one thing the army did better than anyone else in Tibet. Relocate Tibetans. Rip apart the roots people had to their land, and to each other. Proclaim people to be refugees and move them to make room for soldiers or Han immigrants. Tibetans seldom complained. They remembered that the army had once relocated them with cannons and aerial bombs.

"You mean moving towns?"

"Sometimes. I heard about some village up in the mountains. Damned shame. No one said destroy it. Some hot dog in a tank started shooting it from half a mile away. Said he thought it was abandoned, said his crews practice that way."

"Practice?" Winslow snapped. "You mean find an old Tibetan building and blow it up?"

Jenkins inhaled on his cigar and studied Winslow closely, but made no reply.

A phone rang, with a sound more like a buzzer than a ring. A radio telephone, the manager had said. Jenkins's secretary called out his name. Jenkins stood and shrugged. "The venture will compensate," he said, and stepped out of the room.

Shan leapt to the metal table and lifted the top half of the newspaper stack.

"We have to go," Winslow said nervously.

Shan nodded, pulled out the paper dated the week after the stone eye was stolen, folded it, placed it inside his shirt, and returned the stack to the shelf.

As they approached the cleared patch of earth five minutes later the two figures in aprons kept at their work, one now lifting a plastic bucket to fill a round tray with dirt as the second slowly shook the tray. The dirt sifted out the bottom of the tray in fine grains, until there was a small mound under it. Then the man with the bucket shuffled back to the cleared patch and began refilling the bucket. He had nearly completed the task when he looked up and acknowledged Shan and Winslow. He was a Chinese, in his sixties, with thick black-rimmed spectacles and long thick snow-white hair under a broad-rimmed hat. His apron, apparently tailored for the task, had four rows of small pockets. From his belt hung a small nylon pouch, and a holster bearing a small hammer and two thick brushes. He cast what looked like a grimace toward them and returned to the bucket.

Shan wandered to the far side of the patch, where the man's assistant waited with the soil sieve beside what looked like a pile of coats. She was also Chinese, much younger, with very short hair, wearing a tee shirt that said, in English, Bones Are Us.

"Some Tibetans," Shan observed quietly, "think there are things buried in the earth that, once discovered, have the power to change the world."

The young woman cocked her head at him. "Mostly," she replied after studying him for a moment, "the things we find have the power to make your back ache and your hands blister." She accepted another bucket of earth, bending over the sieve with a business-like manner. A blue pottery shard appeared, which the man lifted and inserted into one of his pockets.

"The manager says you found something with writing," Winslow said.

The man looked up in surprise. "Your Mandarin is very good. Most of the foreigners don't even try."

"If you asked," Shan suggested, "some of the villagers might help you. It is a lot of work for only the two of you."

The man looked at Shan with the same curiosity the woman had shown. "They don't like us digging in their valley. The first day we opened the ground, they drove some of their animals over our dig."

"Surely not on purpose," Shan said in surprise. It didn't seem possible that the peaceful villagers of Yapchi would try to damage the professor's work.

The man shrugged. "No one is too welcoming." He lowered the bucket. "I am sorry. I thought you were more of the oil workers. They come and make fun of us sometimes, say we seem to be taking a long time to plant our garden. Or how they could move this dirt out in five minutes, when it takes us five days."

"But you don't work for the venture?"

The elderly Han shook his head. "Our university has a contract with the development bank. The cost will be deducted from the funds advanced to the venture. It is how the banks make sure the proper study is conducted before production ruins the site." He removed his hat and wiped his brow. "I am Professor Ma from Chengdu. This is my assistant Miss Ming."

As Shan and Winslow introduced themselves the professor stepped to the pile of coats and lifted them, revealing a wooden box that had the appearance of an old tool chest. He inserted a key in the padlock that held the box shut, opened it, and extended an object wrapped in black felt toward Shan. It was a heavy piece of bronze, two inches wide, slightly curved, with two rows of writing. The top row was Tibetan script, the bottom Chinese ideograms. Both scripts were heavily ornate, the Tibetan in the special ornate form traditionally used for recording scriptures and sutras. The fragments gave little sense of the original message. Until the communist government had abandoned the tradition fifty years before, Chinese ideograms had been written vertically, from top to bottom, so that the few Chinese characters that appeared on the bronze shard were not connected in meaning. The first character was *lao*, the word for old. The second said *yu*. Jade. The third, broken at the center, was impossible to identify. The ornate Tibetan script eluded him. He thought he saw the word treasure, but could not be certain.

"A samkang," Shan suggested. The bronze shard could have come from a large bronze temple burner.

The professor nodded. "As good a guess as any."

Shan tried to visualize a little Tibetan temple at the head of the valley, trying to translate its teachings into Chinese. The lessons, he thought sadly, had not stuck. He watched as the professor filled another bucket and Winslow carried it to the sieve. "Have you dated the site?" he asked.

"Two or three centuries old at most. There is a layer of char three inches under the surface. A wooden temple, once it burns, leaves so little behind."

"How large a complex?" Shan asked. Those who lived in the temple surely would have known how to find the valley's deity.

"Small," the professor said, pointing to a pattern of holes that radiated out from the cleared rectangle, which he must have used to gauge the extent of the char layer. "One central building, with a small walled yard."

"What happens to your findings?" Shan asked.

"We are allowed one more week," the professor sighed. "Then we write a report and send it to the bank. They have a form we complete, certifying that a comprehensive analysis was performed and that no unique artifacts of importance were discovered. Then someone puts it in a file and forgets it."

Shan studied the rigid set of the professor's jaw. "You've done this before."

"All over the Tibetan regions. Amdo. Kham. Tsang." He was using the old Tibetan names for the lands, not Beijing's. "Good summer projects for my graduate students."

The sound of a heavy truck interrupted the professor. They turned to see Lin's troop trucks driving rapidly along the western side of the valley, abreast of each other, deliberately destroying the spring barley.

Winslow cursed. "I could get on the radio telephone," he said, "tell the embassy that the army is interfering with an American investment project."

"Not," Shan said, "if Mr. Jenkins did not agree."

The professor studied the truck with a grim expression, settled his hat back over his head, and resumed working, as though the appearance of the soldiers meant they could no longer speak.

Suddenly Shan became aware of the drumming again, from high on the slopes, though it seemed farther south and higher than before. Ma paused, not looking up, just staring at the ground with worry in his eyes. Shan recalled Jenkins's strange reaction to the drumbeats. The sound seemed to tug at something inside Ma as well.

"Back to the village," Winslow said. "Right away."

But Shan hesitated, following the American's gaze toward two new vehicles that had appeared at the camp. A white utility vehicle with two men in business suits standing beside it, and a nearly identical black truck parked behind it. "Senior managers from the venture," he suggested. "You could make an official request, ask them to help in locating Larkin's work crew."

"Too risky if they don't—" Winslow began. But Shan was already walking back toward the camp. He heard a curse behind his back, and the American jogged to his side.

Two minutes later they were among the sterile metal trailers, Winslow looking for the new arrivals, while Shan wandered about the camp trying to determine where the Yapchi workers were housed. He inched along the side of a huge dump truck, until he was only forty feet from the white vehicle and the men in suits. The men were Chinese, and they were not talking with Jenkins or anyone else from the venture. They were speaking with the knobs who were camped near the army tents. With a chill Shan recognized one of the men. Director Tuan from Religious Affairs, whom they had left at the stable in Norbu. He leaned forward to inspect the small, elegant lettering on the door of the white truck. Bureau of Religious Affairs, it said, in Chinese only. And with Tuan were four of the men in white shirts who looked like guards.

Suddenly, out of the shadows by the army trucks, Colonel Lin emerged, striding purposefully toward the new arrivals. An instant later the engine of the dump truck that concealed Shan roared and the vehicle pulled away, leaving him in plain sight of the howlers from Norbu. He turned, but out of the corner of his eye saw Tuan dart to Colonel Lin's side. As the two officers conferred in low, urgent tones Tuan and his men began studying the faces in the camp. Shan walked as fast he dared without appearing conspicuous, desperately looking for Winslow, or at least a place to hide. He was just about to round the corner of the first trailer when Director Tuan called out in a shrill voice, "There! That's the one! The one who knows about both! Arrest that man!" One of the white-shirted guards began blowing a whistle. Tuan was pointing at Shan.

Part Three

STONE

CHAPTER TWELVE

There are moments, Lokesh sometimes told him, when the wheel of life spins at double speed, when the predestined lines of so many people converge with events important to each one that life itself seems to explode in a confusion of actions and sensations. Lokesh called such moments karma storms.

Shan was at the center of such a storm now. The howler kept blowing his whistle. Colonel Lin barked furious orders. Workers from both ends of the camp called out in alarm, some shouting that there must be an accident, others that saboteurs were in the camp. Shan bolted around the corner of the office trailer, desperately looking for Winslow. A horn blew, much louder than the howler's whistle, an air horn as loud as that of a locomotive. Workers everywhere stopped and began converging on the compound. The big flatbed truck began coasting away, spilling its cargo of pipes as it moved. The sound of the drum mingled with the noise, beating faster than before. And on the slope above, where the timber crews labored, a huge tree slammed into the earth.

Shan ran, weaving in and out of the trailers, wondering if he dared flee toward Yapchi Village. No, he would be in the open, easily spotted, easily outrun by one of the trucks.

Workers urgently shouted, warning others from the runaway truck, some dodging the rolling pipe, some trying to retrieve the pipe. Shan stumbled to one knee, but workers sped past him, racing after the truck. They seemed to believe the alarm had been sounded because of the truck.

Then, as abruptly as it had started, the horn stopped. The whistle stuttered and slowly quieted. A man called out in an oddly awed tone, in Tibetan, then another in Mandarin, and most of the workers halted and began pointing. On the slope above the camp, at the top of the eastern ridge where the road cut through, two figures stood in a pool of brilliant sunlight, staring down at the camp. A solitary monk and, at his side, a huge yak. The Tibetans whispered excitedly. Shan heard rapid, whispered mantras. Even many Chinese workers stopped and stared, some in confusion no doubt, but some perhaps in reverence, for in Chinese tradition few images were more hallowed than that of the old Taoist monk Lao Tzu walking with his ox.

The voices died away. Everyone seemed to be staring at the unexpected, inexplicable sight on the ridge. Only the distant drumming broke the silence, seeming more than ever like the heartbeat of the valley's deity.

Shan hesitated too long. Suddenly hands grabbed him from behind and pulled him roughly back against the wall in the narrow alley between two trailers.

"Here!" a woman's voice commanded, and shoved something onto his head. She pulled his arm into the sleeve of a green jacket. He stared numbly into the face of the young Tibetan woman, thinking he had seen her before, then Winslow was beside him and with the same angry look the woman thrust another jacket at the American. She tossed them each a hard hat. "Go! You'll ruin everything!" she cried, and pointed urgently toward the wooded slope behind the camp, then sped away, shouting to the furious howlers that she had seen the man running down the road past the runaway truck.

Winslow helped Shan into the jacket and pulled him away at a fast walk. The swarm of workers seemed to part for them as they walked into the open, past the troop trucks. Between them and the shelter of the slope were three army tents. But only two soldiers lingered there, tending a large pot on a cook fire. As Winslow led him forward Shan saw that the American's coat had a word on the back in big English and Chinese letters. Manager. On the helmet he was wearing was stenciled a large numeral one. On Shan's own head was a hard hat identical to those used by the venture workers. They passed the soldiers, who gave them quick nods, then rapidly moved up the slope.

After a quarter hour Winslow finally paused. He took off his helmet and studied it a second, cursed, then laughed. "Who was that masked man?" he said in English.

"I'm sorry?" Shan asked. He was busily scanning the opposite side of the valley. Gyalo and Jampa, for he knew it could only have been them, had vanished.

"A joke. I mean who was that woman who helped us?"

"A lot of Tibetans don't like knobs," Shan said. But he did know who it was. He had finally placed her face while they had trotted along the slope. He had last seen her at the hermitage, the day he had left Gendun performing the death rites for Drakte. The purba runner, Somo.

Perhaps it hadn't just been Somo who had saved them, they realized as they walked around the upper slope toward Yapchi speaking about what had happened. Somo might have released the brakes on the truck, but the air horn had been the signal used for emergencies, or for important announcements by the manager. The horn had confused everyone enough for them to escape. Winslow had been present when Jenkins had used it to summon workers to announce that they would be operating the drilling rig night and day, with double wages for all if they struck oil before May first. "There's a little box with a key lock," Winslow explained as he studied the compound and slowly grinned. "I saw Jenkins open it that day. I thought only Jenkins had a key."

They stopped at an opening in the trees and sat on a rock to let Winslow scan the camp with his binoculars. "Soldiers have the workers lined up," he said. "Probably checking every identity card."

"The soldiers will blame the howlers," Shan speculated, "and the howlers will blame the soldiers and the knobs."

Winslow replied with a dry grin. "Ain't it grand." The American studied the compound. "Maybe especially the knobs. They're pulling out." He handed the glasses to Shan.

He examined the camp in confusion. The knobs from Golmud, from the north, were indeed leaving, and in a hurry, pulling up their tents and throwing them into their trucks, loading equipment under the watchful eye of Director Tuan. Strangely, impossibly, Religious Affairs seemed to be evicting the knobs. As if Tuan was taking over for them, as if Tuan had authority over them. There was something wrong, something confused about who had authority at the camp, just as at Norbu. Perhaps not, he realized a moment later. Perhaps the only confusion was about who had authority over Shan, and Tenzin, and the mysteries that seemed to riddle the valley.

"You will be reported," Shan said in a leaden voice as he lowered the glasses.

"Maybe not. I've been thinking on that. When that Director Tuan saw you, you were alone. And he didn't see me at the gompa with you."

"But he was speaking with Lin. That's why he said it, said I knew about both."

"Both what?"

Shan thought a moment. "Tuan is interested in Tenzin or someone who looks like Tenzin. Lin is looking for the stone and its thief. His best clue is that a group of Yapchi rongpa was found a hundred miles south of here. Tuan saw me with Tenzin. Lin saw me with the Yapchi caravan. He meant both what Tuan is seeking, and what Lin's commandos are seeking. As if," Shan said slowly, "they are seeking different things. Connected but different."

Winslow winced. "Connected through you." He studied Shan, then surveyed the camp again with his glasses. "Even if they wanted to complain about me, what could they say? That an American diplomat was disrupting the oil production? That I am interfering with some campaign they have against Tibetans?"

It was Shan's turn to wince.

"Christ," Winslow sighed. "In the end it's always about that, isn't it," he said, as if just grasping the meaning of his own words. "It never stops, does it? Like some huge Chinese machine that was turned on so many decades ago, and they don't know how to turn it off. It just keeps consuming Tibet and Tibetans."

The drumming began again.

Winslow froze a moment then slowly turned toward the sound, his jaw clenched. "What the hell is that? Some kind of psychological warfare?"

Shan smiled. "A deity drum. I think someone is trying to call in the deity that once lived in the land here." He explained that it was Lepka's drum but that no one from the village was using it.

Winslow shifted to better see the slope above them. "Are you saying it's the one who stole the eye?"

"It could be. But there are lots of Tibetans who might try it, to call that deity back."

Shan remembered the strange way Jenkins had tilted his head, toward the sound. He listened to the powerful beats. It was someone with a strong arm. With a chill, a vision of a demon with powerful arms flashed through Shan's mind. Maybe it wasn't someone who was after the oil company. Maybe it was just the one who was stalking Shan and his friends. Maybe the dobdob had taken the eye and was now calling Shan to be punished, the way Drakte had been punished.

Shan saw that the American's gaze had shifted back to the chaotic scene in the camp. "Lokesh said you used to be an investigator," Winslow said after a moment.

"A long time ago."

"So what the hell is going on here?" the American asked in a hollow voice. "I came looking for a missing woman. And now all this.... What would an investigator say?"

"That investigator interviewed people to discover facts and fit them together to reach a conclusion," Shan replied quietly. "It never works that way here. In Tibet facts are misleading, hard to connect. The Tibetans don't think one thing happens because of another thing, they think everything just happens, because it was meant to be." He saw the confusion on the American's face and pointed to a bird flying between rocks below them. "That lark isn't in the air because it leapt off a branch and spread its wings, or because something scared it. It is just in the air, now. And in the now that existed five minutes ago it was in a tree. They don't see cause and effect, so it can be useless to ask someone why something happened. There is no why of action, there is only action."

After a moment Winslow spoke again. "But for you and me, and a guy like Lin, it's more complicated. We believe in cause and effect." He looked into his hands. "There was a woman in Beijing who loved orphans..."

"Lokesh says I learn things in a contrary fashion, that things should be learned in the heart before reaching the mind. But I must understand things first in the mind, by asking the why of them. Like why someone is hiding on the slope with a drum. Why tools get stolen from Jenkins's garage the night after the eye gets stolen from us. Why Lin is really in Yapchi Valley. Why that ghost lama is wandering around the mountains.

230

Why Melissa Larkin wanted to lose herself here. If we knew the motivation and sequence, we might know everything."

"Sequence?"

Shan pulled the newspaper from his shirt, the paper from the week after the theft of the eye in Lhasa. It was full of articles about the Serenity Campaign. But near the bottom of a middle page was a small notice about a security incident at an army office in Lhasa. An area around the headquarters of the 54th Mountain Combat Brigade had been cordoned off and new security procedures had been posted for all citizens to read. Most of its civilian workers had been dismissed. Four pages later, on the back of the paper, was another article which Shan read carefully. The revered abbot of Sangchi, creator of the Serenity Campaign, had not arrived to give a scheduled speech. Anyone who had seen the abbot was to contact Public Security immediately. The paper he had read at Norbu, reporting the flight of the abbot toward India, had been dated several weeks later. Tenzin had said he had been there when the abbot fled.

"Sequence," Shan repeated. "Looking for connections in the sequence of events." He pointed to the second article. "Like why the chenyi stone and the abbot of Sangchi disappeared the same night. And motivation, like what we learned from Tuan today."

"He didn't—"

"He told us he knows we are connected to the valley, and so is the one he wants, because he came here in his search. But if he was interested in the stone eye he would have been here before, or sent those men in white shirts. I think," Shan said slowly, "that Lin and Tuan seek the same person but the difference is that Lin is looking for him for what he did, and Tuan is looking for him because of who he is."

The two men looked at each other, then stared at the valley for several minutes.

"What did that woman at the camp mean—she said we'd ruin everything?" Winslow asked.

Shan had not realized the American had heard Somo's words but had not forgotten them. Somo was at the oil camp for the purbas, doing something she feared they would ruin. "I don't know," he said.

"Nothing is going to stop the oil," Winslow said grimly, as if he had begun to hate the venture as much as the Tibetans. "It's going to take a deity to do that."

They listened to the drumming for nearly a minute before Shan turned to the American again. "It's not something you should be involved in. You should go. The things that go on here, the things that are going to happen here, you can't do anything about." He realized bitterly that what the American said was true. The huge machine that Beijing had unleashed decades earlier was out of control. Or not out of control exactly, just embedded so deeply in the world Beijing had created that it was impossible to stop.

231

Winslow said nothing. He just gazed at the oil derrick, raised his glasses, and pointed. Several figures in chubas were near the derrick, sitting in a circle. It was the prayer circle, Shan knew. The Tibetans had taken their prayers to the derrick. Perhaps Lepka had told them of the bell hidden there.

Winslow pointed to a second group of figures, a squad of soldiers jogging toward the slope where Gyalo and Jampa had been seen. "I liked that yak," he said in a distant tone as though they were unlikely to see Jampa and Gyalo again. When he looked at Shan a strange anguish was on his face. "If I know about all this, and do nothing, what does that make me?"

"Smart," Shan suggested. "Pragmatic. A survivor. A foreigner who does not have to worry about these things."

Winslow took off his hard hat and examined the number printed on the front and back. "That horse left the stable, partner." He looked absently toward the opposite ridge where Gyalo and the yak had been. They listened to the drumbeat fading in and out as the wind ebbed and flowed. "I was at home on my father's ranch years ago when my uncle was killed by the kick of a horse," he said in a contemplative tone. "I got there just after he was kicked, when my mother was running to call an ambulance, and I knelt beside him, as blood starting trickling out of his mouth. He knew he was dying. He said he didn't mind at all, and no one was to harm that horse. He said if he had to choose between being a good cowboy and just someone who lived a long time, he'd choose being a cowboy every time." Winslow slowly returned the hat to his head, stood, and, without looking back, continued at a steady determined pace along the slope. They had another mile before reaching the village.

Shan gazed at the American, then at the distant, quiet village. All the villagers had wanted was the return of their deity. A great sadness settled over him. It was more than premonition he felt, it was a certainty of tragedy to come. No one could save the valley, for the world was in the control of petroleum ventures and Colonel Lins, who believed that everyone belonged to the new order or they belonged not at all. The American could pretend to hope, but Shan had learned not to pretend anymore. Lokesh and Gendun said Shan suffered even more than the Tibetans from men like Colonel Lin and what they did, for the Tibetans could accept it as part of the great wheel of destiny, but Shan always felt he should do something to change it, and therefore Shan would always live in defeat.

Winslow was out of sight by the time Shan began walking again. The rumble of the derrick drifted through the air, and the sounds of more heavy equipment. A new vehicle approached the derrick in a cloud of dust. He paused to watch it stop behind the tall scaffolding and shuddered again. It was a battle tank. It aimed its turret at the prayer circle, then shut off its engine.

Something inside shouted for him to run, but he could not, he could only stare at the very Tibetan stalement, the tank against the prayer circle. His legs seemed as heavy as his heart and he had to will each one to move again. After a quarter hour he was in the north end of the valley, where the wind drowned out the sounds of the machines. He paused for a moment, trying to clear his mind, then dropped to the ground in the lotus fashion, his back against a tree. There was a calming exercise, a meditation practice, which Gendun called 'scouring the wind.' Let yourself float with the wind, extend awareness into the natural world as a way of reaching the inner world. He needed to be scoured, he thought, he needed more than anything to reach the emptiness that brought the calm, and the calm that brought the clarity. He absorbed himself in the sound of birds, inhaled the scent of the junipers, watched a tiny bee float among yellow flowers, and saw a blue flower bow its head over an orange blush of lichen. After a few minutes a new sensation came to him; he explored it a moment before he recognized it as the smell of fresh paint.

Five minutes later he discovered the source of the scent, a boulder six feet high and nearly as wide, coated over its front surface with red paint. He paced around the boulder several times. The painted surface faced the valley, or more precisely faced the far end of the valley, the derrick and the oil camp beyond. Judging by the many spots of paint on the earth, the paint had been applied in haste, and there had only been enough paint for the front, facing the valley. He was certain it had not been there the day before, or even that morning. It would have stood out in his mind, not merely because of the bright color, but because he had seen such rocks before, usually with faded paint, old paint being overtaken by lichen. In traditional Tibet such painted rocks indicated the home of a protector deity.

He reached out to touch the painted surface and found it tacky, still not fully dry. He searched the base of the rock on his hands and knees. There was no loose soil where a piece of stone might have been buried. There was nothing on the top except a small pile of owl pellets. Someone could have painted the rock to taunt the Chinese. Someone could have painted it to invite a deity to take notice of what was happening in the valley. Someone could have painted it to try to draw a deity back to its eye.

The grass in front of the rock was pressed smooth. He considered the position, with its long open view to the oil camp, and the way the adjacent rocks were arranged in a V shape, ending with the red boulder. Before painting the rock the drummer had sat here, using the rocks to amplify and direct the sound toward the camp.

He walked the ground around the red rock in increasingly wider circles. There was no sign of a horse, only a few bootprints. It could have been, and probably was, only one person on foot. One person carrying a small pot of red paint, and a drum.

A hand on the back of the rock, he paused and closed his eyes. There seemed to be another sound, or at least the remnants of a sound, an odd rushing, as of wind. But there was no wind in that moment. It was like a groan, or perhaps a distant rumbling, or a muffled roar from somewhere closer. Then, abruptly, the drumming began again on the slope above him. He opened his eyes and ran, desperately seeking the source, until he reached the foot of a high cliff and realized the sound came from still higher, inaccessible without circling far around the face of the rock.

He gazed with foreboding back at the red rock. Perhaps, he thought, no one in the oil camp would understand. The soldiers would probably not recognize the significance of a red stone. But then he recalled the latest arrivals at the camp. The howlers would know. The howlers would despise the rock.

The small canyon behind Yapchi was deserted when he reached it. In the village he discovered Winslow on a bench against one of the pressed-earth walls, writing in a tablet of paper, a line of villagers beside him.

"Names and identity-card numbers," he announced when he noticed Shan's inquiring gaze. "If people disappear this goes to the United Nations Commission on Human Rights. The venture at least has to be accountable for the people it dispossesses."

Shan watched as villagers began filing out of the old wooden house, Lhandro at the door clasping hands with each of them as they departed. He walked to the gate of the house and waited until, the last of the villagers gone, Lhandro joined him. The village headman did not know who had painted the rock and was not aware of any red paint in the village. "Our people are saying it is a sign," he said with a flutter of hope, as if he were not certain himself.

"A sign, at least, that the thief may have brought the eye to the valley," Shan observed.

The headman brightened momentarily, then nodded solemnly.

"There was a sound up there, not the drum," Shan said. "Not the drum. A rushing like wind, but not wind."

Lhandro nodded again and began studying the slopes "People say there are portals on Yapchi Mountain, to the bayal. Maybe that is what happened to Gyalo and Jampa," he added pointedly, as though they may have disappeared into one of the hidden lands.

After a few minutes he invited Shan into the quiet house, where they drank tea and ate cold dumplings with Lhandro's parents as Shan explained Professor Ma's project. None of the villagers had known of an old temple, not even in legends. "Dig anywhere in Tibet and you will find something eventually," Lepka said with a sigh. He was stroking the tiny lamb, which lay cradled in his lap.

"Could it be," Shan wondered, "that the deity resided there once? In a small gompa?"

"There has never been a gompa here," the old man said again, in a stern tone. He turned to contemplate the photograph on the altar.

Shan studied the old man. Had he been told the words the oracle had spoken on the mountain? *In my mountains, in my heart, in my blood,* the strange hollow voice in Anya had said. *Bind them, bind them, bind them,* the voice had said, as though speaking of wounded people. *So many dead, so many to die.* What would the words mean to Lepka?

But the old man was no longer listening, no longer part of the conversation. He had joined his wife at the altar, where they had begun chanting their beads.

Shan stepped outside to find a small cluster of people at the far end of the village, past Winslow's bench. Some were on the ground beside an open blanket of yak hair felt, and villagers were dumping baskets of barley grain into the blanket. Some dropped khatas onto the blanket with the grain, and others dropped pots and kettles near the blanket. As the villagers noticed Shan they greeted him with hopeful expressions and stepped back from the blanket. Lokesh sat helping Nyma tie the handles of the pots together. On his old friend's lap was a pencil stub and a long sheet of paper bearing several lines in Lokesh's hand.

His old friend grinned and patted the ground beside him. "I have begun it," Lokesh said in a satisfied tone as he noticed Shan's interest in the paper. "My message to the Chairman in Beijing."

Shan clenched his jaw and stared at the paper. He had begun to think Lokesh had forgotten about his strange pilgrimage to the capital.

"I will read it to him, to that supreme chairman," the old man said with an uncharacteristic edge of stubbornness in his voice. "We will drink tea together and I will explain the way of things in Tibet. I am sure he does not understand."

Shan returned his friend's gaze. It was a new side to Lokesh, the challenge in his eyes, the resistance in his voice. He was warning Shan in his way, for he feared Shan might argue. But Shan turned away and surveyed the landscape, listening to the rumble of the derrick and the distant, defiant beating of the drum. "I am sure he does not understand," Shan agreed.

Shan joined in the packing of the supplies, which were doubtlessly for those who had fled into the mountains. One of the Yapchi women started singing a soulful song. Another knelt behind a young girl and began braiding her hair. From where they sat on the lower slope the village appeared serene and the sound of the derrick was obscured by the song. It had the air of a festival outing, of a picnic.

Suddenly the serenity was shattered by a loud boom, like thunder, and an odd whistling noise in the sky. The woman stopped singing, looking up with a puzzled grin at first, as though someone was playing a prank, or lighting fireworks. Then, several hundred yards away, the slope exploded. "Anya!" Nyma cried out, and ran toward the village.

Moments later Shan found Lhandro at the northern entrance to the village. The headman stared forlornly toward the vehicle now sitting halfway between the village and the derrick. It spat fire, the thunder erupted again, the whistling returned, and the slope exploded again. The tank had advanced and was attacking the deity stone.

"They told us some young officer is training his men," Shan said, as though it might give comfort. But there seemed to be no other words to say. Two more shells were fired, and when the smoke cleared on the slope the deity stone was gone. Not just the stone—an entire patch of the slope was gone, the trees and lichen rocks replaced by a patch of smoldering, shattered earth. The tank spun about and began its slow course back toward the oil camp.

No one spoke of the incident, although some of the older villagers seemed unable to move, and only stared mournfully at the smoking patch of earth. With a stab of pain Shan realized they might have concluded another deity had tried to join them, and been killed by the Chinese. Slowly the village went back to its work. Shan watched, perplexed, as Lhandro's mother and Nyma began hanging scraps of cloth from the sills of windows across to the pen walls or to the ground, anchored with stones. Some were khatas, others small prayer flags. Several villagers were sweeping the entrances to their houses, some even washing the walls. One man held a can of black paint and was painting in huge script, inscribing the mani mantra along the front of his house. Between two houses Shan found a dozen of the villagers in a circle, offering mantras. It was a familiar scene to Shan, sad and uplifting at the same time, the way battles were fought between the Chinese and the Tibetans. Prayer flags and mantras against battle tanks.

As if to complete the festive air, Lhandro ordered a large fire to be ignited in the center of the path, near the entrance to the village. His mother and wife brought a large pot and an urn of butter and set about to make tea for the entire village. They would use the new salt, Lhandro proclaimed, and his mother brought out an old dongma that had been used to churn tea when Lepka was a boy.

As they drank the tea the headman's father told a story, passed down through many generations, of how their house had been built—a long story replete with details of how the strongest trees had been chosen, with prayers spoken to each tree before it was cut; and how the clan members had gone high in the mountains, above the trees to where glaciers lived, to bring rocks back for the foundation, because they had lived so close to the sky deities and knew the language of the wind and could tell it to blow gently over the valley.

A remote sort of happiness settled over the village, a contentment edged with anticipation. Shan saw more than one of the villagers wipe away tears, and several more joined in the cleaning of the houses. The group that lingered by the fire began a new song, softly at first, then growing vigorous, even loud. Lokesh looked at Shan with puzzled eyes. It was, Shan realized, one of Lokesh's traveling songs, a pilgrim's song, a song of lonely wanderers.

236

When the army trucks appeared again, winding their way slowly up the valley, no one in the village seemed surprised. Lhandro sighed, and helped his father back into the house. "They will search in earnest this time," the headman said to Shan and Lokesh, handing Shan his drawstring bag. "You must go up the slope. You have done all you could do here. Take the trail Anya brought you on, from Chemi's village. Someone will find you."

Above them, already on the trail, Winslow waved and turned away at a jog. But they didn't follow. Shan and Lokesh stopped in the shadow of the first large tree above the village and watched as the trucks arrived. The first vehicle turned around, so its rear cargo bay was facing the village path. A soldier pulled back the canvas cover, revealing a dozen soldiers in combat gear. Shan took a step forward, a chill creeping down his spine. Colonel Lin climbed out from the cab of the truck and up into the bay, the soldiers still sitting, as though waiting for a command, and raised a bullhorn to his mouth.

"Citizens of Lujun Valley," he began, and with a sinking heart Shan saw that Lin was reading from a prepared script. "You have been honored to participate in the great economic opening of these lands by the people's government." Lin paused and even from his position two hundred feet away Shan saw a frown on his face. "A new sun is rising, and all the peoples of China embrace you today." Shan remembered his bag, and pulled out his battered field glasses.

The people of the village had stopped their work, stopped their singing and their mantras to gather in the central path, several moving to stand at Lhandro's back as the headman positioned himself between the trucks and the village. A figure emerged from the first house, leaning on a staff, a burlap sack over his shoulder. It was Lepka, walking straighter and with more strength than Shan had seen before in the man. He stepped to his son's side as the soldiers from the second truck produced a folding table and chair and set them up near the entrance to the village, forty feet from Lhandro. A man in one of the green nylon jackets appeared, carrying a clipboard, and settled into the chair. Two men in white shirts appeared and unfolded a small banner fixed to two poles. Serene Prosperity it said in red letters.

"There are new communities, with water pipes and electricity, waiting for you. You may cast off the last chains of feudalism." Lin lowered the paper with an impatient scowl. "You people are being relocated," he barked. "The village is being requisitioned by the 54th Mountain Combat Brigade on behalf of the oil venture. Some of you may obtain jobs in the venture and live in company housing. The others will be moved to one of the new cities." Lin meant the soulless complexes of cinderblock housing with tin roofs that Beijing built around factory complexes. There would be no barley fields, no livestock, no caravans to Lamtso, no elegant wooden houses infused with prayer.

237

"You did not ask us," Lhandro called back. Strangely, his father bent and lifted a thick flaming branch from the fire and held it at his side, like a weapon.

"Of course we did," Lin shot back. "The venture asked the District Council. They approved on your behalf. They are your political representatives."

The wind had died. Lhandro's words came as clearly as those Lin spoke though his bullhorn. "The District Council is all Chinese. They have never been to Yapchi Valley," the headman shouted. "We demand to speak to the Council."

Lin smiled icily. "Be careful what you ask for, comrade."

"No one asked the land," a thin but strong voice called out. "No one asked the land if it wanted to give up its blood, so Chinese could run their cars in Beijing." It was Lepka. Other villagers reached into the fire and lifted burning sticks, like torches. They had no weapons. Surely, Shan thought, they didn't believe they could rid themselves of the army simply by burning two trucks. Even if they tried the soldiers would cut them down. He lowered the glasses and took an anxious step forward.

Lin glared at Lepka, turned and snapped out a command. The soldiers on the benches beside him leapt out and instantly formed a tight rank in front of their colonel.

"You will assemble in a line by that wall," he commanded the villagers. "Have identity cards ready. You will approach the table one at a time."

The villagers did not move.

"You will form a line!" Lin shouted, throwing down the bullhorn. He unsnapped the cover on his holster and his hand settled over the butt of his automatic pistol.

Lepka slowly moved, not toward the table but back toward his house. He began to sing again, in a loud, reedy voice that carried up the slopes. The lonely pilgrim's song. Shan was confused. What was in the bag at his shoulder? It had the shape of a thin box with sharp edges. Other villagers joined in the song and began wandering back among the houses. A woman ran forward and wiped a window clean. Another woman appeared at a doorway, paused to hang a long brown cloth on a peg by the door, and darted around the house.

Two soldiers stepped along the wall near Lhandro, as though to rush past him to grab one of the villagers.

Lhandro raised his hand, and stepped forward to the wall to block the soldiers. Shan saw that he had one hand wrapped around his gau. "Yapchi Village," Lhandro proclaimed in a loud, calm voice, "returns your embrace." And his father threw his torch inside their precious wooden house.

"No!" Shan moaned, and lunged forward as the other villagers threw their torches inside the remaining houses. "We have to stop—"

But Lokesh's hand gripped his arm so tightly it hurt. "Because you and I," his old friend said, the pain obvious in his voice, "have no home, we may long too much for others to keep theirs." Lokesh had understood, not at first, but before the torches were thrown. "It is the only way they can speak with those Chinese," he added in a softer, quiet tone.

"That house is so old," Shan said, in a choking breath. "It is their temple." He pulled again, and Lokesh pulled back, with both his hands now. It was already too late. The dry ancient wood was like tinder. Flames were already leaping out the door. Lepka was hobbling up the path, not looking back. The sack still hung at his side. Shan knew what was inside now. There was one thing, out of all the treasured belongings in the house, that he would not leave behind. The photograph of the Dalai Lama.

The soldiers leapt forward as Lin roared out furious orders. The man in the green jacket pulled a portable radio from his pocket and began yelling into it. A moment later the air horn sounded in the distance.

One of the soldiers by Lhandro slammed a baton into his belly, and the headman fell against the low wall, then sprawled on top of it, clutching his abdomen.

Lokesh pushed forward to help Lepka up the steep terrain as other villagers pushed past. Shan stared at them forlornly. They had no hope now. The soldiers would easily overtake them on the trail and turn them over to the knobs. They had destroyed what had become state property. They had interfered with a priority project for the economy.

A woman paused, the large woman who had taken Shan into the village the first day. "Thank you," she said softly. "We'll have to find our deity somewhere else."

The words tore at Shan. They had given up their village, their valley. They were openly defying the army. And the woman had stopped to thank Shan. His eyes welled with moisture. "Your deity is still here," he said hoarsely, but no one heard.

For a moment a mad thought seized him, that he would climb the cliffs and stay, he would search every rock and he would find a way to bring the wrath of the deity down on the soldiers. But then he looked at Lokesh and the others struggling up the slope. They needed his help.

More trucks sped up the valley. Most of the villagers had already left, Shan realized, thinking back on the circle by the fire. The only old ones had been Lhandro's parents, who had doubtlessly insisted on staying. They had all known. They all planned it. They had lovingly cleaned their houses, the way a body would be cleansed for the death rites. The talk at the fire and the singing had been a way of saying farewell to their beautiful village. Someone rushed by to help Lokesh with the old man. Nyma, in the dress of rongpa woman, a tattered red scarf on her shoulders. A soft bellow came from nearby. Shan turned to see Gyalo and Jampa. Lepka laughed as Nyma helped him onto the broad back of the animal, and the

239

yak and monk moved up the trail at a surprisingly brisk pace, the old Tibetan lifting his hand high in glee. "Lha gyal lo!" Lepka called out and Lokesh, a step behind, echoed the cry.

There was still no chance, he thought bitterly. But Nyma waited, and hurried him through a gap in the high ledge that would have been wide enough for one of the utility vehicles used by the troops. She waved a hand when they were through and two figures rose from the top of the ledge. Shan saw the flicker of a knife blade, and suddenly a rope sprang free and logs and rocks tumbled into the opening, filling it to a depth of several feet. Nyma tossed in a small rock, turned with a satisfied gleam, gathered her robe in her hand, and trotted up the trail. Twice more in the next half mile, where the trail narrowed into tight defiles, figures appeared above them and tossed down rocks and logs to block the path. At the last one Winslow was on top, urgently stacking logs and rocks that were being handed up by a chain of villagers.

Below, no more than a few hundred yards behind, they heard whistles and angry shouts. Winslow hesitated, looking in the direction of the approaching soldiers, then began filling the defile, making the wild hooting sounds Shan had first heard when the American had ridden the wild yak.

"If they know we're on the trail, they will know they can intercept us at Chemi's old village," Shan pointed out. It made no sense. They had nowhere to flee to, no sanctuary to hope for.

"The purbas said it would probably be only Lin and his men. They said they think the howlers and the oil workers will not help," Nyma told him. "Gyalo and Jampa are far ahead by now. The old ones will be safe once they reach the gorge above Chemi's old village. It's like a maze above there, full of caves. The people are splitting up. The purbas said the army won't be that interested in pursuit, that the priority for them would be keeping the oil crews working."

But the purbas hadn't looked into Colonel Lin's icy eyes. They hadn't seen the way he had looked at Lokesh and Lhandro when they had first met, or witnessed his furious explosion when the houses had begun to burn.

He waited as Winslow climbed down from the rocks. "You should go. Run ahead. Help Lokesh if you can."

Winslow frowned, then cursed and nodded slowly. "Adios, partner." He set off at a quick pace up the mountain, leaving Shan alone with Nyma. Shan looked after the strange American. Not only did he not understand the man's last words, he wasn't even sure why the American was there. Melissa Larkin was dead, and Winslow was due back at his embassy.

Someone called out from the rocks below. To his amazement Lhandro emerged, wearing one of the company's green jackets and a safety helmet. It was the jacket Somo had given Shan, the village headman quickly explained as he nervously scanned the slope below. He had hidden it on the other side of the wall, with the hat. In the confusion after the fires started he had rolled over the wall, on top of the jacket, and lain as if unconscious. Minutes later, when the trucks of workers arrived to fight the fires, he slipped on the jacket and hat and mingled with the workers.

They jogged slowly on, the last of the fugitives. Lhandro pulled ahead of them, telling them to stay in the gorge as he set off to find the other villagers. Thirty minutes later they paused at the clearing that opened toward Chemi's ruined village. There was no sign of activity. But there was a sound in the wind, the sound of clinking metal. Shan and Nyma ran, hard, across the clearing and into the upper gorge as the metallic rumble increased and they heard the sound of voices on a radio. A rifle shot rang out. A bullet ricocheted high above them. The army would not want them dead, only in custody. They caught glimpses of figures ahead of them in the gorge, disappearing as the trail twisted out of sight. Then the high rock that towered overhead exploded a hundred feet above them. The tank was shooting into the gorge.

Shan paused for a moment to glance behind. Lin was there, in the gorge, his pistol in his hand, with four soldiers behind him. Only four. But four soldiers with automatic weapons would be more than enough. The soldiers would not shoot to kill, but one of their bullets could easily maim for life. A shot rang out, again over their heads, and another. Shan could keep running but a hundred feet ahead he saw Lokesh and the American, and between them Anya, frequently looking back, terror in her eyes.

The gorge narrowed and turned. They were out of Lin's line of sight, but they had no chance of hiding, no chance of climbing the high, nearly vertical walls to distract or evade the colonel. They reached Lokesh and Winslow, both of whom appeared near exhaustion. Shan put Lokesh's arm around his neck and kept moving, half-carrying the old Tibetan up the trail. Nyma swept up Anya and put the child on her back. They reached a long straight chute of rock and scrambled desperately for the far end. But halfway down it a rifle shot rang out again, then another, and another. Shan saw the shots hit the rock wall, each lower than the one before, each closer. The last one hit a rock a few feet in front of Nyma. With a groan of defeat she stopped and slowly turned.

"Treason!" Lin shouted as he jogged toward them. "Destruction of state property! Sabotage! You will never—" His words were drowned out by a violent explosion above them, then two more in rapid succession. The tank was shooting at the rockface. A hundred feet above them the wall burst apart, shattering violently with each impact. Huge slabs of rock sloughed off the face of rock above the soldiers, who did not look up but stared confidently at their prisoners, their guns leveled.

Lin glanced upward at the last instant. "Fool!" he shouted, and reached for a radio on his belt as he desperately leapt forward. But the debris was on him the next instant. The biggest slabs slammed onto the four soldiers, who had no time to flee or even cry out. There was a muffled scream and a spurt of blood, then the soldiers disappeared. The rock kept falling, groaning, shifting, and falling some more, raising great clouds of dust as it slammed into the gorge. Small, sharp pieces like shrapnel landed at Shan's feet.

Suddenly there was silence. The dust cleared and the soldiers were gone, buried under ten feet of stone. There was no sign except for one arm extending out of the debris at the front, its hand clutching a pistol. Finally the pistol dropped, and the fingers hung in the air, trembling.

CHAPTER THIRTEEN

A cloud enveloped them, a dry, choking cloud that swirled about them as if to warn that their world was changing. No one spoke. No one moved. Then the wind began pushing the rock dust away until it was like an eerie midday fog, thin enough for Shan to see the hand again. The fingers extended from the debris, shook and seemed to reach for something in the air, then gradually stilled.

Anya took a hesitant step forward, and another, slowly walking toward the hand as Shan and the others stood frozen.

"Run," Winslow said in a distant voice. "We should run." But the American did not move.

As the girl reached the hand she gently opened the fingers and clasped her own around the hand. The fingers remained limp at first but then, as if gradually sensing her touch, they returned the clasp, squeezing the girl's hand tightly. Anya fell to her knees and began a mantra.

Shan, still in a daze, found himself stepping toward the girl, lowering himself beside her. A moment later he sensed someone towering behind him, and looked up into the American's grim face. Winslow's eyes were fixed on Anya's hand, and Lin's fingers, desperately trying to hold on, as though he were falling. Shan and Lokesh began pulling away the rocks.

It was more than a quarter hour before they had Lin's body uncovered. Anya had not stopped her mantra, had even entwined her rosary through her own fingers and Lin's. The colonel's face was nearly covered in blood from a long gash that ran from his crown to his left temple. Otherwise he seemed unharmed, except for his right arm, pinned under a long slab of rock. Shan and Winslow tried in vain to pry the slab up, then Nyma began digging underneath it. In a few minutes they were able to slide Lin out, his right wrist bent at an unnatural angle, his hand purple.

Nyma rose and sighed. "A few minutes up the trail are some small trees. I'll get splints." As she turned and jogged away, Winslow picked up Lin's pistol. Without looking at Shan he emptied the small oblong leather case on Lin's belt that contained extra magazines, stowing them with the pistol in his rucksack. Shan stared at the American, who looked up as he retightened the strings on his pack and turned away with clenched jaw to tear his bandana into long narrow strips.

With her free hand Anya wiped the blood from Lin's face with the bottom of her skirt as Lokesh searched in vain for the other soldiers. Nyma returned in ten minutes, and in another ten they had the splints tied around Lin's wrist.

"He shouldn't be moved," Nyma warned. "It's a terrible concussion."

Winslow stood. "All we can do is move him," he stated in a flat voice, meaning no one could stay with Lin, and with the path blocked it was unlikely his soldiers would find him before dark. The American handed Shan his pack and bent, his hands on his knees.

Nyma nodded reluctantly, and helped Shan lift Lin onto Winslow's back.

Shan and the American alternated carrying Lin on their back, until at last they rounded a boulder and Lhandro appeared with two men from his village. Nyma quickly explained. The Yapchi men called their headman out of earshot, gesturing angrily at Lin and the mountains above them. Shan watched as Nyma approached them and spoke quietly. With hanging heads the Yapchi men seemed to apologize to her. They fashioned a rough litter by tying two of their heavy chubas together and began carrying Lin up the steep slope, not on a trail, but over the grassy mountainside toward a gap in the mountain that opened to the south. In an hour of heavy climbing, led by Nyma, they had crossed the gap and were looking out over the long Plain of Flowers where the ruins of Rapjung lay.

Lhandro paused, only for a moment, looking back toward his valley with desolation in his eyes. The village headman did not acknowledge Shan when he stopped beside him. "Our deity is truly blind. We proved that today," Lhandro said in a near whisper, and stepped over the crest.

Nyma and the men from Yapchi plodded on without explanation, taking a goat trail toward a tiny plateau a thousand feet below. Their eyes seemed glazed, their expressions frozen into masks of grief and fear. They had lost their serene village. They had lost their valley. Several of the soldiers who had caused it were dead, and the army would never believe its men had died by accident. Now they were carrying into their midst, to whatever hiding place Nyma was leading them, the demon who had brought all their afflictions.

It had once been a hermitage, Shan decided as they reached the plateau, but a rockslide had destroyed the little retreat. The front wall of a stone hut remained, with empty frames for a door and a window that had looked out over the abyss that began a few feet away—a thousand-foot drop into the labyrinth of gorges at the southern base of Yapchi Mountain. The remainder of the structure was lost in a huge tumble of loose rocks that rose halfway up the back of the wall and continued in a long sweep to meet the steep slope above. On the opposite side of the wedge-shaped plateau was a single gnarled juniper tree, its trunk over a foot wide but no more than eight feet in height. Its branches all pointed southward, toward Rapjung.

"I think they meant for us to go to this place," Nyma announced in a weary, uncertain tone. "They said the place on the south slope once used by lamas. I have never been here but—" Her voice choked off as a man appeared beyond the hut, as though materializing out of the shadows by the rock wall. It was one of the purbas from the canyon at Yapchi, the man with the tattered green sweater. He gestured them toward him with an urgent motion, as though he were fearful of them lingering in the open. He melted just as suddenly back into the rocks.

At the rear of the plateau, its narrowest point, the rockslide had nearly reached the sheer rock face of the mountain. But the catastrophe that had destroyed the hut had not annihilated the rest of the small complex, only buried it. A sturdy door frame stood in the rock debris, like an entrance to a tunnel. Beside it, facing the plateau, a wall of rocks had been skillfully constructed to appear as a continuation of the avalanche, hiding the entrance from all but those who stepped to within a few feet of the rock face. Shan watched the men carrying the litter enter the darkened entrance, then followed them into a low chamber with thick, closely set logs for roof beams, capped by sturdy planks and supported by thick wooden posts, as though its builders had anticipated the rock fall.

Half a dozen pallets lay unrolled along the rear wall of the chamber beside one of the piles of kettles and pans Shan had seen tied together at the village. Nyma ventured through a doorway that led to a room dimly lit with butter lamps, and motioned for the men to bring the litter forward. The second chamber they entered was larger than the first, perhaps fifteen feet wide and twenty feet long, with an open air hole in the roof. Two openings without doors led to small rooms that appeared to be meditation cells. An old faded thangka of the Medicine Buddha hung between the cells. As his eyes adjusted to the darkness Shan saw several shapes rise from the shadows where they had sitting by the back wall. Lhandro's parents were there, and Tenzin, with the three purbas who had been waiting for him at Yapchi. In a corner behind the purbas was the equipment he had seen in the canyon by the village. At the back wall Lepka was examining several large, very old clay jars that appeared to contain dried herbs.

Lokesh and Tenzin did not hesitate as Lin was laid on a pallet. As Shan's old friend bent over Lin's limp form Tenzin collected all the lamps in the room and placed them beside the pallet. Winslow appeared and produced his electric lamp as Lokesh placed three fingers along one wrist, then the other, then the neck.

"Why bring a hostage?" one of the purbas asked with barely concealed anger. "We can do nothing with a hostage. All he can do is betray our secrets."

Lokesh looked toward the door, then back to the fiery Tibetan. "I don't understand. Is there a hostage?"

"This damned officer," the purba growled.

245

Lokesh knitted his brow in confusion. "Ah," he sighed after a moment. "No one brought a hostage. We brought a man who needs our compassion."

The purba with the green sweater, who had been speaking with Winslow, turned to Shan in disbelief. "You took him out of the rocks? You dug him out of his own grave?"

Lhandro's father hobbled over, lowered himself to the floor, and began helping Lokesh as he washed Lin's face, rinsing the cloth in a bowl of water and wringing it out for Lokesh. "You should be grateful to this man," the aged rongpa said.

"Grateful?" the purba spat.

"He is the one who made everyone run so fast. If he had not," Lepka said, "some of us would have been below when those rocks fell, instead of those unfortunate soldiers."

The purba groaned in exasperation, wheeled about, and left the chamber.

Lokesh toiled hard over Lin, washing him, massaging the hand of his broken wrist, repeatedly taking his pulse. As Nyma went outside to look for better splints, Lokesh looked into Lin's ears and mouth, then listened again, his eyes closed, at the pulse on Lin's neck and finally, removing the colonel's boots, at each of his ankles. He washed the wound on Lin's head once more, with a grim expression. Injuries to the crown of the head were especially unfortunate, for that was where, if it had to migrate from the injured flesh, the spirit would depart the body.

"I will make tea, for when he wakes," Lhandro's mother offered.

Lokesh's face was strangely clouded. "This one will not wake for a long time, if ever," he said, then rose stiffly and left the room.

Ten minutes later Shan found him sitting near the front edge of the small plateau, watching the sun set over the Plain of Flowers. Shan studied his friend, trying to understand the melancholy confusion on his face.

"The best healers at Rapjung were those who did not even begin studying medicine until they had spent years of learning as a monk, getting thoroughly familiar with their inner Buddha," said the old Tibetan. "They said that no healer could restore the balance of health in a patient unless there was also balance in the spirit of the healer."

Lokesh almost never complained, but when he did it was always about his own shortcomings. To think that somehow Lokesh felt himself at fault for not being able to deal with Lin's injury brought a stab of pain to Shan's heart. "I remember the lamas in our barracks saying once that if left to ripen to its true nature a soul will inhabit a body for many decades, then one day pop off like a ripe fruit," Shan said, following Lokesh's gaze toward the Plain of Flowers as he spoke. "But they also said that if left to grow in the wrong places spirits could became so rotten they will tumble off prematurely."

Lokesh offered a slow nod in reply.

They watched the sun disappear. The horizon glowed in a brilliant line of pink and gold under a distant layer of clouds.

"It isn't that it may be his time to die that disturbs me," Lokesh said quietly. "It's just that he is dying and I know no medicine, I have no words, I know not even what hopes to express for a man like that, or how to reach his spirit if he dies. There must be millions of Lins in the world and it pains me to so little understand them. I can make no connection with them. Not with me, not with the earth, with the world I know. How can I address the essence inside?" Lokesh sighed. "It makes me feel so incomplete, Xiao Shan. There can be no healing when such gaps exist."

Shan, too, had no words. It pained him deeply to think that the wise, kind old Tibetan was made to feel incomplete by a man like Lin.

They sat in silence as night fell. Shan began to realize how unique the little plateau was, sheltered from the north winds by the immense tower of rock behind it, open to the south, with a view for dozens of miles over the low ranges to the west and south, and beyond them, the starkly beautiful changtang. In Tibetan tradition it would be considered a place of great power. "The hermits who came here," he said at last. "Were they from Rapjung?"

"It wasn't exactly a hermitage. I knew it, or knew of it. There were two places on this side of the mountains, in the high lands above Rapjung. For centuries, every summer the medicine lamas came to them, because of their power as mixing places. There was a place they called the mixing ledge at the edge of a huge cliff, and another nearby called the herb shelf."

"Mixing places?" Shan asked.

"There are medicines that take hours to mix right, because special prayers have to be said over them, special sanctified tools used, with very precise portions to be mixed, in correct sequence, to keep the earth power in them. Once a batch was begun, the mixing could not stop. And for certain medicines the lama had to be in the correct state of mind, which meant they would come and sit in cells or sit out under the night sky until they reached the proper level of awareness. In the summer, I think, with that mountain wall behind to reflect the light, the full moon must shine on this place like no other. The mixing ledge was said to have a healing power of its own, as if the place itself was a medicine."

They watched the vastness of sky and land before them as it surrendered to shadow. Eventually a woman's soft voice called out, close behind them. "There is food."

Shan turned to see Nyma. She seemed uninterested in eating and sat on a nearby rock. "Where will we go?" she asked after a long silence. When neither of her companions answered, Nyma replied to her own question. "The Mountain Combat Brigade is on the other side of the mountain," she said in a brittle voice. "They will think we killed those soldiers. That dobdob is stalking us, probably waiting somewhere on the mountain right now. Down below is Norbu gompa, with all those howlers.

Some of my people feel such hate. Some want to go back and sabotage that oil camp." She looked at Shan. "They have no hope. They have only anger left."

"You know where that would lead," he warned, "if there is armed resistance, even the hint of it, the army will come and stay. Martial law will be declared, and a man like Lin will run the district, for years."

"Sometimes today I have felt anger, too," she confessed. "Our village. Our precious village . . ."

In their frantic flight up the mountain Shan had not considered why she had taken off her robe. To blend in better with the others who were being chased, he had assumed at first, but now he remembered the woman running out of the house at the last minute, pausing to hang a brown cloth on a peg. "Your robe," he said. "You left it to burn."

"It's not mine," Nyma said in a hollow voice. "I am finished with that lie. I am not a nun. If my people had a real nun maybe none of this would have happened."

A small, sad moan escaped Lokesh's lips.

"You can't—" Shan began. "They need you. . . ." But the words choked away as a wave of helplessness washed over him. He saw her turn her head toward the chain of peaks that ran to the west.

A loud hollow croaking noise came from above, the sound of a nighthawk.

"We could follow those peaks into the main range of the Kunlun Mountains. We could follow them for a thousand miles, follow them for months, maybe not see any other person the entire time," Nyma said, with longing in her voice.

Nyma's distant gaze caused Shan to piece together the mental map of the region he had been constructing in his mind. Suddenly he realized where they were, and he knew Winslow would soon reach the same conclusion. They were only two or three miles from where Melissa Larkin had fallen to her death.

Lokesh was asleep beside Lin when Shan and Winslow left the next morning. The American had been studying his map when Shan had finally gone inside to eat the night before, and the two men had not spoken, but Shan was only a few steps behind when Winslow left at dawn and began climbing the long western arm of the mountain.

"You should have stayed and rested with the others," Winslow suggested when Shan caught up with him.

"I need to see for myself," Shan replied.

"But Larkin is my business," the American observed.

"But this mountain," Shan said, "this mountain has many secrets still to tell us. Not just about Larkin."

"I thought everything was finished yesterday."

Shan nodded with a grim expression. "Some things were finished. But I think something else started."

The American's only response was to point to a massive blue sheep, a bharal, standing majestically on a ledge above them, leaning so far over the edge it almost seemed to be floating in the air. Winslow stared intensely at the animal and Shan remembered his story of being called by something to climb up a mountain and retrieve a small stone. The American began jogging up the trail, as if worried he was going to miss something.

Shan caught up with Winslow several minutes later at a strange nook in the rock, a slight recess in a high cliff face, where water seeped out of the mountain fifty feet above and flowed down the nearly vertical wall, not in a waterfall but in a broad, thin glistening sheet of moisture, nearly thirty feet wide, covered with moss and small ferns, falling onto a shelf of stone that appeared to have sloughed off the cliff eons earlier to form a sheltered alcove. Not falling onto the rock itself, Shan saw as he approached. The water fell behind the slab and flowed under it. The effect was of a perfectly level dry shelf bounded by a lush, living wall of plants, protected from the wind but open to the sun. More plants grew in pockets of soil on the shelf itself, plants he had not seen elsewhere on the mountain.

"Look at this," Winslow said in a tone of wonder, and Shan joined him on the other side of a large squarish boulder near the edge of the fallen slab. There were half a dozen flat rocks, each about eighteen inches high and a foot wide, arrayed in a semicircle before three evenly spaced indentations in the stone floor, each of them half-spheres about a foot wide and eight inches deep.

"Who . . . what was . . . how did this get made?" Winslow asked, with wonder in his voice.

Shan knelt at one of the indentations, touching its surface. The stones and holes were not perfectly shaped. They did not appear to be manmade, but they must have been—for mixing medicine. He turned to see the American rubbing his fingers along the flat back of the boulder that shielded the semicircle of stones. The surface, though partially encrusted with lichen, was covered with Tibetan script carved into the rock.

"The herb shelf," Shan whispered, and explained to Winslow what Lokesh had told him, how medicine lamas had once used the mountain.

Winslow seemed deeply moved by the place. He kept rubbing his fingers over the ancient script. "They knew so much," he said, "so much that we don't know. That we'll never know."

Shan sat, tentatively, on one of the stool stones, as lamas had once done. A gentle breeze stirred over the shelf, filled with unfamiliar smells. He smelled something like mint, and something like fennel, mixed with more acrid odors. The power of the place hung over it like a mist, though not in any frightening way. He felt strangely relaxed, and intensely aware. It was a place where healing began.

Winslow called Shan to a patch of moss below the shelf. It had been pressed down recently, by feet, and by reclining bodies.

"Two people," the American said as he squatted by the moss to study it. "Not last night, but recently." He turned and scanned the landscape urgently. Above Rapjung, in a small meadow less than five miles from where they now stood, they had seen two people who sought herbs, the ghost lama and his attendant. The American sprang up and began walking quickly, almost jogging, up the trail.

Twenty minutes later Winslow stopped and looked at a patch of snow high on the slope above them. "Why would Zhu hide?" he asked abruptly. "Why would he sneak around in the mountains without telling Jenkins?" He moved on, without waiting for a reply, walking rapidly until they reached the crest of the long ridge they climbed, where he flattened his map on a boulder. A high cliff jutted out to the west of them, forming a huge vertical wall that ran several hundred yards before cascading downward to the gorges below.

"We never asked where Zhu's team was," Shan said, "where they were when Zhu saw her body. We asked Jenkins about Larkin's team, but not about Zhu's." He studied the landscape. The cliff was the place Zhu had indicated on the map, the place where Larkin had fallen. Someone could have watched Larkin from the slope they had walked up, or from the flat ridge that ran parallel to the cliff, the one on which they stood. But not anyone on official venture business, for the ridge was outside the boundaries of the concession Jenkins had drawn on Winslow's map. Neither Larkin nor Zhu would have been inside their company's concession.

Half an hour later they were on top of the cliff, walking in grim silence, every few minutes pausing to gaze down into the shadows far below. Shan watched apprehensively as the American leaned out over the edge. In spots the footing was hard granite, but in many places debris of shattered rock and gravel lay underfoot. It would not be difficult for someone to slip and fall and certainly possible, even likely, for someone dizzy from altitude sickness to tumble into the shadows far below. Suddenly Winslow pressed his hand to his brow and Shan leapt forward.

"It's okay," Winslow said in a tight voice, pushing him away. "I took a pill."

"Did she have pills?" Shan asked.

"I don't know," the American replied, in a helpless tone. He stared down at a narrow ribbon of water that led away from the bottom of the cliff disappearing into the shadows of one of the gorges that twisted their way south.

Suddenly a patch of color caught Shan's eye; on a small ledge that jutted from the cliff face, a hundred feet away, twenty feet below the rim, a patch of light grey and blue in a pool of sunlight emerged from a tumble of boulders that filled a narrow fissure in the cliff face. He pointed, and Winslow darted away. By the time Shan reached him Winslow had already disappeared into the fissure that led to the ledge. "It's too dangerous," Shan called out. He saw now that the ledge had been formed when a slab of rock had cleaved away from the cliff and wedged itself in the fissure. It could be balanced there, for all he knew, ready to slide away under the pressure of a few more pounds of weight.

But Winslow was already on the ledge by the time Shan climbed into the fissure, and did not acknowledge Shan until he joined him on the tiny unprotected ledge. Shan shuddered as he saw how pale Winslow had become, and followed his gaze toward a body in the rocks. It was a dead bharal, one of the rare blue sheep that were nearing extinction. The animal had probably been dead a week, though it was hard to tell in the dry, cold air.

Winslow reached out to stroke the huge horns. "I thought..." the American began, then his voice drifted away. "I thought they never fell, a sheep like this, I thought their hooves gripped the rock."

Shan inched beside him and pointed to a patch of brown in the animal's neck, where the hair was matted together. "It didn't kill itself by falling," he said. "It was shot."

"Shoot it and leave it here? Who would..." Winslow's voice drifted again. After a long silence he stroked the horns again, then placed a tentative fingertip on the rich coat between the animal's ears. "I was sitting in the airport with a Tibetan bureaucrat, waiting while one of those bodies was loaded on a plane. He thought my job was very funny. He said the one thing Tibet is about, has always been about, is impermanence, and people should know that before coming." Winslow seemed to be trying to explain something to the sheep. "Afterwards I realized he thought it was amusing that people were surprised by impermanence." He began stroking the sheep between the ears, as if it needed comforting.

It felt as though they could not leave the dead animal, as though the beautiful sheep that had died alone, snatched unsuspecting from life in one cruel instant, deserved more. Shan considered the position of the body and the cliff above. The bharal had been on the top of the cliff, at the edge, surveying its domain, not knowing of the ways, until the last instant, when the ways of men had caught up with it.

"Larkin didn't do this," Winslow said, as if he knew the woman.

"No," Shan agreed. "Someone else was here."

The shot had been clean, probably with a high-powered rifle with a telescopic sight. It had not been made by a hunter, for the body could have been easily retrieved. It had been whimsy that had killed the beautiful creature, the act of one who killed because he could kill, a casual act by one who had snapped off a quick shot, laughed, and moved on.

They exchanged a grim glance and when Winslow rose it seemed he had a great weight on his back. He held onto the side of the fissure as though having trouble standing.

"We should do something," the American said, the helplessness back in his voice.

Shan did not reply, but began building a cairn on a flat rock above the sheep's head, exposed to the light and the wind. Working in silence, in ten minutes they had built a narrow two-foot cairn. Shan remembered the old khata, still in his pocket from where he had retrieved it above the oil camp, and anchored it under the top stone.

Winslow nodded solemnly and closed his eyes in what might have been a prayer, then climbed back up to the rim of the cliff. At the top he turned back toward the mixing ledge, apparently no longer interested in searching the cliff, and when they reached the main spine of the mountain he studied his map once more. "Yapchi," he said, "from here, if we could cross those two ridges—" He pointed to two long steep outriders to the north. "It's only four miles." He turned to Shan. "I want to know where Zhu's team is, where the other witnesses are."

An ache of foreboding coursed through Shan as the American spoke, for he knew Winslow was suggesting they try to traverse the treacherous terrain to reach the valley, which by now would be crowded with angry soldiers searching for Lin, but Shan knew the answers to their mysteries lay in the valley and the slopes above it. He offered a reluctant nod and gestured for him to lead the way. Ten minutes later Winslow stopped him with an upraised hand. Between them and the first of the ridges was a deep, impassable gorge not marked on the map. They would not reach Yapchi that day. The American began to turn back, then paused and pointed with a grin. On the crest of the ridge beyond, far beyond earshot, walked a monk and a yak, with the yak in front, as though leading the monk somewhere. Gyalo and Jampa had disappeared, Lepka had explained, after leaving him on the narrow trail that descended to the mixing ledge.

Remembering the bharal, Shan feared for the monk. He was helping the local people, Shan knew, transporting the sick, or supplies, or perhaps just looking for a good meditation rock. Perhaps letting Jampa look for a good rock.

"He's going to visit me, your friend," Winslow said suddenly as he watched the pair move toward the higher elevation.

"Gyalo?"

"Lokesh. He talked to me on the trail yesterday. He wanted to know everything I could tell him about Beijing. He said he had heard there were lights on the street that told you when to walk, and he wanted to know how to read them. He said he will be coming to the city in a few months, and asked if he could sleep on my floor. He asked if I could draw him a map to show where the Chairman lives."

Shan grimaced. "Lokesh doesn't understand."

"No," Winslow agreed. "But he said he is on the path his deity takes him." The American studied Shan's pained expression and shrugged. "I will do my best to watch over him when he comes," he promised, then moved down the trail that led back to the mixing ledge.

Anya and Tenzin were with Lin when they returned, the girl holding his hand again, Tenzin wiping his brow with a wet cloth. To Shan's surprise Lin's head moved, and his eyes fluttered open and shut. "He just does that," Anya whispered. "He doesn't speak. He doesn't focus. I am not sure where he is," she said solemnly. "He may not find awareness again," she added sadly.

But suddenly, as Tenzin wiped his brow, Lin's eyes opened wide. "You!" he groaned, and jerked his hand from Anya to grab Tenzin's neck, squeezing him, pulling him down. Tenzin, strangely, did not resist, even though Lin was clearly choking him. Then, as suddenly as they had opened, Lin's eyes rolled back into his head and his hand went limp, falling onto his chest.

"He has bad dreams," Anya said to Tenzin in an oddly apologetic tone.

Tenzin looked at the girl, expressionless, and began wiping Lin's brow again. A minute later, as Anya rose for fresh water, Shan knelt at the pallet and slipped his fingers into the pockets of Lin's tunic. There was no sign of Lhandro's identity papers. But he pulled out a folded photograph from a breast pocket, which he carried to the doorway to examine in the sunlight.

It was a grainy blurred black-and-white image, probably captured from a security camera. It showed two men in an office hallway, wearing the long work tunics of janitors and carrying buckets and mops. They were facing the opposite direction, but the taller, older of the men had his head slightly turned to look over his shoulder. The first man could have been Drakte. But there was no mistake about the second man in janitor's garb. It was Tenzin. In one of the buckets, Shan suspected, was the eye of Yapchi.

"You need to know something," Winslow said from behind him, with warning in his voice. He was pulling his binoculars from their case as Nyma appeared behind him.

"It's Lokesh," Nyma blurted out, stepping around the American. "Lokesh disappeared." He had left soon after Shan and Winslow had departed, Nyma explained, going down the narrow goat trail that led below, carrying only some cold tsampa and a water bottle, talking, seemingly speaking to people no one else could see. Shan darted out onto the ledge, pulling out his battered field glasses. He could see half a dozen trails as well as several long, gradual slopes where a man could climb without a trail. For the next hour he and Winslow scanned every trail, every flat rock where someone might sit to meditate. Shan ran down the trail where Lokesh had last been seen, stopping often to call his name. Nowhere was there sign of his old friend. Lin's soldiers knew Lokesh's face. If the colonel's men found him they would have no patience, no incentive even to give him to the knobs.

They would work on him, frantically, as long as it took, with any tool they could find, to discover what had happened to their colonel.

Shan sank onto a rock at the top of the cliff, fighting the dark thing that seemed to be clenching his heart. He watched the sun disappear over the distant changtang, losing himself in the dark, threatening swirls of shadow on the horizon.

Suddenly someone touched him and his head jerked up off his chest. He had been asleep. The colors were gone from the horizon. It was nearly dark. Nyma knelt beside him, crying.

"Lokesh?" he asked in alarm.

She nodded, scrubbing away tears with the back of her hand. "He found him. He went into the mountains and found him. Lepka saw them coming, and said we must be near a portal to one of the hidden lands. We didn't understand, but then Winslow saw the two of them on a goat path above. It was Lokesh, walking ahead of him, and turning all the time, as if always trying to coax him forward a few more steps, like a wild animal being tamed." She looked back toward the hidden chambers.

Shan climbed to his feet, confused.

"It's a spirit creature," Nyma said. "It has to be a spirit creature come to save us."

He ran, and stumbled, falling to a knee, picked himself up and ran again. Inside, the main chamber was like a temple, filled with a reverent silence, the air sluiced with incense smoke. Lhandro and his parents sat near the wall, eyes round and excited. The headman's mother rocked back and forth, as Lhandro and Lepka silently mouthed their beads. Winslow sat in the furthest shadows, his countenance lit with an odd, puzzled joy.

At the foot of the pallet sat Lokesh, and at one side Anya still held Lin's hand. Opposite the girl, one hand stroking Lin's forehead, the other reading his wrist pulse, was an ancient Tibetan, older even than Lhandro's father. He appeared frail and strong at once, thin as a reed yet vibrant and serene in his countenance. He wore a tattered quilted worker's jacket over an equally tattered maroon robe, and on his feet were old black athletic shoes that were on the verge of disintegration. A sturdy staff leaned on the wall beside him.

Lokesh gave a small croaking sound as he saw Shan, then he reached out and grabbed Shan's hand in both of his own. Lokesh squeezed it hard, again and again. His friend seemed to be in the grip of some strange rapture. "It's Jokar Rinpoche!" Lokesh said when he was finally able to speak. "From Rapjung," he added, as if the ruined monastery was still routinely sending out old healers. "From before. The same Jokar," he whispered, as though someone might think it was a different incarnation of the lama.

It was the medicine lama, the apparition they had seen in the herb meadow, the lama, Shan knew, who had healed Chemi. He had convinced himself that the lama had to be real, that such a man, despite all odds, was walking the mountains, a flesh-and-blood vestige of another world, not a deity or demon or spirit creature. But in that moment, as the lama turned and lifted his hand toward Shan, for some reason Shan could not comprehend, it seemed his father was reaching out to touch him, and when the lama grasped his hand Shan gasped, and felt his breath rush out.

"Lha gyal lo," the lama said softy, with a small, familiar smile, then turned back to his patient.

They sat in silence as the lama worked, incense filling the room, wind fluting around the rocks overhead. Lepka broke into a low song. The purbas stood in the shadows with wary, bewildered expressions.

Shan rose and stepped backwards into the shadows. In the flickering light he saw Winslow in the corner, still grinning. In the nearest of the meditation cells Tenzin sat alone, and apart, in deep meditation. Shan sat at the edge of the light and studied the lama, and Lokesh—whose face still glowed in wonder, reverence mixed with the eagerness of a young student.

Shan sensed that everyone in the room felt the same detached, otherworldly nature of the moment. It was indeed as though Jokar had come from another world, had been spirited there because he was needed, and was only visiting before ascending again to the deities. The lama was unlike any man Shan had ever seen, ancient yet ageless. When he had touched Shan, in the moment he had sensed his father nearby, something like a surge of electricity had shot up Shan's arm. Sometimes deities visit, Anya had said, and change people's lives forever.

Oddly, the lama was missing the little finger on his left hand. Only a tiny stump remained where one had been. Shan remembered Lokesh speaking of how the medicine makers in Rapjung had sometimes wielded huge cleavers to chop herbs and how young students, before understanding the rhythm of the cleavers, sometimes lost fingers to the blades. It must have happened decades ago.

Shan let his awareness drift and in his mind's eye he was on Rapjung plain, nearly sixty years before, and a young Lokesh was with his old teacher Chigu and with Jokar, as a young healer monk then, perhaps still in training. Behind them in the distance the graceful buildings of Rapjung rose up the slope. Geese flew overhead, and Jokar was exclaiming over a rare herb he had found. A lark flew and landed close by, and it became a boot, and Shan saw four stubby fingers pushed in his face by a man in dark glasses. Realization swept over him like a wave of sickness, and he was suddenly back in the chamber, breathing hard and very cold. He rose unsteadily and stepped outside.

Moments later Nyma caught up with him as he sat with his back against the mountain wall, looking at the sky. "What is it? Are you ill?"

"Not sick," he muttered.

She stared at him then took a hesitant step backwards as though she saw something that frightened her.

"You remember, Nyma, that morning at Norbu when we thought the knobs were going to take us?"

"I will never forget that terrible morning," she answered, and sat beside him.

"The knob doctor was impatient, he was unhappy with Khodrak and the committee, as if they were wasting his time. He had come for a purpose, from far away, not from local Public Security."

"A special squad of doctors," Nyma said, "probably from Lhasa."

"But not just arrived from Lhasa. Gyalo said they had been traveling hard, a long time, from the Indian border." Shan sighed and gazed back at the stars. "The doctor looked at that officer and held up his fingers. Four fingers. I thought he was mocking Khodrak, saying that there were only four of us when there was supposed to be five."

"But they wanted Tenzin."

"Someone wanted Tenzin." Shan nodded. "Khodrak I think, and Tuan. But that knob officer was there for something else. There was a reason that special medical team had been traveling with the knobs. For weeks, coming from near the Indian border. At Norbu Tuan said the doctors were there because of an agitator from India. I thought he meant the resistance, even the Tiger. But he meant Jokar."

"I don't understand."

"His fingers. He pushed his little finger back and held up the other four. A strange way. Most would just push the thumb down and show four fingers. But he used his thumb and three fingers."

"Like Jokar," Nyma said in a slow whisper.

"Not like Jokar," Shan said. "It *was* Jokar he was indicating. He was looking for the medicine healer with four fingers, tracking him with a team that could lure the sick from him with offers of Chinese clinics and hospitals, and find evidence through those who use traditional healers. The government thinks he has stirred up a path of reactionary practices all the way from India."

"If that's true," a voice said out of the darkness, "it would explain why the medicine fields are being burned." Winslow stepped beside them.

"But why?" Nyma protested. "The rumors, the reports. They make it sound like the government is seeking some terrible criminal. He is a healer. He is so important to Tibetans." She looked at Shan and her eyes dropped to the ground. She had answered her own question.

Winslow dropped to a rock and they sat in silence. A new vision rose in Shan's mind: Jokar in a lao gai camp, being flogged by guards as he tried to push a barrow of rocks up a hill.

"He only wanted to teach us again, to bring the healing home," Nyma said finally, in a mournful whisper.

In the morning, Lin was sitting up, leaning against the wall. He seemed incapable of speech, or at least not inclined to speak, but his eyes restlessly watched the Tibetans and his good hand restlessly searched his pockets, making a small pile of their contents. Cigarettes, matches, a whistle, a small key for manacles, and a tiny pouch of ochre cloth tied with a thread. Whenever Tenzin appeared in the circle of light cast by the butter lamps, the colonel pointed at him, sometimes making small grabbing motions like an angry crab, sometimes rubbing his eyes as if to see Tenzin better. Anya still did not leave his side, and she held a bowl of tea from which he sometimes sipped, though he winced whenever he lifted his head to swallow.

Jokar was gone. No one had seen him leave. Lhandro's mother said it was the way of such creatures, that they would just spirit away. Winslow thought he had seen someone walking on the western trail in the grey light of early dawn. Lokesh looked exhausted. He had stayed up nearly all night with Jokar, long after Shan himself had collapsed of fatigue onto a blanket. Shan watched as he tightened the strips of cloth binding Lin's wrist, then, deeply focused, as if unaware of anyone else in the room, pulled a bowl of brilliant white salt from the shadows. Lokesh placed Lin's hand, the hand with the broken wrist, over the bowl, and began rubbing the salt over the hand. It was Lamtso salt, the empowered salt of the sacred lake, and Lokesh was washing Lin's hand in it.

Lin did not react, but simply watched with the same rapt attention as Lokesh while the old Tibetan applied the salt with a kneading motion, then gently wiped the skin clean with a scrap of cloth. When he was done he folded what looked like a prayer scarf around the wrist, tied the arm into a sling around Lin's neck, pushed himself to his knees, and rose. Lin watched him expectantly, and raised his eyebrows, as if he were going to ask Lokesh to stay, but just watched uncertainly as he stepped away. Shan followed him outside to where Lhandro's mother was churning butter tea. The two men took their bowls of tea and walked to the rim of the plateau. Neither seemed to know what to say about what had happened the night before.

"So many times we have climbed up mountains because you thought you saw a giant turtle or a deity with ten arms," Shan finally observed. He had lost count of the number of times, in fact, but he never said no when his friend insisted they climb. "Last night, it was like the turtle was finally there."

Lokesh offered his crooked grin to Shan and nodded. "Those are the words."

"Is it true that you knew him? At Rapjung?"

"I was only a low initiate. But he remembers. We spoke for hours last night about Rapjung and Yapchi Valley, until Jokar wandered away and sat with Tenzin by that old tree. He remembers how I was always with Chigu Rinpoche, how Rinpoche had hoped I would stay to live at Rapjung for training."

No one stayed at Rapjung to live, Shan thought bitterly. "But he escaped before the army came."

"He had been called away by the Dalai Lama's personal physician. In a secret message, when the Dalai Lama fled to India. Jokar was one of the youngest instructors and they wanted him to help establish a new Tibetan medical college in India. All these years that is where he had been, building for a new future in India."

"It's such a long way to come. Hundreds of miles. He appears to have no money." Shan remembered the tattered robe and shoes. "Knobs have been chasing him." But he knew that meant little to Jokar. Once he was on the course intended for him he would be as likely to change it because of knobs as Gendun, or Lokesh. The Beijing Shan would have laughed when told deities protected such men. But there were times it seemed the only explanation.

"He said it is a pilgrimage of sorts," Lokesh continued. "He said if he had money he might be tempted to ride buses and go into towns. He has traveled on foot, always on foot, close to the earth. Eight months now, staying with rongpa here and there, sometimes traveling with dropka and their herds. Healing where he can. Uncovering old roots he said, as though the old ways were still in the land and in the heart of the people and simply had to be discovered again. He makes the old medicines when he can. Sometimes entire villages have sat with him through a night, to hear of the Dalai Lama and of the old days in Tibet and he reminds them of ways of healing they thought they had forgotten."

"But why come here?"

"This is where he spent nearly fifty years of his life, at Rapjung. He was sent there as a young boy while the thirteenth Dalai Lama still lived. In India, he was senior lama of the new school for many years. It was time to finish there, he said. I think now he wants the old school to be born again."

"Rapjung?"

Lokesh nodded. "He says he met other healers while walking from India, that they all know of Rapjung and many asked if medicine herbs still grow there. He said he saw the ruins, but he also saw new buildings." They exchanged a meaningful glance. Jokar did not know about the fire. "He said Tibetans must learn how to stay the same by practicing change." Lokesh paused and nodded again, slowly, as if contemplating the words. "The rumors must be true. Jokar must have come to take the seat of Siddhi, the defiant leader from the ancient tales."

"The knobs have spies in India," Shan said. "They would have learned about such a prominent lama embarking for Tibet to gather the people and restore an institution of the old order. They would consider it the gravest of sins against the government. It is so dangerous for him."

Lokesh nodded. "Duties," he said sadly. There was no need for more words. It had become their own shorthand. Shan had had the same conversation with Lokesh, and other Tibetans, often. Soldiers would do what they had to do, Lokesh meant, and the Tibetans would do what they had to do.

"He would have been safe staying here, for a few days."

"Who could presume to tell him to change his plans? He is visiting all the old places. The herb meadows. The mixing places. While he does so he will look for medicine for the sick colonel."

Shan considered Lokesh's words. "What does he say of Lin?"

"The bone at the top of his head was cracked. But there was something else, worse, from before the rocks fell."

"He was already ill?"

Lokesh nodded heavily. "Heart wind." The tantric medical system Lokesh and Jokar practiced believed that the heart-center was the intersection between the physical and spiritual beings. Not the physical, beating heart as such, but the center of the awareness and life energy. Heart wind meant stress on the heart center brought on by intense anger, fear, or other mental imbalances. Jokar would not address one of Lin's maladies without addressing them all. "There are medicines that could help perhaps, but in such cases all the imbalances are related," Lokesh said.

"Jokar says that heart wind seems to be the most common ailment in Tibet today." Lokesh's gaze drifted toward the trails. He, too, seemed to be looking for Jokar. "He said something else. He said that bringing Lin from the rocks to here, that was part of the healing, too. For everyone."

Shan weighed the words. Jokar meant that it wasn't just Lin who suffered an imbalance, that perhaps they all shared an imbalance, and that for Tibetans to bring a hated colonel from what would have surely been his grave may have begun another healing as well.

"Jokar says there was a small grey plant with heart-shaped leaves that grew on the slopes near Yapchi that would be helpful. He asked me if I remembered the ways of harvesting and mixing."

"I think you should find him, Lokesh," Shan said after they watched a flight of birds leave the mountain, soaring toward the Plain of Flowers. "You should take him to hide, stop him from moving around so much while soldiers are in the mountains. Take him and hide him. For weeks. Speak with him of the old ways. Write them down. For months, if necessary. Until the soldiers leave Yapchi. The purbas would help you."

His old friend seemed to consider the words a long time. "I would not know how to," he said at last.

Shan stared at him. Lokesh not only meant he would not know how to find Jokar, but that he would not know how to ask such a holy man anything. Shan thought of the night before. No one had questioned the ancient lama, no one had asked where he had come from, or why he was there. Because, in the language of Shan's teachers, his deity had become him. It was as if Jokar was indeed a spirit creature, a true Bodhisattva, a Buddha who remained on earth to help others find enlightenment.

"I have to go back to that valley," Shan said. "I have to find the path of that eye if it is there. Because," he said slowly, "I am bound."

Lokesh fixed him with a searching stare. "Sometimes deities are created in the seeking. And the seeking itself may create the path."

Shan returned Lokesh's stare. "You make it sound like I just follow acts of compassion and they will eventually connect me to a deity."

Lokesh answered with his crooked grin.

Shan sighed. "You will be safe staying on the mountain. Someone needs to help Tenzin," he suggested. It would be a way of keeping Lokesh with Tenzin, who was perhaps his safest guardian if Shan could not be with the old man.

"You forget, Xiao Shan. I am bound also." Lokesh looked over the plain. "You should know something else," he said with a strange spark in his eye, excited yet solemn. "Tenzin was speaking. I saw Jokar touch him, and Tenzin's tongue grew back. They spoke a long time at that tree, and when the moon was bright Jokar and Tenzin began working at something, like lamas mixing medicine in the moonlight. After a while I went to investigate. They had a sack of Lamtso salt, and Jokar had ripped off the bottom of his robe and made little squares of it. I helped them, creating little pouches from the squares, filling them with salt and tying them at the top. True earth, Jokar called the salt. Tenzin repeated the words, again and again, smiling like a young boy."

Lokesh stared out at a high cloud. "Tenzin has a strong voice, a voice that would be good for temples. His new tongue knew prayers. Jokar told him of a teaching, from the first lama at Rapjung, the founder, the one called Siddhi. He said all healing was about the same thing, about connecting the earth to the earth inside us all. We took all the pouches to one of the meditation cells. While Lin was sleeping Jokar put one in his pocket. He said everyone in the mixing place should leave with one." Lokesh reached into his shirt and produced one of the small bags for Shan.

"Lin was studying the room this morning," Shan observed as he accepted the pouch. "As if planning something."

"I don't know the state of his awareness," Lokesh said forlornly, as though finishing the thought for Shan. Lin was such a dangerous man. He could still inflict great harm on them all. "Those falling rocks may have done something to the soldier in him." Lokesh was fond of telling Shan stories of cruel people who had experienced close calls with death only to become dramatically different, better people.

As if on cue a cracked, but fierce voice boomed out from the back of the plateau. "Surrender! You are my prisoners! Only if you surrender will we show mercy!" Lin was standing unsteadily, his good hand on the rock wall, his knees about to buckle. He seemed to be shouting at Shan and

Lokesh. Not really shouting, Shan realized, for the rock wall amplified his voice. But trying to shout.

"Perhaps," Shan said dryly, "just one more rock."

Lokesh groaned and leapt up. Lin staggered and dropped to his knees as Lokesh reached him. A thin trickle of blood came from the wound on his scalp.

As Shan reached the two men a small figure darted forth from the shadows, rushing between Lokesh and Lin. "Everyone was sleeping," Anya said in an anguished voice.

Nyma appeared behind the girl. "That old thankga." She seemed close to tears. "The colonel ripped it to pieces."

"Submit! You are my prisoners!" Lin called again in an angry voice, though he had so little strength the words came out in barely a whisper.

"No one," Anya said to Lin in the tone of an impatient midwife, "no one is going to surrender. And no one is going to attack."

Lin looked with an odd, confused expression at the girl, then he fell forward, his good arm clutching at Anya, trapping the girl, so that when he fell she was beneath him, cushioning the fall.

When they had carried Lin's unconscious form back to his pallet, Anya looked up with a determined glint. "You will have to go tell them," the girl declared. "Tell the army we have their colonel. He is important to them I think. They will miss him."

"Little girl," a voice said from behind them. The youngest of the purbas who had come with Tenzin was awake. "Tell them that and they will assume he is a hostage. Tell them anything about him and they will assume it is a trick, or he is a hostage. It will become like war in these mountains. They have so many soldiers they would be like ants on a mound. It is treason to kidnap an officer."

"We kidnapped no one. Ours was simply the way of compassion," the girl said in the soft tone of a lama.

The purba stepped out of the shadows and fixed Anya with an angry stare. "You're old enough to know better. Old enough to go to one of their coal mine camps," the young Tibetan said with fire in his voice. "I'll tell you what we do with your colonel. We carry him to the edge and drop him over, like they have done with so many Tibetans before. Sky burial," he added with a grin.

Suddenly a hand appeared from behind and clasped the man's shoulder. The angry purba seemed to deflate. He frowned, shook the hand off, and turned away. It was Tenzin. The man whom the colonel wanted so desperately to imprison knelt at Lin's side, opposite Anya, and helped her pull the blanket over his unconscious form.

The sun had been up two hours the next morning when Winslow and Shan neared the narrow gap that led back over the range into Qinghai

Province. The lanky American stopped, warning Shan with an upraised hand, and pointed. A solitary figure was hiking along the ridge, a small Tibetan man wearing a derby-like hat with a drawstring pouch slung over his shoulder. They crested the ridge and waited for the man, who smiled cheerfully as he approached.

"You are the ones helping Yapchi," he observed. "The distant ones who came to help." Distant ones. The man meant foreigners. "People all over the mountains are speaking about you, about how you are going to restore the balance," he said in a bright, confident tone. "My grandfather knew distant ones who helped him see things," the man added enigmatically.

Shan paused. Foreigners? The grandfather of a man who lived in the mountains knew foreigners? "There could be soldiers below," he warned.

"I'm not going below," the man said, "I am just bringing water."

Shan studied the small pouch. "Not much more than would fill a kettle." In his pocket, his hand clenched around another pouch, one of the little ochre bags of true earth Jokar had prepared.

"Not even," the man said. He opened the pouch and produced a one-liter plastic bottle. The label it once bore had been torn away. Tibetan script ran along the side, made with a bold black marker. *Sum*, it said, the number three, and below that *chu*, river. "It's going to the sky birthing, for the Green Tara," he said, still in his bright tone, then he returned the bottle to the sack and started down the trail again.

"What did he mean?" Winslow asked as he followed the man with a confused gaze.

"Offerings," Shan suggested. "Perhaps they have decided to invoke the protectress deity called the Green Tara. She is believed to be very powerful."

"A protector deity," Winslow sighed. "Where do I sign up?"

Workers were stretched across the valley as Shan and Winslow surveyed it two hours later. The logging crews had cut a swath nearly three hundred yards wide above the camp. Through their binoculars, tiny figures could be seen scrambling over the tower of the derrick as it kept cutting into the earth below. And at the near end, the south end, by the ruins of Yapchi Village, crews unloaded a truck trailer stacked with freshly sawn lumber.

Each time the American had paused to study his map, Shan had looked back, hesitating. He had been to the oil camp before, and the howlers had tried to take him. Would Somo still be there? Had the intrepid woman been discovered and arrested for helping him? Increasingly, he sensed that helping Winslow find what had happened to Larkin was also somehow helping to find the deity.

They climbed past the little canyon, now empty, where the villagers had hidden, planning to circle the valley along the edge of the band of trees. They were above the derrick when Winslow stopped and looked at Shan.

"Stay up here," the American said. "I'll go in, talk with Jenkins about Zhu's crew, maybe his secretary can help locate them. I'll find them and talk to them without Zhu knowing—" he was interrupted by a sudden sound, the slow beat of a deep drum. It seemed to be coming from directly above them on the slope, no more than a hundred yards away. The two men stared at each other, then Shan took a step toward the sound and Winslow grinned, offering a wave of his hand.

Shan ran. Whoever was beating the drum would not likely hear a few broken twigs or sliding rocks. The pounding grew louder, in a rhythm of two rapid beats and a pause, even more like a heartbeat than before. He was close, he was certain, no more than a hundred paces away, searching the clusters of boulders that dotted the slope.

Suddenly something leapt on his back. A leopard, a voice screamed in his mind, and he was down, claws in his back, his struggling hands batted away violently, his head pressed into the earth. He groaned in fear, his breath rushing out of him, his arms flailing, connecting only with the earth. Then, strangely, his attacker seized his arms behind him and rolled him over.

It was a man, Shan saw through a haze of pain. Was the drum still pounding or was it his own heart he heard? A man he seemed to recognize, who surely recognized him, for as soon as their eyes met the man gasped and released him.

No, it was a bear, the distant voice in his head said. The fog lifted from his eyes and Shan saw it was the Golok bear, Dremu. But not the Dremu Shan had known, for this one was torn and gaunt, a shadow of the prideful Golok Shan had last seen the night the eye was stolen.

Dremu pulled Shan upright, his legs still on the ground, and for a moment his hands lingered, clenching Shan's shoulders in something like an embrace.

"They said you had fled," Shan ventured.

Dremu put his finger over his lips. "Damned soldiers took me," he whispered. "I was riding near the oil camp, in the trees and I didn't know they had soldiers hiding." Shan saw heavy bruises around the Golok's eyes. "They beat me and put me on that work crew, took my horse even, to haul their logs." Dremu looked toward the drumming sound, which continued, louder than ever, very close. "They didn't know who they had caught," he said in a defiant tone. "Thought I was just some rongpa, like those others who just take their orders. I ran away. But first I told those rongpa that their eye was back in the valley, that the eye was watching again."

"Why would you say that?" Shan asked, studying the forlorn Golok. Had Dremu taken the eye, as Lhandro suspected?

"Because the valley's heart is beating again." Dremu, too, stared toward the drumming. "I'm going to get that stone for you, Chinese. So you can make it like the old days." He pointed in the direction of the heartbeat, bent and moved forward, like a predator stalking prey, Shan a few paces behind.

Just as Dremu seemed about to pounce around an outcropping onto the drummer, the Golok jerked back and held his shoulder, wincing with pain. The drumming stopped, and they heard the sound of feet running. He looked in despair at his shoulder, slowly lifting his fingers. "Buddha's breath! I thought I was shot." He bent and picked up a round stone from near his feet, a pebble that did not belong with the sharp granite shards that otherwise lay underfoot. "A sling," he said, with a hint of respect in his voice, as he looked about cautiously.

The slope was silent, and seemed empty now. Dremu rubbed his shoulder, seeming reluctant to follow. In the hands of an expert a sling could be as deadly as a rifle. He bent low and inched around the rock.

The patch of ground on the far side of the outcropping showed evidence of several boots; prints of the smooth-soled boots worn by Tibetans, made with woolen uppers. They were nearly all small prints.

"Children," Dremu announced as he squatted by the tracks. "Two or three children," he said in a puzzled tone. "Maybe one adult. They sat, and knelt," he explained, pointing to several areas where the earth was pressed smooth. The site had been chosen well, with two large slabs of rock behind it to amplify the sound in the direction of the valley. Shan bent and lifted several pieces of grass that lay at the edge of the clearing. They had little knots tied in them. On a small boulder in front, facing the valley, someone had worked with a chisel, trying to cut away a piece of rock, trying to make an elongated hole in front of the rock.

"For the eye," Dremu said over his shoulder, and with a rush of excitement Shan realized the Golok was right. The eye was back in the valley, and someone had been trying to fashion a new home for it. Shan found himself touching the hole, feeling its rough contours. He stared at the crudely worked stone until finally he realized the Golok was staring at him. Dremu seemed to be waiting for orders.

"Some of the villagers thought it was you who took the eye," Shan said. "I can tell them otherwise now."

Dremu scowled. "You mean you thought it, too. Or you would have told them already."

Shan said nothing.

"I wouldn't have done that. Not before you got it back to the valley."

"You mean you planned to take it."

The Golok stared at Shan. "I don't usually plan that far ahead," he said, and offered a hollow grin. "It's just that . . . I think my father and grandfather need me to do something about it. Could you understand that?"

Shan nodded soberly, and the Golok brightened and gestured down the slope. "There were sick people who came to the valley. Some had children. Some of the village children fled."

Shan saw for the first time that Dremu's gau, and the small pouch that had hung beside it, were both missing. "You should get food," he suggested, studying the gaunt man. "And rest." But he didn't know how, didn't know where the other Tibetans were, and who would offer help to the Golok. He could not send Dremu to the mixing ledge, where Lhandro was, who had thrown stones at him. "That monk Gyalo and his yak are in the mountains, on the high ridges. If you can find them they will help you get food. All the others have fled. You should, too, until the soldiers go."

"Not all," Dremu countered.

"You mean the drummer."

"I saw some others on the slope this morning. In the high rocks, moving stealthfully. I think maybe they are trying to damage the oil rig."

"Purbas?" Shan asked with a chill.

"I only saw them from a distance. They moved slow, and without fear, as if they didn't care about the soldiers. Probably they have charms to protect them."

Shan stared at the Golok uncertainly, then, asking him once more to leave for the high ranges, he turned and jogged away. He found a game trail that ran parallel to the valley floor and had trotted northward on it for several minutes, watching for movement on the upper slopes and the shadows of caves, when suddenly two figures appeared on the trail in the distance— not walking so much as strolling, conversing, watching the ground as if hunting for something. Shan faded into the shadows between two rocks. He pushed back as far as he could in the cleft and watched, first with fear, then with confusion as two shadows passed by. One of the figures was singing a Tibetan pilgrim's song.

He scrambled out and leapt forward. "Lokesh!" he called out in alarm.

Thirty feet down the trail his old friend turned and offered his crooked grin. "Good fortune!" Lokesh exclaimed. "You can help us, Xiao Shan." His companion, wearing an amused grin, awkwardly raised a hand in greeting to Shan. Tenzin.

"Help with what?" Shan asked in exasperation, looking about for some place to hide the men.

"I told you," Lokesh said sheepishly. "Looking for medicine herbs. Tenzin wants to learn about herbs too."

"In the mountains, you said in the mountains."

Lokesh waved his hand around the landscape. "The mountains around Yapchi," he said with another grin. "Surely you remember. Jokar Rinpoche said it would help that officer. His heart wind is so distressed he could die."

"Tell me where," Shan said in a pleading voice. "Tell me where and I will get your herbs. Just go back. Now—"

His words choked in his throat. Two green uniformed soldiers stepped around a large tree less than a hundred feet away. From behind the soldiers a figure in a white shirt emerged, followed by half a dozen other Tibetans. Shan recognized the man in white. Director Tuan. Four of the others were oil workers, wearing the green jackets of the venture. But the other two wore the robes of monks.

Tenzin gasped as he saw Tuan, grabbed Lokesh and pointed urgently toward the trees above them, pushing him away from the trail. But another soldier appeared on the slope above, thirty feet away, and began speaking excitedly into a small radio.

A moment later a whistle blew from the direction of the camp. Shan saw more of Tuan's white-shirted guards running up the slope. There was no hope, no chance of escape. The soldiers and howlers had won.

Their captors swarmed around them. Lokesh lowered himself to the ground and began saying his beads. Tenzin seemed frozen, looking from Shan to Lokesh with a grim, apologetic expression.

But it wasn't the soldiers who stepped forward to claim the capture. Instead Tuan pulled a camera from a belt pouch and began taking photographs. Of Tenzin, of Lokesh, of the two monks who trotted forward and stood by Tenzin.

One of the monks grabbed Tenzin's hand in both his own. "Rejoice with us, Rinpoche," the monk said gleefully. "Our teacher is returned to us."

Rinpoche. Shan looked at the monk, more confused than ever. He had called the fugitive Rinpoche.

Tenzin, his face still grim, looked at the monk and sighed. "I am no longer your teacher," he said in his deep, melodious voice. "I am but a novice again, and have found new teachers," he added, and gestured toward Lokesh and Shan.

The monk looked injured. Lokesh stared in wonder.

Tuan grimaced. "The abbot of Sangchi will learn to teach again someday," he declared with a victorious smile, and nodded toward the howler guards as more soldiers arrived, guns at the ready. One of the soldiers stepped forward and in a blur of motion fastened a manacle around Tenzin's wrist. Then he bent, roughly grabbed Lokesh's arm, and fastened the other end of the manacle to the old Tibetan.

"We need you, Rinpoche," one of the monks said with a sob, then, with an impatient gesture by Tuan, the soldiers jerked Lokesh to his feet, cutting off his mantra.

Shan watched, paralyzed with confusion, as Lokesh and the abbot of Sangchi were led down the path toward the oil camp.

CHAPTER FOURTEEN

Shan had learned from the lamas how to confront the lies that had once ruled his life, and how to abandon both the lies and the comfort they had given him. The lie that for twenty years as an investigator in Beijing he had made a difference. The lie that he and his wife, or at least he and his son, would someday be reconciled and reunited. And the lie that his release from the gulag meant he could live the rest of his life in freedom. He had come to accept that he would be returned to a hard labor camp eventually. For Shan, in the life he had chosen it was as inevitable as death, and perhaps above all else, the Tibetans had taught him not only to stop fearing, but to embrace the inevitable.

Yet somehow he always clung to the illusion that Lokesh could not be touched, that thirty years of his life had been enough to give to Beijing. It was an illusion that fed Shan's twisted view of the world, the view that said everything else was worth it, all the suffering could be endured, because a few wise, joyful creatures like Lokesh survived and walked the remote corners of Tibet.

But Lokesh would not survive. He had been taken by the soldiers and howlers, who had been told that the abbot of Sangchi was in the hands of purbas. The two would be kept together, for that was the way their handlers would prefer it. They would use Lokesh, make him suffer to extract whatever it was they wanted from Tenzin. With only one prisoner to interrogate they would eventually resort to chemicals, as they had with Shan in his early days of capture. But chemicals gave unpredictable results, and though few Tibetans would give information under torture, they would often surrender it when a companion was tortured because of them.

He let himself drift down with the crowd that had assembled around the new prisoners as they were conveyed into the camp. No one questioned him. No one came to put manacles on him. Tuan did not even seem to have noticed Shan. The excitement over the discovery of the famous abbot of Sangchi seemed to distract everyone.

He had been so blind. Gendun had known, and Shopo. Someone had died, Gendun had said. He had meant the abbot had somehow died, and Tenzin was trying to find a new life. He recalled Tenzin's first words to him, that day overlooking the red river. It was possible to start a new incarnation in the same body, because Shan had done so. Images flashed through Shan's mind: of Tenzin's anguish over Drakte's death, of the bitter way he had heaved a rock into the lake when Shan had suggested a pebble might capture his guilt, of the days and weeks he had watched the tall Tibetan carry dung. Shan had suspected Tenzin was the infamous Tiger, trying to reform after a life of violence. But some other dark weight had hung around the soul of the abbot of Sangchi, and he had decided to start again. And now they were dragging him back in chains, back to the particular prison he had fled.

As the soldiers led their prisoners past the army tents a loud argument broke out. A beefy soldier whom Shan remembered as Lin's sergeant shouted that the prisoners belonged to the 54th Mountain Combat Brigade. But the howlers kept pushing the two men toward one of the white utility vehicles. Tuan hovered close to Tenzin and stood with four of his men behind him as the sergeant railed, then one of the men in white shirts stepped to the soldier's side, spoke quietly, and handed the man a business card. As Shan stepped closer, trying to hear, a hand closed around his shoulder.

"You must have a death wish," Winslow growled, and pulled Shan away. "Jenkins told me what he knows. Mostly it's that you are number one on the list for the 54th Combat Brigade. They have your name. They think you may be a criminal escapee, that you kidnapped Lin. They're sending more troops in. Looking for Lin, looking for you."

Shan let himself be pulled by Winslow as he watched numbly. Lokesh and Tenzin were being photographed again, standing by the white trucks, wearing leg manacles now, their hands unfettered. For appearances, for the photographs, because the howlers would not want to show the abbot in chains. Shan stared, still perplexed, and did not protest when Winslow pushed him into the bay of a cargo truck and followed him over the tailgate. Shan hardly noticed when the truck began to move. He opened his mouth to call out for Lokesh but his tongue was too dry to speak. The truck passed quickly through the gap in the low saddle of land and the camp was gone.

Shan gazed out the rear of the truck for a long time, half expecting to see the white trucks speeding behind them. Lokesh and Tenzin would go to a Public Security lockup, which would most likely be in the nearest large town. He pulled out the map he had taken from Jenkins's conference room. Wenquan, or maybe Yanshiping. He would get out of the truck at whatever town they passed through. But maybe the soldiers would take their prisoners south, directly to Lhasa. In which case he should jump out at the first crossroads. And do what? Throw stones when the soldiers raced by?

"Best thing we can do is get some sleep," Winslow said as the truck began a steep descent through the long narrow gorge that led out of the mountains.

"Sleep?" Shan asked in confusion.

Winslow gestured at the map in his hand. "It'll be late by the time we arrive. At least seven hours' drive, if the roads are clear."

Shan looked about the cargo bay. It was mostly empty, a few cardboard cartons were stacked against the cab and secured with twine to the slats of the bay. There were ropes and a pile of what appeared to be dirty coveralls, and several empty shipping pallets with the oil company's name stenciled on them.

"Golmud?" he asked in disbelief.

Winslow nodded. "Venture headquarters. Center of operations. Where we can find out about Zhu's crew. Where Jenkins said somebody accessed Larkin's electronic mail account."

"When?"

"Two weeks ago."

"But that was before she died," Shan said in confusion.

"Right. Except she was supposed to be in the mountains on field work at the time. Someone used her pass code at Golmud two weeks ago."

Shan stared at the American and shook his head. "I can't," he protested, and put his hand on the side of the truck to lift himself up. "Lokesh—"

"Lokesh will get little help from you if you are arrested," a woman's voice interjected.

Shan and Winslow both spun about to see a shape rising out of the pile of clothing. Shan stared at the lean, sinewy woman, the only person in the oil camp who had known Lokesh.

"This is Somo," he heard himself say to the American.

"You know her?" Winslow asked in a skeptical tone.

"We met once. We have mutual friends. You saw her, too, handing us jackets and hats."

Winslow nodded with a grin at the purba. "We owe you for that," he said, then looked back at Shan. "So you're saying she's a—"

"A friend."

Winslow nodded again.

Somo stepped forward and sat beside Shan. "We will find out where he is taken. I know he was in lao gai for many years. He will know how to survive."

"Not if they consider him one of those who helped Tenzin hide. The abbot of Sangchi," he said, trying to get used to the thought of the lanky silent man, the gatherer of yak dung, as one of the most prominent lamas in all Tibet.

"Why would you go to Golmud?" Shan asked her.

"I am on the rolls of the venture as an administrative assistant. I have been reassigned," she said with a narrow smile, eyeing the American uneasily.

269

"Winslow has helped us," Shan said, and explained how the American had stopped Colonel Lin from arresting them earlier.

The woman nodded slowly, as if she had realized Shan was inviting her to share her secrets. "I asked for the reassignment. It was part of the plan. I am supposed to... I was supposed to get access to the central computer at the base camp to create a personnel file that showed Tenzin to be a worker in the venture. Then arrange for him to be assigned to a camp in the far north, near Mongolia. From there it would have been simple to get him out. Mongolia, then Russia, then Europe and America. He was supposed to meet important people in the West who can help Tibet."

"But the government was looking on the Indian border," Shan said, and fixed the woman with a pointed stare. "It's where Drakte went, isn't it, during those weeks after he took us to the hermitage. He disappeared. He went south to lay a false trail."

Somo looked into her hands a moment, biting her lip as though Shan's words caused her pain. "The one who planned all this, our leader, he said Drakte was the best for such a job. Drakte went to towns in the south with stories of seeing the abbot on the road at night, always farther south. He even had things of the abbot's, and said Tenzin had traded them for food. So the knobs would find a trail of evidence."

"What kind of things?" Shan asked.

"Personal things, objects which anyone investigating would know belonged to him: A pen case. An old book given to the abbot by his mother. A prayer amulet he had been photographed wearing. Tenzin was told nothing from his former life could stay with him, for even though we might disguise him, its possession would betray him."

Shan fingered the ivory rosary in his pocket. Had Drakte kept one thing, perhaps the most precious thing, to return to Tenzin when he left China?

"Then we changed Tenzin," Somo continued. "The way he walked. We had his hair grow long. We taught him mannerisms of the dropka."

"Should have been foolproof," Winslow said.

"Should have," Somo agreed. "But someone found out. Perhaps someone saw him who we didn't think would recognize him. We thought all the searchers would be in the south. We thought he would be safe at that hermitage, and on the caravan."

"Who?" Shan asked. "Who would have seen him in Lhasa, then again while he was fleeing in the changtang? When did he leave Lhasa? Was there a meeting, a conference where someone from the north would have seen him?"

"That Serenity Campaign. There was a big meeting to launch it. The abbot of Sangchi gave a speech, and two days later he disappeared, before the conference had even concluded."

"Colonel Lin," Winslow suggested. "He came to Yapchi, from Lhasa."

Somo gave her head a slight shake, and frowned. "Most of his troops are in the south still, watching out for purbas taking Tenzin across the border. As if Lin wanted to keep our sham alive. He must have come north because of that stone, because he knew it would be returned to the valley. Because he is obsessed with that stone perhaps."

"No," Shan said. "Not because of the stone. No matter what the Tibetans may think of the chenyi deity, to Lin it is only a stone. Drakte took the stone," Shan said, looking at Somo again. "And he had someone else with him." He unfolded the photograph he had taken from Lin's pocket. "This is why Lin was so interested in the stone—because it would lead him to Tenzin."

Somo stared at him with a hard glint, not of surprise, but of assessment, as if trying to decide how many more secrets she dare divulge. "All right. Tenzin took something, something secret about the soldiers, about the 54th Mountain Combat soldiers. Military intelligence."

"Tenzin?" Shan asked. "He's no spy."

"No," Somo agreed. "I don't know what it was. I don't think they planned it, from the way Drakte talked about it. He was angry at Tenzin for increasing the danger to them. Probably Tenzin wanted to help the purbas with something, because the purbas were making possible his escape."

But to Lin, Shan knew, it would still mean the abbot was a spy. It made it personal. Tenzin had shamed Lin, or even worse, might have information that could harm the entire army. "Lin's trying to cover himself," Shan said, the thought reaching his tongue as it crossed his mind. "He never told his superiors. He's trying to recover the missing papers before the damage is done. If the army command suspected military secrets were in the hands of the fugitive abbot, they would be scouring the countryside, erecting roadblocks everywhere."

"But why would Tenzin think it was safe to come to Yapchi today?" Winslow asked.

"He didn't, not necessarily," Shan said. "Jokar said herbs must be gathered in Yapchi Valley for the healing. I should have known. It was a thing the man Tenzin wants to become would do, a thing Lokesh would do without a second thought."

Winslow fixed Shan with a sad gaze. The fugitive abbot had been captured because an ancient medicine lama had asked for herbs to heal an ailing Chinese colonel. The thought somehow reminded Shan of someone else. "Did you go to that durtro like you said, with Gendun and Drakte?" he asked Somo.

Her face tightened, and she nodded. "Herders came, many herders, and said prayers, and talked about what a brave man Drakte was. Gendun stayed afterwards. He said Drakte was having a bad time of things, and he was going back with Shopo to continue the rites. I think they meant for the full ritual." The traditional death rite period was forty-nine days. Somo watched a range of mountains recede in the distance. "There was

271

something . . . I don't think it meant anything really. But when I was leaving Gendun sought me out. He said we must all learn to understand the dead better. He said to give Shan something, that he had learned something about Drakte." She reached into her pocket and extended a chakpa, one of the bronze sand funnels.

Shan stared at the funnel, struck dumb for a moment by the memory of Gendun teaching him how to use it, then slowly he lifted it from Somo's palm. He examined it carefully, perplexed, then looked inside to see a small slip of paper resting against the inner wall. He slipped the paper out with his finger and read it. He looked up at Somo. "Drakte carried the deity in a blanket," Shan read to his two companions, "but he was learning to unwrap it."

Somo looked at Shan with apology in her eyes, as if she felt she had troubled him with a meaningless message.

"The eye was kept in a little felt blanket," Winslow suggested.

Shan said nothing, but read the paper again, and again. Somo offered an uncertain nod to the American and looked back at the retreating mountains.

"So now what do you do?" Shan asked the woman after several minutes.

Somo did not shift her gaze from the mountains. "When I started from Lhasa three weeks ago, Drakte told me we were doing this to help a Chinese who was going north to help Tibetans. I didn't know about the abbot then, just the stone." She paused and looked at Shan with puzzled eyes. "The abbot and the eye of the deity, in a way they were the same thing."

Shan nodded. "The purbas' help with the eye was just a cover, a way to get Tenzin north in secret. Who would have looked for him on a salt caravan?" He looked up into the woman's face and somehow knew they were sharing the same thought. Drakte had died to warn them, to make sure Tenzin stayed free. Somo was not giving up on Tenzin.

"I am going to the computer as soon as we arrive in Golmud," Somo stated, "in the middle of the night. I will still make Tenzin an employee, under the false name we devised."

"But he's gone," Winslow said.

"It's still my assignment," Somo said in a voice that had grown distant. "And after it's over, whatever happens, I am going to find out about Drakte's killer."

"I think," Winslow said, studying first Shan, then Somo, "it's not over until you find the killer."

They watched the landscape in silence again.

"You can get into the electronic records?" Winslow asked after a long time.

"At university, they made sure I had advanced computer training before returning to teach Tibetan children. With chalk and slate."

Winslow explained about Melissa Larkin, and they spoke together for an hour about the mysteries that had been woven together at Yapchi.

"Did Drakte know that man Chao who was murdered?" Shan asked. Somehow he already knew the answer.

"Yes," Somo said readily. "He was a Tibetan. Many people don't know that, because of the name he took."

"And you knew him also?"

"A month ago Drakte and I were planning to spend two days together by Lamtso. We had been talking about making a family together," she announced in a matter-of-fact tone that caused Shan to turn away, embarrassed, then she paused and looked out the rear of the truck. "But instead, he asked me to go with him to Amdo town, because he had discovered an old friend there we had to meet. He said there would always be time for us to go to Lamtso," she said in a tight voice. "We met at an old stable being used as a garage, and we sat on a bench and ate cold dumplings with his friend, whose name was different when Drakte knew him as a boy. They had me sit in the middle, like a referee."

"What did Chao do? How did he act?" Had it all been a trap to capture Drakte? Shan wondered.

"He was scared. He asked if Drakte knew Director Tuan, like he was warning Drakte. But Drakte just laughed about Tuan. They did not discuss things that were dangerous. Just talk about life on the changtang and things from when they were young. It was just old friends meeting again, that's all. That Chao, he embraced Drakte when we parted and said he was sorry."

"About what?"

"Just that he was sorry. About everything I guess."

"Did Drakte have that ledger with him?" Shan asked.

Somo shook her head. "But afterwards he worked on it all night, because he said he was going to meet with Chao again. I thought at first it was something he was doing for the Lotus Book, to record how the district is so stricken by poverty. It includes every village, every farm, every herding family in Norbu district. Signed by the head of each family."

"The district," Shan said. "Not the township."

Somo nodded. "The Religious Affairs district. The Norbu district that Tuan heads for Religious Affairs."

From a pocket Somo produced a slip of yellow paper and handed it to Shan. "I nearly forgot. Drakte had this in his boot. I keep trying to understand it. I think it came from Chao, but not when I was with them."

It appeared to be a payroll record, with one word handwritten at the top. Dorje, it said, followed by a dash, like it was an address, or person. The dorje was a Buddhist symbol, the small scepter-like object that was sometimes called the thunderbolt to symbolize the teachings of Buddha. Below the name were two columns of handwritten numbers, the first a list of twelve identification numbers, the second a group of twenty. Bureau

273

of Religious Affairs, Amdo, someone had written under the first column, with a check by each identification number in the column. Beside the two top sets of numbers of the first column was written Director Tuan, and below it the single Chinese word *wo*. It meant I or me. It could mean, Shan realized, Deputy Director Chao. Under the second column was written Public Security.

"It's not his writing," Somo said. "Not Drakte's. It must be Chao's. I asked some questions," she said pointedly. "The head of Public Security in Amdo town was reassigned months ago. No replacement was named. Since Director Tuan used to be the head of Public Security here, he offered to be the interim supervisor. He began to consolidate things. Including payroll."

"You mean the knobs here are being paid by Director Tuan of Religious Affairs?"

Somo bit her lower lip as she nodded.

Gyalo had warned about knobs who did not look like knobs. It explained why the howlers in white, military-style shirts all looked like Public Security.

"And one more thing: it looks like payroll data for the knobs in the district. But only fifteen knobs are known."

"What do you mean?"

"I mean the purbas watch the knobs in Amdo town. There have been fifteen stationed out of there for years. We checked with those who clean the barracks. Fifteen based in Amdo, traveling with Tuan sometimes. So there's another five somewhere else. Working in secret."

In secret. The five could be anywhere. They could be wearing robes at Norbu. He remembered the camp Dremu had found above the Plain of Flowers, after the meadow had been burned. Had it been knobs? Shan extended the paper back toward Somo, but she raised her palm to decline, as if the paper frightened her now.

The truck bounced and slid along the rough track until it finally reached the north-south highway and picked up speed, then climbed and descended, and climbed again, through rough, barren terrain, along what Shan knew was one of the highest roadways in the world. He slept, and when he woke they were traveling through a snowbound landscape. After dark, past the snow, the truck stopped at a cluster of rundown mudbrick buildings for gas. The driver filled a thermos with hot water, threw in a handful of tea, and left it in the rear of the truck with two tin mugs and a bag of apples.

Shan slept fitfully, starting awake each time a faster vehicle overtook them. Heavy trucks and buses frequented the road. Twice they passed army convoys which had halted on the shoulder.

Several hours after sunset the air became thick and acrid. Dim sulfur-colored streetlights appeared and the truck began weaving around men and women on bicycles, its horn blaring. They passed blocks of dingy grey buildings and factories belching thick smoke. Shan watched out the back of the truck, standing now, holding onto the frame of the cargo bay. It was China, or at least the China that hundreds of millions of Chinese knew.

"God-forsaken place, Golmud," Winslow observed.

Shan said nothing. God-forsaken perhaps, but it was the closest he had been to China in over five years. There were other smells he noticed mixed with the factory smog. Sesame oil, chili peppers, coriander, fried pork, ginger. A woman rode past on a bicycle, holding a bamboo pole on which were skewered four roasted ducks. A man rode by in the opposite direction, balancing a long rolled carpet on his handlebars. An aged woman on a bench tended a brazier with little spits of roasted crab apples. For a moment Shan fought an urge to just go sit with her, and smell the intermingled diesel and spices, the scent of modern China.

Thirty minutes after leaving the city, under a brilliant floodlight mounted on a tall metal pole they turned onto a broad gravel road wide enough for four trucks. Idled vehicles began to appear on the right side, dozens of vehicles: dumptrucks, bulldozers, towing trucks, truck trailers, cement mixers. It was a huge parking lot for heavy equipment. More floodlights on poles appeared every hundred feet, and they entered what appeared to be a parking lot for trailers identical to those used at Yapchi. Dozens of trailers, over a hundred, Shan estimated, in orderly rows, a city of trailers. As the truck slowed he swung his head out and looked forward. There was nothing else except four enormous cinderblock buildings facing each other, creating a huge square of gravel perhaps two hundred yards on each side.

The truck stopped at the edge of the empty, open square and the driver, after rapping hard on the rear window of the cab, walked away, stretching his arms over his head, without a word to them. They climbed out cautiously, peering about the empty compound. Shan took a few hesitant steps toward the only building whose windows were lit, gravel crunching loudly under his boots. It was one o'clock in the morning.

In the dim orange glow of the sulfur lamps, with a gibbous moon rising over it, the huge yard had the air of a stark, sturdy temple compound in repose. There was a strange vibration in the air, a beating, as of a distant drum. Then suddenly one of the doors of the building he was facing opened and loud rock-and-roll music poured into the yard. Two men staggered into the night, holding onto each other to stay upright, waving energetically at the new arrivals then turning toward the huge complex of trailers.

Shan stood, exploring the strange, unexpected feeling that rose within. He had entered a different world, or at least a world he had not known for years. He had last seen drunken men, had last heard such music, had last walked in the night under such lights, in Beijing, in his prior incarnation.

Winslow tapped him on the shoulder as though he suspected Shan of napping on his feet, then pulled him toward the door the men had exited. They entered a short hallway, lined in unpainted plywood, illuminated by a single naked, intensely bright bulb. The walls on both sides held long bulletin boards which overflowed with papers of many shapes, sizes, and colors, and in several languages. Shan glanced at them in confusion. Monday Night, one said in English, African Queen, Bring your own Leeches. Another said, in Chinese, All Dogs Found in Trailers Will Be Donated to the Kitchen. Lost, One Monkey, the top of another said in English and French. A poster for the Foreign Affairs Branch of the Public Security Bureau reminded foreigners to strictly observe the terms of their entry visas. An announcement in the style of a banner stated that all unassigned workers would be expected to assist in assembling platforms for the upcoming May Day celebration. There was even a bulletin from the Bureau of Religious Affairs reminding venture workers that any religious artifacts found in the field were to be surrendered to the people's government.

The corridor led to a darkened hall that ran the length of the long building, with many doors on either side. Directly across from them was a door marked Infirmary, in Chinese and English. Twenty feet away on the opposite side was a set of open double doors, through which red light flooded out, flickering in time to the music. The sound was almost unbearably loud to Shan, but no other door, no other place in the compound seemed to show any sign of activity. With a mock bow, Winslow gestured them through the doors. Somo stared at her feet self-consciously, and Shan saw her clutch at a piece of turquoise that had appeared in her hand, her remembrance from Drakte, then she swallowed hard and followed Winslow into the bar.

The room, nearly sixty feet long and perhaps twenty-five wide, was jammed with people. No one gave them more than a glance as they worked their way toward an empty table at the rear. At one end was a bar, constructed of unpainted timber, with two men standing in front of shelves stacked with bottles of beer and hard liquor—not just the Chinese mainstays, but Western whiskeys, Russian vodka, French brandy, British gin, and, conspicuously displayed under a small spotlight, a bottle of *hejie jiu,* lizard wine from Guangxi, complete with a dead lizard suspended in the bottle. Men and women, many in green jackets, were raucously ordering drinks at the bar. On a stage at one corner a huge machine with a television screen displayed video images of women in fields of flowers and English words scrolling across the bottom of the screen, with a small ball bouncing over the words. A stout Han man wearing a purple silk shirt sang into a microphone, standing close to the screen, swaying, staring intensely, expectantly, as if he were about to jump into the field to join the women. A small crowd milled about the stage, some jeering, some calling words of encouragement to the man.

Two of the walls were plastered with posters, most of them of handsome men and women with images of martial arts, beautiful mountains, sleek cars, or other handsome people in negligible bathing suits behind them. Each had captions of what Shan assumed were movies, in English, Chinese, or French. He stared at them a moment, vaguely remembering that once he had attended movies, but he couldn't recall where, or when.

At the opposite end of the room where the light was dimmer, there were two tattered sofas and a dozen high stools. Several young women were perched on the stools, as though on display, all wearing heavy makeup, tight low-cut dresses, elaborately styled hair and high boots of brightly colored vinyl. Half a dozen Westerners sat at a table near the stage, burly men with big hands, four of them smoking cigars, one with his head resting in his palms, elbows on the table, as if asleep. With the Westerners was a well-groomed middle-aged Han man wearing a blue dress shirt, who watched the man on the stage with an uneasy smile.

"Mai xiao nu," Winslow announced with a sense of wonder as they sat down, staring back at the overdressed women. It meant women selling smiles. "Mai xiao nu," he repeated with a grin, as if he found the words amusing. When Somo blushed he shrugged apologetically, then declared that he would get them soft drinks and strode toward the bar. Somo looked at Shan, biting her lower lip. She stood and stepped purposefully toward the Chinese man sitting with the Westerners. She leaned over him a moment; he looked up with what Shan thought was relief, offered a gesture of farewell to his companions, and walked with Somo to the door. They stood and spoke for less than a minute until, with a worried glance toward Shan, she followed the man down the corridor.

Shan studied the strange collection of people in the room. His eyes began to sting from the tobacco smoke. A man nearby began belching repeatedly as his companions applauded. Shan could not shake the feeling he was being watched. What had Jenkins called the headquarters camp? Hell on wheels.

Winslow appeared a moment later with three red cans of American soda with a Chinese label, and the two sat uneasily for ten minutes before Somo reappeared with the man in the blue shirt, who distributed key rings with plastic tags like hotel keys to Shan and Somo. Each tag held a letter of the English alphabet and a number. The man introduced himself to Winslow as the administrative manager, and explained that Winslow would be accommodated in the special housing for distinguished visitors. Shan and Winslow exchanged a nervous glance. They were being split up. The American frowned but, as the manager turned and gestured him toward the door, he rose to follow the man. "In the morning," he said uneasily, and soon disappeared out the door with the manager.

"There are separate quarters for female workers," Somo announced unhappily as she downed her drink and pocketed her key.

"I will sleep in that truck," Shan suggested.

"No," Somo said nervously. "It could be moved, even driven to some other camp. And I saw a security patrol in the hallway. Not police or soldiers, just men in brown jackets. But if you're found without a worker's card you'll be taken into Golmud, or worse. They have trouble with thieves infiltrating the camp."

Five minutes later he was wandering along the dark rows of trailers. At the end of each row was a dimly lit sign with a letter. Each trailer had a huge number painted over its center door. He found his assigned trailer, unlocked the door, stepped inside, and found himself standing between two long rows of metal bunkbeds, half of which were occupied with sleeping figures. Two men sat on a cot at one end playing *mah jhong* by the light of a flashlight. Shan moved in the opposite direction and found an empty bunk at the end of the trailer. He was asleep seconds after his head touched the pillow.

It seemed only moments later when someone began pushing one of his feet. He woke with a start, remembering Somo's warning about the security patrols. Sunlight poured through the small metal-framed windows of the trailer.

"Breakfast stops in ten minutes, buddy," declared a young Han Chinese man at his bedside. "Sorry," he said as he saw Shan's nervous reaction. "If you wind up waiting in line most of the day for a job assignment you won't be able to eat until tonight." The man studied Shan uncertainly, wiped his thin, wispy moustache, and shrugged.

Shan mumbled his thanks and followed the man outside, warily studying the long alley between the rows of trailers before stepping beside the young Chinese.

"I saw a truck by the ops center," the Han said. "You must have come in late. From Tsaidam?" he asked, referring to the huge oil field in western Qinghai, one of the most famous in all China.

"Yapchi," Shan said.

The man glanced at him in surprise. "You asked to rotate out of Yapchi? Are you crazy? I hear there's going to be big bonuses there. American," he added. "I love Americans. Hamburgers. Las Vegas."

They arrived at the same big building Shan and his friends had been in the night before, but entered now at the opposite end, stepping directly into a huge messhall. A gust of humid air poured over him as the door closed, carrying with it a mélange of scents: Pickled cabbage. Bacon. Cheese. Black pepper. Cigarette smoke. Eggs. Strong black tea. Fried rice. Coffee. Marinated fish.

Shan wandered around the room until he spotted Winslow sitting at a long table with over a dozen Western men and women, most of them younger than Winslow. A large black box on the table blared loud music. A young blond man with a ponytail pounded out the rhythm with two spoons on his plastic plate. Beside him a thick-set, square-jawed woman with short brunette hair played solitaire. Three others, including two of the men Shan had seen by the stage the night before, were studying a map, unrolled on the table. One was nursing a mug of coffee, the other a thick cigar.

Shan sat beside Winslow, who quietly reported that Somo had not yet appeared. The American gestured toward a line of workers at the side of the hall where attendants in white aprons hovered over steaming metal trays of food. Shan shook his head, and the American handed him a piece of cold toast from his own plate. Shan accepted the toast and reached for a Chinese newspaper near the end of the table. It was published in Golmud, dated just the day before. He quickly scanned the headlines. The authorities were closing in on the reviled Tiger, the reactionary wanted for murdering a Religious Affairs official in Amdo town. Large rewards were offered to citizens who assisted in his capture. A companion article explained that the effort to take the Tiger was a two-pronged campaign against such reactionaries, the second element being the separate search for the abbot of Sangchi, whom reactionaries working for the Tiger had kidnapped to steal him away to the Dalai Cult.

"Mostly Europeans," Winslow reported in a low voice, in Tibetan. "None of them has been here longer than a week. All in from other assignments. Most of them about to rotate out from home base."

Shan surveyed the men and women at the table. They seemed to be studiously ignoring Winslow.

"They have pointed out that of all the foreign countries represented in the venture, the only embassy that has ever challenged the venture on anything is the American."

"You mean your questions about Miss Larkin?"

"No. Environmental studies. Somebody else from the embassy came a month ago, saying the venture was not properly assessing environmental impacts. These engineers say the venture could block further investment by the American partners if we're not careful. There's lots of capital available elsewhere with no strings attached."

The man nearest Winslow pushed his chair back and lifted his tray. "I'll be sure to brush off my tuxedo for next time we dine, Mr. Ambassador," the man said in English, with an exaggerated bow of his head. He studied Shan a moment and turned back to Winslow. "Don't take any shit off of them," he added in a tone that was almost apologetic. "Give one of them an ear and you'll have a hundred hounding you. Every damned one expects us to help with a visa to move to the States."

"I have never expected to depart the worker's paradise," Shan said slowly, in English, fixing the man with a steady stare.

The man returned his gaze uncertainly, then broke into a grin. He looked from Shan to a table at the far corner of the room before grinning at Winslow. "Glad Comrade Zhu has his team on the case," he said, then hurried away.

Winslow and Shan exchanged a worried glance, and Shan found himself slowly surveying the messhall. Workers were rapidly filing out of the chamber. Several of the aproned staff wheeled food carts through a set of double doors while others began wiping tables with rags from buckets that reeked of ammonia. But near a door that opened to the interior of the operations center a slender man with hooded eyes, wearing a stylish brown nylon jacket, leaned against the wall, repeatedly glancing at them as he spoke into a portable radio. Shan rose, slowly, without fully standing, to look toward the corner where the American had glanced. The entire table was occupied by men and women in brown jackets. With a pang of fear he recognized the sleek man sitting at the head of the table, gesturing emphatically as the others listened, as if he were holding court. Special Projects Director Zhu.

Shan ducked down and stared at the table, evoking a quiet curse from Winslow as he explained what he had seen.

"I was wondering," Shan said as he calmed himself. "Why Larkin would come here just to access the computer? Why not do it from Yap-chi?"

Winslow shrugged, watching in the direction of the distant table. "Secrecy. Maybe a better internet connection. They just have that little satellite phone there. Or maybe that's not why she came. Maybe she just happened to check her e-mail while she was here."

"But she came in secret, when she was supposed to be in the field. A two-day journey, here and back. It was important to her. What else is here? What else does this base do?" As if in reply a heavy truck laden with supplies tied under canvas covers pulled past the windows of the messhall.

A quarter hour later they stood at the back of the long building opposite the operations center. Much of the rear of the structure was open, consisting of ten oversized garage bays, several holding heavy trucks undergoing repair. A long loading dock lined the remainder of the building, at which several cargo trucks of varying sizes were being loaded. They climbed the dock, but as Winslow took a step toward the warehouse, Shan put a hand on his arm. "Perhaps we should just watch a moment," he suggested.

"What for?" Winslow asked, casting nervous glances about the facility.

"For the one thing," Shan said.

"One thing?"

Shan gazed intently at the warehouse workers who were supervising the loading. "When I was starting my career in Beijing I worked with an old investigator who said that despite what I had been told in my training at the university the easiest part of the job was knowing who to ask, and where. He said the hard part was inviting those you questioned to give you more than you ask, for if you know what to ask you already have most of the answer. He said there was always one thing in any situation that would open a person up, one thing that was the essence, not the one truth but the one lever to the truth."

"Sort of like the zen of interrogation," Winslow quipped, anxiously watching the workers. Shan asked the American to wait near the door and he slipped into the shadows behind one of the high stacks of crates that lined the warehouse floor.

A few minutes later they entered the warehouse together, Shan holding a clipboard stuffed with papers, Winslow wearing a worn green cap with the symbol of an oil derrick on it.

They stood near the center of the huge open warehouse space, Winslow with his hands on his hips, wearing an impatient expression, an unlit cigar hanging from his lips, Shan looking forlorn. In less than a minute a balding Han man wearing the blue shirt that seemed to indicate senior administrative personnel hurried to their side. Shan had watched the man from the shadows, had seen the way he had obsequiously watched three Westerners who entered the warehouse and darted to assist them, ignoring all else, even the man who had helped Somo the night before, the Chinese administrative manager.

"The accounts for the field teams at Yapchi are out of order," Shan sighed, with a long, exasperated glance at Winslow. Winslow's task, Shan had told the American, was to say nothing, look irritated, and give no clue of understanding Mandarin.

"Surely not," the man in the coveralls stated, nervously looking at the American. He wore an American-style baseball cap, black, with an orange bird on its front. Shan felt guilty about playing to such an obvious, even sad, weakness, but the one thing that most of the venture workers seemed to be obsessed with was making contact with foreigners, for help with immigration.

"I told him," Shan said, "these things are very complex. Multiple deliveries. Sensitive equipment that may be shipped directly to the camp. Sometimes boxes with food supplies and field equipment get confused."

The warehouse manager examined Winslow carefully. The American offered a forced, impatient grin, then glared at Shan.

Shan retreated a step, as if expecting to be hit. "Please," he said in a plaintive tone. "He's been to Yapchi already. He has their records for verification. He's American."

The man nervously motioned them toward a computer terminal on a table in a corner of the warehouse. Moments later he had a screen displayed that read Yapchi: Supply Balances. Shan looked at the screen with a satisfied smile. Running the petroleum venture was as bureaucratic and disorganized as running the army.

The man tapped a few more keys and a subheading appeared: Field Teams. "They all have the same equipment," the man said, pointing at a column on the left side. "Team One," it said. Metallic water bottles, twelve, the listing began. Tent, four man, one. Sleeping bags, four. Butane cooking stoves, one. Fuel cylinders, eight. Rations, sixty meals. Shan quickly scanned the rest of the list. Ropes, axes, mineral hammers, seismic explosive charges. The four-member teams were equipped for five days in the field. "Tell him I know baseball," the manager urged Shan. "They play tapes of baseball games one night a week. Baltimore Orioles," he added in a hopeful tone.

Shan gave an impatient nod in reply. "But one of these field teams left behind some of their equipment."

"Which team number?"

Shan gestured toward Winslow. "What team do you think? The one headed by the American."

Strangely, the man seemed to deflate. "Ah," he said slowly, "Melissa." His eyes clouded.

"You knew Miss Larkin?"

"Sure. I mean—" the man searched their faces warily as if trying to assess how slippery the ground had become. "She brings things for us when she visits. Fossils sometimes. Pretty pink quartz. Once some American sweet biscuits. She is . . ." he studied their faces again, then fixed his gaze on the computer, "easy to remember." When he felt Shan's inquisitive stare, he sighed and continued in a more distant voice. "Once when she was here there was a big storm and the electricity was gone. No one could work. Most people went to the operations center and drank all day. But Miss Larkin, she made a fire here, in a big iron bucket," he explained, pointing to the center of the concrete floor. "Some of us sat around it and told stories. She taught us American songs that day. Row, Row, Row Your Boat," he said in English, having difficulty with the r's. "Jingle Bells. Oh Susannah."

"But that last time she was here, she wanted something special, didn't she?" Shan suggested. "She left food supplies at Yapchi because she had to carry something else."

The man tapped a few more keys at the computer, then sat down heavily on a nearby stool. A new screen appeared, showing resupply orders for the Yapchi camp. "She said she didn't have time to do all the paperwork." He looked around the warehouse, suddenly wary not of Shan and Winslow but of the shadows beyond them. "Said no one would miss them, that months would go by before anyone would ask for them and I could reorder by then. I said only six, but she insisted on taking all twelve."

"Twelve what?"

The man winced. "It didn't make sense. I still think about it sometimes. I still don't understand." He looked into Shan's face with a pleading expression. "I'll have replacements by next month."

"Twelve what?" Shan repeated.

"Dye markers," the man whispered. "Used to mark currents, or measure the flow of water. Where we usually work, in the new fields, it's almost like a desert. The markers were all covered with dust. I reported that they had all expired," he said, as if once he had decided to confide in Shan, as a fellow Han who shared the burden of dealing with Americans, he had to tell it all, "too old to use. I didn't check. Probably true," he added quickly.

"You just did your job. She was a team leader, after all," Shan said and looked at the screen. There was a line blinking at the bottom of the screen, the last entry under Larkin's name. Replenish, it said, and referenced a date. The date was tomorrow. He pointed at the line of text.

"Resupply," the man said hesitantly. Shan leaned over and moved the cursor to the line and clicked the mouse. A new list appeared, with the same date, and map coordinates. Butane fuel cylinders. Blankets. Five hundred feet of rope, and seismic charges. Four cases of seismic charges.

As Shan studied the screen a chill crept down his spine.

"Why, if it's for Larkin's team," he asked slowly, "would you keep this in the system?"

The color drained from the man's face and he stared at the screen a long time before answering. "I don't put the supply assignments in the system, just assemble the supplies for the orders that appear on the screen. That team may still be working. I hear they haven't found her body," the man said in a subdued, worried voice. Then, as he saw Shan's intense interest in the screen, he stood in front of the monitor.

"She asked you to keep the replenish order in the system when she was here," Shan stated. The man had mixed his tenses in speaking of Larkin, using the present tense sometimes even though he had obviously heard of her death.

"No, it's a mistake," he groaned, "just a mistake for this to be in this system. It doesn't mean anything."

"You mean she asked for a special resupply and later someone asked you to take it off?"

The man looked at Winslow with a pleading expression now. "A good woman," he said in broken English. "Row, row, row your boat," he said with a forced smile. "Baltimore Orioles."

"You mean the Office of Special Projects," Shan said.

The words brought a cloud to the manager's face. "He said take her listings off our screens. I must have forgotten this piece."

"Special Director Zhu said take off the resupply request?" Shan asked. "Cancel it?"

The man in the blue shirt hunched his shoulders forward, and seemed to draw into himself, getting smaller. "Not cancel it," the man whispered to his feet, looking more frightened than ever. "Just take it off our screens." He stepped in front of the computer and turned to face the entrance to the warehouse, as though guarding the screen. Or hiding it.

"You mean Zhu found out the replenishment order was still in the system," Shan said slowly, glancing at Winslow, who was busily writing down the map coordinates, "and he said continue with it. But he is taking over the resupply assignment?"

The man's voice had grown hoarse. "Like the rest of us, I guess. He hopes she still lives."

But no, Shan realized as he hurried Winslow out of the building, it was because Zhu hoped to make sure she didn't.

"How could—" Winslow began when Shan had explained his suspicion.

"The dye markers," Shan explained. "We saw the dye markers being used the day before we saw Zhu in the mountains. He told us she had been killed a week before. He filed reports stating as much. But he was lying. She was in the mountains, near us, just the day before. No one else was using the markers. No one else had any markers. Zhu reported her killed to make sure no one else would interfere."

"Interfere with what?"

"I don't know. I think Zhu is going to deliver those supplies. He reported her dead. What if he lied, what if he wanted everyone to give up on her so he could find her? Zhu, and maybe Public Security, had decided she's dangerous. What if it was because he wanted to make her dead now that everyone had accepted the lie that she was dead? Make her dead now, or take her somewhere for interrogation. She's a ghost now. Zhu can do anything and no one would know."

Winslow stared at Shan. "Impossible," he said, but Shan didn't see disbelief in the American's eyes. He saw cold fury, and fear, and a glimmer of helplessness.

Shan surveyed the compound as they walked around the perimeter of the square, stopping by the vehicles they passed to watch the reflections in the window glass. "We can't leave Somo." The man from the dining hall, the one in the brown jacket, now wearing sunglasses, was two hundred feet away, standing by a parked truck, speaking in low tones into his little radio. Across the compound Shan saw two more men in brown jackets, listening to radios, briskly walking toward them now. An open vehicle, a jeep, pulled up beside the men. Zhu was in the front passenger seat, wearing his sunglasses, slapping a knob's truncheon against his palm.

"She has people who take care of her," Winslow said. "Purbas."

"She came with us," Shan said. "We're being watched. Her friends will pick her up eventually. With Tenzin arrested, she can do no more here."

But Shan was wrong. Five minutes later a heavy dump truck moved slowly across the yard, raising a thick plume of dust. It turned so that its path took it between them and their followers. It slowed as it approached. Someone was standing on its wide running board.

"Christ, it's her," Winslow gasped, and instantly the two men darted through the dust cloud to the truck. Somo motioned them onto the board and they leapt, landing on either side of the woman, Shan holding onto the side mirror, Winslow the handle used for climbing into the high cab.

Moments later they were beside the huge lot of idled equipment they had passed the night before. The truck slowed and Somo motioned for them to jump, following them a moment later.

"Why not stay on, get in back?" Winslow asked, brushing the dust from his sleeves.

Somo pointed to the main gate, where the truck was coming to a halt. Two army trucks were parked there, a squad of soldiers deployed on either side of the gate beside several men in brown jackets.

"Checkpoint. Effective this morning, everyone in and out of the base has to be cleared by the army. The 54th Mountain Combat Brigade," she added tersely, as she turned and led them into the maze of equipment, finding refuge behind the lowered blade of a huge bulldozer. They sat in the shadow as she quickly explained that Larkin had indeed been at the base in the past month, when she was supposed to be in the mountains above Yapchi, and she hadn't used the computer just for a few electronic messages to her office in the United States. The American geologist had used the only terminal in the entire venture that had a link to her company's mainframe computer, and for two hours, timed to be in the middle of the night at the company's headquarters in America, she had fed geologic data into the computer.

"But why?" Winslow asked. "She can't have a secret deposit of oil. The oil belongs to the venture. She knows that. What could be so secret? So urgent?"

"More importantly," Shan said, "what could an American geologist lost in the mountains possibly be doing that would cause Zhu to want her dead?"

"Modeling," Somo reported in a puzzled tone. "That's all anyone knows. That's what the big American computer is used for. Modeling geologic data."

"But what the hell is so secret?" Winslow pressed. "She works for an oil company. And why the computer back home?"

"I asked," Somo explained. "Seismic data from the field is inputed and the computer extrapolates mineral deposits, using thousands of calculations and data about known fields. Predicts underground geologic structures. Identifying patterns of mineral tracers to point to big ore or oil bodies." Somo shrugged. "Some geologists use the computer more than others. Larkin had used it before, often. And oil companies are secretive. They don't want others knowing what they're finding," she added.

Shan recalled Jenkins's description of the American woman. Larkin was a perfectionist. "But she would have to get permission," he suggested. "Someone would have had to approve it."

Somo sighed. "Yes and no. There are access codes that have to be fed into the computer to start the program. Entering the codes means you have permission."

"And Larkin had the codes."

"Larkin used code numbers registered in Mr. Jenkins name. But he was at Yapchi at the time."

"Maybe he had approved it," Winslow said.

285

"Or maybe not," Shan suggested. He looked at Somo. "Why would they speak so freely with you about the computer? You're a stranger."

Somo frowned. "Not to everyone."

"Meaning other purbas?" Shan asked.

Somo did not reply.

The roar of an engine suddenly erupted through the stillness of the equipment yard. A grey utility truck sped by.

"They're looking for us," Shan said.

"We're going," Winslow said. "Back to Yapchi."

"There's no transportation arranged," Somo said, searching the yard behind them with a worried expression. "No truck to Yapchi for two days. And even then, the army will be at the gate."

"We have to," Winslow insisted, and his voice dropped. "We have to keep Melissa from dying again."

They sat behind the bulldozer blade for more than an hour, listening to the sound of the utility vehicle moving through the yard and up and down the access road to the highway. Winslow stared absently into the red clay soil beneath them. Shan pulled the ivory rosary from his pocket and rolled the beads between his fingers.

The truck sped by again.

"I asked people here about Tenzin," Somo recalled suddenly. "No word of the abbot of Sangchi being captured or returned to Lhasa. A prominent lama like that, the Bureau of Religious Affairs had a lot invested in him. The head of my school walked out last year in a protest, tried to run away to India. They caught him but he wasn't sent to prison. Sent to somewhere else. Two months later he was back at work, giving speeches about the dangers of reactionaries and leading criticism sessions against other teachers."

Shan considered her words in silence. "You mean political officers might work with Tenzin."

"The government had so much invested him already," Somo said. "I think they will try to rehabilitate him. Reprogram him. Maybe with doctors. Maybe with special religious trainers from the howlers."

Her matter-of-fact tone chilled Shan. He recalled Gendun's words in the hermitage, when the lama had expressed concern over Tenzin. Tenzin was going north, because someone had died. It was the abbot of Sangchi who had died, Shan knew now. But no matter how hard the abbot tried to find a new Tenzin, the government would demand the old abbot back, the tame abbot who had helped so many of their political campaigns.

Shan looked at Somo. It was the slenderest of reeds, only a remote flicker of hope. But if they had not been imprisoned it was possible Lokesh and Tenzin could be found, and saved. He stood up and surveyed the equipment yard. "If no truck is scheduled then we have to find one that is not scheduled," he said in a determined voice.

Winslow sighed, and stood. "First I have to get to that equipment drop site," he said indicating the map in his pocket.

"In the mountains above Yapchi?" Somo asked skeptically. "By to-morrow? Impossible. It's over two hundred miles."

But Winslow was already jogging back toward the compound.

Minutes later they walked down one of the long alleys between the housing units, ducking into the shadows twice when they heard the sound of a truck nearby, then again when a helicopter flew low overhead. It was early afternoon, and the units appeared to be empty, the workers all engaged in jobs, or waiting for jobs in the buildings around the square.

When Shan opened the door to his assigned trailer the unit was lit only by the sunlight coming in the small high windows. But someone leapt up from a bunk at the back of the unit, hastily buttoning his shirt. It was the oily young Han who had taken Shan to the messhall. There was a movement on a bunk behind him and a sleepy face appeared above a sheet, a young woman, naked, with streaked makeup on her face. A single red boot lay on the floor beside the bed. One of the mai xiao nu who had been at the bar the night before. She sat up in the bed looking at them with a surprisingly cheerful expression, slowly raising the sheet to cover her breasts.

The youth looked at Shan nervously, then Somo stepped forward and he relaxed. "Plenty of room for everyone, brother," he offered with a roguish grin. But as the door slammed shut and Winslow appeared, the man's expression tightened. He stared uncertainly at Shan, and shrugged, shifting his gaze to the American.

"I was looking for some clothes," Shan said.

"No one's touched your stuff." The man gestured toward the bunk Shan had slept in.

"I had nothing," Shan said. For the first time he noticed a ring of keys hanging from the man's belt. Perhaps he was the attendant for the unit.

"So see a supply officer," the man said. "At the—" He was cut off by the shrill sing-song squeal of a siren. "Ambulance to Golmud," he said knowingly.

"Who was hurt?" Shan asked.

"Manager in the warehouse. Bad fall. Broke both arms." The man eyed them suspiciously. "Sometimes people have bad joss. They say something wrong and bad things happen. I tell them, don't act like it's different here because of all the foreigners. It's just like the rest of the world."

Shan considered the man's words a moment, then exchanged a worried glance with Winslow. Someone in a brown jacket had caught up with the supply manager, and interrogated him. Probably, Shan thought with a shudder, Zhu himself.

"There're clothes here," the youth said in a new, tentative voice, the voice of one accustomed to bargaining. He gestured toward the other bunks and the lockers that stood between each. "But I'm in charge of the unit. I would get criticized if, say, thieves broke in when I wasn't here." It had the sound of an offer.

Shan looked at his companions. He had no money, and his meager belongings had been left behind in the mountains above Yapchi. Winslow lowered the small knapsack he still carried and looked inside. He frowned, looked up, then studied its contents again. He had given his stove and fuel to Dremu, his food to the children at Yapchi. He pulled out the sleek pair of binoculars. The young man's eyes widened as he accepted the glasses from the American. With the air of a diligent shopkeeper, he hung them around his neck and began unlocking the lockers with his set of keys.

When they left ten minutes later all three wore hard hats, and Shan a pair of brown, oil-stained coveralls over his own clothes. Somo and Winslow wore the green venture jackets, Somo a bulky sweater under hers that gave her the appearance of a thick-shouldered man.

"We still have no plan," the purba complained. "I should go back to the office. I can create some kind of distraction with the computer perhaps."

"No," Winslow said in a conspiratorial tone. "We're doing it cowboy style this time."

The American led them through the maze of trailers to the far side of the compound where two large helicopters sat in front of a small hanger. One of the machines was being loaded with crates of supplies. They had waited only five minutes before the machine was loaded and a trim figure wearing a tight red nylon jacket and an American-style cap over dark glasses strode out of the building, flicking a cigarette over his shoulder as he approached the aircraft. Winslow pointed to a stack of small cardboard boxes. Each of them picked up one and walked toward the helicopter as the man opened the cockpit door.

"They said all cargo was stowed," the man protested, studying them with an impatient gaze as they lowered the boxes onto the tarmac.

"They were right," Winslow replied, then quickly opened the cargo door behind the cockpit and climbed inside, pulling Shan and Somo in behind him before slamming it shut. The cowboy way, Shan thought uneasily.

The pilot sighed, as though he was used to such antics. "Sorry, no riders scheduled today. I get too many headaches from Personnel when I move people around without paperwork." He closed the cockpit door and began flipping switches on an overhead control panel.

"Where you headed?" Winslow asked.

"Camp Nine. Southwest. The British team."

"Perfect," Winslow said good-naturedly. "We're going southwest, too. Near Yapchi."

"Not Yapchi. Not today. Yapchi field drop is tomorrow." The pilot seemed unruffled by the strangers in his craft, but Shan saw that his hand was hovering over the microphone on his control panel. At the side of the hanger were two men in the brown jackets of venture security, their backs turned to the aircraft. The engine was beginning to whine as it warmed up.

"Change in plans," Winslow announced.

The pilot looked back and sighed, lifting the microphone as he did so. "Sorry. I have to get in the air. You want Yapchi, check with Personnel to get the paperwork done. I'll lift off after breakfast." He touched a switch on the microphone and it hissed with static.

"But it's an emergency," Winslow said, still smiling at the man.

"I don't think so," the pilot shot back, impatient now, and raised the microphone to his lips.

"In the name of the U.S. government I requisition this aircraft," Winslow announced in a new, sterner voice. He raised his passport out of his bag.

The pilot lowered the microphone. "Good joke," he said with a shrug. "I like Americans. Just go now and no one knows anything. If I call security it will go badly. Reports have to get filed. Security," he said slowly, examining them more carefully now, "is already really pissed about something."

Winslow pulled out his map and pointed out the coordinates, holding his passport with his fingers against one corner of the map. "A fast chopper like this, wouldn't take much longer for you to slightly change course."

The pilot looked at the passport, frowned, and lifted the mike again.

Winslow pushed it down. "Listen to me," he said in English. "Someone's going to get killed."

"That's it," the pilot said, and pulled away from the American, his hand now on the cockpit door handle.

Winslow sighed and looked at his backpack, sitting at his feet. With a chill Shan remembered that the American had Lin's gun. He glanced at Shan, then extended his passport toward the pilot. "I am an American diplomat—look." He opened the passport to the information page on the inside. "In Beijing, at the embassy, we get memos from security warning us to watch out for pickpockets, because American diplomatic passports are so valuable on the black market in China. Smugglers pay a fortune for them. A good embassy passport, one with five or six years left, can go for ten thousand U.S."

The pilot's hand drifted away from the door, and he accepted the passport for closer inspection. "Seven years left on mine," Winslow said. "I just go back to the office, say it was stolen, and they give me a new one."

"Then they invalidate this one," the pilot rejoined.

"Doesn't affect the value. Black market buyers know they can still use it anywhere that doesn't have automated clearance systems, any border station without a computer uplink to the centralized files. Meaning eighty percent of the world."

The pilot stared at each of them a moment, then grinned, put the passport in his pocket, and engaged the rotors.

You will sense a great rushing like a strong wind when you die, with a floating sensation, and the world will soar around you. The words of the death rite echoed in Shan's mind as they shot over the rough, dry landscape. Wearing the earphones that hung on the back of the seat in front of him, leaning on the small window, Shan found a distant place within and simply experienced the rushing of the land beneath. Riding in a helicopter could be a meditation exercise, he mused, to understand how vast, and transitory, the world was.

The pilot did not argue when Winslow asked him to bypass Yapchi's main camp, coming in low from the west so as not to be seen. He would not, Shan realized, want anyone to know he had departed from his assigned route, which would have been west of Yapchi in any event. As they approached the site Winslow had marked on the map the pilot guided the helicopter low over the mountains, hugging the contours of the ridge, until suddenly Shan realized they were hovering. Winslow and the pilot were pointing to a clearing near the top of the ridge and glancing at the map. Then abruptly, the machine tilted forward a hundred yards, straightened and sank. They touched down hard, Winslow flung open the door and they leapt out. The pilot offered a mock salute, hesitated, looking around the bleak terrain, then examined the three figures beside his machine. He unbuckled his harness and rummaged around the cargo compartment. Moments later he began tossing things out of the open door. Two blankets. A first aid kit. A down vest and, finally, a bag of American potato chips.

Seconds later the machine was gone and they stood alone in the wind on the high ridgetop clearing. Winslow handed the vest to Somo, as Shan gathered up the other items in one of the blankets and slung it over his shoulder, then trotted to the nearest outcropping. He felt strangely uneasy being in the clearing.

"You want to find Miss Larkin," Shan said to the American when Winslow had caught up with him. Somo and I want to find the purbas. I think they may be at the same spot."

"You don't know that," the American asserted. "Christ, everything is a conspiracy with you."

Shan sighed. "In the helicopter I realized something. When Somo told me what Larkin had done with the computer I asked why would anyone speak with Somo about what Larkin did. That was the wrong question. I should have asked why would Somo's contact know what Larkin did, if she had gone so far to preserve her secrecy. There can be only one answer. Because she was with purbas, because purbas are working with her for some reason. That explains why Zhu is so interested in her. A foreigner helping the resistance, the government would—" Shan stopped in mid-sentence. Winslow grinned back at him.

Somo gave a reluctant shrug, but nodded slowly as the two men studied her. "I don't know any details. It's a different project, a different team. Bad security, for everyone to know what the others are doing."

Shan nodded agreement. "Rivers," he said. "We know she is marking rivers. We know Tibetans are collecting water from rivers." He asked Winslow for the map, and traced with his finger each of the blue lines that radiated out of the mountains. He climbed to the top of the outcropping. They could see two of the small rivers, emerging from narrow canyons to flow to the west and south.

"She's expected to be here tomorrow," Winslow said. "She's not here now. And she wouldn't be likely to travel all night in the mountains. So say she's no more than half a day's walk from here." He made a wide circle with his finger on the map. "But to the west she would be out of the Yapchi oil concession," he added.

"Sky birthing," Winslow said. "That man taking the bottle to the Green Tara, he said something about going to the sky birthing." He frowned and searched the horizon.

Suddenly Shan looked up and pointed to the main peak of Yapchi Mountain. "We know where the sky is born," he declared with a grin.

They had been walking for three hours, feeling increasingly uncertain that they could find the place they sought, when suddenly a Tibetan youth appeared, jogging along a trail that ran laterally below them on the slope they were descending. He had no pack, not even a heavy coat, but he clutched something in his hands. Shan looked at Winslow, who was rubbing his temples with a grimace, then at Somo. She grinned, tightened the laces of her shoes, grabbed the bag of potato chips and leapt down the slope.

They watched, Winslow taking two more of his pills, as the purba runner advanced on the youth, but when Somo was still two hundred yards from him, the boy dropped out of sight below a ridge. When Shan and Winslow crested the ridge the American gave a shout of glee, one of his strange cowboy hoots. Somo was sitting with the boy three hundred yards away. As they approached they could see the boy was stuffing the chips into his mouth, speaking in a relaxed fashion with Somo. But before they were within earshot the youth stood, waved at the two men good-naturedly, and began running again.

"He had a bottle of water," Somo said in a meaningful tone. "Only a small bottle of water, for the Green Tara."

They followed the path the boy had taken until, with an hour of light left, Somo raised her hand in alarm. A noise like thunder was echoing off the mountain in front of them. Shan gestured her forward, and five minutes later they stepped onto an open ledge that revealed the source of the thunder far below. Shan pointed toward a tiny line of shadow on the towering rock monolith above them.

"That damned goat trail," Winslow said. "The one Chemi led us on into Yapchi." They stood at the edge of a broad U-shaped chasm filled with mist, the place Chemi had shown them the week before from far above, the place where clouds were born.

Somo pointed downward. On the other side of the gorge, far below, they could see the boy again, following a trail that spiraled down into the mist. Half an hour later, daylight almost gone, they were on the trail, at the edge of the mist, descending toward the thunder sound, warily hugging the wall as they sought footing on the slippery path. What had Chemi said of the place? Some people believed a demon lived there.

"We can't climb back up in the dark," Winslow warned, rubbing his temple again.

Shan eyed the treacherous path uncertainly. "The boy didn't come back," he said, and stepped forward into the mist.

In another few minutes the mist began to clear, and they looked out over a roiling mass of water, a narrow, powerful river that tumbled into the chasm and then, in a violent maelstrom, seemed to boil itself away. There was no outlet. Water was not leaving the gorge, except in the small clouds they had seen drifting skywards.

Somo stared at the strange sight with wide, frightened eyes. "It could be what they said," she offered in a near whisper, meaning, Shan knew, that the strange, powerful place could indeed be home to a demon. He fought a temptation to step back into the mist, to hide in the clouds.

Suddenly a sharp cracking sound joined the thunder, and a piece of the rock wall beside him burst into fragments. An instant later a patch of wall on the other side, by Winslow, split open followed by the sharp whine of a ricochet. Someone was shooting at them.

Chapter Fifteen

Winslow dropped to his knees, pointing toward a hole in the side of the gorge below them, where the barrel of a rifle protruded from the shadow. He began fumbling with his pack, cursing under his breath. Shan, suddenly remembering that the American carried Lin's pistol, pushed Winslow's arm down.

Somo removed her green jacket and called out. "Lha gyal lo!" she cried, one hand in the air, the other conspicuously grabbing the gau around her neck.

A Tibetan man burst out of the shadows, brandishing a long rifle. He stared at them, acknowledging Somo with an angry frown, then motioned them forward with the tip of his weapon. As he stepped down the sloping trail Shan saw that the hole in the rock was actually a wide undercut, ten feet high and thirty long, where the river must have once eroded part of the wall. The man waited for them, exchanged a few whispered words with Somo, and led them toward a deeper patch of shadow which proved to be a heavy blanket hung from a timber wedged in the rock.

They followed a short tunnel, through another hanging blanket, and stepped into a cavern with a high vaulted ceiling, perhaps forty feet wide, lit by several bright gas lanterns.

The boy they had seen above sat near the entrance watching, round-eyed, the activity in the chamber. Two young men, one of them a purba Shan had seen with Tenzin, huddled over a map spread across a flat rock. On a table made of long planks laid across two stacks of flat stones a portable computer sat open, its screen displaying what seemed to be a three dimensional cross-section of a mountain, in many colored layers. Several rifles leaned against the back wall. Beyond the computer, he saw two middle-aged Tibetans bent over two microscopes. A third figure, in a green jacket, leaned over a rack of test tubes, scribbling in a spiral notepad.

Winslow froze and made a small choking sound. The figure in green straightened and turned slowly. It was a woman with unkempt, curly reddish blond hair gathered in a short braid at the back. She opened her mouth as though to speak, but only stared at Winslow, her green eyes puzzled.

"Dr. Larkin, I presume," Winslow said softly in English. For the first time since Shan had known him the American seemed at a loss for words. He just stared at the woman with a small, self-conscious grin. She was shorter than Winslow, though not by much, and perhaps ten years younger. Her high cheekbones would have given her an elegant appearance, but for a sprinkling of freckles on each.

The woman glanced peevishly at the two Tibetans at the map, then at the sentry standing at the entrance. "You're the one from the embassy," she said in English. She stared at Winslow strangely. Not in anger, or frustration, but as if there was something about Winslow that perplexed her. "The one the Tibetans call the cowboy. They said you were gone."

"I was," Winslow said, still grinning. "I came back. To warn you," he added after a moment.

Melissa Larkin frowned, and glanced at the men with the map again. "We are in no danger," she said. "Comrade Zhu did me the favor of already reporting me dead," she added.

"Only to clear the field," Winslow declared. "Comrade Zhu wants you dead again," and then, switching to Tibetan, he began explaining what they had learned in Golmud. The American geologist remained silent as Winslow spoke—pouring three mugs of black tea, but keeping her eyes on Winslow the whole time. One of the men at the map darted to the back wall, returned with an automatic rifle, an army weapon, and disappeared behind the blanket at the entrance.

"A trap?" Larkin asked. "Sounds a bit melodramatic."

"I've worked in China for over five years," Winslow said. "And you have been in China and Tibet almost as long. What part don't you believe? That the venture's given up on you? That the Chinese would want to stop you from working with certain Tibetans? That Comrade Zhu would go to the trouble of coming back into the mountains and not just send the army in? All the others might think you're dead. Zhu knows better, because he planned it, because he lied to me, lied to Jenkins, lied to everyone to make us think that."

Larkin smiled as if amused by Winslow's words. The expression made little indentations on either side of her mouth. Shan searched for the word in English. Dimples. She gestured Somo toward the man who remained at the map, and stepped away to join the purbas in hushed, urgent dialogue.

Shan stared at the computer and racks of test tubes. On the table was another map of the region, with thick lines drawn in several bold colors. He inched closer and studied it. Each line had a number inscribed at its end. One, two, three, through six. He looked up and found the woman in the green jacket, with the green eyes, standing three feet away, staring at him.

"You're the Green Tara," Shan ventured, "the one they bring water to."

"Not my idea, that name. It's embarrassing," Larkin said.

"A protector deity," Winslow said with another grin. He seemed unable to stop smiling. He had come to Tibet for a body and discovered a living woman.

Shan saw that one short line on the map, labeled seven, ran only for an inch on the paper, on the mountain above them, then continued for two inches in red dashes. "You plot river courses," he said in confusion. He spotted several long plastic tubes of colored powder leaning against the back wall. "You drop markers in rivers. But the rivers are already mapped. Why?"

"Not all are mapped," the American woman said. "Not this one. Not the Yapchi River."

"The Yapchi?"

"That's what we call it."

"What's a river in the mountains have to do with oil?"

Larkin sighed. "Do you know how many geologic mysteries remain on the planet? I mean major unknowns. A hundred and fifty years ago the sources of many major rivers had yet to be found. The tectonic plates had not been defined, or even theorized. Many of the world's greatest peaks had yet to be discovered. Vast regions had yet to be mapped. Today, outside the bottom of the oceans, what's left? In all my career I had never hoped to have a taste of such excitement. But then I came to Yapchi camp." Her gaze drifted toward Somo and the other purbas, still speaking in quiet tones. "After four days on this mountain I knew something was wrong. The water coming off the mountain wasn't nearly enough, given the size of the snowpack and dimensions of the watershed."

"You mean you discovered this river? But it's not a river. I mean—"

"It is and it isn't. It's a hidden river. A buried river. The river tumbles down the mountain for three miles and slams into this gorge. It's the wrong place, I thought at first. A fluke of the terrain, maybe just a temporary feature that happened this year because of a rockslide somewhere above that blocked the normal watercourse. Nature doesn't send rivers into deadend canyons."

"You mean it goes inside, underground from here," Shan said. "A new feature for maps of the region."

"Like the Upper Tsangpo." Winslow gave a low whistle. "You'll be famous," he said with a new tone of respect.

Larkin acknowledged Winslow's words with a surprised expression, a nod of respect. A few years earlier a team of American explorers had gained international notoriety by scaling a treacherous, uncharted gorge in Tibet to confirm the existence of a beautiful waterfall that had been spoken of in Tibetan myth.

"But why would Zhu hate you for that."

Larkin looked at the man with Somo then at the two older men at the table, who continued to work at the microscopes, pausing sometimes to lift water from the test tubes with small droppers. "He doesn't like my helpers."

Shan stared at the two Tibetans. They were not purbas, or at least not like any he had known. They looked like professors. Somo appeared at his side. "They are friends," she said pointedly, meaning that no one would offer their names. "Beijing will be furious," Larkin said, her eyes suddenly flush with excitement. "The discovery will be announced overseas, and credited to Tibetans. And if we discovered that it emerged north of the mountains it would be the new headwaters."

The Tibetans all grinned at Shan. Larkin meant that the little river they had discovered would be the new source of the Yangtze, China's greatest river, announced and proven by Tibetans. Beijing would indeed be furious. Beijing would be apoplectic. It was Shan's turn to grin.

An hour after dawn the next day they arrived at the high, remote clearing where Shan, Winslow, and Somo had been dropped by the helicopter the day before. Long rays of sunlight cut horizontally across the windblown ridge. The supplies had not arrived. The two purbas who had been with the map the day before stole away in opposite directions to circle the landing zone. Larkin had not accepted that Zhu wanted to do her harm, but she had agreed to leave early for the supply drop, and had listened with an amused expression to Winslow's suggestion that they might want to test Zhu with a trick. If Zhu were indeed intending to harm Larkin, he would not come in the helicopter with the supplies for fear of frightening her away, and because the pilot might become a witness. He would have himself dropped perhaps a mile away and wait until the helicopter completed the supply drop. The purbas would watch the trail that led to the nearest clearing, the likely dropoff point, while Winslow rigged a decoy. "Be careful. Watch everywhere," Somo warned the two sentries as they began to jog to their post. "We don't know where that hidden patrol is." Hidden patrol. The words caused Shan to survey the rugged landscape again. She meant Tuan's hidden squad of knobs.

Larkin still gazed with amusement as they watched from the rocks. She had seemed touched that Winslow had gone to such lengths to locate her, but although she did not give voice to the point, it seemed apparent she thought she needed no one's help. Yet the two Americans had warmed to each other, preparing the evening meal together the night before, and walking side by side on the trail that morning, sharing stories of home and mindless bureaucrats and experiences in Tibet, laughing softly together sometimes, even pausing to watch a hawk floating in the mountain updrafts.

After an hour of watching from the rocks Larkin gave a conspicuous yawn, casting an impatient glance at Winslow, then produced her spiral pad and began studying her notes.

Somo seemed troubled somehow. Finally she cast an anxious look toward the rocks on the opposite side where the two purbas kept watch, then turned to Shan. "They didn't want me to tell. They don't know you, said you and I were not part of this project. But you have to know. It's just that those bottles of water that go to the Green Tara. Sometimes they come with messages."

"Secrets," Larkin interjected, with a tone of warning.

"Sometimes about movements of knobs and soldiers, and Religious Affairs. Lokesh and Tenzin are not at Yapchi. But for the past two days none of them have moved south into Amdo town or north into Wenquan," Somo reported. "And no helicopters are known to have landed at Yapchi or anywhere else within twenty miles."

Winslow opened his map with a puzzled look, and shared it with Shan. Wenquan was the first town in Qinghai, going north. Amdo was the next town south for anyone going toward Lhasa.

"They weren't taken where anyone would expect," Somo said in a hushed, urgent voice. "Not to jails. Not to Lhasa. Not to the airport to be sent to some other prisoner facility. Not to any known reprogramming facility." There was nothing on the section of highway between the cities, except a short thin grey line intersecting it from the west. "There is only one place," she said, pointing to the end of the line. "Norbu gompa."

It made no sense. But it would make less sense for Religious Affairs and the soldiers to hold the prisoners at Yapchi, and certainly the soldiers knew about Norbu. Shan's mouth went dry as he recalled the political signs at the gompa, the strange, bullying air of the men in white shirts and the predatory gaze of Chairman Khodrak.

"And there's something else, something that has the others confused. The howlers and the soldiers had a big argument at Yapchi. Tuan and one of Lin's officers were shouting at each other the night after Tenzin and Lokesh were taken, and the next morning Tuan and all his men were gone."

Suddenly there was a whistle from across the top of the ridge. A helicopter soared into view, the same sleek machine that had deposited them there the day before. In moments it landed, and two men began unloading several small cartons and nylon bags. In less than five minutes they were done. The men pounded a tall stake into the ground, an orange pennant fixed to the top, and leapt back inside. In seconds the machine was gone.

Winslow leapt to his feet, Somo a step behind him. "I need those supplies!" Larkin called after him, then sighed and sank back against her rock to read her notes.

Ten minutes later Winslow and Somo had returned and the two purba sentries began stealing back along the perimeter of the clearing, having signaled that someone was approaching. The boxes still stood in the center of the field but they had been rearranged. In the center were two figures wearing the coveralls and green helmets Shan and Somo had worn from Golmud. Winslow had fastened a twist of brown grass at the back of one helmet, like a braid of hair. They were dummies, stuffed with the blankets from the shipment, one held up with the stake, the other propped on the boxes. The green figures were slightly bent, as though reading the manifest, their backs toward the path the purbas watched.

"Thirty minutes," Larkin announced impatiently when the purbas returned. "Thirty minutes and I go out and take my equipment." But barely five minutes had passed when one of the purbas snapped his fingers and pointed to the north. Shan ventured a glance around the rocks. Three figures had appeared at the top of the trail, and were bent, running for cover.

"That idiot Zhu probably just wants to pilfer some of my supplies," Larkin fumed. "The little bastard probably sells things on the—" She was interrupted by the sickening crack of a long-range rifle. It shot twice more, and the purbas, their faces drained of color, began pushing Larkin away, down the other side of the ridge.

Shan slipped his head around the rock one more time. The dummies were sprawled over the boxes, one of the helmets in pieces. And from the other side of the clearing strode Special Director Zhu, a hunting rifle perched on his shoulder. His pace was jaunty, as if he were going to collect a trophy.

They dared not take the trail back to the gorge, for it exposed them on a long open slope where they would make easy targets for anyone with such a weapon. Shan led them downward, onto a path at the back of the mountain. In an hour they arrived at the mixing ledge.

Nyma, on a rock near the hidden entrance, called out excitedly, then ran to greet them. As she reached them, however, she paused and looked uncertainly at Shan's companions. She studied Melissa Larkin then turned toward Winslow with a knowing nod. "You never really thought she was dead," she observed solemnly. "I knew that, but to speak of such things could be bad luck."

Larkin smiled awkwardly. She had been deeply shaken by what Zhu had done. She had, Shan suspected, assumed she would go back to the venture when her work with the purbas was done. Now she knew the Special Projects Director would rather see her dead.

Shan quickly introduced Lhandro and his parents, the only occupants of the rooms. They had not seen the medicine lama. Lhandro and his mother served tea as Shan explained what had happened to Tenzin and Lokesh, and the news of Tenzin's true identity. Afterwards Shan found Anya and Lin beyond the gnarled old juniper on a blanket with a bowl of cold tsampa balls, talking and pointing toward clouds. It had the air of a picnic. He stopped fifty feet away. They did not see him. The colonel had his hands together, and the girl was tying a complex pattern of yarn around his fingers. There was an odd noise coming from Lin, as if he were in pain. Shan stepped closer. No, Lin was laughing.

As Shan approached the girl finished her tying. She looked into Lin's face expectantly then pulled one end of the yarn and the entire structure of yarn collapsed. Lin laughed again. Shan stepped forward. They both looked up, startled. Lin frowned and seemed to curse under his breath. Anya patted the blanket beside her and Shan sat.

They did not speak. Anya offered Shan the bowl of tsampa, then pointed at a large bird of prey, a lammergeier, soaring over one of the long ridges below. Shan looked toward the south. Somewhere in the haze near the horizon stood Norbu. Lin pointed to a flight of geese moving in the direction of Lamtso. Once, Shan recalled, Lin had ravaged a line of geese with an automatic rifle.

Suddenly a gust of wind grabbed the yarn on the blanket and carried it to the rocks thirty feet away. Anya sprang up to chase it.

"They took my friends," Shan said quietly.

"That old one, and the tall one who calls himself Tenzin," Lin said. It was not a question, as if he had known they would be taken.

"Tenzin was the abbot of Sangchi, the one who disappeared."

"Fled," Lin snapped. "That's what thieves do. I don't care what the others call him. He is a thief. My thief." He frowned at Shan. "They will never do a hostage exchange."

"No," Shan said in a slow voice, and studied the officer, gradually grasping Lin's meaning. "You are not a hostage, colonel. Not a prisoner."

When Lin turned his head it caused him obvious pain. "You say that because you know I can't leave anyway," he said with a grimace. "I get dizzy when I walk just a few paces. The girl helps me."

"She saved your life. No one would have dug you out of those rocks if she had not been there. The least you can do is use her name."

"They call her Anya," Lin acknowledged in a tight, resentful tone.

"My friends were captured because they went to look for medicine for you."

Lin made a sound like a snort, and his lips curled into a cold smile as though the news pleased him. Anya still chased the yarn up the slope, her uneven gait causing her to stumble frequently.

"If you had asked them to get that medicine, to go back to that valley where your soldiers waited," Shan said pointedly, "they still would have gone."

Lin looked at Shan through squinting eyes, his lips pursing as if he had bit something sour. He said nothing, and his gaze drifted toward Anya, who looked like a child at play now. They watched in silence a long time. The girl seemed to have forgotten them for a moment, as she knelt to look at some flowers.

"The girl shows me things," Lin said. "Anya," he added hesitantly, and turned slowly back to the landscape below. "When they come, I'll see that she is not harmed. She can go back to her home."

Shan stared at the officer. When they come. He meant his mountain combat troops. "She has no home," Shan said, ignoring the threat in Lin's words.

Lin frowned again and watched another skein of geese. "I'll get her some food to take, some shoes maybe. In the mountains you need good shoes."

"Where she lived is burned down. Yapchi."

"Damned fools," Lin shot back. "I didn't make them do that."

"Of course you did," Shan replied, just as quickly. He and Lin exchanged a taut stare, then Lin broke away as Anya called out. She was limping back with the yarn, and a rock she wanted to show them with yellow lichen in the form of a lotus flower.

As he retreated to the back of the plateau, Shan looked up and froze. There was something new in the rocks above, just a hundred yards away, just past where the field of talus started. He climbed a rock for a better view. There was a figure sitting among the boulders. Jokar. The old medicine lama was meditating above them. How long had he been there? No one had seen him for three days. Had he been meditating in the rocks all the time, watching over the mixing ledge and the distant Plain of Flowers? Where, Shan wondered, was his guardian? At the herb shelf there had been signs that two people had slept there.

Inside, Lhandro and his father were arguing. His father, having heard about Tenzin and Lokesh, wanted to return immediately to Yapchi. Lhandro kept telling his father that there was nothing to be done at Yapchi for the two prisoners. As Lepka saw Shan he broke off his dialogue and stepped to the doorway of one of the empty meditation cells, staring into the darkness. "It's the stickmen," the old man muttered toward the shadows. His voice was strangely feeble. "The stickmen never let up."

Nyma glanced at Shan with a sad expression as Lepka stepped inside the cell. "Sometimes he is like this. His mind wanders."

"What does he mean?" Shan asked.

"It's from his childhood," Nyma said. "A toy I think."

"Monsters from his dreams," Lhandro's mother said over Shan's shoulder in a voice tight with worry. "For years he has had nightmares every few weeks, crying out about stickmen," she added. "But this month, almost every night the bad dreams come."

Shan looked about the chamber. Winslow and Larkin were talking excitedly. The two purbas who had come with Larkin were speaking in low urgent tones with Somo about Lin. Shan studied the purbas. Perhaps he had spoken too hastily in telling Lin he was not a prisoner.

How many crimes, how many motives, he thought as he watched Lin, then the purbas. Everything was compartmentalized, as Somo had pointed

300

out. Like Beijing's operations. The knobs had been looking for the medicine lama. The mountain troops had been looking for Tenzin. Tuan and his shadow Public Security squad were looking for the killer of Deputy Director Chao. Khodrak sought a man with a fish. Special Projects Director Zhu had falsely reported Larkin's death so he could stalk and kill her. Why? Because she had been taken under the wing of the purbas, she said. But Shan no longer believed it. Everyone had their own plans, their own mission, and none seemed to know what the others were doing, or why. Shan did not even understand what Jokar was doing. Had the medicine lama really come so far from India only to wander about the mountains above the Plain of Flowers?

"How long has Jokar been back?" Shan asked Nyma.

"Back? We told you. He's been gone since the day you left."

"But I saw him. On the rocks above."

Nyma rushed outside, Shan close behind. Jokar was gone. Had Shan only imagined seeing the lama?

They stepped around the talus, studying the rocks closely. The old man could easily have fallen. In fact it seemed almost impossible to climb to where Shan had seen him.

But when they returned there was an air of excitement. The purbas had quieted. Lhandro and his father wore looks of confused awe. Lhandro's mother was on a pallet, and the medicine lama was bent over her.

"Suddenly he was just there," Lhandro said. "Standing beside my father in the meditation cell, as if he had just spirited there. No one saw him come in. He said my mother should lie down and asked if she was over her stiff knees. Her knees had been stiff, until we brought the Lamtso salt back."

Jokar moved to Lhandro's father, who sat nearby. Close to the butter lamps. In the brighter light Shan saw a discoloration on Jokar's neck, a large dark bruise that he had not noticed before. As if the lama had been beaten.

Jokar touched Lepka's pulse and the two men began speaking, in low tones at first, then in a more relaxed, louder fashion—of Rapjung and how the herb gatherers once came every autumn to Yapchi, how sometimes a lama and student would come for a month to stay and mix medicine.

"I remember a beautiful house there," Jokar said, "like an old wooden temple." His voice was like shifting sand. He kept holding Lepka's wrist as he spoke.

Lepka smiled back. "That house brought serenity to many people."

When the lama was finished with Lepka, he looked at him, and then his wife. "Sometimes," Jokar said quietly, "don't always use that staff of yours. Lean on your wife. She is a strong staff, too."

Nyma sat in the corner, watching Jokar with an expression of guilt and awe. She still wore her rongpa clothes. Shan had not seen her doing her rosary since the day the village burned.

301

The purbas lingered in the shadows of the opposite corner, watching uncertainly. "Are they scared of him?" Shan asked Somo, when she retreated toward the door.

"No. But I'm scared. They seem sure he is the one now, they're saying more purbas should come and guard him."

"The one?"

"The monk who has come to fill the chair of Siddhi."

Shan stared at Somo in disbelief and fear. The frail old medicine lama would never propose aggression against the Chinese. But he might know of the chair of Siddhi and want to go there to speak with the people about the Compassionate Buddha. To the purbas it might make little difference, what Jokar said, as long as he took the seat. A prophesy fulfilled would have much power among the people of the mountains, and the legend could be made to serve the purbas' goals. The legend said the lama who sat in the chair was the leader of revolution. Suddenly one of the young Tibetans from Larkin's team rushed forward and knelt beside Jokar.

"Rinpoche," the youth blurted out, "will you come, will you do this thing for all of us?"

Jokar slowly turned, cocking his head at the man.

"Will you take the chair of Siddhi?" When Jokar replied with only a stare the purba repeated the question in a shaking, excited voice.

The lama offered a small smile and nodded. The purba's eyes flared, and he looked back triumphantly at Somo. He leapt up, fastened a small pack to his back, and ran out the door.

When Jokar stood again he walked purposefully to Winslow, who sat only a few feet from Shan, and sat down. The American grinned, then shot an awkward glance at Shan, as if asking what to do. The lama's hand rose and settled over the crown of Winslow's head, not touching it. The hand slowly drifted along his head, neck, and body, an inch off the American's skin. When he finished the lama sighed, and lifted Winslow's wrist. "The mountains have a hard time with you," Jokar said softly.

Winslow cocked his head at the lama, as if trying to understand. "I'm doing better," he said, grinning awkwardly, as if he had decided the lama was referring to his altitude sickness.

"You have come far for this," the old man said. His deep, moist eyes surveyed Winslow again, settling on the crown of his head. "There is that one black thing. You must get rid of that black thing." He paused again and gazed into the American's eyes. He seemed about to speak again, but sighed. It was his turn to cock his head, as if to better understand something he saw in the American. "You've come far," he said again, and slowly rose.

Winslow stared at the floor. He seemed shaken, somehow. He swallowed hard, and looked up at Melissa Larkin, who returned his solemn stare. He grinned awkwardly. "Feels like far," Winslow quipped, then rose and stepped outside.

Five minutes later Shan found the American sitting by the gnarled juniper tree. "You found her," he said uncertainly. "Now you can go back."

"There's a path I'm on," the American said softly, with an odd curiosity in his voice, the curiosity of one who was confused by one's own actions, or emotions. They stared at the tree together. A small brown bird lighted on a nearby branch and watched them. "I'm meant to be on it. It's just that sometimes it's hard to see it."

There was another mystery Shan had not had time to consider, the mystery of who Winslow was, or who he was becoming. "You came to find Miss Larkin's body," Shan reminded him. "You found her alive. You saved her life. Go. Everything that's left—" he struggled for words. "From here, everything becomes very dangerous."

"Zhu's still out there. What if I left and something happened to her?"

"The purbas protect her. They understand the danger now, thanks to you."

Winslow sighed, and rose to his knees, leaning closer to the bird. "In my heart, I have stopped working for the government," he confessed to the little creature, which seemed to listen carefully. Shan detected a new serenity in the American's voice. "Giving up my passport was like a great weight being lifted from me, somehow. It was part of that path, it was meant to be." He turned to Shan. "And now, what Jokar said. He said I had come far for this. I don't think he meant far like in far from America. But what did he mean, the mountains have a hard time with me?"

"I don't know," Shan said, feeling an unexpected sadness. "Something between the mountain deities and you."

"It's just that I'm not finished in Tibet," Winslow said, still to the bird, which stared directly into the American's eyes.

He turned abruptly and looked at Shan. "I had a dream last night. I was floating over the mountains, more peaceful than I have ever felt. I was holding Jokar's hand, and we were floating over the mountains while he laughed and pointed out his special places. We flew with geese over a deep blue lake," Winslow said in a hollow voice. "At the end I looked at him and I said, Rinpoche, every lama needs a cowboy, and he just nodded solemnly." The American looked back at the bird, which still showed great interest in his words.

"It was just a dream," Shan suggested. If Lokesh had heard about such a dream, he would have asked Winslow if he was sure he had been asleep. Lokesh might have said it wasn't a dream, but an awareness event.

"I think it means I'm supposed to help Melissa and the Tibetans. Help Lokesh and Tenzin."

"I thought," Shan sighed, "that you were supposed to be back in Beijing."

"And tell the bureaucrats Larkin's not dead, but don't worry she soon will be? They probably have a form for it. Report of Future Murder."

303

Winslow looked into his hands. "I know you're not going to give up on Lokesh."

"No," Shan said softly. "Leaving him is not what I do."

Suddenly, from near the rock wall, Nyma called for them in a tone of distress.

"He just stopped," she cried when they ran to her side. Her face was ashen. "He leaned against the wall and sighed, then just slid down it. Jokar . . . Jokar is dead."

The lama was slumped against the wall, one leg thrown out, the other pinned under his body. One of his hands gripped a worn bronze dorje. His face gave no sign of life. Lhandro and his parents were saying mantras at a rapid, almost frantic pace. The remaining purbas knelt in a semicircle around the lama, their faces twisted with helplessness.

Shan squeezed between them. Jokar was not breathing. "So old," Nyma said in an anguished voice. "But no one is here to say Bardo."

His fingers trembling, Shan lifted the old man's hand. Lokesh would know what to do. He arranged his fingers as he had seen his friend do dozens of times. There was no pulse that he could detect at first. But then he sensed something like the flutter of distant bird wings. One beat, and after what seemed an impossibly long time, another.

"Sometimes, a man like that can be called away to speak with deities," Anya said at Shan's shoulder. The others stared at her solemnly but no one offered an argument. If one deity came to Anya to speak, another could easily summon Jokar to speak somewhere else. "Part of him could have been called back to that bayal he came from." Jokar was from one of the hidden lands, she meant. It was, as Lokesh might say, as good a truth as any.

With Nyma's help Shan gently pulled out the leg pinned under the lama's body. The man's flesh was cool; not cold, but not nearly as warm as Shan's.

"He is gone," Lhandro moaned. "It happens like this, the organs begin to stop one at a time."

"He embraced the knowledge," Lepka said softly, at the lama's feet. When he saw inquiry on Shan's face he continued. "It was a teaching from Rapjung, that I heard often when I was young. The greatest gift of being human is the knowing, and the greatest knowing is of death." He gazed at Jokar as he spoke, then turned back to Shan as though he needed to explain further. "It is a great gift, the monks would say, to know of your own impermanence."

No one spoke. Even the mantras stopped. Lepka looked about with an expression of curiosity, as if he had not expected anyone to be surprised by his words.

"Someone should sit at each side, to make sure he doesn't fall," Lhandro's mother instructed quietly, and took one side herself. Nyma took the other. Shan stepped back and saw the worried expression on Winslow's face.

"I have a few pills left," the American offered in a helpless tone. Winslow stepped close to Jokar, one of his hands wringing the fingers of the other. "That herb place. I could go back, if someone tells me what to pick."

Shan studied the lama, then the American, not understanding the strange connection developing between them. "He mentioned the black thing," Shan said. "He told you to get rid of it. That's what you can do."

"I didn't understand," the American said slowly, his eyes shifting back and forth from Shan to Jokar.

"The black thing you carry," Shan said.

Winslow looked into the shadows a moment, sighed, picked up his pouch and stepped outside. Shan joined him, a few steps behind as he walked to the rim of the plateau.

He reached Winslow as the American turned back to look at Lin, who had moved to sit on a rock near the gnarled juniper. They stepped past the ruins of the old hut, out of Lin's view, and Winslow opened his pack. "I thought Melissa might need it, with Zhu still in the mountains," he said apologetically.

Shan did not speak, but pointed to a spot far below where a small chasm created a deep shadow. Winslow reached into his pack, pulled out Lin's pistol, and threw it over the edge of the rim. It soared in a wide arc then tumbled downward for a long time until it disappeared into the shadow. In quick succession the spare magazines followed.

A great bird soared close by, a lammergier that dove to investigate the tumbling magazines, then pulled back and sent a long screech after them.

They wandered back to the medicine mixing room in silence and joined the vigil beside Jokar. The rongpa recited the mani mantra. Larkin and Winslow sat at the lama's feet. Somo cradled one of the lama's hands in her own, lightly stroking it. Anya began singing one of her songs, in a whisper, and, strangely, after a moment, Melissa Larkin began humming in accompaniment, as if the American geologist knew the song. More than thirty minutes passed, when suddenly the fingers of one of the lama's hands rose, and Jokar's body jerked slightly forward, then fell back.

Shan had seen deep meditations, had gone into deep meditation himself, and this was not one. Jokar was somewhere else. The lama's eyes opened, though they seemed to have no life in them. They sparked with energy, then faded. Shan watched, scared. The lama's eyes were glazed. His fingers were extending and contracting, as if they were climbing something. The mantras in the back of the chamber grew louder. The purbas had joined in. Melissa Larkin stepped forward with a bowl of tea and gently pressed its warmth against the lama's arm. His eyes flickered again, and his hand reached out as though to clutch something in the air. Jokar's mouth opened and shut and his head bent back, his jaw clenching as though he were in struggle with something.

The chamber fell utterly silent again.

"It's like he's trying to wake from a deep sleep," Lhandro whispered.

But Shan knew it was no slumber. Jokar had not died, Shan knew, but he had gone to the edge of death, or perhaps somehow death had visited him and he was sending it back. The ancient body had given up for a while, but the essence of what was Jokar fought back, as though it had unfinished business. Lepka started a mantra that Shan had never heard before, a pleading mantra, filled with the name of Yamantaka, the Lord of Death.

Then the lammergeier screeched again, so close it seemed the bird was sitting on the rocks over their heads, and an instant later the lama's eyes lit, and stayed lit, and Jokar was with them.

Winslow emitted one of his cowboy hoots and the medicine lama's eyes grew wide; fully awake now, the lama smiled appreciatively at the American, as if it had been the hoot that had summoned him back. But no one offered another word or sound, until suddenly there was movement behind them. Shan turned to see Lin standing in the shadows. How long had he been there, Shan wondered. Had he understood what he had seen? For that matter, did any of them understand?

Jokar breathed deeply. Nyma offered him the tea.

By the time Shan rose, Lin had retreated outside and was studying the gnarled juniper again, as if he expected it to reveal an important secret, or perhaps provide a bird to come listen to him. Shan saw that the constant anger had faded from Lin's eyes. In some ways he was not the same Lin they had met on the road two weeks earlier. But he knew the short-tempered, predatory Lin was still there, just below the surface of the confused man who sat in the shadow of the tree.

"What that old man did . . ." Lin started in a low voice when Shan sat beside him. But he seemed uncertain how to finish. "In the village where I grew up, they would have called him a witch for doing that."

"It doesn't work," Shan said, putting a hand on the end of one of the twisted branches, "trying to explain the Tibetans according to what we learned growing up in China."

A growl came from Lin's throat, as if he were warning Shan away from such conversation.

"It was Religious Affairs that took Tenzin," Shan suddenly declared. "Director Tuan."

"That Tuan? He had no business—" Lin blurted out. He clenched his jaw. "Only because I wasn't there," he spat.

Shan stared at Lin and nodded. "Because Tenzin was your mission. Not Tuan's."

"We all work for the people's government," Lin muttered.

"But Tuan didn't turn Tenzin over to the people's government."

306

"You don't know that."

"He didn't go north on the highway, he didn't go south. He used no helicopter."

"Spies," Lin hissed. "Those who seek government secrets are executed."

Shan ignored the accusation. "I think the government would have special plans for the abbot of Sangchi. There is the Institute for Advanced Tibetan Studies in Beijing." Shan was referring to a favorite venue for realigning wayward Tibetan leaders, a special school created by Mao Tse Tung for instructing senior Tibetans in the precise application of his doctrine. "There's half a dozen medical institutes where an ailing lama might spend a year or two recovering from a lapse. But he hasn't gone to them, or to prison. He hasn't left the area."

"He owes the army first," Lin growled.

"You mean he owes the 54th Mountain Combat Brigade. What used to be the Lujun Division."

Lin glared at him, as though speaking of such things was traitorous. It was the old Lin. Maybe, Shan mused, remembering how Lin had been with the girl, there was now a Lin for Anya and another Lin for the rest of the world. "He stole things from us."

"A piece of rock."

"And military secrets," Lin said in a low voice, toward the tree.

Shan paused. Lin had at last confessed his real interest in Tenzin and the stone. At last confirmed what Shan and Winslow had suspected. "Tenzin has no interest in military secrets."

"What would you know of such things?" Lin shot back. "The traitors who help him do," he added. "Maybe it was the price of the purbas for helping him. Steal information from me for them to use against the government."

"Tenzin would not make such bargains."

"Motive is unimportant. He took secrets. It's treason." Lin looked at him with a gloating smile. "You know how treason proceedings work. Short trial, quick bullet. I can do it with a military tribunal. Secret. The others will keep looking for him along the Indian border long after I have him in a hidden grave in the mountains."

Shan did not reply, but studied the lichen growing at the tip of the branch. "When you go back, colonel," he said at last, "will you try to find him?"

"Of course. I will find him, I will take him from whomever has him. He's mine. The moment he stole from me his life was forfeit. The howlers can't hide him for long. The howlers are playing in a world they don't understand. They'll have to find another tame abbot."

Shan stared at him, weighing the words. Lin could be right, he suddenly realized. It would explain the strange actions of Khodrak and Tuan and the argument between the howlers and the knobs, then the howlers and the soldiers, at Yapchi. They were delving into the world of public security and state secrets, realms that were normally closed to the Bureau of Religious Affairs. Modern China had its hidden worlds, too.

"When you can walk again without falling off the mountain, you may go," Shan said wearily. "But it could be several more days, even a week."

Lin stared at Shan again, rubbed his temple, and blinked. As if, Shan thought, like Jokar struggling to keep control of his body, Lin was struggling to keep the malevolent colonel in control.

"So you should write a letter," Shan suggested.

"No deals. I told you. Kidnapping an officer means lao gai. Or a firing squad. No forgiveness."

Who will forgive us for keeping you alive, Shan wanted to ask. "Perhaps you would want to tell someone you are alive."

"I have no family."

"Soldiers from your unit are searching, thinking you must be dead. Perhaps you would want to give instructions to Director Tuan and the howlers who have Tenzin."

The suggestion caused Lin to pause. An icy glint returned to his face. "Why would you want this?"

"Because it would be the compassionate thing, to relieve the anxiety of your soldiers," Shan suggested. "Because their reaction to such a letter may tell me where my friend is, the one who was arrested with Tenzin." Because I need to reach them before the army does, Shan told himself, because such a letter might stop Tuan from sending them away.

Lin offered a thin smile that hinted of grudging respect. "You weren't always in Tibet."

"I worked for the people's government for twenty years in Beijing," Shan said. "For the party members who ran the government."

"But then you made a pilgrimage to Tibet," Lin said in a taunting voice.

Shan stared at him, then slowly unbuttoned his sleeve and silently showed Lin his lao gai tattoo. "I went to live with a better class of people," he said softly.

Lin's eyes narrowed as he stared at the tattoo. He gazed a long time at the line of numbers, and his expression shifted several times, with anger, suspicion, disdain, and confusion all crossing his countenance. His eyes did not move, but just stared at the empty air, when Shan pulled back his arm.

After a moment Shan rose. "I'll send some paper out. You know we will read the letter before we deliver it. Say anything you wish. Just nothing about Jokar, and nothing about this place." He had taken five steps when he paused and looked back at Lin, who still stared into the air. "That girl, Anya," he said to Lin's back, "she has no family either."

Lin's head pulled up but he did not acknowledge that he heard.

Unexpectedly, there was laughter at the entrance to the hidden rooms when Shan approached it. Winslow was there, with Anya and Nyma, showing them tricks with one of the braided leather ropes the purbas carried. Having made a loop in one end, Winslow was waving the rope over his head and releasing it to catch things. A narrow rock set on its end twenty feet away. A small boulder on the slope above. Anya, standing still, arms at her side, giggled as the rope dropped over her head and closed about her waist. Shan smiled then stepped inside for Lin's paper, which Lhandro offered to take to the colonel when the rongpa learned what it was for. The young purba challenged Shan's judgment at first, but Somo raised her hand to silence him.

"What it means," she declared with a dangerous gleam, "is that Lin will demand the howlers give up Tenzin and Lokesh."

When Shan wandered back outside, another figure had joined Winslow. Jokar, a playful expression in his eyes, stood perfectly erect as the American lassoed him once, twice, then again. Each time the lama nodded his head approvingly, then finally he asked if he could learn the use of the rope. Shan, Anya, and Nyma watched in amusement as the lama fumbled with the rope, slowly twirled it over his head. He missed his target the first three times, then missed no more, finally asking Winslow himself to stand, laughing as he brought the rope down over the American's shoulders.

"It is like archery," Jokar smiled with an approving nod, "without the bow." Then the old lama asked Anya and Nyma to try to lasso him, which they tried lightheartedly for a quarter hour, until the lama suddenly pointed to a rock in the rubble with lichen in the outline, he insisted, of a horse's head, the sign of Tamdin, the horse-headed protector demon.

Shan and Winslow lingered at the rock wall long after the others were called away by Lepka's announcement that fresh tea had been churned.

"I'm going with you," the American declared suddenly. "To Norbu."

Shan sighed. "It was your passport that protected you. After you gave it up, you have no—"

The American woman stepped out of the door. "For what?" Larkin asked Winslow. "Why would you give someone your State Department passport?"

Winslow grinned at her. "Lost it, that's all. I always lost my homework in school."

Larkin stared at him uncertainly. Her face flashed with color and she bit her lower lip. "We're going to find our friends who were arrested," Winslow said quietly.

"At Norbu," Larkin said. "I heard the purbas say they're at Second House."

"You know the gompa?" Shan asked.

"Some of the purbas speak of it. They say it's where the howlers take sick monks to be healed."

The words sent a chill down Shan's back.

"Some of us were in the mountains last month and saw a monk from

309

Norbu. A monk, and a doctor in a blue uniform. With men who looked like soldiers, in white shirts, carrying small tanks of kerosene on their backs. I joked with them and told them they'd save a lot of trouble if they just used yak dung. But they didn't want to joke."

Shan stared at her and was about to ask what they could possibly have been doing with so much kerosene when someone else emerged from the shadows of the doorway. "We can't just march into that gompa," Somo said in a pained voice, as if she had been arguing with them about going to Norbu.

Shan was about to protest. He wanted no one else to go with him, no one else to expose themselves to the near certainty of arrest by the knobs. But Somo had come from Lhasa to help the fugitive lama, had lost Drakte in the struggle to keep Tenzin safe.

"You'll need people who were there before," Nyma said over Somo's shoulder. She was carrying two bowls of tea, which she extended to Shan and Winslow.

He sighed. Nyma, too, could not be refused. "We must make Director Tuan worried," Shan said. "Make him react somehow," he added and, as Lepka appeared, sipping from his bowl, he explained the letter he expected Lin to write.

"A start," Winslow agreed, "but what else is there at this gompa?"

Nyma spoke of the Public Security medical teams they had seen there, and Lhandro spoke of the nervous monks and the frightening, ruthless manner of the chairman.

"What is it that this Chairman Khodrak wants most of all?" Somo asked.

"He's ambitious," Nyma ventured. "He wants to win the Serenity Campaign. He wants to join the Bureau, people say, he wants to get attention so he will be promoted into the Bureau of Religious Affairs itself."

Promoted. Nyma was right, Shan knew, though he'd never before known of a monk who thought in such terms.

"What he wants right now," Lhandro said in a speculative tone, "is a May Day festival. But no one will go. It's a Chinese holiday."

The information seemed useless. They looked at each other, and looked at the sky. Winslow absently traced the pattern of the lichen with his fingertip.

"Your friend Lokesh," a rasping voice interjected from the shadows, "he told me you teach him the Tao te Ching sometimes."

Shan looked up at Lepka in surprise. The old farmer was speaking of the ancient text of the Tao, the teaching Shan had memorized as a boy. When he nodded, Lepka extended a finger in the sandy soil and began drawing. He made four simple lines, a line of two parts over a solid line, over two lines of three equal parts. A tetragram, it was called, used for designating chapters of the ancient book. The lines signified Chapter

Thirty-six, called Concealing the Advantage. As the words ran through Shan's head he realized he was whispering them to his companions:

> In order to weaken it,
> It must be thoroughly strengthened,
> In order to reject it,
> It must be thoroughly promoted,
> In order to take away from it,
> It must be thoroughly endowed.
> This is named subtle wisdom,
> This is how the weak triumphs over the strong.

"A man like Tuan," Shan said with a nod to Lepka, "must be empowered to be destroyed."

Winslow looked up with a devious glint. "Beware of Greeks," he said, "beware of Greeks bearing gifts."

Larkin shared his conspiratorial grin. "A Trojan horse," she said, then turned to the others in the small circle. "It's a legend," she said, and explained.

They sat in silence, letting the words of the Tao te Ching and the Greek legend sink in.

"Perhaps," Shan ventured, "those who run Norbu must be careful what they ask for."

"And what the rongpa and dropka in the surrounding valleys want most of all," Lhandro suggested, "is a spring festival as in the old days."

They spoke for nearly an hour as the kettle boiled and Nyma churned tea. Somo brought out the other purbas, who listened and nodded excitedly. Somo disappeared through the door, emerging a moment later, strapping on her belt pack. She began running up the trail that led back up the mountain.

"Second House had a beautiful gonkang," a wisp of a voice said from behind them as Somo disappeared.

Nyma gasped. Jokar had materialized among the rocks ten feet away. "And the stable. We used to store herbs in that old stable."

Lhandro and his parents stepped out of the door, followed by all the other Tibetans, who sat near Jokar and listened as the lama spoke of life at Norbu gompa sixty years before. It seemed somehow a perfect ending to their planning, like a benediction. Everyone thought the lama had finished when his eyes drifted out over the plateau and the clouds beyond. He leaned forward, as if studying something, as if he saw old Norbu in the clouds. "There is a place," he said with a slow nod, as if he were walking through the rooms in his mind, "in the cells by the stable, at the rear. A secret place, from when they came for the Sixth." The old lama seemed to have lost touch with reality again.

311

But Shan watched the clouds, too, as the others stood and gathered around the tea churn once more. If Jokar could see the gompa in the clouds, perhaps he could see Lokesh. He watched so intensely he was unaware of anyone approaching until a paper, folded tightly into quarters, dropped against Shan's boot. He blinked and saw Lin, studying the Tibetans with suspicion in his eyes.

"You can't touch those prisoners," he growled, rubbing his temple as he spoke. "If you touch them, if you try to take them, Public Security will shoot you." Lin's voice was still weak but his tone was vengeful. He raised his hand and looked as if he were going to make a fist out of it, but after a moment dropped it to his side and seemed to stagger, as if dizzy. "And if the damned knobs don't, I will," he rasped. "I will arrest everyone here. Arrest you and execute you!"

Part Four

BONE

CHAPTER SIXTEEN

When he scoured his mind of fear and laid back with his eyes closed, Shan felt small ripples of contentment coursing around him. Not his own contentment, for he had yet to find and free Lokesh and Tenzin, but that of the Tibetans who had gathered on the flat plain outside Norbu. Children were laughing, horses neighing, men were calling in expressions of wonder, and throughout all was woven the throaty rumblings of yaks. Occasionally, like the seasoning in some exotic dish, he heard the singing rush of arrows.

He had spent an hour that morning sitting near the makeshift archery range a band of dropka had built beyond the tents, sitting on the spring grass, sharpening his awareness on the arrowpoints. The Tibetans had long ago taught him meditation exercises utilizing arrows and bows, sometimes real, sometimes imaginary, and he had discovered what Gendun meant when he had told Shan that archery was not a sport but a teaching. It was a perfect vehicle for achieving focus, and when he emptied his mind sufficiently he could hear, as Gendun had taught him, not just the drawing of the string, the release of the string, the flight of the arrow and its impact, but also the perfect instant of quiet just before the string was released, when the archer and his implements become one. Nothing in his own life was ever so straight, or true, or quick.

The inhabitants of the neighboring lands had brought Khodrak and Padme their May Day festival. It had taken three days, with messengers running back and forth among the surrounding villages and dropka camps, but now a small town of tents had arisen on the plain adjacent to Norbu. Some rongpa came in old trucks, against which they tied canvas flies to sleep under. Dropka families erected tents of heavy felt. A few rongpa had settled into their traveling tents, white-fringed with blue patterns. Once, Lhandro explained, Tibetan townspeople had routinely taken their families to the countryside with such small tents, to celebrate religious holidays by reconnecting with the land, or to complete a kora of a gompa or holy mountain. Many of the Tibetans had not seen each other for years, and the air was filled with exclamations of greeting. Away from the gompa, away from the solitary white-shirted guard at its gate, Tibetans threw barley flour in the air, a traditional form of rejoicing. So traditional, Shan knew, the howlers would try to stop them if they saw it.

In the truck they had met in the mountains, Shan had listened to a strange debate among Lhandro and the purbas. What did they need most of all to bring the local people to the festival, Somo had asked the rongpa. Yaks, the Yapchi headman had said, and archery. There could be no festival without yaks and arrows. To his surprise, the yaks had been easier to assemble than the archers, for archery had been another of the traditions suppressed by the government. As Shan had watched on the second day from the hidden post the purbas had established on the ridge above Norbu, a small herd of yaks had arrived, some already festooned with colorful ribbons and strands of yarn. The archery range, outlined with rocks aligned toward a series of hardened mud targets, had waited until dropka from the deepest part of the ranges had arrived, the dropka who lived farther from the reach of the government.

He started from his dreamlike state as someone touched his arm, and opened his eyes into Anya's smiling face. She had clasped her hand around his own, and he silently let her pull him to his feet, then toward the makeshift pasture.

"Nearly a hundred!" she said excitedly.

Yaks. She meant nearly a hundred yaks, Shan saw as they stepped among the creatures. As he studied the joyful faces of the other Tibetans who gazed upon the animals, he realized that in the impoverished district such an accumulation was rare, representing a significant portion of the inhabitants' collective wealth.

Anya led him into the center of the herd, patting nearly every animal they passed. Sharing a handful of dried cheese with him, she carefully explained the traditional names for the many color patterns. She pointed to a black creature with white spots. "Yak thabo," Anya explained with a dreamy expression, pausing to rub the yak's ears. "Yak dongba," she said, gesturing toward one with a white star on its forehead. A *kawa* had a white head, a *tsen yak* was golden, and one with asymetrical horns was called *ralden*. Anya finally reached a large, purely black animal which greeted them with a low rumbling in its throat.

"I saw Gyalo arrive last night," she whispered. "He put on herder's clothes." Anya began tying braids in Jampa's hair, showing Shan how to fold and twist the hair, as she explained that he was the rarest of all, a *lha yak*, a perfect yak in every sense, protected by the deities and never to be used to carry an impure burden.

Suddenly he realized that Anya was staring past his shoulder with fear in her eyes. He turned to see that she watched the gate of the gompa, nearly two hundred yards away.

"It's time," she announced, and falling silent once more they walked back to the purba's truck. As they reached the shadows at the vehicle's side Nyma appeared and nodded toward the ridge above the gompa. A figure was running at the crest of the ridge, wearing the green uniform of a soldier. Shan watched as the figure ran halfway down the slope, then he climbed into the shadows of the covered cargo bay to sit beside Nyma, who picked up his battered pair of binoculars. The purbas had positioned the truck so the bay faced the front gate and looked into the compound beyond, toward the first of the two-story structures inside, the administrative offices where Shan and Nyma had encountered the Democratic Management Committee of the gompa.

Nyma studied the compound then handed him the glasses. He could see the soldier's face plainly in the lenses as the figure approached the gate. The rongpa and dropka reflexively hurried away from the figure, as they always did from the People's Liberation Army. Only those in the purba truck knew it was not a soldier, but even with his binoculars he could not tell it was Somo. Her hair was tightly tucked under an oversized green wool cap, the kind used under helmets by the mountain troops. Her uniform was complete but soiled, her tunic slightly torn at one shoulder. A leather dispatch case dangled from her other shoulder. The image was of a seasoned soldier who had been campaigning in the high ranges.

The stern white-shirted Han men who had patrolled the festival camp had done so with disinterested, almost careless expressions. The first day a junior official, not Tuan, had strutted among the Tibetans with a suspicious air, as if he were passing judgment on the assembly. When he had shouted orders for several of the dropka to open their gaus for him the dropka had hesitated. But then the purbas had begun playing East Is Red, one of Beijing's favorite anthems, on a portable tape machine and several children appeared waving minature flags of the People's Republic, supplied by the purbas themselves. The howler offered an icy smile of approval, then waved the dropka away before withdrawing with a smug expression. His casual air had worried Shan. Important prisoners should have made the guards more wary.

But still, a single sentry in a white shirt had been posted at the gates at all times since Shan had begun watching from the rocks above two days before. He took encouragement from the presence of the guard, as he did from the news that the dining hall was closed, but still there was no proof that Lokesh and Tenzin were inside the gompa walls. Somo now ran to the nearest guard, spoke in a low tone as she handed him Lin's letter, then darted away as though there was a crisis in the mountains. Everything went as scripted. She would not linger, for fear of too many questions. She would speak in a low voice, in hope of being mistaken for a man, and she would not look at the guard's face, to make it less likely she could be identified later. The guard stared in confusion after the running soldier a moment, then ran inside the administration building with the letter. Shan leaned forward with his binoculars. No one immediately appeared at the door but there was a movement at the window of the second floor office Shan had seen on his first visit. Less than a minute later, with a flush of excitement he watched five figures emerge and stride hurriedly to the gate:

Director Tuan and Chairman Khodrak with the original guard and two more of Tuan's soldiers. As they reached the gate the guard pointed at Somo's receding figure, now far up the ridge. If they followed, the purbas were ready. By the time the guards arrived at the top of the ridge they would see four figures in army tunics, prompted by hidden purbas with signal flags, moving over the crest of the next ridge, hopelessly out of reach.

Tuan looked as though he was about to order some of his men after Somo, but he looked out over the Tibetan encampment and seemed to reconsider. Instead he spoke to one of the guards and the man shot away, toward the structure behind the administrative building.

Nyma shot Shan a grin. "Lha gyal lo," she whispered. Perhaps it was as much evidence as they could hope for.

Yet still the Tibetans in the encampment expressed reluctance to go inside the gompa. If they were to proceed with their plan they needed help from the rongpa and dropka, help in understanding who might be inside, help in avoiding too much of the howlers' scrutiny. But it was a place of monks, a sacred place, despite the Chinese flags that flew between the buildings, and Lhandro cast discouraging looks toward Shan as the leaders of the gathered clans met with the purbas.

A new set of visitors began moving around the camp, two photographers with several monks, led by Padme, who pressed bits of hard candy into the hands of all the children. Shan followed at a distance, watching as the group paused repeatedly to take photographs: Monks with smiling children on their laps. Monks helping to decorate the yaks. Padme gave new nylon jackets to several adolescents and distributed bottles of orange drink, directing the photographers to shoot pictures of all the joyful faces against the brilliant blue sky, then again with the gompa in the background. Padme found tools and had the monks pose with hammers, pretending to repair the rundown buildings outside the gate.

As Padme led his party back into the gompa grounds, Shan lingered in the shadows beside the purba truck, a new hat pulled low over his eyes. He became aware of an old man staring at the truck, a white-haired Tibetan with a leathery face that bore the scars and wrinkles of a long hard life. The man sat forty feet away, his back against a small mound of felt blankets left beside a dropka yurt. Shan realized that not only had the man been there for hours, he had seen him on another day, operating a sewing machine at the gompa gate the first time Shan had visited Norbu. He saw the man's fingers working, two fingers moving in and out by his knee. It could have been a nervous gesture. It could have been a request for someone to approach, by a man who did not know how otherwise to ask. Shan pulled his hat tight and with small, tentative steps ventured near the old man.

The Tibetan nodded as Shan reached him, and Shan hesitantly sat beside him. There were spies everywhere, Somo had warned. Sometimes monks were found to be working for Public Security. Even older Tibetans were coerced into becoming informants by promises of leniency for loved ones in prison. "They say you came from a Chinese bayal to help us," the man said in a strong but hoarse voice.

A Chinese hidden land. The man meant that people didn't come to help from the normal Chinese world. Perhaps it was true, Shan thought. A bayal known as the gulag. "I would like to find a way to help," Shan confirmed.

The man looked about and produced a folded piece of paper from inside his dirt-encrusted chuba. "I used to work at First House," he announced with a proud smile that showed half his teeth to be missing. "Not a monk, but as a carpenter. Once there was beautiful wood growing on those slopes. Sometimes people still come and ask me to make things. Simple things. A table, a chair, a stool. But paper to draw patterns and designs on is always scarce. A man from the kitchens wanted an altar built for his mother, and asked me to draw it for him, so he could buy the wood. He brought this to draw on, when that Padme left it on a table one night."

It was an oversized sheet, a map, Shan saw, a map drawn by an expert hand, or perhaps traced from a printed map. The old man extended a gnarled finger at several notations. "Second House," he explained, pointing to Norbu, at the bottom of the sheet. "First House and Metoktang," he said. He was indicating the Plain of Flowers and Rapjung. The place names were shown, only in Chinese.

"I read and write Chinese," the man said. "Those men at the gompa like to laugh at me, and I just play along. Fools are always to be pitied. Even that man in the kitchens doesn't know I read Chinese. None of them know I studied at the gompa school, with teachers who said we must learn how to live with the Chinese." The man gave a wheezing laugh and gestured back at the map. "If you wish to understand Second House, this is all you need," he announced.

Shan gazed at him uncertainly, then glanced at the newspaper shed, remembering the defiant words secretly written on the board, and went back to making sense of the other marks on the paper. There was a legend that said Sterilized, depicted with an X drawn inside a circle. There was such an X on the far northwest corner of the Plain of Flowers, marked with a date, ten days earlier. There were at least fifteen more such marks on the adjoining lands, with dates, all within the past two months. On Rapjung gompa itself there was such a mark, Sterilized, with a date nine days before. He recalled Larkin's report of a monk and a doctor in the mountains, carrying kerosene. Then suddenly he understood, and felt strangely weak.

"May the gods be victorious," the old carpenter said softly as Shan rose to take the map to the meeting by the truck, where he quickly explained it to the purbas, farmers, and herders at the same time.

"But there is nothing out there," a middle-aged dropka pointed out,

319

confusion on his leathery face. "Nothing but wilderness. Nothing that could be used against us."

"The howlers would call them olds," Shan said, and he saw several of the Tibetans cringe. "Old herbal beds once used by the lamas. Holy sites used by the lamas from Rapjung. That is what Padme is destroying. We took him to Rapjung and he destroyed the buildings there." He paused as Lhandro explained the terrible night at Rapjung when the reconstruction had been reduced to ashes. They had been wrong about the dobdob, Shan knew now. The dobdob must have stopped Padme, beaten him because he had found the monk trying to burn the herbs. He remembered Padme's reaction when he had seen the reconstructed shrines at the old gompa. He had read reports, Padme had said. He meant Public Security and howler reports. It meant the dobdob was trying to stop the howlers, trying to stop the destruction of the herbs. The dobdob, protector of the virtuous, must have been Jokar's companion, the one they had seen in the meadow with Jokar, the one who was now missing.

Gyalo stepped forward to explain what he had seen inside Norbu. Finally Nyma stood up and quietly asked how many knew Drakte. Nearly every hand went up. By the time she had quietly finished explaining that Drakte had been killed trying to help, there were no more arguments from the farmers and herders. They rose with grim determination and broke into groups as the purbas began explaining their plan.

The special medical team was still at Norbu, its technicians looking fatigued as they wandered out among the Tibetans. It meant that the manhunt for the medicine lama had not stopped, and was staying in the area. Why, Shan wondered? What evidence about Jokar kept them at the gompa? Surely if they had known his destination they would have not wasted so many weeks tracking him in the mountains from India.

Less than an hour after the letter was delivered, Tibetans began forming a line at the gate, some of them holding their abdomens, two purbas wearing arms in slings. The guard would not let them inside. They waited patiently, nearly an hour, before one of the men in the light blue uniforms noticed them and instructed the sentry to allow the sick Tibetans to enter, not noticing the single Han among them, wearing a dirty bandage on his hand and his new broad-brimmed hat pulled low around his forehead.

When he arrived at the rear of the compound, Shan was relieved to find none of the discipline he had seen on his first visit. A rope had been strung along on portable wooden posts outside the makeshift clinic, to shepherd the sick into a line. The medical team worked through the first few patients quickly, with an absent air, giving all of them some form of medication. Those released from the doctors milled about the rear of the compound, speaking with those in line, marveling over the large prayer wheel, even admiring the huge pile of yak dung, apparently untouched since Gyalo had left.

Shan and Nyma drifted away from the line and wandered toward the

320

stable where they had been trapped on their first visit. They stopped at the stable and confirming that no one was watching, stepped into the adjacent structure as Shan slipped off his bandage. The low, decrepit wooden building was old, perhaps older than the stable. Its meditation cells, three on either side, and two at the back, were musty, the air stale. Shan remembered Gyalo saying that the gompa had only a third the number of monks it had been built for.

Of all the human-built places Shan had experienced in the extraordinary lands of Tibet none moved him more than the simple wooden cells he sometimes, rarely, discovered in the country's remote regions, in the few structures remaining from earlier centuries. Here men and women had sat through the centuries, engaged in exactly the same pursuit, with the same feelings, the same yearning for awareness that Shan and his Tibetan friends felt. He had awkwardly described to Gendun one of his first encounters with such a cell as visiting a time machine, for somehow he had sensed the presence of monks who had sat there, three or four hundred years before. But no, Gendun had said, not a time machine, for that implied too much difference between us and them, as if the centuries changed those who sought awareness. It was a bridge, he said, a way of stepping beyond time, eliminating time, reaching for the same plane of awareness that enlightened beings inhabited, without regard to time. He paused, remembering Gendun's words, and for an instant wanted nothing more than to sit and meditate in one of the cells.

"Jokar Rinpoche said it was from the time of the Sixth, when they came for him," Shan said, stepping past Nyma to the rear cells. He was still struggling to see through Jokar's words, still trying to separate those words meant for this world and those meant for another.

"Lhabzang Khan," Nyma said in a distracted tone as she stepped into one of the rear cells. She raised a finger and tentatively touched the old cedar, as if it might crumble. "Lhabzang Khan from Mongolia invaded Tibet and kidnapped the Sixth Dalai Lama. His army came through Amdo on the northern road."

It had been three hundred years earlier, Shan remembered, when the young Sixth had been kidnapped by the Mongolians, with the notion of presenting him as a gift to the Manchu emperor in Beijing. But the Mongols and the Chinese had been cheated when the Sixth had died en route to China.

"Places like Norbu, near the northern road, would have been looted," Shan said, and stepped into the second cell. He began pushing the rear wall along its edges. Nothing moved. He pressed his finger along the length of each seam in the planks. Nothing. No gap in the finely crafted construction. He stepped out of the cell and saw Nyma was doing the same in the first cell. "Someone could come," she said, nervously glancing over her shoulder.

He stepped into the cell with the nun. "Jokar," she sighed, "could just have been speaking about something he saw when meditating, a vision."

Shan nodded in disappointment. There was a little ledge made of two narrow planks built into the side of the cell, where a monk might place a butter lamp and incense burner. He ran his hands along the planks and under them. There was no lever, no switch hidden underneath, no place to hide anything. Finally he ran a finger along the top of the planks, lightly at first, then harder. As his hand approached the rear corner, the end of the back plank dropped half an inch, and the rear wall swung open.

It was a narrow space, no more than three feet wide. As they stepped inside Nyma lit a match. They had no candle, no butter lamp, no electric light. But they also had no time to linger. Nyma extended the match in one direction, then the other. The musty closet ran for twenty feet. At one end was a bench, on which cushions were stacked, at the other shelves.

They had no time to look further. Nyma blew out the match and stepped back into the cell with Shan. He pushed the opposite, raised end of the trigger plank and the rear wall groaned softly and settled back into place, the plank snapping back into position.

Outside, several dropka were turning the huge prayer wheel. An excited dropka asked a passing monk if they could keep turning it past the posted hours, in honor of the holiday. The monk nervously replied he would relay the request to the Committee.

As he walked back around the compound Shan realized there was no sign of the Committee, no sign of Khodrak or Padme. No sign of Tuan. Despite the glimmer of hope he had felt when Lin's letter had been delivered, it now seemed impossible that Tenzin and Lokesh could be there, that the presence of an important prisoner like Tenzin would not be evidenced somewhere in the gompa. There could be other places, he realized in despair, secret places the purbas did not know. The guard at the gate could be there simply because of all the Tibetans camped outside the gompa.

He leaned against one of the old wooden dormitory buildings and slid down the wall to settle onto the earth. Other Tibetans were scattered around the grounds, some saying their beads, others just basking in the sun, perhaps taking a rest from prayers in the lhakang. He watched the windows of the two large buildings. In the center of the floor above the dining hall a man in a white shirt appeared periodically, sometimes looking outside, usually standing a few minutes with his back to the glass. Two pairs of men in white shirts patrolled the grounds, talking energetically, like monks engaged in religious debate. A man in an apron sat on the steps that led to the kitchen, holding a broom upright. Shan studied him. He was younger, more athletic-looking, than the other kitchen workers. His apron was unstained and he seemed little interested in helping with the kitchen labors.

A line of monks streamed out of the rear of the first building, each carrying a small notebook. The wind caught a piece of paper extending

322

from one of the notebooks, sending it tumbling down to the ground. Without thinking Shan rose and grabbed it for the monk. It was a piece of lined paper. Imprinted at the top were the words Feudalism is Regression, and below were handwritten notes, in Chinese. He extended the paper to the monk, who took it from him with an awkward smile.

Out of the corner of his eye Shan spotted a similar piece of paper, crushed and trodden, half-buried in the earth. Something about the peculiar way it was folded drew him to it, and as he bent to lift it from the ground his heart leapt. It was a spirit horse.

He stuffed the paper into his shirt and ventured closer to the kitchen. A worker appeared at the door with a mug of tea for the man sitting outside, who stood and shouldered the broomstick like a rifle. The Tibetan with the tea cowered, and scurried away as the man laughed and took the tea.

Shan wandered the grounds, trying to keep an eye on the central building without appearing conspicuous. In front of him a middle-aged dropka woman gave an exclamation of joy and bent to retrieve another of the paper horses where it had blown against the building. She held the horse in the wind, laughing as it fluttered like a tiny banner.

At the center window on the top, the howler peered out again. Fearing he would be noticed, Shan bent his head and joined a group of dropka, trying to will them to move slower as they passed the building. He chanced another look at the second floor, as they passed the end of the building, studying the distance to the ground. A young man might be able to lower himself from a window at the top and run away. But Lokesh would probably break a bone.

In the front courtyard preparations for the next day's festival began in earnest. A huge flag of the People's Republic had been hung on the front of the administrative building, suspended by ropes from two upper windows. The ropes were not secured inside but on a series of small hooks he had not noticed before, small iron hooks that ran along the sills of all the windows. On traditional Tibetan holidays special thangkas would have been hung from such hooks. At some large gompas special towers had been built solely for the purpose of displaying holy paintings on such occasions. But Chairman Khodrak had chosen a banner of a different kind.

"Special guests," Gyalo reported excitedly when Shan reached the purba truck. "One of the workers in the kitchen was at the archery range. An old man, a carpenter, knew him, and he learned that they have been preparing meals for two special guests who are confined in one of the rooms upstairs." Shan held out the paper horse for Nyma and the others to see, and explained how the military men in white shirts were watching over the second building.

"Who takes the meals?" Shan asked.

"The guards," the monk said in a disappointed voice. "But the guards won't go in to take out the night soil. They want Tibetans to carry it."

They joined in the preparations that afternoon, Shan with his hat pulled low, helping to raise ropes with paper streamers from the administrative building to the wall, then carrying juniper wood to the large samkangs that flanked the gate inside the wall. A loudspeaker announced that the chairman had graciously suspended the rules for the prayer wheel and furthermore the chairman had decided to allow the visiting families to take as much of the yak dung as they might carry, even to the extent of taking loads to their home hearths. Shan greeted the news with a grin, and spent most of the afternoon carrying baskets of the dung with the Tibetans, his face covered in its dark dust, the guards moving away from him as he approached. He passed the kitchen building half a dozen times before he found the guard at the steps bent in slumber, and he paused, futilely watching for movement at the upstairs corner windows. When Shan reported that the guard was napping, Gyalo, who had not dared to enter the gompa since deserting it, picked up a handful of the dung from Shan's basket and powdered his own face with it, then joined Shan with an empty basket. He wore a heavily patched vest, and a necklace of the blue beads favored by many of the dropka, with a broad-brimmed hat that kept his face in shadow.

As they reached the kitchen door, where the guard still slept, the old Tibetan carpenter appeared on the steps and gestured for them to follow him into the kitchen. He pointed to two buckets of fresh water by the inner door, then whispered to a middle-aged Tibetan man in an apron, who picked up a mug of tea and quickly arranged half a dozen sweet biscuits on a plate. They followed the kitchen attendant, each carrying a bucket of water, through the empty dining hall, and up the stairs at the center of the building. The attendant greeted the guard affably, extended the cookies toward him, and nodded Shan and Gyalo toward the door at the end of the corridor over the kitchen, the only door on the hallway that was closed.

There was no lock on the door. They stepped inside quickly and Gyalo closed the door behind them. A small table sat in the center of the chamber, with a pad of paper and two pencils. Two figures lay on straw pallets leaning against the wall under the windows.

"Lha gyal lo!" Gyalo whispered.

Tenzin was in the lotus position, his face drained of strength and color, doing his beads with a weary helpless expression. Lokesh was beside him, his eyes closed, his legs sprawled in front of him, under a blanket. Tenzin stared uncertainly at them, studying Shan slowly, as if he had a hard time focusing his eyes. When he recognized Shan anguish filled his face. "They don't understand," he groaned. "They refuse to believe I have left that life behind. They—"

Shan raised his palm to silence Tenzin. "I know, that man suffocated, and a new man was born."

"But I caused so much sorrow," Tenzin said, and he seemed about to weep. "You can't be caught. . . . Not you, too. There're guards," he warned. "You will be—"

Shan cut him off by gesturing to Lokesh. "What happened to him?" he asked as he studied Lokesh's slumped figure. His friend's hands clutched his beads. He seemed asleep, his breath making a dry rattling sound each time he exhaled.

Tenzin gestured weakly toward Lokesh's left foot. "They had a big clamp," he moaned. "A carpenter's clamp. But that Tuan is no carpenter." He looked up at Shan with a forlorn expression. "I never knew men could do such things," he croaked, with the voice of a much older man. "They made me watch."

Shan lifted the blanket over Lokesh's foot. The ankle was swollen and purple. Something was broken inside it.

"Lokesh didn't say anything, just did his mantra as they turned the clamp. He warned me before it happened that they would do something to him, and that I should not worry, that I should understand it was just a test of faith, nothing more, and he was used to such tests. But the test was for both of us he said."

For a moment a fire raged inside Shan. They had tortured his friend, they had slowly tightened the clamp until a bone had snapped. In a gompa. For what? To find out about Shan? No. It was about Tenzin. To find out about the purbas helping Tenzin. To persuade the abbot of Sangchi to return to the prescribed path.

It was the reason for the light guard. Lokesh could not walk. And the howlers would never expect Tibetans to endeavor a rescue.

"I think I could get out the window," Tenzin said. "But I would not leave him."

"Doctors," Shan said. "There's a medical team here who could help with his leg."

"I asked," Tenzin said wearily. "That Khodrak and Director Tuan, they said they would think about it. First they want me to sign papers, to give a speech, to say I was on retreat to perfect the Serenity Campaign, to state that officials in Lhasa are wrong in suggesting I was fleeing. On retreat to study the integration of Buddhist thought with the characteristics of Chinese socialism." It was an idiom of political officers. Build industry with the characteristics of Chinese socialism. Strengthen education with the characteristics of Chinese socialism. "I told them I had indeed been contemplating that topic," Tenzin said pointedly, gazing forlornly at Lokesh again. "He doesn't complain. Lokesh just does his beads when he's conscious, or sings one of those pilgrim songs. But I think a break like that, it is very painful. He keeps writing a letter with the paper they gave him for self-criticism. A letter to the Chairman in Beijing. He says he is going to deliver it personally. Sometimes he folds papers and asks me to drop them out the window. He said strong horses will come and we can drop out of the window onto them and ride away."

Shan stared painfully at his old friend. "But if they keep you here," Shan said, "they must remain hopeful that you will cooperate."

Tenzin sighed. "Khodrak acts like I am his personal prize. Great for their careers, I heard him say to Tuan, the best thing ever. They've invited a senior delegation from Religious Affairs to the festival."

Shan could not take his eyes off Lokesh. He lifted one of Lokesh's hands and squeezed it. The old man's eyes fluttered open. He gazed dreamily at Shan, then lifted his fingers and touched Shan's cheek, as if to determine if he were real.

Suddenly Gyalo was pulling him away. "The guard is finishing. If he begins to pay attention to us, my friend, we will be in much trouble," he said in a desperate tone.

Lokesh's eyes fluttered shut again.

Tenzin grabbed Shan's arm. "You must understand something. They could come any second," he said urgently, and looked into Shan's eyes with deep despair. "Someone must know this in case we disappear. He went there for me. He died because of me."

Shan and Gyalo froze. The abbot of Sangchi suddenly seemed very old. "Some nights I can't sleep because I see him standing, dying, on that mandala."

Shan swallowed hard. "You mean Drakte. You mean you sent Drakte to Amdo town."

Tenzin nodded. "He was going anyway, but I had asked him to find me one of those Lotus Books, to bring it to me. He went there and the knobs killed him for it. He lost the book. He lost his life, because of me," Tenzin said in a desolate voice.

Gyalo pulled on Shan's shoulder but Shan would not move. He looked from Tenzin's tortured face to Lokesh, then to the paper on the table, and slowly pulled the pouch with the ivory rosary from his pocket. "Drakte was supposed to use all your things to leave a trail in the south. But he kept one thing back." He handed the pouch to Tenzin, who opened it and stared inside.

He heard Tenzin's breath catch, and watched the man's face sag. "My grandfather gave these to me," the Tibetan whispered. "He said they are the only valuable thing a monk should have, because they are his connection to his god."

Shan watched as Tenzin twined the beads around his fingers. "You have to tell them," he said slowly, "tell them you'll make your speech. Tomorrow. You have to play the abbot again," he said apologetically, "for a few minutes more." Then he leaned into Tenzin's ear to explain.

Night had fallen when Shan drifted toward the rear of the encampment, to walk among the stars. But as he passed the dropka tents by the yak herd he was distracted by a strange sound.

"Humm, humm en da rengg," a dropka youth recited in a singsong voice. It had the sound of a mantra, but unlike any Shan had ever heard. He rounded the tent to see a group of dropka, young and old, sitting by a huge yak-dung fire, beside which Winslow was standing. Shan spun about, alarmed that the American would be so careless as to come down from the hiding place on the ridge after they had all agreed it was too dangerous for him to do so. But then he saw two lean men standing at the edge of the circle, facing the gompa. One was close enough to recognize, one of the stoney-faced purbas who had been with Tenzin at Yapchi.

Winslow acknowledged Shan with a grin. For a moment Shan thought he was waving at him, then he realized the American was leading the dropka in song.

"Whur da deaar end nat'lope ply—yy," the dropka continued. It was an American song, in a rough approximation of the English, one of the Western songs approved for the public address systems of Chinese trains: Home, Home on the Range.

As Shan sat near the fire, trying to join in the spirit of the circle, his concern for the American increased. It was too dangerous for him to come to the encampment, even with purbas protecting him. He would be an illegal now, without the protection of his passport, without any identity as far as the authorities would be concerned. Like Shan, Winslow didn't exist now, and if captured he might be made to disappear.

In the dim light on the far side of the fire Shan became aware of another figure, seated on the back of a horse cart, a dour Tibetan man, Shan's age, flanked by two of the purbas he had seen on the ridge. Shan rose and edged around the ring. But when he got close to the cart the nearest purba stepped in front of him. The man on the cart stared at Shan with hooded eyes, showing no greeting, no emotion of any kind. In the firelight Shan could see two deep gutters of scar tissue along the man's cheek, and the flame in his eyes. He saw much that he recognized in those eyes. They were prisoner's eyes, filled with a weary, sad intelligence, but they were also extraordinarily fierce eyes, lit with fury and righteousness alike. Shan had seen the same eyes on thangkas of wrathful protector demons.

Shan took another step forward and the purba's hand closed around his arm like a cold vise, and pressed it against something near his chest. A pistol butt, in a shoulder holster. Shan froze, then stepped back out of the purba's grip, studying the lines of scar tissue on the man's cheeks. It was the one they called the Tiger, he somehow knew, the legendary purba leader with the stripes on his face. The two most wanted men in all Tibet were at Khodrak's gompa.

Shan retreated to the far side of the circle. He wandered out onto the plain, into the comfort of the night, trying to fight the new fear that the Tiger's presence had ignited. An owl called. The mountains on the horizon glistened in the moonlight. The appearance of the purba leader unsettled

327

Shan as much as if knobs had risen out of the fire. The Tiger was not there to help Shan. The Tiger was famed as a man of action. It was said that his mother had been Moslem. Moslems believed in retribution. The Tiger was so hunted, so prominently marked for destruction he could easily have an army of knobs on his trail at that moment. The words Anya had spoken their first night on Yapchi mountain came back to him. So many have died, the oracle had said, so many still to die.

Shan found himself sitting, staring at the sky, beseeching the stars. If only he could just take Lokesh and go. He had no more hope to give the Tibetans, he had no way of seeing through the mysteries that shrouded the gompa and Yapchi Valley. All he could see was the danger.

Time passed, perhaps an hour. Something moved in the darkness, ahead of him. A man, sitting on a rock a hundred feet away, was holding something that glinted in the moonlight, looking not at Shan but out onto the plain.

"The lamas have no patience for me," a deep voice suddenly said behind him. "They say I shouldn't expect to achieve so much in one life-time." It was an extraordinary voice, hoarse and powerful, like a growl but not exactly. How had Lhandro described it? Like someone roaring in a whisper, because the knobs had broken his voicebox.

As Shan turned toward the man with the ravaged face he saw a second guard sitting on a rock, fifty feet away.

"I told them when I was young I had teachers from the tantric schools who taught that with the right practice you could achieve Buddhahood in one lifetime."

Strangely, Shan realized, he had never heard another name for the Tiger. He shifted uneasily, wondering how many more men with guns lurked in the shadows. And how often the Tiger spoke with Chinese in the night.

"I tell them compared with that, what I seek seems so little." The man sat beside Shan and watched the sky a moment. "When you're always on the run, always moving after sunset, the night sky becomes your home," he said, and for a moment sounded very tired. "You have a man who wrote a letter. Colonel Lin is no friend of Tibet. He has been written, more than once."

Written. The Tiger meant written in the Lotus Book, the purbas' compendium of atrocities against Tibetans.

"I would like to spend time with that Colonel," the purba leader said in a businesslike tone. "Take him somewhere. Valuable things could be learned."

Shan felt his belly clench. "Lin is injured," he said weakly. "Why?" he asked, looking into the man's ravaged face. "Why would you bother to speak to me about this? The purbas know where Lin is."

The man said nothing. Something moved in the distance, and one of the purbas with the guns leapt up. After a moment Shan heard the clatter of small hooves, those of a wild goat or gazelle, and the man returned to his post. Shan studied the Tiger. He seemed like another rock in the night, a lonely statue whose face was slowly being etched away by the wind. Shan realized that the Tiger might have answers to many of the questions that had been plaguing him.

"Why are there no knobs here?" he asked suddenly. "Why didn't the knobs take the abbot of Sangchi?"

The Tiger sighed. "The ones who have him are knobs and not knobs. Things are adrift in this district. Even those knob doctors aren't sure who to report to. We intercepted a request they sent to Lhasa, asking for instructions. They want to go up onto the Plain of Flowers to find the medicine lama. But Tuan and that abbot Khodrak want them here."

"But if monks become the political enforcers," Shan said "What can the people do to . . ." his voice trailed off.

"Right," the Tiger said grimly.

"Somo said there are other knobs working for Tuan somewhere else. Five others."

"We can't find them. No one knows where they are. We have tightened security everywhere. No new faces are permitted at any of our meetings now. We have word out all over the district. But those five are not to be found. Everyone is wary, very nervous. It is getting more and more dangerous."

They sat in silence. Crickets sounded somewhere.

"I went to that hermitage where you started but you had already gone," the Tiger said suddenly. "The dropka who were there told us about an old lama taking away the body of Drakte. We followed, and stayed at the durtro until the vultures were done, trying to understand what had happened to him. We talked into the night, and when we awoke your lama was gone, into the mountains."

Had he been wrong about the Tiger? Was he there about Drakte, about finding revenge for Drakte? "I know Drakte was at Amdo town that night," Shan said. "Getting one of the Lotus Books. But why there, why couldn't someone have met him away from the dangers of a town?"

"That damned Serenity Campaign. The howlers are keeping scores for economic success. We laughed about it at first. But this gompa, this Khodrak, decided he had to have the best score in Tibet. And he did." The Tiger gazed at a particularly bright star.

"But it has to be lies," Shan said.

"Exactly. Drakte found out. He had other duties, but he was from this region originally, and he would not allow Khodrak to get away with the lies. It became a personal quest of his, even though I opposed it. When he finished his work for us in the south he roamed through this district to collect the true data. When he found out that a boyhood friend was Tuan's

329

assistant he said it was destined, that he was meant to give it to that Chao. And Chao readily agreed, even said he would trade Drakte something just as good."

"But they were attacked."

"It must have been a trap. To a man like Tuan, Chao would have been a traitor. Chao died, and Drakte was fatally wounded. The Lotus Book Drakte carried was lost."

"How did Chao die, exactly?"

"A stab in the back, wide, like a butcher's knife. They were at a garage. It could have been an ax. Chao died immediately. If Drakte had come to us we probably could have saved him. But he went to you instead."

"You sound convinced they did not attack each other."

"That bastard Tuan must have discovered them. He would have been furious with Chao. Chao could have ruined him. Easiest solution for Tuan would have been to kill them both. He was in Amdo that night, in meetings about the Serenity Campaign. He could kill Chao, say reactionaries did it, and call him a martyr."

They listened to the crickets again. The Tiger pointed out a falling star.

"Why speak with me?" Shan asked again.

"I told you. Because of that colonel. There's a woman back there who speaks like a nun," the Tiger said, "from that village that was burned. She says we can't have Lin unless you agree."

They were silent again, for a long time. "All they wanted was to complete their deity," Shan said in a sad, lonely voice.

"All I ever wanted was to grow barley with my father," the feared leader of the purbas replied, in a tone that seemed to match Shan's.

"That deity has to be mended in the light, not in shadow," Shan said after another silence, and he looked skyward, puzzled at the words that had drifted off his tongue. He heard the purba general sigh, and he waited for an answer, but none came. He turned and saw that the Tiger was gone.

When he returned to the campfire the dropka had retired to their tents and Winslow was huddled with Nyma, Lhandro, and Somo. Somo asked Shan to repeat in detail everything he had seen inside the gompa, and they reviewed their plan once more. Everything was ready, but no one had anticipated that Lokesh could not walk.

"That," Winslow said slowly, sprouting a grin, "must be the reason I am here."

The little bell came from far away to reach him, its first peal sounding like an alarm in his consciousness. Shan sat upright in his blanket. It was before dawn. He had slept fitfully, kept awake by Winslow as Lhandro and Nyma taught him a strange dance step in the shadow of the truck. The bell sounded again. Something inside him had been listening, the lao

330

gai Shan who had learned all the many types of bells, sirens, and whistles used by the knobs and their prison guards, had learned to know which bell summoned guards with rifles, and which brought guards to search their barracks or carry a prisoner to the infirmary. Slowly he realized this bell was to summon monks to their predawn prayers.

He rose and stepped around the sleeping Tibetans and through the grey light toward the gates. A solitary guard leaned against one pillar. Electric lights illuminated the assembly hall. Monks were filing out of the sleeping quarters that lined the two side walls of the gompa and entering the lhakang.

"Two long cars came in the night," a voice said at his shoulder. Somo. "Red Flags I think," she added, referring to the limousines used by many of Tibet's senior officials.

"The Bureau of Religious Affairs," Shan said. "The ones Tenzin said were coming from regional headquarters."

They watched from the truck as the monks streamed out of the lhakang an hour later, carrying benches and cushions to the courtyard in front of the administrative building. A table was brought from the dining hall to the building entrance and by fastening boards to it several monks converted it to a makeshift speaking platform with a wooden crate for a step. A man in a shirt and tie appeared in the doorway with another Chinese flag, which he affixed to the front of the platform. Shan followed the first group of Tibetans into the gompa, the guard watching not the Tibetans now but the officials at the entrance.

The window of the upstairs office opened and a large loudspeaker appeared in it. Anthems began to play, until abruptly someone was addressing them. "Citizens of China," a thin voice said. "We salute you. It is you, the children of industry, who have made us a great nation and who will make us greater still." It was the radio. Someone had patched in the May Day speeches from Beijing. A murmur shot through the courtyard. It was the supreme Chairman himself, addressing the nation.

Padme, wearing his robe over a pair of blue jeans, appeared in the door with an uncomfortable expression, studying the disorganized crowd. He glanced up at the window as though debating whether to turn the radio off, then quickly ordered everyone in the courtyard to be seated on the benches and carpets and listen. It might appear unpatriotic not to stop and listen while the Chairman spoke, and even more so to turn the radio off now that the speech had started. Padme dispatched the guard to command the Tibetans outside the gates to attend, darted inside, and reappeared a moment later, without his jeans, to sit in one of the chairs on the podium. Shan remembered the blue jeans they had seen at the burned patch of herbs, and how Winslow had given the monk the yellow nylon vest from the burned meadow to wear. When they had arrived at the gompa with the injured Padme, he had been recognized from a distance. Because the vest, like the jeans, had belonged to Padme.

A tall distinguished Tibetan appeared, grey-haired, wearing a business suit, closely followed by a stocky Han in nearly identical attire, hurriedly straightening his tie. Emissaries from the Bureau of Religious Affairs. The two mounted on the podium and sat beside Padme. Dropka and rongpa began to arrive in family groups and sat on the carpets near the wall.

Then, as the crowd dutifully stared at the loudspeaker in the window, Shan watched as two men in light blue uniforms carried a stretcher with an old man from behind the central building toward the medical station. He sighed with relief. Tenzin had understood the bargain he had to reach with Khodrak. Shan gestured to Gyalo and the two men inched their way along the wall.

Ten minutes later, neatly attired in the white tunics of the kitchen workers, Shan and Gyalo approached the medical team and announced to a technician sitting by the door that they had been sent for the old man with the bad foot. They waited another ten minutes, then the door of the station opened and a man in blue, a stethoscope around his neck, motioned them inside.

"He's sedated. A bad fall, that one. Had to put on a walking cast to stabilize the bone. He'll need crutches for a month at least." The man hovered over a clipboard with an incomplete form, then someone called for him to join the celebration. Chairman Khodrak was waiting with his visitors. The doctor sighed and tossed the clipboard on the table. Suddenly the technician appeared in the door. The man ignored Shan and Gyalo at first but then he stilled and slowly faced the monk. "He's one of those!" the man cried out, pointing at Gyalo. "One of the banned ones! The chairman must be told!"

The doctor gaped in confusion then stared at the radio handset that sat on the table six feet away. He was leaning forward, seemingly about to reach for the radio, when a rope materialized and settled over the technician, pinning his arms to his side. Before the man could cry out, a wooden post hit him on the head, one of the stanchions that had held the rope outside the clinic. The man slumped to the floor, colliding with the doctor as he leapt for the radio. A long, lanky form sprang through the air and Winslow was on top of the doctor, straddling him. The doctor fought for a moment, tearing at the American's clothes. The American launched an arcing blow with his fist that connected with the doctor's jaw and the man fell back, limp.

Winslow grinned at the two unconscious men and then at Shan and Gyalo. "Like I've been saying all along, what this country needs is a few good cowboys." He was wearing a chuba, with a military wool cap covering his light hair. His cheeks were darkened with dirt. In the early hours of the morning the American and Nyma had climbed a tree at the rear wall and dropped inside.

They quickly bound the two men together with medical tape, taped their mouths, and carried them into the shadows at the rear of the clinic.

332

The rear of the compound was empty. They quickly carried Lokesh past the stable and into the meditation cells, where hands reached out to help him as the secret door swung open. Shan carried the empty stretcher back to the medical station, leaning it against the wall with three others. Moments later he returned to the hidden closet, now lit by Winslow's electric lamp. Lokesh lay asleep on the cushions Shan had seen the day before. Winslow stood with Nyma at the opposite end of the chamber, studying the shelves. In the light of the electric lamp their contents were clearly visible: Peche, over a dozen Tibetan books, were stacked there, each wrapped in a dusty red cloth. Shan fought a momentary urge to examine the old books, took one more look at Lokesh and stepped out into the cell, closing the secret door behind him.

He lingered outside the cells a moment, wondering if he should risk appearing back at the assembly, where his arrival might be conspicuous now that the Chairman was well into his speech. He wandered around the rear of the gompa and worked his way toward the rear of the office building. On the front side of the building the Chairman was still speaking, now about the importance of electronics production, citing factory names and specific worker heroes. Shan had personally attended a dozen May Day speeches in Tiananmen Square in Beijing. They could last an hour or more. He stepped inside. In the entry room a small table was littered with food dishes. A Party newspaper had been dropped in haste on the table. A blue suit jacket hung on a peg in the wall. Slipping it on, he quietly stepped out into the corridor and up the stairs. He passed the office with the loudspeaker in the window and continued to the meeting room, pausing a moment as he saw a sixth robe that now hung on the pegs for dead monks, an addition to the row since his first visit. Gyalo, it said in large script, a deserter from Buddha.

He searched the empty conference room methodically. The closet in the corner was filled with boxes of the plastic dorjes and other small trinkets, as well as a stack of familiar little books with red vinyl covers. Scriptures from Beijing. A black leather satchel sat on a chair beside more maps like the one the carpenter had given him, marking the progress of Norbu's campaign against the old order. The top map was in a plastic jacket, clipped to a large envelope bearing the address of Religious Affairs headquarters in Lhasa.

Beside the maps were sheets from old peche. From the words Shan could make out and the diagrams of plants they appeared to be directions for finding and using herbs. Six feet down the long table was another grouping of old writings, broader than peche leaves, arrayed around a tablet with the familiar caption decrying feudalism. The tablet had perhaps thirty names, in Chinese. Names were being transcribed from the old papers, which were records from an old gompa. They were names of lamas and monks, he suspected. The howlers were recording the names of the former inhabitants of Rapjung and Norbu to see if any of their families survived. Shan had been conscripted for similar tasks during his imprisonment. Refining the socialist context, a political officer had called it, when he had been forced to help cross-reference telephone directories with lists of old gompa members. The surviving families might not be punished, might never know they had been identified. But the party cherished such data, for future reference, for possible leverage when more information or intimidation might be needed. A white sheet was clipped to one peche page, bearing a Chinese translation. Jokar Rinpoche, a summary said, senior instructor at Rapjung and now a senior member of the Dalai Cult. At the top of the sheet someone had written an excited note. *Guru Dorje,* it said, *this is the one,* with the words underlined twice: *he came from Rapjung.* It was why the medical teams were staying. They had discovered Jokar's destination.

A chalkboard had been propped on an easel at the end of the table, on which a list of numbered rules had been inscribed, with a number of cross-outs and corrections, as if they were still being drafted and refined: No contributions shall be made by the people directly to monks or nuns. The managing committee of the gompa must receive and record all contributions. All those who contribute more than two percent of income shall pay a tax equal to one hundred percent of the contribution. Labor contributed to reconstruction of any religious shrine, cairn, or gompa must be reported, valued, and taxed accordingly. Religious Affairs will strictly enforce the requirement that all religious artifacts are the property of the people's government. Those with personal shrines must pay a rental to the government. Gompas will be encouraged to start economic enterprises and will eventually be required to report a profit to maintain their licenses.

It had the sound of a bizarre manifesto, the platform for a campaign that would truly mean the end of religious activity in Tibet.

Shan looked back uneasily at the note that bore Jokar's name. Guru Dorje, it said at the top. It was like an irreverent nickname. Guru was Sanskrit, another word for lama, and the dorje, the thunderbolt scepter, was one of the most important implements of Buddhist ritual.

Below the chalkboard at the end of the table lay a stack of reports with glossy covers. Each was nearly an inch thick and had a plastic spine along its left side. Prosperity Blooms in Norbu District, the title read. Shan stared grimly at the reports, then leafed through the top copy. Computer graphics had been heavily utilized, with graphs and tables and pie charts, most comparing current economic activity in the district with historic performance. The district was a powerhouse of development, the report explained. Barley production had soared four hundred percent. Sheep herds had increased threefold, goats almost fivefold. The severe health problems that had once debilitated the population were gone. Friction between the district's diverse populations had been eradicated.

Beside the reports was a facsimile of a brief letter from Religious Affairs headquarters, congratulating Khodrak and Tuan on their success in the Serenity Campaign and noting that their proposal had met with enthusiastic support in Lhasa and Beijing. Lhasa looked forward to announcing the new institute for Tibetan children that would be awarded to Norbu. An institute. It was why Tuan had referred to needing more teachers, why Drakte had been so upset about Khodrak's falsification of the data. Sign the ledger, Drakte had told the woman at the Lamtso Gar, or all your children will grow up to hate you.

Shan lingered at the door a moment, looking at the blackboard, then stepped back into the still-empty corridor. Drawing a deep breath, he walked into the office, staying in the shadows, away from the window. Over a hundred people sat outside, watching the speaker in the office window. No one, as he had hoped, had dared stay inside to work while homage was being paid to the Chairman. He quickly surveyed the room. Two photographs were taped over a filing cabinet. One was of Tenzin, taken in the conference room where Khodrak had confronted him less than two weeks earlier. Beside it was a photograph from a newspaper, showing Tenzin in a robe, his head shaven, greeting several important-looking Han, over a caption that said the Tibetan people welcome the Vice Premier. Over the door, invisible to those who looked in from the corridor, was a small banner, in Chinese only. Strike Hard. It was the name for one of Beijing's most aggressive campaigns against the Tibetans in recent years, in which the howlers and knobs had temporarily joined forces in another effort to pry Tibet's collective fingers from its rosary.

He glanced at the clock. By now Somo and another of the purbas were dropping down the back wall, wearing uniforms of the 54th Mountain Combat Brigade. Suddenly there was applause, both over the radio and from outside. Shan darted out of the room to a large office occupying the entire end of the floor opposite the conference room, with windows overlooking the courtyard, just in time to see Tenzin being led around the corner by one of the knob guards. The radio was switched off. Standing in the shadows, he watched as Khodrak stood and introduced the important visitors from Lhasa, then stated that it was his great honor to make an announcement that would reverberate throughout the world. The famous abbot of Sangchi, lost for so many weeks, had come to Khodrak, and the abbot had chosen to honor Norbu by announcing to the world, on May Day, on the steps of their own gompa, that he had not been fleeing or kidnapped but had simply been on retreat to better understand the socialist imperative. The assembly stared in disbelief before breaking into enthusiastic applause. The Religious Affairs officials conferred excitedly, then stood and vigorously shook first Khodrak's, then Tenzin's hand. The abbot of Sangchi, Shan saw, wore one of the Norbu gilt-edge robes.

Shan watched, his heart racing, as Tenzin spoke, offering his gratitude to everyone at Norbu gompa. "If I have confused the people of Tibet," he said, "I apologize. Perhaps I myself was confused for a long time. But now, here at Norbu gompa, because of Chairman Khodrak, I have come to clearly understand my path," he said, and looked out toward the northern landscape. "I am a hermit who wanders the countryside," Tenzin said in a melodious tone, "a beggar who travels alone. I left behind the land of my birth and gave up my fertile fields."

Khodrak and Tuan glanced nervously at each other. Tenzin was reciting one of Milarepa's songs, one of the ancient songs Lokesh sometimes sang. The Closing Song some called it, because it was written when the famous teacher lay dying. A dropka ventured forward to the podium and handed Tenzin a khata. Khodrak smiled icily then inched forward as another, then a third Tibetan offered Tenzin prayer scarves. Khodrak looked uneasily at the Bureau officials, rose and stood at Tenzin's side. One of the monks stepped forward with a camera and snapped a photograph.

Shan's gaze drifted toward the wall by the window. Pinned there was another of the maps depicting the sterilization campaign. He turned to study the room. Along the wall by the door was a row of filing cabinets, above which hung a flag of the People's Republic. Past the cabinets, in the corner, sat a cardboard box, its contents covered with dust. They were photographs in uniform black frames, most of which were images taken in banquet halls or on the steps of important government buildings. Tuan was in all the photos. Tuan in a knob uniform, Tuan in a business suit, Tuan with Khodrak, raising glasses with army officers, even Tuan on the Great Wall. He looked up. In any other office these would be trophies, to be prominently displayed. But Tuan had no personal photographs on his walls, no mementos of his career.

A different kind of photograph was pinned to the wall behind a large desk, a glossy picture ripped out of a magazine, of a small cottage on a tree-lined lake with a rowboat pulled up in front of it. Under the picture was a small table with a single drawer. Shan slowly opened it to find a large knife, a butcher's knife, and over a dozen packs of cigarettes. He looked back up at the cottage by the lake. It had the air of someone's retirement dream. He looked at the knife. It could have been used to kill Drakte.

A facsimile page had been left on the otherwise empty blotter of the desk. Shan scanned it without touching the paper. It was confirming that transportation had been arranged for the Norbu delegation to attend the upcoming celebration for the Yapchi Valley oil project, in two days time. Lhasa had decided that the event provided the perfect opportunity for the anxiously awaited award ceremony for the Serenity Campaign. Norbu's new institute would be announced at that time. A photographer would accompany them, and a security contingent.

A small black wire ran from the wall into one of the desk drawers. Shan opened the drawer to reveal a white dial telephone, with an index card of numbers taped to its side. He lifted the receiver to confirm it was live, warily set it down. He opened the drawer below to find medicine bottles, over two dozen bottles of pills. Standing, he paced the room, then found himself back at the desk, lifting the phone. He quickly dialed the first number, listed as the Religious Affairs district headquarters in Amdo town.

A woman answered on the fifth ring. "Wei," she said. It was the universal syllable used over telephones in China, not a greeting, just an anonymous acknowledgment.

Shan froze, about to hang up, then looked at the five digits on the face of the phone and recited them to the woman.

"I am sorry," she said. "Everyone else is at the labor day celebration. If I can help the Director's office—"

"It is a day for honoring heroes," Shan said.

"Yes," the woman replied uncertainly.

"The trip to Yapchi," Shan said. "The arrangements for travel. The Director wanted me to confirm that we received them, to make sure no last minute changes had been made."

"No changes."

Shan turned and looked at the picture of the cottage again. "The Director reminded us that heroes walk among us. It is why he wants the full names and addresses for the five, so they may be properly recognized."

"I'm sorry?"

"The Director has a private meeting with those from Lhasa. He has decided that on a day such as this all of the people's heroes must be honored. Those who work in secret too often get overlooked."

"But you must have—"

"Everyone else is at the labor day celebration," he reminded her. "If you are worried about security I will give you the identification numbers so you can cross-check them," he said, pulling out the paper Somo had given him, and carefully reading out the numbers for the five unexplained entries.

"Very well," the woman sighed. "I will fax the list immediately."

Applause from outside interrupted. Shan hung up the phone, closed the drawer, and darted to the front window. Khodrak was patting Tenzin on the back. Shan began unbuttoning the jacket he had borrowed, turned toward the door, and froze. Director Tuan stood in the doorway, fixing Shan with a ravenous stare.

"I could have you shot," Tuan hissed. "I could have a bullet in your head by nightfall. I have had you checked with the Ministry of Education. Impersonating a government worker. Breaching state security."

"Perhaps you forget you are no longer with Public Security," Shan observed woodenly.

The Director of Religious Affairs opened his mouth to speak, then was interrupted by more applause. "We don't have time to worry about such niceties right now," he sneered, and stepped into the room. "Whatever you are—fugitive, dropout, deserter from the army perhaps?—we will find out. Later we will have time to decide what to do with a man who impersonates a teacher. A vile thing to do. There are places we can keep you in chains until we decide how best to dispose of you." He turned as though to call for assistance.

"I never said I was a teacher," Shan shot back. "You jumped to conclusions. You also said I could be useful. You gave me your card." All he could hope for was to keep Tuan off his stride, buy time for Somo and the others.

Tuan's mouth opened but his words became lost in a sudden fit of coughing. He backed against the wall by the door, his hand pressing a handkerchief to his mouth. When the coughing stopped he closed his eyes a moment as if he had grown faint. As he lowered the handkerchief Shan saw pink spots on it. "What were you doing here?" Tuan snarled, as he stepped away from the wall. Anger still colored his voice but the fire in his eyes had dimmed.

"Watching the proceedings, like everyone else. It would be rude to enter the audience when such a prestigious guest is speaking."

"You knew about him," Tuan said accusingly. "You were with the abbot. He was probably hiding behind the hill that first day we saw you."

"He never told us he was the abbot."

The Director stepped past Shan to the window and stared at Tenzin, still on the platform, then looked back at Shan. "We were going to draw up papers today, to decide who he was going to be if he refused to cooperate. An illegal reactionary. Perhaps the killer of our beloved Chao," he said icily. The threat was thinly veiled. Tuan needed to finish the hunt for Chao's killer, his final victory leading up to the awards ceremony at Yapchi. Tenzin would have been a convenient candidate. Someone else would have to be found.

"But that was a problem for the Public Security Bureau," Shan said, eyeing the open door. "Your problem is winning the Serenity Campaign."

Tuan followed his gaze and sighed, slowly stepped to the door and shut it. For a moment he seemed like an old, weary man, not angry but bitter. "That," the Director gloated, "has already been done. It only remains to collect our prize."

Perhaps that was the mystery he should focus on, Shan thought. Perhaps he had not sufficiently weighed the stakes of the strange game Khodrak and Tuan played. "Your photograph in the Lhasa paper? A congratulatory letter from Beijing?" Such things would seem of little import to a man who kept such trophies in a dust-covered box. He remembered the chalkboard in the conference room, the list that had read like a manifesto. "The institute? A statue in Amdo town?"

An odd light began to shine in Tuan's eyes. "Serenity," he said in a tired voice. "Serenity is all I want." He took a pack of cigarettes out of his pocket and held them under his nostrils as he had the time he met

338

with Shan in the meeting room below. His sickness was in an advanced state, Shan realized. "The problem with everyone in Tibet is that they have been conditioned to settle for less. There are riches here, riches in the ground. Once we become the model, all things will be possible."

We. He meant Khodrak and himself. He meant the district, his district, as a model of development. It was a dusty old paradigm, the use of an enterprise as a political model. The government would pour subsidies into such a model to guarantee its success, to create a propaganda model to demonstrate the correctness of its policies. More than a few of Beijing's most conspicuous models had later proven to be shams, rife with corruption and forged production records. He recalled the photographers and monks posing with hammers, the pictures taken of Padme and his monks with the young shepherds in new clothes, the doctors with young Tibetan mothers. Tuan and Khodrak knew the game well. They had packaged everything, ignoring the truth, ignoring the rules of the Serenity Campaign even, but playing by rules Tuan had learned from a long career in the government and as a Party member. Their institute could quickly become a corporation, and with control of the leading economic enterprise in the region, they would rule a small kingdom.

"My partner arranged for Public Security to be told Chao's killer had gone into Qinghai. That was risky. My former colleagues can be overzealous."

Shan stared at Tuan, trying to make sense not of his words, but of the man himself. He had once been one of those zealous knob officers, and retired. He had gone to seed and sprouted a new career, growing ever harder, more callous, more bitter. More sick. "Your partner is a busy man."

Tuan gave an amused snort. "When you're a thunderbolt you can move fast and strike hard." It had the sound of a tired joke.

Shan clenched his jaw. Guru Dorje, the note had said. Guru Thunderbolt. It was Khodrak's nickname. But Shan had seen the name on another piece of paper, scrawled at the top of the yellow slip Somo had found in Drakte's boot, the compilation of data on Public Security soldiers. "Your partner was asking Chao for information on your payroll," Shan observed, watching Tuan closely. Chao had not intended the payroll slip for Drakte. Perhaps he had it out, showing it to Drakte when the killer came, but the note was meant for Khodrak.

Director Tuan paused. He glared at Shan, not seeming to notice that the fax machine by the desk was humming, was receiving a fax, then looked out at the podium with a forced smile. Strangely, he looked back at his photograph of a lake cottage.

"I liked that Chao," Tuan confessed airily. "He was the only one of my staff who told jokes. He could fix things when herders became uncooperative." Tuan's eyes narrowed. "I found him in that old stable, dead a few minutes, sliced open along his spine like a pig in a butcher shop. I thought the trail of blood was his at first, then I realized he would never have had the strength to rise from that wound. I sent my men to follow but they lost the trail in the mountains."

Shan studied the Director, weighing his words. Tuan was saying, or at least trying to make Shan believe, that he was not the killer. "The one who ran may have not been the killer, he may have been a victim as well."

Tuan shook his head. "We swept the town. Put up roadblocks, stopped all traffic for twenty-four hours. If the murderer had stayed in the town we would have had him."

"You assume the murderer was someone you didn't know."

Tuan shrugged as if disinterested, then studied Shan with narrowed eyes. "I will finish it, I will close this matter myself. Chao was one of mine. It is for me to decide." His words had the barest hint of an apology in them.

Something icy crept into Shan's belly. "Reports have to get written for public executions. Someone in Lhasa will check. They expect evidence in the file."

Tuan seemed disappointed, and he made a fluttering gesture with his hand that seemed to dismiss Shan's suggestion. "After living in Tibet so many years you should know better," he said in a mocking tone. "When you get selected for a government bullet in your skull it doesn't have to be because you deserve it. It's because you were always supposed to die that way." A smug smile appeared on his face, as if he were very pleased with his wit. "It makes things so much easier for Public Security here."

Shan returned his frigid stare. "The Tibetans also say that nothing happens in life that does not affect everything else."

One side of Tuan's mouth opened, exposing a tooth, with a silent snarl. He threw a pencil onto the desk. "The next few minutes will be the most important of your life. I will leave, and send a guard to stand at the door outside. If you try to run he will catch you and we will do things to your feet so you never run again. When the festivities are concluded we can begin anew here, but I will bring others to help. You're not stupid. If you write the right confession before I return, I may decide to keep it and let you live, give you a job after all." He pulled a piece of blank paper from the top drawer. Tuan's tone was not cruel, but casual. He frowned at Shan, then stepped away, closing the office door behind him.

Shan stared at the door a moment, trying to understand the strange man. Nothing in his words had given Shan reason to change his view that Tuan was the killer. But Shan *had* changed his view. It had been in Tuan's tone, his manner, the lack of anger or passion in his voice. He was too casual, too distracted, too weak, to be the one who stabbed Chao and Drakte. But, as the Tiger had suggested, Tuan could have laid a trap, could have stood by with his thin smile and ordered one of his men to do it.

Shan stirred from his thoughts and darted to the front window. Chairman Khodrak was shaking hands with Tenzin again, for the photographers. He ran to the window on the opposite side of the room, overlooking the courtyard between the buildings, and opened the sash. Nothing moved except the fluttering flags. The rope bearing the miniature Chinese flags was tied to an iron hook above the window. He pulled the rope, and pulled again, harder. He leaned out the window, pulling with both hands. The rope broke free of its fastening on the opposite building.

The sound of boots came from the corridor. He paused, ran to the wall behind the desk, grabbed the single page that now sat in the facsimile machine, ripped away the photograph of the serene cottage, then rushed back to the window. Stuffing the papers into his shirt he grabbed the now dangling line of flags and climbed out. A moment later he was on the ground.

The next instant Tenzin and his guard appeared around the corner of the building, moving toward the door of the second building. Shan stepped in behind them. As they reached the door two soldiers of the People's Liberation Army appeared in front of them and reached out for Tenzin, pulling him between them.

"Religious Affairs matter," the guard grunted.

"Not anymore," one of the soldiers snapped. "This man is wanted for breach of military security. Orders of Colonel Lin."

The guard looked back out the door as if hoping to see reinforcements. "Director Tuan has custody. Religious Affairs—"

"I said Colonel Lin," the soldier said, and offered a sympathetic shrug. "We all just take orders, comrade. Take it up with your Director," and turning, pushed Tenzin toward the stairs.

The guard hesitantly retreated, confusion obvious on his face. He turned and examined Shan suspiciously.

"Look at that," Shan said in an impatient tone, and pointed to the downed line of flags. "And on May Day." The guard glanced back inside, then at Shan and the broken line of flags, then muttered something under his breath and walked away.

A moment later Shan met Tenzin and the two purbas in uniform at the kitchen door and rushed them toward the meditation cells. Inside the old building, Shan helped Tenzin quickly trade his robe for the clothes of a dropka, then helped him into the hidden chamber as the purbas disappeared in the direction of the rear wall.

Winslow appeared to be asleep, but Lokesh was wide awake, squeezing Nyma's hand affectionately, like an old uncle reunited with his family as they studied one of the ancient manuscripts. He looked up at Shan with his crooked grin, and Shan set his finger to his lips for fear the old man might cry out.

As Tenzin sat beside him Shan quietly explained that in a moment Khodrak and his men would discover that the holding room was empty. But when the knobs began to search the grounds, someone would call their attention to a strange scene on the ridge above, four men in army uniforms herding a man in a maroon robe up the ridge.

Tuan and Khodrak could not protest too loudly, for fear of being discredited in front of the officials from Lhasa. Even if Tuan pursued with his white shirts, he would arrive too late to find any trace of them on the far side of the ridge, for horses awaited the disguised purbas, which would quickly take them out of sight. He could not spread a wider alarm, because Tenzin was back where he was officially meant to be, in the custody of the army.

Then, as Khodrak and Tuan reeled in confusion Lhandro would announce the people of the region would pay homage to the gompa and its important visitors by staging their own celebration. The Tibetans' long delayed spring festival would begin.

A whistle blew, and a moment later Shan heard boots pounding the earth outside. He settled back against the old wall. Once monks had hidden in here from Mongol invaders he told himself, bringing their most important thangkas and scriptures inside. The thought of the peche still lying on the shelves where they had been secreted, probably fifty years before, somehow comforted him. Treasures could still be hidden, and the arrogance of those who sought to usurp them could still be used as a weapon against them.

Shan watched the festival parade in his mind, as Lhandro had described it. In the front would be adorned yaks, all the yaks in the camp, which the dropka had finished decorating the night before. In the very front, festooned with red yarn and braids would be Jampa, led by Gyalo, the monk Khodrak had declared dead to Buddha, in a festival mask. Dropka in their traditional finery, some of it handed down for generations, would follow, some with hand drums and *damyen*, the traditional string instrument from the changtang. Then there would be dancers, adorned with some of the elaborate headdresses that had been used in *cham* dances, the dances traditionally performed to depict important historic or symbolic events. Finally, for good measure, children would lead their favorite sheep and dogs in the procession. It would be loud and chaotic, which was exactly what Shan and his friends had hoped for.

No one spoke. The boots pounded by again and receded. A voice droned over the loudspeaker, then there was a sound of another voice, loud but not amplified. Lhandro's. There was silence, then the sound of animals. The procession was circling the compound, past the dining hall and lhakang, past the medical station and the prayer wheel. Shan leaned forward, straining to hear. There was a beat that could have been drums, then another louder beat, and Tenzin touched his arm. Someone was tapping the wall outside. He slid clear of the secret door and it swung open. Somo, her face taut with anxiety, helped them out of the chamber.

Outside, as yaks in ornate harnesses streamed past, Lhandro and several others stepped into the doorway to block the view inside, calling out

342

good-naturedly to their friends in the procession. "Lha gyal lo! Lha gyal lo!" The words echoed through the compound.

"Lha gyal lo!" a cracking voice cried behind him. He turned to see Nyma trying to put her hand over Lokesh's mouth.

They carried Lokesh out into the corridor, where Winslow was waiting, bent at the waist, his elbows on his thighs. Somo and Nyma positioned Lokesh onto the American's back then tied him in place with loops of heavy twine around Winslow's chest and waist. Lokesh began to laugh hoarsely. "My spirit horse has arrived," he exclaimed.

As the American stood, Somo draped a blanket around them, covering Winslow up to his chest, fastening the blanket with pins, then suddenly the dancers were there, six of them. Two in costumes of skeleton creatures, the others with headdresses of protector demons. Two of the costumes were made for two men, customarily with one on the other's shoulders, with four arms ending with hands with long claws. The dancers pressed about the doorway and paused as though resting, then slowly continued. But as they did one of the big creatures stopped in front of the door and Lhandro and Somo pulled off the headdress, revealing two of the dropka Shan had seen at the purbas' truck the day before. In less than a minute they had the costume sleeves over Winslow's and Lokesh's arms, the headdress itself balanced on Lokesh's shoulders. Winslow toppled forward out of the building, then found his legs and began dancing down the street. They could hear Lokesh call out his praises for the gods as they walked. Shan turned to see Tenzin being fitted into one of the skeleton costumes just as someone pulled the mask of an angry yak over his own head. Nyma picked up a long narrow bundle wrapped in the jacket she had been wearing. It was one of the peche she and Lokesh had been studying, Shan realized. She cast a knowing look toward Shan, then closed the secret door. They would leave the other peche inside, in the shelter of the fragrant closet.

He could barely see where he was going as he took a step forward, and discovered gratefully that someone was leading him outside, toward the other dancers. In a moment Shan was mimicking the jig of the others, moving three steps forward and one back then one sideways, slowly proceeding toward the gate

Sheep bleated behind him, and the normally moribund monks of Norbu began calling out encouragement for the children in the procession. When they reached the benches by the gate Shan saw that Winslow was slowing. If he fell and the mask dislodged all would be lost.

But they were nearly out, nearly at the gate. Shan stepped closed to Winslow to support him if necessary.

"Again." Padme's voice called over the speaker. "Our distinguished visitors have asked for the dancers again!" Much of the assembly cheered. Shan's heart sank.

He watched Winslow turn, the skull face seeming to stare directly at

Shan. Then, following the lead of the Tibetans, as several monks snapped photographs, Shan, Winslow, and the abbot of Sangchi danced for the Bureau of Religious Affairs.

Thirty minutes later they pulled off the masks in the shelter of the tent by the purbas' truck. Winslow, sweat pouring from his face, looked numb with exhaustion but Lokesh could not stop grinning. He kept waving his arms as he had in the costume, laughing, as Somo and Nyma helped him off the American's back.

Only when Winslow straightened did he seem to notice that his clothes had been torn in the scuffle with the doctor. He lifted the remnants of his shirt pocket, which hung loose, ripped along both sides and examined them with a puzzled expression. "Did I have a card in there?" he asked in a hollow voice.

Shan replied with a slow shrug.

Winslow shrugged back. "To hell with them. We showed the bastards." He made a twirling gesture with his hand at his shoulder, like throwing a rope.

The purbas moved in urgent silence as the final element of the plan unfolded. The decorated yaks milled about the gate. The children played among the benches with the dogs. The dropka with the drums and damyen sat near the podium and played more music while the purbas wrapped Lokesh in a blanket and carried him into the truck, followed closely by Tenzin and Shan. Five minutes later they were pulling onto the road out of Norbu.

Abruptly, behind them a truck in the compound began honking its horn as if it were urgently trying to part the crowd and leave the gompa. Their own truck accelerated.

"They wouldn't chase the army in a truck, not across the ridges," Lhandro said in a despairing voice as the sound of the horn grew closer. "They must be coming for us."

"Somo! Where's Somo!" one of the purbas cried out.

As one of the white howler trucks sped out of the gompa yard Shan's heart sank. He threw a blanket over Tenzin and Lokesh, and watched as the truck overtook them.

But the vehicle did not stop. Five of Tuan's howlers sat inside, impatiently waving them aside as the white truck sped past.

As their old truck slowly rumbled back onto the road a hand appeared on the back gate and Somo swung inside, her face a strange mask of pride and fear.

"I didn't understand why they gave up so easy, why they didn't at least chase after those soldiers," she said anxiously. "So I stayed close to the speaker's platform. Padme ran out with a facsimile, stood by as the officials read it with Khodrak. At first Khodrak just stood there, saying words that no one wearing a robe should ever say. Then he changed, and smiled; said the army would learn now, that perhaps the abbot of Sangchi had been a prisoner they had stole from the army, but now the army had a prisoner who was his by right. He had proof from the old Tibetan books. It would be a grander victory even than discovering the fugitive abbot, he said. There is no one else in all of Tibet who better represents the old oppressive ways, he said." Somo cast a sorrowful look at Shan, then Tenzin. "What a lesson we can make at Yapchi, Khodrak said. What a victory will be ours."

It could mean only one thing. They had left the ancient medicine lama on the mountain with Lin. But Lin's soldiers had finally found their colonel, and now Lin had made good on his vow. He had arrested Jokar.

Chapter Seventeen

The mixing ledge was deserted when they reached it the next morning.

"The soldiers," Somo said forlornly as she walked through the empty chambers with a butter lamp. "They were searching with helicopters. Lin must have signaled them. It's how they must have found Jokar Rinpoche."

Lhandro's parents and Anya as well, Shan thought bitterly. They were all gone. "It means we can't stay," he said. "We need to go back to the water cave." Winslow, Tenzin, and the other purbas had carried Lokesh on a litter to Larkin's cave. Shan, Somo, and Nyma had pushed on with Lhandro to the little plateau.

The meager possessions of those who had been hiding at the mixing ledge were spread around the chambers, undisturbed, as though they had been forced out with no time to pack. The Yapchi headman knelt by his father's empty pallet with a mournful expression. His parents would not survive imprisonment for long. He had left them in a joyful state, communing with the medicine lama, but they had been wrenched away, into a violent, soulless world, a world they would never comprehend. Lhandro touched the corner of the framed photograph, sitting at the head of the pallet, and a small choking sound escaped his throat. His fingers trembled. "Some of the dropka," he said, "call helicopters 'sky demons.'" A sky demon had landed and consumed his parents. It happened that way sometimes. Helicopters came without warning and snatched away someone, who would never be seen again. In ancient days, a dropka once told Shan, sky demons did the same thing, but with lightning.

Lhandro stared at the photograph and opened his mouth, as if to ask why. It wasn't that his parents might be dead that hurt the most, Shan knew, but that it was so incomplete. Lhandro would never know whether to offer death rites, would not know when or where to mourn, or whether to seek them in some prison.

"All we wanted was our deity," Lhandro whispered to the photograph. He collapsed onto his knees beside the pallet, before the Dalai Lama, and began a mantra to the Compassionate Buddha.

Shan studied the room and the pallet. "Why," he asked slowly, "would soldiers leave the photograph like that?"

Somo looked at him, and then back at the image of the Dalai Lama. It was the kind of thing the soldiers hated, the kind of thing they would have thrown against a wall or ground into the earth with a boot heel.

Lhandro looked up in confusion. Somo knelt, studying the contents of the chamber with wary eyes, then shot up as Nyma called in alarm from the doorway.

Two figures approached along the western slope, walking slowly, stopping sometimes to survey the landscape below. Somo gestured the others back behind the rocks until it was clear the approaching figures were Tibetans, both clad in dropka chubas, one, the taller of the two, wearing a derby. With his binoculars Shan saw they were holding hands. Then the strangers stopped and sat on a flat rock two hundred yards away.

Somo sighed. "We can ask those herders if they saw something. But now we have to pack up anything that was left behind. No evidence should be left. If they come back, if they decide this is a purba hiding place, they will destroy it with explosives," she declared grimly, and stepped back inside, Shan and the others following closely.

Five minutes later Shan froze. Strangely, he thought he heard laughter. He looked at Somo, who had stopped, too. They rose from the bundles of blankets they were tying and warily moved outside.

Anya was there, wearing an oversized chuba, kicking an apple like a soccer ball as someone with their back to them tried to block her. It was the man in the chuba and derby who had been walking with her. Kicking the apple, Anya gave a surprised grin and waved at Shan as he stepped forward, then the man turned. Somo gasped. It was Lin.

The colonel froze. The apple rolled past him. Impossible as it seemed, for a moment Shan thought he saw playfulness on Lin's face. But his features instantly hardened and the fragment of a smile left on his face chilled into a scowl.

"Still on the run," Lin said gruffly as Anya ran to Nyma and embraced her. "I knew you wouldn't get far."

"I have a teacher," Shan explained in an even voice, "who says one of my problems is that I never run away." He studied Lin. The heavy chuba, which he now recognized as belonging to Lhandro's father, hung over his army pants. His army shirt had been replaced with a red one, like many of the dropka wore. His eyes were clear, his legs obviously steady. "But sometimes in Tibet," Shan added, "it can be hard to understand what running away means."

"I showed Aku Lin where the pink flowers called lamb's nose were blooming," Anya said, and she stepped in front of Lin as though to protect him. "We found some greens we can cook."

Aku Lin. She had called him Uncle Lin. Shan stared at the girl, and back at Lin, then at Somo. Their presence meant a helicopter had not come. "How long have you been here?" he asked. "Alone like this?"

"Three days," the girl said as she stepped closer to Shan. "The medicine lama said stay with Lin. He said it was how we needed to be," she added in a low tone. She seemed to search Shan's face for something, then Somo's, until, with an expression of doubt, she gazed back toward the brilliant white top of the mountain, as if something was happening she didn't understand.

Shan remembered the joyful expression on the girl's face as she had played with Lin, and the deep laugh he had heard. It could only have been from Lin. It was how Jokar had said they should be. "But they were arrested. Jokar and the others. Where were they taken?"

"Arrested?" Anya cried. "No. They said they would be back soon. They just went to Yapchi," Anya said. "They talked all night about it, first. Once when I woke up, Lepka—" she looked over Shan's shoulder at Lhandro, who had just appeared, and stopped.

"What?" Lhandro demanded. "What was my father doing?"

Anya's gaze became apologetic. "He was crying."

Lhandro looked at Lin, accusation filling his eyes. Lin glared back, his fingers curling, as though he were bracing for a fight.

"No—it was about the valley healing. I didn't understand all of it. It was about old things, when he and Jokar were boys."

"The valley healing?" Somo said. "You mean the people of Yapchi healing."

Anya shook her head slowly. "It was what they said," she explained, and looked at Shan. "The valley. I think they meant our deity. After they spoke, they seemed to have an idea where the deity went." She shrugged. "The next morning they left at dawn." The girl searched Lhandro's eyes as though for an answer. "Stickmen. Jokar said the stickmen would need a blessing."

"Medicine," Lhandro said to Shan, glancing with unmasked anger at Lin. "They must have gone for that medicine. The herbs Lokesh sought."

But Lin looked like he was no longer in need of herbs. He had clearly recovered from his concussion. The splint was off his wrist, which was now wrapped in a strip of cloth.

They stood in silence. Lin glanced at Shan, stepped to the apple and gave it a fierce kick that sent it over the edge of the cliff.

"They have your letter," Shan said to the colonel. "They know you're still alive."

"I will rejoin my men," Lin shot back, as if someone were arguing he would not, then he walked away and sat on a rock beyond the gnarled tree.

Anya looked after him, worry in her eyes. "He had a sister, much younger, but she died. The Red Guard. Then all those years in the army," she said. "Once he spent a year living inside a mountain near India." She looked at Shan and Nyma. "He never learned to honor his inner deity. I think," she said in a sorrowful, but insistent tone, "he never even learned how to find it." She somehow made it sound as though it was why he had been hit by the rocks.

"You must take him below," Somo said in a tight voice. "He is too dangerous. He will cause us great harm if he stays."

Anya looked out over the plain. Shan wasn't sure she had heard.

"My grandfather, before he died, used to take me to the little orchard he had on the slopes." The girl's voice was barely discernible above the wind. "He showed me how some trees grew stunted and bore no fruit when they were not sheltered from the cold. He made little rock shelters for most of them but he always kept one or two without shelter, to remind himself," she said. "Those trees that had to use all their life force to survive the cold never bore fruit."

"Take him down," Nyma said in an insistent voice. She saw moisture in the girl's eyes and she put an arm around Anya, pressing the girl's head against her shoulder. "There is that old chorten on the slope below Chemi's village. We will meet you there at midday tomorrow. It will give us time to go together to Yapchi afterwards. Some of the villagers may have gone back to the little canyon. Maybe we can find what happened to Lepka and Jokar. Maybe if we just speak to those Chinese from our hearts, they will understand," she added, but her voice was full of doubt.

Anya bit her lower lip as she studied Nyma's cool expression.

"They took Jokar Rinpoche," Nyma said, as if to be sure Anya understood.

The girl's gaze drifted toward the ground and she gave a slow absent nod.

As the others continued packing in the hidden chambers Shan found a rock near Lin and sat, watching a hawk soar below them. A wave of helplessness surged through him, leaving him in a sad, hollow place, and he found he could not speak for several minutes.

"When I was very young," Shan said at last, "whenever it snowed, a long line of women with brooms of rushes would march down the street, sweeping it into the gutters. It was never much snow, just a powder, and they would usually come before dawn, when I was lying in bed between my mother and father. We would always wake up and listen, for it was a beautiful sound. The swishing of the brooms was like a waterfall, my mother said, and it made her feel like we were in the mountains. My father called it the passing of the caterpillar, because that was how the line of sweepers looked, a long grey creature with many legs, churning up powder as it walked. Sometimes they sang—not political songs, just simple children's songs about snowflakes and the wind. Sometimes my mother would sing along in the dark, just a whisper. Now I have dreams sometimes, but it's only the sounds, no images, because it was always dark when this happened. I just hear the caterpillar, and it makes me feel peaceful. Sometimes weeks have gone by and the only time I am peaceful, is in those dreams."

349

Lin looked at him with big round eyes and gave a silent nod, as if they had been conversing about sweeper women all along. They sat in silence again. Shan pointed out a line of white birds flying in the distance. Lin kept his eyes on them until they were lost in a cloud.

"She asked me not to shoot any more birds," Lin said in a thin voice and searched Shan's face as if for an explanation.

Shan just nodded.

The colonel turned back to the cloud as if he could still follow the birds. "You can see a long way in Tibet."

Shan nodded again. "All the way back around, a lama told me once."

Lin searched his face again.

"He meant sometimes you see yourself, and your past, differently, after spending time here."

Lin clenched his jaw. "She's never been to a school, you know. Not one day of her life. There are tests she could take. I could get her in a good school. A girl like that, she could have a future." He looked back at Shan. "What kind of life would she have here? These people have been displaced," he added in an uncertain voice, as if he knew nothing of how it had happened, and looked into his hands. "I could get her leg looked at by real doctors."

"Your soldiers," Shan said. "They took Jokar. The medicine lama."

"No," Lin said as if to correct Shan. "Just an old man. He didn't hurt anyone."

Shan looked at him in confusion. It almost sounded as though Lin were defending the medicine lama. "I think it was because those howlers took the abbot of Sangchi."

Lin looked back toward the horizon. "It isn't proper work for soldiers, all this. Our job is guarding the frontiers." He looked at the old tree. "The abbot, he shouldn't have taken that file. I only wanted the file."

"Was it really so important?" Shan asked, watching Lin closely, remembering how the purbas had refused to discuss it.

Lin cut his eyes at Shan and looked away. "Military secrets," he muttered.

"Then why isn't it Public Security that's after him? I think maybe Public Security doesn't know about a stolen file. I think it was about the 54th Brigade," Shan suggested. "Maybe the honor of the 54th."

"Classified," Lin muttered. "Four of my soldiers have died for that secret."

"It was the Bureau of Religious Affairs who took Tenzin," Shan declared, watching Lin for a reaction. "And a monk named Khodrak. Khodrak saw Tenzin in Lhasa, before the stone was taken. He saw him with a former monk named Drakte. I think he saw Drakte again last month, near here, and he started looking for Tenzin."

"A lie," Lin said in a stronger voice. "There was no such report. Or else the search would have come here, instead of along the Indian border."

"Not a lie," Shan said. "Khodrak and the howlers, certain howlers, didn't want anyone else to know. Just like you didn't tell anyone your real reason for coming to Yapchi. There seem to be a lot of officials working unofficially."

Lin scowled and his eyelids slipped downward. It could have been pain, or fatigue, or he could have just been trying to end the conversation.

"The howlers want to take Jokar from your men. Jokar helped to heal you," Shan reminded Lin. "Would you really give him to the howlers?" He stood when Lin did not reply. "You have to go back," he said again. "Tomorrow."

Lin opened the old chuba and stared at his red shirt as Shan walked away. "I can't find my tunic," he said with a frown.

But inside, on Lin's pallet, his tunic lay neatly folded. Shan and Somo exchanged a knowing glance. Somo had worn the colonel's tunic at Norbu. "We have to send people to take him away from here," she said as they stepped back to the doorway.

Purbas, Shan realized. She meant purbas should come and forcibly remove Lin. "No," Shan said. "That would be the worse thing. We must . . ." He searched for the words.

"Trust?" Somo asked. "You want us to trust Lin?"

"Not Lin," Shan said, looking toward the peak of Yapchi Mountain. "Lokesh said this place has powerful healing properties. I think we have to trust the healing."

Somo frowned, then spun about and left the chamber.

A quarter hour later they said goodbye to the little plateau, leaving Lin and Anya with food for only two more meals. Shan nodded a farewell to the colonel, who still sat at the stunted tree. Lin scowled back. Anya stood apart as they left. She had begun one of her songs that had the sound of mourning, and for a moment he tried in vain to read her face, to understand what truth she had glimpsed this time. When Shan looked back she was standing at the very edge of the rim, looking down into the abyss.

The Green Tara seemed to be running a dormitory. Chemi was there, with her Uncle Dzopa, still nearly comatose, and more than a dozen of the Tibetans Shan had first seen at the camp behind Yapchi village. The rongpa were speaking in excited tones of the spring festival and the miraculous escape of the abbot of Sangchi, sitting beside Tenzin, asking for his blessing. People were coming from many miles away, they said, gathering on the mountain, saying what happened at Norbu was a portent of what would happen when the seat of Siddhi was at last occupied.

Shan listened with foreboding, which only increased as he saw Lokesh and Winslow talking in urgent tones with several purbas who arrived carrying packs of supplies. Jokar was still at Yapchi, they confirmed, and even allowed to walk about, although one of Lin's soldiers was always at his side. The camp manager had asked for a doctor to come and examine the frail old lama, but Jokar had refused to be examined. Lhandro's parents were with him, or near him—not prisoners, but refusing to leave him. "They just stay at that dig with that Chinese professor," Larkin reported.

"You were there?" Shan asked. He surveyed the cave again. The laboratory equipment, and the older Tibetan men who had looked like professors were gone.

"On the ridge above," the American woman replied. "Yesterday. Taking measurements. We had binoculars. Many more soldiers are in the camp. They put up a checkpoint, at the entrance to the valley. They want to stop anyone from coming in on the road. They have patrols deployed on the slopes above the camp."

"Measurements?" Shan asked, looking from Larkin to Winslow. "But you're not still looking for oil."

Larkin ignored him. Winslow put his palms up as though to disavow any knowledge. But Shan saw a new map on the rock slab, a map bearing the name of the petroleum venture, a detailed relief map of Yapchi Valley and the route leading from the main highway. He stepped over to it. Along the southern slope of the valley were several new dotted lines, each in different colors. Larkin stepped past him and covered it with a large-scale map of Qinghai Province.

Nyma walked from the group of purbas to Shan. "At the camp everyone says they expect oil tomorrow or the next day," she reported in a tone of resignation.

The words had the sound of an epitaph. It would be over when Jenkins's crews struck oil. The fate of the valley would be sealed. The slopes would be completely stripped of their timber. The fields of barley would be ruined by the venture's machines. The songs of the lark would be replaced with the sound of engines, the fragrance of the spring flowers with acrid fumes.

"Less than twenty-four hours," Larkin nodded grimly. "There is a convoy coming in, of high officials. People from Lhasa, and Golmud, for the big celebration."

Nyma looked back at the purba who lay on the pallet. "Who took the bullet out?" she asked.

"I did," Larkin said. "There wasn't anyone else. He bit a piece of leather rope as I worked. Just in the muscle. Lokesh says his blood is still strong."

Shan looked at the wounded purba in alarm. A bullet. With a sinking heart he noticed one of the army's automatic rifles on the ledge above the man.

He studied Larkin again, remembering how frustrated she had been when they had had to leave the explosives behind. "You can't," he heard himself say with sudden despair. "All these people," he said, gesturing toward the refugees in the cave. "They have suffered enough."

Larkin met his stare. "Cowboy has their names and registration numbers. He's going to make sure they get relocated properly. Next time he's in Tibet, he's going to report back to me."

Winslow looked up, grinning at Shan. Cowboy.

There was a murmur of surprise from across the room. Shan looked up to see six large Tibetan men enter in pairs, each pair carrying a heavy wooden box slung from a stout pole. Larkin stood and stepped forward to help the men stack the boxes at the rear of the cave.

"There was an accident," Somo said at his side, in an uncertain, worried tone. "They were laughing because they said a company truck slid off the road."

Shan stepped away and circled back, away from Larkin, to get closer to the boxes. They were marked in Chinese. Qinghai Petroleum Venture, they said. High Explosives. He wandered outside, fighting the sense of defeat that seemed to have overtaken Nyma and Lhandro, then found Winslow at the mouth of the cave, standing over the churning water of the buried river.

"Some of the Tibetans are very superstitious about this place," the American said. "They say it is a connecting place."

"Connecting?"

"I don't understand all the words I heard. One of them said it was a gate. I think they mean to another universe, one of the hidden lands. The bayal. Melissa said Tibetans believe there are many worlds inhabited by humans, some not visible to most of us, and many different types of heavens and hells. Nyma said years ago, before she was born, an old nun who lived nearby brought her students here and announced she had been called to speak with a deity that lived in the hidden land past this gate. Then she just jumped in."

Shan followed Winslow's gaze toward the maelstrom below. Larkin's secret river. Somehow, he thought, it wouldn't be the same when the geologists put a name to it and fixed it on their maps. In a wild and largely untamed land this was one of its wildest and most untamed parts. It was like a whirlpool, he thought, a dark whirlpool that had sprung up on dry land. He imagined the water rushing down, roiling through its hidden course. Perhaps they were looking at the top of a waterfall that dropped through a vast underground cavern into a lake where nagas lived. Perhaps there was indeed a hidden land beyond, and a hermit in that land was sitting on a rock looking up at the waterfall, wondering about the world that lay above it. Perhaps this was where the chenyi stone belonged. Perhaps in that world deities were not so hard to find.

"Larkin will be in grave danger," he said suddenly, pulling his gaze from the mesmerizing waters, "if she lets her camp become the base for saboteurs."

"She's not just a geologist," Winslow said absently, still watching the water.

"There are only two things they can do with those explosives," Shan pointed out. "Try to attack the camp, maybe ruin it with an avalanche. Or put them on the road into the camp, when that convoy of dignitaries comes. Either way it won't solve anything."

"It's the road. It must be," Winslow said, his eyes heavy with worry. "But they wouldn't deliberately kill all those people. Just block it."

"It will just bring more soldiers," Shan said. "More arrests. Zhu hasn't given up looking for Larkin. When he has soldiers to help he will find this place. When soldiers come the people here won't just be refugees, they'll be treated like enemies of the state. They will come to make arrests, they will come to attack."

Winslow grimaced. He looked back into the cave.

"Some people say that when you save someone's life you become their guardian forever," Shan observed quietly. But he knew the connection between Winslow and Larkin had grown more complex than that.

Winslow sighed. "If my wife had been a geologist," he said toward the cave, in a distant tone, "that's who she'd be." He glanced at Shan with surprise, as though the words had come out unexpectedly. "I don't mean . . ." He stared at the wild water and for a moment Shan thought he saw a longing in the American's face, as if he were thinking of jumping in to explore the hidden land. "I mean . . ."

"It's all right," Shan said quietly. He backed away from the edge and stepped inside, approaching Lokesh's pallet, where his old friend spoke in low tones with Somo. The purba runner was drawing on a paper which Lokesh leaned over excitedly. But when Lokesh saw Shan he pulled the paper away and quickly folded it.

"Lokesh wanted a map of Beijing," Somo explained. "I was there for running competitions. And he's been writing a letter to the Chairman," she added enthusiastically, then paused, seeing the strained look that passed between the two men.

"Shan does not want me to go," Lokesh observed in a matter-of-fact tone. "But not for any good reason," the old man said as he pushed the paper inside his shirt pocket. "Only because it could be dangerous." Once the pocket was buttoned closed, his expression brightened. "We saw many flocks of geese coming here," he announced to Shan, then gave an exaggerated yawn and rubbed the skin above his cast. Shan sighed and lowered himself to the edge of the pallet, leaning against the rock wall.

Falling in and out of wakefulness, he watched the Tibetans in despair. Strangers came and quickly departed after exchanging messages with the purbas. Somo and Winslow sat with some of those from Yapchi and reviewed Drakte's ledger book. One of the farmers laughed as she explained what Tuan and Khodrak had done, and said they must have compiled their data in some bayal.

It was midnight when he awoke to find Lokesh staring at him with his crooked grin. "Who is supposed to be watching whom?" his old friend asked. Shan brought him a plate of cold tsampa and a bowl of tea, and Lokesh spoke energetically of little things, like a grey bird he had seen in the mouth of the cave, dipping itself in a pool of water, and a cloud he had seen that looked like a camel.

The chamber was silent except for the sputter of several butter lamps. Larkin had fallen asleep at her table, her head cradled in her folded arms. Most of the purbas were asleep, the others outside on guard duty.

"She has green tea, the American," Lokesh said, knowing that Shan preferred the green leaf.

Shan studied his friend. It was as if he were trying to avoid speaking of something.

"What are they doing, Lokesh? Larkin and the purbas. I fear for them."

Lokesh looked out over the chamber. "I saw old images painted on the wall in the back. I think that hermits once lived here."

"What are they doing?" Shan repeated.

Lokesh shrugged. "Trying to align the earth deities and the water deities."

Shan sighed in frustration.

"I think they are trying to learn about how miracles are performed," Lokesh added in an excited whisper.

"They have explosives," Shan said, and pointed to the wooden boxes, stacked where the purbas slept.

Lokesh stared at the crates a long time. "I don't know. Nyma and Somo, they wouldn't use avoiders."

Avoiders. It was part of their particular gulag language, stemming from a teaching given in their barracks by an old monk, in his twenty-fifth year of imprisonment, just before he died. Guns were avoiders, he said, and bombs and tanks and cannons. They allowed the users to avoid talking with their enemy, and allowed them to think they were right just because they had more powerful technology for killing. But those who could not speak with their enemies would always lose in the end, because eventually they lost not only the ability to talk with their enemy but also with their inner deity. And losing the inner deity was the greatest sin of all, for without an inner deity a man was an empty shell, nothing but a lower life-form.

Shan looked at Somo and Nyma, both asleep on the floor of the cave. He could never consider them lower life-forms.

"We must speak with those purbas in the morning," Lokesh said in a sorrowful tone. "If a bomb is set off, Jokar is lost forever." Despair flashed across his face, then he settled back into his blanket as Shan blew out the lamp closest to the pallet.

But in the morning the purbas, the American geologist, and the explosives were gone.

"They left three hours ago," Lhandro said in a confused voice. He was standing at the cave opening, as if he had been out searching for them. "They wouldn't speak with me. Except some of the purbas gave me letters for their families. Before they left they sat in a circle and prayed, even the American woman, then they picked up their boxes and left. They made a fire outside." He gestured toward the opening.

Shan and Somo darted out onto the ledge. Against the wall was a small pile of ashes, fragments of charred papers. The maps. They had burned their maps, the notes of their research. As if they had abandoned the idea of publicly announcing the discovery of the river. There was an alarming sense of finality. They had taken the explosives. They had burned their records. The convoy of officials was arriving that morning.

"She left a note," a melancholy voice said over his shoulder. Winslow stood with a small piece of paper, a page ripped out of Larkin's notebook. "Her address in the States, where I should write to tell her parents about her if things don't go well. A special telephone number in Lhasa where people might have information about her. She says no one but me will have that number. She says come back in the summer and we can make a camp at the sacred lake." The American looked up the mist-shrouded trail, toward the grey patch above them where daylight was beginning to show. "If she's still alive. She says a venture supply truck will be leaving for Golmud before noon, to be sure I am on it, because she's an American taxpayer and wants me back at work."

Before noon. Before the officials were scheduled to arrive, she meant.

"Everyone has to go down," Shan said urgently, "get down to the road. Flee." Lokesh looked at him pointedly. Shan realized he sounded like someone else they had heard desperately exhorting everyone to flee. Perhaps Drakte, too, had given up hope. He gestured toward Chemi's uncle, who seemed to be stirring to consciousness at last, and would need help if he were to make it down the mountain. "The soldiers will be swarming over the slopes by tomorrow."

The refugees looked at Shan oddly, as if he had misunderstood something about them, but they began leaving the cavern in small groups, wearing anxious expressions. Shan heard one young farmer call out excitedly. "Siddhi's chair," he declared in a proud, defiant voice. Shan's heart sank. They were going to the high meadow where the other farmers and herders were gathering, waiting, because they had faith, because they believed the old lama would somehow escape and find them to lead them into a new age.

Finally only a handful of the villagers remained, waiting to carry out Lokesh and Dzopa. But when they went to lift the big man onto a blanket to carry him, he called out in protest and pushed away his niece.

"Rinpoche!" the man cried in a tormented voice.

Shan took a hesitant step toward the man. Dzopa blinked rapidly, then pushed his brow as though to stretch open his eyes. He had been cut badly on his arm and taken a concussion when the village was bombed. He had an infection, Chemi had said, and a high fever that made him delirious. Shan had felt sorrow for the man who had left his freedom in India only to return to his village just when it was being destroyed. The delirium had seized him again, and he was calling for a teacher he had left in India.

Chemi spoke rapidly to him, saying comforting words, and handed him a bowl of tea. The man stared at his niece as though he did not recognize her, then drained the bowl. With shaking hands he reached for a pan of tsampa on the floor and began shoving the food into his mouth with his fingers.

"I must find Rinpoche," Dzopa said between mouthfuls, his eyes growing steadier.

"We will get you down to the road today," Chemi said uncertainly.

The man hesitated and gazed at her with wide, hollow eyes. "He made me well again, my niece, all of me. He knows the working of miracles," Dzopa said. Then, more urgently, looking around the cavern he asked again, "Where is Rinpoche?"

Shan stepped to the man's side. "Jokar is below," he said tentatively. "In Yapchi."

"Jokar?" Nyma asked. "But this man—"

Dzopa fixed Shan with a penetrating gaze. His eyes were no longer cloudy. "Jokar Rinpoche is in Yapchi Valley?" The question leapt from his lips in a voice that was suddenly strong and angry. He sighed when Shan nodded. "He always said things were not finished at Yapchi. He said someday there will be great destruction there again, before things are settled." He looked absently toward the huge boots that sat beside his pallet, then slowly reached for them and began to ease them onto his feet.

"How long?" he asked Chemi when he had finished his task. "How long have I been unaware?"

"A week."

The man's face sagged, and he seemed to lose his strength for a moment. "The little blue flowers with the grey leaves that grow along the southern cliffs. Are they out yet?" he asked his niece in a voice that was suddenly small and anxious.

Chemi looked at her uncle in confusion. But Lokesh reached into his pocket and produced a tiny grey stem with a blue bloom.

Pain filled the big man's face as he stared at the flower. He looked as if he were about to cry. Then he sighed and studied the faces about him. "He would have gone with someone from Yapchi Village," he said, and settled his gaze on Lhandro, squinting, studying the rongpa. "You are Lepka's boy?" he asked. "Did he go with Lepka?" He nodded, answering his own question. "He would have gone with Lepka."

357

Chemi knelt and put her hand on his shoulder. "You cannot go to Rinpoche. Soldiers arrested him."

Dzopa's face froze. His eyes seemed to glaze again for a moment, then they grew bright as embers. He stared about the chamber with a challenging, almost threatening expression, then gazed at the cave wall, as though he could see beyond it, as though he were searching for Jokar far in the distance. He reached out for the brazier, only three feet away, and dipped his fingers in it. He began rubbing his cheeks with ashes.

The man's strange behavior was frightening, and Shan took a step toward him, to help the obviously delirious man back to his pallet. But suddenly one of the rongpa by the entrance cried out in warning. Two men charged into the cave, brandishing rifles. One of them slammed his rifle butt into the belly of the man who had shouted, leaving him writhing on the floor. Dzopa moaned and crawled toward the shadows at the rear of the cave. Somo crouched as if about to attack, then one of the men leveled his weapon at her and coolly touched his fleece hat in greeting. The second man, who wore a loose leather jerkin and a black felt hat, leaned his rifle against the table and began examining its contents.

They were not soldiers but nor were they purbas, Shan realized. Zhu. The Special Projects Director could still have men in the mountains. As the man with the lowered rifle herded them together against the wall of the cave, even forcing Lokesh to his feet, his companion began dumping the contents of the table into a drawstring bag. A pack of cigarettes, a metal mug, tea bags, a ruler, pencils. The men were not interested in arresting them, or asking questions.

"Golok!" one of the rongpa spat, and the man with the cap answered with a grin that showed an uneven row of brown teeth. The intruders were thieves.

The man at the table finished quickly, then turned to face his captives, removing his hat to reveal a bald scalp. His eyes flared, and he ran a finger along his thin moustache as he studied them. His gaze fell upon the metal stove Larkin had left behind and he lowered the rucksack on his back, rummaging through it until he produced a similar, smaller stove, into which a blue canister was fastened. He set the stoves on the table, unscrewed the canister, and with a satisfied grin screwed the canister into Larkin's stove. As he stuffed the two stoves into his sack Shan realized he had seen the smaller stove before. He exchanged a glance with Winslow, who also had recognized it.

The man with the moustache ordered them to line against the wall and began searching them, pulling off bracelets, necklaces, and even prayer amulets, dumping them into a smaller pouch he kept at his belt. When Nyma clamped her gau in both hands, refusing to give it up, the second man stepped forward, reaching for his knife.

"Go to hell," Winslow growled, and pulled Nyma behind him.

"No!" a voice boomed from behind the two men as the blade flashed

358

out of its sheath. The Goloks spun about and stared into the deep, empty shadows behind them.

Shan's heart sank. It could only be Dzopa, in his delirium. He would only anger the thieves, and get hurt for doing so. In his weakened condition another injury could kill him.

The Golok with the rifle raised it as though to fire.

"It's only my—" Chemi began, her words choked to a gasp as a wrathful creature lunged out of the darkness. It was a huge man with a grey robe draped over his ox-like shoulders, his cheeks blackened, his eyes ablaze. In his hands was a stout pole, one of the poles used by the purbas for carrying their cargos.

"Ai yi!" Lokesh cried out, and pulled back against the wall, joined by several of the rongpa.

Shan, too, found himself retreating, his throat suddenly bone dry. They had seen the man before, that terrible night when Drakte had died. The dobdob had returned.

The Goloks did not retreat but stared in confusion, the tips of their weapons drifting toward the floor. In their moment of hesitation the dobdob sprang. The pole spun through the air and slammed into the head of the bald Golok, an instant later into the skull of his companion. The two men hit the floor together, slumped, unconscious.

His eyes no longer wild, the dobdob searched for Chemi. "Rinpoche," he said to his niece in a voice like quiet thunder, "sometimes he forgets he is mortal." He said it as if it explained something important.

"You were with him in India," Shan said in a faltering voice, and settled his gaze on Chemi. Her uncle was the dobdob, and the dobdob was the guard companion of the medicine lama. "You came with him from India."

The man did not respond, did not seem to hear Shan. He hefted his new staff in the air, as though to get its balance, pulled his tattered backpack from the floor, then marched out of the cave. His face had the glint of a feral beast.

"My uncle..." Chemi murmured in a strange blend of fear, awe, and even affection as she gazed at the opening of the cave. "I didn't know he could become a..." She looked at Shan. "I didn't even think he could stand."

Maybe he couldn't, Shan thought, not until he had heard that Jokar was a prisoner. Since coming to Yapchi Mountain Shan had begun to realize that there were many ways of healing.

"They were just old stories, about how the men in our family became dobdobs," Chemi said, wonder still in her voice. "But that was all so long ago, from before Rapjung was destroyed. Dzopa used to stand in his barley field and talk about Rapjung, but never about...I never knew. Dzopa was away when it happened, the destruction of the monastery. He had come to our village because my father was sick and never went back."

"He found Rinpoche," Lokesh said, sharing her awe. "In India he found the last lama from Rapjung."

Shan nodded. "They came all the way together, with Dzopa protecting him." He remembered Dzopa's frantic warning about lamas being burned. He had caught Padme trying to burn the Plain of Flowers. He had probably seen the smoldering ruins at Rapjung. "What did he mean when he asked how long Jokar was off the mountain? Why this mountain?"

Chemi stared vacantly toward the pallet where her uncle had lain. "The stories said they were supposed to go, the oldest boy of each family from the villages around Yapchi, to become monk policemen. Enforcers of virtue, my father always called them. He said it was a pledge we made to Rapjung a hundred years ago."

Shan studied the woman, then looked at Lokesh. The two searched each other's faces. It almost sounded as though the families had been told by the lamas of Rapjung to perform penance. But the families had been the victims of the Yapchi massacre a hundred years ago.

"Drakte," Lokesh whispered.

The dobdob had come that night not to kill Drakte but to do what he always did, to protect the only Rapjung lama still alive. Somehow Dzopa had seen Drakte as a threat. Shan remembered the dark bruise on Jokar's neck and the sling the purba had carried. Surely Drakte would not have attacked the lama. But the dropka with Jokar that night had said the lama had been attacked.

"It must have been some terrible mistake," Somo said, as if sharing the same thought. Her voice shook. "People had been following Jokar and Dzopa, and knobs were treating the lama like a criminal." She looked at Chemi, biting her lower lip. "Dzopa didn't kill him," she said as though to comfort the woman.

"He is going to fight those soldiers," Chemi said in a voice heavy with despair. "He is the last man living from my family."

Shan knelt by the unconscious thieves and dumped the small pouch onto the floor. The Tibetans who had been robbed quickly retrieved their belongings, then Shan studied what was left, an assortment of silver chains and other jewelry. He picked up a tiny leather pouch on a long hide thong that seemed familiar. He stared at it a moment, then sorted through the booty until he found a lapis bracelet, and an elegant pocketknife with a folding spoon. He studied Somo a moment, who knelt by Lokesh again, then rose, the knife, bracelet, small pouch in his hand, and retrieved his own sack of belongings.

"Lokesh walks slow with his cast," he said to Chemi, but looking at Lokesh, "Keep him off the steep slopes. And be sure he doesn't stop for tonde today. Make him safe." I will find him, Shan almost added, but knew it was unlikely he would leave the valley, except in manacles.

"You can't go," Somo protested.

Shan looked back at Lokesh with a sad smile. "There is a deity to patch."

Chemi stepped toward Lokesh and knelt at the old man's side as though to confirm she would respect Shan's request.

He saw Lhandro waiting by the entrance for him and nodded at the farmer, then knelt at Lokesh's side. "The rongpa have trucks. Stay with the others. They will find the purbas, and the purbas will get you back to Lhadrung."

His friend reached out and tightly grasped Shan's hand. "We started this together," Lokesh said in a tortured voice.

"And I would never have made it without you, old friend," Shan said, his voice cracking. He squeezed Lokesh's hand then quickly stepped to the cave entrance.

"Things will be better," Lokesh said to his back, "after I return from Beijing, you'll see."

Shan turned a last time and looked into his friend's eyes. "I will never see you again if you go to the capital," he said, fighting a torrent of emotion. He could not stop Lokesh from sacrificing himself in Beijing unless he stayed with him. But he had no hope of saving Jokar unless he went to the valley.

Lokesh grasped his gau with one hand and waved goodbye.

Somo and Nyma were close behind him as he reached the ledge over the water. "Lha gyal lo," he said quietly to them, and looked into Somo's eyes. "You can still get Tenzin north," he said, "still complete the plan. Avoid the oil venture. Go in secret. You must complete the plan," he said, seeing the grim determination on their faces. "Something must be completed," he added, trying hard to keep defeat out of his voice. He took a step toward the trail. The two women matched his step.

He stopped and threw his arms up in frustration. "I have to go," he pleaded. "It's over. Drakte would be pleased that you have saved Tenzin." But they continued to follow him up the trail. Suddenly a figure appeared in the mist ahead of him. Tenzin stood there, gazing at the swirling cloud seeds. A few feet above him stood Lhandro and Winslow, his backpack in his hand.

"North," Shan said, like a plea. "People are waiting outside for you," he said to Tenzin. "In America."

The lama kept gazing at the mist. "There is no path to the north today," he sighed.

"How could it be better for both you and Jokar to be lost?" Shan asked in his pleading tone.

"Going north and leaving Jokar with soldiers, when I had not tried to stop it, if that happened then I would surely be lost," Tenzin said with a small smile.

Shan looked into the swirling waters. Maybe any hidden world would be beautiful, and better, because this one was so painful. They had no chance against the soldiers and howlers. But for the Tibetans it would still be better, for their souls, to be prisoners in the gulag, or dead, than to walk away and abandon Jokar.

"How," Tenzin asked slowly, "can you insist on going while denying us the same opportunity?"

Because, Shan wanted to say, I am the only one with nothing to lose, the only one who will not be missed, the only one with such a huge debt to repay to the lamas. But then Somo grabbed the pouch off his shoulder and ran up the trail.

The purba had gone almost a mile before Shan and Nyma caught up with her. She was standing alone, on a ledge that looked north and west over the rolling, starkly beautiful ridges that led to Yapchi Valley. In one hand she clutched the turquoise stone given to her by Drakte. She was wearing a look he had not seen before, the look of a fierce warrior, the look of a protector demon. A chill went down his spine. Somo seemed to be saying goodbye to something. Was it to the mountains that would forever be changed when the oil started flowing? Or was it to life itself? She was descending to do battle with the Chinese soldiers. He looked at the stone in her hands. Drakte had wanted to be a monk, but Beijing had prevented it. She had wanted to be a teacher, but Beijing had prevented it. Then, because they had both been cast away by Beijing, they had met and fallen in love. But they could not stay together, not in this life, because Beijing had prevented it.

Somo turned with a forced smile, then glanced back up the trail where the figures of Lhandro, Winslow, and Tenzin could be seen in the distance.

An hour later they were walking silently, grim-faced, through the ruins of Chemi's village, toward the chorten where they had promised to meet Anya. When the crumbling chorten came into view, Nyma pointed, relief flooding her face, toward a small figure walking around the chorten, then quickened her pace. Shan and Nyma were less than a hundred yards away when Shan stopped and held up his hand.

"It's her, I know it is," Nyma exclaimed, and began waving to get the girl's attention. She followed Shan's gaze and her hand slowly dropped. Lin sat on the ground forty feet from them, a chuba arranged under him like a blanket. The colonel was watching Anya with a melancholy smile. He wore his uniform, except a small piece of heather extended from his breast pocket. As Shan approached he glanced up and the smile disappeared.

"They say oil should come today or tomorrow," Shan said as he squatted beside Lin. "A delegation of venture officials are on the way."

Lin nodded slowly.

"I remember those snow caterpillars," Lin said suddenly, in a reluctant, hollow voice, as if compelled to continue the conversation Shan had offered the day before. "Suddenly last night I just remembered, how those women swept the snow, like you said. Sometimes little sparrows would be numb with cold and get swept up in the snow. My father would go down to the street sometimes when the caterpillar passed, to check for sparrows. If he found one he would put it in his pocket and we would take it home, then release it in the afternoon when it warmed.

"One day the block captain called a meeting," he continued, referring to one of the watchers who kept political order in residential units. "She had a burlap bag which she dumped on the table. It was dead sparrows, maybe twenty dead sparrows. She said from now on it would be our patriotic duty to collect the sparrows from the gutter after the sweepers passed, and eat them. Because the Chairman insisted that all resources be put to use for the cause of socialism. Then she gave us instruction on the approved methods for killing sparrows."

Shan stared sadly at Lin. He remembered children from his own youth filled with revolutionary zeal, stoning pigeons and seagulls, parading with the carcasses of mice. It was how the Chairman shaped good little soldiers, his father had said bitterly.

"So we killed the sparrows," Lin continued. "We ranged far beyond our block when the snow came, just to find and kill sparrows. One day I caught my father with a live one in his pocket and I told the block captain. I thought it was a joke I played on my father. But that afternoon I came home and there was a meeting. A tamzing. My father was in the middle, with welts on his face, and a sign pinned to his shirt that said reactionary pig. They wouldn't stop until my father killed that sparrow, in front of everyone. He was crying when he did it. The only time I ever saw my father cry."

They were silent a long time.

"Why," Lin said, looking at his hands, deeply perplexed. "Why would I have forgotten that until yesterday?" He glanced at Shan awkwardly, as if he had not intended to speak the thought out loud, then gazed toward Anya in the distance. "She's getting one more tonde," the colonel said. "Said that sometimes old chortens attract good tonde. Says I need one to keep rocks off my head." He spoke in a sober voice, as if he had come to fervently believe in tonde.

Lin turned to Shan and frowned. "I still have orders," he said, as if to correct himself. "People can't be allowed to do things to the government."

"Duties," Shan acknowledged with a small nod, still watching Anya.

The sound of heavy engines echoed up the narrow valley that led to the Yapchi road.

"There was something she did," Lin said, "when we were coming today. There was one of those rock rabbits, a pika she called it. It ran away and stopped about forty feet away. Then she sat and sang a song. She said, sit, Aku Lin." The colonel frowned again, as if displeased with his confessional tone. "She sang this song like I have never heard before.

In Tibetan. I couldn't understand. But the words weren't important. It was like—I don't know, like what it would be if an animal could sing. And that pika came right up and sat in her lap. She picked up my hand and put it on top of the pika. I felt it breathing, like those sparrows when I was a boy." He cut his eyes at Shan. "A silly thing," he added, in a new, gruff tone. "A thing for children."

"A deity song," Shan said. "Anya calls them deity songs."

The machine sound was louder now. "A tank," Lin said in a weary voice. "And two or three trucks. Coming this way."

Shan looked at Lin. Was the colonel warning him, so he and Nyma could flee?

Anya straightened from where she was digging, and waved at them. Shan and Lin both waved back.

"You and I," Lin said awkwardly, "we're the same age I think." He sighed. "I had a letter from my mother before she died. She said two generations had been lost, but that the next one would be ready, the next one had the chance to put it all behind them and find a new way."

Shan stared at the man. They were not the words of an army colonel. He was saying that the turmoil brought by the party and politicians had ravaged men like Shan and himself, and their parents. But Anya was of the new generation.

"A good doctor could fix that leg. I promised to meet her at that resettlement camp in a week or two. I have some leave coming. I am going to take her to a good hospital." Lin spoke in a rush, as if he had to get the words out quickly or they might not come at all. With a strange sensation Shan realized that there was no one else Lin could speak them to, that Shan had somehow become his confessor. "If she wants I will take her to a real school. There are private schools now. I could pay—" Lin spun about. Three figures stood behind them, barely ten feet away. Nyma with Winslow and Tenzin, his dung bag on his shoulder. Lin glared at Shan, as if Shan had tricked him.

"Please," Shan said to them. "You should stay back. Soldiers may be coming—"

"Tenzin has an offer to make," the American announced as Nyma approached and knelt in the grass. "The papers the colonel has been looking for. Tenzin wants to return them."

As he spoke Tenzin lowered the dung bag from his shoulder, knelt, then accepted a pocket knife from Winslow, which he quickly used to cut the threads at the top of the bag. He ripped the double layer of thick leather apart, reached inside, and pulled out a thin sheaf of paper, perhaps ten pages in total.

As Lin stared at the paper a sound like a growl came from his throat.

"It's a report on a disaster," Tenzin said to Lin, as if he had to remind the colonel. "A unit of the 54th Mountain Combat Brigade was inside a mountain on the Indian border, a secret command center, still under construction. The mountain collapsed. Everyone inside was lost, with several million dollars of computer and surveillance equipment. Forty soldiers died. And the Tibetan workers who were being forced to hollow out the mountain. The last part is very sensitive. It says all the workers died. But one old monk survived for a few hours. He was laughing a lot. They thought he was delirious at first. He said the prisoners did it, that they had gradually dug away the support columns, that they had destroyed one of the army's crack units. That none of them minded taking four because it had become the right thing to do." Taking four. It was a gulag term, for choosing to commit the sin of suicide—and the incarnation as a lower life-form that would follow, a life on four legs—instead of continuing the misery of the gulag.

Winslow put his hand on the report and Tenzin released it to the American. Shan stared at the papers. "Old monks destroyed the army's most advanced listening post. This is the secret that the colonel couldn't bear the world to know," Winslow said, looking with wonder at the pages. "Take the report, colonel," he said after a moment, in a plaintive tone, "and give us the lama."

It didn't seem that Lin had heard. His eyes drifted back toward Anya. For a moment it seemed he wanted to ask the girl's advice.

"The report for the lama," Winslow pressed.

When Lin did not reply, Tenzin stood. "Not just the report," he said to the colonel. "You can have the abbot of Sangchi, as well, if you wish. Just release Jokar."

Winslow cursed under his breath, and put a hand on Tenzin's arm as though to pull him away. Nyma moaned and reached out to hold Tenzin's leg.

Lin's eyes slowly shifted back to Tenzin. He seemed about to speak when Anya called out. She was waving at him with something in her hand. Lin leaned forward anxiously. Anya was climbing on the old chorten, as if maybe to better see the machines that were coming.

Beyond the chorten, perhaps half a mile from where they sat, Shan saw soldiers moving up the slope in a tight line. Suddenly there was a whoosh of air, a whining sound, and the slope above them, a hundred yards away, exploded. Shan turned in alarm. Had Somo been there, watching? Surely she would have gone over the ridge by now. Perhaps the tank was sending a warning shot for any Tibetans lingering in the hills, clearing the approach to the valley for the arriving officials. Or had the soldiers heard about the gathering in the high meadow, those waiting for the old lama to lead them in resistance?

Anya was standing now, facing the smoldering patch of earth in confusion.

"Damned fool," Lin muttered, and slowly rose as another shell screeched through the air.

But this one was not aimed up the ridge. It connected with the chorten.

There was a thunderous explosion, and the chorten was no more.

Nyma screamed and ran toward the ruins.

"Noo—ooo!" Lin moaned, and clenched his chest as if he had been shot. "No—ooo!" he repeated in an agonized voice. He rose, took a step forward and fell to his knees.

Shan, staring in horror at the smoking ruins, found himself helping Lin to his feet. The colonel, his face drained of color, lashed out at Shan with his fist, then stumbled down the slope. "Anya!" he called. "Anya come here! Xiao Anya, did they hurt you?"

Shan followed him, his feet leaden, his heart a lump of ice.

Nyma was first to reach the small, limp body lying on the spring blossoms. She seemed not to even notice when Lin pushed her away and knelt beside Anya. She was not bleeding much, Shan told himself, but then he saw the splinter of rock embedded in the base of her neck. The girl's eyes were opened in surprise, but there was no light in them. She had died instantly.

"Xiao Anya," Lin said in a feeble voice, stroking the girl's cheek. "Little Anya," he repeated, again and again. In her hand, clenched almost shut, was a piece of green stone, a tonde for Uncle Lin.

Soldiers approached, then halted a hundred feet away as they saw their colonel. One of them called out excitedly, and began running back toward the tank, which was now visible below. Lin seemed not to notice the soldiers. He lifted Anya's shoulders, pressing her lifeless check against his for a moment, blood oozing out of her wound now. His eyes fixed on the green stone in her hand, and he wrapped his own hand around her limp fingers and the stone. He seemed to have trouble breathing for a moment, and he collapsed, his head buried in her shoulder, his back arching in a long, wrenching sob.

No one moved. No one spoke. Slowly Lin rose to his full height, stiff, his face sagging, and carried the dead girl cradled in his arms, down to his troops.

CHAPTER EIGHTEEN

Who will sing for me when the songbird dies? Who will sing? The words of the oracle echoed in Shan's mind until, numbed with pain, he realized Nyma was speaking them.

"Did she know?" Nyma asked again and again, then grabbed Shan's arm and burst into tears. "Blessed Buddha, she knew. Our little Anya knew this would happen," Nyma sobbed.

She would not leave the ruined chorten. Nyma planted herself in the patch of flowers where Anya had been thrown, scrubbing away her tears, reciting a mantra, not seeming to notice when the soldiers milled about, only staring at the spot among the flowers where the girl's blood had mottled the blooms.

Shan watched, still paralyzed with grief, while the commandos searched the rubble as though looking for more bodies. Several seemed hesitant, looking at the anguished woman, or down the slope at their colonel who had refused to let go of the dead girl, whose blood now ran down his arms and legs. One soldier seemed to recognize Shan, and hung by him, as though waiting for orders to drag him down to the trucks.

Who will sing for me when the songbird dies, Shan heard again.

Then came the shrill call of a whistle, and the soldiers seemed to melt away, jogging down the slope as first the tank and then the trucks retreated in a cloud of dust.

"It may not be safe here," Shan pleaded with Nyma. "I can take you to one of the caves at least." But she gave no sign of hearing. Tears streamed down her cheeks again, and her invocation of the Compassionate Buddha grew louder.

"It doesn't matter," Nyma said in a brittle voice. "Don't you see? Tibetans have no reason to hope. This is what happens to those who hope. We've been abandoned," she said in a haunting tone.

"I have to go to Yapchi," Shan said. He repeated the words, and when she did not respond he turned away and began walking toward the valley, feeling painfully alone, suddenly deeply regretful that he had left Lokesh. Tenzin and Winslow had fled. Perhaps they would reach Lokesh and keep him safe. He kept telling himself that as he climbed, until he stopped, his legs wobbling strangely, and collapsed onto a rock. No one was safe. The army was in the mountains and it was shooting at Tibetans. Gentle Anya, who spoke with lambs, lay dead, because she had wanted to find a charm to attract a deity to the leader of the soldiers who had killed her.

He emerged at the top of the ridge, at a high point between the oil derrick and the village, then found a game trail and began to descend into the valley. Five minutes later he heard someone conversing loudly and crouched behind a rock.

It was Gyalo, speaking with Jampa, briskly walking down into the valley on an adjacent trail, several steps ahead of a long single-file line of grim-faced Tibetans. It looked like a column of soldiers, Shan thought with a start, but then he saw that the implements they carried on their shoulders were shovels and axes and picks. There were at least forty men and women, some of whom he recognized as the refugees he had seen in the cave the night before. Some of them sang songs. Scattered among them were helmets of green, as though Gyalo had found defectors from the venture. Except that they were heading back toward the valley.

Maybe, Shan realized with a sinking feeling, they were soldiers of a sort. He stepped out of his hiding place and the monk greeted him with a warm grin. "The army is still down there," Shan warned.

The monk smiled, and gestured the other Tibetans to pass around him as he stood with Shan and Jampa.

"Please," Shan said, "there's been enough suffering." He explained what had happened to Anya.

The outlawed monk shut his eyes a moment, then looked at Shan and nodded gravely. "That oracle spoke of it." The big yak, who had been studying Shan, gave a massive sigh and looked off into the distance. Gyalo fingered one of the braids twined with bright beads which Anya had tied at Norbu.

"Even if you could undermine the derrick," Shan said, thinking he may have understood the purpose of Gyalo's party, "they would never let you close enough to try."

Gyalo gave Shan a long, slow look, then stepped off the trail toward a ledge that overlooked the southern end of the valley and pointed. Shan followed Gyalo's finger, shielding his eyes with his hand, toward a place perhaps two hundred feet from where the painted rock had been. He pulled out his binoculars. There seemed to be movement in the shadows under the trees.

"We have to release the deity that's trapped," Gyalo explained in an earnest tone. He looked at Shan with a bright expression. "They say you found it, that you solved the puzzle," he declared gratefully, and without another word continued down the trail, pointing out a bird to Jampa as they walked.

Shan looked after the monk and his yak in confusion. He had solved nothing, but he had no time to worry about the monk's strange words. At least, he told himself, the Tibetans would be out of reach if they stayed on the upper slopes. The soldiers might not care if the displaced Tibetans wanted to pass their time digging out boulders from the mountainside.

The ruins of Yapchi Village lay silent as he passed through them, undisturbed except for a small work party that was ripping apart the burnt timbers of the houses and stacking them in one of the stable yards. The sheep that had journeyed with them from Lamtso were in a small pen, several of them gazing at one of their number that hung upside down, skinned and gutted, on a scaffold of timbers. The caravan sheep were being butchered for the oil workers.

As he continued down the path toward the derrick a voice echoed in his head again. You and the Yapchi deity are going to fix the land for us, you are going to make the Chinese leave, Nyma had said at Lamtso. The wave of emotion that surged through him was so powerful he had to stop again. He found himself fighting for breath, and sat again. Anya was dead. Yapchi Village was destroyed. Lokesh had been tortured, and was leaving, crippled, for Beijing. The old lama was a prisoner. Drakte had died. Lin, who alone had the power to take the soldiers away, had not been changed, only hollowed out, turned into a bitter shell of a man. The Tibetans were still going to resist, and lose, with more of them dying or imprisoned. Soldiers had died. The valley was slowly being destroyed. The oil was still going to flow. Not for a moment had they even cast a shadow of uncertainty over that outcome, not for a moment had there been any doubt that those who craved the oil would win. The deity would stay blinded forever.

He could not bear to look at the derrick as he walked past it. It was like a cold metal monster hovering at his shoulder. Workers crawled over it. It whirled and pounded and groaned so loudly that it seemed the machine was indeed fighting the earth.

Beyond the derrick, close to camp, a platform had been built, supported by raw logs taken from the slope above. Along the front of the platform hung a freshly painted banner, declaring in bright red letters, Serene Prosperity. On the far side of the platform workers bent over cans of red paint to complete one more banner, fastened along its top to a long rope. Victory for Lujun Valley, Shan read, painted on a long roll of cloth, with small derricks painted along the bottom, like the religious symbols sometimes arrayed along the borders of thangkas. Chairs and benches stood on the platform, enough for perhaps twenty people, and from its stairs Jenkins directed workers. The manager paused as a utility vehicle appeared in the camp, followed by two boxy black limousines. The convoy of dignitaries had arrived. Shan looked back in puzzlement at the northern slopes, again wondering why Larkin had taken her Tibetans there, not to the road, not to start an avalanche to block the convoy, not to the angry Tibetans who gathered on the mountain, waiting for the lama to lead them.

Shan saw no sign of Winslow or Somo as he walked toward the camp. Perhaps the American was back in the office trailer, arguing with Jenkins. Everything looked normal. The army tents were still at the rear of the camp, bristling with activity. Soldiers ran in and out of tents, shouting. Their lost colonel had materialized. Even Professor Ma continued his digging, with many more helpers now, racing against his deadline, although now they worked under the eyes of a stern sentry, with a heavy staff for a weapon.

But as he walked past the archaeology dig, two hundred feet off the trail, he halted abruptly. It wasn't a soldier guarding Professor Ma, it was the dobdob. He studied the army tents again. No one seemed to have noticed Dzopa. Shan began walking hestitantly toward the dig, recognizing the workers as he approached. Lhandro was there, and his parents, and Jokar, all on their knees, digging earnestly in the square of open soil, now much larger than before. Dzopa stood erect, his staff at his side, a pile of blankets below him, his backpack and Jokar's staff a few feet behind him.

Professor Ma and his assistant both sat beside the opened square of earth with soil sieves, acting as though nothing had disturbed their routine, the diggers alternately bringing their buckets of earth to them, the bench beside them covered with artifacts. Why would Jokar be permitted his freedom, Shan wondered, then with a chill he saw that it was not a pile of blankets at the dobdob's feet but the crumpled form of a soldier. From where Dzopa stood it was no more than fifty feet to a large outcropping at the base of the slope. He must have circled about, and come at the guard from behind. The dobdob seemed to have simply assumed the sentry's duties, however, for neither he nor Jokar seemed to show any intention of fleeing.

Shan picked up one of the trowels by the side of the dig and stepped into the loose earth to help Lepka fill his bucket. The old man acknowledged Shan with a casual nod, as if he had expected him, and continued working. Shan studied the man's face as he dug his trowel into the earth. It was not fear he saw, or the exhaustion he might have expected, it was a deep spiritual pain.

As he emptied his bucket into the professor's sieve, the old Han exchanged a worried glance with Shan. Behind him on the bench were new artifacts. "You were supposed to be gone by now," Shan said.

Curiosity filled the professor's eyes. "I was packing to leave when that old lama came. I didn't stop him when he started digging, and after an hour he beckoned me to his side. He said I must not be in such a hurry. He said my spirit was out of balance, and I needed to tend to my heart wind." Ma gave a small, confused smile. "I stopped packing."

Shan returned the empty bucket and squatted at the bench. There was a little bronze tray for burning incense cones, and metal arrowheads. There were pieces of jade, fragments of a statue. Strangely, one appeared to be the leg of a hooved animal. Not a horse, for the hoof was split. A yak perhaps, or a cow.

Shan looked back at the old lama, and heard Dzopa groan. Jokar's serene face seemed to have gone blank again, as it had that awful hour at the hermitage. His shoulders sagged. The dobdob approached him with a deliberate air and raised the lama's hand with a slow, reverent motion, then cupped the lama's hand around his own mouth and blew hard into it. The lama's eyes fluttered and seemed to struggle for a moment to find focus, then Jokar was back. "It has been exhausting, this journey, has it not, my old friend? I'm ready for a long sleep," he said to Dzopa with an apologetic smile, then resumed his digging.

After a moment the lama paused and stared at his hand then, with a movement that somehow chilled Shan, he touched it with his other hand, running his fingers along it with a look of wonder, as if he had never seen a hand before. A living Buddha, Nyma had called Jokar, a Bodhisattva. In the middle of the chaos and fear the living Buddha was pausing to— what? Marvel at the miracle of the human body?

As the dobdob returned to the edge of the dig Shan saw a new figure beside the bench. Winslow. The American stared at Shan with an uncertain expression. He held a piece of paper. As Shan stepped to his side, Winslow lowered the paper, as though he were thinking of hiding it. Shan eased it out of the American's hand.

"That doctor, he found my card, it fell out of my shirt that day at Norbu." The words came out in a slow whisper as Winslow's gaze settled on the lama. "Guess I offended his dignity."

The paper was a facsimile, directed to the camp managers of all oil venture operations. Sent by the U.S. embassy in Beijing, it gave a description of Winslow and requested that they immediately report his whereabouts. Winslow had lost contact with the embassy and the Chinese government had filed a complaint about criminal activity by the American. Winslow's official credentials had been suspended, and if he was seen he was to be directed to contact the embassy and surrender himself to Public Security, with his passport.

Shan read the message twice. The embassy seemed to be disowning Winslow. If he were not given the cover of his diplomatic immunity, he would be subject to criminal charges before the knobs. Shan looked up to return the paper to Winslow, but the American seemed to have lost interest in it, and was with Jokar now, holding the lama's bucket of soil.

Shan stared at the others in the dig, as confused as ever. They all seemed to see things Shan could not understand, all except Lhandro, who paused every few moments and looked at the others with the same confusion Shan himself felt.

It made no sense. Had Jokar come to the valley to dig? Had he really surrendered himself to do this? He had come back to Yapchi to restore balance. Jokar and Lepka had come together to heal the valley, just as the derrick was about to strike oil, just as the officials were to arrive for the ceremony that marked the end of the valley.

Shan stepped back to Professor Ma. "I don't see your assistant."

"She is finishing the report, in the office," Ma said, with a nod toward the trailer complex. As if, Shan realized, whatever the lama was doing, or finding, did not belong in the report.

"So you didn't find anything important enough to stop the project?" Shan asked in a futile tone.

Ma looked at him as if Shan had told him a joke. "You mean did I find the missing link that explains evolution? Or the tomb of a Chinese emperor?" He gave a thin laugh. "No." He gazed at the open patch of soil. "Not so old really." His eyes drifted toward the small chest where he kept the bronze shard with the Chinese and Tibetan writing.

A loudspeaker in the camp started playing a martial anthem: The East is Red. A line of vehicles appeared over the low saddle of land and descended into the camp.

Suddenly Lhandro grunted loudly and called for the professor. Ma seemed reluctant to go. He looked at Shan with a strange plea in his eyes. Lhandro called out. His fingers were scratching at the soil covering what appeared to be a cylinder, perhaps twelve inches long.

"A piece of pipe," Lhandro speculated. "Sometimes they brought in bamboo to carry water."

It was indeed bamboo, Shan saw as he knelt beside the rongpa, a sturdy piece over two inches in diameter. Shan dug a finger around the end of the cylinder, then abruptly pulled his hand away and looked at Ma, who returned his steady gaze. Lhandro finished the digging and raised his find. It was not a water pipe. It was capped at both ends, and made a rattling sound when he shook it. Shan looked from Ma to Jokar, who solemnly nodded as though to confirm Shan's suspicions. Lhandro saw the exchange, and looked from face to face, searching for an answer to the mystery. His gaze settled on his father.

"He's a good man, that professor," Lepka said. "We have told him things about what has happened to you, and to Shan."

Lhandro took the cylinder to the professor, expectation in his eyes, but Ma simply placed it beside the other artifacts on the bench, without comment. Shan stood, and stepped to the wooden chest beyond the professor and opened it. Inside, beside the felt that covered the bronze shard he had seen before, was another piece of felt. He lifted the top layer. It covered a human skull, with a jagged hole in its temple.

"I don't understand," Winslow said over his shoulder. Shan looked up and followed the American's gaze to Lhandro's father, who rose slowly and sat on the ground at the edge of the dig, rocking slowly back and forth. The American picked up the bamboo canister and shook it as Shan lifted the bronze shard and studied its markings again. He ran his fingers along the Chinese characters.

Shan took the cylinder from the American. He had one of his own, probably older than this one, handed down from his great-grandfather, left for safekeeping with the lamas in Lhadrung. He twisted the top of the cylinder and it loosened, then pulled free in his hand. He dumped the contents onto the bench. Lacquered sticks of yarrow wood, yellow with age.

"Sixty-four," he said in a voice tight with emotion. "There will be sixty-four sticks." He looked up into the confused faces of those around him. "Throwing sticks, for the Taoist verses." He looked back at Lepka. Stickmen, he had said. Lepka had had nightmares about the stickmen. Shan turned to Winslow and quickly explained how the sticks were used to ritually build a chapter number by throwing them and separating them into groups of three, using the grouping remaining after the count to create solid or broken lines that in turn built one of the tetragrams which, in the tables memorized by students of the Tao referred to a specific chapter of the Tao te Ching. Like the tetragram Lepka had unexpectedly drawn at the mixing ledge. "I would throw sticks like these for hours with my father when I was young," Shan said quietly, "and we would take turns reciting the Tao."

He fingered the shard again. Now that he knew what to look for, deciphering was simple. "It is Chapter Seventy," he explained, "in Tibetan and Chinese." He pointed to the characters. "The verse ends here with these characters," he said, and looked to Lepka.

"Evolved individuals wear a coarse covering with precious jade at the center," the old Tibetan recited as he stared at the pile of sticks. Jade. The leg of jade was of an ox. It had been a statue of Lao Tzu, the Taoist sage, with his ox.

Shan continued to search Lepka's face. "When the soldiers came, the Lujun troops, there weren't just Tibetans living in this valley," he said.

The old man shook his head. "My father explained the secret to me before he died," he said, looking at Lhandro with apology in his eyes. "Some Chinese had come, twenty or thirty years before the Lujun soldiers came, to build a small Taoist temple. They were scholars he said, who lived like hermits, trying to explain the similarities between the teachings of the Tao and the teachings of Buddha. To bridge the gaps between our peoples. Monks came from Rapjung sometimes and they would have debates or throw the sticks and recite verses for us. The village would come and listen."

He looked at Jokar, who offered a nod of encouragement. "They weren't any problem, they were peaceful, and built gardens for the herbs that the Rapjung monks used. They spoke of how wonderful it would be if Chinese and Tibetans could work together to study the mysteries of healing, and they themselves took lessons from the lamas." Lepka looked toward the army tents for a moment, then turned his gaze back to the freshly turned soil. "My father was away in the Tibetan army when it happened. He said those monks would probably have tried to stop the Chinese soldiers, too, that they would not have wanted bloodshed. But there was no one left from Yapchi when the soldiers left, no one to defend those Chinese monks. When people came from the villages nearby and found all the bodies, they went crazy."

He looked only at Shan now as he spoke, as if he were confessing, as if it were a story he had to tell to a Han. "My father said probably those Chinese monks were trying to bury the bodies, trying to help. But the people were too angry."

Too angry at Chinese, he meant. People came and became crazed with rage and the lust for revenge. Not soldiers, but the farmers and herders. He looked at the skull in the still-open bench. A hoe could have killed that monk, or a pick.

"They couldn't tell anyone afterwards," Lepka said forlornly, wringing his hands. His wife stood beside him, holding his shoulder tightly. "If word got out about the Chinese monks, the Chinese army would return. So our families burnt the Tao temple and covered it with a barley field." Tears streamed down the old man's face. "Afterwards, the monks from Rapjung heard. They came and said words for the Chinese, for all those who had died. They made the people reopen the grave that had been dug for the Yapchi villagers and bury whatever remains they could find of the monks with the villagers. Made the people who had killed the monks promise to send their first sons to become dobdobs at the gompa, so such a thing could not happen again." He looked at the yak-like Dzopa. Enforcers of virtue, Chemi had called the monk policemen. "My brother went," Lepka said, "but he died at Rapjung when Mao's children came."

Suddenly there were loud voices at the platform, commands for workers to leave the platform and allow the dignitaries to be seated. The chairs and benches were quickly filled with Chinese and Tibetans in business suits. Jenkins's secretary stood at the top of the stairs, welcoming the guests, handing them paper programs, but glancing frequently toward one of the army tents, where a tight knot of soldiers had formed. Lin must be there, with Anya. Other soldiers were moving around the compound, holding their weapons conspicuously.

Professor Ma had opened Dzopa's backpack and produced a blanket from it to cover the fallen sentry but it was only a matter of time before the man revived, Shan knew, and more trouble would begin. An officer from Lin's command climbed onto the stage and stood beside a microphone on a stand, facing the assembled dignitaries as he waved a polished wooden pointer in the air. He was gesturing toward the ruined village, the denuded slopes, even the patch of scorched earth where the painted rock had been. He explained the victorious role of the People's Liberation Army in the opening of the valley, and pointed out the soldiers stationed on the outer perimeter of the camp like a security net.

Shan looked back at the blanket. It was white, heavily soiled but still white, streaked with lines of soot. Dzopa's blanket. Dzopa who had traveled with Jokar from India. Shan's vision seemed to blur a moment, and he saw something else, in his mind's eye. He saw Jokar sitting in the night wrapped in Dzopa's blanket. He saw Drakte running, frantic, in great pain, fleeing from Tuan's howlers, knowing the white-shirted men were pursuing, trying to capture him, perhaps even trying to ambush him. He saw Drakte pause as a white figure appeared before him, saw Drakte fit a stone to his sling and fire a shot into Jokar's neck. The shudder that coursed through his body somehow told Shan that he had glimpsed the truth.

Another figure appeared, striding purposefully up the stairs, watched expectantly by the seated figures. It was Jenkins, now wearing a clean blue shirt and red tie, leading half a dozen others in ties and blue shirts, including two Westerners. As Jenkins stepped aside and gestured his party onto the platform, Shan spotted another group assembling near the platform. Or being assembled. Over fifty Tibetans were being herded by soldiers toward the front of the platform. The forced laborers, Shan suspected, by the way several of them acknowledged Lhandro and Nyma with small, tight nods.

Finally came Special Director Zhu, and an older woman wearing a dark grey suit, and a large-brimmed straw hat against the sun, to sit in the last two seats of the front row. Zhu began to sit, then straightened, squinting toward the dig, toward Shan and Jokar and Tenzin. Even from the distance Shan sensed his sudden excitement and he watched as Zhu called a knob soldier to the edge of the platform and pointed in their direction. The knob took several strides toward the dig, then paused as an army officer called out. The officer bolted up the platform steps, looking toward the southern end of the valley as he spoke excitedly into a handheld radio. After a moment the officer ran to Jenkins and pointed southward with a victorious gleam.

Shan could not hear the conversation, but from the man's excitement, from the way the party in blue shirts raised their hands, clapping in Jenkins's direction, he knew the soldiers had scored one last victory. An army truck sped past, and Shan saw the distant figures of a patrol jogging along the south end of the valley.

"She's okay, Winslow," a deep voice suddenly announced. Jenkins was there, at the side of the dig, studying Winslow with an apologetic expression. "I thought you'd want to know. Larkin's up there, the soldiers say, hiding in the trees with a lot of Tibetans, digging for something. They're bringing her down." The American manager studied Winslow, then shook his head and sighed. "I'm sorry about that fax. If it helps I'll put in a word. You were trying to help, I know." Winslow did not acknowledge him, only stared toward the far end of the valley. Jenkins shrugged and stepped back toward the platform.

A mocking voice called from a distant corner of Shan's mind. Thirteen months of freedom. Four years in the gulag, then thirteen months of freedom. It was the way many purbas lived, he knew, alternating long stretches of lao gai with short intense bursts of work on behalf of their cause.

375

But there was another voice, equally distant at first, shouting at him down a long dark corridor in his mind. The deity rock. Even a small distraction might allow some of the Tibetans to escape, perhaps even taking Jokar with them. If only Tenzin and Jokar could flee, Shan could bear all the suffering to come. He inched toward the crew putting the final touches on the Serenity banner. Without consciously understanding what he was doing at first, he found himself by the stack of paint cans. He leaned and picked up a can of red paint. When he looked up Somo was there, only five feet away, staring forlornly at the line of prisoners coming down the valley through the ruins of the village. He stepped to her side and extended the can of paint. She accepted it with a confused look. They gazed at each other a moment, exchanging the kind of sad, proud gazes soldiers might trade as they were about to throw themselves against impossible odds.

He opened his mouth with a small, sad smile. "Can you run?" he asked.

An intense energy seemed to build in her eyes as Somo considered his question. Then she looked at the can of paint and smiled back. He spoke quietly to her, and an instant later she faded away through the crowd.

As she did so the East is Red anthem exploded through the public address system again and scattered applause broke out as the dignitaries rose to formally welcome a final set of visitors marching from the camp toward the platform. Shan's throat tightened as he watched Khodrak, Padme, and Tuan escorted by a line of the white-shirted guards, each of them shaking hands with many of those in the crowd, acting like guests of honor. This was their day as much as Jenkins's. Khodrak moved slowly, ceremoniously carrying his mendicant's staff, Padme a step behind, carrying the black satchel Shan had seen in the conference room at Norbu.

The professor wandered toward the delegation from Norbu. Shan watched as Ma politely shook hands and spoke, first with Padme, then with Khodrak, who seemed at ease with the elderly Han.

Lhandro stirred from the paralysis that seemed to have gripped those at the dig. "It is dangerous for that professor," the rongpa headman said in a low voice to Shan. "He doesn't know what kind of monk that Khodrak is."

"He senses something important here," a soft, worried voice said at Shan's shoulder. It was Ma's assistant, the young graduate student who had been finishing the report. In her hand was a large brown envelope. "He must go. I keep trying to take him home.

"He was supposed to be the head of the entire university. He was so adored by his students that they would ask him to give extra classes, at night, unofficially." She spoke the words quickly, as if she had been storing them, anxious to tell Shan and his friends. "Five years ago he was ready to be installed as the chairman of the university, but someone from Beijing visited a class and discovered that he was not using the approved history text." She paused to watch a procession move out of the army encampment, a small knot of officers, with Lin at the center wearing a clean uniform. "The professor laughed and said that history was a rich tapestry and the party's history book made it seem like an old grey rag. His students laughed, too, and applauded. But the visitor didn't laugh. They made another professor head of the university, and took away Professor Ma's classes. He is only allowed to do research now."

Shan studied the old Han, who seemed to have recognized something in Khodrak that bore closer inspection. What was the professor doing? Lepka had said he was a good man. In another lifetime he might have been a Chinese monk, trying in his own gentle way to bridge the gaps between peoples.

Although out of earshot, Ma seemed to be speaking affably with the chairman of Norbu gompa. But his eyes roamed over Khodrak, studying his elegant robe, his finely worked leather sandals, the pearl rosary that hung from his belt. After a moment he gestured toward the mendicant's staff, and Khodrak hesitantly extended it toward him. The professor ran his fingers along the fine scrolling of the metal head then, strangely, the two men seemed to struggle for possession of the staff until Khodrak jerked it from Ma's grip and peevishly stepped away, the professor watching his back with an oddly disappointed expression. One of the howler guards rushed to Khodrak's side and leaned into his ear. The chairman looked toward the dig, and his eyes suddenly glowed. They had found Jokar.

The music faded, and Jenkins appeared by the microphone on the platform as though to speak, but his eyes were on the odd drama unfolding by the dig. The crowd seemed to follow his gaze, and gradually grew silent.

Suddenly Ma hurried past Khodrak and stepped in front of Jokar as though to defend him. Another figure materialized beside Ma. Lepka had joined him, as if Jokar, Ma, and he, the three oldest men present, suddenly felt an obligation to resist the chairman of Norbu. Khodrak frowned, then glanced pointedly at Colonel Lin, who stood twenty feet away, as though to will the officer to intervene. Lin reacted by taking a single step toward the professor, so Khodrak stood alone, facing the old men in momentary confusion. He seemed about to gesture toward his white-shirted troops when the professor swept his arm around the site of the dig.

"Tibetans did a terrible thing here a hundred years ago," Ma said loudly.

"Not Tibetans," Lin shot back irritably, and though he seemed about to say more, the words choked in his throat as a look of surprised disbelief crossed his face. He looked at Shan as though for help. Again Khodrak pressed forward. He seemed unable to contain his anger, and his greed, even in front of those who had come to fete him. Or perhaps not, Shan thought. Perhaps Khodrak had decided he had already been anointed by the government, that everything for him had become part of a performance for the dignitaries, a demonstration of new powers.

"This old Tibetan is a criminal!" the chairman of Norbu gompa shouted to Lin, stabbing an accusing finger toward Jokar, then he repeated the words in the direction of the officials seated on the platform.

Shan stepped in front of Jokar, beside Lepka and Ma. Khodrak answered the movement with a sneer. "A master criminal of the Dalai Cult," Khodrak continued in his loud, public-address voice as he pointed at Jokar, "surrounded by his criminal henchmen! Fomenting regression!" He shot an impatient glance at Lin and his troops, looked back at the officials, then straightened and smoothed his robe as he turned in the direction of the platform, his staff at his side.

"Great things will be said about this day," he boomed, "about how the new China routed out the last of the bad elements in this region with the forces of economic development and prosperity!" The chairman of Norbu had apparently rehearsed a speech, and had decided now was the time to give it. He had not counted on Jokar wandering freely, and he had to be sure the world knew Jokar was his. For Khodrak had clearly decided that the day should not be about the oil well, but about his personal victories.

"It is a day of reckoning for this valley, for this region, a day of history for the Bureau of Religious Affairs and Norbu." He pointed to the long single file of figures being escorted at gunpoint down the valley, then to Jokar. "Today we wipe out the criminal elements who have kept this district in the feudal age. Today we start a new life! A new age! They will hear about this in Beijing!" He cast a yearning eye toward the microphone that had been installed on the platform, and one of the white-shirted men leapt to the platform, pulling the microphone from its stand and handing it down to Khodrak, who pointed at the medicine lama again.

Jokar seemed not to notice. He was staring at the top of Yapchi Mountain now, as if he saw something there not visible to anyone else, staring toward the snowcapped peaks with a weary, serene smile.

"A leader of one of the most feudalistic institutions in all of Tibet, one of the most dangerous instruments of repression!" Khodrak's voice boomed across the valley now, and the chairman raised his ever-present mendicant staff in the air as though to punctuate his point. "A conspirator with the Dalai criminal himself! An agent sent from India to subvert the new order!"

A figure swept by Shan in a blur, rushing toward Khodrak. It was Dzopa, his own staff raised in the air now. Khodrak's lips curled and he lowered his mendicant staff, holding it with both hands, its metal head aimed at the dobdob like a spear.

The metallic crack of a gun split the air.

Dzopa spun about, groaned, and crumpled to the ground. The soldiers behind Lin spun about, weapons raised. In the same instant Padme darted to Khodrak's side, and Winslow ran into the crowd of Tibetans. One of the howler guardians held a pistol, still extended, its barrel smoking. Lin furiously pointed at the man, and the nearest soldier lunged and slammed his rifle butt against the pistol, knocking it to the ground, then rested his boot on the weapon.

Dzopa twisted, holding his left calf, which was bleeding profusely. Lhandro darted to the man's side and pressed a scarf against the wound. Jokar took two steps toward the dobdob then was restrained by Lepka, whose hand appeared on the ancient lama's shoulder. Tenzin stepped forward and knelt by Lhandro and the dobdob, Khodrak watching Tenzin with a victorious smile.

Shan's eyes shot back and forth from Lin to Dzopa. Then his gaze locked on the mendicant staff in Khodrak's hands.

"Arrest them!" Khodrak shouted at the guards. "You saw what that man with the staff did. Now his companion reveals himself, that one with the chig! And that Han who conspires with them!" he shouted in a victorious tone, pointing at Shan. "Arrest them all! Traitors! Murderers!"

Chig. Shan looked about in confusion. It meant the number one. He looked back at Lhandro, still on the ground beside Tenzin. The simplest, oldest form of representing the number one in Tibetan writing was an inverted U, slanted slightly to the right. Like the birthmark on Lhandro's neck. His eyes moved from Khodrak to Lhandro. The one with the chig.

Shan became aware of Tenzin moving his arm, drawing something in the earth with his finger, then looking at Shan. A shape of curves. It looked like the Arabic number three, slanted to the left, its bottom extended like a tail. It was a shape Shan knew well, the shape of the curved scar on Drakte's forehead. In Tibetan the symbol meant *nyasha*. Fish. Once the chairman had been looking for a man with a fish.

Khodrak's smile faded as he saw the figure in the dirt, and he turned his back on Tenzin and the dobdob. "Murderers!" he called out again. "Seize them!"

"Murderers?" A voice called out from behind Khodrak. Several of the officials were standing at the edge of the platform now. One of them, a lean older man wearing a grey uniform, examined the chairman of Norbu gompa with a puzzled expression. "You order an arrest?"

"The Religious Affairs officer in Amdo town." The announcement left Khodrak's lips slowly. "It will be written that he was a hero who died for our true cause, who died for the Serenity campaign, who died as an example of how Norbu leads the new order."

It will be written. Khodrak had written lies to win his newfound power. Drakte had written the truth to stop him, and died for it. Shan sensed his legs move and suddenly he was in front of Khodrak, blocking his path to the platform. Khodrak glared and made a shoving motion with his staff. Shan stared at the staff, his gaze fixed now on its head.

"I know the hero who died for the truth," Shan declared.

Suddenly the truck escorting Larkin and the Tibetans began honking its horn as if in celebration, and those on the platform looked away, toward the line of prisoners. But Khodrak and Shan kept their eyes locked together, until abruptly Khodrak lowered the staff, its head leveled at Shan's abdomen, and lurched forward with it. A hand shot out as Shan felt the cold steel touch his stomach. Ma was at his side, hand on the metal shaft head, pushing it back. The horn stopped, and Khodrak withdrew the staff with a satisfied air and stepped around them.

A strange stillness fell over Shan and the professor as they watched Khodrak, then slowly Shan turned to see Ma standing looking into the palm with which he had seized the staff. The professor's palm was sliced open. Blood dripped down his fingertips onto the soil.

It was said by the old Tibetans that sounds accompanied enlightenment, not human words but sounds the spirit somehow knew to use when it was in contact with deities. Perhaps the sound that escaped Shan's lips now was such a reaching out, a strange part-groan, part-exclamation of discovery, part cry of pain.

The professor, who seemed oblivious to his wound, looked at him with sudden worry. "Are you ill?" Ma asked.

Yes, Shan wanted to reply. Ill with the truth. Ill with the heavy knowledge of what Beijing's years of occupation had done to all of them.

But instead someone shouted out in a loud, steady voice. "One yak," the voice said sternly. "Only one yak. Lamtso Gar has one yak." Shan almost began looking around before he realized it was his own voice. "Eighteen sheep. Five goats," he said, remembering the way the woman at the lake had proudly pointed out her entry in Drakte's ledger. "And two dogs."

Khodrak halted. The color of his face shifted, pale at first, then flush with anger. The chairman of Norbu was suddenly in front of him again, raising his staff, now slamming the butt end of it into Shan's belly. Shan collapsed onto his knees, holding his belly, fighting for breath. But not taking his eyes off those on the platform, turning as though trying to address the dignitaries, the Tibetans, and the soldiers all at once.

"Last year," Shan shouted, gasping, looking at the platform, "a child died of starvation there."

"Coward!" Khodrak snarled. "We are the examples of the new way. We came to be celebrated." He turned. "Tuan!" he snapped, and the Director appeared, followed by four white shirts who seemed eager to close on Shan. But then Shan pulled a piece of paper from his pocket, and unfolded it: the photograph of the cottage by the lake he had taken from Tuan's office. He extended it like a weapon. Tuan, only ten feet away now, halted, the color draining from his face.

Lin uttered a sharp syllable and soldiers flanked the white shirts, making it clear they should go no further. It was a little thing, Shan thought, of minor consequence to Lin. He was just allowing Shan to hang himself in front of the dignitaries.

If Khodrak was not certain whom his audience should be, Shan at least knew who his was. He struggled to his feet and stepped closer to the platform as Khodrak glared, first at Shan, then at Lin. "The people of the district compiled their own report of economic activity. A report based on the truth. The people must have a voice, too. When they sought to present it to Deputy Director Chao in Amdo town, Khodrak killed Chao, then killed the Tibetan who brought it."

Incredible as it seemed, Shan realized the only audience that would listen to him was the one before him now, an audience of soldiers who distrusted knobs, and howlers who distrusted knobs, and knobs who distrusted both; an audience in which those not from Lhasa and the Ministry feared those who were, who would tolerate his accusations because they were all seasoned in the language of accusation, and had been taught that suspicion and fear and blame were the foundations of power. Most no doubt assumed Shan would be in manacles after his speech, but just as certainly everyone was wondering whether they might hear something that might enhance their own power.

"Killed them with the very staff he carries. Measure it and you'll see it matches the wound that killed Deputy Director Chao." Shan had no doubt now that it matched another wound, one he had seen, the terrible gash in Drakte's abdomen that the purba had tried to mend with coarse thread and a tent needle. Drakte had fled Khodrak, had fled from Amdo town, but the blow Khodrak had inflicted had finally killed him at the hermitage. And killed their sacred mandala.

The line of detainees from the end of the valley was closing, and would be at the camp in five minutes. Melissa Larkin would be there, face to face with Zhu.

There was movement behind Shan. Professor Ma was there again, with Shan; two Chinese against the Tibetan chairman of Norbu gompa. The professor said nothing, but turned his hand outward, where the officials from Lhasa, in the front row, could plainly see the blood dripping from his hand. One of them, the stern woman in the grey dress gasped and spoke into the ear of a man beside her.

"Lies!" Khodrak shouted. "You have no proof!" He looked back uncertainly at his guards, penned in by the soldiers, and then at Tuan, who still stood as if paralyzed. It seemed as though Director Tuan had suddenly given up. But Shan knew he had given up long ago. Tuan had never shared Khodrak's energy, or goals. Shan's visit to Tuan's office had cracked open a door in Shan's memory, down the dark, distant corridor that represented his Beijing incarnation. For Inspector Shan, who had specialized in corruption investigations, the evidence had been obvious. Tuan's ambitions had been more modest than Khodrak's. He had only wanted to retire before he died of his disease, to go to his modest cottage, financed by the phantom soldiers he had put on his payroll.

"You were in Amdo to stop the true records of the township from

381

reaching the Bureau," Shan continued, "to stop Deputy Director Chao from receiving such records and passing them on to Lhasa. But then you recognized the Tibetan who was there, delivering those records. You had seen him in Lhasa with the abbot of Sangchi, the night the abbot disappeared. You realized it probably meant that the abbot was not in the south. But you never told anyone in Lhasa. You let the search continue in the south because you had your own plan to capture the abbot. Find the abbot and let him proclaim the success of your campaign. Not the Serenity Campaign. Your campaign. Not Lhasa's campaign. Not Beijing's campaign. A new campaign to take over enforcement at gompas from Public Security, with a new security force formed within Religious Affairs. A force like the one you founded with Director Tuan, without authority from Lhasa." Ultimately the top officials would care little about the murders. But Khodrak had committed a crime far worse than murder. He had conspired against an official party campaign. He had been disloyal.

"Lies!" Khodrak hissed again. "You will see," he said to the platform, "I have saved for you the greatest prize of all." He turned, searching the crowd, calling for Padme. "The proof of all their treason!" The young monk pushed back into the crowd and reappeared with the black leather satchel, which Khodrak hastily opened, producing a large bundle wrapped in cloth, which he triumphantly handed to the woman at the front of the platform.

As the woman in grey took the bundle two more of the dignitaries joined her, watching over her shoulder as she unwrapped it. When the cloth fell away Khodrak gasped and seemed about to strike at Padme with his staff. But Padme, too, stared at the contents with disbelieving eyes. It was Drakte's battered account book, which Shan had last seen at the cave the night before. The woman leafed through the pages then glared at Khodrak.

The woman seemed to shake with anger. Then she removed her straw hat. "Soldiers from Public Security," she barked out. "Reveal yourselves in the next sixty seconds and you will avoid punishment. This is an order from your general!"

The howlers needed no prompting, no discussion. Some cursed, some groaned, but all quickly shed their white shirts and trotted away, toward the camp. Two men in the official grey tunics of Public Security marched to Khodrak and Padme. Khodrak stared at the woman, leaning on his staff, gripping it with both hands, the color drained from his face. Another knob approached Shan, hand extended. Shan gave him the photograph of the cottage, still in his hand, the folded facsimile with the phantom names that Shan knew would tie back to Tuan, and finally the slip of paper Chao had given to Drakte the night before he had died. The knob studied Shan uncertainly, then looked back at the woman on the platform, who extended her hand for the papers to be brought to her.

Suddenly Padme pointed to the slope where Larkin and the Tibetans had been working. "The pagans!" he shouted with a strange mix of anger and hope in his voice, and darted through the soldiers, still pointing at the slope.

Somo had reached the place where Larkin had been digging, Shan saw, for a boulder there was now covered in bright crimson paint. The deity had revealed itself again.

Lin shook his head wearily and spoke to an officer at his side, who sprinted toward the army encampment. Most of the officials in the stand continued to watch earnestly, as if everything they were witnessing had been all part of the planned entertainment.

With a creak of metal the battle tank emerged from the shadows by the oil camp, its officer standing half out of the hatch on the top of the turret. It halted a hundred yards from the camp, its barrel quickly shifting to the range, and fired three shots in rapid succession.

The side of the mountain at the south end of the valley instantly exploded, as it had when the tank had attacked the first deity rock, raising a haze of dust and debris over the slope. But the third shell struck with a much larger explosion than the first two. Larkin's crew had been busy not only digging, but planting the explosives there. The tank officer stared in confusion and raised a pair of binoculars toward the ball of fire and cloud of debris that followed, then shrugged at Lin. Several of those on the platform clapped, apparently pleased with the way the army had punctuated the ceremony with fireworks.

Lin stared, first at the slope, where the dust was rapidly clearing, then at Shan.

Suddenly Lin's mouth fell open and he, with most of the crowd, gasped as they saw the massive creature that had appeared at the edge of the dig. Jampa stood there, smelling the exposed earth. The yak slowly stepped to the chest where Ma stored his artifacts and sniffed at it, touching it with its nose. While everyone watched the animal in silence, it stepped slowly forward, directly between Shan and Khodrak, past Lin, then stopped and stared at the distant slope. It cocked its massive head, then raised its nose high in the air and gave a long, extraordinarily loud bellow. Everyone seemed to be staring at the animal, some in amusement, others with somber, awed expressions, as though they sensed the yak was trying to communicate with them, or with something in the mountains. As if in reply a muted thunder came from the distant slope. Not really like thunder, Shan realized, but like a rumbling from inside the earth.

"Earthquake!" one of the venture workers cried out.

Still no one moved. All eyes followed those of the mighty yak now, to the slope, where the rumbling seemed to increase in intensity, the sound of pressure building. An odd muted rushing sound like a small eruption could be heard, followed by a blur of movement on the slope.

The brittle silence continued, broken at last by Jenkins, who leapt from his seat on the platform as he stared with sudden alarm at the slope.

"Jeeee—sus!" the American manager cried in a desperate voice, then vaulted from the platform and began running toward the nearest truck, barking out orders for the bulldozers to follow. He paused at the truck door to look at the scene. "Mother fucking army!" he shouted, firing each syllable like a shot from a cannon then, looking at his perplexed workers, pointed to the slope. "Go! Go! Go!" he yelled, and leapt into the truck.

Binoculars appeared in Lin's hands. He stared in confusion, but for only a moment, and when he lowered them there was something like awe in his eyes. He looked at Shan, his eyes momentarily filled with sadness, then he hardened again and spoke rapidly to the officer beside him, who lifted a small radio unit and began barking orders. Soldiers began running toward the derrick. Lin leaned toward the officer again, and after a moment of hesitation, disappointment clouding his face, the officer spoke into the transmitter. The soldiers escorting Larkin and the Tibetans, only a hundred yards away now, jogged away from the column. Their former prisoners seemed not to notice, for they were running to Larkin's side, cheering and pointing toward the slope, some of them waving khatas in their hands.

Lin looked at the glasses in his hand, then stepped to Shan's side and slowly extended them.

But Shan did not use the lenses to examine the site of the explosion. Instead he desperately searched the slope for any sign of Somo. If she had lingered at the rock she could not have survived. There was no sign of her.

"I don't understand," Professor Ma said over his shoulder.

"The deity has spoken," Lhandro offered. He stood a few feet away, supporting his father, who gazed at the slope with a huge grin, tears streaming down his face. Beside them Jokar knelt at the wounded dobdob's side, speaking in low tones, his hand resting on the crown of the Dzopa's head. Strangely, the dobdob pointed to the yak.

"Water," Shan said, his own voice filled with wonder. "There was an underground river, and now it has been released." The words seemed so simple, the reality so impossible. Melissa Larkin had never been trying to locate her hidden river for the mere sake of geology. She and the purbas had been trying to find it in the hope they could use it against the venture, to alter the course of the oil project.

Trucks roared up the valley, some packed with workers, others pausing to pick up workers by the platform, still others speeding by with piles of shovels, picks, and buckets in their bays. The people on the platform began drifting away, confused, asking when the ceremony would continue. Except for the knobs who had shed their white shirts; they stood in a tight group, listening with shocked expressions at the woman on the platform, who pointed fingers and seemed to be hissing at Khodrak. When she finished Khodrak was enclosed in a small knot of his former guards who, appearing eager to prove their remorse for straying, wrenched away his staff and pulled him toward one of the white Bureau trucks.

384

"The contour of the valley," Shan said with a sigh, watching as first Jampa, then Gyalo, stepped to Jokar, "means the water will go to the derrick, the lowest point." The dobdob clutched at Jokar's arm a moment, then released it with a sound like a sob, and with the monk's help the lama slowly climbed onto the yak's broad back. Lin stepped slowly to the edge of the dig and conspicuously turned his back to Lepka and the others who sat by it. Shan looked at Gyalo again and recalled the monk's strange words on the slope that morning, that Shan had solved the puzzle. All Shan had done was to tell Lhandro that he had heard a strange rushing noise in the ground near the first deity rock. Gyalo led Jampa and Jokar away, up the ridge, unnoticed amidst the chaos at the bottom of the valley.

Shan looked back at the dig. Tenzin had disappeared into the trees.

"But surely just a little water can make no difference," Ma said.

Shan stared up at the snow-covered peak in the distance. "No, just a delay. But perhaps over time it may not be a little. That depends on the mountain," he said, and realized his words sounded like he was speaking of a deity.

Jenkins certainly did not dismiss the threat. He could see the American in the binoculars, standing on the back of a truck near the village ruins now, shouting out orders as the bulldozers crawled toward the end of the valley. The venture manager was going to build a dam, to divert the water from his derrick. But a small river was already pouring down the slope near his truck, spreading across the barley fields in a dozen small rivulets.

When Shan turned back Nyma was tending to Professor Ma's torn hand as his assistant poured water over it. Lepka kept staring at the water covering the fields of barley. "Sometimes it's hard to know what deities want," he heard the old man say.

Suddenly a hand covered with streaks of red was raised in his face and he looked into Somo's gleaming eyes. "I saw Winslow," she said. "He said our Drakte can move on now. He said you did it."

Winslow. "Where is he?" Shan asked.

"On the slope, jogging back up." Somo pointed to the saddle of land. Gyalo and Jokar were halfway up it now, and as he watched the unmistakable form of the American joined them. Winslow was leaving, fleeing at last.

"I wanted to thank him," Shan said. "For putting that ledger in Padme's satchel." He had last seen the account book in Larkin's cave, but he remembered how the American had come with his backpack, and how Winslow had darted into the crowd when Padme had left his satchel on the ground. He watched Winslow moving up the slope, then saw more figures scattering over the saddle of land. The Tibetans who had been with Larkin.

"Where will they go?" he asked Somo.

"To that meeting place," she said. "Where the people wait for Jokar."

Shan stared with new despair at the retreating figures. She meant the chair of Siddhi, the rebellious monk, where, after what had happened in the valley, the Tibetans would be more inclined than ever to resist the government. "Jokar would never abide violence," he said with a sinking heart and turned. But Somo had vanished.

He took a step toward the saddle of land and another, filled with dread again. Nothing had really changed. The authorities would not only capture Jokar, they would take many Tibetans with him. He took a deep breath, and began jogging. Then the drumming began.

Lhandro was at Shan's side as he began running toward the slope opposite the saddle, toward the sound, toward what Shan hoped was the deity stone. But the rongpa slowed as they reached a small ledge that overlooked the valley floor, a hundred feet up the slope. The water had reached the derrick, forming a small muddy pond around it. The workers had stopped and were staring at the water. One man jumped off and ran toward the source of the water, splashing in the rivulets that coursed through the fields, then stopped, sank to the earth, arms upraised, kneeling in the mud, his hands clenched in fists.

Lhandro hesitated, looking with anguish at his precious valley, which was in chaos. Shan put a hand on his shoulder. "The water will stop," he assured the rongpa, "it is letting Jokar and the others have one more chance, that's all," he said, as though a deity had planned it all along. Confused by his own words, he turned and continued running as Lhandro headed toward the ruins of his village. The sound of the double beat, the heart drumming, seemed close now, almost directly above the center of the valley, not far from where Shan had begun chasing the runaway khata on his first day there. But he ran at an angle, parallel to the valley floor, as if he were another of the workers dashing toward the floodwaters. After a few hundred yards he edged close to the wooded tier on the slope, then darted into the shadows of the trees and began quartering back and up the slope.

He climbed above the source of the sound and worked his way down. It was muted now, because the drummer had again chosen a position in front of large flat rocks facing the valley, so muted Shan began hearing voices. They were high pitched, and seemed to be laughing. Suddenly he slipped on loose scree, and tumbled headlong, stumbling, righting himself as he hurtled between low shrubs. He found himself on his knees before two playful children, a boy and a girl of nearly the same age, the girl with crude bandages on her hands. They seemed familiar somehow, and at first he thought he had seen them at Yapchi Village. But then they both gasped at him, clearly recognizing Shan, and looked toward a figure ten feet away, squatting in the rocks, staring down at the valley. The boy darted to the man, who turned and stared at Shan with wide, surprised eyes, then his gaze shifted to a flat rock near where the children had been playing. On the rock sat the eye of Yapchi.

The man stood. It was Gang, the Chinese caretaker of Rapjung. He looked ragged, and exhausted, his hand also still bandaged from his burns. He offered no challenge, and said nothing as Shan stepped past him to look at the rocks below.

A man sat with the big drum, pounding it with two sticks with leather pads at the end, watching the valley with a wild gleam in his eyes. Shan slid down the side of the rock and had sat by the drum before the man noticed him. The pounding faltered, then stopped.

"It's Shan," Dremu said, as if someone else was there. The Golok's mouth hung open and he looked at the rocks above him.

"You found them," Shan observed. "The drum and the eye."

Dremu nodded soberly. "This is what we needed, when I was in the mountains with my father all those years ago."

"I think you lied when you said you were taken by the venture work gang," Shan said. "Those two Goloks tried to steal from us."

Dremu seemed to shrink. He hunched his shoulders forward and wrapped both arms around the drum as if he were going to fall. "That was before," he muttered.

"Before what?"

The Golok just hugged the drum, looking at Shan's feet. "They're not my friends," he said after a long silence. "They are wild, like leopards. At first I thought if we worked together we could make enough money for the next winter. It was okay when we just stole from the oil company. But when they met me here and said they were going to steal from the Yapchi farmers I tried to stop them. They beat me and took everything I had, even my horse."

Shan reached into his pocket and pulled out the leather pouch, the lapis bracelet, and the knife with the spoon, and placed them one by one on the rock in front of Dremu. The Golok stared at them, then with a reverent expression picked up the pouch. "I had nothing left but the rags on my back. That was before..."

Before what? Shan almost asked again, but somehow he knew the answer. Dremu meant before the deity began speaking to him through the drum.

There was movement around the edge of the high rocks, and Gang approached them, supported by his son. In Gang's bandaged hand, extended toward Shan, was the chenyi stone.

"This man," Dremu said, "was almost dead. First I found his family looking for him, crying, thinking they had lost him forever, thinking he had gone to kill you. Then we found him, beating the drum, looking crazy, not able to talk. By then the drum was drumming him." Dremu looked at Shan uncertainly. "I couldn't...I didn't..."

"You did well," Shan offered. "You kept the deity."

Gang pushed his son away and stumbled toward Shan. He held out the stone in both hands, appealing to Shan with his exhausted, glazed eyes, and was wracked by a sob. He began crying, convulsing with tears, able to control himself only enough to step forward and drop the chenyi stone into Shan's hands.

Shan gazed at the stone, then surveyed the chaos in the valley below. He felt empty, drained, uncertain where to go, what more he could do. After a long time he raised Gang's hand in his own and returned the stone to him. Then Shan picked up the two drumsticks, exchanged a solemn look with Dremu, and began pounding the deity drum.

CHAPTER NINETEEN

Dremu stared in disbelief, twisting his head from side to side as if to better see Shan. A smile gradually broke across his weary face and he showed Shan how to make the quick one-two beat, the heart sound. They watched, the drum pounding, the children laughing, as more derrick workers jumped off, splashing, into the huge puddle of water that was growing around their machine. Shan watched his hands pounding the drumskin without conscious effort, and found himself drifting to a place he did not recognize, watching his hands as though they belonged to someone else. He had heard of monks in old Tibet using such sounds, not just in ritual but in meditation exercises. The throbbing of the drum became the throbbing of his own heart and the echo that came back to him seemed to come not from across the valley but from somewhere else, a faraway place where something huge was stirring to the sound, rolling over as though to awaken, the way a mountain sometimes rolls over.

It was as if one of Lokesh's karma storms was roiling the valley, as if everything that could happen was happening, changing too fast to be understood, too sudden for the pain of it all to be fully sensed. He could not stop beating the drum. The drum was beating him.

He lost track of time, but eventually became aware of Gang standing close to him, staring with his head cocked, his eyes not bitter or angry, only empty and pleading. Shan handed him the sticks and stepped back. An hour or more had gone by. The speaking platform below was empty, and the dignitaries were gathered at the tables, having their banquet as though unaware of the water that still flooded their derrick or, more likely, unconcerned, because they knew the water would soon recede and the derrick would resume drilling.

The derrick itself was empty, and the muddy pond at its base was perhaps three hundred feet across. But the waters seemed to have stopped flowing. A new pond had appeared at the end of the valley, where Jenkins had built a rough levee by bulldozing the surface soil of the barley fields into a long, low bank.

Shan studied Gang, who seemed to have drifted to the same place the drum had taken each of them before. His eyes lost their focus. His hands gripped the drumsticks despite his still-healing burns, gripped so tightly his knuckles were white, as if he wasn't holding sticks but a lifeline. The embittered Han had attacked Shan, he knew now, had attacked him and taken the eye.

But why? Because he thought Shan had not earned the right to return the eye? Because he simply could not believe there could be another Han who was virtuous? More likely, because he had spent most of his life trying to redeem himself, to prove himself to the Tibetans, then seen the most visible proof, his reconstructed shrines, go up in flames.

Shan wandered to the valley floor, mingled with the workers who still seemed to be running everywhere with shovels and hoes. A truck sped by carrying logs from the camp stockpile. Soldiers in mud-caked uniforms jogged toward the base camp and were being herded into two troop trucks that waited below the derrick. Shan watched as the first of the trucks sped away, racing through the camp and out of the valley.

"Too late to beat the knobs," Shan heard someone say with an air of amusement. A broad-shouldered Tibetan in grease-stained coveralls stood ten feet away, speaking to no one in particular.

Shan ventured closer to the man. "Those knobs already left?" he asked.

"Their prize isn't the oil well," the man observed in a bitter voice. "For them a hundred resisters will beat an oil well every time."

Shan closed his eyes and fought down a wave of fear. There was a meadow somewhere; a small, high meadow where Tibetans waited for Jokar, where they expected to find new strength in resisting Beijing—a leader who could be respected like no other, who would become a new symbol, a modern-day Siddhi. Somo and many of the purbas must be going there now, waiting for Gyalo to bring Jokar. Some of the purbas had guns.

When he reached the trees on the far side of the valley, Shan ran. He did not know where the meadow was. All he could do was go up, east toward the highest spines of the huge mountain, praying he would see a sign or meet Tibetans on the way who might lead him to Jokar. He jogged until his side raged with pain then stumbled into a stream.

As he knelt in the water, he looked about, gasping. The distant drumming from Yapchi began to seem hollow, and he began to hear it as a sound of frustration, not hope. No deity had come, no compassion had been found. And now, he thought as he splashed the frigid water on his face, when the soldiers or knobs found Jokar at a secret rally against Beijing, they would show no mercy.

"Lokesh!" he heard someone shout, again and again, until he realized it was himself. No matter how urgently he wanted to find Jokar, another part of him was still desperately thinking of Lokesh, who would soon begin hobbling toward Beijing, where he would be killed or imprisoned.

He launched himself out of the water, following one goat path, then another, always seeking the paths that would take him still higher. An hour passed, then another, and he began to recognize trails. He had circled far below Larkin's birthing water cave and was climbing again, near where

Chemi had brought them over the mountain on their first day in Qinghai. Rounding an outcropping, he froze. A huge black drong stood in a clearing a hundred feet away, staring warily at him. But then he took a step forward and saw the red ribbons in its neck hair, some of which Shan and Anya had tied.

"Jampa," he called softly, and stepped to the animal's side. Why was the yak here, and alone?

Then with a chill he saw craters in front of the yak. Jampa's large black eyes seemed to be studying the craters, and for a terrible moment Shan thought Gyalo and Jokar had been attacked. But then he recognized the terrain. There were three craters, evenly spaced, in a straight line, and directly above them towered the snow-capped pinnacle of Yapchi Mountain. It was where they had first met Zhu, where the seismic charges had killed a flock of birds.

Shan stroked the yak's neck and surveyed the landscape. The high meadow where the Tibetans waited for Jokar must be near. The yak must have delivered Jokar and wandered away. But there was no sign of anyone, no sound of equipment, no shouting from soldiers, no cracking of rifles. Nothing but the wind. And two geese flying high over the ridge, toward the south, over the massive backbone of the mountain, toward the sacred salt lake. He watched the geese until they were out of sight, then walked along the edge of the clearing. A tapering rock column, perhaps twenty feet high, rose from the northern edge, and on its base was a shadow of the mani mantra, the vaguest remains of words painted there many decades before. Like a signpost in a way, or a greeting. As he touched the ancient script he thought of the Rapjung lamas. They had come across the mountain to Yapchi for herbs, to debate with the Chinese monks. Yapchi Valley, as isolated as it seemed from the south, was even more cut off from the north, and so had become part of Rapjung's flock, a garden of herbs in a way for the lamas. And the Tibetans on this side of the mountain had inscribed a greeting to the lamas who came down to them. All that had ended on a terrible day a century earlier.

He paced around the windworn column of rock. At its narrow top, incredibly, was a remnant of a prayer flag, a piece of red cloth. He wandered back along the clearing, still searching, climbing up the slope for a view of the top of the column, now two hundred feet away, and of the secret meadow that must lie beyond. As the top came into view he stared disbelieving. It was not a prayer flag.

"Gyalo!" he called out. The monk was on the column, sitting lotus fashion, staring forlornly at the sky. Shan called repeatedly as he jogged back toward the clearing, but the monk gave no sign of hearing. Jampa himself seemed unconcerned about Gyalo. Yet the yak did seem concerned about something. The great beast was at the south end of the clearing now, and Shan thought he recognized sadness on its face. He walked to it, stroking its neck again, trying to understand.

Gyalo and Jampa had come here, but no farther. They had been bound for the high, hidden meadow, for those who waited for Jokar to sit on the rock called the chair of Siddhi. Jokar, perhaps Winslow, had been with them but now were gone. The monk and yak did not seem upset or alarmed, just sad and puzzled. The yak's huge, liquid eyes gazed at Shan expectantly then, facing the high spine of the mountain it made a loud sound. Not a bellow, or a snort, but a loud wailing cut short by an intake of breath, like a sob.

Shan gazed at the yak, at the forlorn monk on the column of rock, then began running up the treacherous goat trail.

The sun was low in the western sky, washing the vast rock wall with a thin rose color by the time Shan found the narrow cleft in the rock where they had taken refuge from the helicopter the day they had first crossed Yapchi Mountain. Inside the cleft the stillness was like that of an ancient temple. No wind blew. No bird called. The dim light was the only evidence of the outside world.

He followed the wall on the left into deepening shadows, past the little stone pillar with dust encrusted prayer flags, until suddenly he heard a wet, hissing sound. He froze, studying the shadows, until he made out two legs stretched across the path in front of him. It was Winslow.

The American was so weak he seemed to have trouble raising his head to greet Shan. "Dammit, Shan, you have . . . to learn . . ." The American's words were punctuated with ragged gasps. He sounded as though he were suffocating, ". . . to stop investigating."

Shan reached along Winslow's legs to the side pocket where he carried his electric light. As Shan switched it on his heart sank. A pink froth oozed out of Winslow's mouth, and was dripping onto his shirt. He stared at the American. There was no time for talk. He frantically searched the other pockets of the American's pants until he found his pill bottle. It was empty.

"Took . . . the last one four hours ago," Winslow gasped. "He had to come. I wasn't going to let him try it alone. I carried him the first mile. Almost didn't make it. Old Jokar . . ." Winslow seemed to be forcing himself to smile, but the effort ended in a grimace. A wet, rasping rattle came from his chest. "He had to help me sometimes, let me hold on to his staff. I helped him, he helped me. We couldn't have made it without each other," the American said in a tone of wonder. He moaned, and tried to raise his hand to his head, but failed. "My head . . . I never knew it could hurt like this. . . ." His eyes fluttered open and shut several times.

Shan wiped the froth from Winslow's face. It meant pulmonary edema. His lungs were filling with fluid. The head pain meant cerebral edema.

"We have to get you down," Shan said. His words came out in choking breaths. There was nothing to be done for Winslow, except descend the mountain, on the tiny, treacherous goat trail, in the dark.

Winslow seemed to struggle to keep his eyes open. "Go . . . check on Jokar."

Shan glanced up at the darkest part of the shadows ahead, which marked the entrance to the cave. "Jokar would want you to go down."

Something touched Shan's hand. Winslow's fingers, grasping Shan's. He had the strength of a baby. The only thing that broke the silence was the American's wet, labored breathing.

Winslow's fingers trembled. "What's that sound?" he gasped. "Like wind."

There was no sound, no movement except the American's labored breathing. More of the pink froth dribbled down his chin. "I'm beginning to understand it," Winslow whispered. "This whole impermanence thing. It's a gift, like the old lamas said."

The words hung in the air like a prayer.

"I will get you down," Shan insisted, choking down his helplessness.

"Not a chance," Winslow said in a strangely serene voice. "Not on that path. I would just kill us both. Hell I can't even stand, let alone walk. You try to carry me, we both fall."

Shan followed Winslow's eyes to the top of the mountain, visible at the top of the huge fissure. It was illuminated in a brilliant golden light cast by the setting sun, as if they were in a tunnel that led upward to the heavens.

"Jokar knew before," Winslow gasped. "I mean he knew before coming up here. He knew that day he touched me."

Shan remembered the haunted look the lama had when he laid his hands on the American that day at the hermitage.

"I understand now," Winslow said in his weak, croaking voice. "Everything has been about leaving it all behind, hasn't it?"

Shan stood and pulled on Winslow's arm to lift him. The American, much heavier than Shan, barely moved. He stared at Winslow. The American had given up on his job, given up his passport, given up his possessions, given up his grief for his wife, given up everything that came before, the clutter of his life below. It was true. Since the day Shan had met him, when he had been defying death by riding the yak, the American had been leaving everything behind.

"I think you . . . should go check on Jokar. Take the light. Then we can go down, no problem."

Shan reluctantly stepped over the American's legs "We are going down that path. We can just crawl a little at a time. You'll be better when we descend."

"I'll be better. You win," the American whispered, and his fingers made a tiny motion that seemed to be a gesture toward the cave.

Inside there was a musty odor of incense that had not been there before, but the chamber was empty and no incense burned. Shan stepped to the healing thangkas and looked briefly at each one, trying to calm

393

himself. At the long thangka where the collection of dorjes lay, a new one sat beside the sandalwood dorje, one of bronze, burnished with decades of rubbing. Nearby, leaning against the wall, was something else. A long wooden staff, as worn and weathered as the dorje. On the ledge beside the dorje he saw two small dust-encrusted shapes he had not noticed before. He reached out for one, shaking away the dust. It was a small bone, perfectly shaped. Shan cleaned the second. It seemed to be a rock, until he realized how light it was. He studied the objects again and discovered he had been wrong. The rock was a carefully crafted piece of bone. And the bone was an exquisitely carved stone.

Shan pulled aside the thankga, releasing a stronger smell of incense. As he expected, there was a tunnel behind the old painting. He followed it at a sharp downward angle for nearly a minute before it leveled into a low, broad chamber. A second large thankga hung at one of the sides: a representation, not of the Medicine Buddha, but of a fierce protector demon, Rahula, a wrathful deity with several heads and a serpent body instead of legs.

Shan grasped the gau around his neck then stepped behind the thangka. To the right a long wide ledge, three feet high, ran the length of the narrow, forty-foot-long room, as straight and square as a bench. To the left, at the center of the wall, was a small altar of polished, deftly fitted wood, with a sixteen-inch golden Buddha, behind the traditional seven offering bowls. He slowly approached the altar. The four bowls that were meant to hold water were dry and crusted with dust. A single stick of incense and the stub of a candle burned beside the bowls on a polished stone tray. On either side of the altar were several large clay jars, some nearly two feet high, filled with dried herbs.

He stood in front of the Buddha, still clutching his gau tightly, and stared at it a moment before turning to face the lamas. He counted fifteen of them sitting on the long ledge then moved to the far end where the row started with a figure in a robe of coarse sackcloth, a stone bowl for mixing herbs at his side, his hands folded neatly on his legs around a string of coral beads. Not his hands exactly, but the bones of his fingers and the shriveled parchment-like skin that covered them. The man's head, little more than a skull covered with the same parchment, tilted back in a slight grin. One of the first of the lama healers, who had probably come to sit inside the mountain three or four hundred years before. Shan walked slowly along the wise old men. Some wore brocade robes and had gold urns at their sides, although most wore the robes of simple monks. At the foot of one lay a stack of wood blocks for printing a teaching.

Then the line ended, near the entrance, and he was gazing into Jokar's face. The old lama was struggling no longer. He had come home. He had finished what he had set out to do when he left India. That's all it was, Shan knew now, with a strange, sad warmth. There had been no conspiracy. He had never intended to lead the Tibetans in resistance or stir up political controversy. There had been no motive other than to find closure to a long life well lived, to leave his bones in honored company, to give his bones to the mountain they all cherished.

Jokar wore a serene smile on his face, which was so peaceful he seemed only to be in slumber. Shan touched the lama's hand, wrapped around his rosary. The warmth had left it, but it was not yet cold. The lama's other hand was resting on the leg of the shriveled man beside him, a figure with short white hair and a small wooden mixing bowl cradled in his lap. Jokar had known him. Lokesh had known him, too. Shan's old friend had recognized the sandalwood dorje in the antechamber as that of his old teacher, Chigu.

He gazed back on the tomb. It had probably been only an hour since Jokar had placed the candle on the altar and lit the stick of incense. The lama had climbed onto the long stone bench with his colleagues, clasped his beads, and the leg of his old friend, then drifted away for the last time. Inside Yapchi Mountain treasures were buried, Dremu had said.

Shan used the last of his water to reverently fill the offering bowls on the altar, before he suddenly remembered the American. He paused by Jokar a moment, then walked, backwards, to the thangka, climbed back to the entrance chamber and stepped outside, into the dusk. Winslow was nowhere to be seen.

He searched frantically with the electric light, first at the deep crevasse beyond the stone pillar, then outside, on the path. There was no sign of the American anywhere. He must have dragged himself down the treacherous path, to make sure Shan would not risk his own life in trying to help him. The trail was empty but dim, with no more than a hundred yards visible in either direction. He stepped down the trail several yards, then peered over the edge with the light. Nothing was visible, nothing but blackness. It was nearly a thousand feet to the bottom.

Returning to the cleft, he extinguished the light and studied the sky. Stars were appearing overhead, and below. A wind blew, and he realized his cheek was suddenly cold and wet. He wiped away a tear then stepped back into the cleft and began searching every corner, every indentation in the rock wall.

Five minutes later he saw the tip of a boot, above his head, jutting out from a long, high crack in the rockface that ended a few feet off the ground with a flat rock like a shelf, looking out over the entrance to the cave. Shan pulled himself halfway up the rock and lit the shelf with the flashlight. Winslow was sitting on the small shelf, the rock wall pressing against each shoulder.

"We must go now," he called out urgently, but the American was studying the shadows beyond Shan's shoulder and seemed not to hear. Shan scrambled up the rock and reached out to wipe the froth from the American's face again, then pulled back with a shudder. The froth was cold. Winslow's eyes, still open, had gone beyond seeing.

He dropped to the American's side. A long wracking sob shook Shan's body. So many times Shan had wanted Winslow to return to his embassy, so many opportunities had come and gone for the American to find safety. Just a phone call, just a word at the Golmud base, just a request to Jenkins at the oil camp. He could have escaped. But each time he had chosen to stay.

After a moment Shan realized there was a bundle on Winslow's legs, wrapped in black cloth. And over the cloth, clenched in the American's hand, was a note. Shan gently lifted the paper out of the lifeless fingers. It was nearly illegible. The American had written it at the very end, in English, with trembling fingers, in the dark. Shan studied it for several minutes before he could decipher the words.

By all that's holy, leave me here to watch over them. Tell no one but Melissa. Let the others wonder, my last little joke on the world. It's not so bad, Shan. I think I'm getting the hang of this impermanence thing. This is where I belong this time. Every lama needs a cowboy.

Shan sat a long time, fighting the dark, hollow thing he felt inside. Death was an old acquaintance. Death didn't scare him, it just intimidated him, it made him feel so unprepared, so incomplete, so wasteful of what his Tibetan friends called the precious human incarnation.

He sat until the dark thing lifted from his heart, until he could bear to look into Winslow's eyes, until it seemed they were just friends silently watching the night fall. He studied the American once more, read the note again, and he knew that in his own way Winslow had found what he had been looking for.

At last he rose, pulled the bundle from Winslow's lap, crossed the American's lifeless hands over his legs, and pushed his eyelids closed. He hesitated a moment, then searched the American's pockets to find the tiny pouch of salt prepared by Jokar. He placed the pouch in Winslow's hand, closed his fingers around the true earth, then climbed down.

Winslow had realized what was behind the long thangka, where Jokar was going. He wanted to watch over the old ones. He wanted to stay by all that's holy.

Shan found himself wandering back inside the mountain with the bundle Winslow had been holding when he died, the bundle taken from Padme's satchel, switched by the American for the accounts that had proven Khodrak's lies. He felt as though he were being led, walking like a blind man toward the tomb chamber to deliver the bundle. It was Winslow's spirit, Lokesh would have said, asking Shan to show him the way to the lamas, to deliver a final offering. In that moment Shan would not have disagreed.

On the altar the candle still flickered, almost at the end of its wick. He set the book at the bottom of the ledge, studying the lamas again. The flickering light seemed to give movement to the faces of the old men.

"He decided not to leave you," Shan whispered to Jokar. "That American, he came far," he added, remembering the lama's words to Winslow at the mixing ledge. Afterwards Winslow, shaken by the lama, had told Shan of his dream, of flying through the air with Jokar. Maybe that's where they were now, floating over the mountain, laughing at the surprise they had dealt those below. Shan thought of the two geese he had seen soaring over the mountain.

"It's such a perfect place to finish," a deep, disembodied voice observed suddenly.

Shan gasped and stepped backwards, as though struck, his heart racing as he gaped at Jokar.

Then a tall, gaunt figure stepped through the door, his face so weary, his eyes so wide, so much emotion on his features, it took Shan took a moment before he recognized Tenzin.

The abbot of Sangchi pulled a candle from his pocket and silently stepped to the altar to light it from the dying wick of the one already there. Placing the candle on the altar, he turned and surveyed the figures on the ledge. "You found the chair," he whispered in an awed voice, and slowly walked down the line of dead lamas, pausing before each one, his lips moving in silent prayer, until he reached the far end, the oldest of the old ones, the one with the grinning skull and the sackcloth robe.

"What do you mean?" Shan asked as Tenzin studied the oldest of the dead lamas.

"Siddhi was the first," Tenzin replied, "the first teacher at Rapjung. Lepka told me something at the mixing ledge, after he heard those purbas talking about Jokar as a leader of rebellion. He said the purbas misunderstood, that Siddhi was a teacher who embraced the Medicine Buddha, that he didn't organize the people to fight the Mongols, he organized groups to be missionaries among the Mongols, to spread the way of compassion." He looked back at Shan. "Jokar would never allow his name to be used for violent means. When he said he would take the chair of Siddhi, this is what he meant."

The chair of Siddhi. They were standing before the chair of Siddhi, and Siddhi's descendants, the chair of the gentle old men who had spent their entire lives keeping humans connected to the earth inside them.

Tenzin dropped to his knees, then lowered his chest to the floor, prostrating himself, praying with his mouth an inch from the floor. After more than a minute he rose and gently kissed the edge of the ancient sackcloth. Then he rose and repeated the action in front of each of the remaining figures, until he joined Shan in front of Jokar.

"The purbas said we would just go north," Tenzin said quietly, staring at Jokar's split, tattered black canvas shoes. "They said they had it all planned. I would escape through Russia and go on to America, where people would give me a house and ask me to give speeches sometimes."

Self-revulsion echoed in his words. A single tear rolled down his cheek. "The stone eye was my cover. A party of purbas stealing north, escorting me would eventually be noticed. But the eye, traveling with ordinary Tibetans . . . ," Tenzin glanced at Shan, ". . . that man Tiger said with them I could go north and no one would suspect.

"I never planned to take those papers from Lin. Drakte had taken me there, Drakte had stayed at my side all that week during the Serenity conference, wearing a monk's robe, keeping me safe from all the howlers, making sure I did nothing to inadvertently reveal my intention. That Khodrak kept coming up to me, saying he was the most fervent supporter of the Campaign, that he thought it was the work of genius. He must have known about my being in his district because he saw Drakte with Chao that night." Tenzin fell silent a moment and stared at the lamas. "That report was there on Lin's desk when Drakte and I went for the stone and I began reading it. The month before, Religious Affairs had given me a speech to read before a youth congress in Lhasa. I told those youths that there were no Tibetans in slave labor camps, that such stories were made up by the Dalai Cult to poison the minds of Tibetans. Then there was the paper in Lin's office, proving me wrong. I just kept reading that paper as Drakte pulled at me, when we had the eye in our mop bucket and we were supposed to flee. Finally, to get me to leave, he told me to keep it. He said, what did I expect, it was what the purbas had been telling me."

Tenzin searched Shan's face. "They made me lie to those children. I had never believed the stories about slave labor, of old lamas still in prison, or of monks buried alive in their gompas. I knew I had to leave when they told me I was to become a director of Religious Affairs for all of Tibet, because they would never again let me be an abbot, or a monk. But even then, even when I had decided to leave, I never believed so many horrible things could have . . ." His voice drifted off, and he looked back at Jokar, apology in his face.

"At that hermitage, with Gendun and Shopo, we spoke of things, and more purbas came. Drakte showed me how all the numbers at the back of Lin's report were registration numbers for people: one set for soldiers; one set for prisoners, mostly old monks who had been imprisoned for twenty years and more, the Tibetans who had dug out that mountain, knowing they were going to die in it." Tenzin gazed down the row of lamas and lowered his head, as if in shame.

In the end, Shan knew, it wasn't simply that the abbot of Sangchi had been blind to the atrocities of the Chinese but that he had been blind to the inconspicuous, but profound, faith and courage of men like Lokesh and Gendun and Jokar, of prisoners who chiseled away the interior of a mountain knowing all along it would entomb them.

"When Drakte told me about the Lotus Book I asked him if he could get me the names of those brave Tibetans from the mountain. After a week he brought me the names." Tenzin sighed heavily. "I asked him if he could get me one of the Lotus Books, to borrow it so I could write the names of those people in and sign my name to it." He stared into his hands. "I only wanted to prove myself, to declare to the world that I was finished with those who made slaves of others. It was a prideful thing to do. I got Drakte killed. Since that night at the hermitage I see him in my nightmares. Sometimes when I meditate, his face comes to me. It was never worth his life."

"Drakte didn't die for you. He died for the truth."

"Finding the truth is supposed to be a struggle of the spirit, not of the flesh," Tenzin said heavily.

The words seemed to echo down the cavern. In the dim flickering light it seemed to Shan some of the long-dead lamas in front of them were sighing.

"I remember what Drakte said that night. He kills the thing he is, he said of the killer. That monk who calls himself chairman," Tenzin said, as though he would not speak Khodrak's name, as though he still could not believe what had happened at Amdo, "he destroyed everything an abbot is supposed to be. And then that night he killed them both. Over the ledger."

"I don't think Drakte was there just to give Chao the ledger. I heard Gendun speak with Drakte once. He told him, if you really want to change the howlers, just read them the Lotus Book. I think he was going to do that, before bringing it to you. I think he was teaching himself to put down weapons, reaching out to his deity."

"What do you mean?"

"Somo gave me a message from Gendun about Drakte. She didn't think it was important. But Gendun thought it was very important, and I know now it was. He said Drakte carried the deity in a blanket and was learning to unwrap it. Somo thought it was about the stone eye. But Gendun meant Drakte, that Drakte was struggling to use the ways of compassion. He was opening up his own deity, and he chose to deal with Chao the way that Gendun would have, not the way a purba would."

The silence in the cave tomb had the texture of the night sky.

An image floated through Shan's mind of Drakte sitting in the night with the Religious Affairs officer, speaking to him of the Tibetans' suffering, trying to convert him to the ways of compassion. Like the missionaries Siddhi had once sent against an enemy. But the scene continued to unfold in his mind, taking him where he had been trying not to go. For in his heart he now knew what had happened in the garage. Khodrak had appeared. Take a moment, he probably said, and encouraged Chao and Drakte to sit on the floor to pray their beads, walking around them as he had in the stable at Norbu. The two Tibetans would not have refused an abbot. That was when Khodrak had stabbed Chao in the back with his mendicant's staff. He kills prayer, Drakte had said.

"What would you think," Tenzin said after another long silence, in a voice full of despair, "if you saw what we have made of the world?" He was speaking to the dead lamas.

The silence washed over them again, like a physical force, somehow holding them there. Shan's mind cleared, and he probed his awareness, finding his meditation mind for the first time since they had sat at the mandala. Time passed, perhaps a quarter hour or more. Suddenly the pungent smell of ginger swept over them, and his father was there beside him, for the first time in months, and then his father was talking, not with Shan, but with Jokar, and the two men were standing at the far end of the chamber like two old friends, waving at Shan, before stepping into the blackness beyond.

When he became aware of his surroundings again Tenzin was staring at a sheet of paper in his hands. It was a long list of names.

Something pulled Shan to his feet and he found himself stepping to the cloth bundle, which he retrieved and extended toward Tenzin. "You asked Drakte to let you record them," he said, and unwrapped the bundle. It was a heavy leather-bound book, on the cover of which someone had worked a lotus flower.

Tenzin stared at the book, then at Shan, and solemnly accepted the volume. "Winslow took it," Shan explained. "He switched it for that account book. It is the one Drakte was bringing to you. Khodrak took it that night in Amdo."

Tenzin hefted the book in his hands, and stared at it again before opening the cover. He slowly leafed through the pages to the first empty page, near the end, then pulled a pencil from his pocket and began to write. He worked for nearly an hour, at first with Shan reading the names of the dead prisoners for him to transcribe, then alone, sometimes looking up, studying the dead lamas. When he finished he stood and laid the book on the altar, staring at the little golden Buddha. Finally he looked at Shan expectantly. "It is written," he said quietly.

"It would be foolish to try that trail at night," Shan said slowly, looking back at the book. Tenzin studied him a moment, then pulled another three candles from his pocket, placed them beside the solitary candle on the altar, and took up the book again.

The two men settled beside each other in front of the altar, under the candle, facing the lamas, and Tenzin handed the book to Shan.

The Lotus Book was written in many hands, in several languages, in pencil and ink and even, Shan saw, in watercolor. He turned to the first of hundreds of entries, glanced at Jokar, and cleared his throat.

"The first writing is dated fifteen years ago this month," Shan declared in a gentle tone, and began to read. "I was not always this frail old woman without a family, without a house, without a monk to pray with, without children to laugh with, even a dog to lick my hand," the first line said.

"But this is the story of how it came to be, beginning on the day the Chinese killed our sheep..."

And so they read, for hours they read, passing the book back and forth, replacing each candle as it sputtered out, their voices cracking, pausing sometimes to wipe away tears. Gompas were scoured off the earth by the Red Guard. Monks died under torture. The populations of ancient mountain villages were transported to the jungles to make way for Chinese open-pit mines. Five-hundred-year-old Buddhas were melted down to make bullets for the army. Parents were executed in front of their children, and Tibetans were sent to prison for celebrating the Dalai Lama's birthday.

Shan lost all track of time. He had to pass the book to Tenzin when he came to entries about the 404th Peoples Construction Brigade, his lao gai prison, and the names of the many Tibetans who had died there. At last, incredibly, they were at the final pages and Shan recognized Tenzin's handwriting. He took the book from Tenzin to finish reading.

"The enslavement of our land and people remains unabated after five decades," the entry began. It continued with a description of the mountain fortress and the way the slaves conspired to destroy it, and at last the names of those who had died in it. The words were strong and fierce, although not as strong and fierce as those of the very last entry.

"Thirty years ago a young Tibetan graduated as the top student at the only school in his county that allowed Tibetans to study beside Chinese children. Because his parents had joined the Communist Party, he could speak Chinese well and was sent to university in China, even promised a lucrative job when he returned. The job was with the Bureau of Religious Affairs, and one day they brought a robe to him and told him he was to become the political officer of an important gompa. He found much about that gompa that appealed to him and when they asked him to transfer to another five years later he asked to stay to continue his monastic training.

"That monk became me, someone different from the political officer who started at that gompa, but still a favorite of the government, which saw to it I became the youngest abbot ever appointed in Tibet. I made that gompa a showcase for assimilated Buddhism, and by way of example taught the country how socialism could empower Buddhism. I tried to embrace the Buddha but first, for many years, I embraced the Chinese government as my protector. When they asked me to preach against resistance, I did so at the top of my lungs, because the government was the great benefactor of Tibet. When they launched a campaign for economic emphasis in religious affairs, I suggested it be called the Serenity Campaign, and I launched that campaign with a speech at my gompa.

"Then one day I saw an old man who was supposed to be painting a chapel and I criticized him for working so slowly. He smiled and said he did the best he could. He showed me his hands, which had no thumbs. He had been a lama once, he said, but the Chinese soldiers had cut off his thumbs with pruning shears so he could not say his beads. We talked for hours that day and the next day he brought a young woman who told me more, about her brother who was imprisoned for having a photograph of the Dalai Lama, and the next day that woman brought a man she called a purba."

The passage continued for several pages, with Tenzin's recollections and confessions about revered teachers he had helped send away to Beijing for political instruction after speaking in support of the exiled government, of helping the government redraw maps to eliminate reference to pilgrimage sites, even of how he had learned from two old lamas named Gendun and Shopo that compassion could be shaped out of sand. They had showed him how to start over, Tenzin wrote, by learning to respect yak dung.

"I sinned against my people and my soul," the last paragraph read. "My government lied to me and I lied to my inner deity. I used up much of my human incarnation to help make others' lives miserable. When you speak of enemies of Tibet speak of the abbot of Sangchi. When you speak of lower creatures trying to burrow through darkness to light speak of a pilgrim named Tenzin."

Shan stared at the closing words a long time before he closed the book. When he finally rose he laid the book beside the Buddha, in full view of the Rapjung lamas. "I think it is dawn," he said quietly.

Tenzin, looking gaunt and hollow again, followed him along the line of the old men, paying homage to each with a prayer, then they climbed out of the chamber, leaving Jokar in his beloved mountain, resting at last on the chair of Siddhi.

CHAPTER TWENTY

W hen Shan and Tenzin crested the ridge above Yapchi three hours after sunrise they stopped, staring in confusion. The valley had been transformed. Not only had Jenkins's levee failed, water was still pouring down the slope in a long, steep cascade. It had washed the soil away until it found bedrock, creating a new riverbed down the slope. The little pond around the derrick had become a huge body of water, nearly a mile long.

Shan paused, leaning on the staff in his hand, Jokar's staff. He had not intended to bring the staff away from the burial cave but without conscious effort his hand had closed around it as he stepped back in front of the large thangka, as though the staff had willed itself into his hand. He had paused uneasily, studying the weathered staff that had served the medicine lama for so many decades, then he had hefted it and carried it out. Jokar and Shan knew someone who needed a staff.

"The valley is being made again," Tenzin said in a tentative, perplexed tone.

Shan sat on a rock, a sense of unreality washing over him. The army and the venture were surely going to stop the water, to plug the cascade on the mountainside. But a war had been waged in the valley, and they had been defeated by the mountain. Workers drifted toward the camp, dragging tools behind them like broken soldiers leaving a battlefront. A bulldozer lay on its side near the bottom of the slope, half submerged in the new riverbed where the bank must have collapsed. The derrick was in the middle of the little lake, listing nearly thirty degrees, the valley floor underneath it destabilized by the water.

The only work underway seemed to be at the camp itself. The field where the celebration had been planned was a chaotic mass of men and equipment. The rope for the banner had broken loose so that the tattered Serenity slogan flew high in the sky, like a kite. Workers were frantically throwing ropes, barrels, buckets, and tools into the cargo bays of trucks. Half the trailers were gone. As Shan watched, a heavy truck gunned its engine and eased one of the trailers up the road that led out of the valley. The venture was retreating.

"They were going to make a miracle," Tenzin said in an awed voice. "It was what Lokesh said in Larkin's cave."

Shan studied the contours of the valley. It was indeed being made again. When the lake reached the northern end of the camp the road would become its outlet and the road itself would be washed out, converted to a stream, cutting the valley off from any access by trucks or tanks, or any other vehicle. At its southern end the water would reach to a few hundred yards of the village ruins. It had already turned the small knoll with the burial mound into a little island. At the rapid rate the water was accumulating, in a few more hours it would entirely cover the mound and reach the digging, the site of the Taoist temple. The wound that had lain open for a century would at last be sealed. *Wash it, bind it, bind the valley,* the oracle had said with their beloved Anya's tongue.

Shan discovered that Tenzin had folded his legs under him and was sitting with his head cocked, mouth half open, his eyes full of wonder.

There were others gripped by the same spell farther down the slope, sitting on a ledge overlooking the oil camp. Shan found Jenkins there, with Larkin and a dozen others who had the look of venture managers, including two wearing the suits of the visiting dignitaries. Tibetans, too, slowly drifted toward the ledge, all looking at the camp with the same confused expression.

When Melissa Larkin saw him she stood and approached him on unsteady legs. Shan sat and waited for her.

"They said you had gone to look for Winslow, and Jokar," Larkin said. "I was worried. Cowboy had such a strange look in his eyes last night. Like he was being pulled apart, or pulled away."

"I found him," Shan said quietly. "He had run out of his pills. He's not coming back. There was a place he had to go to with Jokar."

Somehow Larkin understood. Her legs gave way and she sat heavily beside him. Her hand went to her mouth and she bit a knuckle. Tears welled in her eyes. Her head sagged and she buried it in her arm, braced against her knees.

"He wanted you to know, only you," Shan said when she finally looked up.

Larkin smiled through her tears. "I thought he was just some lunatic bureaucrat when I first heard about him. Then when we met, it was..." Her voice drifted off and she stared at the birthing lake. "There was this connection between us. That night up in the mixing ledge, he said that maybe we had known each other in another incarnation. I thought he was joking. But lately I don't know what's a joke and what is..." She looked away a moment and rubbed her tears away on her sleeve. "He told me about his wife. I told him how my fiancé had died in an avalanche. I warned him, I didn't think I could ever again..." Tears streamed down her cheeks. Jenkins, sitting thirty feet away, stared at her absently. "He came to collect my body but in the end...because of me," she sobbed.

"No," Shan said. "It was where he was meant to be," he added, and told her of Winslow's note. This is where I belong, this time, the American had said. "He would have come," Shan ventured, "to see you at that sacred lake."

Larkin nodded, gave a forlorn smile, then stared back at the lake. "Nothing happened the way I expected," she said toward the water. "Even this," she said, nodding toward the water. "We never expected so much water."

"Once, when I was young, I had a teacher," a frail voice said.

They turned to see Lepka standing close, gazing at them with sad, moist eyes. "He said there were places on earth where souls are magnified, ripening places he called them, because souls ripen faster there. He said when many people gather in such places it feeds the power of the ripening place, so that great events can happen, and the lives of many people get settled. He said this was such a place, and it was why the lamas never called it Yapchi Mountain, why they had their own name for it, an old name that has been lost. No one has used it for many years."

Lepka looked back toward the snowcapped peak, then squatted by them, lowering his voice. "But my father knew it. It was a long name in an old lama's dialect that meant the Place Where the Spine of the Earth Protrudes. My father just called it Bone Mountain," he whispered. "Sometimes when old lamas finished ripening," he added, "that's where they would go to sleep."

Shan returned Lepka's sad smile, and invited him to sit beside them, watching the valley as it changed before their eyes. "I think that Winslow," Lepka said to the American woman, "he and Jokar Rinpoche are in some bayal, laughing together right now." Larkin put her hand in the old man's, and squeezed it tight.

"What will you do?" Shan asked the American woman.

Larkin looked out over the water. "I was going to try to get back to him, to Cowboy. I guess I'll just go home. Zhu doesn't really want me dead, just out of Tibet." She turned and gazed back at the top of the mountain for a long while, squeezing Lepka's hand the whole time.

"I never would have believed it if I hadn't been here," a deep voice said over their shoulders after several minutes. Jenkins had risen and was standing behind them, staring at the lost derrick. "It's finished. Lost nearly all the heavy equipment when the levee broke. Lucky to get the trailers out in time." It seemed he had decided he owed Shan a report. "I had a furious call from the States, they wanted to know what happened." He gazed at Shan as if about to ask him what had happened, then shrugged. "I said it was just unstable geology."

"No," another voice interjected. Somo had appeared, her feet and pant legs streaked with mud, but her face lit with a serene expression. "I think it is the opposite of that."

Strangely, they all seemed to understand. Jenkins gave a sound like a snort and offered a melancholy smile to the purba. She was suggesting it was the way the geology was supposed to be, the way the mountain could be expected to act once it understood what the humans were trying to do to it.

"It's a loss, the entire damned project," Jenkins said. "All that mud, all that water. Hell, we hadn't even hit the oil yet. Economics will never support a project here now," he said with an inquiring glance at Larkin. "Jesus," he added, staring over his ruined work. "Jesus." He looked back at Shan. "The Tibetans from that village say that deity spoke. They say they are sorry it was so inconvenient for us, but he just spoke." Jenkins shook his head. "It's not my job to speak with deities," he added wearily. "I keep hearing that drum in my head. I'm tired of taking things out of the earth. I'm going home. But first I have to write a report." He shook his head and sighed. "I'll call it an act of god."

"There was someone looking for you, Shan," Larkin suddenly remembered. "I think all those Tibetans who were fleeing, or going to that meadow. I think they just came here when the news spread." She pointed toward the opposite slope, where a makeshift camp of Tibetans had appeared.

Shan stood on uncertain legs and began jogging down the slope. He found Lokesh sitting at the shore of the rising lake, washing stones. "Touch the water," he said excitedly. "It is different water." It was his tonde. Lokesh was washing his charm stones in the water.

Shan bent to the water and touched it, cupped it in his hands and washed his face. The liquid seemed to tingle his skin somehow. Perhaps there was carbonation in the water, from its being pushed deep into the rock. "Already people are saying these waters have great powers," Lokesh added.

Shan handed his friend the staff he had brought from the cave. The old Tibetan stared at it, then slowly, as if it might be painful to touch, he laid his fingertips on it, the way he might take a pulse. "I hope they had time to settle in," his old friend whispered, and Shan saw the sudden sadness in his eyes.

Settle in. "Yes, they settled in," Shan said, and wondered how many of the Tibetans knew. Lepka and Lokesh both seemed to have understood where Jokar and Winslow had gone, as if they had been able to read something in the two men that had been invisible to Shan.

One of the two army trucks remaining in the camp pulled out, behind a heavy truck towing the last of the trailers. The second army truck began moving but suddenly turned at a right angle toward the center of the valley, along the edge of the water. It stopped near the center, a hundred feet from where Shan stood, and the two soldiers in the front seat seemed to argue about something. Then the engine died and four soldiers climbed down from the bay. They moved slowly, without their usual aggression, with none of the usual fire in their eyes. They formed a small group at the tailgate, working something out of the bay, then abruptly cleared to the opposite side of the truck, and Lin appeared from behind them, alone, holding a long bundle wrapped in a bright white sheet. He looked at the Tibetans on the shore of the lake, who stopped what they were doing and stood, silently watching him. As Lin began walking toward Shan, Lhandro and Nyma stirred from where they stood in one of the ruined fields and approached warily. Lokesh pulled himself up with the staff.

As Lin bent to lay the shrouded figure on the soil near Shan, Lhandro stepped forward, arms extended, and accepted Anya's body. Lin silently surrendered her, his hand lingering on the girl's covered head. "She should be with her people," he said in a whisper. He swayed for a moment, as if about to collapse. "But don't give her to those birds," he said to Lhandro. "Please," he added in his brittle voice. "I couldn't stand to think she'd been taken by the birds."

No one spoke for a long time. The water lapped near their feet.

"The valley can make room for our Anya," an old man said, and Lin turned to nod as Lepka stepped into their small circle. "There are also remains of Chinese, from that temple." Lepka lifted an object in his hand. A shovel. "I need your help," he said to Lin.

The colonel stared, his eyes squinting as if he had trouble seeing what it was Lepka held.

"I need your help, Xiao Lin," Lepka repeated gently, and pointed to the base of the slope, where several tall trees cast their shade. The old man turned with his shovel and the colonel followed him with small steps and downcast eyes, like a confused boy.

Xiao Lin, Lepka had called Lin. Little Lin. Shan looked back at the soldiers. They stared at their colonel, some with fear, some with anger, some with wonder.

As the two men dug in silence, Nyma released the cloth from Anya's face, letting the dead girl's long black hair stir in the wind. Nyma sang softly, the way Anya had sung her deity songs, as she tied the long strands in a braid. More of the villagers arrived, but none with a shovel. They watched from a few feet away, until suddenly Professor Ma was at the grave holding his box of relics. The villagers watched for a moment, then stepped forward to help as the old Han laid the box on the ground and began lifting from it the pieces of bone he had recovered from the Taoist temple. They wrapped each bone in a cloth, in khatas and kerchiefs pulled from the women's heads, and each villager took one of the shrouded bones and sat with it, speaking a mani mantra over it as the professor stepped to the hole and accepted the shovel from Lepka. He scooped the soil for several minutes as Lin and Lepka watched, then offered the tool to Shan. After several minutes of silent digging Shan was about to hand the shovel back to Lhandro when he looked up to see a line formed by the grave. Other Yapchi villagers were there, young men who must have been in the work crew, and Gyalo and Chemi, and at the end the Americans, Larkin and Jenkins.

They worked for over an hour, Lin sometimes taking turns with the

407

shovel, other times standing with his grim, sagging expression, working the fingers of one hand. Shan saw a flash of green in the hand. It was the stone Anya had found for him at the chorten, the tonde she had uncovered for Uncle Lin. Just when Shan thought the grave was done, Lin gestured for his troops to come forward. The soldiers had stood by their truck the entire time, watching uneasily, but when they arrived at the grave no words had to be spoken. A young Chinese soldier solemnly extended his hand for the shovel and dug for ten minutes. When he was done tears streamed down his cheeks. One of the Tibetan women pulled him to her, and he cried on her shoulder.

Each of the soldiers dug, and when they were done two of them stood in the grave and accepted the bone relics from the Tibetans, arranging them reverently in the earth along the perimeter of the hole. When the relics were all deposited one of the soldiers paused, then wrote four names on a piece of paper and set it under one of the relics. The names of the four dead soldiers he explained in a whisper. At last Nyma kissed Anya's head and covered her face again. Lepka and Lhandro lowered her body to the soldiers.

The shovel was passed around again, to fill the grave, then stones were laid over it. A cairn would be built, Shan knew, and perhaps one day a chorten. The silence as they stood by the grave was broken occasionally by a short prayer, or a quick word of remembrance.

Lin said nothing over the grave, stepping away with a distant, hollow expression, pausing only to silently hand Lhandro the identity papers he had taken two weeks earlier. But when Shan turned he saw the colonel standing by the truck looking expectantly at him. "I sat in my tent with her all last night," he said when Shan and Lhandro approached. Then, on the hood of the truck, he solemnly unfolded a military map and pointed to Yapchi Valley. They were looking at the provincial border region, with new red markings drawn across a large area. "An order was issued this morning," he said in a weary voice. "From here—" he indicated a point immediately north of Norbu, the line of small ridges above the gompa, "north to the provincial border is now a hazardous materials zone. No one is permitted entry. Not the army, not Public Security. No access. Not even Religious Affairs," he said pointedly, in a voice that gained strength. He saw the inquiry in their faces. "I told central command it must be so, because of what I discovered when I was out there." He spoke in a flat voice, as though he were at a military briefing. "I will have signs erected."

Shan and Lhandro stared at Lin in disbelief. The red hash marks covered an area of at least a hundred square miles, an area as large as a township.

"And those men from Norbu. That Tuan was taken away by Public Security. Corruption like that, by a senior official," Lin said, shaking his head. "He's finished. Khodrak, they're taking him to a special knob institute," he said, and seemed to suppress a shudder. He meant a knob medical institute, where wayward officials were held, usually for years; where government doctors tried to cure their antisocial tendencies with drugs. "He won't be back."

Lin folded the map and handed it to Shan, searching Shan's face a moment. Shan nodded slowly, and then Lin produced an envelope from his pocket, handed it to Shan and silently stepped toward the cab of the truck.

"I don't understand," Nyma said, at Shan's shoulder.

"Rapjung gompa and the Plain of Flowers has been liberated," Lhandro said in a disbelieving voice as he watched the soldiers climb into the rear of the truck. "For Anya."

Shan glanced back at the truck. Lin was at the cab door staring at someone sitting on the running board. It was Dremu, returning Lin's stare with a doubtful yet somehow stubborn expression.

"This man says we killed his grandfather," Lin said wearily as Shan stepped to his side.

"Not you exactly." Shan saw that Dremu nervously fingered the small leather pouch that hung on his neck. "It's just that . . . It's just that a Golok clan refuses its tribute."

Lin looked at Shan in confusion, but Dremu seemed to carefully ponder Shan's words. He nodded solemnly, dug into the pouch and pulled out a single heavy gold coin. He stood and raised the coin toward the northeast, high, as though showing it to someone in the distance, then extended the coin to Lin with two hands, like a ceremonial offering.

"He is paying us?" Lin asked as Dremu wandered away, an unfamiliar expression on his face. Not serenity, but probably the closest the Golok had ever been to serenity.

"Returning it. That coin belonged to the Lujun."

"What do I do with it?" Lin sighed.

Shan recalled how Lin had used the stone eye. "You need a new paperweight," he suggested.

Lin raised his brow, then his gaze drifted toward the grave. After a moment the engine roared to life. Without another word he climbed into the cab and the truck sped away, the colonel still watching the grave through the open window.

Shan opened the envelope Lin had given him and read the single page it contained.

"What is it?" Nyma asked.

He read again, uncertain how to answer. "Somebody died," he said, and watched the truck climb out of the valley.

The silent, reverent mood of the Tibetans continued the rest of the day as the last of the venture employees retreated from the valley. Some watched as the waters of the lake lapped near the new grave. Others helped with cooking fires lit in the ruins of Yapchi Village.

When they had finished their evening meal, everyone stepped back to the lake, sitting beside it until the sun set. Other Tibetans began to arrive, the remnants of those who, misunderstanding, had gone to the upper slopes to wait for the old lama. They touched the water and spoke excitedly, some cupping it in their hands to drink, others filling bowls and tipping the water over their heads.

Shan sat near the dying embers of a fire beside Lokesh as a new silence overtook the camp. A dog barked and he looked up to see a purba, one of the hardened young men he had seen with a gun at Norbu. The purba nodded first to Shan, then to Tenzin, and stepped aside. In the shadows behind him stood the man with the striped face, the Tiger.

"It's time," the purba general announced to Tenzin in a terse voice. "On the other side of the hills there is a truck waiting to take you north."

Tenzin studied the hard features of the purba's face. "I've gone far enough," he said quietly. Shan followed his gaze into the shadows. There were others with the Tiger, five or six others waiting in the night.

The rough, guttered tissue of the Tiger's face moved up and down as he repeatedly clenched his jaw. He shot an accusing glance at Shan. "People need the abbot of Sangchi on the outside. We have plans."

"The abbot of Sangchi no longer exists," Tenzin declared, then slowly surveyed the ragged group. Nyma, who had not stopped crying since the burial. Gyalo, who silently stroked Jampa's nose. Dremu, sitting in the shadows, staring uncertainly at the fire. Dzopa, the big dobdob, lying on a blanket, his horse-like face downturned, still filled with the pain of losing Jokar. "People need me here," Tenzin said. "We—" he embraced those around him with a sweep of his arm. "We are going to rebuild a gompa. We are going to build a place where Tibetans can learn to heal." He glanced toward Shan then turned back to the purba. "I made a vow to some old men in the mountain."

"Rapjung?" the purba asked in an impatient, disbelieving voice. "That old place can never—"

"If there is going to be a new Tibet," Tenzin replied, "it must be built on the old."

"But the army will come," the Tiger protested. "The howlers will come. Anyone trying to build a gompa will be arrested."

"No," Lokesh said brightly, "that colonel, he has made Rapjung a hidden land."

Tenzin grinned at the old Tibetan. "With strong backs and strong hearts we can build anything," he said. As if to emphasize the point Jampa took a step forward and snorted. "Rapjung gompa was never destroyed, only its buildings. Jokar Rinpoche taught us that. It was just a treasure that had to be uncovered again."

"The government will still look for you. The army. The howlers, they hate you now. They will seek you out as a political enemy now."

"No," Shan interjected. "They will not." He pulled out the paper Lin had given him. "Anya's Chinese uncle wrote a report." Shan read it to them. It was dated the evening before, when he and Tenzin had been in the lama's cave. It explained that while in the mountains looking for reactionaries, Colonel Lin had encountered the abbot of Sangchi, had even captured him and confirmed his identification. But the abbot had tried to escape. There had been a struggle and before Lin's own eyes the abbot had fallen off a high cliff into a gorge. Colonel Lin was writing to certify that the abbot was dead.

"That Zhu filed a false report about Melissa Larkin dying," the purba leader pointed out. "They know he lied."

"This is a colonel in the army," Shan said. "A decorated colonel from an elite unit."

The purba sighed and nodded, conceding that no one was likely to challenge Lin's report. He surveyed the Tibetans who stood by Shan. "All our plans," the Tiger said in a dark voice. "All the people," he added, looking at Somo now. "Drakte," he said pointedly.

"Drakte," Somo said slowly, as she stepped to Tenzin's side, "would have said he and I should build a gompa."

The purba leader stared at her in silence. He studied each of them, then gave a final nod to Shan. "Lha gyal lo," he said quietly, and slipped away into the shadows.

But one of his followers lingered, and stepped to the edge of the firelight. It was Melissa Larkin, wearing a fleece cap and a herder's vest. "I'm staying," she said to Shan, with a new glint in her eyes. "There is much more to understand about how the earth works in Tibet." She began to turn, then paused. "Someday Beijing will discover there is a new headwater for the Yangtze," she added, before she followed the Tiger into the night.

Shan watched the fire with the others for a few more minutes, then wandered into the night himself along the water, watching the stars, until suddenly he saw a flicker of light halfway up the slope. A small campfire. He searched the landscape around him, making sure no one followed, then walked quickly toward the light.

When Shan rose at dawn, he found a dozen Tibetans standing at the edge of the village ruins looking down into the valley. Dremu had appeared and was pacing back and forth as if, like the others, he had grown wary of approaching the water. Shan walked along the line of Tibetans, searching the faces of Nyma and Lhandro, who stood at the front, then Nyma sighed and he followed her gaze to the water. In the rapidly brightening light he began to understand. The making of the lake was finished. During the night the waters had risen above the gap at the end of the valley and were flowing out, past the saddle of land. The lake had reached its natural level, and the buried river was still pouring out of the side of the mountain. The derrick had fallen, disappearing under the water, and the burial mound was now submerged. The debris at the camp had been covered. The lake was serene. The sediment had rapidly settled, so the waters seemed made of deep blue crystal.

Strangely, Shan remembered Larkin's words about meeting Winslow at the sacred lake. He had thought she'd meant Lamtso. But she, above all, had known the water and the rocks and the contour of the land. She had known it would shine like a blue star in the mountains, like one of the lakes the Tibetans called sacred.

They gathered around their cooking fire and spoke of what it meant, then watched solemnly as Shan brought a small object wrapped in felt to the fire. With a knowing look Lokesh extended his open palms and Shan laid the object on them and opened the bundle.

"Victory to the gods," Nyma murmured.

Lepka and Lokesh smiled and nodded, as if they had always known Shan would return the eye in the end.

"Who was it?" Lhandro demanded. "Who attacked you?"

"The eye has come back," was all Shan would say. "It has been watching over the valley for many days."

"Yes," one of the villagers whispered. "We heard it."

The Tibetans gathered close to touch the chenyi stone with tentative fingers, and offer it prayers.

Then Nyma stepped away from the group and stared at Shan. "But here we are," she said with eyes suddenly round and wide. "It's been the biggest mystery all along."

The words hushed everyone. All eyes turned to Shan, who stared at Nyma. Oddly, he realized he was grinning. Something in her words seemed wonderful to him. Despite the murders, the lies, the destruction— the real mystery for Nyma still was where to seat her deity.

"But I know the place now," Shan declared. "The mountain has made the kind of place where deities like to live," he said, and asked Lhandro if he knew where poplar saplings might be cut.

Two hours later a small procession moved to the water's edge, where a coracle had materialized, hastily made of poplar boughs and skins. Two narrow paddles, carved from planks saved from the houses, were in the little boat. Shan unwrapped the eye's felt blanket for the last time and held the jagged stone over his head. Excited murmurs rippled through the assembled Tibetans.

"The virtuous Chinese," someone in the crowd said admiringly. The words caused Shan to pause a moment, reflecting on all that had happened in Yapchi Valley. Perhaps, in the end, the virtuous Chinese who had saved the valley had been Colonel Lin. Or perhaps the virtuous Chinese had been found in pieces of Lin and Gang, Ma and Shan.

As Shan bent to pick up a paddle the crowd fell silent. Confused, he studied the expectant faces, then realized that they did not expect him to go alone. He handed the first paddle to Tenzin, and lifted the second, surveying the faces, then stepped to the side of the small crowd and extended the paddle to a small gaunt man who hovered in the shadows with his wife and children. Shan had found them the night before, huddled with the drum and the stone, and convinced them the time had come to end their hiding.

Gang accepted the paddle without speaking and the three of them stepped into the coracle, the assembly solemn and silent.

"It's like a precious jewel," Tenzin said of the beautiful water.

Gang repeated the words.

They paddled to the center of the lake to a spot between the derrick and the burial mound, now under many feet of water, then Shan motioned to Gang. The sullen man's face seemed to change, and he took the eye from Shan with a joyful expression. He extended it toward the people on the shore, then lowered the chenyi stone into the water and released it. Shan watched the stone, tumbling downward in the sparkling crystal water, turning blue in the filtered light, then it was gone. *Deep is the eye,* the oracle had said, *brilliant blue eye, the nagas will hold it true.*

When they returned to shore Lepka and Lhandro waited with bowls of tea. They stepped past a small circle of men and women chanting a mantra to sit on a blanket in one of the barley fields as Tenzin asked Gang about his construction work at Rapjung. Shan lay back in the warm morning sun and gradually slipped into sleep.

It was more than two hours later when he became aware of movement along the lake, the laughter of children. He sat up and looked, rubbing his eyes, at a scene so surprising it took a moment for him to understand. Strands of prayer flags had materialized near the lake, suspended between poles and rock cairns. Logs were moving along the valley floor from the venture stockpile, each carried by three or four Tibetans, men and women alike. There were new faces, many new Tibetans. As he watched, a small group appeared on the saddle of land and began running down the slope toward the lake. A chain of people carrying logs moved along the shore of the lake. At the water's edge each team stopped as a woman, an unfamiliar nun, dipped a bowl in the lake and spilled water on the log, like a baptism.

He tentatively approached the nun, but halted thirty feet away. It was Nyma. She had found a robe, and cut her long braids, cropping her hair close to the scalp in the fashion of a convent. Her eyes sparkled as she saw Shan. She had decided she could be a real nun after all. He offered a small wave, and with a smile she pointed to the south end of the valley.

The logs were not going to the ruins of Yapchi village, as he had assumed, but beyond, to the trail up the mountain. A child laughed and Shan turned to see Gang's daughter, riding one of the logs like a horse, as three sturdy Tibetan men joyfully carried it. The trees taken by the venture were all going to Rapjung. They were being carried over the mountain to build the new gompa.

413

"We held the last circle," Nyma said excitedly when he reached her. "The prayer circle we started in the canyon. They never stopped, they said. They went to a cave high above the valley and continued, night and day. With the eye back they knew they could finally stop. I joined them at the edge of the water, and when they had finished I asked them to help me cut my hair," she declared serenely.

Below the lake, near the village, Shan found Lokesh sitting on a rock, speaking with Lhandro. Lokesh was pointing to the fields as Lhandro listened attentively.

"No more barley," Lhandro announced as he saw Shan. "Now it is going to be like the old days, just medicine herbs for Rapjung. And Lokesh gave us drawings," Lhandro exclaimed, "so they can rebuild the herb gardens at Rapjung the way they used to be. People will bring in new soil, in baskets, from the valleys. We will send some from here."

"Drawings will help," Shan said hesitantly, "but it would be even better for them to have someone there who knew the old gompa."

Lokesh fixed him with a level stare. "That is where you will find me, in a year's time. Maybe less."

"We have little money but we offered to give it all to him," Lhandro said, "for buses to Beijing, to bring him back quickly. But he refused. He said he must journey as a pilgrim to Beijing. When he gets hungry he says he will beg. He says monks used to beg and it is an honorable thing to do."

Shan turned toward the lake, trying to calm himself. In all the years he had known the gentle old man this was the only thing that had ever come between them. But there was no room for argument, for Lokesh had been spoken to by his inner god. "It's going to be difficult," Shan said quietly, "with that bad foot."

"I have Jokar's staff." Lokesh pointed to the length of weathered wood at his side.

"The road to Golmud is treacherous," Shan said in a tentative voice. "Let me at least go with you that far, old friend." He sensed an odd taste of fear on his tongue, fear that Lokesh would say no. "Then I will leave, I will go find Gendun. I need to get him some new boots."

The old Tibetan smiled. "Of course. You can help me improve my Chinese on the way. I will need to speak better Chinese when I reach the capital. I will be ready to leave in the morning."

"So soon? Surely there are many diagrams to make for Gang and Lhandro."

"Which is why I did not leave this morning," Lokesh said stubbornly.

Shan saw the challenge in the old man's eyes. "Tomorrow morning," he agreed.

More and more Tibetans arrived, herders and farmers who had come to see the miracle for themselves. Tents were erected, and Lokesh sat in front of one with Lhandro, making drawings from his memory, drawings

414

of gardens, of buildings and the special joinings of wood used in the roof eaves, even the details he remembered from the carving on the door to the printing room. Nyma appeared, cradling a long bundle, which she unwrapped on a blanket. It was the peche from the secret room at Norbu.

Lokesh paused and touched the top page with a trembling hand as he scanned the words printed there. "A history of Rapjung," he said in a quivering voice, and squeezed Nyma's hand as she showed him pages with maps and plans of buildings.

In the frenzy of activity Shan lost sight of Tenzin. He finally found him in the small canyon behind the ruined village, sitting in a large circle of Tibetans with Dzopa, his leg bandaged, on one side, and Gang on the other. Dremu sat on a rock above them, like a sentry. Below him was Somo, staring at two objects in her hands, a pocketknife with a spoon, and a lapis and silver bracelet. Dremu had returned the payment she had made at the hermitage.

The Tibetans in the canyon were speaking of work parties and supplies. Shan sat on a rock behind Tenzin and studied the group. All of the others were older, most sixty years or more. One man said he had been a stone mason, another a painter of thangkas, another a maker of incense. Three were carpenters, two metalworkers who once had worked full time making prayer wheels.

"You can work full time once more," Tenzin observed in a tentative voice. "But we have no money to pay wages."

"Money?" an old man quipped. "We heard about that howler's report. They said we were wealthy already." The laughter that erupted around the circle suddenly died as a stranger appeared at the edge of the circle, a tall lean Han with long white hair. Several of the Tibetans shot accusing glances at Shan.

"I am no good at woodworking," the Han said in a strained voice, using Tibetan. "The only time I built a stone wall it came out crooked. But I can make books. That gompa once made books, important books." It was Professor Ma, looking greatly fatigued. "I left the valley," he said, looking at Tenzin and Shan, "but after five miles I climbed out of the truck. Jokar, he said I must do something about my heart wind." The words brought a sudden stillness to the canyon.

"I will come if you will have me," Ma said after a moment. "I have no home in China anymore." An older Tibetan woman made a place for him in the circle. "It's just that when I make books," he said as he sat, "I would like to make them in both Tibetan and Chinese. And sometimes," he added, pulling a familiar bamboo canister from his pocket, "I would like to talk about the Tao."

Lokesh and Shan left before dawn, while the others still slept. As they left the valley the last stars of the night were twinkling on the surface of the lake, and the reflected blush of dawn made it seem as if the water were glowing. In the dim light he made out two figures at the far side of the lake, watching them. Even from the distance Shan knew it was Tenzin and Lhandro. The former abbot of Sangchi, who had died and been reborn, and the farmer who had lost his valley and found it again. The two men raised their hands in farewell, and lifted a long pole with a prayer flag attached to its end, as if in salute.

Tenzin had knelt by him when Shan had settled into his blanket the night before, and stared at him in silence so long Shan had asked if he needed to grow a new tongue again.

"I do not know if ever again I will have a journey such as that we have been on," Tenzin had said at last, closing both his hands around one of Shan's, pressing hard. "But if I do, I pray you will be with me."

When they stopped to eat cold tsampa on a flat ledge lit by the early rays of the sun, Lokesh was buoyant, speaking first of how Rapjung would look when he returned in a year's time, and then of how Somo had told him of a noodle shop in Beijing where he could get tsampa.

"There is a place I used to go," Shan said in a tentative voice. "A Taoist temple. The monks there will give you food and a pallet if you have no money. They may remember my name."

Lokesh looked at Shan warily.

Shan sighed. "I will draw you a map."

Lokesh uttered a sound like a laugh that echoed off the rocks, and Shan sensed the wall that had risen between them was melting away. They spoke in eager voices about Shan's old neighborhood and the dangers of walking in a city with so many automobiles.

Finally they packed away the food, and Lokesh lifted himself on the staff. "I am going to Beijing!" he shouted out, for no apparent reason. But when he took his first step the staff would not move. He pulled it, hard, but it did not budge. It was stuck in a fissure in the rock.

Lokesh stared at Shan, his eyes wide as he rubbed his white whiskers. "Was that crack in the rock there before?" he asked in a whisper. "I did not see it before."

"I don't know. I suppose so," Shan said in confusion.

Lokesh pulled again, to no avail, then let Shan try. The staff was lodged firmly in the stone. Lokesh twisted it, and pushed it, and pulled it again. Still nothing.

A strange cloud settled over the old Tibetan's face, and he sat on a nearby rock, staring at the staff—Jokar's staff—that held fast, protruding almost vertically from the ledge.

"I could bring some water to put on the stone," Shan suggested.

"It's not that," Lokesh said in a grim tone, and he began a mantra. After five minutes he tried the staff again, without effect. He wrapped both hands around the end of the staff, and stared at the top of Yapchi

Mountain. "There are people to be healed in Beijing," he said in his loud voice again. "They have heart wind there, an epidemic of heart wind." He tried the staff again, without luck.

"I will find something else for a staff," Shan suggested. "You can lean on my back until then."

Lokesh did not look at him, just shook his head grimly. He spoke another mantra, looking at the mountaintop all the time as if conversing with it. Nearly a quarter hour passed, then he tried the staff again, without moving it. Finally he hung his head on his arms, still raised around the staff, and sighed. He looked back at Shan with a weary expression. "I never expected this," he said, and turned back to sit on the rock again. He stared into his hands for nearly five minutes, then rose to the staff again and fixed the mountain with a deliberate stare. "I will not go to Beijing to see that Chairman," he offered in his loud voice. He twisted the staff and it came free.

"All right," the old Tibetan said to Shan after examining the staff for a long time. "We will do it your way."

Shan cocked his head in inquiry.

"You know," Lokesh sighed. "We'll have to keep patching deities one at a time."

Shan said nothing, but picked up their bags and followed Lokesh as he hobbled down the trail. His old friend studied Yapchi Mountain while he walked, then picked a purple flower which he examined in silence.

After half a mile Lokesh paused again. "If we go to Rapjung," he called back, "we have to go on the low trail, the easy trail, because of my foot. I am sorry."

They walked along the stream until they reached a small rise in the land, where Lokesh raised his hand for Shan to stop, lowered himself onto a wide boulder, and reached into his pocket. His letter to the Chairman appeared in his hand and Shan watched, perplexed, as Lokesh unfolded the letter and seemed to read it. Then Lokesh straightened the paper over a rock and carefully began making new folds in it. He labored over the paper for several minutes, then hobbled to the top of the rise, his back to the wind. Shan followed, and as his old friend raised the paper in his extended arms Shan recognized it. Lokesh had crafted it into one of his spirit horses. He waited for Shan to reach his side, extended the horse over his head and released it. The paper floated lazily in the breeze, then suddenly a gust seized it and the paper soared away, scudding high toward the northeast horizon, toward Beijing.

"That Chairman in Beijing," Lokesh said in a cracking voice, "he could be driving in the mountains someday. His limousine could break down and he could be stranded. When he finds my paper it will work its magic. So he can travel to a new place on a good Tibetan horse."

They watched the paper until it was a tiny dot in the sky, and then it was gone. Lokesh turned back toward the old flooded road and without a word stepped away. For a long moment Shan watched him hobble across the rough landscape, then silently followed.

They had walked for another hour, following the rush of water from the valley, when Lokesh paused again, putting both hands on his staff as he studied the rock formations at the top of a low ridge across the stream, half a mile away.

Shan recognized the expression on his friend's face, and set the bags down.

"That rock," Lokesh said slowly, squinting toward the ridge, rubbing the white bristle on his jaw. "It is very like a formation my mother described once. She said it was actually a turtle deity just pretending to be a rock, that it would soar over the mountains at night." He looked at Shan with apology in his eyes. "She said it spoke the words of Buddha."

Shan studied the swift, shallow stream that separated them from the ridge, and the vast open landscape beyond. "It's going to take us a long time to get to Rapjung, isn't it?" he asked his friend.

Lokesh shrugged. "I could collect herbs along the way," he suggested, and extended his staff to Shan as he balanced on his good foot. "And you need to learn how to look for tonde."

Suddenly, unexpectedly, Shan smiled. Anchored to the earth by the lama's staff, he bent to let Lokesh climb onto his back, stepped into the stream, and set off in search of the turtle Buddha.

Glossary of
Foreign Language Terms

Terms that are used only once and defined in adjoining text are not included in this glossary.

Amdo. Tibetan. One of the traditional provinces of Tibet, constituting the northeastern lands of historic Tibet. Renamed Qinghai Province by the People's Republic of China.

Bardo. Tibetan. A term used for the Bardo death rites, specifically referring to the intermediate stage between death and rebirth.

bayal. Tibetan. Traditionally, a "hidden land," a place where deities and other sacred beings reside.

bharal. Tibetan. A "blue" sheep found in high elevations in Tibet, today almost extinct.

chakpa. Tibetan. A bronze funnel used to convey sand onto a mandala sand painting.

chang. Tibetan. Tibetan beer, typically made of barley.

changtang. Tibetan. The vast high plateau which dominates north central Tibet.

chenyi. Tibetan. Literally, "right eye."

chorten. Tibetan. The Tibetan word for a stupa, a traditional Buddhist shrine including a conspicuous dome shape and spire, usually used as a reliquary.

chuba. Tibetan. A heavy cloak-like coat traditionally made from sheepskin or heavy woolen cloth.

dhakang. Tibetan. The assembly hall of a monastery.

dobdob. Tibetan. Traditionally, a monk policeman, employed in large monasteries to maintain discipline.

419

doja. Tibetan. A red cream, derived from whey, used by nomads on the skin as a shield from the high-altitude sunlight.

dongma. Tibetan. A wooden churn traditionally used to churn buttered tea.

dorje. Tibetan. From the Sanskrit "vajre," a scepter-shaped ritual instrument that symbolizes the power of compassion, said to be "unbreakable as diamond" and as "powerful as a thunderbolt."

drong. Tibetan. A wild yak.

dropka. Tibetan. A nomad of the changtang; literally, "a dweller of the black tent."

dungchen. Tibetan. A long ceremonial trumpet.

durtro. Tibetan. A charnel ground, where Tibetan dead are dismembered in preparation for feeding to vultures.

gau. Tibetan. A "portable shrine," typically a small hinged metal box carried around the neck into which a prayer has been inserted.

Golok. A Tibetan tribal people who traditionally inhabited the Amnye Machen mountain range in south-central Amdo Province.

gompa. Tibetan. A monastery, literally a "place of meditation."

gonkang. Tibetan. A protector deity shrine, often found in monasteries.

goserpa. Tibetan. Literally, "yellow head," one of the terms used to refer to any foreigner.

khata. Tibetan. A prayer scarf.

kora. Tibetan. A pilgrim's circuit, a circumambulation around a holy site.

lama. Tibetan. The Tibetan translation of the Sanskrit "guru," traditionally used for a fully ordained senior monk who has become a master teacher.

lao gai. Mandarin. Literally "reform through labor," referring to a hard-labor prison camp.

lha gyal lo. Tibetan. A traditional Tibetan phrase of celebration or rejoicing; literally, "victory to the gods."

lhakang. Tibetan. A Buddhist chapel or temple.

mai xioa nu. Mandarin. Literally, "women selling smiles," a slang term for prostitutes.

mala. Tibetan. A Buddhist rosary, typically consisting of 108 beads.

mandala. Literally, a Sanskrit word for "circle." A circular representation of the world of a meditational deity, traditionally made with colored sands. (Tibetan: *kyilkhor.*)

mani stone. Tibetan. A stone inscribed, by paint or carving, with a Buddhist prayer, typically invoking the mani mantra, *Om mani padme hum.*

mani wall. Tibetan. A wall made of mani stones. Traditionally, pilgrims visiting a shrine would add a mani stone to such a wall to acquire merit.

mudra. Tibetan. A symbolic gesture made by arranging the hands and fingers in prescribed patterns to represent a specific prayer, offering, or state of mind.

naga. Tibetan. A deity that is believed to reside in water.

nei lou. Mandarin. State secret; literally, "for government use only."

peche. Tibetan. A traditional Tibetan book, typically unbound, in long narrow leaves which are wrapped in cloth, often tied between carved wooden end-pieces.

purba. Tibetan. Literally, "nail" or "spike," a small dagger-like object with a triangular blade used in Buddhist ritual.

Rinpoche. Tibetan. A term of respect in addressing a revered teacher; literally, "blessed" or "jewel."

RMB. Mandarin. Renminbi, a unit of Chinese currency.

rongpa. Tibetan. A farmer.

samkang. Tibetan. A brazier, often found in monasteries, used for burning fragrant woods.

tamzing. Mandarin. A "struggle session," or "criticism session," typically a public criticism of an individual in which humiliation and verbal and/or physical abuse is utilized to achieve political education.

tangzhou. Mandarin. Comrade.

Tara. Tibetan. A female meditational deity, revered for her compassion and considered a special protectress of the Tibetan people.

thangka. Tibetan. A painting on cloth, typically of a religious nature and often considered sacred.

tonde. Tibetan. Small relics excavated from the ground, thought to hold particular power or bestow blessings.

tsampa. Tibetan. Roasted barley flour, a staple food of Tibet.

Author's Note

While *Bone Mountain* is a work of fiction, the struggle of the Tibetan people to maintain their spiritual and cultural identity is all too real. There is indeed a Bureau of Religious Affairs which deploys a small army of bureaucrats against the practice of spirituality and ritual in everyday life and licenses monks based on their political, not their religious, faith. The lands of Tibet have suffered as severely as its people. It is no coincidence that Beijing's maps refer to Tibet as Xizang, its Western Treasure House. Sacred mountains have been deforested then leveled for their mineral content, scores of thousands of Chinese miners have displaced traditional farmers and herders and more than a few Tibetans have been imprisoned for trying to prevent bulldozers from despoiling their sacred grounds.

For over a thousand years Tibetan medicine drew from a vast pharmacopoeia of Tibetan herbs and Buddhist teachings to uniquely integrate the spiritual and physical aspects of healing. Sophisticated medical colleges taught noninvasive diagnostic methods and treatments unknown in the West. That rich legacy has been largely annihilated in the Chinese occupation, many of its treasured texts and teachings lost forever. But a handful of medicine lamas did indeed survive by fleeing to India, where they quietly labor to piece together the remnants of those important traditions.

Readers interested in learning more about the struggle of the Tibetan people will find excellent overviews in Tsering Shakya's *The Dragon in the Land of Snows* and John Avedon's *In Exile from the Land of Snows*. Many powerful autobiographical tales by or about Tibetan survivors have become available in recent years, including *Ama Adhe: The Voice that Remembers*, by Ahde Tapontsang and Joy Blakeslee, Sumner Carnahan's *In the Presence of My Enemies,* David Patt's *A Strange Liberation: Tibetan Lives in Chinese Hands, Born in Lhasa* by Namgyal Lhamo Taklha, and *The Autobiography of a Tibetan Monk* by Palden Gyatso. The forces at work against Tibet's natural environment are comprehensively reviewed in *Tibet 2000: Environment and Development Issues*, available from the International Campaign for Tibet. Introductions to the remarkable traditions of Tibetan medicine are offered in Terry Clifford's *Tibetan Buddhist Medicine and Psychiatry*, and *Healing from the Source* by Dr. Yeshi Dhonden. Lastly, readers who wish to further explore how Tibetan Buddhists blend sand and deities would find a valuable starting place in David Cozort's *Mandala of Vajrabhairava*.